JACQUELINE CAREY

KUSHIEL'S MERCY

GRAND CENTRAL
PUBLISHING

NEW YORK BOSTON

This book is a work of fiction. Names, characters, places, and incidents are the product of the author's imagination or are used fictitiously. Any resemblance to actual events, locales, or persons, living or dead, is coincidental.

Grand Central Publishing
Hachette Book Group
1290 Avenue of the Americas
New York, NY 10104
Visit our website at www.HachetteBookGroup.com

Grand Central Publishing is a division of Hachette Book Group, Inc.
The Grand Central Publishing name and logo is a trademark of Hachette Book Group, Inc.

Printed in the United States of America

Originally published in hardcover by Hachette Book Group
First mass market edition: June 2009

10 9 8 7 6 5

OPM

ACCLAIM FOR

JACQUELINE CAREY'S EPIC SERIES

KUSHIEL'S MERCY

"Sensual prose and graphic eroticism make this fantasy saga particularly appealing . . . Highly recommended."

—***Library Journal***

"Few tales of star-crossed romance offer as much delight and satisfaction as Jacqueline Carey's Kushiel series. Sexy, tragic, and always suspenseful, these novels are notable both for their impeccable characterization and their startling plot twists. KUSHIEL'S MERCY . . . will keep book lovers glued to the pages as this final novel in the Prince Imriel series races to its rousing conclusion."

—SciFi.com

"4 Stars! Both thought-provoking and compulsively readable . . . Imriel and Sidonie's love for each other and their country shines through to the glorious end."

—***Romantic Times BOOKreviews Magazine***

"Excellent characterizations . . . superb."

—***Midwest Book Review***

"If you like alternate history, alternate sexuality, and crazy international intrigue, you won't be able to resist KUSHIEL'S MERCY." **—io9.com**

"Engrossing . . . A terrific read."

—MonstersAndCritics.com

more . . .

"One of the best episodes in a consistently top quality fantasy series—don't miss it!" **—BookLoons.com**

"4 Stars! A very good conclusion to the second Kushiel trilogy." **—HippoiAthanatoi.com**

KUSHIEL'S JUSTICE

"Wonderful . . . fascinating . . . Imriel de la Courcel [is] one of the most interesting fantasy protagonists in a long time. Carey's setting is nuanced and complex . . . Top Pick!" ***—Romantic Times BOOKreviews Magazine***

"Carey brings Alba vividly alive again . . . A multilayered plot and Imriel's complex inner life as he struggles with pain and loss in the present while trying to make peace with the past hook the reader but good."

***—Booklist* (starred review)**

"A moody tale of violence and divided loyalties . . . Events are clearly building to what promises to be a spectacular climax in the sixth volume."

—Publishers Weekly

"Wow!" ***—Philadelphia Weekly Press***

"Unforgettable characters who live out their lives, whether blessed or cursed by the gods, against a background of high passion, complex intrigues, and subtle magic."

***—Library Journal* (starred review)**

"Another fantastic feast, spiced with the exotic tastes of a variety of unique cultures, blended with the familiar characters we have grown to care for, and a few new faces as well. I can't wait for more." **—BookLoons.com**

KUSHIEL'S SCION

"Magnificent . . . credible and gripping, this is heroic fantasy at its finest."

—*Publishers Weekly* (starred review)

"Intelligent, sexy, heartbreakingly human . . . Carey at her intoxicating best." **—*Booklist* (starred review)**

"Evocative . . . Her exotic alternate earth, set in a Renaissance-like time of cultural flowering and sensual gratification, provides a lush backdrop for a cast of compelling and fascinating characters."

—*Library Journal* (starred review)

"Skillfully rendered, sensual, and thoroughly engrossing . . . This will appeal to newcomers and fans of the first trilogy alike." ***—Kirkus Reviews***

"Haunted by sex and death, permeated with ambiguity, uncertainty, and tentative knowledge, it's also a grand adventure." ***—Locus***

"[An] utterly fantastic novel . . . Carey's settings are beautifully realized and . . . the author never loses sight of what makes these books so wonderful: the characters . . . Top Pick!"

—Romantic Times BOOKreviews Magazine

OTHER BOOKS BY

Jacqueline Carey

*Naamah's Kiss**
*Santa Olivia**

Kushiel's Legacy

*Kushiel's Justice**
*Kushiel's Scion**

Kushiel's Avatar
Kushiel's Chosen
Kushiel's Dart

The Sundering

Godslayer
Banewreaker

*Available from Grand Central Publishing

Acknowledgments

As another trilogy draws to a conclusion, I'd like to express my gratitude to everyone who's contributed to its success. Thanks to my agent, Jane Dystel, for her wise advice and unfailing support. Thanks to everyone at Grand Central (a.k.a. Hachette Book Group, a.k.a. Warner Books), and especially to my editor, Jaime Levine, for her dedication and enthusiasm. Thanks to all the booksellers who've done so much to hand-sell the series. And as always, thanks to my readers.

ALBA
THREE SISTERS
AZZALLE
KUSHETH
NAMARRE
TERRE D'ANGE
CAMLACH
THE FLATLANDS
SKALDIA
L'AGNAGE
City of Elua
SIOVALE
EISANDE
La Serenissima
Milazza
ILLYRI
CAERDICCA UNITAS
Lucca
Tiberium
Montrève
Marsilikos
EUSKERRIA
Amilcar
ARAGONIA
New Carthage
CARTHAGE

NORTH
THE CHOWAT
HELLAS
EPHESIUM
CYTHERA
Tyre
KRITI
The Temenos
MENEKHET

Dramatis Personae

House Montrève

Phèdre nó Delaunay de Montrève—Comtesse de Montrève
Joscelin Verreuil—Phèdre's consort; Cassiline Brother (Siovale)
Imriel nó Montrève de la Courcel—Phèdre's foster-son (also member of the Royal Family)
Ti-Philippe—chevalier
Hugues, Gilot (*deceased*)—men at arms
Eugènie—mistress of the household, townhouse

Members of the D'Angeline Royal Family

Ysandre de la Courcel—Queen of Terre d'Ange; wed to Drustan mab Necthana
Sidonie de la Courcel—elder daughter of Ysandre; heir to Terre d'Ange

Alais de la Courcel—younger daughter of Ysandre

Imriel nó Montréve de la Courcel—cousin; son of Benedicte de la Courcel (*deceased*) and Melisande Shahrizai

Barquiel L'Envers—uncle of Ysandre; Duc L'Envers (Namarre)

House Shahrizai

Melisande Shahrizai—mother of Imriel; wed to Benedicte de la Courcel (*deceased*)

Mavros, Roshana, Baptiste Shahrizai—cousins of Imriel

Members of the Royal Court

Ghislain nó Trevalion—noble; Royal Commander; son of Percy de Somerville (*deceased*)

Bernadette de Trevalion—noble, wed to Ghislain, sister of Baudoin (*deceased*)

Bertran de Trevalion—son of Ghislain and Bernadette

Amaury Trente—noble, former Commander of the Queen's Guard

Julien and Colette Trente—children of Amaury

Raul L'Envers y Aragon—son of Nicola and Ramiro (see Aragonia)
Denise Grosmaine—Secretary of the Presence

Alba

Drustan mab Necthana—Cruarch of Alba, wed to Ysandre de la Courcel
Breidaia—sister of Drustan, daughter of Necthana
Talorcan—son of Breidaia
Dorelei (*deceased*)—daughter of Breidaia, wed to Imriel
Sibeal—sister of Drustan, daughter of Necthana, wed to Hyacinthe
Hyacinthe—Master of the Straits, wed to Sibeal
Grainne mac Conor—Lady of the Dalriada
Eamonn, Mairead, Brennan, Caolinn, Conor—Lady Grainne's children
Brigitta—Skaldi wife of Eamonn
Urist—commander of the garrison of Clunderry
Berlik (*deceased*), Morwen (*deceased*)—magicians of the Maghuin Dhonn

Cythera

Ptolemy Solon—Governor
Leander Maignard—D'Angeline expatriate
Deimos—sea-captain

CARTHAGE

Astegal, House of Sarkal—General of Carthage
Jabnit, House of Philosir—gem-merchant
Sunjata—Jabnit's assistant
Bodeshmun, House of Sarkal—Chief Horologist
Gillimas, House of Hiram—magistrate; member of the Unseen Guild
Maharbal—innkeeper
Kratos, Ghanim, Carthaginian Brothers One and Two—bearers
Gemelquart, House of Zinnrid—noble; member of the Unseen Guild

ARAGONIA

Roderico de Aragon—King of Aragonia
Justina—member of the Unseen Guild
Esme—bath-house attendant
Nicola L'Envers y Aragon—noble; kin to Queen Ysandre
Ramiro Zornín y Aragon—noble; kin to King Roderico
Serafin L'Envers y Aragon—son of Nicola and Ramiro
Rachel—D'Angeline chirurgeon
Liberio—army general
Aureliano—army captain

Marmion Shahrizai—D'Angeline exile
Paskal—guide
Leopoldo—Duke of Tibado

EUSKERRIA

Janpier Iturralde—ambassador
Bixenta—keeper of the guesthouse
Nuno Agirre—messenger
Gaskon, Miquel—soldiers

OTHERS

Brother Thomas Jubert—Priest of Elua
Claude de Monluc—Captain of the Dauphine's Guard
Lelahiah Valais—Queen Ysandre's chirurgeon
Emile—proprietor of the Cockerel
Quintilius Rousse—Royal Admiral, father of Eamonn
Favrielle nó Eglantine—couturiere
Bérèngere of Namarre—head of Naamah's Order
Amarante of Namarre—daughter of Bérèngere
Diokles Agallon—Ephesian ambassador; member of the Unseen Guild
Jean Le Blanc—noble
Tibault de Toluard—Marquis of Toluard (Siovale)
Roxanne de Mereliot—Lady of Marsilikos

Jeanne de Mereliot—daughter of Roxanne; chirurgeon
Oppius da Lippi—captain of the *Aeolia*
Lucius Tadius da Lucca—friend of Imriel's
Claudia Fulvia—Lucius' sister; member of the Unseen Guild
Maslin de Lombelon—former lieutenant in the Dauphine's Guard
Henri Voisin—captain in the D'Angeline Navy
Marc Faucon—lieutenant in the D'Angeline Navy
Gilbert Dumel—D'Angeline barge captain
Antonio Peruggi—Caerdicci trader
Isabel de Bretel—Baronesse of Bretel

HISTORICAL FIGURES

Benedicte de la Courcel (*deceased*)—great-uncle of Ysandre; Imriel's father
Baudoin de Trevalion (*deceased*)—cousin of Ysandre; executed for treason
Isidore d'Aiglemort (*deceased*)—noble; traitor turned hero (Camlach)
Waldemar Selig (*deceased*)—Skaldi warlord; invaded Terre d'Ange
Necthana (*deceased*)—mother of Drustan
The Mahrkagir (*deceased*)—mad ruler of Drujan; lord of Darŝanga
Jagun (*deceased*)—chief of the Kereyit Tatars

Gallus Tadius (*deceased*)—great-grandfather of Lucius

Cinhil Ru (*deceased*)—legendary leader of the Cruithne

Donnchadh (*deceased*)—legendary magician of the Maghuin Dhonn

Kushiel's Mercy

One

There are people in my country who have never travelled beyond the boundaries of Terre d'Ange. Indeed, there are many who have never left the province in which they were born; contented crofters tilling the land, tending orchards, or raising sheep, never venturing farther than the nearest market.

Betimes, I envy them.

Already, as a young man, I have gone farther than I could have imagined as a boy daydreaming in the Sanctuary of Elua where I was raised. It did not begin by choice—as all the world knows, I was abducted by Carthaginian slave-traders, sold into slavery in Menekhet, and from thence taken to the land of Drujan, ruled by a madman who consorted with a dark and ancient god.

It was a short time ago as historians reckon such things, but a long time ago in my life. I will never bear those memories lightly, but I have learned to bear them. Since that time, since I was rescued and restored, I have ventured as far south as Jebe-Barkal and lost Saba; and as far north as Vralia, an unlikely kingdom arising in the harsh glory of the cold north.

I have been wed and widowed.

I have become a father, almost.

And I have fallen in love, which is somewhat altogether different. It was not with my wife, Dorelei, although she was worthy of such devotion and in the end I did come to love her. Love of my wife is what drove me to Vralia, seeking justice on her behalf. I found it, too, although it was not entirely what I expected. Still, the man who killed her is dead, and his skull lies buried beneath her feet in Alba.

But there is a difference between loving and being in love—that maddening passion that expands the heart and exalts the soul, that shakes the heavens and roils the depths of hell. That, I have known but once. Betimes I wish it was with Dorelei and her thoughtful, gentle ways. Betimes I wish it was with anyone, anyone else. A crofter's daughter, a merchant's son. Anyone whose station in life would raise no alarms. Who would allow me to stay in one place, to live and love and be happy. Whose bedchamber would not become a political battleground, raising the unwelcome spectre of my treasonous mother and her eternal scheming.

Anyone but Sidonie.

It wasn't, though.

And I knew it.

I knew it in Alba, when I was still bound by strange magics, struggling to shed my youthful self-absorption and fulfill my duties as a man. We hadn't been sure, Sidonie and I. Too young, too uncertain. What had begun between us was always more than casual dalliance, although I daresay she knew the stakes better than I did. My royal cousin, Sidonie de la Courcel, Dauphine of Terre d'Ange, eldest daughter and acknowledged heir of Queen Ysandre.

The one person in the world I could not love without raising suspicion.

I knew it was love, real and enduring; we both knew it. When it began, Sidonie asked me, *Imriel, tell me truly,* she said. *How much of what lies between us is just the lure of the forbidden?*

I couldn't answer it, not then. I didn't know. I knew I wanted her, fiercely. I knew there was a dark fire in her depths that fed my own desires. I didn't know about the aching abyss of tenderness and yearning that would open between us, unassuaged by time or distance. Nor, I daresay, did she.

We discovered it together.

And when Dorelei and my unborn son died, Sidonie and I both bore a measure of guilt for it. If we had been more certain, more courageous, it would never have happened. *Love as thou wilt,* Blessed Elua's precept commands us. We hadn't dared. We took the sensible route and waited. We'd feared to throw the realm into turmoil.

Well and so, it happened anyway.

There was no triumphal reception in the City of Elua when we returned from Alba after overseeing the burial of the skull of the man who killed my wife and son. Still, D'Angelines will do as they will. A great many of them turned out in support the day we rode into the City, cheering wildly. There were Tsingani and Yeshuites among them, too, for which I take no credit. For their part, it is Phèdre they adore; Phèdre nó Delaunay, Comtesse de Montrève, my foster-mother, a heroine of the realm. For as long as I live, deserved or not, I will coast on the goodwill she and her consort, Joscelin, have engendered among folk who long for heroes.

But there were others, too.

Not many, but enough. Knots of folk, here and there,

amid the throngs. Men and women of middling age, sporting black armbands, eyes hard and faces grim. Where they congregated, the cheers were dampened. As we passed, they held out their hands, thumbs outthrust, rotating their hands to give the ancient signal of Tiberian imperators.

Thumbs down.

Death.

"Why?" I asked Sidonie as we rode. "Who are they?"

Her face was pale. "Families of her victims."

I swallowed. "My mother's?"

"So they reckon, yes. Families with loved ones who died during Skaldia's invasion." Sidonie met my eyes. Hers were dark and troubled. Cruithne eyes, the only sign of her mixed heritage. "It's a reminder that your mother was condemned to execution and escaped it. They have a right to their anger, Imriel. No one said this would be easy. Are you willing to face it?"

"You know I am. Are you?" I asked softly. "The cost you bear is higher."

Somewhat shifted in the depths of her black eyes, a certitude settling into place. Her slender shoulders were set and squared. "Yes."

"Then I stand beside you." I kneed the Bastard. My speckled horse snorted and pranced, jostling alongside Sidonie's palfrey. I reached out to lay my hand over hers briefly. "Always. For as long as you will have me, and longer, I will stand at your side."

She squeezed my hand. "I know."

Neither of us knew for a surety what we would face upon our return. The Queen was opposed to our union, that much was certain. Whether or not she would actively seek to part us, not even Sidonie could say.

Our company parted ways in the City of Elua. Phèdre and Joscelin, along with their loyal retainers Ti-Philippe and Hugues, would retire to Montrève's townhouse. I meant to continue on to the Palace with Sidonie and her personal guard. I'd had quarters there, once. Queen Ysandre had granted them to me herself, delighted with my impending marriage to Dorelei, niece of the Cruarch of Alba. Of course, she'd not known I was already in love with her daughter.

She knew now. I didn't know if my quarters still existed. I didn't even know if I'd be welcome at the Palace. Still, there was no way to find out but to try.

"You're sure?" Phèdre asked, searching my face. "You could stay with us and send word to Ysandre seeking audience. It might be easier."

I shook my head. "I'm too old to hide behind your skirts, Phèdre. Or your sword," I added to Joscelin.

He snorted. "When did you ever?"

It made me smile a little. "Well, the cloak of your heroism, then. I need to face this myself. Anyway, I've broken no law, committed no crime."

Phèdre sighed. "As you will, love. I'll send word to Ysandre myself. Mayhap she's ready to hear reason."

They had been away as long as I had, Phèdre and Joscelin; bound first on a mysterious errand, then setting out in pursuit of me after learning I'd nearly been killed in Alba and was hunting the man, the magician, who had done it, who had slain my wife and our unborn son. If anyone could make the Queen hear reason, I thought, it would be Phèdre. She had been the one to expose my mother's treachery in abetting the Skaldi invasion, and she had been the one who gave the testimony that condemned my mother to death.

But when I thought about those folk on the street, their thumbs pointing downward in a stark reminder that Melisande Shahrizai had evaded justice, I wasn't so sure.

"Mayhap," I said. "We'll see."

She hugged me in farewell. "Come to dinner on the morrow and we'll talk. Everyone will want to see you."

"I will," I promised.

I turned in the saddle to glance after them as they rode toward the townhouse. If Phèdre and Joscelin could weather everything that fate had thrown at them, I reckoned Sidonie and I had a chance. Sidonie caught my eye when I turned back and read my thoughts.

"It's just politics," she said. "Not hordes of Skaldi, shape-shifting magicians, or deadly madmen bent on destroying the world."

"True," I said. "There is that."

As it transpired, I needn't have worried over our reception, which was cordial and proper. After all, Sidonie was returning from a state mission, representing her mother in Alba—and it was true, I'd done naught wrong. I was a Prince of the Blood in my own right, returning from avenging my wife, the Queen's own niece by marriage.

"Welcome home, your highness." The royal chamberlain greeted Sidonie with a deep bow. "Your mother awaits you in her quarters as soon as you have had a chance to refresh yourself."

Sidonie inclined her head. "My thanks, Lord Robert."

The chamberlain accorded me a bow only slightly less formal, as was fitting. "Welcome, Prince Imriel. Your quarters are in readiness. Her majesty will send for you at a later time to express her gratitude in person for your brave deeds."

"My thanks," I echoed.

Well and so. Sidonie and I glanced at one another. She tilted her head, smiling slightly. "Go on. I'll send word to you."

"All right."

I watched her walk away, surrounded by her guard in

their blue livery with the pale stripes. We'd scarce left one another's side since being reunited in Alba—truly reunited. We had years of lost time to make up. But we had agreed that once we reached the Palace, diplomacy and tact would serve us better than flagrant public displays of passion. So I watched her go, took a deep breath, and made my way to my quarters.

That was something, anyway. If Ysandre had maintained my quarters within the Palace, she didn't mean to accuse me of sedition.

They were pleasant quarters, nicely appointed, with a fresco of Eisheth gathering herbs on the ceiling, and a balcony overlooking one of the gardens. I sent a chambermaid to order a bath drawn, then wandered the rooms, waiting for the bath to be filled and servants to bring the trunk with my clothing and possessions that had been in our train.

I lingered in the bedroom, overcome by memory. The bed was larger than I remembered; I'd grown accustomed to a smaller scale in Alba. I twisted the knotted gold ring on my finger without thinking, clenching my fist until it bit into my palm. It was here that Sidonie had given it to me. But in truth, this bedchamber held more memories of Dorelei.

Gods, I'd been an ass to her!

"I'm sorry, love," I murmured. "You made me a better man in the end. I'll try to be worthy of it."

It had been Dorelei's last wish to send me back to Sidonie. I'd done it, although I hadn't wanted to. She'd been right to do it, though. If I hadn't, if I hadn't seized that bright thread of hope and joy . . . I don't know what would have become of me. I might have become a cold and bitter monster, like the vision I saw of our grown son. I might have died in the far reaches of Vralia, bereft of all reason to live. Such things are never given to us to know, and in my experience, it is best not to meddle.

That had been a year ago.

A year since Ysandre de la Courcel found me kneeling, heartbroken, in her daughter's embrace. A year since she burst into fury, speaking words that singed my ears. I'd left the City of Elua that day. Two days later, I'd departed on the trail of the man who killed my wife, the bear-witch who'd nearly taken my life, too. But in those few days, Sidonie and I had done a fair job of overturning the entire Court.

Now I was back.

The servants brought my trunk. I unpacked my things myself. There wasn't much aside from clothing: a leather-bound book of love letters that Sidonie had given me, a wooden flute that had been a gift from Hugues, and a flint-striking kit. Everything else, I carried on me. My sword and dagger. The etched vambraces Dorelei had commissioned for me. Sidonie's ring. The gold torc that marked me as a prince of Alba. Drustan mab Necthana, the Cruarch of Alba, had given it to me himself when I wed Dorelei there. And in the purse at my belt, a smooth stone with a hole in the center; a croonie-stone, the *ollamhs* called it.

It had been part of the bindings that protected me from Alban magic, and I carried it for remembrance. I never wanted to be bound like that again, ever. The bindings had protected me, but they'd severed me from myself, too.

Never again.

And yet if it hadn't been for that binding, I might have spent all my days with Dorelei aching and miserable, seething in discontent. I might never have learned to love her, and grown from a pining, self-absorbed youth to a man in the process.

Or she might not have been slain.

I would never know.

"Prince Imriel?" The chambermaid appeared in the

doorway, startling me out of my reverie. "Your bath is ready."

"Thank you." I racked my memory. "Delphine, is it not?"

"Aye, my lord." She bobbed a curtsy. "I'm . . . We were all very sorry to hear of Lady Dorelei's death. She was kind."

"Thank you," I repeated. "Yes, she was."

The chambermaid hesitated, sympathy and avid curiosity warring on her pert features. "Is it true that you, that you and . . . ?"

"Yes," I said.

"Oh!" Her eyes widened. "Well, then . . . well."

"Indeed," I agreed gravely.

Politics and gossip, the lifeblood of the D'Angeline Court. I dismissed Delphine from the bathing-chamber, sinking into the warm water and enjoying a few minutes of luxurious privacy before I heard a familiar voice arguing at the door to the antechamber. I listened, smiling.

"He's right," I called out at length. "You may admit him."

"Name of Elua!" My cousin Mavros Shahrizai strode into the bathing-chamber and glared at me, hands on his hips. His midnight-black hair was loose and rippling, his blue eyes vivid with emotion. We bore an unmistakable family resemblance. "Do you never think to send word? We worry, you know."

I stood in the tub, dripping. "Hello, Mavros."

"Idiot." He gripped my bare shoulders and gave me the kiss of greeting, then held me away from him, gazing with a critical eye at the pink furrows of flesh that ran at a raking angle from my right shoulder to my left hip. "Gods, it's worse than I reckoned. You didn't tell me that bastard nearly gutted you."

I shrugged. "I lived."

His fingers flexed, digging into my shoulders. "Idiot. He's dead now, right? You brought his head home in a bag?"

"And buried it in Clunderry," I said. "Oh, yes."

Mavros let go of me, fetching a stool and dragging it nearer the tub. "Finish your bath and tell me about it."

For as long a journey as it had been, there wasn't much to tell. It had been a slow, plodding hunt. I'd been shipwrecked on the Eastern Sea and lost weeks stranded on an isolated island while we salvaged and repaired our damaged ship. I'd been mistaken for an ally of raiding Tartars in a Vralian village and thrown in gaol. I'd managed to escape, and followed Berlik to the place where he'd sought refuge, spending countless days attempting to find him in the trackless wilderness.

In the end, he found me.

"So he wanted to die?" Mavros asked when I finished.

"Yes," I said. "To make atonement."

"Huh." He thought about it while I dried myself and slipped into a dressing-robe. "Do you reckon it worked?"

"I don't know." I knotted the robe's sash. "What he did . . . as awful as it was, I came to understand it. He thought it was the only way to spare his people."

"From the future your son would bring," Mavros said slowly.

"Yes." I shivered, remembering the vision. A young man, his features a mixture of mine and Dorelei's, but bitter and cruel. Armies raging over Alba, blood-sodden fields. Women and children dragged from their homes, houses put to the torch. Men hunted like animals. The standing stones and the sacred groves, destroyed. "I'll tell you one thing, Mavros. I'll not defy Blessed Elua's precept again and I want nothing more to do with strange magics. All I want is to be left in peace for a time."

"Good luck." His tone was wry.

"I know," I said. "Sidonie."

"Is it worth it?" he asked with genuine curiosity.

I turned the gold ring on my finger. Despite everything, the love I felt for her was undiminished. The soaring exaltation, the inexplicable *rightness* of the fit. The shared laughter and talk, the common, ordinary happiness. And somewhere beneath it, a sense that this was important and needful. I couldn't explain it. I only knew it was true.

"Yes," I said simply.

"Well, you know House Shahrizai stands behind you," Mavros said. "Although things being what they are, our support might not be terribly helpful."

"So I noticed." I gestured, pointing my thumb downward.

"*Mmm.*" His face was introspective. "You and Sidonie . . . it raised old fears, opened old wounds."

"You *do* know I've no aspiration toward the throne?" I asked.

"Oh, I do." Mavros glanced up at me. "But I'm not the one you need to convince. There are a few thousand of those, starting with her majesty the Queen." As though summoned by his words, there was a knock at the outer door—one of Ysandre's guards, come to fetch me to audience. Mavros laughed humorlessly. "Well, and here's your first chance."

After bidding Mavros farewell and donning clean attire, I accompanied the guard to my audience with Ysandre. It was early evening and the Palace was beginning to come alive with what revelries the coming night would hold: private fêtes, wagers in the Hall of Games, mayhap a performance in the theatre.

I endured the gauntlet of stares and whispers. I was used to it; it had been my lot since I had first returned to Terre d'Ange as a child. I met the stares, returned them with a level gaze, trying to read the faces behind them.

Some were sympathetic.

A few were hostile and guarded.

Most were simply curious.

I wasn't sure if it would be a state reception or a private one. It turned out to be somewhere between the two. The Queen received me in her private quarters, but Lady Denise Grosmaine, the Secretary of the Presence, was in attendance, which meant whatever transpired would be documented for the Royal Archives.

I entered the Queen's salon and bowed low.

"We welcome you home, Prince Imriel." Ysandre's tone was even. Careful.

I straightened. "My thanks, your majesty."

Ysandre de la Courcel had ruled Terre d'Ange since before I was born. She'd assumed the throne when she was no older than I was now, and she'd had a long time to learn to school her features into a polite mask. But I was Kushiel's scion, and I could see a measure of what lay behind the mask—hurt, betrayal, and anger. It hadn't gone away since I left. It had settled into a deep place inside her.

Still, she was the Queen, and a very good one.

"We—" She paused, then continued, her voice firm. "*I* wish to thank you for avenging the death of my husband's blood-kin. I wish to tell you that Drustan, that the Cruarch of Alba, sent a letter commending you for your courage and persistence. We are both grateful to know that the spirit of Dorelei mab Breidaia will rest peacefully thanks to your efforts."

"As am I," I said quietly. "She was my wife. She would have been the mother of my son. I pray they are both at peace."

The Secretary of the Presence recorded our words, her

pen scratching softly on paper. I gazed at Ysandre. Sidonie had inherited her mother's fairness, although Ysandre's hair was a paler hue. She had inherited her mother's cool, reserved beauty. But she had not inherited a kingdom on the verge of being invaded and conquered due to the treachery of Melisande Shahrizai.

Ysandre inclined her head. "You may go."

I spread my hands. "Your majesty . . ."

Her expression hardened. "We will discuss the *other matter* at a later date. There will be a Priest of Elua seeking an audience with you to discuss these things. I recommend you grant it."

I opened my mouth to make a reply or an appeal, then thought better of it and inclined my head. "Of course, your majesty."

With that, I was dismissed.

Outside of Ysandre's quarters, I leaned against the wall and exhaled hard. Ah, Elua! Love shouldn't have to be so *hard.*

"Prince Imriel?" a cheerful voice asked. I squinted at the speaker. One of Sidonie's guardsmen, a short, wiry lad with dark hair. He grinned at me. "That bad, eh? Her highness sent me to fetch you."

"That's the best news I've had all day," I said.

His grin widened. "Thought you might think so."

The guard, whose name was Alfonse, led me to Sidonie's quarters. It was the first time I'd entered them openly as her acknowledged lover, and it felt strange. I half expected to be halted. But no; Sidonie's guard was loyal, and it seemed Ysandre wasn't minded to intervene, at least not overtly, not yet. I suspected it had little to do with tolerance for the situation, and more to do with fear of driving Sidonie into open rebellion.

Sidonie's rooms were larger and finer than my own.

There was an abundance of candles lit against the encroaching darkness. Covered platters sat on the dining table, and the succulent aromas seeping from beneath the domes made me realize I was hungry.

"I hope you don't mind." Sidonie, seated on a couch, set down the sheaf of letters she was reading. "I thought it might be nicer to dine in my chambers than face the gawking horde on our first night."

"It's perfect," I said. "And I'm ravenous."

"*Mmm.*" She rose with deft grace. "How was Mother?"

"Cordial." I caught her hand. "How did you find her?"

Sidonie kissed my throat. "Formal."

I ran a lock of her hair through my fingers. "She wants me to speak to a Priest of Elua."

She nodded. "I told you I'd been working to gain the support of the priesthood while you were gone. If they're convinced that what's between us is genuine, it will make it harder for her to oppose it."

"And I'm to convince them? Seems I'm expected to do a good deal of convincing these days." I traced the line of her brows, so similar to my own. "What of you?"

"Oh, I've already done my part, at least with the priesthood." Sidonie turned her head to kiss my palm, then smiled at me. "They're sure of *me.* Now it falls to you to convince them that this isn't part of an evil scheme to gain the throne by seducing me and winning my heart." She took my hand in hers, kissing the tips of my fingers.

The pulse of desire quickened in me. "Anyone fool enough to think that doesn't know you very well," I said, my voice sounding rough in my ears.

"True." Sidonie glanced up at me, then slid my index finger into her mouth and sucked on it, just long enough to turn desire's pulse into a throbbing, thundering drumbeat. Her black eyes sparkled with wicked amusement. "But, then, most people don't."

I made a wordless sound, stooped, and scooped her into my arms. Sidonie laughed softly, looping her arms around my neck as I carried her toward the bedchamber, kissing her.

"I thought you were ravenous," she teased.

I nudged the bedchamber door open. "It can wait."

Two

So began our life of uneasy stalemate at Court.

Sidonie and I neither hid nor flaunted our relationship. Everyone knew, of course. But since Ysandre had chosen, at least for the time, to treat it as though it didn't exist, it wasn't discussed openly, at least not in earshot of anyone who might report to the Queen.

It was discussed a great deal in private. It was discussed with glee by young nobles engaged in the Game of Courtship, many of whom were surprisingly supportive, reveling in a tale of tragic romance. They were too young to remember the Skaldi invasion, which had happened before I was born. Melisande Shahrizai was only a name, a story. She'd been in exile for over twenty years, first in the Temple of Asherat in La Serenissima, and then vanishing to Elua-knows-where.

But there were plenty of others old enough to remember, and many of them discussed it with mistrust and suspicion. Not all of them. For every D'Angeline who regarded me as the potentially traitorous spawn of Melisande Shahrizai and Benedicte de la Courcel—who had only escaped being convicted of treason by virtue of dying before he could be tried—there was another who regarded me as the foster-son of Phèdre nó Delaunay and Joscelin Verreuil, undeniably heroes of the realm.

Phèdre did meet with Ysandre. She had been the Queen's confidante for a long time, and she could be damnably persuasive. Not this time.

"She claims I'm too close to the matter to be an objective judge when it comes to Imriel," she said, frustrated.

"She has a point, love," Joscelin observed. He put up his hands in a peaceable gesture when Phèdre raised her brows at him. "You and I and everyone under this roof know that you're right. But in Ysandre's mind, you'd defend Imri under any circumstances."

"She's scared." I toyed with one of the quince tarts that Eugènie had made in honor of my visit, the second visit that week. "For ten years, she's had people like Barquiel L'Envers telling her that she was nursing a serpent in the bosom of House Courcel. Now it looks as though I've proved them right."

"Sinking your fangs deep into her heir's tender breast," Ti-Philippe commented.

I flushed. "In a manner of speaking."

He eyed me with amusement. "Or not."

"Well, she'll have to listen to the priesthood if they choose to speak on your behalf," Phèdre mused. "That was a shrewd thought on Sidonie's part."

"What do you plan on telling them?" Joscelin asked.

I shook my head. "I've no idea."

I had indeed received a request from Brother Thomas Jubert, the senior member of the Great Temple of Elua here in the City, summoning me to an audience in two days' time. I had agreed to it readily. At the time I'd not felt apprehensive, but as the meeting approached that began to change.

If the priesthood did choose to give us their blessing, well and good. It wouldn't change much in political terms, but it might go some way toward swaying the hearts of those in doubt, and it would make it difficult for Ysandre to move toward outright opposition.

And if they didn't, it would seal the opinion of those who opposed us. And it would make it a great deal easier for Ysandre to issue an edict ordering her wayward heir to choose between me and her inheritance.

I didn't know if she would. And I didn't know what Sidonie would do if she did. All I knew was that I didn't want to find out. If I could rip out my heart and show it to the priest, I thought, it would be simple. If I could live out my life before his eyes, show him I intended no harm and aspired to nothing more than spending the balance of my days at Sidonie's side, it would be simple.

But I couldn't, and mere words seemed an inadequate tool.

"How did you do it?" I asked Sidonie the night before my meeting with the priest, pacing the salon. "Convince him?"

"I spoke from the heart." She smiled slightly. "At considerable length. I think mayhap I wore him down."

"But what did you *say*?" I asked.

"I'm not sure it's right to tell you." Sidonie regarded me, her expression unreadable. "And even if it is, I can't lend you my words, Imriel. They won't help. You have to find your own."

"I know. I know." I halted my pacing and sat on the couch beside her. "But it would help me to hear it, truly."

"All right." She drew her knees up beneath her gown, lacing her arms around them. Her dark Cruithne gaze rested on me. "I said a lot. It's probably for the best I don't remember half of it." Her smile came and went in a quick flicker. "I don't want to swell your head. In the end . . ." She lifted her chin, her gaze moving off into the distance. "Why you? That's the question, isn't it? Why is this worth sowing unrest in Terre d'Ange?"

I nodded and kept silent.

"Blessed Elua doesn't join hearts without a purpose." Sidonie knit her brows. "Since I was old enough to know my own name, I've known I was my mother's heir. I've grown up learning and understanding the responsibilities that entails. And until . . . until that night, the Longest Night, when I first kissed you, I'd scarce done a single thing that wasn't in keeping with those duties. Not one action, not one deed, not one misspoken word."

"Very proper," I murmured.

"Mmm." Her gaze shifted back to me. "Imriel, you are the one person in the world, the only person in the world, my mother would forbid me. And yes, I did think in the beginning, mayhap it was only that. Some long-stifled act of rebellion. But it wasn't. So, why? Surely there must be purpose in it." Her voice dropped, softening. "Love chooses. We don't, not always. I could have chosen anyone, anyone else, and I would have learned nothing of the terrible might of love, the power and sacrifice. What manner of D'Angeline would I have been, then? What manner of person?"

"You would be you," I said. "Always."

Sidonie tilted her head, her gaze sliding away once more, contemplating somewhat I couldn't see. "I'm not so sure. This land, this realm of ours, at its worst . . ." She shook her head. "We can be a vain, proud, and insular people. I know it. I've felt it all my life." Her mouth quirked. "I hear what people say. Cruithne half-breed. And the worst of it was always leveled against Alais, not me, just because of the way she looks. It hurt more in a way because I couldn't protect her from it. She's my younger sister; we share the same blood."

"I know," I said quietly. "And pride in it on both sides. So you should, Sidonie." I touched the torc at my throat. It had been a proud day when Drustan gave it to me. "I understand."

"I know." Her dark gaze returned. "My mother and father, D'Angeline and Alban, a love-match despite themselves, uniting two realms. Phèdre and Joscelin, *anguissette* and Cassiline Brother, facing untold danger. Anafiel Delaunay, keeping his oath after so many years, honoring his lost love. Ah, Elua!" Sidonie drew a deep breath, eyes bright with unshed tears. "At its best . . . at its best, Terre d'Ange has a great deal to teach the world about the nature of love and how we might best live our lives." Her voice grew stronger. "And I do not think I would ever have understood that if I had not fallen in love with the one person in the world it was not *proper* to love."

I stared at her, the hair on the back of my neck prickling.

"I had a long time to think while you were surviving shipwrecks and gaol and endless hunts through the trackless wilderness." Sidonie wiped her eyes impatiently, adding, "You can close your mouth now."

I did. "Sidonie . . ."

She uncoiled, reaching for me. Her hands sank deep into my hair. Her face was close, so near our breath mingled, and her expression was fierce. "So now you know. But I don't want to talk anymore. I don't want to *think* anymore. Not here, not now."

I obliged her.

Our love-making wasn't gentle that night. Betimes it could be. Betimes it wasn't. That night, for the first time since we had been reunited, Sidonie and I waged love like war. I took her on the couch. I carried her to the bedchamber and I took her there. I left marks on her skin. She left marks on mine. And in the small hours of the night, when the full moon rose outside our balcony, I watched her sleep, peaceful as a babe, her bare skin silvered by the slanting moonlight.

"Sun Princess." I traced the line of her spine, from the nape of her neck to the cleft of her buttocks. My throat felt tight. "I don't have the words. I wish I did. I just don't ever want to be without you."

Sidonie murmured in her sleep. I lay down beside her, fitting the curve of my body around hers, drawing up the sheet to cover us both. My arm settled around her waist. Still sleeping, she hugged it to her.

Why do we fit so well together?

"I'll try to find words," I whispered, and slept.

On the morrow, I went to meet with the priest at the Temple of Elua. A smiling young acolyte met me in the vestibule, kneeling to draw off my boots.

"Brother Thomas will meet you in the inner sanctum," he said.

It is an old place, one of the oldest in the City, quiet and peaceful; a roofless sanctuary with pillars marking the four corners and ancient oaks flanking the effigy of Blessed Elua. The trees were old, too. The only living thing in the City more ancient was the oak tree in Elua's Square in the exact center of the City, said to have been planted by Elua himself. I walked barefoot over lush grass to approach the effigy, kneeling to press my lips to the cool marble of his foot.

"Imriel de la Courcel," a voice said behind me.

I rose and turned. "Brother Thomas Jubert?"

The priest inclined his head. He was a big man and younger than I'd expected, not yet sixty, with black hair and pale grey eyes that reminded me of Berlik, the magician of the Maghuin Dhonn who had killed Dorelei. The thought made me uneasy, which his words did nothing to allay.

"Come." Brother Thomas beckoned. "I would speak with you, as would others."

I raised my brows. "Others?"

He folded his hands in the blue sleeves of his robe. "Elua's priesthood does not speak for all his Companions."

"I see." I followed him into the temple, down a corridor. Somewhere, a woman's voice was raised in song, merry and incongruous. Brother Thomas led me into a pleasant atrium garden, set about with chairs and couches.

Representatives of all the orders of Elua's Companions were there—or at least all save one. Naamah's priest clad in scarlet, Azza's in a saffron tunic with a crimson chlamys. A Priest of Kushiel clad in black robes, wearing the bronze mask of office. A Priestess of Eisheth in sea-blue, and Shemhazai's in a scholar's dark grey robes. A Priestess of Anael in brown, tied at the waist with a rope belt. A Priest of Camael in a forest-green surplice, his sword hanging at his side.

"No Cassiline Brother?" I asked Brother Thomas.

He smiled faintly. "We do not believe the Cassiline Brotherhood speaks for Cassiel. I believe you have some familiarity with that notion."

"I do." Joscelin had been a Cassiline Brother, a warrior-priest of the order. He had broken his oaths of loyalty, obedience, and chastity for Phèdre's sake. He believed in the end that his path was in accordance with Cassiel's wishes. I believed it, too.

"Please be seated." Brother Thomas gestured. His expression was grave again. "Understand, Imriel de la Courcel, that we have little liking for this process. We are servants of Blessed Elua and his Companions. We concern ourselves with matters of the soul, the heart, the flesh. Of love, desire, and divinity, growth and healing, penance and redemption, wisdom and mortal striving. Not politics."

I took a seat. "And yet you summoned me here, my lord."

"Yes." He sighed. "Your dilemma is a political one, but it touches on matters of the spirit."

No one else spoke, all of them watching silently. I felt unpleasantly as though I were on trial. "What would you have me say, my lords and ladies?" I asked, spreading my hands. "Or what is it you wish to say to me?"

They exchanged silent glances.

"I wish to say this," Brother Thomas said quietly. "We will listen to the words you say here today. Once we have come to consensus, I will advise the Queen accordingly on this as a matter of spirit. I will give no advice in the matter of politics."

I shrugged. "Nor would I expect you to."

"That is well, then." Brother Thomas inclined his head. "Speak."

I hadn't expected this. I had expected . . . what? A more intimate conversation, a priest's gentle questioning leading me to divulge the secret truths of my heart. I wondered if Sidonie had known, and suspected that she had. I wished she'd given me warning, though I supposed that would have somehow tainted the procedure. I wasn't sure if I was more annoyed or impressed with her integrity.

"I love her," I said slowly. "Sidonie. And I could give you a hundred reasons why, a hundred things about her that surprise and delight me, but the truth is that, in the end, I don't *know* why." I paused, but no one spoke. "My lords, I know no one who has done more in the service of love than Joscelin Verreuil. When I first came to love Sidonie, I didn't trust my feelings, not wholly. We were young and fearful and uncertain, and we both knew full well the risks involved in our liaison. I asked Joscelin how it was that he knew for a surety that he loved Phèdre. He said that he had tried doing without her." I smiled a little to myself, remembering. "He's not a man of surpassing eloquence, but he speaks to the point."

"You took this as advice?" the priest inquired.

"I did. And in defiance of Blessed Elua's precept, I chose duty over love. I fulfilled my obligation to the Crown and wed the Cruarch's niece. You know well what followed." I swallowed hard at the memory and made myself continue. "If I could unmake that choice, I would. And yet I cherish what small good can be gleaned from the horror. To do otherwise dishonors the dead. I learned a great deal about the true nature of love from Dorelei mab Breidaia. I learned a great deal about myself and what it means to be a man. And I learned that for good or ill, I do love Sidonie de la Courcel with an abiding passion that time, distance, or dire magic cannot alter."

They were silent.

My heartbeat quickened. "My lords, for two years, since first we knew we loved one another, Sidonie and I have been parted. It's led to naught but misery for far too many. I cannot unmake my choice or undo the tragedies that ensued, but I can seek to trust Elua's wisdom as I should have done before." I turned out my hands, pleading. "Is it too much to believe that the gods wish us to be happy?"

Another glance was exchanged.

"Do you claim that your happiness is worth throwing Terre d'Ange into chaos?" Brother Thomas asked in a dry tone.

"Do you claim we are the ones responsible for sowing chaos when we are but following Elua's precept?" I asked sharply. "*Love as thou wilt.* If the Queen forbids our union, she is violating the one tenet we are all of us taught to hold dear, and guilty of heresy. That's the crux of the matter, is it not?"

"It is the reason we are listening," the priest replied. "But you have not answered my question."

I tilted my head and regarded the sky. It was a clear summer day, sunny and bright. A flock of swallows veered across the blue expanse overhead, graceful and free. "My happiness," I murmured. There was a taste of bile in the back of my throat. "No, my lord. When you phrase it thusly, how can I say yes? And yet . . ." I shook my head. "I've had so very little of it."

The assembled group stirred. "Of happiness?" Brother Thomas asked gently.

"Yes." My voice broke on the word. I gazed at his face, feeling uncommonly weary. "My lord, let us be honest with one another. In the end, it doesn't matter what I say to you here today, what advice you give the Queen. All it can grant is a small respite, a measure of time. I know this. The wounds my mother caused cut too deep, and there are no words that will sway the wounded heart of Terre d'Ange, only deeds."

"Deeds," he echoed, his expression sharpening. "You speak of deeds?"

"Yes, my lord. One deed in particular." I took a deep, shaking breath. "There is a burden ahead of me I have to shoulder if I am to prove myself to the Queen and the realm. And I will. I'll try. But Blessed Elua, I'm *tired*!" I laughed humorlessly, raking my hands through my hair. "In a scant twenty-one years, I've lived enough for three lifetimes. Is it so much to ask for a small respite?"

Brother Thomas studied me. "You know the burden you face? This deed you have not named?"

"Yes, my lord," I said wearily. "Of course I know. Somewhere in my heart, I suppose I've always known."

Unexpectedly, the Priest of Kushiel rose. "What I have heard suffices," he said, his voice muffled by the mask.

He bowed in my direction, sunlight glinting off the bronze planes. "He speaks the truth of his heart."

"I concur." Naamah's priest and the Priestess of Eisheth spoke simultaneously, rising and exchanging laughing glances. "It may be there is healing in it," Eisheth's priestess added.

The Priest of Naamah smiled at me. "Of a surety, there is desire."

Shemhazai's priest leveled a shrewd, thoughtful gaze at me, then stood. "Yes," he said. "I cannot fathom the wisdom of it, not yet. But I do not deny the knowledge."

"I see no harm here," Anael's priestess said simply, rising.

Azza's priest stood, tossing his chlamys over his shoulder. "If it is pride that speaks, it is earned," he said. "No more can I say."

The last to rise was the Priest of Camael. He was the oldest among them, with a warrior's posture that belied his lined face and age-silvered hair. "I like this least among you," he said slowly. "For there is too much in it that threatens the strength of Terre d'Ange. But I will not say he does not speak true, and that is all you have asked of me."

"So be it," Brother Thomas said.

One by one, they inclined their heads to him and departed. I got to my feet and watched them go, my heart feeling at once heavy and light. I had spoken the truth, but it was a cruel, harsh truth, and not one I welcomed. Love came at a price. If Terre d'Ange was not to bear the cost of it, I would have to do it. The deed that had been left unspoken. "Is that all, then?" I asked the priest. "What happens now?"

"It is enough," he said somberly. "And what happens now depends entirely on the will of her majesty Queen Ysandre."

Three

We found out soon enough what Ysandre willed.

Brother Thomas served us better than I would have reckoned. He paid a visit to the Palace with a dozen members of the temple in tow, serene priests and priestesses in their blue robes and bare feet. The Queen granted them a private audience. What was said in her chambers, no one knew for sure, but all had seen them arrive.

Speculation swirled, and a day after the meeting, Ysandre announced that there would be a public audience in the throne hall at three hours past noon on the morrow.

"Do you think she'll heed their advice?" I asked Sidonie.

"Elua, I hope so," she said fervently.

"And if she doesn't?" I watched her expression change. "I know it's your choice, Sidonie. But I have a voice in it."

"You have a very pleasant voice." She kissed me. "Not in this."

"We'll see," I said.

The audience was enormous. The throne hall was a vast

space, big enough to swallow up the two hundred chairs placed toward the front of the room for peers of the realm. There were at least three hundred peers in attendance, and many hundreds more ordinary citizens, jostling for standing room.

It was easy to see the realm was divided. Sidonie and I were seated in the first realm of peers to the right of the Queen, as was befitting our status. Those who chose to sit or stand on the right side were allies and supporters. House Montrève, of course. House Shahrizai. Sidonie's personal guard. My old friends Julien Trente and his sister, Colette, now wed to Raul L'Envers y Aragon, who was also there. And too, although he wouldn't meet the Queen's eyes, their father, Lord Amaury Trente. Gerard de Mereliot, representing the Lady of Marsilikos. Marquis Tibault de Toluard, the avid inventor, who maintained a friendship with Joscelin. A number of young peers I didn't know by name.

There were Tsingani and Yeshuites among the throng, too; and adepts of the Night Court, hundreds of them, glittering and lovely. It tugged at my heart for reasons I couldn't explain.

But there were others, too. The left side of the throne hall was nearly as crowded, and there were victims of the Skaldi War among them, sporting grim expressions and black armbands. And, of course, the contingent wouldn't be complete without Duc Barquiel L'Envers, who had long detested me for inexplicable reasons of his own.

At the precise hour, a horologist struck a gong. An impressive silence fell over the hall, broken only by the faint creak of hinges as the great doors at the rear of the hall were closed. A pair of guards opened the doors to the inner throne chamber and Ysandre emerged.

The Queen mounted the dais and stood before the audience, tall and fair, her carriage erect and regal. Sidonie lacked her mother's height, but she had the same carriage. I wondered if Ysandre had the same capability as her daughter for utterly abandoning it in private. Somehow, I didn't think so.

"All rise for her majesty Queen Ysandre de la Courcel!" the herald called.

Those who were seated rose, bowing or curtsying. The packed throngs toward the rear followed suit. Ysandre inclined her head.

"All be seated for her majesty Queen Ysandre de la Courcel!"

We sat.

Ysandre took the throne. She looked tired, shadows under the violet eyes that were nothing like her eldest daughter's. A gold crown with delicate spires sat atop her fair hair. For all that it was finely wrought, it carried a visible weight. I felt an unwanted pang of guilt and sympathy. I couldn't even imagine what Sidonie must feel.

"My lords and ladies, good folk of the realm." The Queen's clear voice carried in the stillness. "Even in the annals of Terre d'Ange, I imagine this is an unwarranted occurrence," she continued more softly. There was an edge of sadness in it. "I daresay it is known why I have called this audience."

There were nods and murmurs all around.

"So." Ysandre gathered herself. "Sidonie de la Courcel, my eldest child and heir, the Dauphine of Terre d'Ange, desires to be united in love with her kinsman, Imriel nó Montrève de la Courcel. Is this still your claim?" she asked Sidonie.

Sidonie rose, according her mother a second curtsy. "It is, your majesty."

"And is it also your stated desire?" Ysandre asked me.

I stood and bowed. "It is, your majesty."

Ysandre nodded. "I am advised by the priesthood of Blessed Elua that your claim is worthy," she said slowly. "And here before those assembled, I swear in Blessed Elua's name that I will not forbid your union."

There were gasps, hisses, and a few quickly stifled cheers.

Ysandre raised her hand. "However." Her voice hardened. "I am advised by many others that this union is a dagger that cuts at the heart of Terre d'Ange. Let me say this." She looked squarely at me. "Imriel de la Courcel has served the thrones of both Terre d'Ange and Alba with honor. I do not accuse him of sedition. But when I look upon the faces of those here assembled . . ." Her gaze drifted over the crowd. "I see a thousand anguished memories of lives lost on the fields of Troyes-le-Mont, memories you children cannot begin to compass. I see fear and suspicion, a canker eating at the heart of the realm. I see old hatreds roused, old wounds bleeding, and the seeds of discord being sown."

There was a genuine ache behind her words, and I did not think she took any pleasure in the fierce nods of agreement from those assembled on the left of the hall. I'd had my differences with Ysandre, but I'd never doubted she loved Terre d'Ange.

"Blessed Elua cared naught for crowns and thrones," she said quietly. "Those words, I am told, were spoken by Melisande Shahrizai."

The mention of my mother's name evoked another hiss.

Ysandre raised her hand for silence a second time. "It is true," she said. "It is also true that Blessed Elua cared naught for the trappings of mortal society, the conventions and rules by which we bind ourselves." She closed her eyes briefly. "*Love as thou wilt.* It suffices unto itself." Opening her eyes, she gazed at Sidonie. "That I grant you, my love," she murmured. "Love as you will. But if you declare him your consort, know that I will not acknowledge it. There will be no legal binding. And if you wed him . . ." The Queen's jaw tightened as she forced the words out, sorrow in every syllable. "If you wed him, I will disinherit you."

In silent acquiescence, Sidonie inclined her head.

"This I swear in Blessed Elua's name before all here assembled." Ysandre's voice sharpened. "Do you hear and acknowledge it?"

"I do, your majesty." Sidonie lifted her chin and gazed at her mother. "Is there aught that might make you recant this vow?"

"Need you ask?" Ysandre said wryly.

Sidonie held her gaze without blinking. "I would hear you say it before all here assembled."

The hall was deathly silent. I felt Ysandre's gaze shift, felt the weight of it fall upon me. Felt the unwanted burden settling on my shoulders.

"Yes," she said gently. "Of course. Twenty-some years ago, on the blood-soaked battlefields of Troyes-le-Mont, Melisande Shahrizai was convicted of treason and sentenced to execution for conspiring with the Skaldi warlord Waldemar Selig to conquer Terre d'Ange. That death, she evaded." Her throat worked. "Imriel de la Courcel, do you find your mother and bring her to justice, I will recant this vow and grant every blessing to your union."

There it was, then.

The burden.

I bowed deeply for a third time, holding it. The silence in the hall persisted. I straightened and met the Queen's eyes. "I hear and acknowledge your words, your majesty."

Ysandre inclined her head. "That is all."

The Queen made her exit through the throne chamber, but it took a long time for the crowd to disperse, mingling excitedly to discuss the news. Sidonie's guardsmen hovered close, mindful of the hostile element, and Joscelin took care to position himself at my side while we waited for the throng to thin. But there were no threats, only a long, bland stare from Barquiel L'Envers that didn't disguise the seething dislike beneath it.

"What in Elua's name is the matter with him?" I muttered.

"A lifetime of plans gone awry." Sidonie watched him. "You missed the last one. He'd hoped to convince Mother that I should wed his youngest son."

"*What?*"

"Oh, yes." She nodded. "To forge a great alliance with Khebbel-im-Akkad. Truth be told, I don't think the Lugal would consider sending one of his heirs to Terre d'Ange for aught less."

"What did your mother say?" I asked.

Sidonie smiled faintly. "She told him he forged a great alliance with Khebbel-im-Akkad when he wed his only daughter to the Khalif's son, and if he thought the realm would stand for her half-Cruithne heir wedding a half-Akkadian prince, he'd lost his wits." She gave me a wry glance. "At least no one questions the purity of your bloodline."

"Generations of incest," Mavros said cheerfully, approaching us with our cousin Roshana beside him. "At least on House Shahrizai's side. Nice to see you're carrying on the tradition."

"I'm glad you're pleased," I said.

In truth, Sidonie and I weren't *all* that closely related. My father had been her great-granduncle, brother of King Ganelon de la Courcel. It made us first cousins, I supposed, but there were two generations between us.

Of course, it was also true that my father had gotten me late in life, embittered by a lifetime of intrigue in La Serenissima, obsessed with the idea of putting a pure-blooded D'Angeline on the throne, and seduced by my mother's wiles. When I was a babe, he and my mother had been part of a plot to assassinate Ysandre. It very nearly worked, too; it would have, had it not been for Phèdre and Joscelin.

Strange to think, if it had worked, I would likely have inherited the throne by now. I would be the King of Terre d'Ange, and Sidonie would never have been born. The thought made me shiver.

Small wonder half the realm mistrusted me.

Sidonie touched my arm. "Let's go somewhere quieter."

I nodded. "I think that would be wise."

The crowds had thinned enough for us to make our way out of the throne hall, escorted by guards and accompanied by a small entourage. We adjourned to one of the smaller salons in the Palace, used for private fêtes. Sidonie looked pale. I would rather have spent this moment alone with her, and I daresay she felt the same, but those who had supported us publicly risked the Queen's displeasure. It would have been ungracious to dismiss them as mere props. I sent one of the Palace understewards to fetch wine and refreshments.

"So . . . are we celebrating?" Julien Trente asked uncertainly after the wine had been poured.

I shrugged. "We're not lamenting."

"What happens now?" Mavros perched on the arm of a couch, swinging one leg. "Do you pack your trunks and head off to La Serenissima to follow your vanished mother's seven-year-old trail?"

"*No.*" Sidonie's voice was fierce. She drank half the contents of her winecup, her color returning. "Not now. Not yet. Not after two years of fear and uncertainty, wondering if Imriel was alive or dead."

"What, then?" Roshana asked mildly.

"My thought is this." I glanced at Phèdre. "I mean to write to the Master of the Straits and beseech his aid. He can search for her in his sea-mirror. If she is anywhere on D'Angeline or Alban soil, he will find her."

Mavros blinked in surprise. "You think he'll do it?"

"Oh, yes." Phèdre answered his question, and well she might. The Master of the Straits, the waters that divided Alba and Terre d'Ange, could cause the waves to rise and lightning to strike at his command. He had also once been a Tsingano lad named Hyacinthe and her dearest friend. Like me, he owed her a debt he could never repay. "I am quite sure of it."

"Do you think she *is*?" Roshana asked.

"It's possible." I smiled wistfully. "Alba, I doubt, but mayhap Terre d'Ange. Of a surety, it would make matters a great deal easier. And if she's not, at least I'll know where *not* to look."

"In time," Sidonie murmured. "Gods, I hate this."

"So do we all, your highness," Mavros said with a rare note of genuine sympathy in his tone. "Believe me, House Shahrizai does not relish its role in your plight."

"Will they support me in this?" I asked him. "You know it means my mother's death."

"Yes," he said without hesitating, and Roshana nodded in agreement. "There may be a few who are uncomfortable with it. It goes against the grain, turning on family. But what she did is unconscionable. Her sentence was just. No one likes it, but no one denies it."

"Our kinsman Marmion Shahrizai *did* turn on her years ago," Roshana reminded him. "And Duc Faragon sent him into exile for it."

"Duc Faragon sent Marmion into exile because he caused the death of his sister Persia," Phèdre said thoughtfully. "Not for trying to bring Melisande to justice." She was silent a moment. She had known my mother very, very well. I tried not to think about that. "You know, I wouldn't put it past her to contact Marmion."

"Seeking vengeance?" I asked.

Phèdre shook her head. "No. He was always terrified she would, of course. But Melisande's too cool-headed for vengeance. That's part of what made her so damnably deadly. If anything, she'd use his guilt and regret to turn him back into an ally." She glanced at Raul L'Envers y Aragon. "Is Marmion still in Aragonia?"

"Oh, yes." Raul nodded. "He's among the King's favorite drinking companions."

"Mayhap your mother will make some discreet inquiries." Phèdre smiled. "Lady Nicola had a certain fondness for him once upon a time."

"My mother is a woman of varied tastes," Raul said diplomatically. "I will ask. I am told that matters are uneasy in Aragonia these days and tongues are wagging in all directions."

"Uneasy?" I asked.

"Carthage," he said briefly. "The Council of Thirty has elected a new general, young and ambitious. There are rumors that he means to move against Aragonia and reclaim it for Carthage." He smiled sardonically. "All the Carthaginian ambassadors deny it, of course, and I am told the King accepts their gifts and believes their smooth lies. But my brother, Serafin, is worried."

"Terre d'Ange stands with Aragonia," Sidonie assured him. "We have not forgotten that when Skaldia invaded, Aragonia came to our aid."

Raul gave her a brief bow. "Aragonia knows no better ally than Terre d'Ange."

I shuddered. "Let's not discuss Carthage further today."

He gave me an apologetic look. "Of course."

It was unreasonable to hold an entire nation to blame for

the actions of two men; nor did I. Still, I could not forget that the men who had abducted me and sold me into slavery were Carthaginian. It is not the sort of thing one ever forgets.

We spoke for a while longer, speculating and planning. Although I'd rather have been elsewhere, alone with Sidonie, there was a comfort in knowing we had friends and allies. And, too, what was said here today would be carried forth as rumor and gossip. Terre d'Ange would know that I was not sitting idle, that foreign dignitaries and the Master of the Straits himself were assisting me.

I hoped Hyacinthe's search would be lengthy.

I hoped against hope that he might find her.

In my heart, I didn't believe he would. But it would buy us time to enjoy this brief respite, Sidonie and I, before the suspicion grew that I was merely biding my time, going through the motions of looking into the mystery with no intention of actually searching for Melisande, let alone bringing her to justice.

When it came to that point . . . ah, Elua.

I knew what had to be done. It was the one secret I'd kept from Sidonie. Not a-purpose, not really. It was the sort of secret that got people killed. Before I wouldn't have dared risk it. We were too young and uncertain. Now it was different. She'd stood up to her mother and defied half the realm for my sake. There could be nothing less than complete honesty between us, dangerous or no. I owed her nothing less.

I would have to tell her about the Unseen Guild.

Four

I told her that night.

I could have waited. Elua knows, I wanted to. We'd won a victory of sorts that day, albeit a bitter one. By the time we retired to her chambers, Sidonie was tired and drained. I wanted nothing more than to hold her in my arms and safeguard her sleep.

Instead, I laid a burden on her.

"Sidonie," I said softly when we were alone together. "There's somewhat I never told you about my time in Tiberium."

She paused in the act of brushing her hair. "Oh?"

I sat cross-legged on her bed, turning the knotted gold ring on my finger. The ring had been her gift, a symbol of the ties that bound us, and of other ties, too. On the night of her seventeenth birthday, I'd lashed her wrists to the bed-posts with a golden cord and tormented her with pleasure until she begged me to take her. I suspected there would be no such love-play tonight. "You know the tale of Anafiel Delaunay?"

"Yes, of course." She frowned. "Why?"

Anafiel Delaunay, born Anafiel de Montrève, had been her grandfather's lover and a poet of some renown. Long before any of us were born, they had studied together in Tiberium. There had been a falling out between them when Prince Rolande's betrothed was killed and Delaunay wrote a satire implicating Rolande's new bride in the death, none of which particularly mattered anymore. What mattered was that Delaunay had sworn an oath to protect Rolande's daughter, the infant Ysandre. And he had kept it, long after Rolande's death in battle.

The Whoremaster of Spies, his detractors called him. Anafiel Delaunay had adopted two children into his household, training them in the arts of covertcy, and later, courtesanship. He was long dead, and so was one of them; two more casualties of my mother's plotting.

The other was Phèdre, who had kept all his promises and more.

I swallowed. "Who taught Anafiel Delaunay the arts of covertcy?"

Sidonie stared at me. "I never thought to wonder."

"Well," I said. "I did. And I found out."

I told her then. The truth, the whole truth, of what had befallen me in Tiberium. How I'd made inquiries. How I'd been seduced by Claudia Fulvia, the wife of a Tiberian senator, seeking to recruit me for a secret organization she called the Unseen Guild. A consortium of spies, reporting to persons in places of power all across the world, capable of influencing great events. They had attempted to recruit Anafiel Delaunay when he was a young man in Tiberium, training him in the arts of covertcy.

In the end, he had refused them.

So had I.

"It was a choice," I said hoarsely. "Swear allegiance, or refuse and keep their secrets."

"And you chose the latter?" Sidonie asked.

"Yes." I took a deep breath. "But there's more. I told you about Canis?"

"The man who took a spear for you in Lucca." Her eyes were dark and unreadable. "The one who said, 'Your mother sends her love' before he died."

"Yes." I told her the whole truth of that tale, too. How Canis, who had seemed only an odd philosopher-beggar, had given me a clay medallion with the image of a lamp on it. How I'd learned in the Temple of Asclepius that there were words etched around the edge in a code invented by a blind healer. *Do no harm.* And how, when at last I'd confronted Claudia Fulvia about it, she had admitted that it meant a member of the Unseen Guild had placed me under their protection.

"Your mother," Sidonie said flatly.

"I think so," I murmured.

Sidonie rose without comment. She went to the balcony doors, gazing out into the summer night, her arms wrapped around herself. She was wearing a dressing-robe of thin, cream-colored silk, so fine I could see the silhouette of her body through it. "Why didn't you tell me this before?"

"Because you didn't want to discuss the issue of finding my vanished mother until we had no choice," I said. "And because you could get killed for knowing it."

She turned. "I'm the heir to Terre d'Ange with a handpicked personal guard, not some fainting flower to be coddled from the world's dangers."

"The Guild employs assassins," I said. "If Canis had been one, he could have killed me in my sleep a half a dozen times."

"Yes, well, you're not particularly careful of your safety." Sidonie studied me. "It's a fanciful tale. Do you believe it?"

"Do you remember the medallion I wore on the Longest Night?" I asked. She nodded. "It was a replica of the one Canis gave me. I wanted to see if anyone at Court recognized it."

"And did they?"

"No." I shook my head. "But the Ephesian ambassador who was visiting did. Diokles Agallon. He offered an exchange of favors. He said if I told him where and how I got it, he might be able to tell me where it originated."

"What did he want in return?" Sidonie asked.

I smiled slightly. "For me to push the Sultan's suit for your hand."

She didn't smile. "I take it you declined."

"Sidonie . . ." I spread my hands. "At that moment, I realized I didn't want anything to do with it. All I wanted was you. All I could *think* about was you. And at the time, no, I hadn't thought so far ahead as to reckon that one day, the price of it would be bringing my mother to justice."

"Does my mother know about this?" she asked.

"No," I said. "Phèdre didn't reckon it worth the risk. Not with so little knowledge. She's the only person I've told, and she's said naught to anyone but Joscelin, and mayhap Hyacinthe. I left the choice to her. She's been trying to learn more."

"Well, I can't *not* tell her, Imriel," Sidonie said. "It's a matter of state. I can't withhold that from her."

"I thought you might feel that way," I said. "Sidonie, listen. I don't know the extent of the Guild's power and influence, but I do know they're real. Enough to be dangerous. Do as you must. Only please, please bid your mother to tread lightly in this matter. I am truly afraid that if she shows her hand, they might act."

She sighed. "Imriel, why does everything in your life have to be so infernally complicated?"

"I don't know," I said humbly. "I wish it wasn't."

"Gods!" Sidonie blew out an exasperated breath, casting her gaze toward the ceiling. "Blessed Elua, if there is some divine purpose in this union, I hope and pray that you will reveal it to me one day."

I kept silent.

"Are you harboring any other secrets?" she asked me.

"No," I murmured. "Not a one. Have I lost your trust?"

"No." Sidonie's mouth quirked. She crossed the room lightly, climbed on the bed, and knelt astride my lap. "No." She took my face in her hands. "May Blessed Elua and his Companions have mercy on me, I do trust you. As I love you, I trust you."

I slid my hands up her warm, silk-covered back. "Promise?"

"Yes." Sidonie kissed me. "I do. Irrationally, maddeningly, utterly."

"Always?" I whispered.

"Always and always." She kissed me again, her tongue darting between my lips, then sat back on her heels to regard me, a complicated mixture of sorrow and love in her dark eyes. "I promise."

On the morrow, Sidonie requested a private audience with her mother. They met for a long time, long enough that my relief was mingled with apprehension. I spent the better part of the day drafting my appeal to the Master of the Straits, trying not to worry.

In the afternoon, one of her guards came to fetch me—Alfonse, the one who'd come before. I hoped he brought word from Sidonie, but I was wrong. "Captain de Monluc wonders if you'd pay him the courtesy of a visit, Prince Imriel," he announced.

"Is aught amiss?" I asked.

He looked surprised. "I don't believe so, your highness. Should there be?"

"No." I shook my head. "And please, call me Imriel."

"Imriel." Alfonse tasted the word, then grinned. "All right."

I'd never been comfortable standing on ceremony. I wasn't raised to be a Prince of the Blood. I'd obey the protocols when I had to, but I preferred to dispense with them whenever possible.

Alfonse led me to the wing of the Palace that housed the barracks of the Dauphine's Guard, which in truth were generous and comfortable. Most members of the Palace Guard came from the ranks of the lesser nobility—younger scions unlikely to inherit lands of their own, hoping to make names for themselves in the service of the throne and earn a reward, or mayhap make a wealthy love-match.

The captain of Sidonie's guard, Claude de Monluc, was one such—although he'd fallen in love with a chambermaid, not an heiress. I knew that much about him and little else, except that he seemed serious and competent, and he'd cared enough for the chambermaid to wed her.

The full complement of the Palace Guard numbered five hundred, but only fifty of them were personally attached to Sidonie's service. That day, it seemed half of them were lounging in the common room of the barracks, tending to their equipment, playing games of chance, drinking and flirting with servants and sundry guests. There was a pause when I entered, the captain's men watching curiously.

"Prince Imriel." Claude de Monluc was seated on a hassock, running a whetstone down the edge of his sword. He rose, sheathed his blade, and gave me an exacting bow. "Thank you for coming, your highness."

I inclined my head. "You're welcome, my lord captain.

Is there some danger I should be aware of? Your men seem sufficiently at ease."

"No." De Monluc hesitated, frowning. He was a tall fellow with blond hair and cool blue eyes, an expression that sought to keep its own counsel. "I thought we should talk, you and I. Will you join me in a tankard of ale?"

I shrugged. "Why not?"

We retired to a quiet corner with a pair of chairs drawn up to an unlit brazier. A barracks attendant brought over a pair of foaming tankards. I hadn't seen them poured. I gazed at the ale, then at de Monluc's face.

"Do you fear poison?" he asked in a dry tone.

"No," I said thoughtfully. "No, you're a man with a sense of honor, albeit a rigid one." I took a healthy drink. "And anyway, 'tis you who mistrusts me."

He gave a short laugh. "I cede the point, your highness."

"I'm not interested in playing games," I said mildly. "And I'd sooner have you call me Imriel."

De Monluc's lips tightened. "You're blunt. Will you give me an honest answer to a blunt query?"

"I might," I said. "It depends on the query." I watched suspicion creep into his expression and rolled my eyes. "Elua's Balls, man! I'll not lie, if that's what you're asking."

A muscle in his cheek twitched. "Do you seek my post?"

"Your post?" Whatever I'd expected, it wasn't this. I stared blankly at him. "The captaincy of the Dauphine's Guard? Why in the world would I want that?"

"Well, the last man to share her highness' bed did," de Monluc observed. "But I reckon you might have reasons of your own." He studied me with his cool, blue gaze. "You've enemies at Court. Taking command of the Dauphine's Guard and creating your own personal army would be a shrewd step. It would afford you a measure of protection."

I returned his gaze. He looked away, taking a sip of ale.

It didn't matter. I could see the aching lines of pain and sorrow beneath the distrust. "You're one of them," I said. "You don't wear the black armband, but you are, aren't you? You lost family at the battle of Troyes-le-Mont."

"It didn't . . ." De Monluc paused. "My father. I was ten."

"I'm sorry," I said quietly.

He was silent a moment. I waited.

"I'm not one of them," he said at length. "Not one to reckon a man should be judged by the deeds of his forebears. I talked to men who served under you in Alba, Urist and some of his fellows. They thought well of you."

"I thought well of them," I said.

Claude de Monluc glanced at me. "So do you want it or no?"

"Are you good at your job?" I asked.

He straightened, stung. "I am. I *earned* this post, my lord, and I am loyal to her highness. These men . . ." He gestured. "They're off duty, your highness. We completed drills this morning. There is no license here, if that's your thought. We know our duty. Any one of us would lay down our lives to protect the Dauphine."

There were shouts of agreement from a few guardsmen within earshot who forgot to pretend they weren't eavesdropping.

"Is he good at his job?" I asked them.

"Too good, my lord," one called amid rumbles of laughter and agreement.

"A strict taskmaster?" I asked. "Willing to share every hardship? Given to painstaking measures of precaution when it comes to the Dauphine's safety?"

"By the seven hells, is he ever!" Alfonse said fervently.

I raised my brows at Claude de Monluc. "Well, then. I have no interest in your post, Captain."

He flushed. "I'm sorry."

"Don't be," I said. "After Maslin de Lombelon's ambitions, and with the gossip surrounding me, I don't blame you for wondering . . ." A thought struck me. "Do you and your men drill on horseback?"

"What?" De Monluc looked startled. "No, only on foot. We're guards, not cavalry."

It was Maslin's name had made me think of it. We had a long history. He had been the second in command of the Dauphine's Guard, and, briefly, Sidonie's lover. After they had quarrelled, he'd set out to find me in Vralia, determined to prove to her that he loved her more than I did. Instead, he'd found out a great deal about himself, including the fact that his feelings for Sidonie were a dubious mixture of yearning, ambition, and idealized romanticism.

And that I, on the other hand, truly did love her.

"You should," I said. "The men who attacked me in Vralia were mounted. Maslin thought he could handle them, but good as he is with a sword, he doesn't fight well in the saddle."

"And yet he saved your life, did he not?" de Monluc asked in confusion. "Or so I heard."

I hadn't said any more than that publicly, reckoning it was true enough in its own way. "He did," I said, lowering my voice. "Of a surety, I would likely have died if he'd not been there. But let us say I had more of a hand in my own salvation than Maslin would have liked." I laughed at the memory. "He told me that he was hoping I'd have to spend the rest of my life knowing I owed every breath I drew to him."

"He said that?" De Monluc stared. "And you think it's funny?"

I shrugged. "In its own way, yes. Anyway, 'tis a serious weakness. What if Sidonie were attacked in the middle of a hunting party or riding from some pleasure jaunt?"

"Do you think there's reason to fear such a thing?" he asked.

"Elua, I hope not!" I shuddered. "Still, people are capable of terrible things, my lord, and I daresay there are a few out there willing to blame Sidonie for the unspeakable sin of falling in love with Melisande Shahrizai's son. Why not take every precaution?"

"You've a point," de Monluc said.

Another thought struck me. "Ask Barquiel L'Envers for assistance," I suggested. "Blessed Elua knows I can't abide the man, but I've always heard he fielded an excellent light cavalry." I laughed again. "Tell him it's because you mistrust my intentions and you want Sidonie's personal guard trained to deal with any possibility. He'll leap at the chance."

"I'll do that." Claude de Monluc drained his ale. "You're not exactly what I expected, Prince Imriel de la Courcel."

"Imriel," I said.

He nodded. "Imriel."

I finished my ale and rose. "I nearly lost my wits when my wife was slain. If anything like that were to happen to Sidonie . . ." It was so awful to contemplate, I couldn't find words. "I don't know." I shook my head. "I couldn't live through it twice. I'd die. And that's really all you need to know about me, my lord de Monluc."

"Claude," he said, rising and putting out his hand.

I clasped it. "My thanks. Let me know what arrangements you make. If you don't mind, I'd like to train with your men, so long as it's not L'Envers himself doing the training. I could use some lessons on fighting in the saddle."

"Of course." He smiled. "Sounds like you managed well enough in Vralia."

I smiled back at him. "Oh, I was on foot."

He stared. "On foot?"

I laughed. "I spent half my life being taught by Joscelin Verreuil. Would you expect aught else?"

"Apparently I did," he said.

I left the encounter feeling better. I didn't expect to earn the loyalty and trust of Sidonie's guard, at least not easily, but I'd settle for a measure of respect, and I thought mayhap I'd won it today from Claude de Monluc. It wasn't his job to protect me and I didn't expect that either, but it would be good to feel confident that if there was a dagger hurtling toward my back, a guard would shout a warning.

And it least it hadn't been a summons to speak with Queen Ysandre for failing to tell her about the Unseen Guild, although it made me uneasy that Sidonie hadn't returned yet. I put the thought out of my head and sat down at her desk to complete my letter to the Master of the Straits.

I was just finishing when she returned. I glanced up, trying to decipher her expression. "Was she angry?"

"No." Sidonie looked bemused. "She knew."

I blinked. "She *knew*?"

"Mm-hmm." She sat on the couch. I dusted my letter to Hyacinthe with sand and went to join her. "Phèdre told her everything before she and Joscelin departed on their mysterious errand." Sidonie glanced at me with a flicker of amusement. "The one we don't want to know about."

"Do *you*?" I asked.

"Gods, no." She rolled her shoulders. "We've got burdens enough, you and I."

I shifted to rub her neck and shoulders. "You were gone a long time."

"We had a good discussion." Her voice was soft and low. "The first in a long time. *I* was angry. She should have trusted me with the knowledge."

I pressed my lips to the nape of her neck, inhaling her scent. "Why didn't she?"

"For many of the same reasons you didn't, so she said." Sidonie sighed. "Because it's dangerous. And because there's no proof and naught to be done about it without stirring the waters. Spies will be spies, she said. We have spies, too, you know."

I blew in her ear. "Oh, do we?"

Sidonie wriggled. "Do you want to talk or . . . ?"

"Both." I let go of her and reclined on the couch, folding my arms behind my head, smiling at her.

"Elua, you're insufferable!" With an agile movement, Sidonie turned and stretched atop me, propping her elbows on my chest and resting her chin on folded hands. "Yes." She gazed down at me. "We have spies, although not so extensive a consortium, and none successful enough to find your cursed mother. But you recall the situation in Carthage that Raul mentioned? Mother is concerned about it. Aragonia has been a loyal ally."

"Carthage," I echoed, shifting my hips so that my phallus, erect and aching in my breeches, pressed against the warm cleft between her gown-clad thighs. "Where an ambitious young general threatens war."

"He's not . . ." Sidonie writhed against me. "At this point, there's no . . ." I unfolded my arms and reached down to grasp her buttocks, pulling hard. She shuddered and narrowed her eyes at me. "Why in the name of all the gods do you find it so perversely arousing to discuss politics while making love?"

"I don't know," I murmured. "But you want me inside you, don't you?"

"Yes," she whispered. "Gods, yes!"

It had been this way between us since the beginning, and neither of us could say why. The desire between us was like an oil-soaked rag, ready to ignite at a single spark. And yet it was more than that, too. We reflected one another, the bright mirror and the dark. Sidonie sat back on her heels, undoing the laces of my breeches. I pushed her skirts up around her hips, tugged her underdrawers down. She took my throbbing phallus in hand, fit me to her slick opening. I pushed.

We fit.

She sank onto me, sighing. I filled her.

"So it was a good talk," I said.

"Yes." Sidonie rocked atop me, her eyelids flickering as I dug my fingernails into her buttocks. "I think . . . I think mayhap the truth of it is she was waiting to see if you would tell me on your own. About your mother and the Unseen Guild."

I jerked my hips upward. "And I did."

"You did," she agreed. "Eventually."

"You were the one who didn't want to face the cost of winning your mother's blessing until we had to," I reminded her.

"True." Her pace quickened. "I need to not talk for a moment."

A moment; many moments. I watched her face transformed with pleasure, alight and incandescent. It never failed to shock and thrill me, how utterly and thoroughly my cool, collected cousin was willing to surrender to complete abandonment. We hadn't even begun to test the limits of it. I watched her ride me to climax, again and again, waiting a long time to join her.

"Mmm." Sidonie collapsed on my chest. "Also a good talk."

I ran a few strands of her hair through my fingers, watching her blurred, black gaze sharpen, coming back from wherever pleasure took her. "Do you suppose it will always be like this between us?"

Her lips curved. "Always?"

I nodded. "Always and always."

Sidonie kissed me. "Gods, I hope so."

Five

The months that followed were among the best of my life. They weren't perfect; Elua knows, nothing ever is. Not in my life, anyway. But this came close.

I'd won the respite I'd prayed for. The Queen had made her pronouncement; the gauntlet had been cast. I had countered. My letter to Hyacinthe was dispatched by courier; the Master of the Straits made a prompt reply. There was a debt of honor between us, he wrote. I had played a crucial part in Phèdre's quest to find the Name of God and free him from his curse. I had ventured into the depths of distant Vralia to avenge his wife's niece. Of course he would search for Melisande in his sea-mirror.

Word was leaked. The adepts of the Night Court were more than happy to comply. Gossip whispered in the bedchambers of the Court of Night-Blooming Flowers made its way to the Palace Court and out into Terre d'Ange. The Master of the Straits himself was aiding my quest.

For now the realm was content to watch and wait.

And I was content to be with Sidonie.

We spent the better portion of our days apart. After their long talk, Ysandre didn't exactly relent, but she thawed considerably. Sidonie had duties, many of them tiresome. Whenever Ysandre was otherwise committed, she stood in her mother's stead, hearing suits brought by foreign dignitaries, the quarrels of members of the noble Houses, the complaints of the citizenry.

She had a good head for it. Although she was young—only nineteen, a year past gaining her majority—Sidonie had spent her entire life learning statecraft. She had an acute memory and the ability to recall in a heartbeat the most obscure detail of any legal or historical precedent she'd ever read—and she had read extensively. Supplicants thinking they stood a better chance of swaying the Queen's young, untried heir were shortly disillusioned.

For my part, I did my best to take on the mantle of responsibility I'd long avoided. I was a peer of the realm, and I had estates I'd neglected all my life. I was a member of Parliament, capable of influencing decisions that had bearing on the whole of Terre d'Ange. I spent a great deal of time simply trying to inform myself. It seemed for every person reluctant to speak with me, there were two others eager to bend my ears in different directions.

Claude de Monluc kept his word, and much to my amused delight, Duc Barquiel L'Envers dispatched the Akkadian-trained captain of his own guard to teach the Dauphine's Guard how to fight in the saddle. Since he didn't know me by sight, I was free to take part, posing as a nameless guard among guards. I spent many hours on the drilling-grounds, learning the niceties of cavalry warfare: how to shoot a short bow from the back of a horse at full gallop, how 'twas better to slash and cut on a forward charge than risk lodging one's blade, how to use one's mount's momentum to best advantage and avoid engagement, when to trust blindly to a rearward thrust.

The Bastard loved it. He had the makings of a good warhorse.

And I was good at it. I daresay I had been for a while; as I'd told Claude, I'd spent half my life being taught by Joscelin. Still, it would always be Joscelin against whom I measured myself, and there was no contest. He was better than me. He always would be. Once I might have cared. I didn't, not anymore.

Heroism be damned. I wanted only to be sure Sidonie was safe.

Later, at Claude's request, I asked Joscelin to teach the Dauphine's Guard a few rudiments of the Cassiline discipline. Not all of it, of course. True Cassiline Brothers begin their training at the age of ten, and for ten years, they do nothing else. Claude's men were skilled swordsmen in the traditional style, and it would have made no sense for them to unlearn everything they already knew to commit to a discipline that would take ten years to master. Still, there were some useful maneuvers that they could add to their repertoire, like the overhead parries for defending against a mounted enemy while on foot.

It was . . . fun.

With the sense of an extended truce in what Sidonie called the Battle of Imriel settling over the Court, a spirit of revelry returned. Drustan mab Necthana arrived later than was his wont. Sidonie and I attended his reception together. After that, daring young nobles began to throw private fêtes, inviting us to attend together. Julien Trente was the first, although I happened to know it was Mavros who put him up to it, reckoning it wouldn't have been seemly for House Shahrizai to be the first to celebrate. But after Julien came Lisette de Blays, who was one of Sidonie's ladies-in-waiting, a pretty young Namarrese noblewoman with an impudent sense of humor.

After that there were others. It became somewhat of a fashion. Sidonie and I weighed the invitations with care, seeking to accept only those that were sincere and genuine, begging off on those who merely sought to create spectacle. In public we were circumspect, even in the midst of frivolity and license.

Betimes it wasn't easy. Whatever the nature of the fire Blessed Elua had lit between us, it continued to burn unabated. It had survived time, distance, enchantment, and grief, and it survived familiarity, too. There was an invisible cord binding us together. In the midst of a crowded room, I always knew where she was. If I closed my eyes and listened hard, I could almost feel her heart beating, drawing mine as inexorably as a lodestone draws iron.

I could make it quicken with a single whispered word in her ear and watch the pulse beat faster in the hollow of her throat. And all it took was one laden glance under her lashes, and my blood ran hot with desire. Still, we never acted on it in the presence of others.

Alone, it was different.

The nights were ours.

After we talked of exploring love's sharper pleasures, I turned to Mavros for counsel. If there is one thing the Shahrizai understand, it is discretion. I trusted Mavros enough to arrange a private Showing for us featuring adepts of Valerian House and Mandrake House engaging in love's sharper pleasures. It was customary to attend the Night Court for such things, but there were other arrangements that could be made, private townhouses with pleasure-chambers.

"Do you really think this is necessary?" Sidonie asked me.

"I do," I said. "For both of us."

"It frightens you," she said softly. "Still."

"A bit." I was honest. "I saw too much darkness in Daršanga. Death sown in the place of life." The mere mention of the place made me swallow, tasting bile and worse. "For a long time, it made me fear my own desires. It's different with you. But I need to be sure this is somewhat you truly wish to explore, because if it's not, if we do and you discover the reality's nothing like the fantasy, and you want naught to do with it . . ." I shook my head. "I promise you, I'll wake screaming in the middle of the night, dreaming of the Mahrkagir. Only it's *my* face he'll be wearing."

"I know." Sidonie took my hand. She was one of only three people I'd ever told the whole truth about what befell me there. "I'll go."

I gazed at her. "It doesn't frighten you at all, does it?"

"No." She smiled a little. "I told you, I trust you."

I squeezed her hand. "That's what frightens me."

Sidonie raised her brows. "Trust *me*, then."

She was right, of course. In the Night Court, there were elaborate contracts spelling out what was or was not permitted during the course of an assignation. That was part of what I wanted her to see and understand. Still, in the end, the essence of the exchange was trust, the surrender and acceptance of it. The more complete the surrender, the more wholehearted the acceptance, the more powerful the exchange.

And that, no mere Showing could teach.

We went, though.

It took place in the townhouse Mavros had rented. It was much like the Showing I had attended with him at Valerian House, only more discreet. The staging area was behind a veil of sheer, transparent silk. It was dimly lit, but the viewing area was completely dark. None of the adepts performing would be able to see who watched them. There were no attendants, only Mavros, serving as the host.

Sidonie and I fumbled our way to one of the reclining couches, trying to hush our laughter. We took our places. I slid my arms around her, resting my chin on her shoulder. I wanted to be able to feel her every reaction.

"You may begin," Mavros called.

We watched.

It was the same, but different, so different! The only other time I'd attended such a Showing, I'd been abominably drunk, wallowing in misery. And even then, it had been good. Now . . . Elua have mercy, it was so much more.

We watched the pair of Valerian adepts enter the staging area and kneel, *abeyante*, heads bowed and hands clasped before them. We watched the Mandrake adepts stride onto the stage. "Strip," one ordered ruthlessly.

The Valerian adepts obeyed.

I felt Sidonie's breathing quicken, her ribcage rising and falling beneath my encircling arms. I could tell by her subtle responses whether or not what she was viewing pleased and aroused her.

Most of the time, it did.

A few times, it didn't.

I took note of everything. It was beautiful; it was all beautiful. These were Naamah's Servants, reveling in their art—and it *was* an art. There was a calculated beauty to the arc of a Mandrake adept's arm as she swung the flogger. There was a pattern to the emerging welts, a rhythm to the gasps and pleas. Every pose struck had its own beauty, its own internal tension. Every order, every plea was part of a ritual. Still, I took note. The blindfold, yes; the gag, mayhap not. The crack of the whip, the slap of the tawse, the smack of the paddle—yes. Even the keen whistle and sharp cut of the cane.

"Really?" I whispered in Sidonie's ear.

"Mmm." There was a smile in her voice. "We'll see."

One of Mandrake's adepts tossed a rose, gave an order. A Valerian adept crawled on all fours, retrieved it in his mouth. He raised his head for approval, lips bleeding from the stem's thorns. His mistress retrieved it, stroked his cheek with the rose's petals. He bowed his head, kissing the tips of her boots. I felt Sidonie's body tense.

"No?" I murmured.

"No." She tilted her head back. "I'll kneel for you, but I won't crawl."

I stroked her hair. "Good to know."

When it was over, after I gave Mavros a purse to present to the adepts as a patron-gift, all three of us shared a cordial in the salon. For the first time, he looked at Sidonie with frank curiosity. She returned his regard with perfect equanimity.

"Did you enjoy the Showing, your highness?" Mavros inquired, studiously polite.

"Very much so, my lord Shahrizai," she replied, echoing his tone exactly. Mavros narrowed his eyes at her, trying to decide if she was teasing him. Sidonie laughed and finished her cordial, then got to her feet. "Yes, Mavros," she said in her own voice, bending down to kiss his cheek. "Thank you for arranging it. I'm glad Imriel has a kinsman he can trust."

"Of course," he said, bemused. "You're welcome."

We didn't act on what we'd seen that night, nor for several nights. I wanted to approach this with a mind clear of other images, and a heart purged of fear. I made offerings at the temples of Blessed Elua and all his Companions. In the Temple of Kushiel, I stood for a long time, simply gazing at the effigy's face. I had come once to offer penance, making expiation for the lives I'd taken in Lucca, for all my dead. I hadn't been there since.

Kushiel's marble arms were crossed on his breast, his

rod and flail held in either hand. His gaze was fixed on the distance, his features stern and calm. There was a trace of sorrow in his marble eyes, hinting at a compassion beyond the mortal compass. I thought about Berlik of the Maghuin Dhonn, whom I had killed in Vralia. He had knelt beneath a barren tree, bowing his head as the snow swirled around us. After I'd killed him, I'd wept.

I hadn't done penance for his death. I didn't think it would be fitting. That one, I was meant to carry.

And I thought, too, about Sidonie. About her strength and determination, and the unexpected desires that accompanied them. About the wondrous gift of her trust, and what I needed to do to be worthy of it. Trusting her, trusting myself. That was the hardest part of all. The thought of engaging in violent play with her thrilled me to the very marrow of my bones, so deep it made me shudder, stirring echoes of my worst fears. It was a dark, surging desire, tinged with cruelty and laced with tenderness.

I wanted it.

Blessed Elua, I wanted it.

And I loved her.

Somehow it made all the difference in the world. There in Kushiel's temple, I gathered up all my fear, took a deep breath, and let it go.

Sidonie knew. We had dined apart that evening. The Queen was entertaining an ambassador from Euskerria, a territory that lay betwixt Aragonia and the south of Terre d'Ange, and she wanted her heir present. The dinner ran late, and I was in her chambers before she returned, thoughtful and talkative.

"Imriel, you spent your childhood in Siovale," she said in absent-minded greeting. "What do you know about . . ." Her voice trailed off as she glanced around the salon. It was ablaze with candles.

"The Euskerri?" I suggested.

Sidonie nodded.

"Not much," I said. "In the south, they were made scapegoats in the same way the Tsingani were, blamed for goat stealing and the like. I daresay there's as much truth to it. Do you want to talk about it now or later?"

Her throat moved as she swallowed. "Later."

"All right." I put down the book I'd been reading. "Take off your clothes."

"Here?" she asked.

"Here." I cocked a brow at her. "The drapes are drawn, Sun Princess. There's no one here. You've ridden me on this very couch. Are you suddenly overcome with modesty?"

"No." Sidonie shook her head. Amber drops hanging from her ears shivered, catching the light. "It's just . . . different."

"Yes," I said. "It is."

I didn't say anything else, only watched her. After a long moment, Sidonie began to disrobe, unlacing the bodice of her gown. Her fingers trembled a little and her breath was beginning to quicken. The air between us felt charged. "What . . . what do you want me to do with this?" she asked, the satin folds of her gown overflowing her arms.

"Put it there." I nodded at the arm of the couch.

Sidonie obeyed. The candlelight gleamed on her bare skin as she returned to the center of the room, naked and vulnerable. I made myself breathe slowly, trying to rein in my desire.

"Kneel," I said. She knelt, neat and composed, her hands folded in her lap. "Clasp your hands behind your neck." She obeyed. The pose arched her back and thrust her breasts outward. I closed my eyes briefly. "Have you chosen a *signale*?"

She shook her head. "No."

"Think about it." I picked up my book. "When I ask, you will tell me."

The silence grew and stretched between us. I glanced up a few times to find her watching me, intent and wondering. Each time, I returned to my book. It was a treatise by a Hellene philosopher on the nature of love. I made myself read the words, but for all I grasped of their meaning, it might as well have been written in Ch'in. The candles burned steadily, wax dripping.

"Imriel." Sidonie's voice sounded small. "I'm bored and my arms are getting tired."

I shot her a hard look. She returned it with a mixture of defiance and uncertainty. I closed my book, marking the page with one finger. "We can put a halt to this here and now."

Her chin rose. "No."

I smiled. "Good girl."

I waited a long time. I could feel her watching me, the cord that bound us together drawn taut. But Sidonie didn't speak again, not even when her arms began to quiver with the strain of keeping them raised, hands clasped as I'd ordered. At last I put down my book and crossed over to crouch before her.

"I love you," I said to her. "You know that I would never harm you."

Sidonie nodded, her eyes grave and unfathomable.

"Go into the bedroom," I said. "There's an item in the bedside cupboard that wasn't there before. Bring it here."

She lowered her arms and rose unsteadily. I caught her elbow. Desire flared at a single touch. I let her go. Sidonie gave me a quick, flickering smile, then went to obey. She returned with a short braided whip, kneeling without asking and laying it at my feet. The black leather shone dully. It was lambskin with a long, soft tassel at the tip. I stooped to pick up the whip, then circled her, letting the tassel trail over her bare skin and watching her shiver.

"What did Amarante tell you about seeking pleasure in haste?" I asked.

Her breasts rose and fell, breath quickening again. "If you rush too quickly through all the pleasures Naamah's arts offer, they will lose their savor."

"Even so." I nodded. "If you're good, once a month, I will add a new item to the cupboard. If you're not . . ." I paused. "I'll take one away."

Sidonie made a sound that might have been acknowledgment or protest.

"I don't want you growing jaded on me, Sun Princess." I gave the whip the slightest flick, the soft tassels snapping against one rosy nipple. It didn't hurt, but it provoked a startled gasp. "I want to keep you sated for a long, long time." I thrust the braided haft of the whip through my belt and crouched in front of her again. "Out there, you belong to the realm and your duty. In here, you're *mine*. Understand?"

Our gazes locked. "Yes."

"Good." One by one, I undid the pins that held her hair coiled atop her head. It fell in a honey-gold cascade over her shoulders. She looked younger and even more vulnerable. "Tell me your *signale*."

Her voice was low, but steady. "Always."

"Always." I laughed softly. "Always and always."

Sidonie nodded, the hint of a smile hovering at the corner of her mouth. There was nothing but trust in her eyes.

I put two fingers beneath her chin, raising it, and kissed her. Her lips parted for my tongue, her body straining toward mine. I wrenched my mouth away with an effort and stood, breathing hard.

"Stand over there," I said roughly, pointing toward a low chair. "Bend over and grasp the arms."

And, ah, gods and goddesses! She did. I stood behind her, my heart hammering in my breast. My mouth was dry with desire, my palms sweating as I clutched the whip. Her loose hair hung about her face in tumbled locks of gold. The tips of her breasts brushed the chair's cushion. I flicked the whip, lightly, lightly. Once, twice, three times. The soft tasseled end kissed her buttocks, light and teasing. Sidonie caught her breath.

The air between us crackled.

"You like that." I drew near and trailed the tassel down the length of her spine, the cleft of her buttocks. I slid one hand between her thighs, fingering her. Gods, she was wet! "Spread your legs. Wider."

She did.

I shuddered, struggling for control. "That's how much you want this." I withdrew my hand, found her mouth, slid my fingers over her lips. She turned her head, sucking obediently. "Isn't it?"

She made a muffled sound of agreement.

It nearly sent me over the edge.

I pulled away. "I'm going to whip you in earnest now," I said, my voice sounding hoarse and strange to my ears. "Until you beg me to stop. And when you do, I'm going to take you where you stand, hard. Understand?"

"Yes," she whispered.

I did.

Elua have mercy, there are no words for such a thing. Sidonie bore it for a long time, longer than I would have expected, legs spread and arms braced, head lowered, shuddering in the throes of violent pleasure. I took it slowly, plying the whip gently, taking it to the edge of pain and backing away, over and over. A flush spread over her creamy skin. I pushed her harder, farther. Over the threshold, into the realm of pain. The whip cracked, laying harsh kisses on her vulnerable flesh. Red welts rose on her flushed skin. I wanted to lave them with my tongue, easing her pain. I wanted to skewer her and split her open.

She began to cry.

She begged.

And I took her as I'd promised—hard. *I* was hard; ah, gods! I'd never been harder in my life. I could barely get my breeches down. Wet, so wet. I pushed into her; I *slammed* into her. I buried myself in her. Her cheek scraped the chair's cushion. Her nails dug into its wooden arms. I felt her flesh convulse around me, over and over. I didn't care. I drove into her, groaning aloud, until I spent myself in one long, excruciating spasm of pleasure, filling her with my seed.

I barely caught her as she sagged, easing her to the carpeted floor. There I held her, panting, waiting for my hammering heart to slow.

"Are you all right?" I asked when I could talk.

"Yes." Sidonie lifted her face toward mine, slowly returning from a faraway place. "I'm fine." She wound a lock of my hair around her fingers and gave it a sharp yank. "A little sore. Very sated. Are you?"

"Yes." I laughed. "Gods, yes."

"Good." She drew a long, shuddering breath, brushing absently at the tear stains on her face. "How odd. I didn't expect to cry. It didn't hurt *that* much."

"It's not about the pain," I said.

"No." She was quiet a moment. "No, it's not, is it?"

"No," I agreed.

Sidonie glanced down at our entangled limbs. "Imriel, are you still wearing your boots?"

I pried them off, kicking off my breeches. "I was in a hurry."

Her quick smile came and went. "So I noticed."

"I love you." I tightened my arms around her. "Elua help me, I love you so much it hurts."

"I know." Sidonie kissed my throat. "I do, too." She shuddered again, a latent tremor of pleasure running through her. "Gods! That's a sharp spice. I'm not sure I'm ready for a steady diet of it."

"Occasional cravings?" I suggested.

"Oh, yes." She gave me a look that set my heart to hammering again. "Definitely."

I slid one arm under her knees and scooped her into my arms, rising and heading for the bedchamber. Sidonie laughed softly, kissing my face, her fingers working at the buttons of my shirt. I hadn't bothered to take that off, either. Her body was naked and warm in my arms, nestled contently against mine. I could have carried her forever, except for the urgent, rising need to be inside her again.

"I thought you were sated," she said.

I tossed her onto the bed. "So did I."

Six

Summer gave way to autumn.

Drustan returned to Alba, where matters were still unsettled in the wake of Dorelei's death. It was uncertain whether or not Sidonie's younger sister, Alais, would wed Talorcan, Drustan's heir.

A lot of things were uncertain.

Aragonia was uncertain, fraught with rumors of a Carthaginian invasion. Euskerria was uncertain, fraught with rumors that the House of Aragon meant to press the Euskerri into battle to defend against a possible Carthaginian incursion, struggling to establish their territory as a sovereign state. Queen Ysandre, trying to negotiate between the two, worried about the succession in Alba, worried about her own recalcitrant heir, was uncertain.

I, on the other hand, had never been more certain in my life.

Ah, Elua! Those were good days and better nights.

Some were gentle and sweet and tender. Others . . . weren't. Together, Sidonie and I embarked on an exploration of the full spectrum of all of the pleasures of Naamah's arts. Neither of us tired of the other. Neither of us could get our fill. For two years, for too long, we'd been parted. Again and again, we made up for lost time.

And again and again, I was filled with amazement and wonder. I'd spent so long fearing my own nature. Now I could scarce remember why. The nightmare of Daršanga was a long, long way away.

Sidonie was fearless, but she wasn't reckless. She didn't hesitate to use her *signale.* The first time it happened, the first time she gasped, "Always!" I found myself responding instantly. I didn't even need to think—the word penetrated the madness of desire, halting me like a brake thrown on a runaway wagon. I soothed her until she caught her breath and told me to continue. Before it happened, I'd been apprehensive. Afterward, it was easier. The threshold had been crossed. Nothing terrible lay on the other side.

I learned to trust myself, even as Sidonie trusted me.

It was such a strange and unlikely thing, this trust between us. We had spent so many childhood years disliking one another. Sidonie had been cool and dismissive, filled with mistrust. It had always galled me.

Things had changed slowly . . . and then all at once. We'd bickered at a fête and I'd pledged loyalty to her on a perverse impulse. She hadn't believed me, but she hadn't entirely disbelieved me, either. Then came the day of the hunting party, when we startled a wild boar and Sidonie's horse had bolted. I'd gone after her, found her thrown. There had been a rustling in the wood. Thinking it was the boar returning, I'd flung myself atop her, seeking to bear the brunt of its tusks.

And everything had changed.

In hindsight, it was a wonderment that I hadn't ravished her then and there, with her willing encouragement. But it was only the beginning of my realization that my infuriatingly composed cousin wasn't at all what she seemed. And I hadn't been anywhere near ready to embrace my own nature. I'd run away from it, reckoning myself damaged goods.

Not anymore.

The scars of the damage were still there. They would always be there. I bore scars, figurative and literal. The faint tracks of old weals, administered by a whip that was never intended to bring pleasure. The puckered scar of a Tatar branding iron that had gotten me thrown in gaol in Vralia, mistaken for a horse-thief.

They were nothing to the scars Berlik's claws had left on me, but they were emblems of a wound that had cut as deep as Dorelei's death. In Tiberium, a Priest of Asclepius had told me to learn to bear them with pride. Even a stunted tree reaches for sunlight, he'd said.

I'd found mine.

And I didn't want to leave her.

Word came from the Master of the Straits. He had completed a search of Alba and found no trace of my mother. He pledged to spend the winter searching every inch of Terre d'Ange for her, gazing into his sea-mirror, and promised a report in the spring. It was a slow process, he wrote, easy to locate someone when one knew where to look, but tedious and exacting when one didn't. We made certain this bit of gossip was disseminated.

I discussed the matter at length with Phèdre, who knew Melisande Shahrizai better than anyone else. When spring came, unless by some miracle Hyacinthe actually found my mother, I would be bound to act.

"You know," Phèdre said with some asperity, "*I* wanted to go after her when she first vanished." She gave Joscelin a sidelong glance. "You refused to allow it. Now her trail's seven years' cold."

"If you'd found her then, how would Imriel prove himself

now?" he asked reasonably. "Mayhap this happened for a reason."

"I refused, too," I reminded her. "I didn't want *her* past dictating our lives anymore. And I certainly wasn't planning on falling in love with Sidonie."

"That still puzzles me a little," Joscelin mused.

I laughed. "You're one to talk."

"True," he agreed.

"Well, we could start in La Serenissima," Phèdre said thoughtfully, ignoring our comments. "They kept her secrets well at the Temple of Asherat, but of a surety, someone there knows. Mayhap they'd be willing to talk after so long."

"We?" I said.

She gave me one of her deep looks. "You didn't suppose we'd let you go alone."

I glanced at Joscelin, uncertain.

"This time she's right," he said. "You came too damnably close to dying in Alba while we were half a world away. I'll not run that risk again."

It made me feel immeasurably better. "So it's a start. What else?"

"Follow the tale," Phèdre said simply. "It's not much, but it's somewhat."

"The Bella Donna," I murmured.

Joscelin rolled his eyes.

My mother had spent almost fourteen years claiming sanctuary in the Temple of Asherat in La Serenissima. In Tiberium, I'd learned that an odd cult of faith had sprung up around her presence there: the Bella Donna, the beautiful woman wrongfully accused, mourning her lost son. It was said that the goddess Asherat-of-the-Sea, herself a grieving mother, had taken pity on her, dissolving the walls of her sanctuary-prison, so that the Bella Donna could go in search of her missing son.

What the tale failed to take into account was that I had in fact been found for some years before my mother vanished. And it wasn't Melisande who had found me and brought me out of darkness, but Phèdre.

My mother *had* sent her, though. That much was true.

"Stories feed on kernels of truth," Phèdre said pragmatically. "There have to have been sightings. And then there's Menekhet."

"Menekhet?" I echoed.

She nodded. "She counted Ptolemy Dikaios an ally. I'll warrant he knows somewhat." Her brows furrowed. "I'll warrant he's a member of your Unseen Guild, too. If ever there was a candidate ripe for covertcy and intrigue, it would be Pharaoh of Menekhet."

"It's not *my* Guild," I said automatically

"What about your senator's wife?" Joscelin asked. "Claudia Fulvia."

I shook my head. "Claudia didn't know anything beyond what she told me. I do believe that much. I daresay her masters didn't trust her with more than she needed to know." I grinned at the memory. "Claudia had her skills, but discretion wasn't among them. I'd reckon the Ephesian ambassador a better wager."

"Diokles Agallon," Phèdre said aloud, remembering.

I shrugged. "He offered a trade of favors. When I refused, he bade me remember his name. He implied that few within the Guild would be willing to make such a trade. And Canis *did* have an Ephesian accent." I frowned. "Or somewhat close to it, at any rate."

"I'd sooner hunt across Caerdicca Unitas than chance your owing favors to the Unseen Guild," Joscelin observed. "From what I've heard of them, it seems an unnecessary risk."

"Would you say the same if it meant leaving Phèdre for months on end?" I asked. "Mayhap years?"

"I . . ." He hesitated. "I don't know."

"Whatever you choose, we will aid you," Phèdre said steadily. "No matter what."

I smiled at her. "My thanks."

I talked about these matters with Sidonie, too. We talked endlessly about all manner of things, and if half our discussions ended up in bed and breathless, we simply picked up the threads of conversation in the morning.

Elua, it was good.

So many things in my life had been *hard.* Since I'd been abducted as a child, life had dealt me blow after blow. I'd borne them. I'd survived. As Urist, the commander of the garrison at Clunderry, had noted when we'd been shipwrecked together, I had a knack for surviving. I'd struggled with guilt, struggled against strange magics, struggled to become a good man. But this . . . this was so blessedly *easy.* It seemed manifestly unfair that I would have to walk away from the best thing in my life.

"You can't let the quest make you bitter," Sidonie said once when we were lying in bed together, talking in love's afterglow about things to come. "Unfair though it is."

"I'm trying," I said.

She smiled. "You're doing well. It's a lot to ask."

I rolled onto my back. "Well, this deed pays for all. After this, no more."

"A lavish wedding, mayhap." Sidonie propped herself on her elbows, gazing at me. "In time, children."

"Children." I ran a lock of her hair through my fingers. "Yours and mine."

The shadow of Dorelei and the son I'd lost lay between us, but Sidonie didn't speak of it. We both knew. Neither of us ever forgot. "It's going to be hard, you know," she said instead. "Your mother."

"I know," I said. "Even with all she's done."

"She's still your mother," she said.

I'd only ever met my blood-mother twice. The first time, I hadn't known who she was. I'd been ignorant of my own heritage, a Sanctuary-raised fosterling, ignorant of my own face. I'd thought she was wonderful.

The second time, I'd known.

That time, I had despised her.

I still did. Since the day Phèdre, Joscelin, and I had ridden out of Drujan and Lord Amaury Trente had greeted me as Prince Imriel de la Courcel, turning my world inside out, I'd lived my life under the poisonous cloud of Melisande Shahrizai's monstrous, unspeakable treason. She had been condemned to death before I was born, before I was even conceived. There was no doubt in my mind that she deserved the sentence, none at all.

And yet . . . she had loved me. I didn't doubt that, either. A few years ago, I'd finally steeled myself to read the letters she'd written me during the long years of her exile in the Temple of Asherat. And I could not forget that the woman I was meant to bring to justice had also been a doting mother, filled with fierce, unexpected love, counting my infant fingers and toes.

I stared at the ceiling. "How do you suppose it will be done?"

"After so long?" Sidonie's voice was gentle. "I imagine she'll be asked to make a confession, then given a choice."

"Poison or the blade?" I asked.

She nodded. "A swift-acting poison."

"And the body displayed," I said dryly.

"Probably." Sidonie didn't flinch. "Imriel, I hate this, too. On some level, I daresay even my mother hates it. You wanted a voice in this choice. If it hurts that badly, if you want me to step down . . ."

"*No.*" I rolled onto my side, grasping her upper arms hard enough to bruise. "No. I want you, all of you, but as you're meant to be." I flexed my fingers, then let go with an effort. "Wife, mother, and Queen, Sidonie. Nothing less."

She brushed a lock of hair from my brow. "'Tis still a high price."

"I'll pay it," I said. "Any price."

We fell to kissing, then, rolling in the tangled bedsheets. Every time I thought my desire was spent, I found it wasn't. This time, this respite, was short and precious. Autumn was tipping toward winter. Come spring, I would be forced to choose a course of action. But not yet, not now. What my mind denied, my body knew. I nudged Sidonie's knees apart, settled between her thighs. I felt her body accepting mine. Sank into her like I was coming home.

Love.

You will find it and lose it, again and again.

No.

"No," I said aloud.

"No?" Sidonie's voice, bemused. Her hips rose to meet mine, nails digging into my buttocks, urging me deeper.

Alais' voice in my memory.

I think she's going to need you very badly one day.

"No," I repeated, saying it to the Priest of Elua who had uttered that long-ago prophecy, saying it to Alais with her dreams and dire forebodings. I shook my head, dispelling all their warnings and fears. "No, no, *no.* I'll do it. I'll pay the price. Only don't leave me."

"Never," Sidonie gasped.

"Stay with me?" I pressed.

"Always." Her back arched; it was a promise, not a *signale. "Always."*

Seven

Life continued apace.

Swift, too damnably swift. The bright blaze of autumn's foliage flared and dimmed. Leaves turned brown and dry, loosed their moorings. In the mornings, the garden where I practiced the Cassiline discipline, telling the hours, sparkled with hoarfrost. The members of Sidonie's guard watching me huddled in woolen cloaks.

It was the one time of day I always had a pair of her guards in attendance, the one time of day I was otherwise alone and isolated. It had been Claude de Monluc's idea, not mine, and Sidonie swore she hadn't asked it of him. If there were any complaints among the guards, I never heard them. I was glad of their presence.

There hadn't been any threats, but there was a lingering uneasiness beneath the truce. During the nights, it was easy to forget. During the days, there were reminders.

One came in the form of a ridiculous suit pushed all the way from the provincial court of Namarre to the Palace Court. I held among the estates of my inheritance the duchy of Barthelme, located in the province of Namarre. The seneschal had reported the suit to me—some incident of a vassal lord, the Baron Le Blanc, claiming I had violated an obscure clause in his charter of tenure that granted him a tithing exemption on Muscat grapes.

As it happened, it was true. The Duc de Barthelme who had signed the charter some three hundred years ago had been possessed of a surpassing fondness for Muscat wine and had waived the customary tithe in favor of an annual keg of the barony's finest. Generations later, an enterprising successor to the duchy had managed to evade the clause in favor of a monetary tithe, and the clause had eventually been forgotten altogether until Jean Le Blanc uncovered it.

According to my seneschal, the matter had been settled in the provincial court. The bailiff's ruling had been favorable to Le Blanc. The records were surveyed assiduously, and Barthelme was assessed a fine for a hundred and eleven years' worth of illegally gathered tithes.

The incident stuck in my mind because it had been a sizable sum, and when I'd told Sidonie, she'd laughed and said it was a good thing she wasn't in love with me for my wealth. I'd given it no more thought until Sidonie brought it up again.

"You remember your old friend Baron le Blanc?" she said one evening. "He's back."

I stared at her. "The fellow with the Muscat? Whatever for?"

We were dining in her chambers. Sidonie shrugged, spearing a piece of roasted capon. "Lost revenues on a hundred and eleven years' of tithes."

"It was a stupid clause," I said.

"It was," she agreed. "But that's not the point. The Namarrese bailiff ruled that since the Barons of Le Blanc collected revenues on a hundred and eleven years' worth of their finest

Muscat in lieu of tithing it, he's no right to complain. Not unless he's prepared to deliver a hundred and eleven kegs of Muscat to you. Now he's demanding a hearing *Ex Solium.*"

Any D'Angeline peer who felt himself wronged by the regional judiciary had a right to demand a hearing from the throne. It was an old law, but one seldom used for frivolous matters.

I raised my brows. "Is Ysandre going to hear it?"

Sidonie shook her head. "I don't know how it passed through the Court of Assizes, but it did. He's hired a persuasive advocate. Even so, they decided it wasn't worth Mother's time, so it landed on my plate. I'm to take the hearing as a representative of the throne."

"A suit brought against me as the Duc de Barthelme," I observed.

"Mm-hmm." She tapped her fork idly against the rim of her plate. "Passing odd, is it not?"

"It is," I agreed. "Will you hear it?"

"Gods, no!" she said fervently. "No, I'm not about to walk into that trap. I pleaded lover's bias in the matter, and threw it back to the Court of Assizes. Let the Chancellor make of it what he will. If Le Blanc persists, his silver-tongued advocate can pitch his suit to my mother and find out how well she enjoys having her time wasted."

I frowned. "It *is* odd, though."

"Yes," Sidonie said. "It is."

Baron Jean Le Blanc never did get his hearing and his suit was withdrawn for reasons that were never made clear. Still, rumor circulated in its wake. My detractors whispered that it was proof that I was exerting undue influence over Sidonie.

It troubled her, and me too, although mostly for her sake. In many ways, we were still coming to know one another as adults. If I'd learned nothing else about Sidonie, I knew for a surety that she had a keen sense of justice and a determined adherence to the rule of law, instilled in her by both parents, amplified by her own sensibilities.

As much as I loathed to mark the passage of time, I was almost glad when the autumn days turned to winter, shortening, and the Longest Night drew nigh.

It was a time of license and sheer revelry, and although it had its roots in a tradition older than the coming of Blessed Elua, it was one D'Angelines had adopted wholeheartedly.

It was sacred.

It was joyous, too.

For me it held a special significance. Three years ago, on the Longest Night, I had kissed Sidonie for the first time. It had all begun in earnest that night. I still shuddered at the memory of her gold-masked face lifting toward mine, our lips meeting. My Sun Princess. The next year, the next Longest Night, I'd passed in Alba. I'd knelt in the snow, keeping Elua's vigil. That was the night Dorelei had finally surmised to whom my heart belonged. The following year . . . that, I'd passed in Vralia, hunting Berlik. I'd no idea when it had fallen, not for sure. It might have been the night I killed him, or it might have fallen afterward.

This would be our first time together, truly together.

"Night and Day," Favrielle nó Eglantine pronounced. "I see no other choice."

"No?" Sidonie asked mildly. "After all, I've already—"

The couturiere's eyes narrowed. "None." Snapping her fingers, she uttered an order to one of her assistants. "Bring the fabric."

It was gorgeous beyond all expectation. One bolt was black velvet, a black so dense it seemed to absorb light. The other was silk. It was a pale gold hue, almost white, like the radiance of the sun at high noon; but to describe it thus does it no justice. It flowed like liquid sunlight, shimmering with its own inner brilliance. Favrielle handled it with reverence.

"I discovered this in the stores of Eglantine House when I was fourteen," she said. "No one ever dared use it. When I first had my own salon, I nearly beggared myself to buy it." She smiled wryly. "And then *I* never dared use it."

"It's beautiful," I said sincerely.

Favrielle held up a length. "It is the *essence* of daylight itself." She sniffed. "Not some tawdry cloth-of-gold." She shot a challenging glance at Sidonie, who hid a smile.

"It's remarkable," Sidonie said. "Truly."

"I thought, mayhap, one day Joscelin Verreuil would consent to attend the Queen's fête with Phèdre instead of keeping Elua's vigil," Favrielle mused. "I would have done it for them. But you'll do, the two of you."

I kissed her cheek. "Thank you, Favrielle."

She glowered at me. "Go away, now."

The days grew short; the nights grew long. In the salon of Favrielle nó Eglantine, seamstresses sewed feverishly. Our costumes took shape.

Night and Day.

Our fittings were held separately. I didn't see Sidonie's costume until the Longest Night. Mine was exquisitely simple: breeches and a doublet of unadorned black velvet, flat and fathomless. One of Favrielle's endlessly patient assistants spent hours brushing my hair and tying hundreds of tiny crystal beads into it. When she was done, it fell over my shoulders like a cloak of the night sky itself.

"Perfection," she said, tying my mask in place. It was a simple domino of muted silver, a crescent moon rising like horns on my brow.

When at last I saw Sidonie, it took my breath away. I'd dressed in my own quarters. Her guards came to fetch me that we might enter the ballroom together. All I could do was stare at her.

It was simple, too—and subtle, infinitely more subtle than the Sun Princess costume. The pale silk glowed with soft luminosity, unadorned, clinging to the curves of her body in a way that made my mouth go dry. She wore long gloves of the same white-gold fabric, but her creamy shoulders and the length of her back were bare. Her golden hair was coiled in an artful coronet, a radiating sunburst affixed to the back of her head. Behind the softly gilded domino, her eyes looked like pools of night.

"Do you like it?" Sidonie asked.

"You look so beautiful it hurts," I said truthfully.

She smiled. "So do you."

It should have been a perfect night.

It wasn't.

For a long time, it promised to be. There was a little hush when Sidonie and I made our entrance, but it passed. This was the Longest Night, a time for joy and revelry. We had a good many friends and supporters amid the throng, and even Ysandre managed to greet us with considerable aplomb. Phèdre was there, of course, escorted by Ti-Philippe.

"Elua!" she breathed. "So *that's* what Favrielle's been hiding."

I laughed. "She said she would have used it for you and Joscelin if he'd ever consented to attend."

"No." Phèdre shook her head. "No, it's perfect for you. Both of you." She kissed me lightly, smiled at Sidonie. "You look splendid together."

We drank *joie*, danced and mingled with friends, sat at the laden table and dined together. As the hour of midnight drew nigh, the usual sense of anticipation mounted. There were no surprises this year. The horologist called the hour, and the great hall was plunged into darkness. The Winter

Queen hobbled out of her false crag, leaning on a blackthorn staff. The Sun Prince entered in his chariot to a drumroll and resounding cheers, pointing his spear at her and restoring her to youth. The oil-soaked wicks were lit, light returning in a sudden blaze.

Sidonie released her breath in a sigh. "I never tire of the spectacle."

"Neither do I." I touched her cheek. "You *are* my sunlight, Sidonie. The sun in my sky and the moon in my heavens. All that's bright and good in my life." I smiled. "And a little bit that's dark, too."

"You're uncommonly sentimental," she observed.

"I'm uncommonly happy." I spread my arms. "And a little bit drunk."

She laughed and caught my hand. "Dance with me."

Catching sight of us returning to the dance floor, one of the musicians grinned and gestured to his fellows. They switched smoothly into a slow, romantic melody. As we danced, I thought about all the Longest Nights I had known. I thought about the fact that a year ago, I'd been in Vralia. I thought about all the times I had danced with Sidonie. The first time, it had been on the Longest Night, too. That was when we'd bickered and I'd given her my oath on impulse.

It seemed impossible now, remembering how formal and careful we had been with one another. Sidonie had held me at a distance. I'd scarce touched her. Later, after we'd become lovers, we'd struggled to recapture that sense of cool formality. At the fête for her seventeenth birthday, we'd tripped over one another's feet, absurdly awkward in our efforts to disguise how well our bodies knew one another, how well we moved together. It made me laugh aloud to remember it.

"What's funny?" Sidonie asked.

"Nothing." I whirled her. "Only that I love you."

She smiled. "Oh, that. 'Tis enough to make the gods laugh."

Now it was the Longest Night, and it was a simple, blessed pleasure to hold her in my arms with no barriers between us—no mistrust, no awkwardness, no pretense. The music swooped and swirled in long, poignant arcs. We danced effortlessly. Tomorrow the world of politics and its burdens would be awaiting us. Tonight there was only music and *joie*.

And us.

The song ended, and another began. We stood without moving; night and day, reflecting one another. Sidonie gazed up at me. " 'The lover showers kisses on the face of the beloved' ," she quoted softly from the *Trois Milles Joies*.

" 'Like petals falling in a summer rain' ," I finished, kissing her.

"*Whore!*"

The epithet was harsh and shocking. A violin screeched to a halt. A very drunken lord costumed as a Tiberian imperator staggered onto the dance floor, his purple-edged robes disheveled, a laurel wreath askew on his dark hair.

"Whore!" he repeated, spitting the word at Sidonie. "You robbed me for his sake. Everyone knows."

Sidonie's guards were trying to push through the throng, but everyone on the dance floor was pressed tight around us, eagerly watching the spectacle. I edged my body in front of her. "Who in the hell *are* you, man?"

"Your *neighbor*," he spat. "Your *vassal*, my greedy, treasonous, pandering liege!" He waved a flask, his tone turning bitterly sardonic. "Care for a swig of Muscat?"

"Jean Le Blanc?" I asked.

"Everyone knows!" He pointed at Sidonie, swaying. "You. You wouldn't even hear my suit. Everyone knows. Walking around all day, looking like butter wouldn't melt in your mouth. Spreading your legs for that traitor-spawn, rutting like an animal all night. Your guards talk. They laugh. Everyone knows."

"That is a cursed lie!" Claude de Monluc squeezed through the crowd, his hand on his sword-hilt, his face flushed with fury. "Your guards don't talk, my lady," he said to Sidonie. "And they certainly don't laugh."

Jean Le Blanc sneered. "Don't deny the rutting, do you?"

"No one denies the rutting, my lord." Sidonie's voice was cool and remarkably calm. "That's why I refused to hear your suit. Apparently your advocate chose not to waste my mother's time with it." She studied him. "Did someone suggest otherwise to you?"

He looked away, uncertain.

I followed his gaze and saw Barquiel L'Envers grinning. He caught my eye and gave me a mocking salute. "Oh, Elua and his Companions have mercy on me!" I said in disgust. "Is this what you've been reduced to, L'Envers?"

"He said . . ." Le Blanc swayed. "His advocate said . . ."

"Listen to me, you thrice-cursed idiot." I grabbed a handful of his white robe and shook him. "He put you up to this, didn't he? Pushing your suit after it had been settled fairly. Lending you his advocate. Why?" I tightened my grip. "More of my damned mother's legacy?"

Le Blanc had turned pale, but he found a measure of his dignity. "It's not old history. Not to some of us. I fought at Troyes-le-Mont, but I couldn't protect my own family." His mouth worked. "My wife . . . my wife was raped. Many times. She killed herself."

I let go of him. "I'm sorry."

"No, you're *not*!" he said in anguish. "Dancing and laughing and kissing—"

"And rutting," Sidonie murmured.

His hands tightened into fists. "Don't," I said to her. "My lord, believe me, I'm sorrier than you know, but we have no quarrel here. You were urged to bring a foolish suit and misled about its outcome." I pointed at L'Envers. "He took your grief and turned it to his own purposes for what amounts to little more than a childish prank. So tell me, my lord, where your anger lies."

"I don't know," he mumbled.

"You're drunk," Claude de Monluc said crisply. "Drunk, and a disgrace to the Court. Her highness has acted correctly in all legal matters, which is all that need concern you. You may apologize and leave."

"I can't." Le Blanc glanced at Sidonie. "I just . . . can't."

He left, though, miserable and stumbling, a pathetic figure. No one accompanied him, least of all his patron L'Envers. I felt sick at heart.

"*Uncle.*" Queen Ysandre's voice sliced through the crowd, filled with rare fury. Her guards cleared the throng. Glittering in wintry white, her mask discarded, she confronted L'Envers. "You go too far," she said grimly. "Urging that poor man to profane the Longest Night."

"Ysandre . . ." he said in a placating tone, gesturing at Sidonie and me. "They flaunt—"

"*I don't care!*" Color rioted on her cheekbones. "They're in love. I don't like it; you don't like it. No one likes it, except mayhap the Night Court and folk too young to remember. But Name of Elua! It's the Longest Night, and I *will* have peace in my Court. Since you've broken it, you may take your leave."

If it was a contest of wills, L'Envers lost. He bowed stiffly and departed.

"Thank you," Sidonie said quietly to her mother.

"Don't." Ysandre rounded on her. "Just . . ." She drew a

sharp breath, her violet gaze settling on me. "Find her," she said simply. "I'm willing to place resources at your disposal once you do. Whatever it takes to bring Melisande Shahrizai to justice, I will provide. Bribery, diplomacy, force of arms. Only *find her*, Imriel."

"I will," I promised.

Eight

Winter's grip on the land began to ease.

I wrote to Diokles Agallon, the Ephesian ambassador, a member of the Unseen Guild.

It was a calculated risk. I was circumspect in what I wrote. I promised nothing; I didn't dare, not knowing what he might ask. I didn't mention my mother by name. I alluded to our conversation in roundabout terms. I implied that if he had learned aught of the origins of a certain medallion, I might be willing to ply whatever influence I wielded in exchange for the knowledge.

Might.

I made no promises.

"You did make one promise," Sidonie reminded me, dark eyes grave. "You promised Alais a puppy come spring."

I winced. "I'd forgotten."

She kissed me. "She's like to forgive you. She's got larger matters to consider."

Of a surety, that was true. Unlike Sidonie, I'd always regarded Alais as a sister, a true sister. And although she was young, she was older now than Sidonie had been when first I'd begun to fall in love with her. Alais was still affianced to her own cousin in Alba, Drustan's nephew, Talorcan. The wedding had been postponed a number of times.

Everything had been so certain once.

The lines of succession in Alba were matrilineal. Terre d'Ange had feared losing its foothold. That was why Ysandre and Drustan had pressed me to wed Dorelei, Talorcan's sister. Our son would have been his heir.

Our son, the monster.

Now Alais was pressing for change. She was willing to wed Talorcan . . . but she wanted assurance that their children would inherit.

"I don't blame her," Sidonie said. "'Tis a rule based on men's mistrust of women and fear of being cuckolded. I daresay there are any number of Alban women who would support her in this, and a few men, too, when you come to it."

"Drustan's thoughts changed after he became a father, didn't they?" I asked.

She nodded. "He can't do it, though. It's tied too closely to Maelcon the Usurper's revolt."

It was yet another event that had happened long before we were born. The old Cruarch's son, Maelcon, had seized the throne and overturned the old traditions of succession. Drustan, the Cruarch's nephew and heir, had fled into exile among the Dalriada. In time, with the aid of the Dalriada—not to mention Phèdre and Joscelin—Drustan had raised an army of his own and taken the throne back. He had restored the matrilineal lines. There would be a fearful outcry against the hypocrisy if he overturned them now.

"Gods." I groaned. "I know it's not old history to those who lived it, but I get infernally tired of having our lives shackled to the past."

"I know," Sidonie said with sympathy. "Believe me, I do.

But it won't be forever, or at least not all of it. Mayhap the Ephesian ambassador will have a swift reply at a cost we're willing to bear."

"Mayhap," I said. "Claudia said there were factions within the Guild, and I got the sense Agallon was no ally of my mother's. If he had been, he would have known the medallion's origin and dangled it before me as a surety, not a possibility. I pray he can discover it, and I pray he's willing and eager to betray her, because that's exactly what we need."

It had been one of the factors, a big one, in my decision to contact Diokles Agallon. Ysandre had made her decree in a public forum, heard and acknowledged. By now, all of Terre d'Ange knew, and gossip had doubtless spread beyond our borders. There was simply no way my mother was unaware of it. And while I had come to believe that she did indeed love me in her own way, I didn't think she was likely to wait patiently for me to find her and fetch her back to Terre d'Ange to be executed, a notion that made me queasy when I contemplated it.

No, if I tried to trace her trail, years old, amid a tangled maze of allies and enemies, Melisande would know. She would know my next step before I took it. It would be child's play for her to stay a step ahead of me.

Taking her by surprise was our best chance. And even at that, even if Agallon *did* betray her, even with Ysandre's promise of aid, I didn't expect it to be easy.

The decision came at a price, though. Seeking to bargain with the Guildsman might have been the most expedient course with the best chance of success, but no one could know of it. Sidonie told her mother; Ysandre extracted a promise that I'd not grant any favors without her consent. And I told Phèdre and Joscelin, of course. Beyond that, we didn't dare tear away the Unseen Guild's veil of secrecy.

I had been allowed to walk away from the Guild, but there was a price for that, too. Silence. Claudia Fulvia had been clear; if I revealed the Guild's existence and what little I knew of the extent of their vast web, my life—or worse, the lives of my loved ones—was forfeit.

Spies will be spies, Ysandre had said; but I'd seen a measure of their influence in Tiberium. When it suited their purposes, the Guild had provoked a dangerous riot. I remembered Claudia, careless and dismissive. *Starting a riot's one of the easiest things in the world.* Even with her warning, I'd gotten caught in it and nearly died. Of course, that was because Bernadette de Trevalion had hired a man to kill me to avenge the death of her brother Baudoin, whom my mother had betrayed—yet another delightful piece of Melisande Shahrizai's legacy—but it would have been terrifying anyway.

And my comrade Gilot, who had served House Montrève since I was a boy, *had* died. Not that night, not then and there, but it was the injuries he sustained in the riot that killed him in the end.

So we kept our silence.

And people began to wonder at my lack of action.

Spring blossomed. A letter came from the Master of the Straits. Hyacinthe wrote with regret that he had found no trace of my mother anywhere on D'Angeline soil. Wherever she was, it was beyond the limits of the gaze of his sea-mirror, which could not see past the lands bounded by the Straits. This news, we did not divulge.

But people began to wonder.

Of her own initiative, Phèdre elected to write once more to old acquaintances and allies among the Stregazza in La Serenissima, pressing them to make one last inquiry into Melisande's disappearance from the Temple of Asherat there. As a stopgap measure, it wasn't much, but at least it might serve to provide a viable explanation for any information we *did* learn without compromising the Guild's secrecy.

Sidonie's birthday came and passed; mine fell a few weeks later. The celebrations were muted. After the ugliness of the Longest Night, we'd fallen back into the habit of being circumspect in public. Jean Le Blanc hadn't been entirely misled. There *were* a couple members of the Dauphine's Guard who had been indiscreet, gossiping about what they suspected went on in the bedchamber when they were posted outside her quarters. Claude de Monluc had been furious, had wanted to dismiss them altogether. Sidonie, cool-headed and pragmatic, had refused.

"Gossip's not a crime," she observed.

"Lack of loyalty is," de Monluc said in a grim tone.

"There's no shame in aught done in love," Sidonie said, unperturbed. "And no sin in gossiping about it. But matters are tense and I'd sooner be served by men with sense enough not to throw oil on fire. Let them serve in the regular Palace Guard. Give them my thanks and a generous purse. Make the same offer to any who want it."

Claude obeyed her order.

There were three men who took it; there were thirty who applied for their posts. Young men, mostly, half in love with the notion of our star-crossed romance. They doted on Sidonie, which startled her a bit.

"No one's ever *doted* on me before," she mused.

"You've never defied half the realm for the sake of love before," I said. "And I think they're beginning to suspect you don't exactly have ice water running in your veins."

She laughed. "True."

The nights . . . Elua, the nights were still wonderful. Knowledge that our time was beginning to dwindle lent a constant sense of urgency. Still, I could feel the tensions at Court rising.

There were moments of respite. In an effort to keep at least half my promise to Alais, I went to Montrève to choose a puppy for her from that spring's litter. Long ago, I'd given her one of Montrève's wolfhounds. Alais and the dog had been inseparable, but the dog had been killed at Clunderry, torn open by a swipe of the bear-witch Berlik's claws.

Sidonie accompanied me, her mother reckoning that having the both of us out of sight for a few weeks might help reduce the sense of unease.

It was strange and wondrous having her there. We rode together, exploring the places I'd loved as a child. I took her to the spring-fed pond hidden in the mountains. I told her about how my cousin Roshana had sought to teach Katherine Friote, the seneschal's daughter, and me a Kusheline game of courtship, teasing with a quirt of braided grasses. How I'd been unable to bring myself to do it.

"Show me," Sidonie said, eyes sparkling.

I did.

There in the meadow, I plaited long stalks of grass. I stroked her soft skin and bade her to keep still and quiet, rewarding her with kisses when she obeyed, punishing her with the quirt when she didn't. The memory stirred all that old, aching adolescent yearning, banishing the fear that had accompanied it. I ended up tumbling her there in the meadow, the sun warm on my naked back, the sweet scent of bruised grass rising all around us.

We rode home adorned with wreaths of flowering bindweed vine, butterflies trailing in our wake, members of the Dauphine's Guard following at a discreet distance. At times like that, it almost seemed it would be worthwhile to give up the quest in favor of a flawed joy. To allow Sidonie to step down, to return to the City of Elua and say to Ysandre, *Forgive me. It's too hard, too much to ask.*

We didn't, though.

Instead, we chose a puppy; or I did, in consultation with old Artus Labbé, the kennel master, who would see to the pup's training. We spent time with Phèdre and Joscelin, who had elected to accompany us. There at Montrève, with no duties to attend to, no constant presence of judging eyes, Sidonie was more at ease. I saw them begin to see her as I did. Not so much Phèdre—Elua knows, there wasn't much hidden from her—but Joscelin.

One night, after much pleading on my part, he reenacted a famous performance from the time he had been disguised as a travelling Mendacant with Phèdre and Hyacinthe. He hadn't done it since I was a boy. We all laughed until we wept. And when we had done, I prevailed on Sidonie to re-create an imagined scene from the youthful courtship of Ysandre and Drustan, somewhat she and Alais had concocted between them as children.

It was wickedly funny—Sidonie had a knack for mimicry. She emulated her mother at her coolest, uttering declarations of undying passion and high-minded romance in a crisp, exacting tone, until even Joscelin was wiping his eyes.

"I think I begin to understand," he said to me that night.

"You ought to," Phèdre said in her mild way. "When all's said and done, she's a bit like *you*, love."

It was true, although I'd never thought on it. Sidonie's habitual composure was as much a part of her as Joscelin's Cassiline discipline. When it was laid aside, it could be an unexpectedly delightful thing. And yet she was a bit like Phèdre, too. Not an *anguissette*, no. I don't think I could have borne it. But she was fearless in her desires, and utterly unapologetic.

Gods, those were good times.

When we returned to the City of Elua, there was another glad surprise awaiting us. Amarante of Namarre, who had served as a lady-in-waiting, among other things, to Sidonie for a number of years, had returned to take service in the Temple of Naamah.

Her mother was a priestess and the head of Naamah's Order. During the year she had been gone, Amarante had been fulfilling her own final duties before taking her vows. She had spent a year wandering Terre d'Ange, serving Naamah. Now she was back, and a priestess in her own right.

Mavros threw a fête in her honor, staging it to accord with our return.

He had long maintained an obsession with Amarante, which I knew. I do believe he genuinely liked her. I also knew that he had sought her out once her term of Naamah's Service had begun. What had passed between them, no one knew for certain. I knew what Amarante had predicted, because Sidonie had told me.

It won't be what he wants, Amarante had said. *But it will leave him wanting more.*

More than that, Sidonie hadn't cared to know.

It was the first time I found myself jealous; and to my surprise, there was a certain smoldering pleasure in it. I'd known about Amarante for a long time. In some ways, her claim superseded mine; she had been recruited to instruct Sidonie in Naamah's arts. And she had done a damnably good job of it. Still, it stung to see Sidonie's eyes sparkle for someone else, even if that someone had shining hair the color of apricots, apple-green eyes, and plump lips for kissing.

"I've missed you," Sidonie murmured.

"Oh?" There was a teasing undertone to Amarante's reply, although it was uttered with her usual unearthly calm, which had only deepened during her absence. "I'd hardly thought you'd have time."

Sidonie laughed, and said somewhat too low for anyone else to hear.

Amarante glanced at me, lips curving. "If it's what you want, of course."

Mavros punched me hard in the shoulder. "I hate you," he said cordially. "Only know that, cousin. I hate you with the blistering heat of a thousand fiery suns."

The three of us passed the night together; and it was a night impossible to describe, except to say that it was surpassingly beautiful, and when it was over, there was no jealousy left in me. Priests and Priestesses of Naamah are trained in the same arts of pleasure as adepts of the Night Court, but the year of Service they undertake differs. Afterward, they are free to choose patrons or lovers at will. When Naamah stayed beside Blessed Elua during his wanderings, she gave herself to strangers that he might eat, to the King of Persis that he might be freed. During their year of wandering, Naamah's acolytes are forbidden to refuse anyone who seeks them out of true longing, that they might better comprehend the sacrifice of the goddess who lay with mortals.

And in turn, Naamah graced them with desire.

I could feel her presence lingering over Amarante like a touch, a claim, and a blessing at once. A mantle of grace lay over us that night: love, desire, and selflessness all intertwined. There were no violent pleasures, only tender ones, but I learned somewhat of myself. I learned I was capable of sharing and being shared, of holding fast and letting go all at once. And I realized I was surpassingly grateful that Amarante *had* returned, albeit altered. She had long been Sidonie's closest confidante, her safe harbor. I was glad she would be here while I was gone.

In the morning, Sidonie was thoughtful. "I knew it was time to send you to Naamah," she said to Amarante. "I didn't know she would keep so much of you for herself."

Their eyes met in a manner born of long familiarity, and

Amarante smiled. "I held a little back. I'll always be there when you need me."

"Soon, I hope," I said.

She didn't mistake my meaning. "There's no word of your mother yet?"

I shook my head. "We're waiting on word from La Serenissima."

"I hope it comes soon," Amarante said quietly.

It did, although it didn't come from La Serenissima.

It came only a few days later, in the midst of sufficient uproar at Court that it easily passed unnoticed. If tensions in Terre d'Ange were internal and simmering, they were external and rising to a boil elsewhere in the world. Alba's future remained unsettled. Queen Ysandre had been unable to broker any lasting peace between Aragonia and the Euskerri, and now fighting had broken out between them in the mountains south of Siovale. Delegates from both nations were beleaguering her—the Aragonians begging her to honor her alliance and stay out of the matter, the Euskerri begging for acknowledgment of their sovereign rights—and the Siovalese lords worried that the fighting would spill across the border.

In the midst of *that* came the news that a sizable delegation from General Astegal of Carthage—who had thus far done not the slightest thing to justify the rampant unease his appointment had provoked—was lying off the shores of Marsilikos, begging leave to sail up the Aviline River and pay tribute to Queen Ysandre.

And I got a letter.

To all appearances, it was a love-missive, written in a feminine hand, tied with ribbon and scented with perfume. It was delivered to the barracks of the Dauphine's Guard.

It wasn't the first of its kind. We'd both gotten them; it was a popular pastime at Court. This one was unsigned. It contained an innocuous love poem written on thick vellum . . . but there was a series of subtle notches and lines etched along the edges of the vellum. I fingered them, thinking back on the day in the Temple of Asclepius when the priest had taken my hand and shown me similar notches etched in a clay medallion.

"Who delivered this?" I asked.

Claude de Monluc shrugged. "Some Tsingano lad. He said a lady in Night's Doorstep paid him." He grinned. "Not intrigued, are you?"

"Gods, no!" I laughed and showed him the letter. "It's not signed, that's all. One never knows if it's a prank."

"Like as not it's just another high-spirited young noblewoman," he suggested. "Drunk enough to take a dare, sober enough to realize she'd regret it in the morning."

"Like as not," I agreed.

Since Sidonie was in conference with her mother, I went straightaway to the townhouse. Phèdre and Joscelin were still in Montrève, but Eugènie admitted me to Phèdre's study without question. I knew Phèdre had found a reference for the blind priest's system of notation, but it took me forever to locate the moldering old Hellene medical tome in which she'd found it. Doubtless Phèdre could have laid her hand on it in a heartbeat, but she wasn't the most organized archivist in the world.

Once I finally did, I laid it open on her desk, studied the maddeningly intricate chart of slashes and crosshatches it contained, and set about transcribing the message.

It was painstaking work and I daresay I made a few errors, but eventually the gist of it came clear.

I do not hold the answer you seek, but one of Carthage does. If the Queen receives their tribute, he will tell you.

"Carthage," I muttered. "It *had* to be Carthage."

Giving Eugènie my thanks and a fond embrace, I took the letter, the transcription, and the musty old Hellene volume, stowed them in my bags and headed for Night's Doorstep, where the portly Emile presided over a tavern called the Cockerel. He was a Tsingano half-breed who had been one of Hyacinthe's boon companions many years ago, and he was unfailingly loyal to House Montrève.

"I need a quiet word," I said to him.

"For you, my *gadjo* pearl?" He clapped my back. "Anything."

Emile listened while I told him I'd received a mysterious love letter delivered by a Tsingano lad, that I wanted to talk to the boy and learn what he could tell me of the woman who'd given it to him. And that I wanted it done in secrecy.

"I will find out." Emile studied me with disapproval. "Already you philander?"

"No!" I shook my head. "But I fear mayhap it's a plot to make her highness believe otherwise."

"Ah." The lines of reproach smoothed from his fleshy face. Emile laid a finger alongside his nose. "Like the other time, eh? Do not fear. The Tsingani will always keep your secrets and seek to ferret out the secrets of those who would harm Phèdre nó Delaunay's son. We do not forget who freed Hyacinthe from his curse."

"There's another matter," I said. "Can you find someone discreet to ride to Montrève and fetch Phèdre and Joscelin?" Emile hesitated, and I fumbled for my purse, setting it on the table. "For a generous fee, of course."

The purse vanished. "Of course I would do it for free." Emile smiled broadly. "But all things are possible for a fee, *chavo*."

"My thanks," I said, rising.

Strange but true, I trusted the Tsingani more than I

trusted most of my peers. Most D'Angelines held them in a measure of suspicion, although it is better now, I am told, than before I was born. In fairness, the Tsingani did take a certain delight in bilking outsiders whenever possible, but they could be fiercely loyal friends. Of a surety, they'd been that to Phèdre—and to me. It was a Tsingani *kumpania* that had reported seeing Carthaginian slavers with D'Angeline children in tow long, long ago. If not for that, I would have been dead years ago.

I rode back to the Palace and awaited Sidonie.

When at last she entered her quarters, she took one look at my face and stopped dead. "What is it?"

I showed her the letter. "Word's come."

Nine

Ysandre took the news better than I would have reckoned.

We met in private, just the three of us. She glanced briefly at the text of the letter itself, then examined the vellum edges, lingering over my transcription and checking it against the chart in the Hellene book. At length, her fair brows rose.

"That's it?" she asked. "I accept Carthage's tribute, and some mysterious agent of the Guild will divulge Melisande's whereabouts?"

"So it seems," I said.

"It's not much of a favor to ask," she observed.

"I know." I spread my hands. "Your majesty, I can't say why the Ephesian ambassador would ask such a thing in such a covert manner."

Ysandre leveled a hard gaze at me. "Give me your best guess."

"I don't *know*!" I said in frustration.

"A favor may be transferred if all parties are in agreement," Sidonie said pragmatically. "I imagine the Guild must deal in such currency. For some reason, Diokles Agallon has transferred his favor to Carthage. He seeks to align himself with their interests, which, at the moment, appear to be courting your favor."

Ysandre tapped the vellum, her face thoughtful. "He's wary, though."

"He is," Sidonie agreed. "Carthage is poised to make a gambit. If it succeeds, and the axes of power shift in their favor, well and good. If it fails, he may yet distance himself—and Ephesium—from it."

I felt hopelessly over my head. "What gambit?"

"Therein lies the question," Ysandre said in a wry tone. She tapped the vellum idly again, thinking. "I must confess, I am curious about this General Astegal, and I'm weary of trying to settle the bickering of Aragonia and those damned Euskerri. I'd cede sovereignty to the Euskerri over the D'Angeline territory they want if Aragonia would do the same, but there's no reconciling them. And I've half a mind to hear Carthage's suit anyway. We've had poor relations with them since . . ." She glanced at me, her face softening. "For a long time."

"Carthage still practices slavery," I pointed out.

"So do many nations," Ysandre said gently. "But at least there has been no further traffic in D'Angelines. Imriel, I thank you for your candor in bringing this to me. I have promised a reply to General Astegal in a fortnight's time. I have taken counsel with the Royal Admiral Quintilius Rousse, who sees no harm in their overture. I will take counsel with Drustan when he arrives, convene Parliament, and give my answer."

"Father's late this year," Sidonie commented.

"Yes." Queen Ysandre eyed her. "Our children are a trial to us."

The days that followed were fraught with tension. Emile

in Night's Doorstep located the Tsingano lad who'd delivered the missive, but the boy could tell me nothing useful about the lady who'd given it to him. A foreigner, he said, but he couldn't guess from what nation. She'd asked him to deliver it because she was leaving the City in haste, or so she claimed. I spoke to the City Guard, but any number of foreign women had come and gone in the past two days. In the end, it didn't really matter how the message had arrived. What mattered was what we would decide regarding it. And so we waited. We waited for Drustan to arrive; I waited for Phèdre and Joscelin to arrive. The Carthaginians awaited a reply. Quintilius Rousse awaited word to bring it. Alba awaited a clear line of succession. Parliament awaited a voice and a vote.

Everyone was waiting, waiting.

I felt myself wound tight and restless. For the first time, things went awry between Sidonie and me in the bedchamber, our desires staggering out of rhythm. She wanted reassurance, and I sought to lose myself in violent pleasure.

I ignored her protestations for too long, too far.

"*Always!*" Her voice cracked like a whip, one hand wrenching away the blindfold of black silk she wore. She glared at me. "Imriel—"

I dropped the tawse paddle, dropped to my knees. "I'm *sorry*!"

"Imriel . . ." Sidonie sighed, cupping my face. "I know. The world's all out of kilter, isn't it?"

"Yes," I whispered. "Sidonie . . ."

"So we'll set it right." There was a world of tenderness in her voice. "I asked you for this, do you remember? Tonight, you do what *I* say. Do you trust me?"

"Always," I said hoarsely.

She handed me the blindfold. "Put this on."

I obeyed, tying it behind my head.

"Present yourself," she said, and I clasped my hands behind the nape of my neck as I'd taught her to do. I heard her pick up the tawse and circle me. My skin prickled. I was still wound tight and I didn't want this, not now, but I was willing to bear it in atonement. The edge of the tawse scraped along my skin. My muscles tightened further. "I don't mind giving my *signale* when we're caught up in play that's gone too far," Sidonie said. "Or when I find my imagination exceeds my appetite." She tapped me lightly between the shoulder blades with the paddle's edge, and I flinched. "But you just weren't listening to me tonight, were you?"

"No," I whispered.

"You do make a lovely picture like this." There was amusement in Sidonie's voice. "But I'm not going to punish you." The tawse fell to the carpet with a soft thud. She tugged off the blindfold, tangled her fingers in my hair. I blinked up at her, feeling the heat of her body, breathing in the scent of honeyed musk. "I'd never ask aught from you that you didn't wish to give freely and joyously, Imriel."

"If you want—"

"Oh, hush." She gave my hair a tug, then smiled and touched my lips. "There will be other times. But as long as you're on your knees, you may do penance. Lengthy, lengthy penance."

That I did, freely and joyously. And she was right. I lost myself in her pleasure and hers alone, worshipping her with lips and tongue until she cried out, fingers clenched in my hair, and I had to grasp her hips to steady her.

And when it was done, when I couldn't wring another spasm of pleasure from her, I felt calm and at peace. Mayhap we couldn't set everything that was wrong in the world to right, but as long as all was well between us, it was enough.

Sidonie's grip eased, and she gave a long, shuddering sigh. "Good boy."

Still on my knees, I grinned at her. "You're an easy mistress."

It was the following day that everything began to converge. Drustan and his escort of Cruithne arrived at last. Phèdre and Joscelin returned from Montrève. The Queen and Cruarch spent a day closeted in consultation, while I did much the same with my foster-parents.

"I don't like it." Joscelin shook his head. "'Tis too easy."

"I know," I said. "But I can't fathom where the risk lies."

"Nor can I." Phèdre rested her chin on her hand. "He asked naught but that Ysandre accept Carthage's tribute? There was no implication that it implied a favor, a bribe?"

I showed her the letter and my transcription. "None."

She studied it absently. "Well, mayhap Melisande's made herself a thorn in Ephesium's side somehow, and Agallon saw an opportunity to get rid of her and curry favor with Carthage at the same time."

"Yes, but why does Carthage have a sudden burning desire to pay tribute to Terre d'Ange?" Joscelin asked. "If this General Astegal does mean to move against Aragonia, does he really think Ysandre can be bribed into looking the other way?"

"He might reckon it worth a try," Phèdre said. "History is full of precedents."

"Well, it's a sizable tribute," I said. "At least according to Quintilius Rousse."

"What does Rousse say about the risk?" she asked.

I shrugged. "He's not worried. There are only six ships, lightly armed. He's got half the Royal Navy holding them at bay. He's willing to follow them up the Aviline, and recommended Ysandre bring the bulk of the Royal Army inside the walls of the City."

"I still don't like it," Joscelin said.

"Be as that may, my love," Phèdre observed, "we're not

the ones to choose. We can advise Ysandre to be wary, but Parliament has the final say."

It was true, but it was also true that no one with a seat in Parliament—with the exception of me and Sidonie, who had gained a vote upon reaching her majority—knew about the Unseen Guild. I didn't know if that mattered, if it should play a role in my own decision, and if so, what?

Phèdre and Joscelin spoke to Drustan and Ysandre in a private audience. Sidonie and I discussed the matter endlessly. After hours of talking, none of us were any the wiser.

Ysandre convened Parliament.

There were seventy-two members all told: ten hereditary seats for each of the seven provinces of Terre d'Ange, the Queen, and her heir. When a sitting regent didn't have an heir of age, they were allotted two votes. A simple majority of those present would constitute a binding vote. If there was a tie, the regent's vote decided the matter.

It was rare to have the full complement of members present when Parliament was convened, and if the matter was a delicate one, many members chose to abstain; but for that session, we very nearly did. Those unable to attend sent a properly authorized delegate. Word had leaked out across the realm that the Carthaginian tribute was impressive, and curiosity and greed made for a powerful incentive.

It was an open session in the Hall of Audience, every seat along the long, curved tables filled, and a throng of avid onlookers pressed together in the back of the hall. The place was buzzing like a beehive, but it fell silent when Ysandre, seated at the center of the table, raised her hand.

"An offer lies before us," she announced. "Lord Admiral, will you present it?"

The Palace Guard cleared a path for the Royal Admiral Quintilius Rousse. He strode into the hall with a rolling seafarer's gait, bluff and hearty despite the grey salting his ruddy hair. There was a chalice tucked under one arm. He swept a deep bow, then placed it on the table before Ysandre.

"Your majesty, august peers!" His voice boomed in the hall. "I bear greetings from Astegal of Carthage, Prince of the House of Sarkal, appointed General by the Council of Thirty. He wishes to pay tribute to Terre d'Ange on behalf of Carthage."

Ysandre eyed the chalice. It was wrought of translucent red carnelian, the stem shaped like a pair of clasped hands, the base adorned with gold. "Why?"

Quintilius Rousse cleared his throat. "There is a letter. May I read it?"

She inclined her head. "Please do."

I knew what it said; Ysandre had already read it, of course, and so had Sidonie.

"Since I was a boy," Rousse read aloud, rather badly, "I have longed to see for myself the splendors of Terre d'Ange and its Queen famed for her beauty; and yet, the shadow of misfortune has hung between our two great realms, born of deeds carried out by people too low to mention. I come at the behest of the Council of Thirty, anxious to dispel this shadow and restore amity between us."

"Keep reading!" someone shouted when he paused.

Rousse cleared his throat again. "For myself, it would suffice to gaze upon the fabled white walls of the City of Elua, and gaze on your face. I dare to present this small token, this chalice, in the hope that the clasped hands wrought thereon might prove emblematic of a restored amity between us." He squinted, holding the parchment at arm's length. "It in itself is a mere token, emblematic of the gifts the Council of Thirty wishes to bequeath to your majesty and her people, to evince the sincerity of Carthage's desire. These gifts are as follows . . ."

In his resounding voice, Quintilius Rousse read a long litany of the tribute-gifts that Carthage offered. Gold, gold in abundance. Ivory and salt. Spices, exotic seedlings gathered from many places. Bolts of cloth dyed Tyrian purple. Furniture made of fragrant woods.

I watched the avid faces of my peers and felt uneasy.

". . . and as your majesty's horologists will doubtless have informed you, a great event is pending. With your permission, my own horologists will consult with yours to show you a great marvel," Rousse finished.

Excited murmurs arose.

"Hold!" Ysandre said crisply. "What great event?"

There was a delay, then, while the Court horologist was sent for and found. I listened to the peers gossiping among themselves, stirred by the manifest Quintilius Rousse had recited. At length, the horologist arrived, bowing apologetically.

"Forgive me, your majesty—" he began.

Ysandre waved one hand dismissively. "No doubt you've informed me. I've been distracted. What event?"

He was a small fellow, sweating and anxious. "It is the belief among those of us who study the stars and the planets that in three weeks' time, the full moon will pass through the earth's shadow, and its light shall be dimmed."

"She *has* been distracted," Sidonie murmured beside me.

"Is this an omen?" Ysandre asked.

"No!" The horologist shook his head. "No, no, no. Merely a natural phenomenon, your majesty."

"And what marvel might we expect to see?" she asked.

The horologist licked his lips. "Although I have not seen it for myself, it is said that the moon takes on extraordinary hues while it lies beneath our shadow. Beyond that, I cannot guess." A scholar's hunger surfaced in his features. "All knowledge is worth having. I would be eager to partake of the wisdom of Carthage's horologists."

Ysandre inclined her head. "Thank you, my lord," she said, adding to Quintilius Rousse, "You may continue."

Rousse read the remainder of the letter aloud: more fulsome compliments, nothing of substance. No indication that this visit was aught but what it purported to be, a grand diplomatic overture. I suppose that was to be expected, and the more subtle overtures would follow if Ysandre accepted Carthage's tribute. Still, I couldn't shake a sense of lingering unease.

A period of open discussion followed, but it was already clear that the promise of extravagant gifts and a marvel to follow had swayed the majority of the peers. There were a few who argued against accepting the offer, fearing it would suggest we meant to abandon our alliance with Aragonia, but others pointed out that, despite Aragonia's fears, Carthage had not lifted a finger in its direction.

And there were a few—Barquiel L'Envers among them—who were deeply suspicious of Carthage's motives.

"You know they want *something* for this, Ysandre," he said, sounding remarkably practical. "Alliance, a promise of non-interference . . . or somewhat else." His gaze rested briefly on Sidonie. "Why not send a delegation to meet with them in Marsilikos and find out what it is?"

"They're bound to reveal their hand one way or another," a Siovalese duchese observed. "Here or there, what does it matter?"

"I don't know," L'Envers muttered. "But I don't like it."

I didn't either. For once, I was in agreement with Barquiel L'Envers. Somewhat in this offer didn't sit right. But it held a promise for me far greater than any gilded treasure or celestial marvel—secret knowledge of my mother's whereabouts, the ability to cut through the Gordian knot of her intrigues at a single, swift blow instead of spending torturous years trying to unwind it.

And then it would be done.

I would be free. Free of her taint, free of her long shadow. Free to wed Sidonie and spend the rest of my life with her without incurring suspicion and bitterness. And she would be free to spend it with me without having to endure the contempt of those who reckoned she was weak enough to have been seduced by the cunning blandishments of a traitor's son, or an endless series of suits from foreign princes who reckoned her fair game.

So I voted to accept Carthage's offer.

Sidonie did, too.

It wouldn't have mattered. It wasn't even close. There were only four votes against acceptance, and seven who abstained. By the time Ysandre cast her vote, it was merely symbolic. She hesitated, conferring quietly with Drustan one last time. Although the Cruarch of Alba had no vote in the Parliament of Terre d'Ange, he always sat at Ysandre's side to counsel her when he was present. I saw him give his head a slight shake. Like the rest of us, Drustan had been unable to find sufficient cause to spurn Carthage's overture.

Ysandre cast her vote for acceptance.

It was decided.

Carthage was coming.

Ten

A bit over two weeks later, on a bright, sunny day, six Carthaginian tribute-ships sailed up the Aviline River to dock at the wharfs of the City of Elua, preceded fore and aft by D'Angeline war-ships.

It was a considerable spectacle. The Carthaginian ships had massive sails striped crimson and white, gilded figure-heads in the shape of horse-heads, lions, and serpents. Even the railings were elaborately carved. Bare-chested rowers manned the oars, oiled skin gleaming in the sunlight.

"Slaves," I murmured to Sidonie.

There was a tall fellow in the prow of the lead ship, clad in a scarlet tunic with a long cloak of Tyrian purple, a slender fillet of gold around his head. Even at a distance, I could see he had strong features. His thick black hair was swept back from his temples, and he wore a narrow beard dyed scarlet.

"And that, I suspect, would be General Astegal," she commented.

The ships were docked. Sailors swarmed, securing their moorings. General Astegal bowed deeply in the direction of Ysandre and Drustan, but made no move to disembark. Instead, the rowers laid down their oars and set about unloading chest after chest of tribute.

The crew came from various nations. Many were olive-skinned Carthaginians. Others were a tawnier hue, and there were Nubians and Jebeans, too, with dusky skin and woolen hair. I touched my rhinoceros-hide sword-belt, thinking of distant places and old friends.

At last, when the wharf was heaped with treasure, a score of soldiers carrying gilded spears descended from the flagship, saluted the Queen and Cruarch, then formed a double line. Astegal of Carthage, Prince of the House of Sarkal, appointed General of the Council of Thirty, made his approach, sweeping another low bow.

"Well met, General Astegal," Ysandre said. "We welcome you to the City of Elua."

Astegal straightened and smiled. His teeth were very white. "I thank you for the honor, your majesty. Carthage thanks you. It is an honor merely to gaze upon you and your fair city." His D'Angeline was accented, but excellent. He bowed again, this time toward Drustan. "It is a double honor to be received by the Cruarch of Alba."

"Small as we are, Alba can but aspire to be the recipient of Carthage's mighty generosity one day," Drustan said wryly.

Astegal laughed. "I pray it may be so, your majesty." He turned to Sidonie, offering yet another deep bow. "Surely you must be the Dauphine, with your mother's beauty and your father's eyes."

"Well met, my lord." Her tone was neutral.

"Ah." He smiled at her. "So young to be wary of flattery, your highness! I did but speak the truth."

"And in surpassingly good D'Angeline, too," she observed.

He spread his arms as though to embrace the entire City.

"It is as I wrote. I have long dreamed of this moment. I have worked and studied long and hard to bring my dream to fruition." Turning to me, he gave another bow. "You, I think, are also a member of the royal family?"

"Imriel," I said. "Well met, my lord."

"Prince Imriel, of course." Astegal put out his hand, his expression turning grave. "I hope that during my time here, I may make some atonement for the unconscionable acts of my ill-gotten countrymen. And once we have put the past behind us, perhaps you will do me the kindness of showing me your city's fabled pleasures." He winked, showed his white teeth in another easy grin. "You strike me as a young man of good appetite."

He had a firm grip and his sword-hand was callused. For all his diplomat's charm, I thought, this man was a soldier. He was a few inches taller than I, and some ten or twelve years older. Young and ambitious, the rumors had said.

"Of course, my lord," I said politely, wondering if there was some hidden message behind the request. "I do not blame Carthage for the acts of a few miscreants."

Astegal smiled. "Excellent!"

There was a grand procession from the wharfs to the Palace. Behind us, slaves continued to work at unloading the other ships, under the supervision of various Court officials who would attend to the other Carthaginian dignitaries and horologists disembarking, all of it taking place under the watchful eyes of a full contingent of the Royal Army. Commonfolk lined the streets, gazing in awe at the spectacle.

As we rode in an open carriage, Astegal offered a running litany of praise: for the gracious lay of the City, for the skill of its architects, for the beauty of its folk. Flattery, but it stopped short of unctuousness. He seemed sincere in his praise, glad to be here, at ease in his own skin.

I tried to read aught beyond it, and couldn't.

When we reached the Palace, he fell silent a moment, gazing at it, then gave his head a little shake. "Lovely. Who would have thought a structure so vast could hold such grace. Mayhap your majesty will consent to send architects to advise ours."

"Carthage comes courting Terre d'Ange's *architects*?" Ysandre inquired.

"Of course." Astegal smiled. "Among other things. Terre d'Ange has grown bolder and more adventurous under your rule, gracious lady, opening its doors to new friendships and alliances, creating strong bonds." His gaze lingered briefly on Drustan. "It is my wish that Carthage do the same. There are many ways in which we may profit one another," he added, and his gaze slid toward Sidonie.

It made my teeth grate.

Sidonie didn't take his gambit. "Our horologists are eager to learn of this celestial marvel you promise."

"Oh, yes." He nodded. "You have the wisdom your gods bequeathed you, but Carthaginian horologists were studying the skies long before your Elua roamed the earth. We may learn much from one another. And if nothing else"—he made a graceful, self-deprecating gesture—"it is my hope that we shall all part as friends, enriched by our mutual interests."

"I'm sure we will," Sidonie agreed, and I had to stifle a laugh.

All throughout the day, the Palace bustled with activity. Tribute-gifts were carted and displayed in the great hall, dignitaries, horologists, soldiers, and slaves were lodged, tables were laid, harried servants hurried on endless errands. There was to be a grand fête that night with over a hundred peers of the realm, a handful of Cruithne, and all of the Carthaginian dignitaries and horologists attending. Astegal had expressed the hope that he and Ysandre would share a drink from the carnelian chalice, pledging one another's health and toasting to the shared future of our nations. He had also promised one final tribute-gift, a surprise not listed in the manifest and kept veiled until the fête.

"Do you truly intend to prowl the Night Court with him?" Sidonie asked in the bath, as we began to prepare for the evening's festivities, enjoying what was likely to be our last time alone together for many hours.

I grinned at her. "Jealous?"

She wrinkled her nose. "Curious."

"I can play escort without partaking if need be." I caught her arms and tugged her toward me. Water sloshed over the edges of the tub. "If he's an agent of the Guild, it may be he's seeking a private moment."

Sidonie settled atop me. "What do you make of him?"

"I'm not sure yet." I clasped her buttocks, shifting her to gain a better angle. She made a small, satisfied sound as I entered her. "You?"

"I don't know." Her hips rose and fell, slow and delicious. "I don't dislike him. I expected to."

"Just don't agree to wed him," I suggested.

Sidonie laughed and kissed me. "I won't."

Afterward, clean and dried and dressed in finery, we attended the fête. It was a gorgeous affair, albeit a chaotic one. Very few of the Carthaginians spoke D'Angeline. Punic was their native tongue, although all in attendance spoke Hellene, which was used as a common tongue among traders. Many of the D'Angelines spoke Hellene, but not all, and none of the Cruithne did.

As a result, conversations were difficult, and those of us who did speak Hellene were often forced to do double duty, making introductions and translating. My Hellene was good; one advantage of being Phèdre nó Delaunay's foster-son was that I'd been taught to read and speak in a number of tongues. Still, it was exhausting, and I will own I felt relieved when a plump Carthaginian fellow hovering near the veiled treasure introduced himself to me in D'Angeline.

"I am Jabnit of the House of Philosir," he announced with an exacting little bow. "And I have already learned you are Prince Imriel. Well met, your highness."

"Well met, my lord," I replied.

"Oh, no lord!" His black eyes twinkled. "Merely a well-connected merchant." Jabnit patted his considerable belly. "Well-connected and well-fed."

"Too well-fed," a light voice said in amusement.

"Sunjata!" The merchant glanced around. "Come meet the prince."

A young Nubian man stepped around him and bowed gracefully. He was of middling height and slender, with plum-dark skin and gently rounded features. "It is an honor, your highness."

"Sunjata is my assistant." Jabnit patted his shoulder with the same comfortable familiarity with which he'd patted his own stomach. "Tell the prince of our role in this venture. I spy a servant with a laden platter of delicacies."

"Who will care for me if you stuff your belly to bursting, you old glutton?" Sunjata asked, but there was fondness in it. "Go, go."

"Your role?" I asked politely as the merchant waddled away.

"The House of Philosir provided the gems for the gift to be unveiled this evening." Sunjata looked at me under his lashes. "At a considerable discount, for the privilege of being part of this excursion. But surely you cannot be interested in that."

Somewhat in his manner, in the smoothness of his skin, in the light timbre of his voice struck an old chord of memory in me. I had known eunuchs in Daršanga.

My reaction was subtle, but Sunjata read it. "Ah, yes," he said with a seeming ease that didn't quite belie the bitterness beneath it. "There is something we share in common, is there not? I too fell into the hands of Carthage's slavers as a boy. Only in my case, the effects were more . . . lasting."

"I'm sorry," I said quietly.

His slender shoulders moved in a shrug. "I don't begrudge you your manhood. 'Tis no fault of yours that mine was taken. And I am a free man these past few years, insofar as I may call myself a man. Jabnit is a fair patron." He gazed after the merchant, then back at me. "And I am rude and insolent," he said, putting out his hand. "Thank you for your kindness."

I took his hand. "Of course."

He squeezed my hand, his thumb pressing on mine. I glanced down involuntarily. Sunjata sported a silver signet ring on his thumb, a lamp carved on the seal. "Perhaps we will speak again later," he said, releasing my hand. With one deft, unobtrusive gesture, he twisted the ring, hiding the seal against his palm.

I met his gaze. "I would like that."

For the balance of the evening, my thoughts were in a whirl. Exactly what I had expected of the Unseen Guild, I couldn't say, but it wasn't a eunuch in the employ of a gem-merchant.

And the night only got stranger.

A sumptuous meal was served, although I ate without tasting, distracted by my own thoughts and the sight of Astegal, several seats away, paying court to Sidonie in a manner light-handed enough to be inoffensive. She was being pleasant without encouraging him. Elua knows, it wasn't that I was worried about her loyalties, but I was on edge, and it only made me edgier.

Fortunately, I was seated across from the Chief Horologist, who spun a tale compelling enough to prevent anyone from noticing my distraction. He was a kinsman of Astegal's; Bodeshmun was his name. Another tall fellow, older, grave, and serious, with deep-set eyes and a long black beard. In a sonorous voice, he described the promised marvel, in which twelve silver-backed mirrors were to be placed around the walls of the City, and one great mirror in the very center.

"When the moon is wholly obscured," he said, "the light is such that when one gazes into the great mirror, one sees reflected all that is hidden between the stars."

"Why not simply gaze at the sky itself?" Tibault de Toluard inquired, knitting his brows in perplexity. He was a Siovalese lord with a considerable knowledge of science. "Why use a mirror? Surely a reflection is less true than the thing itself."

Bodeshmun turned his head. "Silver has the quality of revealing much that is hidden. Have you not found it to be so?"

"Not especially," the Marquis de Toluard said frankly.

The horologist smiled into his beard. "You will."

"What may we expect to see, my lord?" Roxanne de Mereliot, the Lady of Marsilikos, asked with interest.

"Ah, no!" Bodeshmun laughed deep in his chest. "I will not spoil the surprise, my lady. Let the secrets of the cosmos reveal themselves."

After the meal was concluded, at least one secret *was* revealed. Ysandre, good-natured, acceded to Astegal's request, at least in part. They both drank to one another's health from the carnelian chalice, although she stopped short of toasting the shared future of Carthage and Terre d'Ange. Astegal seemed pleased nonetheless. He called for the veiled treasure to be brought forth. The silk draped over the large square frame was whisked away to reveal what appeared at first glance to be a painting in a gilded frame.

A painting that glittered.

Not pigment, but ground gems in pure form, used with exacting care. It depicted a tall, black-haired man with a scarlet beard and a blonde woman, standing before a tree, their hands clasped in friendship.

"Thank you, my lord," Ysandre said, sounding surprised. "It is surpassingly lovely."

Astegal bowed. "As are you and your land, your majesty."

I glanced down the table toward where Phèdre was seated. In the midst of this polyglot mayhem, I'd not had a chance to speak with her or Joscelin all night. Her head was tilted and she wore a faint, familiar frown, as though she were listening for the strains of a distant sound no one else could hear. But when I caught her eye, she merely shook her head, perplexed.

I knew the feeling.

The gem-painting was placed on an easel in a position of honor. The tables had been cleared of all plates and platters, but the wine and cordial flowed freely. And I found myself approached for a second time that evening.

"Prince Imriel." A hawk-nosed Carthaginian I'd not met earlier approached. He bowed deeply, addressing me in Hellene. "I am Gillimas of the House of Hiram, magistrate to the Council of Thirty." He placed a gilded, gem-studded coffer on the table. "It is our wish to present this small token to you in acknowledgment of the unpleasantness you endured at the hands of our countrymen."

"Thank you, my lord," I said.

He shrugged. "A small token. The wood is cypress from the isle of Cythera."

"Cythera?" I echoed.

"The fragrance alone tells the tale," Gillimas said.

I opened the coffer. The inner lid was also worked in gold, but the coffer itself was bare wood. The scent of cypress wafted out, and from the inside of the lid, the image of a lamp leapt out at me. Both caught at my memories. A barrel outside an incense-maker's shop, Canis the beggar giving me a clay medallion with a lamp on it.

"Very nice," I said slowly.

"Oh, it is nothing, nothing." Gillimas made a dismissive gesture. "A mere token, fit for storing letters."

I ran my fingers over the edge of the coffer's lid, feeling for hidden messages. There were none. "It gives a pleasant aroma."

"The cypresses of Cythera are legendary," he agreed. "Have you been there?"

"To Cythera?" I shook my head. "No."

Gillimas favored me with a careless smile. "Mayhap you should go."

I closed the lid. "My thanks. I'll think on it."

His smile deepened. "Do."

The evening wore on and on, into the small hours. I did my part, conversing pleasantly in several tongues with myriad people, trying to collect my reeling thoughts. Out of the corner of my eye, I kept a lookout for the eunuch Sunjata, but it seemed he had been present only to attend his merchant-patron. All along the edges of the great hall, Carthaginian treasure sparkled. Ysandre had pledged to divide it among the members of Parliament.

Everyone was happy.

My skin crawled.

I wanted . . . what? I didn't know. I wanted a moment alone with Gillimas, with Sunjata, a chance to shake the truth from them. I got neither. I wanted to talk to Phèdre. Cythera. It made sense. A small isle, but it had been ruled in its time by many different folk. Hellas. Ephesium. I'd never been able to place Canis' accent, his history. It had held somewhat of both.

Gillimas made sense as a member of the Guild.

So who the hell was Sunjata?

"So?" In her chambers, in the bed we shared, Sidonie propped herself on one elbow and regarded me, her unbound hair falling over her shoulders. "Did you learn aught this evening?"

"Sun Princess," I murmured, running a lock through my fingers. "Yes and no. I'm confused."

"Don't worry." She bowed her head, her hair trailing over my skin, her lips tracing a line of kisses along the pink scars that furrowed my torso. "Sleep. We'll sort it out in the morning, you and I."

Love.

Loss.

My fingers tightened on her. "Gods, I hope so."

Sidonie yawned, settling her head on my shoulder, fitting her body to mine, where it belonged. "We will."

"Please," I whispered, wrapping her in my arms. "Ah, Elua. *Please.*"

Eleven

"Cythera," Phèdre said. "Interesting."

"Is it?" Joscelin asked.

"Ptolemy Dikaios' wife was Cytheran," she reminded him. "And we know Melisande was in league with him."

Joscelin eyed her. "You do keep an ungodly amount of information stored in that beautiful head, love."

"Precious little else regarding Cythera, I'm afraid," she said. "Except that it's an Akkadian holding. Mayhap the Khalif will prove willing to assist us."

"Assuming my mother actually *is* there," I said. "Elua! I wish these damned people would speak plainly."

After talking with Sidonie, I'd sent a polite message to Gillimas asking if he could tell me aught more about the coffer's history. I'd received a prompt, polite message in reply saying no, he was unable to tell me more, but if I wished, he would be honored to speak with me regarding any other matter. And I'd sent a message to Sunjata asking if I could meet with him regarding a commission of gem-stones, and received a polite reply saying that he and his employer were busy assisting the horologists with their preparations, but that he would be honored to meet with me after the spectacle, which was to take place three days hence.

It was enough to drive me mad.

"I'll see what I can learn about Cythera," Phèdre promised.

"Be discreet," I said.

She laughed. "Aren't I always?"

"Send Ti-Philippe down to the wharf taverns to sound out Rousse's sailor-lads," Joscelin suggested. "He's always glad of a chance to drink and dice with sailors, and they trade gossip from ports all over the world. Since all of Terre d'Ange knows we're trying to find Melisande, no one will find it suspicious, although he might want to get them good and drunk before he steers the conversation toward Cythera."

Phèdre blinked at him. "That's an excellent idea."

He grinned. "Credit a lifetime of listening to your intrigues."

Ti-Philippe agreed readily. He'd been a sailor himself once, long ago, under Rousse's command.

Beyond that, there wasn't much to be done at the moment. Sidonie reported the latest developments to her mother, who replied that the matter would have to wait for discussion until the Carthaginian delegation had departed. For my part, if I found I had no choice but to strike out for Cythera on the dubious message implied in Gillimas' gift, I damned well wasn't going to do it until the Carthaginians were gone.

They made me nervous.

The day after the fête, Astegal had a private meeting with Ysandre and Drustan. He made a candid offer for Sidonie's hand, pointing out that a strategic alliance between Terre d'Ange, Alba, and Carthage would make for an axis of unparalleled power in the west.

"With Aragonia caught betwixt and between," I observed

when Sidonie told me, having gotten a full accounting from Ysandre.

She nodded. "Carthage dreams of empire. He didn't deny it. Mother says he pointed out—very smoothly—that under pressure from three strong nations, Aragonia could easily agree to become a vassal state without a drop of blood spilled."

"Aha!" I said. "So that's what this is about."

"Mm-hmm." She looked troubled. "There was the implication that matters could go very differently if we declined this offer, and that the blood of slain Aragonians would be on Terre d'Ange's conscience."

I whistled softly. "That's damn nigh blackmail. Aragonia was right to be worried."

"He didn't *quite* say it," Sidonie said. "But it was there."

"Tempted?" I asked.

"No, of course not," she said, but her expression was still troubled. "It's just . . . Elua! If it comes to that—and I pray it doesn't—I'm bound to think it now." She took my hand, twisting the knotted gold ring I wore. "What if I could have averted it? How many more people have to die for our happiness?"

"Sidonie." I caught her fingers, stilling them. "It happened last time because we didn't trust ourselves. Will you risk betraying Blessed Elua's precept a second time?"

"Do you know what else Astegal said?" She laughed humorlessly. "He said it had come to his attention that I had already taken a lover. He said that he had the utmost respect for the customs of Terre d'Ange, and that if I wished to surround myself with a bevy of beautiful young men, he had no objection so long as I took care not to conceive aught but heirs of his blood."

I stared at her. "He didn't."

"Oh, he did." She was silent a moment. "It doesn't matter.

Terre d'Ange cannot allow itself to be coerced into betraying its allies and supporting Carthage's imperial aspirations. It's just . . . ugly."

"Very," I agreed. "What did Ysandre say to him?"

She smiled ruefully. "She told him that while Terre d'Ange has indeed grown less insular under her rule, D'Angelines hold their descendance from Blessed Elua and his Companions as a sacred trust. That it was already a matter of considerable concern that her heir was half-Cruithne, and that she couldn't possibly betray that trust further by seeing me wed to aught but a pure-blooded D'Angeline, or the peers of the realm would rise in rebellion."

I stroked her hair. "I'm sorry."

"It's all right." Sidonie shrugged. "It was the best response in diplomatic terms. It may even be true. Father backed her." She gave a quick smile. "She said beyond that, he didn't say much. Just sat and listened with that quiet, deadly look on his face that makes grown men squirm."

"I know that look," I said. "Did Astegal squirm?"

She shook her head. "Not much. He's a cool one. He thanked them for hearing his offer, expressed hopes that whatever the future held, these new friendships would continue . . . the usual diplomatic pap, all very cordial. No further mention of bloodshed in Aragonia. Mother's chosen to keep this quiet for now. She'll take counsel with Parliament after Astegal's gone."

"Huh." I thought about it. "I'll be glad when this is over."

"So will I," Sidonie murmured. "But I don't like thinking about what comes next. I wish those damned Guild people weren't so secretive and evasive."

"I wish the whole lot of them would fall into the sea and take my damned mother with them," I said, and she laughed.

The following day, I found myself with diplomatic duties of my own. It seemed Astegal had been entirely sincere in his desire to sample the pleasures of the Night Court, and in desiring my company while so doing.

We set out from the Palace in the early hours of the evening; Astegal and I and a half dozen other Carthaginian lords, escorted by a score of Sidonie's guardsmen. It was to have been the Queen's Guard escorting us, but Claude de Monluc had intervened and come to an arrangement.

"You don't have to do this," I'd told him. "It's not your duty."

Claude had leveled a hard gaze at me. "Palace gossip says this Astegal's made a bid for her highness' hand. He knows she's in love with you. No, I'm not *your* man, but I'm Sidonie's, and I know for a surety she doesn't want you dead by mysterious misadventure. I'm not willing to entrust this duty to men whose loyalties are uncertain."

I smiled. "You sound like Joscelin."

He laughed. "I wish!"

We went first to Eglantine House, where we were treated to an extraordinary feast, entertained all the while by dancers, tumblers, singers, and musicians of surpassing skill. Several of the Carthaginian lords succumbed to their charms. I explained to them in Hellene the laws regarding consensuality, to which they readily agreed, and after which I made arrangements with the Dowayne. Astegal reclined on a couch, taking it all in through half-slitted eyes.

"You lead a good life here," he observed.

"We do, my lord," I agreed. "But what passes here is sacred, too."

"Of course." His gaze slid sideways toward me. "No doubt you heard of the offer I made. I hope you do not take it amiss."

I spread my hands. "Politics."

He nodded. "Nothing more."

After Eglantine House, we went to Bryony. Dusk had fallen and the evening was balmy, the air soft on one's skin. Gillimas of Hiram was one of the lords attending this night's venture. I was hoping by the night's end he would be sufficiently drunk to speak candidly to me. At Bryony House, where money is reckoned an aphrodisiac, I bribed an adept to see that his winecup was never empty.

It was a good investment. The Carthaginians, who had built an empire on trade and lost it through military overreach, loved Bryony House. They were willing to wager on anything: who could out-drink the other, which lean-muscled, oiled adept might wrestle the other into submission, whether or not an adept could peel an apple in a single, coiling strip. And they had a fine time doing it, encouraged all the while by Bryony's adepts.

"You fatten our purses at Carthage's expense," commented Janelle nó Bryony, the Dowayne. "My thanks."

I smiled at her. "You fattened mine, once."

"True." She traced a finger down my chest. Once upon a time, the Dowayne of Bryony House had lost a bet to me. "At the time, I didn't know your heart was given elsewhere."

"Nor did I." I caught her hand, halting its progress. "Now I do."

"You're faithful to her?" she asked.

"Unless requested to be otherwise," I said, thinking of Amarante.

Janelle nó Bryony laughed and kissed me. "You inspire us, Prince Imriel. The Night Court stands behind you." Her eyes sparkled. "And if there is any truth in gossip, it may be that her highness will not prove adverse to certain adventures in the future."

"Probably not," I agreed.

An idea was beginning to take shape in my mind. There

had been debate over which of the Houses to visit. Astegal had wished to experience the genius of Eglantine House and the carnival atmosphere of Bryony. After some deliberation, he had settled on Jasmine House for our final destination.

The central tenet of Jasmine House was pure, unadulterated sensuality. It was palpable, too. It struck like a wave the minute one was ushered into the salon of reception. It was an undulating space, filled with semiprivate niches. The floor was piled with thick Akkadian carpets and massive cushions on which patrons and adepts reclined. Fretted lamps hung low from the ceiling, wrought with images of love-making. Incense and opium burned in tiny braziers, and servants circulated with wine, cordials, and delicacies.

With the assistance of Claude de Monluc, I got the Carthaginians settled in a niche, happily drinking wine and reviewing those adepts willing and available to serve them, and begged a private word with the Dowayne, Yolande Caradas.

"I have a great boon to ask, my lady," I said.

"Oh?" Her brows rose. She was a stunning woman, with perfectly straight black hair that fell to her waist, and a mouth made for sin. "I'm . . . curious."

I'd never heard anyone invest so much sensuality into so few syllables. It made the room feel hot. "That man, the hawk-nosed fellow." I nodded slightly toward Gillimas. "I wish to have a quiet word with him without General Astegal's knowledge."

"Why?" Yolande asked.

I shook my head. "'Tis a matter of state I cannot reveal."

"Covertcy." Her generous mouth curved. "He seems quite taken with Marielle. I'll have her fetch you to her chamber when they have concluded their pleasure. Will that suffice?"

"Perfectly," I said. "I'm in your debt."

"That's a nice place to have you," Yolande Caradas said.

It wasn't long before the Carthaginians had made their selections. Astegal *was* ambitious; he'd chosen two adepts, a dark-haired girl with smoldering eyes, and a young man with full lips and a wiry panther's grace. They seemed pleased at being selected. I had to own, he wasn't a bad-looking man, and I might have found him charming if I didn't know about his ambitions and his veiled threats.

"Surely you're not abstaining," he said to me, his arms slung around the adepts' shoulders.

"I am, my lord," I replied. "I'll await you here."

Astegal shrugged. "How very unlike a D'Angeline."

I met his gaze squarely. "You don't know us as well as you reckon."

"No?" He smiled lazily. "Well, I'll know you better after tonight, eh? At least two of you."

I inclined my head. "Naamah's grace be on you."

One by one, they retired to private chambers, all except a certain Lord Mintho, who had fallen asleep and was snoring peacefully on the cushions. He'd been one of those who had taken his pleasure at Eglantine House, so I didn't reckon he'd be too sorry in the morning. All of them were fairly well drunk except mayhap Astegal, and I was pleased to see that Gillimas was weaving on his feet as he left, the girl Marielle laughing and tugging his hand.

I didn't have that long to wait. A good deal less than an hour had passed before Marielle came to fetch me. Claude gave me a sharp look. I put my hand over his mouth before he could speak.

"State business," I murmured. "I need to talk to him without Astegal's knowledge and I can't do it at Court. There are things he may be willing to tell us about Carthage's true intentions. As you value your commission in the Guard, keep your mouth shut."

Claude gave a slow nod. I took my hand away, rose, and followed the girl.

"You'll not get much out of him," she said when we reached the inner corridors, her tone smug. "He's snoring like a babe." Marielle tossed her hair. "Patrons shouldn't come to Jasmine House wine-sotted. They tire too quickly for us."

"I'm sure they do." I smiled at her. "Don't worry. I'll wake him. What of General Astegal?"

Marielle glanced down the corridor. "Now, there's a man knows what he's about. By the sound of it, he'll be busy awhile."

"Excellent." I fished in the purse at my belt for two gold ducats. "This is for your assistance," I said, giving her one. "And this is for your silence." I fixed her with a stern look. "Lord Gillimas' life could be in danger if Astegal learns he's provided us with secret information. Understand?"

She nodded, chastened.

I kissed her cheek. "Good girl."

I let myself into her bedchamber, closing the door quietly behind me. Gillimas was sprawled on the bed, mouth open and snoring. I picked up one of the pillows strewn about and took a deep breath, approaching the bedside. In one swift motion, I straddled him and shoved the pillow over the lower part of his face.

Gillimas woke thrashing and terrified, uttering muffled cries. I pinned his arms with my knees and pushed hard against the pillow. His chest heaved and his fear-stricken gaze found my face.

"Listen to me," I said in Hellene. "Because you will die if you don't. You're in the Night Court of Terre d'Ange, Gillimas, surrounded by *my* allies, escorted by *my* men. I can smother you here in this bed, and the girl will swear your heart gave out during love-making. Understand?"

His bare feet flailed ineffectually against the bedding.

"Struggle if you like." I leaned more weight on the pillow. "You think Jasmine House isn't used to hearing a few odd thumps and cries? All I want is a straight answer in plain language. Will you give it?"

He did struggle awhile longer, but he was growing weaker. At length his eyelids flickered in a way I took to indicate assent. I eased the pressure on the pillow. "I'll let you breathe," I said. "But one shout, one lie, one evasion, and it's over. You have one chance. Understand?"

There was a pause before Gillimas' lids flickered again.

I lifted the pillow a few inches. "Is my mother on Cythera?"

He drew a long, ragged gasp of air. "Yes!"

I held the pillow at the ready. "Where?"

"Governor's mistress," he croaked. "Paphos."

"Thank you." I sat back on my heels and regarded him, setting the pillow aside. "Name of Elua, man! That wasn't so hard, was it?" I clambered off him. "Why in the seven hells didn't you just *tell* me?"

"Not how the Guild works," Gillimas said shortly. He glared at me, his chest rising and falling hard. "Not with outsiders."

I helped him sit upright. "Well, it ought to be."

He smiled bitterly. "It's not."

Twelve

It was a long night.

I had to credit Astegal; he got his money's worth. It was near dawn when he emerged, looking heavy-lidded and pleased with himself. And in fairness, the adepts he'd chosen seemed pleased enough. The Dowayne was pleased; I'd given her a generous donation for her assistance. I daresay everyone was pleased except Lord Mintho, grumbling sleepily over missed opportunities, and Gillimas of Hiram, although he gave no indication of it.

For my part, I was delighted.

My mother was in Paphos on the isle of Cythera, mistress to the Governor. I had the information I needed. Now all I needed to do was figure out how to act on it without tipping my hand. Ysandre had promised assistance, and I meant to hold her to it.

I was a little concerned about Gillimas, but not overly. He was a Guildsman and a magistrate of considerable standing, and he'd been careless. I doubt my bluff would have worked if I hadn't caught him unaware, sotted, sated, and sleeping, but I had and it did. He could admit to it, or he could keep his mouth shut and let the Unseen Guild believe I'd assembled the cryptic pieces of their puzzle myself. If I was lucky, mayhap Ti-Philippe's inquiries would turn up somewhat that would lend credence to the notion.

Either way, I knew.

I couldn't bear to wait. With dawn breaking over the Palace, I woke Sidonie and told her, watching her sleepy eyes widen in shock.

"You did *what*?"

"It was worth it," I said. "I got the idea in Bryony House when I realized that for once I was surrounded by supporters and loyal guards. It was the perfect time to bluff."

She shook her tousled head. "What if Gillimas had called it?"

I grinned. "Well, it would have put him in the position of having to explain why I was trying to smother him in a D'Angeline pleasure-house without exposing the Guild. I daresay *that* thought flashed through his mind, too."

"Still," Sidonie murmured. "It was a big risk."

"I know," I said. "But now we know. And as soon as these damned Carthaginians stage their damned horologists' celestial mirror-show and leave, we'll all sit down, pool our knowledge of Cythera, and make a plan."

Sidonie frowned. "What about the eunuch? What was his name? Sunjata?"

I flopped down on the bed beside her and closed my eyes, feeling weariness from the long night settling into my bones. "To hell with the eunuch. If he has a message for me, let him deliver it. I'm not chasing him."

"Well, he is rather fetching," she said with unexpected humor.

I cracked one eye open. "Not half as fetching as you, Princess. By the way, the Dowayne of Bryony House expressed the hope that you and I will partake in certain adventures in the future."

"Mmm." Sidonie leaned down and kissed me. "Let's get our future in order first."

The horologists' spectacle was to take place on the morrow. The mood in the City was festive, and the City itself was ungodly crowded. An unwarranted number of peers had chosen to stay to witness the spectacle. Scientists and engineers poured into the City, many from Siovale, skeptical but curious. Ghislain nó Trevalion had the entire Royal Army billeted within the walls of the City. Quintilius Rousse had a dozen war-ships anchored in the Aviline River, and his lads thronged the taverns.

It seemed like the only preeminent figure *not* in the City was Barquiel L'Envers, who had withdrawn in disgust to his estate in Namarre, having never abandoned his opposition to the Carthaginian delegation. Even the other members of Parliament who'd opposed it had lingered, drawn by curiosity. Not L'Envers. In truth, I didn't blame him, but I welcomed his absence nonetheless.

The day before the spectacle, Sidonie and I rode out to observe the preparations, accompanied by her guard.

I must own, I was at least a little curious. The event itself was to take place in Elua's Square, the exact center of the City. The horologist Bodeshmun was there, overseeing the placement of the great mirror, directly in front of the ancient oak tree said to have been planted by Blessed Elua himself.

"No," he said absently, making a measurement with a piece of string on which a bead was strung. "No, no, no! It must be *perfectly* level."

Slaves groaned, lifting the mirror from its tripodal base. One crawled beneath it, adjusting the tripod, and the mirror was lowered again.

"That is one damnably big mirror," Claude de Monluc observed.

It was. I gauged its diameter as at least five armspans' length; a vast pool of silver, reflecting sky and oak leaves. There were symbols worked around the silver rim, representing the twelve Houses of the Cosmos.

Bodeshmun measured again and grunted. "Better." He glanced down at one of the symbols, then strode a few paces, an unlikely figure in his black beard and a long robe. He raised his thumb, sighting along an unseen line. Half a league away, atop the white walls of the City, an answering mirror flashed. Bodeshmun squinted at his thumb. "Two degrees west," he said curtly. "Send a runner."

One of the slaves departed at a run. We lingered, watching, while the process was repeated, then began anew with the next symbol.

"It seems a complicated business, my lord," Sidonie said at length, still seated astride her white palfrey.

"Yes, your highness." Bodeshmun glanced up at her from beneath heavy brows, then gave a short, perfunctory bow. A multifaceted green gem that hung on a chain around his neck swung briefly into view, catching the sunlight. "The secrets of the heavens do not reveal themselves easily," he said in his deep voice. "One must be diligent and exacting. But I promise, you will find the results well worthwhile."

She inclined her head. "I'm sure I shall."

He smiled in a way that made my flesh prickle. "You will."

For the first time since we'd become lovers, Sidonie and I argued that day. All the way back to the Palace, we quarrelled.

"I don't like it," I said. "Can't you talk Ysandre into calling it off?"

"On what grounds?" Sidonie asked reasonably.

"I don't *know*!" My voice rose in frustration. "It smells bad, Sidonie. I don't know why. I just know it does."

"It's not enough." Her back was very straight in the saddle. "Half the realm is here to observe this. We need some evidence of bad faith on the part of Carthage to deny them."

"Astegal's intentions—" I muttered.

"Were spoken plainly." Sidonie scowled at me. "Imriel, I don't like it either. But we've accepted their gifts. We've heard their suit, and they accepted our refusal with seeming good will. If Carthage *does* move against Aragonia, yes, everything changes. But they haven't, not yet."

"They will," I said darkly.

She sighed. "And we will deal with it when they do. What are you afraid of, Imriel? The City is bursting at the seams, filled with our soldiers and sailors. What can Carthage possibly do?"

"I don't know," I whispered. "That's what scares me."

"Well, stop scaring *me*!" she retorted.

We were irritable enough with one another that when Sidonie answered a summons from her mother on returning to the Palace, I went to the Hall of Games to distract myself. I found Mavros playing piquet with Julien Trente and a young Siovalese baron, and joined them. I played badly and lost rather more money than I'd intended by the time the game broke up many hours later.

"So what's your problem?" Mavros inquired after Julien and young Baron d'Albert had departed for the Night Court, purses fat with my coin.

"Nothing." I shrugged. "This business with Carthage has me on edge. I just want it to be over." We were drinking wine, and I swirled my cup, scowling into it. "I asked Sidonie to have her mother call off the spectacle. She refused. We argued."

"So?" Mavros asked.

"We never argue," I said.

"That's a bit odd in and of itself, don't you think?" he asked.

I shrugged again. "We did enough of it growing up. Not now. It feels wrong."

Mavros sighed. "Look around you, Imri. The City's full to bursting with folk eager to see the spectacle. Our new Siovalese friend was fair twitching with excitement. Carthage has been generous. What do you expect?" His voice softened. "Go tell Sidonie you're sorry and make it up with her. You're lousy company when you're brooding."

I stood. "You're right."

He grinned. "Good man."

Halfway to Sidonie's quarters, I was met by Alfonse, who had been sent to fetch me.

"Sidonie," I said when I entered the salon. "I came to say—"

"Imriel, I'm sorry," she said at the same moment.

"—came to say I'm sorry," I finished. Both of us laughed. I reached out my hand. "Come here."

"You're right." Sidonie twined her fingers in mine. "Somewhat about this sits wrong, and Mother agrees. She wouldn't have Ghislain and the entire army here if she didn't. But I asked, and there's simply no cause to cancel without reason."

"I know," I said. "Mavros said the same thing. He also thinks it's odd that we never quarrel."

She smiled wryly. "I'm sure we will when we can afford the luxury. Right now, we've got the entire realm doing our quarrelling for us."

I slid my hands around her waist, drawing her against me. "What shall we quarrel about when that blessed day arrives?"

"Oh, I don't know." Sidonie looped her arms around my

neck, gazing up at me. "I'm sure we'll find something. Everyone does."

I kissed her, long and deep. "We're not everyone."

"No," she murmured. "We're not." Her arms tightened around my neck. "Imriel, will you take me to bed? No games tonight, just us."

I scooped her into my arms. "Love, I will do anything you wish."

We made love for a long time that night, until the almost-full moon stood high above the balcony outside her bedchamber, silver light spilling through the open doors and drenching our bed. Afterward, we lay for a time watching it, both of us wondering. Wondering what lay in the spaces between the stars. Wondering what the morrow would bring, and wondering what would follow.

At length, Sidonie rolled over to face me. "I love you," she said. Her shadowed eyes were wide and grave, and the moonlight behind her pinned a silvery halo on her love-tangled hair. "Very, very much."

Elua, she made my heart ache.

I wound a lock of her hair around my fingers, feeling it catch on my knotted gold ring; a living echo of the gilded cord that bound us together. "Always," I said. "Always and always."

Despite my misgivings, I slept soundly that night.

I woke with a vague memory of my dreams, of beseeching Hyacinthe to fill the night sky with clouds that they might blot out the moon and ruin the Carthaginian horologists' spectacle. For the space of a few heartbeats, between sleeping and waking, I thought it was true, and my heart grew lighter. But then I opened my eyes to find the bedchamber filled with sunlight, and Sidonie, fully dressed, standing at the end of the bed and regarding me with amusement.

"Lazy boy," she said with affection.

I smiled at her and patted the bed. "Come back and join me?"

"I can't," Sidonie said ruefully, shaking her head. Gold shivered and glinted. Her hair was coiled in a coronet and she was wearing the earrings I'd given her for—Elua!—her seventeenth birthday, it had been. Golden suns, miniatures of the pendant she'd worn on the Longest Night the time I'd first kissed her. "I'm to attend a meeting between General Astegal and the Euskerri delegation."

I yawned and stretched. "Are the Euskerri intriguing with Carthage now?"

"Trying." She eyed me. "You needn't look so tempting."

"This scarred thing?" I asked flippantly, gesturing at my body.

"Mm-hmm." Sidonie's lips curved. "That very one." She stooped to kiss me, her lips lingering on mine. "I'll see you later."

It was a strange day and it passed slowly. I felt caught between warring moods, my apprehension at odds with last night's tenderness, and all of it overshadowed by the vast change looming on the horizon.

I dined that afternoon at Phèdre's townhouse. I didn't tell the whole story of how I'd coerced Gillimas, but I reported what I'd learned from him. In turn, I learned from Phèdre that the Governor of Cythera was one Ptolemy Solon, a kinsman of the Pharaoh of Menekhet, although he ruled under the auspices of Khebbel-im-Akkad.

And I learned from Ti-Philippe, when he joined us a bit later, that there were rumors among the sailors about the Governor's mistress.

"The same story?" I asked. "The Bella Donna?"

Ti-Philippe pursed his lips thoughtfully. "Not exactly. But the isle of Cythera was once sacred to the Hellenes as the home of their goddess of love and desire. It is rumored that her likeness has returned in mortal flesh."

"That would be your mother," Phèdre said calmly.

I groaned. "Isn't she a bit old for it?"

Phèdre raised her brows at me.

"I'll not say much in Melisande's favor," Joscelin intervened with rare diplomacy. "But I will say one thing. Among a folk renowned for beauty and aging with grace, she does stand out."

"What do you reckon is our best course?" I asked, steering the conversation onto safer shoals.

We talked for a while about plausible tales we could concoct to send a fleet of ships to Cythera to apprehend my mother without alerting her in advance, while at the same time maintaining the goodwill of Khebbel-im-Akkad. By the time I departed for the Palace, afternoon was finally wearing on toward evening.

There was a small formal meal that night with the Carthaginians, which I attended as a member of House Courcel. I was in no mood for small talk, and it seemed to drag on forever. All I wanted was for this night to be over, so I could lay aside my fears and at last address head-on the shadow that had been hanging over Sidonie and me for the past year.

It wasn't until we were lingering over glasses of cordial that the Court horologist came, quivering with excitement, to report that the hour was nigh. Even at that, Astegal assured us that we had well over an hour's time before the moon would be completely obscured. Not until that moment would the effects be visible.

"How long will it last?" Drustan inquired.

"At least an hour." Astegal smiled. "The heavens move slowly in their stately dance. There will be ample time for you to bask."

"Or ample time for many to glimpse the marvels you promise," noted Ysandre, who had dispatched a contingent of the Royal Army to ensure that matters proceeded in an orderly fashion, and as many folk as possible were able to share the spectacle.

Astegal accorded her a brief bow. "Her majesty is a generous ruler."

We left the Palace in open carriages, escorted by the Queen's Guard. In the courtyard, one could already see that it had begun. The full moon stood high overhead, a faint shadow beginning to blur one edge. The sight made me profoundly uneasy.

The streets of the City were packed with folk gazing at the night sky, talking in excited tones. It was a good thing that Ysandre had sent the Royal Army to secure Elua's Square, because a solid wall of people surrounded it. If Ghislain's soldiers hadn't held a corridor open, we'd have had a difficult time getting through. By the time we did, the encroaching shadow had eaten a good chunk of the moon.

It was an unnerving sight. The outer rim and the missing piece were still faintly visible, dull and red, the color of drying blood. Near the oak tree, the vast silver mirror gleamed. The angle of the moon was such that it was reflected perfectly in the mirror.

We were given places of honor around the perimeter of the mirror, as were a select number of other folk. I was pleased to see that Phèdre and Joscelin were among them.

There, we waited.

And waited.

And waited.

It was indeed a slow and stately dance. We peered into the mirror, gazed at the sky. We ceded our places briefly to others, letting them catch a glimpse. We strained our eyes gazing toward the distant walls of the City, trying to spot the other twelve mirrors. The bloody stain spread slowly over the moon, creeping gradually toward total obscurity.

There was only a thin sliver of silver-white moon yet visible when a voice at my ear whispered, "A word, your highness. Behind the oak. Believe me, it is more important than this so-called marvel."

The damned eunuch.

I turned, but he was already gone, a lithe, dark figure slipping through the throng. I glanced at Sidonie beside me. She was absorbed in watching the mirror, but she looked up and met my eyes.

"Sunjata," I murmured, too low for anyone else to hear.

"*Now?*" she asked in disbelief.

I nodded. "I'll be right back."

"Be careful," she said.

I grabbed the nearest person behind me, a surprised Siovalese engineer. "Have a quick look," I said, squeezing past him. "It's nearly time."

I left him stammering thanks and worked my way through the throng to the far side of the oak tree. Sunjata was there, pressed against it, barely visible in the shadows. I made my way to him, forced against him close as a lover due to the crush of people. His dark eyes gleamed, inches from mine.

"What the hell do you want?" I said through gritted teeth.

The crowd surged. Sunjata swayed, steadied himself with a hand on my waist. I felt his lips at my ear once more. "I'm sorry."

"For wha—" I began.

Pain, thin and piercing, seared my side. It felt like he'd driven an enormous needle into my kidneys. I tried to gasp, but my tongue was cleaved to the roof of my mouth. The sky overhead whirled, rotating around the bloody moon. Ice-hot fire ran in my veins.

"Listen to me," Sunjata whispered urgently. "I'm sorry. This was the only way to shield you from it. You're going to lose your wits. It's madness, but it will pass. The fever will break in a month."

The needle was withdrawn.

Cold flames continued to race through my veins. It felt like my skull was on fire. I tried to raise my hands to claw at it, but my knees were threatening to give way beneath me. Sunjata grasped my shoulders, holding me upright.

"Go to Cythera," he hissed. "Ask Ptolemy Solon how to undo what's done here tonight. He may even tell you." He released my shoulders, and I began to slump.

Somewhere, an emerald glow arose.

Brightness flashed.

The crowd gave a collective gasp.

I heard it, but I couldn't speak. Couldn't see anything but the roots of the oak tree that were rushing up at me, gnarled and writhing. A tangle of serpents. Deep in my throat, I mewled with fear. Serpents. Roots. I scrabbled at them. A dark hand caught mine. There was a tug on my finger, somewhat removed. A tangle. A knot of gold. A hand knotted in my hair, lifting my head.

"I'm sorry about this, too," Sunjata whispered. "But I don't dare disobey. It's a hard business serving two masters."

He let go my hair. My head fell. All around us, no one noticed, staring rapt at the bloody sky or shoving for a peek at the mirror.

"You're lucky your mother loves you," the eunuch whispered. "Go to Cythera." And then he was gone and madness took me.

That was the last thing I understood for a long, long time.

Thirteen

I had gone mad before.

When Dorelei was slain, I lost my wits. I remember bits and pieces of that terrible night. Running through the woods, my sword in hand. Charging the bear. Berlik's blow laying me open. Dorelei, dead.

I don't remember much of what followed, which was a mercy.

This was different.

I lived in a world of fever-racked terror. I knew no one. Not the ones who found me after the moon's shadow had passed. Not the ones who took me back to the Palace and tended me. Not myself. I knew only that I lived in a world bent on destroying me.

Things came alive.

Sweat-damp bedsheets sought to strangle me. Fat globules of wax slid from candles to scald my skin. Demon-filled shadows lurked in every corner.

My voice came back. I screamed and ranted until my throat was raw. The fever ebbed and flowed. My strength came and went in waves. When it came, I tried to escape. I struggled with my captors. A tall man with blond hair held me down.

They tied me to my bed, tied my wrists and ankles. I strained at my bonds until my muscles threatened to burst and my ligaments to crack. I bent my back like a bow. A dark-haired woman wept. I cursed her.

"I have to go to Cythera!" I shouted at her. "Let me go! *I have to go to Cythera!*"

She laid a cool compress on my brow, her hot tears falling on my face. They burned.

"Let me go, you weeping bitch!" I raged.

They didn't. They kept me there, day after day. When I was weak, they untied me. So I learned. I feigned weakness. One day, I broke free. I burst past them, laughing like a madman. They didn't expect me to be that quick.

They caught me, though, caught me in the hallway. Men with sheathed swords barred my way. I don't know why they didn't draw on me. Too slow, too stupid. The tall man grabbed me from behind, pinning my arms. I thrashed in his grip, cursing him, but he was strong.

"I'll take him," he said to them.

"You don't have to do this, Joscelin," one of them said. "Let us do it."

"He's my son," he said in a low voice. "At least in my heart."

I laughed and spat on the floor. "You wish!" I shouted. "My father was the north wind and my mother was a jackal!"

The tall man didn't answer, only tightened his grip. I struggled and kicked and scratched until others came to help him. They wrestled me into bed, tied my limbs. I went limp and stared up into his summer-blue eyes, hating him.

"Joscelin," I crooned. "That's your name, isn't it? I'll remember it." I rolled my head, rolling my gaze around the chamber. "She's your woman, isn't she? The weeping bitch." I saw fear in him and laughed. "You're scared of me, aren't you? Too scared to kill me. You ought to, you know."

"Imriel." He gazed at me with red-rimmed eyes. "Try to sleep."

"I have to go to Cythera!" I shouted at him.

Somewhere, the woman wept.

"Later, love," the tall man said gently. "When you're well."

I tugged steadily at my bonds, feeling the ropes bite into my skin. A serpent-tangle, fibrous teeth. Gnawing my flesh until it was blood-slick. "I'll cut out your heart," I said to him. "*Joscelin.* I'll get free, and I'll do it. I'll take your woman." I bared my teeth at him, inspiration coming from deep inside me. "I'll take her with my rusted iron rod, I will, and I'll make her beg for it like the whore she is."

He turned away with a choked sound, fists clenched.

Oh, that had hit hard, it had! I laughed.

"Joscelin." *She* was there, weepy-eyed, gentling him. "It's not his fault. He's borne too much for anyone's lifetime. Something broke inside him."

They held one another, consoled one another.

I jeered at them.

Days came and went. Others came and went. A tall woman with fair hair, a studied look of worry in her eyes. A man with a face like a blue mask and eyes like polished stones. Some bitch pretending to be a chirurgeon, a liar who called me cousin. People I didn't know.

I hated them.

I hated them all.

"I *will* kill you!" I raged, my fever spiking. I yanked at the ropes that bound me. Blood and sweat mingled. "All of you! I need to go to Cythera!"

"Hush, love." The dark-haired woman sat beside my bed. She had dark eyes, too. A scarlet mote swam on the outskirts of her left iris, vivid as a rose petal. For some reason, it maddened me further. She dipped a cloth in cool water, laid it on my fevered brow. "It's all right, Imri."

Since I couldn't move my limbs, I snapped my teeth at her.

Liars and hypocrites. They pretended to know me, pretended to be kind. They talked in worried tones, prayed and moaned and wept over me, but they kept me tied like an animal. They tried to feed me broth, and I spat it back in their faces. My body grew weak and wasted, ravaged by fever.

I memorized their names.

I would make them suffer for treating me like this. I plotted ways to kill them, ways to torture them before they died. I told them in exacting, foul detail, relishing the pain and fear it evoked in them. Day after day, I tormented them, while my body grew wasted and the ropes etched bloody channels into my wrists and ankles.

And then I woke up sane.

It was the moonlight that did it, a silvery wash of it spilling over my bed, so bright it woke me in the middle of the night. My bedsheets were soaked with sweat, but my body felt cool. I turned my head and gazed through the balcony doors. There was the full moon, round and bright as a silver coin.

It's madness, but it will pass. The fever will break in a month.

It had.

And I remembered everything.

My stomach seized. I turned my head and vomited, but nothing came out save a trickle of bile.

"Imriel?" In a chair in the corner, a shadowy figure

stirred and rose. Phèdre wiped my mouth tenderly with a clean cloth, eased the soiled pillow from beneath my head. "It's all right, love."

"Oh, *gods*!" I whispered, my eyes burning. "Oh, Blessed Elua and his Companions have mercy on me, ah, gods! Phèdre, I'm *so sorry*!"

She went very still, a moonlit statue. "For what, love?"

"Everything I've said and done in the past month," I said wearily, exhausted past the point of shame. "It's all right. It's passed. The fever's gone."

Phèdre kindled a lamp. In the warm glow, I could see her beautiful face was tired and worn, shadows like bruises beneath her eyes. She swallowed visibly, not quite daring to hope yet. "Do you know who you are?"

"Yes," I said. "Your foster-son, Imriel nó Montrève."

She covered her face with both hands, drew a shuddering breath. "And where you are?"

"In the bedchamber of my quarters at the Palace." I flexed my stiff hands. "Tied to my bed because I've been a stark raving lunatic since the last full moon."

"Oh, Imri!" The anguished tone of hope in Phèdre's voice nearly broke my heart. She laid a hand on my brow. "Is it true?"

Tears trickled from the corners of my eyes. "I promise."

"Joscelin!" Her voice rang out, filled with urgency. "*Joscelin!*"

He came at a run, startled out of sleep. For the past month, they'd been taking turns keeping watch over me. "What is it?"

"The fever's broken." Tears gleamed on Phèdre cheeks. "He knows himself."

Joscelin turned his bloodshot gaze on me. "Truly?"

"Yes," I whispered. "Joscelin, you look like hell. You look worse than I did when you found me in Vralia."

"Oh, *Elua*!" Joscelin dropped to his knees beside the bed. There were tears in his eyes, too. "I thought we'd lost you. Wherever it was you went, I didn't think you were coming back."

"I'm back," I said hoarsely. "I just wish I didn't remember."

He shook his head. "Don't . . . just don't. It was the fever talking."

Phèdre sent a guard to fetch the Court chirurgeon while Joscelin worked at the ropes binding me to the bed. My struggles had rendered the knots impossible to untie, and he had to saw at them with a dagger, working with tender care not to further injure my abraded flesh. Between the two of them, they helped me sit upright, propped against pillows, and drink a cup of water. I was so weak, Phèdre had to hold the cup for me. I could feel the water blazing a cool trail into my shrunken belly.

"Thank you." I leaned back against the pillows and closed my eyes, exhausted by the effort. "Where's Sidonie?"

There was a brief silence.

"Sidonie?" Joscelin asked in a puzzled tone.

I opened my eyes.

"Like as not in Carthage by now." Phèdre refilled the cup from a ewer. "Why, love?"

"*Carthage?*" I stared at her. "No."

"To wed Prince Astegal," she reminded me, holding the cup to my lips.

"No." I pushed it away feebly. "No, no, no! Have you all lost your wits?"

Their faces fell. "It's all right," Joscelin said to Phèdre. "He knows himself, and us. The rest will come."

"I just thought . . ." she murmured.

"I know," he said.

"No!" I shouted at them. "Gods above, *I'm* fine!" I saw

the fear in their eyes and caught myself, falling silent. I made myself look at the memories of my month-long madness.

Sidonie wasn't in them.

This was the only way to shield you from it.

"Astegal," I muttered. "What did you do? What did they do, those damned Carthaginians? What did they do?" I repeated, addressing Phèdre and Joscelin. "The full moon, the mirror? What did they *do*?"

"Hush." Phèdre stroked my cheek. "It's all right, love."

"What did you see in the mirror?" I demanded.

They exchanged a glance, faces softening. "It was a marvel," Joscelin said, wonder in his tone. "The invisible ties that bind all things in the cosmos . . ." His voice trailed off.

"No," I said dully. "It was a trick. It was some vast and terrible enchantment, and I was protected from it only because the eunuch stabbed me with something that sent me mad." I laughed in despair. "Madness as a shield against madness. Now I'm sane, and you're raving."

"You're sick," Phèdre said gently.

"I'm sane," I said. "Sidonie loves me. She defied her mother and half the realm for my sake. She would never wed Astegal. And Terre d'Ange would never betray its alliance with Aragonia to unite with Carthage."

Phèdre shook her head in sorrow and went to meet the chirurgeon.

Somewhat was wrong, terribly wrong. Filled with terror, I held my tongue and suffered myself to be examined by the royal chirurgeon, Lelahiah Valais. She confirmed that the worst of the fever had broken, bandaged my injuries, and recommended strong broth and a great deal of sleep. I heard them speak in hushed tones about my continued delusions.

"Do you think it's because he was taken by Carthaginian

slavers as a child that he harbors such a peculiar grudge?" Joscelin asked the chirurgeon.

"Oh, yes," Lelahiah said. "I'm sure of it. And to be fair, I've heard there are folk outside the City unhappy with the Queen's decision."

"People are always fearful of change," Phèdre murmured. "But what do you make of his claim about Sidonie, of all people?" She sounded perplexed. "I wouldn't say they disliked one another, but they've never been close."

"Mayhap that's why." The chirurgeon lowered her voice. "The mind is a strange place, my lady, and we cannot examine its workings the way we examine the body's. I understand he was very ill after his wife was slain and his wounds turned septic. Mayhap one spell of madness evoked another, and somehow in his thoughts, he has replaced the loss of his wife with a loss that is less painful to him."

Less painful.

Sidonie.

I stared at the moon outside my balcony. A month ago, I'd made love to her by moonlight. Now she was gone. Gone to Carthage, gone to wed Astegal. Gone of her own volition, it seemed. Was I mad? I had been. I'd said things that made me cringe inside. I didn't trust myself. But I loved Sidonie. I knew I did. And she loved me. I could feel her absence like a wound. I remembered her. Everything about her. Everything we had done together. Her scent, the taste of her skin. The faraway look she got in the throes of pleasure. Her voice. *Always and always.*

My head was full of voices and memory.

Gods, I was tired.

Alais' voice, her grave face the day we'd spoken atop the ramparts of Bryn Gorrydum. *I think she's going to need you very badly one day.*

That damned eunuch, Sunjata.

Go to Cythera.

Ask Ptolemy Solon how to undo what's done here tonight.

I closed my eyes. "Whatever it is, I'll do it," I whispered into the darkness. "I'll come for you, love. I promise."

FOURTEEN

My strength returned slowly.

It wasn't as bad as it had been after Dorelei's death. I wasn't wounded, save for the suppurating abrasions around my wrists and ankles, a bitterly ironic reminder of the bindings I'd once worn as a protection against enchantment. But the fever and lack of nourishment had left me weak.

And I was surrounded by madness.

Everyone in the Palace believed it. Terre d'Ange—and oh, gods, Alba too—had made a pact with Carthage. Sidonie had gone away to wed Astegal, escorted onto the Carthaginian flagship with great fanfare.

No one remembered our affair.

It had been erased from memory as though it had never existed. Mavros came to visit me when he learned I was recovering. I begged him to rack his wits. He had been the first person to know, the one who had helped from the very beginning. All he could do was gaze at me with sympathy and shake his head.

I wanted desperately to get outside the City, but in the

first days of my recuperation, I barely had the strength to get out of bed. On Lelahiah Valais' orders, I was kept in relative solitude. Only family members were permitted to visit me. I wasn't allowed to hear aught that might disturb me and feed my delusions. Servants and guards were given strict orders not to discuss sensitive matters in my presence.

Still, I heard wisps of conversation here and there, enough to gather that there was widespread dismay beyond the City's walls. It gave me a thread of hope.

And then, some five days after my fever broke, I overheard a careless guard remark to a chambermaid as she entered my quarters that Ysandre and Barquiel L'Envers were engaged in a shouting match in the throne hall.

L'Envers hadn't been in the City the night of the full moon.

I struggled into my clothing, trembling with exertion, and made my way into the salon. "I need to talk to him," I said. "*Now.*"

"Oh no!" the guard said in alarm. "That's not possible, your highness."

"The hell it's not," I said. "Get out of my way."

He blocked me. "Send for Messire Joscelin and Lady Phèdre," he said urgently to the maid. "They're in the throne hall with her majesty."

She nodded and fled.

I found my sword-belt and drew my blade. My arm shook. "*Get out of my way.*"

The guard put his hands up. "Don't do this, your highness. You're ill."

I gritted my teeth. "I just want to talk to L'Envers. Stand aside, man!"

He did.

I pushed past him, sword in hand. Elua knows, I couldn't blame them for trying to protect me from myself. The madness had made a monster of me. I would never be able to forget. But it was gone now, or at least banished into wherever it is that such things lurk in the dark, unplumbed depths of the soul.

At least I prayed it was.

Trailed by the anxious guard, I staggered out of my quarters. Down the hallway, down the wide marble stair that led to the ground floor of the Palace. I took a two-handed grip on my sword, keeping it angled before me. People shrieked and ran. They'd heard tell of my ravings. More guardsmen came, forming a wary circle around me. I ignored them and staggered onward.

The doors to the throne hall were closed. I could hear raised voices behind them. With both hands, I pointed my sword at the guards posted there. "Admit me."

They paled. "We can't, your highness," one said.

My knees wobbled. "Just do it!"

Someone grabbed me from behind, pinning my arms as Joscelin had done. Someone else wrestled the sword from my hands. I cursed and struggled, borne down under the weight of several guards.

The doors to the throne hall opened with a crash and Barquiel L'Envers strode out, his face white with fury. He stopped short at the sight of me struggling with the guards, fixing me with a look of disgust.

"Some great undying love affair *that* turned out to be," L'Envers said in contempt, then turned on his heel and strode away, followed by a retinue of his own men-at-arms.

"Wait!" His words rang in my ears. A rill of terrified strength ran through me. I thrashed and flailed my way free, got my feet under me, and ran after him.

L'Envers turned and drew his blade. "Keep your distance, lunatic," he said coldly. "I swear to Elua, I *will* run you through."

I managed to halt before I impaled myself. "You remember," I gasped. "Sidonie and I. You remember it."

"Unfortunately." His violet eyes narrowed. "Do you?"

I nodded, panting. "Can we speak, my lord? Please?"

He was silent a moment. "Fetch his blade," he said at length to one of his men, and to me, "Come with me."

On any other occasion, the last place in the world I could imagine wanting to be was alone with Barquiel L'Envers in his private quarters, surrounded by men loyal to him. Today, I was desperately grateful to be there. He sent his men out of earshot, ensconced me on his couch, poured me a generous draught of brandy, then poured one for himself, and sat opposite me.

"Speak."

I had nothing left to lose. I told him everything.

Claudia Fulvia, the Unseen Guild and their threats. Canis and my mother. My letter to Diokles Agallon, the bargain. Carthage. The eunuch Sunjata, Gillimas. What had happened the night of the full moon. Ptolemy Solon and Cythera. My month-long madness, and the madness I'd awoken to.

"Sodding Carthage," L'Envers said when I'd finished. "I knew it."

"Then I'm not mad?" I asked.

"You were." He studied me. "Barking-mad, from the sound of it. But in this, it's hard to say." He quaffed his brandy and refilled it, regarding the glass. "Truth be told, I heard rumors of this Guild of yours years ago in Khebbel-im-Akkad, though I couldn't vouch for them. Of a surety, the whole damn City is convinced, man, woman, and child, that Carthage is our new best friend, and the Dauphine of Terre d'Ange made a love-match with a Carthaginian prince and sailed away merrily with him. You're right about that. Somewhat was done to them."

"But it's only the City?" I said hopefully.

Barquiel L'Envers snorted. "The City, and all who were in it that night. Damn nigh all of Parliament. The Royal Army and its commander. The Royal Admiral and a good number of his men. The Cruarch of Alba."

I felt sick. "All the powers of the realm."

He nodded, looking aged and weary. "And Ysandre's minded to dispatch the army to the Aragonian border in support of Carthage's threat." He scrubbed his face with one hand. "I tell you, lad, if this is some elaborate scheme of your mother's to place you on the throne, I've half a mind to go along with it. I'd sooner see Melisande's treasonous spawn warming his arse on the throne than my own niece acting as Carthage's pawn. And outside the City walls, there are hundreds of thousands of folk who'd agree."

"I don't think it is. The eunuch said he served two masters." I shook my head. "Anyway, it doesn't matter. I can't stay here."

"Oh?" L'Envers raised his brows.

"Sidonie needs me," I said simply. "I have to go."

Barquiel L'Envers looked at me for a long, long time, an incredulous expression slowly dawning over his worn features. He gave a short, choked laugh. "Oh, Blessed Elua bugger me! You actually *love* her?"

Tears stung my eyes. "Very much so, my lord."

"Blessed Elua bugger me," L'Envers repeated, bemused. "So what in the seven hells do we do, Imriel de la Courcel? Raise an army? Wrest Quintilius Rousse's fleet from his control and sail against Carthage? How do we do it without setting off a civil war in Terre d'Ange?"

"We can't," I said. "We have to break the spell."

"Cythera." He raked a hand through his short-cropped hair. "You're sure that part's not a fever-dream?"

"As sure as I can be. Sunjata said the fever would break in a month, and it did. I have to try," I said. "I'll grovel and beg, if that's what it takes. If Ptolemy Solon knows how to undo this, I'll do whatever is needful. But I need your help to get out of the City, my lord."

"If it's *not* a piece of your madness, you know damned well what he'll ask for," L'Envers said wryly. "A pardon for Melisande Shahrizai."

I was silent.

L'Envers sighed. "I wish to hell I knew whether or not to believe you."

"I'm not lying," I said stiffly.

"No." He eyed me. "No, I don't think you are. But I'm not sure you've got your wits back altogether, and of a surety, I'm not convinced you aren't a pawn in some unknowable scheme of your mother's. Are you?"

You're lucky your mother loves you.

"I don't know," I said honestly. "If I am, can it truly be worse than this?" He didn't answer. I sipped my brandy, thinking. "Send to Alba, my lord. There's still one member of House Courcel fit to sit the throne. Alais. If you raise a large enough delegation of D'Angelines and Albans alike to petition Ysandre and convince her that there's somewhat amiss, if you *reason* with her instead of shouting, mayhap she'll be willing to let Alais assume the throne until we can undo what was done."

"Alais!" L'Envers said in surprise. "That slip of a girl?"

"She's second in line for the throne," I pointed out. "And she's gained her majority; she turned eighteen last winter."

"True," he mused.

"She has the Master of the Straits' ear," I added. "If there's anyone Drustan might listen to, it's Hyacinthe. I'm sure he would help. He's a deadly force unto himself, and he knows a good deal about magic. So do the *ollamhs*." I thought about Berlik. "So do the Maghuin Dhonn, for that matter. It's worth asking."

"Anything else?" L'Envers asked, only slightly sardonic.

"Scour the Royal Archives," I suggested. "The Secretary of the Presence will have recorded Parliament's last session and . . . and the public audience wherein Ysandre bade me to bring my mother to justice if I truly wished to wed Sidonie. There has to be written evidence that casts doubt on Carthage's claims and proves the truth. You can recruit scholars from outside the City to compile it."

"While you sail off to Cythera to reunite with your mother and Carthage goes unchecked," he said.

I spread my hands. "Do you have a better plan?"

"Unfortunately, no," L'Envers muttered, rising to pace the room. "You have a point. At the least, it might stall Ysandre from sending the army against Aragonia without setting off a civil war. And there would be a legitimate heir on the throne." He halted. "No pardon for Melisande. A pardon's unacceptable." A look of profound distaste crossed his features. "However, I suppose we could offer to commute her sentence to exile in exchange for Ptolemy Solon's assistance."

My heart leapt. "Then you'll help me?"

"Gods, I must have lost my own wits." His mouth twisted. "I swear to Blessed Elua, if you fail in this, if you prove false or a dupe, I will make it my life's work to hunt you down and kill you." His violet eyes were deadly serious. "No intrigue, no ploys. I will kill you and bear whatever punishment follows."

I thought about Astegal in Jasmine House, his arms slung around a pair of adepts. Smiling as he emerged at dawn, heavy-lidded. I thought about Sidonie in his bed, ensorceled, spreading her thighs willingly for him, urging him into her. My muscles knotted, trembling with fury.

"Duc Barquiel," I said in perfect sincerity, "if I fail in this, you're more than welcome to kill me."

He gave a curt nod. "What do you need?"

I told him. I didn't need much. Money. My horse, my sword and vambraces, some supplies. Mostly I needed to get out of the City of Elua and to Marsilikos without someone sending guards to retrieve me for my own safety.

"Can you ride?" L'Envers asked pragmatically. "You look half-starved and weak as a day-old kitten."

I shrugged. "I'll manage."

He snorted. "I'll arrange for passage by barge. Think you can convince your keepers to let you make a healing-offering at Eisheth's temple in three days?"

"I think so." I smiled ruefully. "It's not a bad idea, actually."

"All right." There was noise in the corridor outside L'Envers' quarters. He turned his head. "Ah. That would be someone come to make sure I've not gutted you, I suspect. I'm surprised it took so long." He put out his hand. "Eisheth's temple, three days."

I rose and took his hand. "Thank you, my lord."

Barquiel L'Envers tightened his grip. "Just don't fail."

Fifteen

It wasn't hard to convince Phèdre and Joscelin to take me to Eisheth's temple; indeed, they thought it an excellent idea. I'd regained enough strength that Lelahiah Valais reckoned the outing would do me no harm, and Phèdre and Joscelin both thought it a hopeful sign that I realized I was yet in need of healing.

I felt awful about it.

I hated to betray their trust. As if I hadn't reason enough to love them, they'd stood by me during my madness, tending me with care while I ranted and raved. The things I'd said were seared into my memory. And when I'd come out of it, they'd welcomed me back with heartbreaking joy, forgiving every word without a thought.

Now I was leaving.

I couldn't see any way around it. I'd tried, over and over, to convince them of the truth about Carthage. Elua knows, they had to have doubts. Barquiel L'Envers wasn't alone. Although he was the only one to take it up with the Queen thus far, there was a realm full of bewildered folk outside the walls of the City.

But they wouldn't hear it, not from me. The madness that had protected me worked against me. I *had* been insane—barking-mad, as L'Envers had said, frothing at the mouth. And every memory that contradicted the beliefs that Carthage's magics had instilled was gone, vanished. When I reminded Phèdre of her research into Cythera, when I reminded Joscelin how he'd thought of sending Ti-Philippe to scout among Rousse's sailors, they looked grave and worried, and quietly changed the subject.

I could imagine the memory that it evoked.

Me, tied to a bed and screaming about Cythera.

They would never let me go, not now. Mayhap in time I could wear them down. Once L'Envers assembled a delegation, once they realized that outside the walls of the City, my seeming delusion was shared by thousands, things would begin to change. But even at that, my tale would seem half-mad. L'Envers was willing to take a chance on it only because he was desperate and he didn't care if I lived or died. There was no way I could prove the truth of my tale. Folk outside the City could attest to my relationship with Sidonie, my quest to find my mother. Not the existence of the Unseen Guild, shrouded in deadly secrecy. Not the admission I'd forced from Gillimas of Hiram. And of a surety, not my encounter with Sunjata the night of the full moon. It would take a long, long time before any of that began to sound like aught but fever-dreams to anyone caught in the grip of Carthage's spell.

I couldn't afford to wait.

Not while Astegal . . . ah, gods! I couldn't bear to think on it.

So I gave up and behaved like a model patient. I spent the long, tedious hours of my recuperation writing a letter expressing my apologies ten thousand ways over. Begging forgiveness. Telling them I loved them. And three days after my meeting with Barquiel L'Envers, two of the people I loved best in the world escorted me gladly to Eisheth's temple, where I meant to betray them.

The temple was built around a spring whose waters were said to have healing properties. It was an expansive and gracious place. Many people came to stay for days at a time, partaking of the healing waters. The head priestess met us in the temple courtyard, a brown-haired woman of middle years, clad in sea-blue robes. I recognized her; she had been present at my hearing in the Great Temple of Elua, when all the orders of Blessed Elua and his Companions had elected to acknowledge Sidonie's and my love. She gave no sign of having met me before.

"Be welcome, Prince Imriel," she said, bowing. "May you find healing here."

My eyes stung. "Thank you."

I turned to Phèdre and Joscelin. It was a bright day, the sun pinning a silvery cap on Joscelin's fair hair, illuminating the scarlet mote in Phèdre's dark eyes. They were smiling, happy, unaware that the world had fallen to pieces all around us. My heart ached at what I was about to do.

"I love you," I said to them. "I love you both."

"We'll be here." Phèdre stretched to kiss my cheek. "You have your offering?"

My throat tightened. "I do."

"Drink deep," Joscelin advised me.

"I will," I murmured, blinking away tears.

And then I left them, Phèdre and Joscelin, the parents of my heart, to entrust myself into the hands of a man who'd wanted me dead since I was born. I followed the priestess as she led me into the inner sanctum, a rocky little garden. There was the spring, bubbling gently, lined by moss-covered stones on which votive candles burned, their flames almost invisible in the sunlight. There was the effigy of Eisheth: the figure of a woman, half again as large as life, kneeling beside the spring, her hands cupped. Streaks of green moss reached up her marble flanks. Her cupped hands held the ashes of other offerings.

"Make your offering." The priestess pressed my shoulder, pushing me gently to my knees. "Drink, and seek healing."

I knelt and she left me.

Eisheth's head was bowed, curtains of marble hair hiding her features. Humble. The mossy stones were damp beneath my knees. I fumbled for the packet tied to my belt, poured an offering of incense into her cupped hands. Hyssop and cedar gum. There were wax tapers piled neatly at her feet. I took one, kindled it at a votive, and lit the incense. A sweet thread of smoke arose from her palms, bluish in the sunlight.

"Merciful Eisheth, grant me healing," I whispered. "Grant it to us all."

I cupped my own hands, dipped them into the spring, and drank. The water was cool, with an acrid mineral tang. I drank deep.

"Ready, highness?" a man's voice whispered behind me.

It was one of L'Envers' guards, beckoning from the entrance, a grey cloak folded over one arm. He didn't have to tell me to hurry. I crossed quickly over to him and donned the cloak, pulling up the hood to hide my features.

"This way." He steered me down the wide corridor, then turned into a narrow hall used by the initiates and acolytes who served the priesthood. I could tell, because he pointed to the crumpled figure of one on the floor. "Mind the body."

I stepped gingerly over it. "You didn't . . . ?"

The guard shook his head. "He'll have a lump on his skull, that's all."

I was relieved. Barquiel L'Envers had a name for being ruthless. At least he was efficient, too. His guardsman navigated me with swift certitude down the back hallways of the temple. Once we had to duck into a storage room filled with strips of willow bark while a pair of acolytes passed, but we managed to exit the temple by the postern gate. There was a plain carriage waiting, another guard at the reins.

"Get in." The first guard opened the carriage door and gave me an ungentle shove. He followed as I slid across the seats, shouting to the driver, "Go!"

The driver snapped the reins and the carriage lurched into motion. "My thanks," I said to the guard.

"Don't thank me." His face was shuttered. "I'm just following orders. It's a sodding mystery to me why his grace is helping you."

"Love of country?" I suggested.

"How on earth is packing you off to some strange isle supposed to help?" His expression slipped a little to reveal utter bewilderment. "No mind. Like as not, he's finally found a way to get rid of you."

"Like as not," I agreed, wondering if it was true.

The carriage took us to the wharf. Barquiel L'Envers was there alongside a sizable merchant-barge, drumming his fingers impatiently on his sword-belt. I dismounted from the carriage, careful to keep my hood up.

"Everything's there." L'Envers jerked his chin at the barge. "Your horse, your things. Passage paid to Marsilikos. After that, you're on your own."

I took a deep breath. "Thank you, my lord."

"The captain and crew are sound," he said. "They were outside the City when it happened. I paid them to keep their mouths shut, and they're scared enough to do it. If you need help in Marsilikos, try the Lady's daughter. She wasn't here for it, either."

"I will." I hesitated, then fished the letter I'd written out of an inner pocket. "I don't have the right to ask you any further favors . . ."

L'Envers lips tightened. "Just ask."

"This is for Phèdre and Joscelin." I handed him the letter. "I didn't divulge any details. And I know you can't give it to them yet. Not until I'm well away, not until you've raised a sufficient delegation that they might, *might* listen, instead of accusing you of abducting me. But it's important to me. I owe them my life. I owe them everything I am."

He took it. "What else?"

"Sidonie," I said softly. "If I fail, if I've been misled . . ." My voice faltered. "You're welcome to seek vengeance against me, I don't care. But please . . . no matter how it seemed, she didn't go willingly. Not really."

Somewhat in L'Envers' worn, chiseled face softened. "I know."

I swallowed. "Whatever you can do to save her."

"Imriel." Barquiel L'Envers hands settled on my shoulders. "She's my blood. Why the hell do you think I wanted to protect her from you so badly?" His fingers flexed, biting deep. "I'll do whatever I can."

"Thank you," I whispered.

He let me go. "Get out of here."

I went.

Shrouded in my cloak, I boarded the barge. I wasn't such a fool as to trust L'Envers wholeheartedly; before we cast off, I made certain all was as he'd promised. It was. The Bastard was belowdeck, looking profoundly discontented. I lingered briefly, cupping his whiskered muzzle in my hand. My saddlebags were stowed in a cabin, neatly packed. There was a generous purse. My sword-belt and my dagger were there. I buckled my weapons in place, my fingers shaking with the effort. Still, it made me feel stronger.

I went to tell the barge captain all was in readiness. He was a taciturn Eisandine fellow, uneasiness lurking behind his eyes.

"You're sure you want to do this, your highness?" he asked.

Sunlight sparkled on the Aviline River. I could see the distant walls of the Palace gleaming. Somewhere in the City behind us, Phèdre and Joscelin were strolling the outer gardens of Eisheth's temple, beginning to get worried. Mayhap they were already alarmed, alerted that some intruder had struck down a young initiate and I was nowhere to be found.

And somewhere in Carthage, Astegal, a prince of the House of Sarkal, appointed General of the Council of Thirty, preened his scarlet beard and dreamed of empire, basking under the ensorceled gaze of *my* girl Sidonie. Whom he might or might not have wed by now. Who did not love him, but had gone away with him willingly.

I ground my teeth. "I'm sure."

The captain—Gilbert Dumel was his name—gave the order. "Oars away!"

The moorings were loosed, the ropes tossed aboard the barge. Deft sailors leapt across the gap. Rowers bent their backs, groaning with effort. L'Envers and his men were gone, nowhere in sight.

Another departure, another leavetaking.

Gods, I was tired.

The grey cloak puddled around me. I heard members of the crew murmuring, speculating. I bowed my head like Eisheth, splaying one hand on the sun-warmed boards of the prow to brace myself.

Love.

You will find it and lose it, again and again.

A Priest of Elua had told me that long ago. It was true. There were so many loves in my life I had found and lost. So many treasures that had slipped through my fingers. Not this. I wouldn't allow it.

Not Sidonie.

Sixteen

The barge made steady progress down the Aviline. I kept to myself, spending long hours practicing the Cassiline discipline in an effort to regain my strength, while the green banks of Terre d'Ange slid past us.

Gilbert and his men gave me a wide, wary berth. They'd heard the stories in the City. Prince Imriel gone mad, tied to his bed and raving. I might have seemed sane enough now, but my wrists were still circled with healing scabs.

They kept their word, though. No one betrayed my presence. I supposed that was one good thing about finding myself under the patronage of Barquiel L'Envers. He wasn't a man anyone wanted to cross.

And, too, they were scared. Somehow, Carthage had managed to strike at the very heart of Terre d'Ange, and no one knew how.

As the days passed, I grew stronger. I'd fought back from worse. Berlik had nearly killed me; this was nothing.

Fighting despair was harder.

Even as my body slowly healed, the sense of weariness

persisted. It had nothing to do with overexerting myself. It was a fear that I'd been given one burden more than I could carry. I *had* failed in Vralia. I'd given up and prepared to abandon my hunt for Berlik. In the end, he'd come to me.

This was different, though. I'd wanted vengeance for Dorelei, very much. I'd wanted to let her spirit rest peacefully. I'd needed to assuage my grief. And I'd wanted to do my utmost to ameliorate the shadow of guilt that lay between Sidonie and me. Still, I could have lived with the failure, bitter and awful though it would have been.

Not this one.

So I pushed my body until my muscles quivered, taking a grim solace in my returning strength. I forced myself not to think about Sidonie and Astegal. It was too dangerous, filling me with fury and despair, making me fear for my sanity once more. There was darkness lurking in me, spilled out by the prick of a eunuch's needle. I couldn't give in to it.

We reached the wide mouth of the Aviline, opening onto the sea. The barge turned east along the coast, making for Marsilikos. I gazed out at the vast expanse of water to the south, thinking about the lands that lay beyond.

Cythera.

Carthage.

Like Tiberium, Carthage had ruled a vast empire once. Long ago, in the days before Blessed Elua wandered the earth, Carthage had conquered Aragonia. It had made alliances with our forebears in the land that would become Terre d'Ange; it had marched on Tiberium. Armies of both nations had fought one another to a standstill.

In the end, the pendulum had swung. Carthage's army had been vanquished on Tiberian soil, its dream of empire destroyed. Tiberium's star had risen for a time, until it too had fallen.

Now Carthage sought to rise again, armed with dire magic.

It could be stopped, though. I had to believe it. Whatever the horologists had done, it wasn't as deadly as what I'd witnessed in Drujan. The Âka-Magi there had used madness as a weapon to destroy an entire Akkadian army, turning it against itself. They had been able to kill with a thought. And Phèdre had managed to bring them down nonetheless—Phèdre, Joscelin, and the brave folk of the zenana.

I had to believe.

The gilded Dome of the Lady was shining brightly the day we reached Marsilikos. The harbor was busy, filled with an unwarranted number of Quintilius Rousse's ships. His men were swarming everywhere. I didn't dare roam the docks, seeking passage to Cythera. Once the Bastard was unloaded, I thanked Gilbert and his men and took my leave of them. I rode into the city, struggling with my fractious horse, sweating beneath my concealing cloak. I'd regained a good measure of strength, but not nearly as much as I'd have liked.

The streets of Marsilikos were filled with uneasy talk. I took a room at a modest inn and gave a false name. I paid a lad to carry a note to the Lady of Marsilikos' daughter, Jeanne de Mereliot, then sat in the tavern, drinking ale and eavesdropping.

All the conversation was the same. Roxanne de Mereliot, her son, Gerard, and every member of their retinue had returned from the City of Elua under the conviction that Terre d'Ange was Carthage's ally, speaking in vague, glowing terms of a marvel they had witnessed, speaking happily of the love-match between Astegal and Sidonie.

No one could fathom why.

There was speculation about a bribe of unimaginable proportions, fueled by the accounts of Carthage's generous gifts. Here and there, a few stalwarts insisted that it had to be some ploy Ysandre and Drustan had concocted to confuse Carthage, lulling them into complacency, but no one could explain how that would play out in a manner that would justify Sidonie's sacrifice.

And there were whispers of dark magic performed beneath a bloody moon, about Carthage itself, a land with gods terrible enough that they had once demanded the sacrifice of babes and children.

I listened, gritting my teeth until my jaw ached.

It wasn't long before the tavern-lad returned with a message from Jeanne de Mereliot, bidding me to meet her in all haste at the Academy of Medicine. I'd nearly forgotten she was a chirurgeon in her own right. She was of Eisheth's line, with healing in her blood.

Since it wasn't far, I made the journey on foot, cloaked and sweltering in the heat, pushing my body to further endurance. There weren't many folk in Marsilikos who could put a name to my face for a surety, but there were a few. I'd ridden with Gerard de Mereliot and an escort of the Lady's men once. With my luck, I'd be sure to encounter one of them.

For a mercy, I didn't.

At the Academy, I presented myself as Cadmar of Landras. It was the name of a boy I'd known long ago when I was a child in the Sanctuary of Elua. I don't know why it was the first thing I'd thought of when I'd given a false name, except that it was a piece of my past no one would ever connect to Imriel de la Courcel. I'd warned Jeanne in the note I'd sent, and I was escorted to her study without question.

"Im—" Jeanne caught her breath at the sight of me, barely catching herself before saying my name. We had passed a night together once, or at least several hours of one. Eisheth's mercy takes many forms. Her smoky grey eyes widened.

"You look . . ." She shook her head. "Thank you," she said to the attendant who had escorted me. "You may go."

"Well met, Jeanne," I said when the door had closed.

"You look awful," she said gently.

"I've looked worse," I said. "Believe me."

Jeanne regarded me with a chirurgeon's concern. "You were very ill. You shouldn't be travelling, Imriel. Not like this."

"I wasn't ill." I found a chair and sat. "I was stark raving mad, Jeanne. But it passed, and now I'm the only living soul who was in the City of Elua the night the moon was obscured who *doesn't* believe that Carthage and Terre d'Ange are allies, and Sidonie de la Courcel fell in love with a Carthaginian prince."

"So your letter suggested." Tears shone in her eyes, born of frustration and weariness. "What in Blessed Elua's name *happened* that night?" Jeanne gestured helplessly around her study, which was piled high with books and scrolls. "I've been looking for answers; we all have. But there's nothing in history to guide us, no account of thousands of folk succumbing to the same delusion at the same time."

"It was a trick," I said. "A spell."

"You saw it?" she asked. "What they did?"

The hope in her voice hurt. I shook my head. "I saw very little. A man drove a needle into me." I touched my side. "Here. He told me I would go mad, but it was for my own protection. He said the fever would break in a month. And he said to seek out Ptolemy Solon in Cythera, who would know how to undo what was done. That's why I'm here. I need your help booking passage to Cythera."

"A needle." A strange expression crossed Jeanne's face. She stooped before me, laying one hand on my brow. "Have you any idea how that sounds?"

"Yes." I caught her hand. "But it's true. There's nothing

wrong with my memory. I remember *you.* You came to my room and offered me respite. Eisheth's mercy. You opened all the windows. I remember, Jeanne. Your black hair spread on the pillow like sea-grass, the cool wind blowing over my skin. You were gentle and kind, and I needed that so much. When you left, you laughed and told me Eisheth had a fondness for beautiful sailor-boys."

Her fingers stirred in mine. "Remembering that doesn't make this true."

"But what if it is?" I asked simply.

She didn't answer right away, but began rummaging through the texts piled on every surface of her study, her face fierce with concentration. I sat quietly, watching her.

"Here," Jeanne said at length, thrusting an ancient, cracked tome at me, marking a passage with one finger. It was written in Hellene.

I read it.

To induce madness, forge a needle of silver that has never seen daylight, one handspan's length. Bathe it in the sweat of a lunatic's brow mixed with the effluvium of a horned toad. For one year, expose it to the light of the full moon. When plunged into the vitals, it will induce madness for the duration of the moon's cycle.

My blood ran cold. "What is this book? Where did you get it?"

"It's a compendium of occult ailments by Cleon of Naxos," Jeanne said. "He spent years gathering tales of folk rumored to have been afflicted by witchcraft." She shrugged. "No one's ever given it credence, but there was a copy in the Academy library. A curiosity, I suppose. I pulled it only out of desperation."

"Does Cleon of Naxos suggest cures?" I asked.

"No." Regret darkened her gaze. "He died some two hundred years ago. There's a note at the end of the compendium stating he meant to compile a volume of occult cures, but so far as I know, he never did."

"Damn." I closed the book. "Well, it's somewhat." I remembered the searing pain of Sunjata's needle plunging deep into my flesh and shivered. A madman's sweat and toad-slime. Gods.

"Are you sure you're all right?" Jeanne asked.

"I'll manage." I handed the book back to her. "Jeanne, listen. It was Barquiel L'Envers who helped me get this far. He's the only ranking peer of the realm who *wasn't* in the City that night. He's planning to raise a delegation to petition Ysandre to step aside and let Alais assume the throne until we can find a way to undo this."

"L'Envers helped you?" Her voice held an incredulous note.

"He's desperate, too." I smiled briefly. "Or eager to be rid of me. Tell him about this. If nothing else, it's one more piece of proof that I'm not remembering fever-dreams. And mayhap there are other texts no one's ever heeded that might hold other answers."

Resolve strengthened her features. "It's worth looking."

"Will you help me get to Cythera?" I asked.

Jeanne gave me a long look. "I shouldn't. I'm not sure it wouldn't be violating my chirurgeon's oath."

"Do no harm," I said softly, thinking of Canis' medallion. "My lady, believe me when I tell you that you will do me far greater harm if you withhold your aid."

"The Dauphine?" she asked with sympathy.

I nodded, suddenly bereft of words.

Jeanne sighed. "I'll do it."

"Thank you." I caught her hands and kissed them. "Thank you. Thank you."

"You're welcome." Silence fell between us. Jeanne de Mereliot freed one hand, touched my cheek with that healing gentleness I remembered so well. Her grey eyes were clear and grave and lovely. "I keep a private chamber here at the Academy if you'd prefer to stay here tonight." She smiled a little. "I promise you, it's much tidier than my study."

Respite.

Eisheth's mercy.

I understood what she was offering, and I wanted it more than I would have reckoned. A blessing to carry with me, a memory of grace to ward off the memories of madness that racked me with shame. A night's haven, a talisman against the thoughts of Sidonie in Astegal's bed.

But it would blur other memories, too.

Sidonie, silvered by moonlight, her face in shadow. The sweat of love-making drying on our skin.

I love you. Very, very much.

Always, I'd said. *Always and always.*

I needed to cling to it. It was that memory which lent me purpose and courage. I couldn't afford to let go of it, to lessen it in any way. I was afraid I'd fall apart if I did.

"You are as kind as you are beautiful," I said to Jeanne. "And there is a large part of me that would like nothing better. But, my lady, I'm very much afraid that your kindness would prove my undoing."

She smiled again, but there was sorrow in it. "Then I'll send word to Cadmar of Landras at the inn. Promise me you'll have a care for yourself."

"It's a long sea voyage," I said. "I'll have naught to do but rest idle."

Jeanne frowned, a belated thought occurring to her. "Why is L'Envers sending you alone and in secret? Do you reckon he *is* hoping to be rid of you?"

"I don't think so, no." I shook my head. "It's a long story, and there are parts of it that are dangerous to know. But the one who drove the needle into me, the one who bade me go to Cythera and seek out Ptolemy Solon—my mother sent him. He told me as much."

She drew a sharp breath. "*Melisande?*"

"The same," I said wryly.

"Why?" Jeanne asked in bewilderment.

"She's Solon's mistress," I said. "I'd learned that much on my own. Beyond that . . ." I shook my head. "Blessed Elua alone knows. But if he's willing to help, it's only because I'm her son."

"Melisande," Jeanne repeated. "Name of Elua!" She gave a short laugh. "What a piece of irony that would be if Melisande Shahrizai's intrigues provided the key to Terre d'Ange's salvation."

I hadn't thought about it in those terms.

Irony be damned. Let the gods laugh, let old scores be settled, let old wounds heal. I was sick unto death of them anyway. All I wanted was to undo this madness. I wanted to erase this grief and confusion that haunted the land. I wanted Terre d'Ange back. I wanted the memories of my loved ones back. I wanted Sidonie back.

Back in my arms, back in my heart, where she belonged. Where we fit so well together.

"I pray they do," I said.

"So do I," Jeanne murmured. "Elua forgive me, but so do I."

Seventeen

Around midday on the morrow, a message arrived from Jeanne de Mereliot.

I'd gone for a ride in the early hours of the morning, taking the Bastard outside the city into the countryside, where I could fling back the hood of my cloak and give him free rein to stretch his legs, working off the pent frustrations of our barge trip.

I shouldn't have taken him. It had been pure selfishness on my part. I knew I had to do this alone. Still, it felt good to have the companionship of one living creature.

The Bastard was blown by the time we returned, his nostrils flaring and his spotted hide damp with sweat. I tipped the ostler at the inn an extra coin to be sure he was well-tended.

Inside, the message awaited.

"Messire Cadmar?" The innkeeper passed me a sealed letter. "For you."

I read it and laughed.

Jeanne had booked passage for me aboard the *Aeolia,* the self-same Tiberian ship that had brought me to Marsilikos . . . how long ago? Not quite four years. It felt like a lifetime. But then, I had lived a lifetime in those few years.

The *Aeolia* was scheduled to depart at dawn the next day. I passed a quiet evening in Marsilikos, nursing tankards of ale and dining on lamb shanks, listening to the continued profound confusion and dismay on the part of my compatriots.

It hurt.

They hurt.

They were scared, bewildered, and confused. It worried me. I prayed that L'Envers was able to keep his temper in check, that the delegation he assembled was able to make Ysandre see reason. Because if they weren't, fear and confusion would begin to give way to anger. L'Envers, the minor lords, and the commonfolk had numbers on their side, but Ysandre had Ghislain nó Trevalion and the Royal Army. If things got ugly, they could get very ugly.

I slept poorly that night, my dreams troubled, and woke in the dark hour before dawn. A yawning chambermaid fetched me bread and honey to break my fast, and then I fetched the Bastard from the inn's stable and made my way to the harbor.

The sky was beginning to lighten by the time I arrived, and I found the *Aeolia* without any trouble. There was a familiar rotund figure giving orders on her decks.

"Greetings, Captain Oppius!" I called from the dock.

He leaned over the rails, plump chin quivering. "You!"

"Cadmar of Landras," I agreed.

Oppius da Lippi's shrewd eyes narrowed. "Well, if you're her ladyship's mysteriously urgent passenger, we'd best get you aboard before someone recognizes that spotted hellion you ride, man!"

Elua, I was an idiot. To be sure, there were other spotted horses in the realm, but the Bastard was fairly distinctive looking—enough so that if there was any kind of search afoot for poor Prince Imriel who'd lost his wits and gone missing from the City, a man wearing a hood and cloak astride a spotted horse in this heat would be an easy target for suspicion. It was sheer dumb luck that I hadn't been noticed earlier.

It made me realize that despite my protestations, I wasn't thinking at the height of clarity these days. I dismounted and unslung my saddlebags, making myself breathe slowly while Oppius' men hurried to lower the plank. Of course the Bastard balked at being led aboard, and I had to use my cloak to bind his eyes. Step by trembling step, bare-headed and exposed, I managed to coax him up the plank and into the hold, all the while conscious that the sun was rising and sailors were beginning to stir around the harbor. I didn't permit myself to heave a sigh of relief until we were both safely aboard, the Bastard was hidden from view, and I was able to don my cloak.

"So." Captain Oppius strolled toward me with his rolling waddle as I emerged from the hold, pale and shaking. He extended his hand. "Cadmar of Landras, is it?"

I clasped his hand. "Until we're at sea, yes."

"Heard some odd things about you." Oppius tilted his head. "In fact, there's precious little news out of Terre d'Ange these days that isn't odd as all hell."

I nodded. "I know, my lord captain. All too well."

Oppius studied me long enough that I began to grow anxious, then his plump face broke into a grin. "Well, you don't seem like you're raving, and the gods above know if there's anyone in this city with a sane head left on her shoulders, it's the Lady's daughter." He clapped my shoulder. "Let's go to Cythera."

I'd ridden out one of the worst storms of my life in a ship

under Oppius da Lippi's command. He was an able captain, one of the best, and though his men mocked him gently behind his back, they respected him and worked with cheerful efficiency. We were underway in short order.

Once we cleared the harbor where the last of Quintilius Rousse's ships was anchored, I shed my cloak. I stood in the stern of the ship, getting accustomed once more to the roll of the deck beneath my feet, the snap and rustle of the sails, watching the golden Dome of the Lady dwindle behind us.

Another departure.

Another leavetaking.

It was to have been the last voyage I ever undertook in my life, this journey to Cythera. The one that paid at long last for all my mother's sins. One way or another, I'd meant to return with Melisande in chains, leading her to her execution. I hadn't looked forward to it. Sidonie was right; it *was* a lot to ask. But I would have done it. For our sake, yes; and for the sake of all those who had fallen during the Skaldi invasion, for the sake of those who survived and endured. Claude de Monluc, who had lost his father. Grainne, Lady of the Dalriada, who had lost her twin brother. Poor, pitiful Jean Le Blanc, whose wife had taken her own life after the abuse she'd suffered at the hands of the Skaldi.

All of them.

And now, instead, I was setting out to beg my mother's aid to save Terre d'Ange and everyone I loved. It wasn't a piece of irony. It was somewhat so far beyond irony, so vast, that I couldn't even comprehend it. All I could do was pray, helplessly, that Melisande Shahrizai did indeed love her son that much.

It was a long journey, but at least the weather held as summer wore on toward early autumn. We followed the warmth, heading southward along the coast of Caerdicca Unitas. I kept my promise to Jeanne and didn't press myself as hard. I kept up the Cassiline disciplines, but I didn't practice obsessively.

Bit by bit, my strength and endurance returned. The ship's cook was decent, and Oppius urged me to dine in the captain's quarters with him. I ate well, putting on weight and muscle, until I began to look like myself and not a victim of famine. When I went shirtless in the sun's warmth, my ribs no longer protruded. My skin grew brown, contrasting with the shiny pink scars.

You needn't look so tempting.

This scarred thing?

The first time he saw me bare-chested, Oppius let out a low whistle. "Jupiter Optimus! What happened to you?"

"It's a long story," I said.

He shrugged. "We've time."

I spent long hours dicing and talking with Oppius. I learned that the *Aeolia* had been in port to pick up a shipment of Namarrese wine that had never arrived, mysteriously diverted to Carthage. Jeanne de Mereliot had found him at loose ends, willing to take a commission to carry a single passenger to Cythera. She'd paid him a great deal of money to do it. I hoped I'd be able to make good on it someday.

Over the course of our journey, we spent a good deal of time speculating about Carthage. I told Oppius what I knew, leaving out the Unseen Guild. I'd not told anyone but L'Envers about the Guild. If there was a danger, I reckoned at least he could take his chances.

To my surprise, Oppius wasn't inclined to disbelieve me. "Bad magic," he said, making a sign against ill luck. "Sailors are a superstitious lot, but we've seen a lot of odd things in our time. I don't like the sound of this. If Carthage conquers the west, they're going to turn their eyes eastward."

"What do you know about Ptolemy Solon?" I asked him.

Oppius pursed his lips. "A bit. In Cythera, they call him the Wise Ape."

"The what?" I said, startled.

He grinned. "The Wise Ape. He's got a name for being a deep scholar, dabbling in all manner of arcane study. Got a name for being ugly as sin, too. But fair," he added. "Cythera's been plagued by troubles in the past. It's been occupied so many times, you'd have Hellenes and Ephesians at each other's throats, Akkadians trying to quash them all. It's been peaceful since Solon was appointed Governor."

"What about a mistress?" I asked.

"Ah, yes." Oppius steepled his fingers over his belly. "The Paphian goddess come back to earth to unite with her divine husband. Venus and Vulcan, the goddess of love and the twisted smith. I've heard that rumor." He gave me one of his shrewd looks. "Your mother?"

"Hard to credit," I said. "But so it seems."

We rounded the tip of Caerdicca Unitas and turned eastward. Carthage lay somewhere behind us. Carthage and Sidonie. I could feel it like a tug on my heart. The farther I sailed from her, the more it ached. Memories haunted me. We'd made love in the bathtub the day Astegal had arrived in the City of Elua. *I don't dislike him,* Sidonie had said, sliding atop me. *Just don't agree to wed him,* I'd said in reply.

Gods.

She'd laughed and kissed me, promised me that she wouldn't. And then the world had changed beneath a bloody moon, and Sidonie had sailed merrily away with Astegal while the entire City cheered and I lay tied to a bed, chafing my wrists and ankles raw, screaming about Cythera.

I wanted Astegal dead.

I'd wanted men dead before. Berlik. He had killed Dorelei, killed our unborn son. I'd sworn vengeance on him. But in the end, I'd understood what he had done, and why. In the end, he sought his own death as penance, and I'd wept after I'd slain him. I hadn't told many people that.

There were others.

There was the Mahrkagir. His death had seemed unthinkable—his very name meant "Conqueror of Death." I'd prayed for it, though. We all did in the zenana. I'd prayed, too, for the death of Jagun, the Tatar warlord who had made me his plaything, put his brand on me. I'd felt awe at the Mahrkagir's death, but I'd gloated over Jagun's.

And there was another man who had stolen a woman and forced her into marriage, the Duke of Valpetra. Gods. I'd played a role in his death. I'd not even known the man, but I'd hated him for what he'd done. After he'd taken her, he'd stood before the Prince of Lucca, the girl's wrist clamped in his hand, and threatened to kill her. I'd ridden them down and cut off his hand at the wrist, freeing her. Helena. That was her name. I hadn't known her, either. But I remembered the searing look of despair and pride on her face.

In an awful way, this was worse.

Astegal hadn't taken Sidonie against her will—he'd taken her will away. Her mind, her very heart. All of her. He had violated her in the deepest, most profound sense. It terrified me to think what it would do to her. All of that fearless lack of inhibition, that frank, fierce passion that startled and delighted me to this day . . . Blessed Elua have mercy, if Astegal destroyed that, if he made Sidonie despise herself for it, I would kill him slowly.

Days passed, one by one.

Cythera drew nigh.

The sight of the isle's rocky coastline struck me like a fist to the gut. My mother was there. I hadn't seen her since I was eleven years old. When I had, I'd thrown her crimes in her face, and then I'd left. And in all the thinking I'd done on this long voyage, I hadn't let myself think about actually seeing her in the flesh. Now I did. It made me feel sick and uncertain.

"You all right?" Oppius laid a hand on my shoulder as the harbor of Paphos hove into view on a fair morning.

My nails bit into the ship's railing. "We'll see."

It was a small place, Paphos, smaller than I'd expected. A pretty little harbor city nestled in the lee of a mountain range. It looked peaceful. There were a few trade-ships, many fishing vessels. A small fortress guarded the outer entrance to the harbor, and beyond it was a modest palace. A palisade running the length of the harbor, a lively marketplace. Pleasant-looking villas, apartments of pale golden brick. Temples. The sunken bowl of an open-air theatre.

I tried to imagine my mother strolling the palisade with a man ugly enough to be nicknamed the Wise Ape, flanked by attendants with parasols. I shook my head. I couldn't do it.

We sailed into the harbor unchallenged. Oppius ordered the sails struck and we went to oars, gliding toward the docks. A handful of mounted men emerged from the fortress, riding along the palisade. By the time Oppius' men had secured the *Aeolia,* they were waiting for us.

"State your business!" the leader called in Hellene.

"Gods, this feels familiar, doesn't it?" Oppius murmured to me. "Delivering a passenger," he called back to the Cytheran harbor-master. "But I'm eager for trade if there are contracts to be had."

The harbor-master laughed. "Oh, always. Come ashore, then!"

My legs trembled as I disembarked. Now that I was here, I wished I had another day to think and prepare. I braced myself for the harbor-master's reaction when he saw Melisande Shahrizai's face reflected in mine.

It wasn't quite what I expected.

He whistled through his teeth. "Ah, I see! One of *hers,* eh?"

I wasn't sure how to answer. "I've come to petition the Governor."

"Solon, eh?" The harbor-master blinked. He was a slight fellow with pock-marked olive skin and an accent that reminded me of Canis'. "All right, then. No doubt he'll see you. He's always interested in curiosities. You're that, no doubt." He watched the Bastard being led ashore. "Nice horse. What's your name?"

"Cadmar," I said. "Cadmar of Landras."

Eighteen

The harbor-master, whose name was Mehmed, had one of his men direct me to a suitable lodging-house; it was not an inn, but a gracious villa overlooking the western edge of the harbor, surrounded by bougainvillea and tall, swaying date palms.

It was owned by a widow named Nuray. Her eyes widened at the sight of me, but she said nothing, only bowed and escorted me to my quarters, which were airy and pleasant and well-appointed.

I was in the city of Paphos, breathing the same air as my mother.

It felt very, very strange.

Mehmed had promised to bear word of my request to Ptolemy Solon. Oppius had promised not to set sail without my blessing.

I tended to the Bastard myself, refusing the aid of Nuray's stable-lad. The Bastard suffered my attentions, eyeing me with a look of deep reproach.

"I'm sorry," I said to him. "Truly."

What had I been thinking? I shouldn't have subjected him to a lengthy sea voyage. It hadn't been necessary. I hadn't wanted to be alone, that's all. Weeks without exercise, without sunlight. The Bastard was in worse shape than I was now.

And why had I given Mehmed a false name? I wasn't entirely sure. *One of hers*, he'd said. *One.* What did that mean?

I didn't know and it made me uneasy. I didn't trust myself. Driven by the memories of my madness, the urgency of my cause, I'd been careless. I thought about Bodeshmun the horologist, aligning his mirrors in the City of Elua with exacting care. Thought about him smiling into his beard when Sidonie and I reviewed his preparations, sure in his knowledge of what was to come.

I couldn't afford to be careless.

I couldn't afford to make mistakes.

So I waited. I availed myself of the villa's baths. Nuray sent a laundress for my clothing, all of it salt-stained and foul. While it dried in the sunlight of a hidden courtyard, I sat on a terrace above the harbor, wrapped in a thick linen robe, and ate a luncheon of grilled octopus, potatoes cooked in olive oil, and sausage seasoned with coriander. I watched waves breaking over a rock formation westward, foam jetting skyward. There was a place, only a few leagues away, where it was said the Hellene goddess of love had first touched mortal soil.

I inhaled the sea air, the same air my mother breathed. A moist, salty tang, sweetened by blooming flowers and ripening fruit. Salt and sweet. My mind wandered. I remembered kneeling for Sidonie, wearing her discarded blindfold. The tap of the tawse between my shoulder blades. Her fingers, loosing the fabric of the blindfold, forgiving me. Her scent, salt and honey. The smile in her voice as she bade me do penance. Ah, Elua! The *love* in it. I'd done my penance with pleasure.

The taste of her.

Gods, it hurt.

"My lord?" A Cytheran voice speaking Hellene, the same soft accent that blended different cultures. It belonged to a young woman, one of Nuray's servants. "There is a message for you."

The sun sparkled on the sea. I straightened. "Yes?"

She bowed. "The Governor wishes you to dine with him this evening. He will see you at sunset."

When it came time, I went.

I was apprehensive. I didn't know what to expect. I rode the Bastard along the palisade, pacing him slowly. The sun was hovering low over the harbor, drenching everything in liquid gold. Somewhere, my mother was here. I wondered if I would see her tonight. The thought made my skin prickle.

The palace was a charming structure built for pleasure, not defensibility. Its high, arched doors and windows took advantage of the cool sea breezes. I was received courteously and escorted into a salon overlooking the harbor, the setting sun framed in its windows.

Ptolemy Solon was there.

Alone.

The Governor of Cythera was a small man with brown skin and a wizened face, coarse silver hair. One could see at once where the nickname had come from. His brown eyes were round and luminous, ringed by wrinkles. Wrinkles bracketed his wide mouth. Ugly, yes. Also very difficult to read. He regarded me without speaking.

I bowed to him. "Well met, my lord. Thank you for your hospitality."

"Cadmar of Landras," Ptolemy Solon said mildly. "Do you know, that had me stumped for the better part of an hour." He tapped his skull. "And I never forget anything. Landras. It's where you grew up, yes?"

"Yes," I said.

"Well." The round eyes blinked. "Well met, Prince Imriel de la Courcel."

I fought the urge to glance around. "Thank you, my lord."

"You may call me Solon." He gave a quick smile. "She's not here, if that's what you're wondering."

I relaxed a little. "It is."

"She's *here,* of course. On Cythera." Solon poured wine from a ewer into two cups. "But she maintains her own villa. I thought it best if we spoke first in private. You did say you'd come to petition me, and I'm quite interested in taking the measure of a young man callous enough to betray his mother unto her death, yet with the incredible temerity to beg her aid when his plans went awry." He beckoned. "Come, sit and take a glass of wine with me."

I accepted, taking a seat at the table beneath the window. He sat opposite me. "Are you aware of her crimes?"

"Oh, yes." He took a sip of wine. "Still."

I gazed out the window. Ships bobbed in the harbor, the sun-drenched water making it seem as though they floated on a lake of fire. "What would you have me say?" I asked. "Yes. I accepted a charge to bring my mother to justice. Thousands of people died because Melisande Shahrizai committed high treason. She was condemned to death before I was even born. I can't go anywhere in the realm without someone calling me traitor-spawn, without someone telling me how a loved one died for my mother's sins. I can't wed the woman I love." I looked back at Solon. "And yes, my plans went awry. And now, quite frankly, I'm desperate."

He sipped his wine. "At least you're honest."

"Did you send Sunjata?" I asked.

"Not exactly." The light of the setting sun glimmered in his round eyes. "He's your mother's doing."

"Did you forge a silver needle and lave it in the sweat of a madman's brow and the slime of a toad?" I asked wryly.

The sunlight in his eyes flared. "Did it work?"

I showed him the healed scars around my wrists. "I had to be tied to my bed."

Solon examined the scars. "Interesting," he mused. He patted my hand. "I'm sorry about that. It was the only way I could think of. And to be perfectly honest, I wasn't sure it would work. The needle *or* the madness," he added. "You'll have to tell me what it was like."

"Horrible," I said briefly. "Will you aid me if I do?"

The sun's bottom rim dipped below the horizon, its light shifting from gold to orange. "I haven't decided," Solon said in a candid tone. "It depends on you and what you offer. It depends on your mother and what she wishes. It depends on the axes of power and knowledge involved in the situation."

"The Unseen Guild?" I asked.

He pursed his lips. "No, no, no. I've naught to do with *them*." He waved a dismissive hand. "Oh, I know all about it, of course. My kinsman Ptolemy Dikaios made me the offer long ago. I accepted the training, but I refused to swear allegiance when it was over. Much like yourself, yes?"

"Not exactly," I said.

Solon shrugged. "Knowledge is power. And yet power corrupts. Not all who wield it, but most. Still, I had a hunger for knowledge. And so I decided long ago that I would seek it out. That I would gather and amass it, and assign myself the greatest challenge of all: to wield it seldom or never in the service of my own desires."

I raised my brows. "That, my lord, is passing odd."

"Do you think so?" He blinked. "And yet consider your mother. *She* amassed great knowledge. She used it as a tool to further her own goals. She plunged a nation into war. She tore her own family apart. In the end she lost everything."

Those weren't exactly the words of a man besotted. I frowned, unsure what to make of Ptolemy Solon. The sun sank lower beneath the horizon. A young woman in loose, flowing robes came with a taper to kindle the lamps.

"There is a fruit that grows south of Carthage," Solon said when the girl had departed. "When it is green, it is poisonous. Only when it has fully ripened may it be safely eaten. I sampled it once in my younger days. There was a heady sense of danger in it. Once I'd eaten it, I craved more. Your mother is like that fruit."

"I see," I said.

"Not entirely." He tilted his head. "I grow old. I thought myself beyond the point of succumbing to such temptations. The fruit, I withstood. My vow to myself, I have kept. But to my chagrin, I find I am unable to resist the delicious, sinful pleasure of groveling at your mother's feet." He laughed at my expression. "Ah, Imriel! The world is full of unexpected delights."

"Elua knows that's true," I muttered.

The upper rim of the sun vanished beneath the sea, leaving a ruddy glow behind it. Servants came with covered dishes, lifting the domes to reveal grape leaves stuffed with rice and lamb, fillets of mullet in wine, crusty bread, and a creamy pink sauce made with fish roe. Solon sniffed appreciatively, his broad nostrils widening.

"Happiness," he said.

I took a long drink of my wine. "Happiness, my lord?"

"It is the highest form of wisdom." Solon tore off a piece of bread, dipping it in the roe sauce. He chewed slowly, savoring it. "That is the totality of what I have learned in my pursuit of knowledge, Imriel de la Courcel."

I tried the roe sauce, emulating him. It was salty and delicious, velvet on the tongue. "Oh?"

Solon popped a grape leaf–wrapped delicacy into his mouth. "Oh, yes. I have applied this learning here in Cythera since I was given the governorship." His jaw worked, and he swallowed with obvious pleasure. His brown eyes glowed. "I've sought to make my people *happy.* I've listened to the concerns of all and brokered peace among them. I've implemented just laws. Do you know, any man, woman, or child sold into slavery in Cythera must be paid a fair wage? Fair enough that they might buy their freedom in seven years' time."

"Sunjata," I said.

He nodded with glee. "Even so!"

"Solon." I pushed my plate away. "I am interested in your thoughts. Indeed, I spent some months in Tiberium studying philosophy with Master Piero di Bonci, and I would have gladly spent longer. Another time, I would like nothing better than to discuss the virtues of happiness with you. But my country has been torn apart by Carthage's magics. Terre d'Ange hovers on the brink of instability. And Sidonie de la Courcel, whom I love beyond all reason, has been ensorceled into believing she is meant to wed an ambitious Carthaginian general—"

Solon speared a piece of poached mullet with his fork. "She did."

My voice rose. "When?"

He chewed and swallowed. "Some two weeks ago. I imagine Carthage will have launched their invasion by now. We ought to get word any day."

Sidonie had married Astegal.

I felt sick.

"Eat." Solon pushed my plate back toward me. There was sympathy in his wise ape's face. "I've a feeling you're going to need your strength. Undoing Carthage's spell won't be an easy task."

I stabbed at my fish. "Then you'll help?"

"I might." He braced his elbows on the table. "What are you offering?"

I forced a bite of mullet down my throat. "My mother's sentence commuted to exile."

"No pardon?" Solon asked.

"No," I said shortly. I thought about riding into the City upon returning from my excursion to Vralia. The black armbands, the down-turned thumbs. The hard, anguished stares on the faces of the bereaved. "No pardon."

He nodded. "I'll think on it. Will you see her willingly?"

"Does she have the final say?" I asked grimly.

"No." Solon blinked at me. "She has the first say, but the final say is mine. I freely confess myself a man besotted, but it has not bereaved me of my wits." He gave a slow smile. "I believe I am the first man to say no to your mother from time to time. And oddly enough, I do believe she respects me for it."

I took another bite of mullet. "I'll see her."

"Good." He swabbed another piece of bread with roe sauce. "Because I would have surely refused my aid if you hadn't. One of her people will come to fetch you in the morning. I hope that you will not be unkind. This will be a long and anxious night of waiting for her."

I fought down a surge of impatience. "I will try, my lord. But I have passed a good many anxious nights myself of late."

"Of course," Solon said. "I understand."

"No." I shook my head. "I don't think you do. You've built a pleasant place here on Cythera. Imagine it altered overnight at a single stroke, plunged into uncertainty and confusion. Imagine my mother leaving you gladly for a man you despise. Imagine knowing that all her formidable will and intelligence have been violated and turned against her. Because if Carthage succeeds in Aragonia and Terre d'Ange, this will be only the beginning. Astegal dreams of empire. Cythera would be a pretty plum."

Solon snorted. "Would Carthage be a worse master than Khebbel-im-Akkad? One overlord is much the same as another. You speak as a man whose country has never been a vassal nation."

"True." I set down my fork. "And I would like to remain thus. Do you wish me to beg, my lord? I will." I got out of the chair and knelt at his feet. "You spoke of happiness. For the first time in my life, I had it. And it has been snatched away from me. I beg you, please, to tell me how to undo what was done. I will give you anything in my possession. I will do anything in my power that you wish."

"Anything." His round eyes glinted. "What if I told you I knew of a spell that could give one man the semblance of another? What if I asked for your beauty in exchange for my ugliness? Would you give it?"

"Yes," I said promptly.

Solon's brows rose. "Truly?"

I sat back on my heels and spread my arms. "Take it."

"Hmm." He regarded me a moment. "You're fortunate that I have spent my life adhering to the wisdom of restraint. Or perhaps merely that your mother would take it amiss to find me wearing her son's face." He shook his head. "I don't want your face, Imriel de la Courcel. What I want is to choose wisely in this. If I aid you, there are those who will recognize my handiwork. Undoing the spell will be difficult. If you fail, it is I—and Cythera—who will pay the price."

"I won't fail," I said.

"Stubborn." Solon smiled a little. "Much like your mother. And impulsive, much unlike her. Sleep, and go to see her.

Whatever you think of her, Melisande is not made of stone. For ten years and more, she has grieved deeply, knowing what befell you when you were taken as a child, knowing what role her own actions played in it. I do believe it is the pain that finally taught her a measure of compassion."

I got wearily to my feet. "I hope so."

His eyes glinted again. "Given that she appears ready to forgive you for seeking her life, I do believe I am right."

Nineteen

I spent a fitful night, tossing restlessly in my bed at the widow Nuray's lodging-house, going over my conversation with Solon in my mind. I didn't think it had gone well. He was an odd and disconcerting man.

Small wonder my mother liked him.

At least it was better than dwelling on the sure knowledge that Sidonie had wed Astegal. I couldn't think about *that* without a tide of black, murderous rage rising in my heart, and the feeling was uncomfortably close to my madness.

I rose early and broke my fast, then spent the better part of an hour practicing my Cassiline forms in Nuray's garden, trying to quiet my mind. I forced myself to focus on the movements; telling the hours, they called it. Step after flowing step, tracing arcs with my blade. It worked well enough that I didn't notice my mother's messenger enter the garden.

"Interesting, that," an insouciant voice said. "What do you call it?"

I halted and turned, then stared.

It was a young man around my age. He'd spoken in Hellene with a native accent, and he wore billowy trousers caught at the ankles and an embroidered Cytheran vest, but he was D'Angeline. His face was narrower than mine, and his eyes a lighter shade of blue, but the stamp of House Shahrizai was there in the angle of his cheekbones, the sensuous mouth.

One of hers.

"Telling the hours," I said stupidly. "It's a Cassiline practice."

"Cassilines!" He snapped his fingers. "I'd forgotten about them." He came over to greet me, extending a hand. "I'm Leander, by the way."

"Imriel." I clasped his hand, frowning in perplexity. "Are we . . . kin?"

"Distantly, by way of the wrong side of the blanket." Leander laughed. "It's a long story." He studied my face. "By the Goddess! You *are* her son. You look just like her."

"She's no goddess," I said wryly.

"Touchy, touchy." He arched one brow. "It's just a saying, my lovely. Very common in these parts. I wasn't speaking of her ladyship."

I bit my tongue on a sharp retort and sheathed my blade. "Have you come to take me to her?"

"I have." Leander inclined his head. He had the blue-black Shahrizai hair, too. It was plaited in a handful of braids, caught up at the crown of his head. "Come with me."

My mother's villa lay in the foothills of the mountains, a short ride from the city proper. As we rode, Leander told me somewhat of his history, or rather, his family's history. Many years ago, Melisande's father, Casimar Shahrizai, had embarked on an illicit affair with the wife of another Kusheline lord, the Baron de Maignard. During their affair, Victoire de Maignard had gotten with child and delivered a boy. Casimar had demanded she acknowledge the boy as his. Being of Azzallese descent and proud, Victoire had refused. They had quarrelled bitterly.

"So." Leander's generous mouth twisted. "Casimar ruined my family."

"How so?" I asked.

"With money." He shrugged. "He got my great-grandmother's husband to invest in a scheme that left him penniless. House Maignard was destroyed. The Baron killed himself in shame. My great-grandmother's family shunned her for her folly. House Shahrizai turned their backs on her. She became a laundress."

He went on to tell me how my mother had heard the story as a child. When she came of age and into estates of her own, she sought out the fallen Maignard clan and offered to buy them out of penury. The price for her generosity was their loyalty to her and her alone.

"Great-grandmother Victoire accepted it," Leander said cynically. "Even Azza's pride would bend under the weight of a thousand vats of laundry. Our family's been in your mother's service ever since."

"You don't mind?" I asked.

"Why should I?" Leander gestured expansively. "Oh, I know, I'm meant to think exile from Terre d'Ange is a hell unto itself. But look around you, man! It's a little paradise here. I've lived here since I was a boy. All of that other business happened long before I was born. And I'll tell you . . ." He fingered a ruby stud in his earlobe and smirked. "Your mother's a generous patron."

"I'm sure she is," I muttered.

Leander drew rein. "All right. You want to hear a piece of Maignard family lore?" His expression hardened. "By all accounts, Casimar Shahrizai was a nasty piece of work. He was charming, but vindictive as all hell. He spent an ungodly amount of money to ruin the old baron. When your mother made her offer, she swore in Kushiel's name that she would never act out of mere spite. Insofar as I know, she never has."

I didn't know what to say.

"So." Leander shrugged again. "Now you know."

It was a strange feeling. I'd never thought of my mother as a child, as someone's daughter. I'd never thought about the forces that had shaped her, like a charming and vicious father. I couldn't help but feel a creeping sense of admiration for the young woman she had been. Laying the groundwork for plans that would eventually shake the realm to its core. Adhering to her own twisted principles of integrity.

And a sense of loss, too—for the person my mother might have been if she hadn't been so goddamned ambitious.

All of us had monsters hidden within us.

I'd seen the face of mine in my madness, turning me against everyone I loved, relishing their pain. I'd seen a future in which my son, Dorelei's and my son, had become a tyrant, cruel and ruthless.

We reached the villa. It was a sprawling place, sunlit and gracious. The foothills were terraced, grapes ripening on the vine. The scent of cypress wafted down from the mountains. Leander and I dismounted in the courtyard. A cheerful Cytheran stable-lad came to take our mounts. Leander ruffled his hair, gave him a kiss on the cheek. The stable-lad ducked his head and smiled.

"All is permitted in her ladyship's household," Leander commented.

He led me through the villa. It had mosaic tile floors that were exquisite, depicting the Hellene goddess of love in various adventures. I heard the sound of laughter. A young woman darted from a hallway, her eyes blindfolded, and blundered into Leander. He laughed and caught her shoulders.

"Leander," she said decisively, raising her blind face and sniffing. "I know your pomade."

"Well done." He kissed her brow. "Hurry!"

A dark-skinned young man emerged from the hallway, his eyes bound, stumbling after her. Leander stepped deftly out of his way. "Ah," he said with a trace of melancholy. "He puts me in mind of Sunjata."

"You know him?" I asked.

"Very well." His mouth quirked. "We trained together, Sunjata and I. 'Tis a barbaric custom, gelding. It happened at Carthage's hands. Now her ladyship seeks to acquire them earlier, before it can be done. And his apish lordship has banned it at her urging, at least on Cythera."

The sound of laughter receded.

I heard a fountain instead.

"Here." Leander halted at the entrance to an inner courtyard. His light-blue eyes met mine. "I will go no farther with you. Her ladyship awaits."

I entered the courtyard.

I saw her.

Phèdre was right. My mother's beauty hadn't dimmed. It had only changed again. Melisande lifted her head and gazed at me, tears brightening her glorious eyes, the deep blue hue of a twilit sea. There were faint lines etched at the corners, a few threads of bright silver strewn in her black hair. There was somewhat else, too. A well of sorrow and regret, a humanity that had been lacking. A goddess rendered mortal by time and compassion, all the more poignant for it.

My mother breathed my name. "*Imriel.*"

I walked toward her. "Mother," I said, my voice sounding strange to my ears. I had never called her that. I'd never called anyone that.

She touched my cheek, her fingers hesitant. "You look older than I expected."

"Twenty-two," I said, my throat tight. "But on most days it feels like more."

"I know," she said quietly.

I took a deep breath, trying to loosen the tightness. "I don't . . ." I spread my hands. "I don't know what to say. You know why I'm here." She nodded without speaking. "Solon accused me of callousness and temerity. I told him it was desperation. But you sent for me, too. Sunjata did your bidding. Knowing that I'd sworn to bring you to justice, you sent for me. So . . . here I am. Begging for your help." I licked my dry lips. "And I will tell you what I told Solon. Terre d'Ange is willing to commute your sentence to exile. I can't offer more than that on behalf of the realm. But anything else in my power, anything you wish of me, I will do."

Curiosity raised my mother's winged brows. It made her look younger. "What do you imagine I might ask for?"

"I don't know." I glanced around the courtyard. Flowering shrubs blossomed in profusion. The fountain splashed merrily, water sparkling in the sunlight. "Me," I said. "You might ask me to join you in exile."

Melisande's curious expression didn't change. "Would you?"

An invisible band around my chest tightened. I thought about Astegal and his heavy-lidded smile. Sidonie. Phèdre and Joscelin gazing at me in perplexity, their memories stolen. The rising tide of unease on the streets of Marsilikos, Quintilius Rousse's ships in the harbor. "Yes," I said, tears stinging my eyes. "If it meant undoing Carthage's spell."

Unexpectedly, she laughed, a mixture of humor and sadness in it. "Ah, Elua! Imriel, I've given you enough reasons to hate me already. Why would I choose one more?" My mother shook her head. "Come. Sit and listen a moment."

There was a curved marble bench near the fountain. We

sat on opposite ends of it. Melisande gazed at the falling water.

"I mean to persuade Solon to aid you," she said without preamble. "And I believe he will. I wish you to know that I expect no gratitude for it. Not from you, not from Terre d'Ange. I do not imagine this will buy me forgiveness."

"Are you making atonement?" I asked her.

Her gaze shifted to me. Gods, she really was beautiful. "Perhaps, in a way. Although you may not believe it, I do love Terre d'Ange. I could have controlled Waldemar Selig if he had proved victorious. I would have built somewhat glorious in the aftermath and turned his victory into my own."

"Dreams of empire," I murmured. "You'd like Astegal of Carthage."

She gave a faint, wry smile. "Probably. But I don't care to watch him usurp the country I once dreamed of ruling."

"A true patriot," I observed.

"No." Melisande shook her head. "I don't pretend to that. Still, there are ways in which I have changed. When you were taken . . ." She fell silent a moment. "I learned what it was to suffer. To hate. To be filled with fury and helplessness. To regret. And afterward . . ." She looked away. "Phèdre nó Delaunay told me I did not wish to know what befell you in that place. And yet I was torn between a fear of knowing and a need to know. In the end, I couldn't bear it. I found a Caerdicci woman who had been there and had her sent to the Temple of Asherat. She told me." She looked back at me. "And then it was worse."

"You wrote to me," I said. "You wrote that if you could undo what was done to me, you would do anything in the world."

The shadow behind her eyes lightened. "You read my letters?"

"Yes." I propped my elbows on my knees, clasping my

hands between them. "Not for a long time, not until years after you disappeared. But I did. At first I tried to burn them," I added. "After that, Phèdre kept them for me."

"Phèdre." My mother's rich voice held too many things to decipher. She gazed into the distance. "The gods must laugh. And yet I begin to think mayhap they hold a shred of mercy for me. I cannot take back my deeds. I cannot undo your hurt. But this at least I can do, and pray that it leavens the burden of regret. So you see, I do not pretend to selflessness."

"That's good," I said. "Since it has the added benefit of removing the sentence of death hanging over your head."

"True." Her brows rose again. "But if I had not acted to protect you, it wouldn't have mattered. You would have forgotten all about your vow."

I studied my clasped hands, thinking about a world in which I had forgotten my promise to bring my mother to justice. Forgotten *Sidonie*. "Will you answer a question truthfully?" I asked. "Could you have prevented it? Carthage's spell?"

My mother didn't answer for a long time.

I lifted my head and gazed at her.

"No," she said finally. "Not without Solon's help. I only knew the rumors Sunjata passed to me. It was Solon who pieced them together. He's studied a great many arcane arts." She gave another wry smile. "But he kept the full truth of it from me, knowing it would mean you wouldn't come seeking my life. All I asked was that whatever it was, he find a way to protect you."

"Solon," I muttered. "I could kill him for that."

"I suggest you don't," Melisande said. "Since he's your best hope."

I eyed her. "What would you have done if you *had* known? Would you have let it happen?"

"I don't know," she said with surprising candor. "What if I hadn't? What would you have done if I had persuaded Solon to tell me how to avert it? Sent a warning? Would you have believed me?"

"Yes," I said slowly. "I believe I would."

"And would you have still sought to drag me back to Terre d'Ange to be executed?" Melisande inquired.

It was my turn to fall silent. "I don't know," I said at length.

"So." Her shoulders moved in a graceful shrug. "Life is filled with things we may never know. And although you have not asked it of me, I grant you forgiveness for seeking my death."

"I didn't relish the prospect," I said.

"That's nice to know." My mother sounded more amused than not. Whatever else was true of her, Leander was right. She wasn't vindictive. She cocked her head. "Ysandre's *daughter*?"

"Did you laugh?" I asked.

Her generous lips twitched. "What do you think?"

I smiled despite myself. "It's not a ploy, if that's what you're wondering. I love her. I've loved her for a long time. For years we kept it a secret, hoping it would pass. It didn't. And I truly will do whatever is needful to get her back."

The early-autumn sun poured down on us, warm and golden. My mother reached out and touched my hair, running a lock of it between her fingers.

I let her.

"What's she like?" Melisande asked.

"Sidonie?" I smiled again. "Dorelei said once that she was like a house without a door. It's not true, though. Not really. She's very . . . contained. But there's a fierceness in her. Once it's tapped, it's . . ." I shook my head. "I don't know. She's determined. Passionate. Loyal. Funny, too. Most people don't know that about her. I didn't, not for a long time." My smile faded. "And she's Astegal's wife."

My mother stroked my hair. "Not for always."

"No." I straightened my shoulders. "Her always is *mine*."

Melisande withdrew her touch and regarded me with deep, abiding sorrow. "Will you do me one kindness? I know you're impatient. And I will send word to Solon seeking his aid immediately. But I would like it very much if you would pass this day with me. I would like, very much, to hear about your life."

As much as I wanted to hate her, I couldn't.

Not in the flesh.

I could feel the bond between us, blood-deep. I was her son. I had fought against it in more ways than I could count, and there was a great deal of me that owed nothing to her. I was as much Phèdre's son, as much Joscelin's, as I was hers and my father's. But deep in my marrow, I knew her touch. I knew she had carried me in her womb. I had read her letters. I knew she had nursed me at her breast, counted my infant fingers and toes, sung me crib-songs, suffering no one else to usurp those duties.

"I will," I said.

My beautiful, damnable mother settled her glorious gaze on me. "Thank you," Melisande said simply.

Twenty

It was a pleasant day.

I would be lying if I said it wasn't. I'd never understood how my mother had gotten so many folk willingly involved in her intrigues, but the truth was she was a charming and brilliant woman, unexpectedly candid and self-aware. One found oneself wishing to please her out of unthinking instinct.

To be sure, her household doted on her. It wasn't just the members of the Maignard clan, of whom there were half a dozen. It was everyone. The Cytheran servants. The freed slaves, many of whom were her pupils.

I learned that my mother was a master in the Unseen Guild, and aspired to go no higher. Once, she had. She had learned of the Guild's existence from Anafiel Delaunay many years ago, when he was distraught over the death of Prince Rolande de la Courcel and careless enough to confide in her. She had sought out the Guild on her own and risen quickly within its ranks. If her gambit with Skaldia hadn't failed, or the attempt to assassinate Ysandre, she would have risen much, much higher.

Now she contented herself with dabbling. She bought slaves who struck her fancy and gave them their freedom, offering them positions within her household with generous pay. A few took their freedom and fled, but most stayed. In time, she made an offer of Guild training and far greater wealth to those she deemed quick-witted and loyal enough to be useful to her. Then she sent them forth to spy on her behalf.

Over the course of the day, I learned a few things about the Guild. I learned that there were indeed factions within it. Alliances were formed. Ephesium, looking over its shoulder at powerful Khebbel-im-Akkad, favored the rise of Carthage. Most of Caerdicca Unitas, remembering the lessons of history, opposed it and sought ties to nascent Skaldic states. I learned that the Guild's origins lay in the east, and that their influence was weak in the western realms.

Mostly, though, I talked.

I talked for hours.

Many of the details of my life she knew. Her spies in Terre d'Ange—and their identities was one thing she *wouldn't* divulge to me—had kept her well informed. But Melisande wanted to hear about my life from me.

And I found myself talking about things that surprised me. How the difficulty of being her son was compounded by measuring myself against the extraordinary heroism of my foster-parents. How I'd learned to let go of that for good when I'd accepted failure in Vralia. How I'd felt in Clunderry after Dorelei and I had learned to love one another on our own terms, watching her belly swell with our child. How I'd grieved for their deaths. How I'd gone from sheer hatred and a cold desire for vengeance to feel a measure of compassion for Berlik at the end.

When I'd talked myself dry, my mother was very quiet for a time. We were seated in her salon, drinking a cool white wine made on the villa's grounds. Blue twilight was beginning to fall outside.

"You're a good man," Melisande murmured. "Elua knows, if I did one good thing in my life, it was binding myself to a promise to allow you to be raised by Phèdre nó Delaunay and that damned Cassiline of hers."

"The only gift I would accept from you," I said, remembering what Phèdre had told me. "I thank you for it."

She glanced out the window. "It's growing late. Will you pass the night here?"

There was a yearning hunger in the question, and fear, too. I found myself wanting to assuage both. I was in her debt. It would be easy, so easy, to offer the simple balm of my presence. And yet in the back of my mind there were black armbands and down-turned thumbs. There was a blood-soaked battlefield. Waldemar Selig had begun to skin Phèdre alive there.

"I can't," I said.

Melisande inclined her head. "I understand."

And so I left to await word from Ptolemy Solon. The stable-lad that Leander had made blush brought the Bastard around. My mother escorted me to the courtyard herself. In the twilight, her beauty deepened. I thought about her likeness hanging in the Hall of Portraits at the Palace. In her youth, she'd had a beauty as keen and as deadly as a blade. Now, oddly, it cut deeper. Sorrow became her.

"I'll see you on the morrow," I said awkwardly. "No doubt you'll wish to be a part of this intrigue."

A wry edge returned to her voice. "No doubt."

I hesitated, holding the Bastard's reins. He was unusually compliant, still out of sorts from the lengthy sea voyage. "Mother . . . why did you name me Imriel? I've always wondered."

"*Eloquence of God.*" A smile touched her lips. Melisande Shahrizai tilted her head, regarding me in the twilight. "Because when you were born, for the first time, I understood it. *Love as thou wilt,*" she said, musing. "I have always adhered to the precept of Blessed Elua in my own way. And yet, until you were born, I didn't truly know what it was to *love* another living soul. Beyond thought, beyond reason. And I thought, for once, that the gods were speaking clearly to me."

I swallowed hard. "I see."

She didn't answer, only laid a hand on the back of my head. I bent toward her and felt the touch of her lips on my brow. "Tomorrow."

"Tomorrow," I echoed.

I rode away in the gathering dusk, my thoughts in turmoil. Unlike Carthage, unlike Alba or even Drujan, there were no arcane arts practiced in Terre d'Ange. And yet, in the space of a single day, I had nearly fallen under my mother's spell, born of nothing but her own singular presence.

It had been a pleasant day.

I wrenched my thoughts away, turning them westward. Toward Carthage, toward Sidonie. I wondered what the nuptial ceremony had been like. I tortured myself with thoughts of Sidonie, willing and eager in Astegal's bed. I felt the spell of my mother's presence dissipate, hard resolve settling in its place.

Still, her kiss lingered.

As I drifted into sleep in the widow Nuray's house, I found myself wondering if I would ever see my mother again once I left Cythera. And I wasn't sure what I wanted the answer to be.

On the morrow, I rose to find a summons from Solon awaiting, bright and early. I wasted no time, breaking my fast with a couple of ripe apricots, then riding over to the palace.

Ptolemy Solon was awaiting me in his library, which was one of the largest I'd ever seen. The main chamber was vast, with a high ceiling, tall windows at one end, doors at the other, and twin facing walls lined with bookshelves, ladders propped against each wall. There were alcoves with cubby-holes for scrolls, and smaller, locked chambers.

In the center of the main chamber, there were long tables suitable for study. Solon was seated at the head of one such table, a book of blank parchment and a pen and inkwell before him. My mother was seated at its opposite end. The vast space dwarfed him, while it seemed to suit her. Nonetheless, it was Solon who glanced up and bade me enter, brown eyes bright in his wizened face.

"Good morning, my lord," I said, hesitating. "Mother."

"Come." Solon patted the table. "Sit. Between Sunjata's tales of a great mirror being forged and the coming occlusion of the moon, I knew enough to guess at what Carthage intended. Not enough to be certain how it was done. I will need to hear everything you can remember about Carthage's visit. *Everything*."

I approached and took a seat. "I am most grateful for your aid, my lord."

"I'm sure you are." He shot an inscrutable look at my mother, who smiled and raised one brow. Solon gestured at a tray on the table containing a pitcher of water and an array of pastries. "Eat. Drink. Tell me everything."

I helped myself to a cup of water, flavored with lemon and honey.

And I began to talk.

I told them everything, commencing with my letter to Diokles Agallon. Once again, I didn't have anything to lose. There wasn't much about the Guild my mother didn't know, and I reckoned what she knew, Solon knew. I told them about Agallon's reply, Carthage's request. The discussions that had followed, Parliament's vote. Carthage's arrival, the exaggerated gift of tribute.

"Wait." Solon halted me. "Describe the tribute-gifts in detail."

I did to the best of my ability. I hadn't been paying overmuch attention, being more concerned with Carthage, but Phèdre had taught me to train my memory well. I recalled Quintilius Rousse's deep voice reading the manifest: gold, ivory, and salt, spices, and seedlings, Tyrian purple cloth, furniture.

"And there was the chalice he sent in advance," I said, remembering. "And the painting presented at the banquet."

Solon's round eyes blinked. "Describe them."

I described the carnelian chalice with its joined hands in which Astegal and Ysandre had drunk to one another's health; the painting made of ground jewels depicting the two of them with their hands clasped in friendship. Solon pursed his lips, his pen scratching on parchment.

"Continue," he said when I had finished. "From the point of their arrival."

I told him about the banquet where the painting had been unveiled, Sunjata's overture, the gilded coffer, and Gillimas' veiled words about Cythera. I related Sidonie's account of Astegal's offer for her hand, his veiled threats regarding Aragonia, and Ysandre's diplomatic refusal. My evening in the Night Court with Astegal and the other Carthaginian lords, and my near-smothering of Gillimas to force plain words of truth from him, watching my mother's lips twitch.

"You needn't look amused," I said to her.

"He brought it on himself," she said complacently. "A skilled Guildsman ought to know better than to mince words with a desperate D'Angeline in love."

"Is he?" Solon asked her.

Melisande gazed at me. "So it seems."

"A mother knows her child." Solon gestured at me. "Continue."

I told him everything I could remember about observing Bodeshmun's preparations the day of the occluded moon. Solon halted me numerous times, pressing me for details. He brought out a book with symbols of the Houses of the Cosmos. I racked my memory, struggling to place them exactly as they'd been aligned on the great mirror in proximity to the mirrors on the City's walls. His pen scratched furiously, sketching a diagram.

"Again," he said when I had finished.

I told him again, this time dredging up the exact words he'd said to Sidonie. The brief bow he had accorded her. A green gem on a chain swinging into view.

Solon's nostrils flared. "Describe it."

I tried, but I'd seen it only briefly. All I could tell him was that it was the size of a child's fist and multifaceted.

"Were there symbols incised on the facets?" he asked.

I shook my head. "I couldn't tell. But I *did* see a flash of emerald green the next night, when it happened."

He held up one hand. "Don't rush. Continue."

"After we visited Elua's Square . . ." My voice faltered. "Truly, there wasn't aught of significance until the following evening."

"How can you be sure?" Solon asked.

My mouth was parched. I took a long drink of water. "Sidonie and I quarrelled. I was uneasy. I wanted her to beg Ysandre to call off the spectacle. She didn't think it was possible without cause. We made up our quarrel that night." I traced a water-ring on the table with one finger, remembering the feel of her moon-silvered skin against my bare flesh. I hadn't thought about the fact that our argument might have played some role in this. "It was the first time we'd argued since we'd become lovers. Do you think it's significant?"

"No," Solon said gently. "I don't. Continue."

I relived the night of the spectacle for him. The endless dinner that had preceded it. The details of every dish I could recall. The carriage-ride to Elua's Square, the throngs that packed the City. The moon's slow, steady occlusion, and its eerie red hue.

The long wait, the crowds jostling around the mirror.

Sunjata's whisper in my ear, following him.

In a dispassionate voice, I told him all I could recall. Standing pressed together beneath Elua's Oak. The searing pain of the needle driven deep into my vitals, the rush of icy fire in my veins. Falling, the world whirling. Sunjata's voice, telling me to seek Ptolemy Solon's aid. An emerald glow, a flash of brightness. A gasp from the crowd. Sunjata's hand tugging the ring from my fingers. Roots writhing like serpents. Sunjata's voice apologizing for serving two masters. Telling me I was lucky my mother loved me. Telling me to go to Cythera.

And then the tide of madness swallowing me.

"Again," Solon said.

I closed my eyes and told him again, shutting out the sound of his pen scratching, shutting out everything. This time, there was nothing new. When I had finished, I was drained. I opened my eyes. "Do you wish to hear about the madness now?"

Solon began to reply, then caught my mother's warning glance. "No," he said in a circumspect tone. "Later, perhaps. Tell me about the ring. Is it significant?"

Tired as I was, I almost laughed. Sidonie had given it to me before I'd wed Dorelei. When I'd struck out from Skaldia into the unknown in search of Berlik, I'd sent the ring back to Sidonie with a message that I would return to claim it.

And when I'd been stuck waist-deep in a Vralian snowbank, bone-weary and frozen and ready to die, it was the thought of that promise that had kept me moving.

I'd reclaimed it in Alba. At long last, Berlik's skull was interred, letting Dorelei's spirit rest peacefully. Sidonie had taken the ring from its resting place on a chain around her neck. She'd undone the clasp and let the chain fall, slid the ring onto my finger. And we had made love like gods, filled with wonder and awe.

"Yes," I said. "Oh, yes."

"A love token?" Solon pressed. "From the Queen's daughter?"

I stared at him. "What do you suppose? Yes."

He shrugged. "I needed to be sure."

"Be sure." I turned to my mother. "What did Sunjata mean about serving two masters?"

A frown knit her graceful brows. "'Tis a long story. To shorten it, Sunjata is a journeyman in my service. But as far as the Guild in Carthage knows, he is a gem-merchant's assistant who has been secretly recruited by a Guildsman named Hannon."

"A horologist," Solon added.

"Why did he take my ring?" I asked.

Melisande shook her head. "At a guess, I'd hazard it was an order he feared to disobey without exposing himself. As to *why* the order was given, I can't say."

"I can." Solon tapped the pages of the book before him, no longer blank, but filled with scribbled notations and charts. "But it will take some doing. This was not a simple spell. It was not *one* spell. I suspect there are a multitude of magics combined here. Horology, symbology, and something else rare and powerful. There is a wide array of lore I must consult to be certain."

"How long will it take?" I asked him.

"It will take as long as it takes," he replied.

I gave a brief nod of acknowledgment. "Can you undo it?"

"*Undo* it?" Solon pursed his lips. "No. It does not lie within my power, and even if it did . . ." His voice trailed off. "Well. It doesn't. But I do believe I can provide *you* with the keys to unlock each link of this chain."

I stood and bowed. "That will suffice."

"Suffice!" He laughed dryly. "I told you, even in this I take a risk. No one else could unknot this puzzle. Carthage will know."

"You could have prevented it," I said softly. "And that, *I* know."

Solon's gaze darted to my mother's face. Her expression was neutral. "Yes," he admitted. "And I aid you now for the same reason I withheld the whole truth from Melisande. Because I have become a fool in my dotage, and I do not wish to lose her." He flapped one hand at me. "Now go, and let me work."

I went.

TWENTY-ONE

While Ptolemy Solon consulted his library and collected toad-slime and fever-sweat, or whatever it was he did to plumb the mysteries of Carthage's magic, I passed more time in my mother's company.

"Tell me," I said to her the first day. "Did you actually threaten to leave Solon if he didn't aid me?"

"Yes," Melisande said in a calm voice.

"Why?" I asked.

We were dining in another inner courtyard of her villa beneath the cool green shade of a grapevine-laced lattice. There were marks on the tile where Hellene-style couches had been removed, replaced by an oval table with two chairs. I knew without being told that my mother had ordered the couches removed because I wouldn't be at ease reclining in her company.

"Let us say I have become a fool in my dotage, too." Melisande gave a self-deprecating smile, glancing around. "I don't wish to lose this, Imriel. But strangely, it is more important to me to make what amendments I might for all that you have suffered."

"It wasn't all your fault," I said.

"I know." She rested her chin on folded hands, gazing into the distance. "And yet. 'Tis a strangeness, truly. I never took pleasure in seeing others suffer against their will, but it never troubled me overmuch, either. It was merely . . . information."

"Fault-lines to exploit," I suggested cynically.

"Yes." Her glorious gaze returned to me. "You see them?"

"I do." I stuck my fork into a spear of tender asparagus, chewing it slowly. "But like Solon, I choose not to exploit such knowledge for my own gain. I do not think merciful Kushiel intended us to use such a gift lightly."

Her tone was unreadable. "So young to be so wise."

I shook my head. "A lifetime of struggling against your legacy. I find it hard to believe you never took pleasure in the suffering of others."

"Ah, well, *suffering*." Melisande gave her graceful shrug. "When it is offered up in tribute, it is another matter. To feel another surrender his or her will unto yours, to bend it until it breaks . . . there is majesty and beauty in it."

For the first time, her words made my blood run cold. They were so matter-of-fact. I set down my fork, my appetite waning.

"It bothers you to hear this," my mother observed. "Have you never been tempted?"

I thought about the first time I'd given free rein to the dark desires in me, and the morning after that first encounter at Valerian House, when I'd caught Phèdre's wrist in anger, felt her pulse leap beneath my thumb, and I'd *known*. I thought about the horrible, unthinkable threats I'd made during my madness. I'd hated the people I loved best in the world. And

I would have taken pleasure in making them suffer against their will. I would have taken enormous pleasure in it.

"Yes," I said shortly.

Melisande cocked her head. "And yet?"

"As a child, I saw death sown in the place of life," I said. "And I think if I were to surrender wholly to my own darkest desires, without the bright beacon of love to guide me, I would become all that I despise."

"Me," she said quietly.

"No," I said. "Worse."

We were both silent a moment. Melisande pushed her own barely touched plate away. A young man who looked to be of mainland Hellene blood, tall and fair, emerged from the recesses of the villa to take our plates away, pausing briefly for a nod of approval that wasn't forthcoming. Lost in thought, my mother merely gestured absently. He looked a bit crestfallen as he departed.

"You said you've changed," I said, watching him go. "Does it trouble you now to observe others suffering against their will?"

"Other than you?" She returned from wherever her thoughts had taken her. "Probably a great deal less than it should, but considerably more than it did."

"That's comforting," I said.

Another graceful shrug. "I am as the gods made me, Imriel. I'm doing my best."

Since it seemed to be true, I didn't press her, but changed the topic. "Do you love him?"

Melisande smiled. "Solon? In my own way."

"Quite a change from having one of the most beautiful courtesans in the realm kneeling for your leash," I commented.

Her brows rose. "Phèdre told you about that?" she asked, sounding genuinely shocked.

"Gods, no!" I said. "Mavros did, when we were younger."

"Sacriphant's son," she murmured. "I heard you'd become friends." Melisande's gaze shifted back toward the distance. "Yes and no. Phèdre nó Delaunay is the only *anguissette* in living memory, and Kushiel's hand lay heavier on her than on any I have read about in history." Her mouth quirked. "And unfortunately, she was a good deal more persistent and resourceful than I reckoned, although in the end I had cause to be grateful for it."

"You have no idea," I said.

"I have enough." She paused. "But Solon . . . Solon, you see with the shallow eyes of youth. He is a homely man, yes, but the breadth of his knowledge and the acuity of his intellect are staggering. And it is an exhilarating pleasure to have one of the greatest minds in existence laid in supplication at one's feet."

"Do you plan on attempting to break his will?" I asked.

"No," Melisande said simply. "No, there is a time when I would have tried it for the sheer joy of the challenge. Now . . . I am not entirely sure I would win. And I am not entirely sure it would please me if I did. Ptolemy Solon and I enjoy one another. After the tedium of my years claiming sanctuary in the Temple of Asherat, I am content to be . . . content." She looked amused. "You're full of questions. Are there more?"

"Yes." I met her gaze and held it. "What fault-lines do you see in me?"

My mother looked at me for a long, long time. The mantle of sorrow settled back over her. "Many," she said at length, her voice gentle. "Fault-lines of grief and loss and despair, and fault-lines of pride and yearning. A strong, bright vein of indomitable courage and strength that with the wisdom of experience, even I would be reluctant to cross." Reaching across the table, she touched my cheek. "Imriel. I swear to you, in Kushiel's name, that I would never do aught to exploit you. And I keep my promises."

"I know," I said. "So do I."

Melisande nodded. "What do *you* see?"

I looked into her.

I saw passion and pride, humor and ambition. Regret and sorrow. A surprising reserve of measured joy, and a chilling amorality. A profound capacity for impersonal cruelty. Unexpected generosity. A lack of conscience, and a growing awareness of that lack. Thoughtfulness. Curiosity.

Me.

I was my mother's fault-line. I was the kernel of vulnerability at her core. I could hurt her far, far more than she could ever hurt me. And she could be hurt through me. What I suffered hurt her. She had loved others in her own way, and there were profound ties there, most especially to Phèdre. That bond, I daresay only the gods themselves understood. But I was the only person she had ever loved with all the deep, abiding wonder and ferocity of her mortal soul.

I pitied her.

It hurt; it hurt us both. I was the first to look away. I knew myself, and I was sane. I took no pleasure in her pain.

"Now you know," Melisande said in a low, steady voice.

"Yes." I took a deep breath and forced myself to meet her gaze. "And I am grateful for your love, Mother. Despite everything, I am grateful for it."

Her generous lips curved in a smile. "Let us hope that it is enough to bring down Carthage."

"Let us." There was a pitcher of cool white wine on the table. I filled both our cups, hoisting my own in toast. "Between the two of us, let us hope."

No word came from Solon that day. I returned to the widow's lodgings and passed the night there. In the morning,

Leander came to fetch me, finding me in the garden once more. This time, I heard him enter and halted my exercises.

"Word from the palace?" I asked.

He shook his head, braids dancing. "Her ladyship thought you might fancy an excursion to the Shrine of Aphrodite. 'Tis only a league or two."

It was a kind thought. I was restless and impatient, eager to be *doing* instead of waiting. At least this would serve to keep me occupied; and too, it was always wise to pay respects to the gods of a place. I had the Bastard saddled, and Leander and I set out, following the road eastward along the Cytheran coast.

I had to own, it was beautiful here. It was autumn. In Terre d'Ange, there would be a chill in the air, a promise of frost to come. Here in Cythera, it was warm and sunny. The wind off the sea tangled my hair, making me envy Leander his braids. The folk we passed saluted us cheerfully. The Bastard, recovered at last from his ordeal, pranced and snorted.

"Good-looking horse," Leander observed, eyeing him.

"He was a gift," I said. "From the House of Aragon."

He whistled. "That's got to sting, thinking on it, what with Terre d'Ange betraying its alliance."

"It does, in fact." I looked curiously at him. "Does it trouble *you*?"

"Truly?" Leander shrugged. "Not really. Blessed Elua wandered the world without a care. Why shouldn't I?"

I couldn't think of a reply, so I didn't give one.

It took a little over an hour to reach the shrine of the goddess, situated on a windswept promontory overlooking the sea. It was built in the classic Hellene style, simple and elegant, open to the elements. Myrtle grew in abundance around it, the sun-warmed leaves releasing a pleasing fragrance. Bees droned around the flowering shrubs. There were vendors in the plaza in front of the temple steps selling incense, honey, oil, and votive offerings. On Leander's advice, I bought a flagon of sweet oil and a piece of honeycomb.

A priestess in a white chiton greeted us at the top of the steps, small, dark, and plump, with a smile at once merry and mysterious. We made an offering of coin and she directed us toward the rear of the temple.

I'd thought to see an effigy there, but instead there was a black stone on a plinth, as large as a tall man's torso, its surface polished and gleaming. I gave Leander an inquiring look.

"It fell from the sky thousands of years ago," he murmured. "Much like the genitals of the castrated Ouranos from which foam-born Aphrodite was begotten. You're to anoint it."

Although I couldn't have said why, it *felt* ancient. Older than the temple, worn smooth by countless generations of hands. I poured the flagon of oil over the top of the stone, then squeezed the honeycomb. Honey dripped, gliding over the oil.

Honey-gold, onyx-black.

I thought of Sidonie and my heart ached with longing. I rubbed the honey and oil, spreading it over the smooth black rock. "Divine Aphrodite, I pray you accept this offering," I whispered. "If there is mercy in your heart for the plight of lovers, I pray you look kindly on my quest."

The stone felt warm beneath my hands, oil-slick and sticky with honey. It was peaceful and strangely erotic, and beneath it lay a sense of waiting stillness. When I had finished, the plump priestess approached with a basin of water and a linen towel. I washed and dried my hands while she gazed at my face.

"Such sadness," the priestess said softly. "Did a woman break your heart?"

"No," I said. "But the world threatens to."

She shifted the basin under one arm and took my right hand, pressing it to her warm breast. "If your heart knows its true desire, you must trust it."

I nodded. "Thank you, my lady."

With that, she let me go and departed. Leander stared after her. "Huh. I've made a dozen offerings and no one's ever said such a thing to me."

"Do you know your heart's true desire?" I asked wryly.

He looked at me under his lashes. "Well, no. But I'm familiar with quite a few others."

Outside the temple, we bought sausages and olives and boiled eggs from a food vendor, eating them in the shade of a fragrant stand of myrtle. I was quiet and thoughtful. Leander watched me curiously.

"What's it like?" he asked. "Being in love."

"It's awful." I smiled. "And wonderful. Betimes you feel like your heart's going to burst into a thousand pieces, flaying your chest wide open. Betimes you feel like you could leap off a cliff and take wing. And then it changes. It puts roots into you, deep and enduring. It becomes a part of you."

"Huh." Leander wiped his hands on his loose breeches. "Hard to fathom."

"You'll know it one day," I said.

"Mayhap." He rose with careless grace. "Shall we go?"

We returned to Paphos together. Leander hummed as he rode. For the first time, I found myself wishing I'd brought the wooden flute that Hugues had given me. I hadn't played it since I'd avenged Dorelei's death. Too many memories. I hadn't thought of it when I'd beseeched L'Envers' aid, and I daresay he would have laughed at me if I'd asked for it. But it had been a comfort to me in Alba; and in Vralia it had saved my life. I tried to recall the charmed tune of the Maghuin

Dhonn that I'd played, the one that had sent everyone in the gaol to sleep, allowing me to escape with Kebek, the young Tatar.

I'd forgotten it.

I listened to my memories, moving my fingers. If I *had* a flute, I thought, mayhap I might be able to recall it. What the mind forgets, the body remembers. By the time we approached the gates of Paphos, I had resolved to visit the market in search of a skilled craftsman.

"Leander—" I began.

"Hsst!" Leander raised one hand, peering forward. "Shabaq?"

A lean figure sitting cross-legged beneath a lemon tree rose and crossed over to us. I recognized him as the young man playing the blindfold game in my mother's household. He laid a hand on Leander's stirrup, flashing a white grin.

"Her ladyship sent me to look out for you," Shabaq said cheerfully. "His apish eminence awaits you at his palace."

Leander glanced at me. "Shall we—"

I didn't wait to hear the rest of it. I nudged the Bastard's flanks with my heels and gave him his head, all thoughts of flutes and stones and honey forgotten, pedestrians scattering before our onslaught.

Ptolemy Solon had found the key.

That was all I needed.

Twenty-two

There is good news and bad news." Solon spoke in a hushed voice. We were meeting in the room where I'd first met with him, overlooking the sea. "The good news is that there is a very simple way to break Carthage's spell." He pointed out the window at the bright harbor. "The spell is bound to Terre d'Ange. Its effects cannot cross the sea."

My heart leapt. "So Sidonie—"

He shook his head. "That's part of the bad news. I fear she has been bound with a different spell, a simpler spell."

"My ring," I said grimly.

Solon nodded. "That is doubtless one part of it. Astegal bears your love-token. He will have placed some token of his own on her to seal the bond."

My mother stirred. "But in Terre d'Ange, all that is needful to break the spell is to ferry everyone affected across the sea? Mayhap to Alba?"

"Yes and no." He looked apologetic. "Forgive me. I do believe I overstated the good news. The problem is twofold. Unless the spell is undone, it will reclaim anyone who returns to D'Angeline soil. Of greater concern, there is malevolence at its core. Any attempt to struggle against it will cause the spell to tighten like a snare, and those caught within it will grow angry and violent."

I thought about Ysandre shouting at Barquiel L'Envers. "So logic and reason will prove little use."

"I fear you would have a very difficult time convincing anyone caught in Carthage's coils to sail away in pursuit of their sanity," Solon said.

I frowned. "Quintilius Rousse had put to sea. It didn't restore his wits."

"Did he cross to a foreign shore?" Solon asked.

"No," I said. "He was anchored in the harbor."

"Not far enough," he replied. "One would have to cross the sea itself." Solon opened a large book on the table, its pages dark with age, and pointed to an engraving. "*This* is what lies at the heart of the spell."

Melisande and I gazed at the image. An infant lay on a slab of rock in a desert, a gaping slit in its belly. Beside it was what appeared to be a whirlwind sprouting horns, fiery eyes, and four reaching arms with clawed hands. A robed man hid behind a boulder, watching.

"This tells how to make a *ghafrid-gebla*." Solon ran one finger from right to left along a line of unfamiliar script. "It requires a flawless gem, emerald or ruby, cut into twelve facets, with the symbols of the twelve Houses of the Cosmos etched onto its facets. The jewel is placed in the belly of an infant. When the *ghafrid*"—he tapped the image of the whirlwind—"devours the infant, the magus utters a word of binding, trapping the *ghafrid* in the very stone it has swallowed."

I stared in sick fascination. "What exactly is a *ghafrid*?"

"It is what we call an elemental," Solon said. "A desert spirit. Very powerful, capricious, and cruel. Once it is trapped within the stone, it must do its master's bidding." He looked thoughtful. "Understand, this is very difficult to do. The infant must be alive when it is devoured. And given that one must slit its belly to insert the jewel, this is a tricky proposition."

I swallowed. "I begin to perceive the wisdom in your restraint of exercising knowledge, my lord."

"Indeed," my mother murmured. "So the business with the moon and the mirrors mattered naught?"

"No, no." Solon shook his head. "It's all part and parcel. This is a puzzle with many pieces. The placement of the mirrors established the compass of the spell, setting the framework for binding the entire City and all in it. The occlusion of the moon increased its power a thousand-fold. And the painting you described defined the essence of the spell. Each piece is important. But this"—he tapped the engraving again—"this is the key."

"How so?" I asked.

Solon smiled. "To undo the spell, all you must do is free the *ghafrid*. And to do this, all you must do is take possession of the gem-stone and speak the word of binding, which is also the word of unbinding."

My mother eyed him wryly. "Somehow I suspect you've overstated the good news once more."

He spread his hands. "I have no way of knowing the word. Bodeshmun—I'm sure this is his work—would have chosen it." He turned back a page, pointing to an image depicting a drawing of a *ghafrid* with a single word inscribed beneath it. "Symbology. Somewhere, likely on his person, Bodeshmun possesses a similar image. It is necessary to maintain the bond."

I studied the page. "What if the image were destroyed? Would that free the *ghafrid*?"

"Well reasoned," Solon said approvingly. "But alas, no.

It would merely bind the elemental into the stone for all eternity."

"Why wouldn't Bodeshmun do so?" Melisande inquired. "It seems simpler."

"Oh, because the *ghafrid* would go mad with rage," he said cheerfully. "Violently, horribly mad. And because Bodeshmun would be bound to it, he would slowly succumb to madness himself. No, no. He'll keep the talisman safe until such time as he deems it reasonable to release the *ghafrid*. It's a dangerous business, trafficking with elementals. I suspect he plans to free it at some point, perhaps when Carthage's ascent is secure and the Queen's daughter has provided Astegal with a few heirs."

"*That*," I said, "will not happen."

Solon glanced at me, sobering. "Forgive me. It's begun, though. I heard word late this morning. Carthage's fleet has set sail for Aragonia." He cocked his head. "The good news is that General Astegal has left his young bride in Carthage. So I suppose that reduces the chances of begetting an heir, unless she's already with child."

I gritted my teeth. "So in order to undo Carthage's spell, I need to obtain the word of binding and unbinding, which Bodeshmun is likely to have on his person. Is that correct?"

"Yes." He nodded. "And speak it in the presence of the *ghafrid-gebla* once you have claimed possession of the stone."

Irony piled on irony. I'd travelled to the far ends of the earth with Phèdre and Joscelin to find the Name of God, a word capable of binding an angel. Now it seemed I sought a word that would loose a demon from its bindings. The bright mirror and the dark reflected one another: good and evil, the sacred and profane.

I sighed. "And the stone lies in Bodeshmun's possession?"

"No, no." Solon pursed his lips. "That I neglected to

mention. The gem must remain in Terre d'Ange to be fully effective. Bodeshmun will have hidden it somewhere."

"What if it were removed?" my mother asked with interest. "Would it diminish the effects?"

"Diminish, yes," Solon said. "Undo, no."

"You should have said that at the outset," I muttered. "What about Sidonie?"

"Ah!" His wizened face brightened. "Now that's easy. She's safe beyond the *ghafrid*'s reach. All you need to do is obtain the ring from Astegal, find his token, and remove it from her."

"Another ring?" I asked.

"Perhaps." Solon shrugged. "A ring, a necklace, a pair of eardrops, a ribbon. . . . whatever it is, it will be something of significance that he's given to her and bade her never remove. A ring is likely. If you were able to obtain even one of the tokens, it would weaken the binding."

I rose to pace the room, restless. "So Sidonie is in Carthage. Astegal is, or will be, in Aragonia. Where's Bodeshmun?"

"I don't know," Solon admitted.

"Carthage," Melisande said. She met his glance with amusement. "Oddly enough, I received word this morning, too."

"Then I need to go to Carthage," I said slowly, thinking. "I'll send word to Barquiel L'Envers. I can tell him to try his damnedest to get Ysandre and anyone who will go to Alba—"

"Or Aragonia," my mother interrupted me. "Let him agree to send the Royal Army and all of Rousse's fleet in support of Carthage's invasion. It won't matter. Once they're on Aragonian soil, the spell will lose its hold, yes?"

"Oh, well reasoned, my love!" Solon said in delight.

"Aragonia, then," I agreed. "And I'll tell him to find that thrice-cursed jewel and take it with him, away from the City.

But I need to go to Carthage." I paced, still thinking. "There are two pieces of the puzzle there, Bodeshmun and Sidonie. And I can reach her. I *know* I can. I was bound by magic in Alba. I never forgot that I loved her. Even through the bindings, I knew it."

"Imriel." The gentleness in Melisande's voice halted me. "You can't go. Bodeshmun knows you."

Solon blinked. "That's true. Perhaps Sunjata—"

"*No.*" I raked a hand through my hair, still wind-tangled. "I don't trust Sunjata. He's the one who took my ring. If he's caught serving two masters, he's not like to risk himself on Sidonie's behalf." I narrowed my eyes. "Solon, you said you knew a spell that could give one man the semblance of another."

"Yes." He furrowed his brow. "But a mere glamour will not suffice to fool Bodeshmun. Ordinary folk, yes. Not a magus." He hesitated. "Unless it were done so that you believed it yourself."

"Is that possible?" I asked.

"It is." Solon's tone was reserved. "But it is dangerous. Of a surety, you would risk losing yourself."

"Solon," my mother murmured. "I think this unwise."

"Who would I be?" I asked him, ignoring her.

"Leander would be a good choice," he said without looking at Melisande. "Your mother has trained him well. He knows Sunjata. Carthage is likely to accept him as my emissary, since the infernal Guild knows of our circumstances here. And he's bored and ambitious and handsome enough to consider seducing Astegal's wife."

I nodded curtly. "So I'd think myself Leander?"

"You would," Solon confirmed. "Until such time as the spell was broken. It would be necessary to create such a key." He rubbed his chin, thinking. "A kiss, perhaps?"

"From Sidonie?" I asked.

The Wise Ape of Cythera studied me. "Are you that confident, Imriel de la Courcel, that this woman you love, this cousin of yours, will succumb to your charms no matter what face you wear, no matter who you believe yourself to be?"

"No," I said softly. I thought about my encounter in the temple that morning, the priestess pressing my hand to her breast. *If your heart knows its true desire, you must trust it.* "No, my lord. But I am very, very sure that I love Sidonie enough to take any chance."

Melisande sighed. "I mislike this. Imriel, you've suffered one ordeal of madness. Your mind is fragile."

I laughed shortly. "What happened to that bright vein of indomitable strength you spoke of yesterday?"

"There are limits to what the mortal mind was meant to bear." Her face was grave. "I fear you challenge them."

I glanced at Solon. "What do you say, my lord?"

He shrugged. "As I said, it is dangerous. There is a chance you would succeed. There is a chance that you would fail, but that this Duc L'Envers will succeed in your stead with the keys I have given you, and you could be thus freed from the spell. And there is a chance that your wits would snap, and you would spend the balance of your life believing yourself to be Leander."

"I'll take it," I said.

Twenty-three

That evening, I acceded to my mother's wishes and passed the night at her villa. I couldn't maintain the will to refuse her, and in truth, if this was the last night in which I would know myself for many days, I didn't wish to spend it alone in rented lodgings.

I was scared.

After what had happened in Alba, I'd sworn I'd never suffer myself to be bound by strange magics; and it was true, the memory of my madness was fresh and raw. The prospect of losing myself filled me with dread. But the prospect of doing nothing was worse. Someone had to get to Bodeshmun, and while Sidonie was in Astegal's thrall, she was in danger. Mayhap it wasn't immediate, but the moment aught went awry with Carthage's scheme, Sidonie became a hostage in deadly earnest.

I wrote a long letter to Barquiel L'Envers, detailing everything I knew. I tried to compose a letter to Phèdre and Joscelin, but in the end, I couldn't think of anything I hadn't already said. I settled for asking L'Envers to tell them I loved them. I paid a visit to Captain Oppius of the *Aeolia*. I released him from his pledge to wait for me, and he promised to see my letter delivered. Beyond that, I told him only that I would be staying on Cythera for a time.

Melisande was unwontedly quiet and subdued. Although she misliked the plan, she had consented to assist. Leander had been told. He had no real quarrel with it, although he was envious and a bit irritated that Ptolemy Solon had sent a request for all his clothing.

"Why not simply send *me*, my lady?" Leander asked Melisande. "It's a good deal simpler and less risky. And I wouldn't have to purchase a new wardrobe."

"If it were my choice, I would," she replied. "But this is Imriel's."

"I have to try it," I said. "I'll go just as mad if I don't."

Leander studied me. "You know, once you're convinced you're *me*, you won't give two figs for the girl."

"We'll see," I said.

Melisande and I dined alone, and I couldn't have said what we ate, although it was good. I was sufficiently on edge regarding the morrow's prospects that I forgot to be uneasy in her company. She spent long moments watching me without speaking.

"Is there nothing I can say to dissuade you?" she asked me at last, when the dinner plates had been cleared and cups of a strong Cytheran cordial served. "Leander is right. The risk is unnecessary."

I sipped my cordial. "I can reach Sidonie. He can't."

"She won't *know* you," Melisande observed.

"It doesn't matter." I shook my head. "We'll find one another." I gazed toward the west, where Carthage lay. "Alais told me once that she thought Sidonie would need me very badly one day. And Sidonie . . . when she met with the combined priesthood of Elua and his Companions, she told them that Blessed Elua doesn't join hearts without a purpose. I believe it's true."

"Will I ever see you again?" my mother asked.

I looked back at her, at her grave, beautiful face illuminated by lamplight. A mortal goddess who carried her sins lightly, her sorrow heavily. What emotions I felt, I couldn't name.

"I don't know," I said quietly. "I'll not make any false promises."

Melisande nodded. "If you find it in your heart to see me again one day, I would like it. I would like it very much."

Against all expectations, I slept soundly that night, beneath my mother's roof in a pleasant guest-chamber on sheets of the finest Menekhetan linen. I slept without dreaming and woke feeling oddly lighthearted.

Today I would surrender everything.

Everything I had, everything I *was*. I would let go of all of it, placing myself and all my trust in the hands of my mother's lover, the dangerously clever and unfathomable Wise Ape of Cythera. Laying it all on the altar of love. In the end, that was truly where my trust lay. Not in Ptolemy Solon's spells and arcane knowledge, but in love. In the precept of Blessed Elua. In Sidonie's pledge.

Always and always.

She was the one who had taught me to trust. To trust her. To trust myself.

I did.

The mood stayed with me as we rode to the palace after breaking our fast; Melisande, Leander, and I. His presence was necessary for the spell. I breathed deep of the warm, salt-tinged air, filling my lungs. Reveling in the knowledge of myself, soon to be relinquished. I patted the Bastard's spotted neck with bittersweet affection.

"You'll have to stay here," I said to him, watching his ears swivel. "I'm sorry. I shouldn't have brought you. I wasn't thinking. But I can't take you to Carthage. Bodeshmun's seen you."

The Bastard snorted in disgust.

"You'll take care of him for me?" I asked Leander.

He nodded, sunlight winking on his ruby eardrops. "Of course."

My mother said nothing.

At the palace, Ptolemy Solon was awaiting us in the chamber overlooking the sea. All of Leander's clothing was there, clean and pressed with a hot iron, neatly folded. Solon looked unspeakably weary, his eyes bloodshot.

"This," he said, "is a damnably difficult spell." He flexed his cramped hands. "One thing must always be bound to another. I have been sewing all night, which is not an activity to which I am accustomed. You need not know the details, but suffice it to say that this enchantment has been bound into every fiber of these garments."

"I'm to wear Leander's attire?" I asked.

"Indeed." Solon stifled a yawn. "For therein lies the spell, bound to it stitch by stitch. Do you expose yourself to anyone in your full nakedness, that person will see you for your true self, then and thereafter."

"What if he beholds himself thusly?" Melisande asked in a low voice.

"He would see himself truly," Solon admitted. "But only were he to regard himself naked in a mirror. I do not recommend it, Imriel. For you would perceive yourself to be Leander trapped in Imriel's form, and it would tax your wits."

I shrugged. "I'm not given to looking in mirrors."

"I am," Leander murmured.

"Well, I recommend against it." Solon gathered himself. "Strip and don his clothing."

I stripped.

It felt odd. I heard my mother catch her breath as I tugged the shirt over my head, baring my scarred torso.

"Oh, gods," she breathed. "*Imriel.*"

"A souvenir of Alba," I said with a lightness I didn't feel. The gravity of what we did here was settling into my bones. I slid my arms into one of Leander's vests, tugging it into place. "As I said, a great deal of what I've suffered is no fault of yours."

"It's just . . ." Melisande shook her head. "Elua have mercy."

I unlaced my breeches. "I pray he does."

Once I was fully attired in Leander's clothing, Solon bade me sit cross-legged on the floor, strewn with cushions. I did, and he sat opposite me. "You must go now," he said to Leander and my mother. "Leander, you I will send for in some time, for you must recount your memories for Imriel once he is entranced. Melisande . . ." He paused, sorrow etched in his homely face. "Bid your son farewell."

My mother sank to her knees before me, cradling my face in her hands. "Come back, Imriel," she whispered. Her touch was warm and soothing, and there were tears in her glorious eyes. "If not to me, at least to the world."

"I will," I said. "I promise."

She kissed my brow. "Blessed Elua pray you keep it."

She went.

Leander went.

Ptolemy Solon and I faced one another. "Breathe deep," he advised me. "Breathe deep and listen. Close your eyes. Take my words into you. *Listen.*"

I obeyed.

"Close your thoughts and quiet your mind," Solon said in a low, calm voice. "Hear nothing but the sound of my voice. Think of nothing but my words. My voice is a warm sea of light, soft and mild. You are drifting atop it, safe and warm. Let yourself go. Let yourself drift . . ."

It was warm in the room and I could feel the sunlight flooding through the window. Solon's voice continued to speak, low and pleasant, almost droning. I listened. I began to feel drowsy and a little bored. I began to wonder how long it would take, then forced myself to stop wondering. I listened, floating atop the sea of Solon's voice. Elua, if nothing else, the man had the patience of a stone. To spend the entire night sewing, of all things, and then this endless talking . . .

Listen.

I made myself listen.

On and on he went. I passed beyond boredom and relaxed. My body felt heavy and inert, but inside, I felt light. Lighthearted. Floating on a sea of light. There had been enough darkness in my life. Too much. This was nice.

". . . and now it is time to put Imriel away," Solon's voice told me. "Time to make him small. Small like a grain of sand, like a tiny, tiny seed. Make him very small, a tiny seed."

I agreed. I made Imriel into a tiny seed.

"Tuck him into the farthest crack of your mind," Solon's voice continued. "Hide him where no one will see him. A tiny seed, safe and hidden."

I hid Imriel away.

"Forget he is there," Solon instructed me. "Until the moment your lips touch Sidonie's, you will forget Imriel is there. When you kiss her, you will remember. Until that moment, you will forget. Forget."

I forgot about Imriel.

"Sit quietly in peace," the man talking to me said. I obeyed, hearing his joints creak as he rose, the sound of a door opening. "Come in," he said to someone. "You may begin. Tell him the story of your life. I will speak over your words. Pay it no heed."

"Where do I begin?" the new voice said.

"Begin at the beginning," the first one said.

"All right." The newcomer took a deep breath. "I was born in Kusheth about a year after the Skaldi War ended, and . . . hells, my lord Solon, I don't remember all that much about the first five or six years of my life."

"It doesn't matter," the man he'd called Solon said. "Say what you do know."

"The first thing . . . the first thing I remember is when my little sister Darielle was born. She was a red-faced, wrinkled, squalling thing, and everyone doted on her because Mother had given up on getting with child again after so long . . ."

The newcomer's voice went on and on, joined by the man called Solon's.

"Hear and remember," Solon said. "This is your story. You are Leander Maignard. When you awake you will know this to be true. Each word is a stitch in the garment of your life. Hear and remember. This is your story. You are Leander Maignard. Each word is a stitch in the garment of your life. When you awake you will know this to be true."

". . . really, life didn't get interesting until her ladyship sent for us to make a household in Cythera, when I was ten or so. All these years, she'd provided for the Maignard clan, but I'd begun to think it would never amount to more than that . . ."

"This is your story. You are Leander Maignard. Each word is a stitch in the garment of your life . . ."

". . . the day we stepped off the ship, my father said, 'We're never leaving.' He serves as her ladyship's master of vineyards, but then, I was always more ambitious . . ."

". . . word is a stitch in the garment of your life. When

you awake you will know this to be true. Hear and remember. This is your story. You are Leander Maignard."

It should have been irritating, listening to both of their voices at once, but it wasn't. One wound around the other. I listened to the newcomer's endless narrative unspooling, while Solon's calm voice continued, stitching in and out, fashioning it into the garment of self I would wear when I awoke.

It went on for a long time, but I didn't mind. Solon had told me to sit quietly in peace, so I did, listening to the story of my life unwind until at last the spool was almost wholly bare.

"Halt," Solon said to the newcomer. "Do not recount these last days."

"Glad to oblige," the other said wearily.

"I'm forgetting . . . ah. Eardrops."

"*Must* you?"

"Yes." Solon's voice had grown hoarse, but he sounded amused. "I've never seen you without them. Surely they will serve as a last line of defense against the perils of nudity. Where did I put that needle?" And then, to me, "You will feel no pain." He pinched my earlobes lightly, one after another. Afterward, they felt heavier.

"Am I finished, my lord?" the other asked.

"You may go," Solon agreed. "Remember, keep out of sight."

"I know. I know."

I heard him leave and heard the door close. I sat quietly in peace.

"Open your eyes," Solon said to me. I did. The room was filled with late-afternoon sunlight. "You are Leander Maignard. You are departing on the morrow for Carthage to attempt to seduce General Astegal's wife and break the spell that binds her, and to find the key to the *ghafrid-gebla* that

Bodeshmun possesses." He went on to explain this to me in considerable detail. "Do you understand?"

"Yes, my lord," I said politely.

Solon gave me a tired smile. "In the morning, you will awake and know this to be true. You will forget this day. Sleep."

I slept.

Twenty-four

The crow of that damnable rooster that the cook insisted on keeping around woke me with a start. I'd slept long and hard. For a moment, I felt strange to myself, my heart racing. Then I remembered why.

Today I sailed for Carthage.

By the Goddess, it was about sodding well time her ladyship gave me somewhat meaningful to do! As much as I loved Cythera, it ate at my pride to cool my heels while others were given more interesting assignments.

And this was a big one.

I'd never have admitted it to her ladyship's son, not if I valued my life, but in my heart of hearts, I was a little bit glad that Carthage had ensorceled the Dauphine and half of Terre d'Ange. It was horrible, of course. But it was exciting, too. And there had been precious few opportunities for her ladyship to deploy D'Angeline spies without rousing suspicion.

This . . . this was perfect.

And now that her sentence had been commuted to exile,

there was no fear of exposure. At last we could play the game as it was meant to be played; and I would be at the very heart of it, a veritable lynch-pin in the scheme. I had the opportunity to seduce a Princess of the Blood and bring down a budding empire.

It was a delicious thought. It was so delicious that I permitted myself to lay a-bed a few minutes, contemplating it and stroking my phallus. I wondered what the half-breed Cruithne princess looked like, although it didn't really matter. I could rise to any challenge.

The household was stirring.

Duty beckoned.

One couldn't have luxury and adventure alike. With a sigh, I left off my musings and my pleasure. I rose, braided my hair, donned my clothing, and went to face the day.

"Leander." Shabaq intercepted me on my way to the kitchen. "Her ladyship wishes you to break your fast with her in the arbor."

"Truly?" I said in delight.

He smiled. "Truly."

It *was* true. I found her ladyship awaiting me in the latticed arbor, sipping a cup of hot bitter *kavah*. I bowed deeply to her, holding my bow. "My lady, you honor me. I pray I prove worthy of your trust in this matter."

Her gaze, so terrible and beautiful and sad, rested on me. "As do I."

I marked, as she had taught me, how her hand trembled a bit returning her thin porcelain cup to its saucer. "Do you doubt me?"

"No," she said softly. "Sit and dine with me, Leander."

I did.

There was fresh, crusty bread still warm from the oven, honey and preserves, and heartier fare, too. Sausage flavored with coriander, eggs cooked with goat cheese and herbs. I ate with a good will, mindful that I'd be dining on salt pork and beans during the voyage to Carthage. Her ladyship watched me, scarce touching her food.

"Have you questions?" she asked me.

I shook my head, chewing vigorously. "Have you advice?"

"Yes," she said simply. "Be careful."

I swallowed a mouthful of cooked eggs and smiled at her. "I will be. I will be the soul of discretion. I will be the perfect courtier, I promise. I will court the D'Angeline princess and make her love me. And I will ferret out all of Carthage's secrets on your behalf." I hesitated, glancing around. "Is he here?"

Her throat worked. "Imriel?"

"Yes." I lowered my voice. "Your brooding son."

"No." Her ladyship Melisande Shahrizai de la Courcel shook her head. There were tears—*tears!*—in her glorious eyes. It made me want to kneel and comfort her. "No, we thought it best if he wasn't here for this."

I nodded. "Of course, my lady."

When we had finished—which was to say, when I had eaten my fill—we departed for the harbor. Everything was in readiness. My mother, who ran her ladyship's household, had seen to the packing of my things. All my garments were laid in a cedar chest, neatly folded. I embraced her fondly, resting my chin on her head. She returned my embrace awkwardly.

"Don't be frightened," I said to her. "All will be well."

She avoided my gaze. "I'm sure it will."

"Women, eh?" I said cheerfully to my father, clasping his callused hand. He gave me a grave nod.

"Have a care for yourself," he murmured.

"I will." I ruffled my sister's hair. Darielle, fifteen years of age and deep in her ladyship's training, wrinkled her nose at me. "You too, brat."

"*You're* the brat," she retorted.

"No." I grinned at her. "Today I'm a handsome young D'Angeline lord who happens to be in the service of the Governor of Cythera, and I'm off to pay tribute on his behalf to General Astegal's poor, lonely young bride."

We rode in procession down to the harbor, where the Wise Ape's flagship awaited. Solon was there himself, looking uncommonly sober. I put on a solemn expression, mindful that this was a serious matter. It wasn't that I didn't appreciate the gravity of the situation—all the gods of Terre d'Ange and Cythera knew, one didn't rise far in her ladyship's estimation by being frivolous and careless. It was just that I felt like a hawk about to fly free of the tether.

I greeted Solon with a deep bow. "Good day, my lord."

His apish eminence inclined his head. "Good day, Leander Maignard. I am pleased that you have consented to carry the congratulations of Cythera to Carthage's young princess. Doubtless it will gladden her heart to see a fellow countryman."

"I will do my best to convey your goodwill, my lord," I said gravely. It was all for show, of course, but outside the veil of discretion that existed in her ladyship's household, one had to be circumspect.

"Captain Deimos has orders to give you every assistance," Solon said, indicating the man beside him, a tall, lean fellow with piercing eyes. The captain and I exchanged greetings. "The tribute has been loaded." He smiled faintly. "I trust you will find sufficient funds, gifts, and bribes."

"I'm sure you've been more than generous, my lord," I said.

Solon handed me a packet of letters. "These are letters of introduction to various Carthaginian lords of my acquaintance. I cannot say of a surety which you will find in residence, and which will have joined Astegal's campaign."

"I'm sure it will suffice, my lord," I replied.

There wasn't a great deal more to be said. Captain Deimos' sailors loaded my belongings. Solon glanced at her ladyship. "Have you words in parting?"

Her ladyship stood, tall and splendid as a goddess, and although she'd taught me to read faces, I couldn't read hers in this moment. For the first time, it struck me—*truly* struck me—that this was a grave trust indeed. Cythera ran a serious risk in this scheme. If I failed, if I was caught, the consequences could be dire. I was leaving her to wait and worry, while her poor, besotted son chafed at his inactivity and I went off to attempt to seduce the woman he loved.

It made me feel strange in my skin.

"Be safe," her ladyship said in a low voice. "Nothing more."

"My lady Melisande," I said to her, "I swear to you in Blessed Elua's name that I will make you proud."

She shook her head. "Just be safe."

It was a peculiar moment. I took it to be a final warning against taking any unnecessary risks, probably one that was well merited, given my exuberant spirits. I noted it duly.

And then it was time to go.

I boarded the flagship, waving a final farewell to those gathered on the docks. Solon had moved to stand at her ladyship's side, and though he looked smaller and more wizened than ever next to her, she had laid a hand on his shoulder as though to draw strength from him. It was curious, and it made me feel oddly melancholy.

Then Captain Deimos gave the order to raise the anchor and set to oars, and the ship began to move. Our prow nosed seaward and the harbor began to fall away behind us, taking my melancholy with it.

I was bound for Carthage.

Her ladyship needn't have warned me against unnecessary exuberance. By the end of our first day at sea, my initial rush of excitement had settled into a more calm, calculating frame of mind. I examined the manifest of tribute that Solon had provided. He really *had* been generous. Gods above, the old ape doted on her ladyship! A lifetime of caution and restraint, and he was throwing it all to the wind, risking Carthage's ire—and a considerable amount of money—in a mad scheme like this.

And to whose benefit? That was the part that made me shake my head. Terre d'Ange and its spell-beleaguered Queen, who had insisted on pressing for her ladyship's execution. Her ladyship's own son, who, until Carthage struck and he desperately *needed* her help, had seemed perfectly willing to see her executed if it meant he got to wed his princess.

Yet her ladyship and Solon were aiding him.

Love makes fools of us all, I supposed. Solon loved her ladyship. And she loved her son Imriel, and bore a strong measure of guilt in the bargain. I'd heard the tales of what he'd suffered as a child, and I had to own, it sounded awful.

One had to wonder about *him*.

I knew what slavery had done to Sunjata. It had made him bitter. And as much as I loved his caustic wit, there were times when I wondered what he would have been like if he'd not been taken. He'd come from a line of warriors. He remembered his father dressing for battle, tall and strong, laughing deep in his chest. Teaching him to throw a spear, to lift his heavy shield. I knew how much it hurt Sunjata that that had been taken from him. One skirmish gone awry, and his father was dead and he'd become chattel.

Imriel . . . Imriel was different.

Well, of course he hadn't been gelded. Two quick cuts of a slaver's knife, and good-bye to the ballocks. Small wonder Sunjata was bitter. He'd been eleven years old. But from what I'd heard about the mad ruler of Drujan, Imriel had cause of his own to harbor soul-twisting bitterness, ballocks or no. And I hadn't sensed that in him.

Anger, yes. Of course he was angry. Either Astegal of Carthage had stolen his beloved, or he'd been unexpectedly thwarted in playing a very, very deep game to place himself on the throne of Terre d'Ange. I wondered which was true. If it was the latter, he played it very well.

But then, he was her ladyship's son.

Such were the intriguing puzzles that occupied my mind during my voyage to Carthage.

I pored over the manifest, making notes in my mind about which items were suitable for what purpose. Good hard coin was always suitable for a bribe, and I'd need a fair bit of it to set myself up with a decent household. There were various baubles and trinkets that might suffice for lesser personages. I might need them to gain access. Access to the Dauphine Sidonie, access to the magus Bodeshmun. Access, in time, to Astegal himself. I went over the things that Solon had told me.

So much to be done.

There was a very fine chess set listed in the manifest, with jeweled pieces of onyx and ivory. That, I decided, was meant for the princess. It was an excellent opening gambit. Once the opportunity to present it was established, I could offer to match wits with her and enjoy a game together.

Sidonie.

My thoughts kept returning to her. I couldn't help but

wonder what she was like. Weak-minded, I thought. Surely, to fall so thoroughly under the influence of her ladyship's son—and then to abandon him for Astegal—she must be weak-minded.

Well and good.

Weakness could be plied, most especially when it failed to know itself. In Astegal's absence, I would ply her. I would woo her. I would find her fault-lines and break her wide open, gently turning her against herself—or at least against Bodeshmun's spell. After all, it was for her own good, more or less.

Gods, that was an intoxicating thought.

And Imriel deserved it.

That was another thought I'd never dare voice in his presence—nor her ladyship's. It was true, though. What manner of son sought his own mother's life? Oh, I knew what she'd done, or at least what the world claimed she had done. They didn't grasp the scope of her vision. And Melisande Shahrizai had kept her word, at least to the Maignard clan. The rest of the world couldn't claim as much. When her ladyship gave her word, she meant it.

Always.

"I *will* make you proud, my lady," I vowed aloud.

And to myself, I vowed silently that I would succeed on my own terms. I liked, very much, the idea of being the lynch-pin of this mad scheme. The thought of bringing down Carthage single-handedly made me shiver to the marrow of my bones. But too, I relished the thought of cuckolding Imriel de la Courcel. Of exposing him as a hypocrite, mayhap even excising her ladyship's single weakness. Him.

Once I had ensconced myself betwixt the Dauphine's thighs, that would do it. I'd strip her bare of Astegal's token. I'd claim her, albeit temporarily, for my own. I'd plunder her to the core and make her mine. I'd been taught the arts of the bedchamber. I was of Kushiel's bloodline, albeit not so pure a strain. I would make her crave me, bend her pliable will. I'd leave my own mark on her.

Of that, at least, I was sure.

The only thing I couldn't fathom was why the thought made my heart ache.

That made no sense at all.

TWENTY-FIVE

"Carthage!"

The cry came from the crow's nest, was taken up aboard the ship. Captain Deimos flung out one lean-muscled arm, pointing the way.

"Carthage," he echoed.

It was an elaborate harbor; and well it ought to be, since Carthage sought to dominate the western world. We showed our papers, and after they'd been examined for a long, hard time, we were granted passage and glided into the wide canal that led to the harbor proper, going to oars.

I craned my neck.

Carthage.

I'd heard the gossip. Carthage was a walled city, her earliest walls built to withstand a Tiberian invasion centuries ago, added to many times. I hadn't credited the size of those walls. I had to own, I nearly goggled at the sight. They were at least fifty feet tall, and there were entire garrisons built into them. There were stables that housed *elephants*, by the Goddess. Astegal may have taken Carthage's fleet and the bulk of its army overseas, but he'd hardly left her ill defended. I couldn't imagine anyone assailing those walls.

"Big place," Captain Deimos remarked.

"That it is," I agreed. "I'll need to take lodgings in the finest inn Carthage offers, at least until I can arrange for a proper household."

He nodded. "I'll speak to the harbor-master."

What a pleasure it was to have so many of Cythera's resources at my disposal! I leaned on the ship's rail, gazing at the city, which spilled down a steep hill toward the sea. There were temples, an immense bath-house, an amphitheater. No great palace, merely villas that grew finer and finer the farther up the hill they were. Of course, Carthage was an oligarchy, lacking a single ruler; although as I understood it, Astegal's appointment as General gave him a tremendous amount of power.

But Astegal wasn't here.

I wondered which of the villas belonged to the House of Sarkal. I was eager to pay tribute to Astegal's young wife, left to languish while her martial husband went off to conquer Aragonia. And I wondered how *that* venture was going.

Well, there was one way to find out. While Deimos spoke with the harbor-master, I disembarked and strolled the docks, getting used to the feeling of solid ground beneath my feet once more. There was a group of sailors dicing in the shadow of a Carthaginian ship.

"Greetings, lads," I said to them in Hellene. I untied the strings of my purse and fetched out a silver coin. "What's the news out of Aragonia?"

They glanced up at me with suspicion. "A D'Angeline asks?" one said.

I shrugged. "Not exactly. I'm a long-time exile in the service of the Governor of Cythera. We've got no dog in this fight."

"General Astegal routed the Aragonian fleet at New Carthage," the sailor said, putting out his hand. "He's occupied the city."

"Huh." I put the coin in his grimy palm. "Any indication Aragonia means to surrender?"

"Nah." The sailor shook his head. "Army's withdrawn to the north. Looks like a long slog."

"My thanks." I fished out another coin. "What of Terre d'Ange?"

They exchanged grins. "You *have* been gone a long while, my lord," the talkative sailor said. "Don't know, except the whole country's damn well flummoxed and at each other's throats. Meanwhile, Astegal's pretty little royal bride sits here waiting patiently for him to return."

They all laughed. I found myself hating them with unexpected intensity.

"Excellent." I smiled broadly and paid the man his second coin. "Many thanks, my friends."

He pocketed it. "Don't mention it."

By the time I'd strolled back to the ship, Deimos had arranged for my lodgings at an inn the harbor-master had assured him was the most fashionable. He'd hired porters and a palanquin, which I was also given to understand was the most fashionable mode of transport. A very efficient fellow, Captain Deimos.

"Very good," I said to him. "Where will I find you if I've need?"

He jerked his chin at the ship. "We'll bunk on board until you've arranged for proper lodgings and the cargo can be unloaded."

"Of course." I fetched a smaller purse out of the inner pocket of my vest and handed it to him. "Make sure your lads have a chance to entertain themselves."

"We've been paid," Deimos said, but he took it nonetheless. "How long do you reckon we'll be here?"

I glanced up the hill, past the sprawl of townhouses and multistory apartments, toward the costly villas. "As long as it takes. Does it matter?"

"Not really," he said. "Just curious." Deimos lowered his voice. "What exactly is the old ape up to, anyway? He seems deadly serious about it."

Days at sea, and the man picks a crowded harbor to ask. Gods above, people could be stupid. I gave him my blandest smile. "Spreading goodwill, my lord captain, that Cythera may be left in peace, untouched by any trouble. Happiness is the highest form of wisdom."

"So I've heard," Deimos said dryly.

I clapped his shoulder. "I'll send word."

The porters and the palanquin-bearers were waiting. The latter lowered their poles, allowing me to step lightly into the palanquin. As soon as I was seated, they raised the poles and began moving forward at a smooth, steady trot. The porters followed, carrying my trunks, and a sealed trunk I'd found that bore an engraved plate with Sunjata's name. I'd no idea what was in it, but it wasn't listed on the manifest, and I'd thought it best to take it with me. Some business of her ladyship's, no doubt.

We passed a sanctuary dedicated to the goddess Tanit, who I understood presided over Carthage along with Ba'al Hammon, and a vast, open space marked by a multitude of carved stelae. One of the porters freed a hand to touch his brow in a gesture of deference.

"What is that place?" I inquired.

"It is the tophet," he said. "Many children are buried there." After a moment, he added, "Not for a very long time. The gods have been merciful."

What a thought! I couldn't imagine gods cruel enough to

demand such a sacrifice. "Do you have children?" I asked the porter, curious. "Could you offer them if the gods demanded it?"

"I have a son." He jogged along, holding Sunjata's trunk balanced atop his head. "To save my people from famine or conquest? If the gods demanded it, yes."

"I think I'd find a gentler god to worship," I murmured.

The porter shrugged, or made a gesture that would have been a shrug if he hadn't been carrying a heavy trunk on his head. "What use is a gentle god?"

It was an interesting question; oddly, it made me think of the shrine of Blessed Elua in our garden when I was a boy. There had been a field of . . . no, not poppies. I'd no idea what had made me think of poppies. Elua's effigy had stood beneath a trellis laced with climbing sweet-pea vines. My mother used to send me out there to pray and contemplate when I'd done something bad, like poked Darielle with a pin to make her scream. I'd usually fall asleep, basking in the scent of sweet-peas, feeling safe and content beneath Elua's enigmatic smile.

I supposed Blessed Elua was a gentle god.

"I'll think on it," I said to the porter, who merely grunted.

They took me to an inn on the slopes of the hill, which was indeed quite acceptable. The proprietor was an unctuous fellow, dressed in loose robes of good quality, jewels flashing on his fingers.

"Maharbal is here to serve you, young lord," he said with a bow, then paused. "My lord is from Terre d'Ange?"

"By birth, yes." I smiled at him. "But no, my lord is from the Governor of Cythera, and it is there that my loyalties lie." It was true enough in its own way, so long as his purpose accorded with her ladyship's. "Leander Maignard. I come bearing gifts of goodwill for General Astegal's bride." I gestured loosely toward the harbor. "They'll be transported once I've arranged for a proper household, naturally."

"Naturally." Maharbal touched his fingertips together. "I would be pleased to assist your lordship. As it happens, I have a cousin . . ."

"There's always a cousin," I observed.

"Indeed." His smile faded somewhat. "I think you would find her accommodations most suitable for a D'Angeline lord of style." He cocked his head. "How passing odd that you find yourself in the service of Cythera."

"'Tis a long, long story." I spread my hands. "His eminence thought the young princess might take kindly to seeing a fellow countryman. One *without* loyalties to Terre d'Ange." Another broad smile. "Although of course the princess need not know this. It is understood that there is some delicacy to the situation."

"I see," Maharbal said dubiously.

I laughed and patted one of the nearest trunks. "Don't worry, good Maharbal. My papers were inspected in the harbor. I have letters of introduction from Ptolemy Solon to a dozen of Carthage's luminaries. You or your cousin won't find yourself harboring a D'Angeline spy, if that's what you fear."

"Of course not!" he protested. "Come, come, let me show you to your chambers." He snapped his fingers for a servant. "Have his lordship's things brought."

Well, of course he feared I was a spy. I'd watched the suspicion emerge when I'd blunted the edge of his greed with the comment about his cousin. It was bound to emerge sooner or later, so best to get it out of the way. And people were predictable. Confronted with the very suspicion in the forefront of their thoughts, they'll deny it almost every time, even though it's written on their faces.

And the ironic thing was that I hadn't exactly lied. I *was* in Ptolemy Solon's service for this mission. But even among those members of the Unseen Guild in Carthage who knew of her ladyship's existence, I doubted anyone would suspect that the Wise Ape of Cythera was sufficiently besotted to risk such a dangerous venture as I was undertaking; and moreover, that her ladyship would implore him to risk it on behalf of the son who'd recently sought to have her slain.

I couldn't fathom it myself.

A gentle god, indeed. Mayhap not.

I followed Maharbal to a pleasant suite of rooms, complete with a pert little serving maid to attend me. She eyed me with interest, not particularly caring if I was a spy. I winked at her and wondered how close-knit the web of intrigue that bound Carthage's servants and slaves was. To wit, if I bedded the chambermaid in Carthage's most fashionable inn, would this bit of gossip find its way to the princess' household staff? And did they gossip with their young D'Angeline mistress?

Mayhap, mayhap not.

Best to be circumspect. As her ladyship had said, *just be safe.*

It was growing late in the day. I had the chambermaid show me to the inn's modest bath, declining with regret her offer of assistance. The evening air held just a touch of coolness. I luxuriated in the warm waters, washing the salt grime from the long sea voyage off my skin, unbraiding and washing my hair, letting it float on the surface of the water. When I climbed out of the pool, clad in naught but my ruby eardrops, there were a handful of peeping gazes. I stood beside the pool, shaking water out of my hair.

"See anything you like, ladies?" I called.

Most of them giggled and scattered. My chambermaid came forward, blushing, to proffer a linen robe.

"If my lordship wishes . . ." she whispered.

"He does." I lifted her chin with two fingers. "But I have

duties to attend to, my peach, and I am weary from my journey." I kissed her lips, feeling them part beneath mine. "Another day, mayhap."

The chambermaid trembled a little. "Do you promise?"

I smiled into her eyes and lied. "Of course I do."

Later, the words haunted me. Unfulfilled desire made me restless. I tossed and turned on my sheets, which were not so fine as those in her ladyship's household. I should have bedded the chambermaid. After all, who would find that odd? Like as not, it was odder that I'd refused. After all, I wasn't meant to be coming to Carthage with the intent of seducing the Dauphine. Not so far as the world knew, not so far as she knew. There was no reason I shouldn't bed a willing girl. It might even have had *more* impact if the princess knew, later, that I'd eschewed all others, ostensibly in love with her. On the other hand, if I established myself as a rake, whatever dragons Astegal had left guarding his household would hardly be inclined to allow me access to his wife.

Gods, this was more complicated than I'd reckoned.

Why did the lie trouble me?

Because, I decided, it wasn't worthy of her ladyship. Despite all the vitriol leveled at her, she lied very seldom, and only to a purpose. And she never made false promises. She maintained her own unfathomable standards of integrity. And although she did not demand that of her people, it irritated me that I'd fallen short of it for so little reason.

I resolved to do better. I would give the chambermaid some little trinket and an apology; like as not, that would suffice to thrill the lass. And as far as slaking my desire went, I'd err on the side of discretion.

After all, that wouldn't be a problem. I hadn't seen Sunjata for a couple of years, but I couldn't imagine that much had changed between us. And for a surety, one couldn't ask for a more discreet lover than Sunjata.

Twenty-six

In the morning, Maharbal escorted me to his cousin's villa. It seemed the lady's husband was a minor Carthaginian lord and a captain in the service of General Astegal's army. While he was away, she had retired to their country estate, and Maharbal saw no reason why the villa should remain empty when there was a tidy profit to be turned.

I liked it. It was a bit small, but then I was accustomed to her ladyship's vast and labyrinthine estate. The mosaic floors were of good quality and the frescoes on the walls were tasteful. The gardens were pleasant.

It wasn't in the most elite neighborhood, but it was clearly a neighborhood of quality. The surrounding villas spoke of well-to-do families, ambitious without being grasping. Nothing ostentatious, but nothing overly modest. If I wanted to be careful and discreet, this struck just the right tone.

As an added advantage, the lady in question had left a handful of her household behind to tend to the maintenance and security of the villa. All I'd need to hire were bearers for a palanquin.

"My cousin's servants would be at your service, naturally," Maharbal said, pointing out this fact.

I pursed my lips. "I prefer to oversee the hiring of my own household."

He sniffed. "I assure you, they are more than competent."

I glanced around. "It's rather small."

"You are but one man," Maharbal observed. "It is space sufficient for a small family."

"Ah, but I may wish to entertain while I'm here," I said. "One could not hope to dine with more than a dozen folk."

Maharbal shrugged. "I suspect you'll find that many of his eminence's acquaintances are not in residence during wartime."

We played the game for a while longer; then I relented and expressed grudging interest. Maharbal made an outrageous offer, which I countered. After copious haggling, we came to an accommodation.

"Very good," he said. "If you wish, I would be pleased to accompany you to the slave-market to purchase bearers. I can tell you which merchants are reputable, and which beat or starve their wares."

An edge had crept into his voice. I sensed Maharbal was testing me, waiting to see if I would protest out of delicate D'Angeline sensibilities. "Excellent!" I gave him a bright smile. "Let's go at once."

Maharbal bowed. "Of course."

We proceeded to the slave-market in the inn's double palanquin. In my opinion, it was a singularly stupid and inefficient manner of travel. I'd sooner ride astride or in a carriage, or even go on foot, which would be just as swift and considerably less jarring. But it was clear, travelling the streets of Carthage, that no one of quality walked. The only folk I saw on horseback appeared to be couriers, and many of the streets were too narrow to admit a carriage.

So, palanquins.

The slave-market was in a forum lined with voluminous silk tents. Maharbal gave his bearers leave to rest in the shade at one end of the forum, while we strolled and perused the wares.

"Will you be wanting a girl?" he asked. Without waiting for an answer, he pointed at a tawny lovely with a defiant gaze. "Amazigh. They're desert folk. Stay away from them. The women are as like to stab you as kiss you."

"No girl." I shook my head.

"Ah." Maharbal raised his brows. "A boy?"

"No," I said firmly. "My friend, it's been over ten years since I've set foot on Terre d'Ange, but there is one part of my heritage I retain. I'll not take anyone, man or woman, as an unwilling bed partner."

"A man of scruples," he said with amusement. "I see."

"Oh, one or two," I replied easily.

Maharbal laughed. "Somehow, I suspect that getting willing bed partners is no obstacle for you, my lord. Come, let's have a look at the brute muscle. Strytanus keeps a healthy stable."

We strolled over to a blue tent where the slave-merchant Strytanus did indeed keep a healthy stable.

I'd been to slave-markets before, but only in her ladyship's company, and only knowing that any slave purchased on Cythera would serve no more than seven years' time, which really wasn't much worse than the custom of indentured service in Terre d'Ange. And, of course, any slaves purchased by her ladyship were given their freedom and the opportunity to enter her service, which served the dual purpose of assuaging her ladyship's deep-seated remorse for her son's suffering, as well as building her loyal network.

This was different.

Carthage had no such laws. Most of the slaves sold here would live and die as slaves, unless by some chance they were clever or useful enough to rise very, very high in their master's estimation. And anyone being sold for brute muscle was unlikely to stand such a chance.

"Where are you from?" I asked an older hulking fellow with a squashed nose.

"Hellas," he said briefly. "I was a wrestler."

"What happened?" I asked.

He eyed me warily. "Lost too many matches and fell into penury. Why do you care?"

"Hey!" The slaver Strytanus struck him across the broad shoulders with a narrow rod. "Mind your tongue."

The wrestler didn't flinch, but his gaze slid away from mine.

I talked to a few others, a process the slaves, slave-merchant, and Maharbal found quite bizarre. In the end, I settled on the wrestler, a pair of lean, hungry-looking Carthaginian brothers who'd known a lifetime of deprivation, and a fierce Amazigh with a branded cheek who refused to talk.

"You're mad," Maharbal said affably. "The Hellene's too old, the Carthaginians are malnourished—through no fault of Strytanus', I'll hasten to add—and the Amazigh's like to slide a dagger between your ribs."

I smiled at him. "We'll see."

Strytanus had grown distracted by a new customer, a Carthaginian lady seeking a pretty boy to decorate her household. She was contemplating a slender lad of some ten or eleven years, with curly black hair and fear-stricken eyes.

"Is he biddable?" she fretted.

The slave-merchant spread his hands. "My lady, I make no claims. He is Aragonian, one of the first fruits of the spoils of war. You asked for *pretty* and he is that. If he is wise, he will be grateful for your gentle mercy."

"Yes, yes." The woman waved one hand. "Does he at least speak Hellene?"

"I fear he does not," Strytanus said in an apologetic tone.

She tilted her head, considering the boy. He stared back at her, wide brown eyes filled with terror and incomprehension. For some reason, the sight made me feel sick inside.

"I think not," the Carthaginian woman said decisively. She gestured to her attendants. "Next!"

The boy gazed after her as she swept away toward the next tent full of human merchandise, unsure what had transpired. Knowing only that he was alone in the world, friendless and bereft.

"Forgive me." Strytanus approached, bowing. "You have made your choice, my lord?"

"Indeed." I wrenched my gaze from the Aragonian boy.

Strytanus noticed. "Is my lord . . . interested?"

"Alas, no." I forced a smile. "Shall we talk?"

We haggled over the bearers I'd chosen. In the end, I daresay I got a fair price, since I'd chosen men the slaver was eager to dispose of. Not so good a price as I might have gotten. I was distracted by the boy.

"Very good," Strytanus said smoothly when our deal was concluded. "I shall have them delivered to your household in a matter of hours."

I inclined my head. "My thanks."

Our business finished, Maharbal and I departed. I felt the Aragonian boy's eyes burning holes in my back, starved for some word or gesture of kindness. I wished I could have spared him. But I'd already told Maharbal I wasn't in the market for aught but bearers. And as the slave-trader had said, he was but the first of many. The spoils of war. There would be others.

Many others.

I could best help them by completing my mission. By undoing Carthage's magics—those that bound the princess, and those that bound Terre d'Ange itself. For the first time, it began to feel like a noble cause. It was a novel sensation, and one I quite enjoyed contemplating.

We ventured to the inner harbor and located Captain Deimos aboard the Cytheran flagship. I made arrangements to have Ptolemy Solon's tribute-gifts delivered to the villa I had rented. And then, back to the inn, where Maharbal made arrangements to have my things delivered and his bearers to escort me. He bade me farewell, covering my hands with his own. "If I may be of further service . . ."

"Of course." I pressed his hands warmly. "You have been most helpful."

He bowed. "We seek to please."

I gathered my things, making them ready for the porters. I spied the chambermaid I'd rejected lurking around a corner. I gave her a cheap gilt ring set with a flawed garnet.

"A token," I said somberly. "For your beauty. An apology for the lack of what might have been."

The chambermaid beamed at me. "My lord is too kind!"

I smiled at her. "I try."

It was a relief to get free of the place. Gods above! It took so little time for folk to attempt to set hooks in one. I rode in Maharbal's palanquin to his cousin's villa, then dismissed his bearers with a word of thanks and a few copper coins.

The servants at my new villa were bustling about, dusting, waxing, and scouring with an alacrity that I daresay they'd not shown since their mistress departed. I wandered the rooms and the grounds, familiarizing myself with the place. The chamberlain, a sober fellow named Anysus, assured me that he would be pleased to procure anything I required. After the cloying manner of Maharbal, I was pleased by his demeanor.

Everything arrived in good order. My possessions, sent from the inn. The tribute-gifts, under the watchful eye of Captain Deimos and his men. Deimos gave me the name of the dockside inn where they would take lodging, and I assured him I'd send word if I had need.

My bearers arrived, looking sullen and suspicious. The steward Anysus took charge of them and led them to the servants' quarters. I'd told him I wanted them washed and fed on arrival. I waited until they were eating, then went to have a word with them, closing the door of the small room in which the household servants dined. The aroma of lamb stew filled the space.

"Listen, lads," I said to them. The Carthaginian brothers put down their spoons with pained looks. I laughed. "Go ahead, keep eating."

They hunched over their bowls, shoveling down food. The Hellene wrestler waited, regarding me with equanimity. The Amazigh continued eating, slow and measured, his gaze hooded.

"I'm a stranger here," I said. "And this place, these servants . . ." I waved my hand. "Rented. I'd like to know I've a few loyal men at my side. Give me that, and I'll pledge you your freedom when I'm done here."

"Where would we go?" one of the brothers asked in bewilderment.

I shrugged. "Wherever you like. You can stay here, or you can return to Cythera with me. You'd be given a position there."

"What's your business?" the Hellene asked cynically. "A danger to us, I'll wager."

I'd chosen him for the shrewdness in his gaze. The brothers were desperate, which would serve well enough. The Amazigh . . . I don't know. A bit of a whim, a hunch. Mayhap a desire to irk Maharbal.

"Not if you keep your mouth shut," I said candidly. "I'm here to pay tribute to General Astegal's new bride and meet with members of the Council of Thirty. All his eminence the governor asks is that I return with assurances that his position is secure should Carthage turn its gaze toward the east. Assurances best kept quiet, given that the governor serves at Khebbel-im-Akkad's pleasure."

"Ah." His eyes glinted. "Politics."

"Indeed," I agreed.

"You want to buy our loyalty."

"I do."

A wide smile spread over his ugly face. "Good enough. It's yours, my lord."

"Will there be food like this every day?" a Carthaginian brother asked plaintively.

I propped my elbows on my knees. "Every day."

It was good enough for them. The wrestler pointed at the Amazigh. "What about him?"

I looked thoughtfully at the desert tribesman. He returned my gaze without blinking, eating steadily and managing at the same time to look as though he would indeed be pleased to knife me. "Do you speak Punic?" I asked the brothers, who nodded. "Ask him if he does."

The older complied. The Amazigh gave a curt affirmative reply.

"Ah." I smiled. "Tell him of my offer."

There was a long exchange. At the end of it, the Amazigh's eyes glittered with fierce tears. He leapt up from the table and poured out a long utterance in Punic. The wrestler rose and positioned himself to defend me—by the Goddess, I'd made a good choice there!—but the Amazigh ignored him and knelt. To my astonishment, he took both my hands and kissed them.

"Um." The older of the Carthaginians blinked. "He says if you promise to give him his freedom, he pledges loyalty with every drop of blood in his body."

I looked into the man's glittering eyes. "In Blessed Elua's name, I swear it."

The Carthaginian repeated my words. The Amazigh let go my hands and bowed his head, touching his brow to the ground.

"Excellent." I stood. "Do you know your way around the city?" All of them shook their heads. I pointed at the wrestler. "What's your name?"

"Kratos."

"How long do you think it would take you to learn Carthage's streets, Kratos?" I asked him.

"A day." He shrugged. "Perhaps two."

"Start when you've finished eating," I said. "Come back when you're done." I thought for a moment. "Take him," I added, nodding at the Amazigh.

"He might flee," Kratos observed. "*I* might flee."

I smiled. "You won't."

Twenty-seven

I spent the balance of my first whole day in Carthage sorting through letters requesting audiences from various personages, placing them with the letters of introduction that Solon had given me. I'd used my time aboard the ship wisely.

One letter I hadn't written, and that was to the princess. I wasn't sure why. On the ship, it had seemed to me that there was some perfect choice of words that was evading me, and I'd resolved to put off the task until I was on solid ground, hoping I'd be able to think more clearly.

Now it seemed a foolish notion. I was Ptolemy Solon's emissary. Her highness would see me or refuse me on that basis alone. Still, the feeling persisted. I pushed it firmly away, uncorked my inkwell, and wrote out a courteous and polite request for an audience with her.

Kratos and the Amazigh—whose name I later learned was Ghanim—returned ere nightfall. I was pleased to have my conviction confirmed. Carthage had strict laws for dealing with runaway slaves. The brand on Ghanim's face suggested he'd already made one such attempt, and I'd determined that he'd put enough stock in my promise not to risk another. Kratos, I thought, had too much sense.

Still, 'twas always a pleasure to be right. If I'd been mistaken, I'd have been out naught but the cost of a pair of slaves. With this gamble, I'd won another measure of their loyalty, purchased with simple trust.

I had a brief word with the steward Anysus regarding the delivery of my letters on the morrow, a task he readily agreed to oversee. I gave orders that my new slaves were to be fed heartily three times a day and provided Anysus with funds to cover all additional expenses that this expansion of the household would entail.

Once that was done, I felt my plans were settling nicely into place. I dined alone and found that the villa's cook was perfectly adequate. And then I retired to my private chambers and rummaged through Solon's tribute-gifts until I found a ring that fit me nicely, a heavy band of gold set with a sapphire. Using the tip of my little belt knife, I was able to prize the gem from its setting.

Perfect.

With the last of my preparations complete, I took to my bed and slept.

On the morrow, I rose feeling refreshed and full of anticipation. Anysus had already departed, bearing my letters. Kratos had accompanied him of his own initiative to enhance his knowledge of the city. I admired the gesture, although it set my plans back a few hours. So be it. I needed to practice patience. This was not a task that could be rushed.

At length they returned. Anysus reported that a mere six of the lords were in residence, but that he thought they would be very pleased to receive Ptolemy Solon's emissary in the next few days.

"Excellent," I said. "What of her highness?"

He made an ambiguous gesture. "That I cannot say, my lord."

"Ah, well." I raised my brows. "Is General Astegal so protective of his new bride that he forbids her visitors in his absence?"

"Not exactly." Anysus hesitated. "Let us say that his kinsman Bodeshmun serves as the gatekeeper. He is . . . selective."

I shrugged. "We'll see. Tell me, since I find myself idle in the meanwhile, might you recommend a reputable gem-merchant?" I showed him the gold ring with its empty setting. "The stone was lost at sea, and I would feign replace it. The ring was a gift from a lady who would be angry to see I'd been so careless."

"Of course." He recommended several, including Jabnit of the House of Philosir, which was what I'd been hoping to hear.

"Very good." I smiled at him and pressed a gold coin into his hand. "You've been extraordinarily efficient and helpful, Anysus. I can see why the lord and lady of the house place such trust in you."

A slight flush of pleasure touched his cheeks. "Thank you, my lord."

I made my first outing with my new bearers that morning. They did a tolerable job. Kratos might have been past his prime, but he was still as strong as an ox. The Carthaginians panted a bit, but they were determined and eager to prove themselves, and they'd gain strength on a good diet. Ghanim was as steady as a rock.

Kratos led us to the jewelers' district, and we located Jabnit's establishment without any difficulty. A little bell attached to the door gave a merry tinkle as I entered. A young woman emerged from the rear of the building, her eyes widening at the sight of me.

"Good day," I said pleasantly. "I've come to see about replacing a lost gem-stone."

"Of course!" Her hands fluttered. "Please, my lord, sit. I will fetch the owner."

There were fine carpets on the floor, strewn with cushions and set with a low table. I sat cross-legged on a cushion, waiting, until the plump gem-merchant came waddling hastily to attend me. He gave me a startled look, as though he'd not believed the girl when she'd said a D'Angeline lord had strolled into his parlor.

"Welcome, welcome!" he exclaimed, bowing. "I am Jabnit of Philosir. How may I serve you, my lord?"

"Leander Maignard of Cythera." I inclined my head. "Emissary of his eminence, Governor Ptolemy Solon." I slid the ring from my finger. "This stone was lost, good Jabnit. I seek a replacement."

"I see." With difficulty, Jabnit lowered himself to a cushion. "Sophonisba!" he called sharply. "Bring tea. And pastries, a tray of pastries." He examined the ring while the girl complied, setting fragrant cups of sweet tea and a tray of honeyed pastries on the table. "What manner of stone?"

I sipped my tea. "A sapphire. Deep, deep blue to match the eyes of the lady who gave it to me. She will be most wroth to find it missing."

"Ah!" Jabnit beamed. "A love-token. Fear not, we shall find its very likeness." He clapped his hands. "Sophonisba! Tell Sunjata to bring a selection of sapphires."

"My thanks, good Jabnit," I said.

The gem-merchant popped a pastry into his mouth. "Not at all."

Out of the corner of my eye, I saw Sunjata enter. I saw him pause briefly, a slight hesitation only a Guildsman would have caught. Our eyes met. His full lips moved in the faintest twitch. I wondered if he'd suspected it was me when the girl announced my arrival. He bowed silently, then lowered a silk cushion strewn with several sapphires to the table.

"Sit, sit!" Jabnit waved hand at him. "For goodness' sake, you know the wares better than I do, Sunjata."

"As you wish, my lord." Sunjata sank to the cushions with fluid grace, legs crossed.

Jabnit reached for another pastry. "Go on, tell him."

Calm and professional, Sunjata described the various gems to me, one by one, pointing out their flaws and merits. By the Goddess, he really *had* become proficient; but then, he'd always learned quickly. I watched his dark, slender fingers dance over the cushion, picking up this stone and that one.

"This would fit the setting well," he murmured in his clear voice. "Little alteration would be required. Does it match your lady's eyes?"

I smiled at him. "I nearly think it does."

"I could have it ready for you on the morrow," Sunjata said.

"Might it be possible to have it delivered?" I inquired.

Sunjata smiled back at me. "I would be honored to deliver it myself. Where are you lodging?"

I told him, then watched him depart after promising to deliver it in the morning.

"Such a gifted young man!" Jabnit said cheerfully. "He can be a merciless scold, but he was on good behavior today." He nudged me with one elbow. "Very popular with the patrons, too."

"I'm sure he is." I returned my thoughts to the matter at hand. "So! How much will this lighten my purse, good Jabnit?"

He named a figure, and I haggled long enough to make a good show of it. I stayed for another cup of tea, consenting to alleviate Jabnit's curiosity about my presence in Carthage as an emissary of Ptolemy Solon's, then left feeling well pleased with myself.

"Home, my lord?" Kratos asked, rising.

"Home," I agreed, climbing into the palanquin.

I returned to find a reply awaiting me from one of the Carthaginian lords, an old scholar named Hamilcar, inviting me to call on him at my leisure. He wasn't one of the Council of Thirty, but he'd known Solon when they were boys, and he sounded eager to speak with me. And one entry into Carthaginian society, accepting me as Ptolemy Solon's legitimate envoy, would ease the way for others.

They would come.

Bodeshmun . . . Bodeshmun might be the toughest nut to crack, guarding access to the princess. But I'd a feeling curiosity would wear him down. Like my lord Solon, he was a man who valued knowledge above all else. In the end, I thought, it would get the better of him. Then all I had to do was convince him I was harmless, and exactly what I seemed. And on the morrow, I'd have the benefit of Sunjata's advice on how to do that very thing.

All in all, it had been a good day.

On the morrow, I idled in my private chambers until Anysus came to announce Sunjata's arrival.

"Excellent," I said. "Pray, send him in. I've a mind to speak with him regarding another commission."

The steward bowed. "As you wish."

He left and returned shortly with Sunjata in tow. This time, Sunjata's handsome face was perfectly composed. Not until the door was firmly closed behind him and we heard the steps of Anysus departing did he smile.

"Well, well," Sunjata murmured. "Leander Maignard."

I grinned. "Pleased to see me?"

Sunjata came forward and put his arms around my neck, kissing me. His lips were as soft as a woman's, but firmer.

"Yes," he said. "And curious as hell." He tilted his head, regarding me beneath long lashes. "What in the name of all the gods is her ladyship up to?"

"Destroying Carthage," I said softly.

His brown eyes widened, lit by a sudden spark of hope and bitter ferocity. "Do you jest?"

I shook my head. "Not today."

"Tell me." Sunjata's body tensed. "Tell me everything."

I led him into the farthest reaches of my chambers, where there was no risk of being overheard. He sat cross-legged on my bed opposite me and listened without a word while I told him all of it. How Prince Imriel had survived his madness and come to Cythera to beg his mother's aid. How her ladyship had persuaded Solon to give it. The details of the intricate web of spells binding Terre d'Ange and its young princess, and how they might be dismantled.

Some of it, of course, Sunjata knew—he'd been the one to alert her ladyship to Carthage's plans. But he hadn't known the inner workings of the horologists' magics nor the extent of what they had planned, only bits and pieces of their preparations, gleaned through his supposed apprenticeship. It was Solon who'd guessed at what Carthage intended and sent the charmed needle he'd used on Prince Imriel, and Solon who had now determined how the spell might be undone.

"Do you truly mean to attempt this?" he asked me.

"Of course," I said in surprise. "Why ever not?"

"It's dangerous." His eyes were shadowed.

I took his hand. "So is what you do."

"I'm merely a spy." Sunjata's full mouth twisted. "Eyes and ears. Does her ladyship ask more of me?"

"Only your counsel," I said. "Well, or so I think. She sent a trunk for you." I rose and fetched it. "Here."

I watched him open it, picking the lock with an easy skill I envied. There was a letter on the top. Sunjata unsealed it and read what was written there. It took him some time, and I guessed it was written in coded language. He sat motionless, only his lips moving silently. Once, a little tremor ran through him. When he had finished, he bowed his head slightly, then straightened. He put the letter back in the trunk and closed it without meeting my eyes.

"Bad news?" I asked.

"No." His gaze shifted to my face, his expression as guarded as I'd ever seen it. "But it's naught I can tell you, Leander."

"All right," I said gently. "What *can* you tell me? I've learned that Bodeshmun guards access to the princess. How might I convince him I'm harmless?"

Sunjata's expression eased somewhat. "Flatter him," he said. "Let him believe Ptolemy Solon is amazed at his achievement and wants a report on the effects. Bodeshmun's as clever as the devil, but there's a spark of vanity there."

"Good." I nodded. "How about the princess herself? Does he keep her under lock and key?"

"Not exactly." He tapped his lower lip in thought. "He's . . . careful. She's no prisoner, but she's insulated and fed lies. I don't believe she's any idea what's happening in Terre d'Ange. You'll have to convince Bodeshmun you've not the slightest intent of telling her."

"I will," I said. "What *is* happening in Terre d'Ange?"

"Nothing good," Sunjata said soberly. "The last I heard, the Queen's accused her kinsman of fomenting rebellion."

"The Duc L'Envers?" I asked, searching my memory. He nodded. "Are they at war with one another?"

"Not yet," Sunjata said.

"The prince was to send L'Envers a letter with Solon's advice," I said. "If the Queen can be convinced to send Terre d'Ange's army to Aragonia, it will remove them from play."

"Perhaps." He sounded doubtful. "I fear the advice may

come too late. She's not likely to commit her forces overseas if she fears a coup at home."

I shivered a little. "What a fearful thing it would be to have one's wits stolen."

"Yes." Sunjata gazed at me. "Fearful." He gave himself a shake. "Ah. Your ring." He reached in his purse and brought it out. "That was a clever piece of subterfuge."

"Thank you." I took it from him. "I'm not bad at this, am I?"

"No," he said wistfully. "Not at all."

A silence fell between us.

"So." I cocked my head. "Jabnit implied that you were wont to tryst with patrons. Is it for business or pleasure?"

Sunjata's mouth twisted in another cynical smile. "What do you think? It's always business, Leander. Her ladyship's business . . . sometimes even the House of Philosir's business. Happy patrons are generous customers." He laughed harshly. "No one thinks of a eunuch's pleasure."

I touched the smooth curve of his cheek. "I do."

"Yes." Unexpected tears brightened his eyes. "You always did."

"Only did?" I leaned forward to kiss him lightly. "Must it be *did*?"

I didn't press him; one didn't press Sunjata. He was proud and he'd been used badly before her ladyship found him. I didn't know what manner of lovers he had endured here in Carthage. But we had known each other well, once. And if I couldn't give him back what had been taken from him, I'd been able to show him the beauty in what remained. He'd always said no one else had done that for him. So I waited.

"No," he said at last. "All right."

"If you don't—"

Sunjata reached for me, kissing me with fierce passion, his tongue sliding past my lips. We tumbled on the bed together, half wrestling, tugging at one another's clothing. I wanted to go at a leisurely pace, but he was unwontedly hurried and urgent at first.

"Slow down," I teased, easing his shirt over his head. I kissed his sleek dark-brown chest, slender and hairless as a boy's. "You're the one who told me men always rush too fast."

"I can't," he whispered.

He did, though. When we were both naked, Sunjata grew quiet and still, gazing at me in the sunlight spilling into the bedchamber. His fingers stroked my hair, undoing my braids until my hair fell loose and waving over my shoulders.

"Take out your eardrops," he murmured.

I laughed. "Now?"

He nodded. "I want to see you mother-naked."

Giving him a quizzical look, I complied.

Sunjata gazed at me for a long, long time, lips parted as though to drink in the sight of me. I let him, wondering what in the name of the gods was going through his mind. But then, I often did. "You can put them back," he said at last. "It was a mistake."

I did. "Better?"

He didn't answer, only closed his eyes and reached for me again.

Twenty-Eight

In the days that followed, I spent a pleasant afternoon drinking palm wine and listening to the old scholar Hamilcar reminisce about his youth and the intellectual shooting star that had been Ptolemy Solon when he had tarried in Carthage and studied in her academies. I received more invitations in response and attended a dinner party hosted by Gemelquart, a prince of the House of Zinnrid and a member of the Council of Thirty.

He was a shrewd, well-informed fellow who wasn't taking part in Astegal's campaign due to a childhood illness that had left him with weak lungs. According to Sunjata, he was a Guildsman, though I liked to think I would have discovered it quickly for myself. There is a certain tenor one learns to listen for when someone asks a question to which the answer is already known.

"So tell me," Gemelquart said with deceptive ease. "How *does* a D'Angeline come to be in the bidding of the Wise Ape of Cythera?"

"Oh, 'tis a long tale of treason and exile, hardly fit for

dinner conversation." I glanced at a nearby lamp and offered one of the Guild's coded phrases. "That burns with a passing clear flame, my lord. Is the oil pressed locally?"

His eyelids flickered. "Yes, indeed."

I smiled at him. "I thought so."

Gemelquart chuckled, then coughed. "I see. And what does Cythera hope to accomplish by your presence here?"

"I merely bring assurances of Cythera's goodwill." I spread my hands. "Inadvertent or no, Carthage's actions have served to resolve a certain . . . dilemma. For that, we are grateful. If I may be indiscreet, let me say that whatever the future may bring, we hope this goodwill is reciprocated."

"Of course." Gemelquart steepled his fingers. "The Governor of Cythera enjoys a happy situation."

"He does," I agreed. "And he would be loath to see it change."

"Doubtless." The Carthaginian lord looked amused. "Well, you may surely tell Ptolemy Solon that Carthage has no designs on his happiness. Perhaps someday in the future he may return our inadvertent favor, given his intimate knowledge of the workings of Khebbel-im-Akkad."

I hoisted my winecup to him. "Doubtless he would be pleased to do so, were his happiness assured."

Gemelquart gave a wheezing laugh. "Yes, yes!" He lowered his voice. "Tell me, is *she* as beautiful as the rumors claim?"

"Yes," I said simply, picturing her ladyship. "She is."

"Ah." He sighed. "I'd hoped so."

It was an exhilarating feeling, like walking balanced atop a very high ledge. I'd seldom felt more alive than I did intriguing in Carthage. And the feeling only intensified when I got my first look at Sidonie de la Courcel.

The idea was Sunjata's. I'd not yet received a reply from her or Bodeshmun or any representative of the House of

Sarkal. But through his own sources, Sunjata learned that the princess was dining at the house of a certain Carthaginian lady on a particular evening. He came to the villa to inform me.

"There's a fashion among some of the young men left in Carthage to pay tribute to her," Sunjata told me, lying propped on one elbow. "Loitering in the streets outside the Sarkal villa to catch a glimpse of her."

"That's unexpectedly charming," I observed.

He shrugged a shoulder. "Don't put too much stock into it. It's some scheme Astegal dreamed up to reinforce the notion that this is a love-match that has all of Carthage charmed. He wants her kept happy and ignorant."

"Thoughtful fellow," I said. "He didn't manage to get her with child before he left, did he?"

"Apparently not." Sunjata smiled wryly. "Though not for lack of trying, I understand. You *do* realize that she thinks herself in love with him, Leander? She's not about to fall into your embrace, lovely creature though you may be."

"Oh, I know." I folded my arms behind my head. "But she's *not* in love with him. That truth is in there somewhere. And I'm hoping that I bear just enough resemblance to her beloved Imriel to unlock it. We're kin, you know, albeit distantly."

"Yes." Sunjata gazed at me. "I scarce had a chance to speak with him in Terre d'Ange. You spent time with him. What's he like?"

"Prince Imriel?" I thought about it. "Intense. But I suppose he was rather desperate when I met him."

"Do you think he actually loves her?" he asked.

"I don't know," I said slowly. "Gods above, it would be unlikely as all hell. But if he doesn't, he's as skilled a player as her ladyship, which is entirely possible." I freed one arm and reached out to run my fingers through the soft cloud of Sunjata's hair. "Anyway, it doesn't matter, does it? What matters is whether or not *she* loves him, and given that she defied her royal mother and half the nation, I'd say she does. Or at least thinks she does," I added. "It may be nothing more than a girlish infatuation."

"No." Sunjata rolled onto his belly, propping his chin on cupped hands. "I don't think it is. And I think he does love her."

I smiled at him. "I didn't know you had such a romantic streak."

"There's a lot you don't know," he replied. "So, do you want to have a look at the lady in question?"

"Why not?" I said. "It can't hurt."

At the appropriate hour, I summoned my bearers. We went to the flower market, I in my palanquin and Sunjata walking alongside it. There, I bought a great armload of roses and a basket. I put Kratos and the lads to work plucking the roses and filling the basket with petals while Sunjata and I visited a wineshop. Kratos thought I was mad—and I daresay the others did, too—but he did it willingly enough.

The sun was low in the sky when we made our way up the hill to Astegal's villa, drenching Carthage in golden light. The villa was easily three times the size of mine, although most of it was hidden behind high walls. There was an imposing gate with a marble arch above it set with a seal depicting the House of Sarkal's insignia, a stylized hawk. A handful of young men were gathered there. They gave us curious looks, but asked no questions as we took places among them.

I tucked the basket of petals beneath my arm. "Let them see how a D'Angeline pays tribute to a woman," I said to Sunjata.

We didn't have long to wait. The gilded light was just beginning to deepen to amber when the princess' palanquin appeared. It was an ornate affair, large and heavy with gold leaf, the sides worked with the same hawk insignia. The bearers were all of a height, strapping fellows in scarlet tunics. Four additional men flanked the palanquin. They were an odd sight, clad in flowing indigo robes, their heads and faces wrapped in burnooses, swords hanging from their belts.

"Amazigh," Sunjata murmured. "Very fierce, and when they give their loyalty, they mean it."

"So I noticed," I said. "These are loyal to Astegal?"

"Very."

The young Carthaginian admirers began to cheer as the palanquin came through the gates. I caught my first glimpse of its inhabitant. Her profile held a young, delicate beauty. Honey-gold hair coiled atop her head, a few curling locks hanging loose.

"She's fair," I mused. "Fairer than I expected. One wouldn't suspect she was half-Cruithne."

"Gods, D'Angelines can be insufferable," Sunjata muttered.

"Jealous, my dusky plum?" I shot him a quick smile. "I spoke of her coloring. My father took me to see the Cruarch's entourage pass once when I was a boy. They're not as dark as you, but believe me, there wasn't a fair-haired head among the Cruithne."

"Perhaps there's been a cuckoo in the Queen's nest," he said.

"Perhaps," I agreed.

At that moment, the palanquin paused to allow the princess to acknowledge the cheers. She turned her head, smiling graciously at her admirers.

"Or perhaps not," Sunjata commented.

Her eyes were black. For no earthly reason I could conceive, that fact hit me like a punch to the gut. Her gaze shifted, meeting mine as though I'd called her name. Her smile turned puzzled. If I'd felt before as though I walked atop a high ledge, now it seemed to me that the drop below had suddenly become infinitely deeper.

I stepped forward and bowed, then reached into the basket and grasped a handful of rose petals, tossing them high into the air. Petals rained down between us. We gazed at one another through the shower.

"Ho!" One of the Amazigh came over and grabbed my basket. He rummaged briefly in it, searching for a hidden dagger or somewhat. I stood stock-still, staring at the princess. She returned my gaze, frowning with bemusement. And then the Amazigh thrust the basket back at me and gave an order, and the palanquin moved on.

I stared after it, long after the other seeming admirers had drifted away.

"Well." Sunjata's light voice interrupted my reverie. "If you sought to give the impression of a man besotted at first sight, I'd say you did a fair job of it."

I shook myself. "Do you think so?"

"I do." There was an inexplicable edge of sorrow to his tone. "And I'll venture to say her young highness took notice of it."

"So it seemed." I cleared my throat. "Well. We'll see what this brings. Will you come back to the villa with me?"

Sunjata shook his head. "I think not. I'm meeting early on the morrow with Hannon, my purported master in the Guild." He smiled crookedly. "I'm to report on *you*, as a matter of fact. The pompous dolt thinks I've been very clever to get myself into a position to spy on you."

"Oh, excellent," I said absently. "I revealed myself as a Guildsman to Gemelquart of Zinnrid the other night. He thinks I'm here to assure the Council that Ptolemy Solon merely wishes to be left in peace with her ladyship and will happily cooperate with Carthage to that end."

"Good." Sunjata nodded. "I'll confirm it. The gods know, it's a good deal more believable than the truth."

"True." I felt strange and thoughtful, unaccountably stirred by my first sight of the woman I meant to seduce. Excitement and anticipation, I reckoned; but there was an odd tinge of melancholy, too. Like as not, I was overtired from all my intrigues. "Could you have ever imagined the old ape would take such a risk for love?"

"You wouldn't?" Sunjata asked.

I shuddered. "Gods, no!"

He reached out and touched my cheek. "Don't be so sure," Sunjata murmured. "I suspect we're all capable of things we couldn't have imagined."

I caught his hand and kissed his fingers, ignoring a sidelong glance from a passing palanquin. After our first tryst, it had occurred to me that there was a considerable benefit in having Carthage—or at least Bodeshmun—believe I was enamoured of Jabnit the gem-merchant's assistant. Harmless. I'd worry later about convincing the princess otherwise.

"Tell me what you learn," I whispered.

"Don't I always?" Sunjata asked.

"Always," I echoed. The word seemed lodged in my chest, heavy as a stone. "Always and always. Actually, no. You don't."

"Ah." His fingers slid from mine. "Well, we all have our secrets."

With that, Sunjata took his leave of me. It was growing late, twilight falling. In another half an hour, one would need a torch to navigate the city. I stood outside the gates of Astegal's villa, watching Sunjata walk away from me. My bearers waited patiently beside my palanquin.

"Home," I said to them, seating myself.

They bent their backs to the poles and lifted, hoisting

me. Clever Kratos with his squashed nose, offering no comment. The Carthaginian brothers, growing stronger by the day. Ghanim. I'd have to ask him about the Amazigh who guarded the princess.

Sidonie.

I said her name aloud, tasting it. "Sidonie."

It felt good on my tongue.

I said it again. "*Sidonie.*"

My bearers trotted. Blue dusk was settling over Carthage, stars emerging as pinpricks in the veil of night. I closed my eyes. Behind my closed lids, I saw her face. Perplexed. A shower of petals falling between us.

Black eyes.

Why did it make my heart ache?

"Sidonie," I whispered for a third time, my head lolling. Petals fell. Her dark gaze met mine and held it, hard and intense. I searched for a word and found it. "*Always.*"

Twenty-Nine

Bodeshmun's response was swift.

He'd had my letter requesting an audience with the princess. Sidonie. He'd doubtless had spies watching me, Sunjata ostensibly among them. I was certain he'd received a full report from Gemelquart. Whether or not Bodeshmun was a Guildsman, I didn't know. Even Sunjata was unsure. It didn't matter. Like Ptolemy Solon, Bodeshmun was filled with knowledge beyond the Guild's scope. The Chief Horologist made his own rules, and it seemed my appearance among Sidonie's admirers had goaded him into action. He summoned me to a private audience the following afternoon.

Of course, I responded promptly. I brought with me the gift of a book of arcane lore I'd found in the tribute manifest, guessing it was intended for the magus.

"So." Bodeshmun accepted the book with no visible reaction. He regarded me with deep-set eyes. "You seek audience with my kinsman's wife on behalf of the Governor of Cythera."

I bowed to him, exacting and correct. "Yes, my lord."

His eyes narrowed. "Why?"

I spread my hands, helpless. Harmless. "May I speak freely?"

"Please do," Bodeshmun said curtly.

"Much of the world wonders what strange manner of madness has befallen Terre d'Ange," I said. "They speculate and murmur, wondering, wondering. Surely you must know there is one man in the world who does not." I gave him another deep bow, this time with a flourish. "My lord Bodeshmun, his eminence Ptolemy Solon wishes to confess himself to be truly and profoundly amazed. You are the architect of a spell the scope and impact of which he could never have envisioned."

A smug, satisfied smile touched Bodeshmun's lips. "Oh, he'd dream it, all right. It's just he'd never *dare* it."

"That may be so," I said diplomatically. "Nonetheless, his lordship is sincerely impressed. And, I daresay, a bit envious. He is eager for a firsthand report of the workings of your charms."

"Oh?" His heavy brows rose. "Were Solon that eager, he'd have sent you to Terre d'Ange. Plenty to see there. But the Ape of Cythera is in no hurry to curry favor from the half-mad Queen, is he? No, he's sent you sniffing around Carthage for reassurances."

"Well, no. There is that. And there is another matter." I lowered my voice. "He knows about the demon-stone, my lord. The . . ." I snapped my fingers. "Oh, I can't remember the word. Any mind, 'tis the other he can't fathom. How you've managed to bind the princess all the way across the sea." I smiled disarmingly. "D'Angelines are notoriously difficult to sway in matters of the heart, as my lord Solon knows all too well."

It was a calculated gamble. My grasp of the workings of

magic was tenuous. Still, if I understood correctly, much of the spell that bound Sidonie hinged on Prince Imriel's stolen ring. There were plenty of folk who could have described the preparations for the spell that bound the City of Elua. Aside from Sunjata, who was ostensibly doing the bidding of his Carthaginian masters, no one but the prince himself knew about the ring. I prayed like hell that knowledge of the prince's arrival on Cythera hadn't gotten out. Of course if it had, like as not all of this was in vain, so I reckoned it worth a try.

It hadn't.

Bodeshmun smiled again, a broad gloat that sat ill on his grave, bearded face. "Does Ptolemy Solon seek a means to keep his mistress in line? He'll have to look elsewhere. I'll not divulge my secrets."

"Oh, of course not." I returned his smile. "But if I might meet with the princess . . ."

His smiled vanished and Bodeshmun gave me a look meant to quell. I looked suitably quelled. It wasn't hard. He was an imposing fellow.

"Sidonie," he mused. My heart gave an unexpected thump at her name. I ignored it and concentrated on looking quelled. Bodeshmun rose and paced the room, his hands clasped behind his back. "Yes. That was a clever stunt you pulled last night."

"I merely hoped to hasten her response," I murmured. "It had been some days since I sent a letter requesting an audience."

"Her *highness* had not yet received your letter," Bodeshmun said, pronouncing her title with distaste. "I had not made a decision regarding Ptolemy Solon's unlikely emissary."

"His lordship thought the princess would be comforted by a D'Angeline face," I said.

"Comforted, and apt to spill secrets she doesn't know," he said cynically. "Believe me, Leander Maignard. She's not got the least inkling of what was done to her." Bodeshmun's gaze dwelled on my face. "And I've every intention of keeping it that way."

"Well, of course!" I said in surprise. "My lord Bodeshmun, you are singularly well-informed, and I trust you're aware of my lord's situation. To be blunt, the continued peace of my lord Solon and her ladyship Melisande rests on the princess' continued ensorcelment."

Bodeshmun gave his head a shake. "I never thought to see the day Ptolemy Solon would become a fool for love," he said half to himself.

"Nor did I," I admitted. "But her ladyship is a singular individual. And, I may add, pleased and grateful that she no longer has a vengeful son seeking her life."

He studied me. "I understand he's gone missing. Does she know his whereabouts?"

"No." I met his gaze, willing my expression to one of perfect clarity and transparency. "No. She knows the shock of your spell broke his wits. And yes, of course we know he vanished. Unfortunately, her own spies within the City were in considerable disarray in the aftermath and were unable to trace him. Has there been word?"

"No," Bodeshmun said shortly.

I nodded. "Well, my lord Solon keeps a guard posted, just in case. Who knows where his madness may lead him? There were rumors he spoke of Cythera in his ravings. And to be truthful . . ." I lowered my voice again. "No mother prays for a child's death, not even her ladyship. But I do not think Solon would grieve if the poor mad prince met an untimely end." I put a finger to my lips. "That is between us."

"I see." Bodeshmun resumed his pacing.

I refrained from interrupting him, watching him guilelessly. The Chief Horologist wore long black robes, dense and concealing. There was no way of telling where on his person the talisman Solon had told me about was hidden. At a guess, I'd venture to say an inner pocket. He'd want to keep it close. I wondered if he slept with it. I wondered what vices he had. It wasn't going to be easy to get at him. I entertained a brief vision of Bodeshmun and I getting blind drunk together at a wineshop, of helping him stumble home, putting him to bed and undressing him.

Not likely.

"You present a dilemma, Leander Maignard," he said abruptly. "I would prefer to send you away. Unfortunately, your appearance last night has piqued the princess' curiosity." Bodeshmun gave a tight smile. "Which is considerable and plaguing. Now I am of two minds as to what to do."

I shrugged. "Oh?"

"It is imperative that she be kept content." He unleashed another quelling stare. "Her willing presence here is key to confounding Carthage's enemies. And I am unsure whether or not *you* would prove an amiable distraction or a dangerous goad."

"Yes, I see." I smiled. "Well, as to that, I cannot say. But if you wished to advise me on how best I might serve as a distraction, I would be pleased to comply. Our interests here are the same."

"Except for Solon coveting my secrets," Bodeshmun observed.

"Well, yes." I laughed. "Except for that."

More pacing. Bodeshmun's robes swirled. Twice, he touched his chest absentmindedly. I marked it, wondering if that was where the talisman was hidden. Clever or no, I suspected he wasn't a Guildsman if he'd given himself away like that.

"You must not speak of Terre d'Ange," Bodeshmun said,

coming to a decision. "She believes that all is well there. She believes that the war in Aragonia was provoked by an act of aggression on their part. And she believes that when it is concluded, in time, she and Astegal will preside over a vast and peaceable empire." He smiled sourly. "And perhaps they shall when it is sufficiently subdued."

"What of her former beloved?" I inquired.

"She has no memory of him," he said. "None at all. It was necessary. And I will ask you not to speak of anything that might touch on it, including Solon's mistress."

"What mistress?" I said lightly.

"I am not jesting." Bodeshmun's face hardened. "I don't care what tale you conceive that places you in Ptolemy Solon's service without mention of Melisande Shahrizai, but you will do it." He bent over me and took my chin in his hand. "Listen well, Leander Maignard. If you fail in any of these things, I will have your eyes put out and that flippant tongue torn from your head. Do you understand?"

My shudder was unfeigned. "Yes, my lord. I do."

"Good." He released me. "Remember it."

I left the audience shaken, which was probably a good thing. Sunjata was right; this was a dangerous business. I was going to have to tread very, very carefully with Princess Sidonie. I had to find a way to reach her, but if Bodeshmun suspected what I was about, I didn't have any doubt that he'd carry out his threat.

I was on my own here.

And if I failed . . . if I failed, Ptolemy Solon would be placed in a very difficult situation, forced to explain my actions to an angry Carthage. But me, I'd just be blind and tongueless.

Not a pleasant thought.

Thirty

The next day, I received official word from Sidonie de la Courcel, Dauphine of Terre d'Ange and princess of the House of Sarkal, that my request for an audience had been granted and that I might call on her on the morrow. It was written on thick vellum in a neat, tidy hand, the letter sealed with the hawk crest of the House of Sarkal.

I wondered if she'd written it herself.

I had one of the chambermaids polish the chess set with its ivory and onyx pieces until their jeweled eyes gleamed. I summoned Ghanim and one of the Carthaginian brothers—I had a bad habit of forgetting which was which—to translate and asked about the Amazigh who guarded the princess.

Ghanim spat on the floor.

"No friends of his, I take it?" I asked the Carthaginian brother.

There was a long exchange in Punic.

"No," he said eventually. "They are men who betrayed their brothers for gold and promises. They are men who sold their honor cheaply. Ghanim was betrayed, too. His brother stole his wife and accused him falsely of murder. That is how he became a slave. He means to seek revenge once you free him."

Well and so, there wasn't much to be learned here. Ghanim stared fixedly at me, his eyes glittering. I felt an odd sense of kinship with him. After all, in a strange way, I was seeking to avenge another wronged man.

"Soon," I promised. "I don't mean to stay here forever."

The day passed slowly. Patience, patience. I willed myself to be calm. The ledge I walked was high and narrow. On one side was Bodeshmun's threat. I could still feel his strong fingers gripping my chin. And on the other side . . .

Sidonie.

I kept seeing her face in my thoughts, that dark, perplexed gaze. I wanted . . . gods, I *wanted.* I didn't even know what. I wanted to hear what her voice sounded like. I wanted to know if Bodeshmun was right, if she had no inkling of what had been done to her. I couldn't imagine it was true. Surely there must be bits of awareness in there. A haunting shadow, a sense that something was wrong.

Or perhaps not.

I took especial care with my appearance on the day of my audience with her. I brushed my hair until it gleamed, applied a pomade I'd discovered among the villa's owners' toiletries, plaited it in careful braids. The weather was growing a bit cooler, and I rummaged through my trunks, selecting a sleeved tunic of deep crimson silk and a pair of loose striped breeches. I decided the latter was too gaudy and abandoned them for a dark, more somber pair. Then I reconsidered, and put the striped breeches back on.

"Leander," I muttered to myself in the mirror. "What ails you?"

My mirrored face gazed back at me without comment.

I blew myself a kiss. "Charming and harmless. For now, that's the course."

Sunjata paid a call on me before I departed. He regarded me with quiet hilarity, his nostrils flaring. "Did you bathe in a vat of perfume?"

"It's a pomade I found," I said. "Mine ran out. Too much?"

"That would be putting it kindly," he observed. "And I fear it's a woman's scent, not a man's."

There wasn't enough time to wash it out. I sighed and scrubbed at my hair with a clean linen towel, trying to remove the worst of the scent. It helped, but it rendered my careful braids frazzled. I unplaited them, gave my hair another rub, and started over. "Any news?"

"The good news is that you seem to have played Bodeshmun well," Sunjata said. "To hear Hannon talk, he's satisfied that you're harmless and easily dealt with. Old Blackbeard's quite tickled at the notion that he's stymied Lord Solon."

"What's the bad news?" I asked.

"You may not have much time here," he said soberly. "Astegal's on the verge of having New Carthage thoroughly secured. The rumor is that he's considering wintering there and sending for the princess."

I paused mid-braid. "When?"

"A matter of weeks."

"Well." I continued braiding. "I'll just have to work quickly and find a way to get myself invited to New Carthage. I need Astegal's ring anyway. Have you begun creating a replica?"

Sunjata shook his head. "Not yet."

"You'd better make haste." After our first tryst, I'd asked him to create a replica of the ring he'd stolen from Prince Imriel, and I was rather irked to find that he'd not yet begun.

He was quiet a moment. "It's a lot of risk, Leander.

Bodeshmun's talisman. Astegal's ring. And you don't even know what you're looking for on the princess."

"No." I grinned. "But that will be the fun task."

His voice rose. "It's not a jesting matter."

"I know." I finished my braids. "Believe me, Bodeshmun impressed that on me quite strongly yesterday. I have no desire to lose my eyes and tongue, and if I'm jesting, it's because I'm nervous inside. But, Sunjata, I have to try."

"Why?" he asked.

"Because . . ." I frowned. The reasons I'd set out with seemed distant and a bit childish now. A grand adventure, a chance to spread my wings at last. The desire to humble the brooding prince and expose his hypocrisy. Even the desire to make her ladyship proud. Instead, I thought of the Aragonian boy in the slave-market, his stricken face. The princess in the palanquin, fed a diet of lies. Terre d'Ange, land of my birth, teetering on the brink of civil war. "I just do."

"Just be careful," Sunjata said.

"So her ladyship bade me," I replied.

"Yes." His expression was unreadable. "She cares very deeply for you."

"Do you think so?" I smiled. "It's a nice thought."

With that, I collected the pretty inlaid box that contained the chess set, summoned Kratos and the lads, and went off to my audience with the princess, wishing I wasn't so damnably nervous and unsettled.

At the villa of the House of Sarkal I was met by a polite steward who escorted me into a sunlit salon that overlooked a garden. The scent of lemons wafted through the tall, arched windows, mingling rather unfortunately with the overly sweet floral odor of pomade still clinging to my hair.

"Please be comfortable," the steward said, indicating an alcove with a low table and chairs. "I will inform her highness of your arrival."

I sat and waited. Once, I heard footsteps and rose to bow, but it was only a maidservant bringing a cup of sweet mint tea. I sipped it slowly, waiting. Wishing I didn't reek subtly of rotting roses. Wondering if the princess was playing some game, making me wait. Gods, I wished I'd taken the time to wash the pomade out of my hair.

And then she came, one of her Amazigh guards trailing behind her.

She wore a gown of pale yellow silk, a necklace and earrings set with canary-yellow diamonds. Her hair was coiled in a coronet, glinting in the sunlight. A golden girl, but for the shock of those black, black eyes.

I rose and bowed, my heart thudding.

"Messire Maignard, I pray you forgive my rudeness," she said, speaking Hellene with a near-flawless accent. A light voice, cool and controlled. I had an immediate urge to know what it sounded like unstrung with passion. Instead, it took on a hint of amusement. "I fear I was in the midst of a lesson, and my steward chose to wait rather than inform me that my mysterious D'Angeline had arrived."

I laughed. "Not so mysterious, I fear."

Her brows rose slightly. "Do tell."

I accorded her another bow. "As my letter indicated, I am in the service of his eminence Ptolemy Solon, Governor of Cythera." I lifted the inlaid box and opened the lid. "He sends his congratulations to you and Prince Astegal on the occasion of your nuptials, and this small token of Cythera's goodwill."

"This is lovely." She took a piece from the box, examining it. An onyx knight, his ruby eyes sparking. "You must convey my gratitude to his eminence. It is a thoughtful gift."

"Do you play?" I asked.

"Yes, of course." The princess smiled. Her lips were pink, the sort of shape that begs to be kissed. The spark of lively intellect in her dark eyes suggested it wasn't something to be undertaken rashly. "But it's a rare man thinks to gift a woman with a game of wits. And you continue to be mysterious, Messire Maignard." She returned the knight to the box and gestured at the chairs. "Pray, sit and tell me. How *does* a D'Angeline come to be in the service of Cythera's governor?"

I set the inlaid box on the table. "His lordship is a rare man." I waited until she sat, then sat opposite her. Her Amazigh guard remained on the opposite side of the room, but he watched us with folded arms, his expression hidden behind the folds of his burnoose. Princess Sidonie ignored him. I cleared my throat. "My lord Solon is kin to Pharaoh of Menekhet. My father served as the master chef to the D'Angeline ambassador in Iskandria."

She tilted her head. "Marcel de Groulaut?"

"No." The question threw me off stride. I blinked, trying to remember the timeline for the tale I'd concocted and what I knew of Terre d'Ange's presence in Menekhet. "Before him."

"Ah." The princess thought a moment. "That was the Comte de Penfars, I think."

"How do you know that?" I asked stupidly.

Sidonie de la Courcel raised her brows, higher, this time. "Messire Maignard, since the day I gained my majority, it has been expected that I should be prepared to assume the throne of Terre d'Ange at a moment's need. To that end, I am reasonably well informed about the workings of my own nation."

I flushed. "Of course. Forgive me."

Her lips quirked. "Rare men are . . . rare. But pray, continue."

Gods, it galled me. I'd expected . . . what? A victim, a hapless pawn, easily manipulated. She wasn't. Spell-bound and ignorant, yes. But still, disconcertingly self-possessed and acutely intelligent. I stammered through my tale of how Ptolemy Solon had come to dine at the Menekhetan ambassador's home and grown enamored of his chef's cuisine, wooing him away, thus establishing the Maignard clan on Cythera.

When I finished, I was sweating; and very much aware of the aroma of my ill-advised pomade hanging in the air.

"So you've never known Terre d'Ange?" the princess asked.

"No." I shook my head. It wasn't going to be easy to avoid speaking of Terre d'Ange when she brought it up herself. "No, but Cythera is beautiful. Mayhap you'll visit one day."

"I'm sure that would be very pleasant," she said politely.

"Yes, indeed." Hot and uncomfortably aware that I was failing at being charming, I fanned myself, waves of scent wafting from me. Her expression turned slightly peculiar. "Ah, gods!" I blurted. "My lady, forgive me. I fear I've doused myself in a most cloying pomade. Believe me, I regret it."

She laughed.

It was an unexpectedly deep-throated laugh, rich and resonant. My heart rolled over in my chest, whispering the word "always." Her black eyes came to life, sparkling at me. "And why did you do that, Messire Maignard?"

"Because I was anxious," I murmured. "Because you are very, very beautiful, your highness. And by the presence of yon glowering guard, I suspect you have a jealous husband."

"Actually, Astegal is quite reasonable," the princess said with amusement. "The guards are merely for the sake of appearances. As I recall, at one point during our courtship, he told me I was welcome to keep a harem of beautiful young men if I chose."

I eyed her, trying to tell if she was teasing me. "And do you?"

"Are you volunteering?" she asked.

"Would you have me?" I countered.

A wicked smile flickered over her face. "Not smelling like that."

I flushed a second time. "I'm *sorry*, my lady!"

"No, I apologize." She laughed. "You're ill at ease and I'm baiting you unfairly. In truth, Messire Maignard, my husband is a rare man himself, and I've felt no temptation to test the boundaries of his tolerance."

I felt a profound pang of sorrow. "Not even a little, Sidonie?"

Why I'd called her by name, I couldn't say. It was wildly inappropriate . . . and yet, something shifted between us. She gazed at me, frowning like someone trying to remember a forgotten tune. I held her gaze, my heart hammering in my chest, suffused with a strange tenderness. Fear, hope, desire? The air between us felt charged, as though lightning were about to strike.

And then she closed her eyes and shuddered, and it passed.

"Oh, gods!" I said in anguish. "Forgive me. That was appallingly overfamiliar. I'm sorry, your highness, I don't know what came over me. Will you please forgive me?"

"I think I'd better." A wry edge crept into her tone. "I deserved no less for baiting you. Are you always this graceless and blunt in practicing the art of flirtation, Messire Maignard?"

"No," I said. "Are you always this acerbic?"

"No." It was only one syllable, but it was accompanied by that same wicked little smile: a quick, maddening flicker.

"Ah." I fanned myself and glanced at her Amazigh guard.

He stared impassively back at me. "You mentioned a lesson. May I ask what your highness is studying?"

"Punic," she said. "One can get by with Hellene, of course, but I find it unwise not to at least attempt to learn the mother tongue of a land. In fact, that was one of the reasons my mother replaced the Comte de Penfars as the ambassador to Menekhet. She discovered he'd not bothered to learn Menekhetan after the Comtesse de Montrève and her consort were there to . . ." The princess blinked, her voice trailing off. A perplexed frown creased her brow.

Oh, hells.

"On their quest to free the Master of the Straits, was it not?" I inquired. "Even in Cythera, we heard of it."

"Yes, of course." Her brow cleared, though a touch of uncertainty lingered. "I imagine you would have, given his eminence's ties to Ptolemy Dikaios."

I sighed inwardly. "Indeed."

Gods above, I felt like a rabbit in a field of snares. How exactly was one to avoid speaking of Terre d'Ange to a woman raised from birth to inherit its throne? And all the topics that touched on Prince Imriel's life . . . all the very things I needed to reach her, the very things Bodeshmun had forbidden me to discuss.

Which left flirting as the only safe ground, except that I was stumbling over my own feet there, awkward and graceless.

"Are you well?" the princess asked. "You look pained."

"I think it's the pomade," I said. "Your highness, his eminence has asked me to conduct other business in Carthage, and I will be here for some time yet. If I were to promise to scour myself quite thoroughly, is there any chance that I might beg another audience of you? Mayhap to play a game of chess?"

She laughed. "Do you promise to be as unwittingly amusing?"

I winced. "By the Goddess, I hope not."

"I rather enjoyed it." Her eyes sparkled. "It's a pleasant change of pace from the usual bland courtesies."

I rose and bowed to her. "Very well, my lady. If the life-blood of my dignity serves to brighten your days, then by all means, puncture it. Bleed me dry of every peck of self-respect, and I shall languish at your feet, a glad fool."

"Ah." She rose. "Eloquence surfaces."

"Belatedly," I admitted. "Truly, your highness, I'm terribly sorry for the impropriety. And if you give me a chance to make amends, I will be most grateful."

"Come tomorrow afternoon," the princess said. "We'll see how you fare at chess."

"Thank you." I smiled at her. "Very much indeed."

She smiled back at me, sincerely, this time. "You're welcome. And Messire Maignard, you may stop apologizing. There was somewhat I quite liked about the way my name sounded when you spoke it, although I couldn't for the life of me say why."

Nor could I.

I bowed again. "Then I wish you would do me the kindness of calling me Leander, and I aspire to the honor of using your name one day in earnest friendship."

She inclined her head. "On the morrow."

Thirty-one

I walked out of the House of Sarkal's villa feeling more profoundly disoriented than I had in my life.

Sidonie.

Why in the name of all the gods and goddesses in heaven had she had such a disturbing effect on me? I'd played the most dangerous man in Carthage like a master, then tripped over my own tongue when sparring with a young woman who'd had a large piece of her memory ripped from her.

All my expectations had been wrong. Weak. I'd thought she'd be weak-minded. Why? Because she'd fallen prey to Carthage's magic, I supposed. I was an idiot. I'd sought to flatter Bodeshmun, but the truth was, he *had* wrought a spell sufficient to impress even Ptolemy Solon. It had ensorceled an entire city. I'd have been a victim had I been there. And Sidonie . . .

Well, she wasn't bound by the *ghafrid-gebla*. Not here. It was a simpler magic, awful and powerful in a different way. It was the very force of her love that had been turned against her. Two days ago, I'd doubted. I hadn't been sure that love was genuine.

Now . . .

A girlish infatuation. Gods! No, no. If I'd ever met a woman who knew her own mind, it was Sidonie de la Courcel.

Except for the parts she didn't.

It was in there, I thought. I could *see* it. That perplexity, a sense of something missing. Something withheld, something denied. Knowledge trapped within her. Like a butterfly battering its wings against a glass jar.

I wanted to smash that glass.

I wanted to free her. I wanted to kiss her until she couldn't breathe. I wanted to taste her, to bury myself in her. I wanted, desperately, to find out what lay behind that quick, wicked smile.

I wanted to kill Astegal.

A rare man . . . gods! Oh, yes, it took a rare man indeed to set a country against itself, to abduct a young woman and turn her against her will with dark magics. All to further his own ambitions. Dreams of empire. And he'd been doing his best to get heirs on her. Soon he'd send for her again.

I gritted my teeth at the thought.

I was losing my damned mind.

"Halt!" I called to my bearers. They lowered the palanquin, and I climbed out. Kratos regarded me skeptically.

"Are you well, my lord?" he asked.

"Well enough," I said shortly. "I need to walk. I need to clear my thoughts."

He shrugged. "As you will."

I stalked alongside the empty palanquin, reliving the encounter in my mind. All right. I'd acted a perfect dolt. That was good and bad. Harmless, yes. The gods above knew I'd reinforced that belief. I'd amused and distracted her.

Bodeshmun would be pleased. From what I'd seen, he had cause to worry. A butterfly's wings, battering. A considerable and plaguing curiosity.

She thought me a dolt.

I hated that fact.

But there had been that moment, that charged moment. When I'd crossed the line of propriety, called her by name as though we were intimate. Asked her a question I'd no right to ask. It had struck a chord within her. I'd *seen* it. And she'd never given an answer.

I whispered her name. "Sidonie."

My heart leapt at the sound of it.

I pressed my own fist against my chest, willing my pounding heart to subside. It felt strange and heavy to me. A stone lodged in my chest. It ached. It threatened to drag me down into deep waters. It threatened to burst and splinter. I breathed slowly and deeply, thinking on the lessons her ladyship Melisande had taught me.

Bit by bit, the feeling eased.

"Name of Elua!" I said aloud. "I'm not even sure I *like* her."

The following morning, I'd arranged to meet Sunjata at the baths. They were massive, laid out in the grand Tiberian style, although the architecture itself was Carthaginian. I found Sunjata in the palaestra, stretching his limbs. Ordinarily, I thought, it would likely be a crowded place, filled with young men wrestling and boxing with one another, practicing for foot-races, but it was quite empty today. I reckoned a good many of Carthage's athletes were serving in Astegal's army.

"Run with me?" Sunjata asked in greeting, nodding at the footpath circling the exercise arena.

"A lap or two," I said. "You know I can't keep up with you for long."

He merely shrugged. For as long as I'd known him, Sunjata had had a fondness for running. It gave him a sense of freedom; and too, eunuchs had a propensity to gain weight as they grew older, their figures growing more womanish. Sunjata would never let that happen. He wasn't vain, but he was proud.

After I'd limbered, we set out on the footpath together. Sunjata paced himself slowly so I could match him stride for stride.

"So," he said when we'd reached the far end. "How was your audience?"

"Aside from the fact that I reeked of attar of roses?" I asked, and he laughed. "Gods, I don't even know what to say. I found myself acting an idiot, and she spent most of the time laughing at me."

"Did you gain a second audience?" Sunjata asked.

"I did that much," I said glumly. "But I'll have to summon considerable more charm if I want to be reckoned aught but a performing lap-dog."

"Lap-dogs don't give Bodeshmun cause for concern," he observed. "Which is to the good." We fell silent on reaching the central stretch of the arena, waiting until we were out of earshot of the few folks availing themselves of the palaestra. "What did you think of her?"

"Disconcerting," I said. "She's quick-witted and bored. I can see why Bodeshmun's worried."

Sunjata increased his stride. "What did *you* think of her, Leander?"

I pushed myself to match his pace, feeling my muscles warm and loosen. It came easier than I remembered. Our bare feet thudded softly on the path. "I'm not entirely sure of that, either. But whatever it is, I find myself thinking a good deal too much of it."

Another stretch of silence. I could hear Sunjata's breathing, steady and even. I matched him breath for breath.

"Perhaps you're falling in love with her," he said when next we reached the turn at the far end of the footpath.

"At one meeting?" I laughed. "Don't be absurd."

"At a glance," Sunjata said. "At a single, devastating glance that stripped clever Leander Maignard of all his smooth beguilements and left him standing in the street, staring after her palanquin like a man besotted."

"That only happens in poets' tales," I scoffed.

He gave me a sidelong glance. "Are you sure?"

I opened my mouth to reply, but Sunjata pulled away, his effortless stride increasing once more. Irritated, I pulled abreast of him. My lungs were working hard now. He pushed his pace and I struggled grimly to keep up with him, running too hard for conversation. Another lap, then another and another. My lungs felt like they were bursting and I had a stitch in my side. Even Sunjata was breathing hard. Still, I managed to keep up with him this time.

"There!" he gasped at last, slowing to a panting halt. "See, I told you. We're all capable of things we can't imagine."

I braced my hands on my knees, trying to catch my breath. "You're out of practice."

"Not so." Sunjata shook his head. "This is my one great escape. I suspect you've been training at somewhat."

I eased myself upright. "Not that I recall."

Sunjata gave me one of his opaque looks. "Let's get you into the baths. I can still smell that damnable pomade."

We passed a pleasant time lingering in the baths. I kept my promise to Princess Sidonie and bathed thoroughly, washing my hair several times over. Afterward, we bought food from one of the many vendors there and dined while strolling the colonnade. I felt an unaccountable excitement rising as morning gave way to noon.

"I've got to be on my way," I said to Sunjata outside the baths. "Shall I see you later?"

"I'll meet you here on the morrow." He smiled wryly. "I've a commission to work on. A particular ring."

"Ah, I see," I said. "Good. Tomorrow, then. But why don't you come to the villa? I had some business I wished to discuss."

"I prefer this," he said.

"Fine." I threw up my hands. "As you wish."

"Leander." Sunjata caught my arm as I turned to go. He lowered his voice. "Listen . . . whatever you're feeling for her, don't fight it. It might be exactly what you need."

"I'm not," I said. "It feels more like it's fighting *me*."

He let go my arm. "That may very well be true."

Before I could ask what in the world that was supposed to mean, Sunjata turned on his heel and set off at a brisk walk. I let him go. There was no reasoning with him when he was in an obstinate mood.

Besides, I had a date to keep.

Once more, I presented myself at the villa of the House of Sarkal. This time, I was bade wait a moment before I was escorted within. When I was, I found the princess already awaiting me, seated in the sunlight alcove and pondering the chess board. One of the Amazigh had taken up his customary position, his presence warning me to be discreet. Today the princess wore a silk gown the color of apricots. The decolletage wasn't low enough to be unseemly, but I could see the swell of her breasts. My mouth went dry.

"Leander Maignard." Her gaze flashed up at me.

I nearly greeted her by name. I swallowed it and bowed. "Your highness."

"Are you thoroughly scoured and ready to match wits?" she asked.

"Both, my lady."

"Well, then." She smiled and gestured at the table. The chess board was positioned so that I would be playing white. "The opening move is yours."

I sat opposite her and moved an ivory pawn. "So it begins."

The princess mirrored my move with an ebony pawn. A heavy signet ring glinted on her right hand. I marked it, remembering she'd worn it yesterday, too. "Tell me, Leander Maignard, how do you spend your days when you're not entertaining bored royalty? What business is it that his eminence of Cythera wishes you to conduct?"

I slid a second pawn onto the board in a deliberate gambit. "Lord Solon merely wishes me to obtain assurances of Carthage's goodwill."

She gave me a sharp glance. "Does he fear he has cause for concern?"

"Your husband is an ambitious man," I said ambivalently. "His eminence is merely being cautious."

"I see." She declined my gambit, advancing a second pawn of her own in a countering move. "Believe me, Astegal has no ambition beyond securing the peaceable future of both our nations, and Carthage did not seek this quarrel with Aragonia. Once it is settled, he will look no farther."

I said nothing.

"You doubt me," the princess observed.

I glanced past her at the Amazigh guard. Between swathes of blue cloth, his eyelids flickered. This one, I thought, spoke more than Punic. "Of course not," I lied. "Indeed, I have received similar assurances from one member of the Council already. I'm simply seeking to concentrate on our game."

She sighed. "A courtier's reply. Very well then, let us play."

We played for a time in silence.

I found myself thinking about Sunjata's advice. I watched

the princess contemplate the board. The contrasts in her face elevated what might have been mere prettiness to beauty. Her features were fine-cut and delicate, but her eyebrows were drawn in a firm line. Not heavy, not by any means. Only strong enough to offset the delicacy, to create a suggestion of determination and vulnerability combined. A captivating contrast, like the one between her gilded fairness and those night-dark eyes.

"Messire Maignard," she said. "You're staring at me."

Hot blood scalded my face. "Oh, gods! I'm sorry. Please forgive me."

"Again?" she asked in amusement.

"I'm a chef's son," I said helplessly. "I've spent almost all my life on Cythera, and yes, I'm staring at you like a provincial rube. Please."

"All right, I forgive you." There it was again, that brief, wicked smile. Honey and gall. "Only because you blush so prettily. It's your move."

I closed my eyes and said a silent prayer for forbearance, then bent my attention to the chessboard.

On the boat, when I'd found the chess set listed in the manifest, I'd entertained some idea of flattering her by losing a-purpose. Playfully demanding a rematch, mayhap. I'd envisioned myself very much in control, smoothly cajoling while the hapless young princess giggled and blushed. Instead, *I* was blushing like a maiden, while the princess uttered barbed witticisms. And I very much suspected if I didn't best her in this game of wits, I'd seal her impression of me forever as a tame lap-dog.

She played well, but she played a cautious and meticulous game. I'd been doing the same, trying to draw out my time with her as long as possible. Now I went on the offensive and played boldly, giving the impression of being rash and distracted. Several moves later, I made a ploy that appeared careless. This time, the princess took my gambit and walked into a trap.

"Ah." Realization dawned on her face before the endgame was played out. She studied the board for a moment, seeking an avenue of escape, then reached out and tipped over her king. "You've won."

My brow was sweating. "You underestimated me."

"So I did." She continued to study the board, retracing her steps and committing her misstep to memory. "Will you give me the courtesy of a rematch?"

"Of course." I began gathering pieces to reset the board.

"It grows late." She touched my hand. "Tomorrow, perhaps."

A spark leapt between us.

I felt it, and I knew, I *knew* she felt it. Her eyes widened, their darkness blurring. I wanted to close my hand on hers, pull her to me. Scatter the chess pieces, drag her to the floor. Pull the pins from her hair until it fell in glorious disarray, tear every scrap of fabric from her body. Rip the necklace from her throat, the earrings from her earlobes. Lay her bare, break the spell. Kiss her until I bruised her lips, take her there amid the scattered chess pieces.

Under the watching eyes of her Amazigh guard.

I drew my hand back as though her touch had burned me. "Tomorrow would be lovely."

The pulse beat visibly in the hollow of her throat, but there was no other sign she was unnerved. Her voice was cool and calm. "The same time, then?"

I rose and bowed. "I would be honored."

I made myself meet the gaze of the Amazigh as I left. Clear and transparent, I told myself, clear and transparent. I gave him a nod, a careless smile. He didn't return the smile, but he accorded me a brief nod. There was no suspicion I could see in his eyes or the narrow strip of his face visible.

Whatever had passed between the Princess Sidonie and me, it had gone unnoticed.

One touch.

A single glance . . .

Blessed Elua was not a gentle god.

Thirty-two

"Well played, your highness." I tipped over my king, acknowledging defeat.

Princess Sidonie inclined her head graciously. "My thanks. It was a hard-earned victory. Who taught you to play so well?"

It was the fourth game we'd played over the course of as many days, and the first that she'd won. Since that first time, under the watching eyes of her guard, we had been careful not to inadvertently touch; and she'd been as careful as I had.

She *had* felt it, I was sure.

"My . . . mother," I said.

Her eyes danced. "Are you sure? You sound uncertain."

It had been her ladyship who'd taught me, of course; or at least taught me to play *well*. Chess was a useful game to learn, although it had its limits. In a true game of intrigue, every piece on the board would be a live player, filled with weaknesses and flaws. Still, it had its merits.

"Yes, of course," I said. "She's a great knack for the game."

"Does your mother also serve in Cythera?" the princess inquired.

"She's Ptolemy Solon's mistress," I said, conflating one lie with another. Her brows rose. I smiled ruefully. "In truth, I suspect her wit and beauty held as much appeal for my lord Solon as my father's cuisine. They have always been discreet, but my father, may Elua bless and keep him, died two years ago. Since then, the liaison has been openly acknowledged."

"Ah." She nodded. "Which is why his eminence holds you in such high esteem."

"Not the entire reason, I hope," I said.

Her smile was genuine. "I'm sure it's not."

My heart gave one of those involuntary leaps. I almost wished she wouldn't smile at me like that. It actually *hurt.* I busied myself setting up the chess board for another game, watching her out of the corner of my eye. "Your victory was swift, my lady. Do you wish to play again?"

"No." The princess rested her chin on one hand. Sunlight glinted on her signet ring. "I'm growing weary of chess, Leander Maignard."

"Just Leander," I said.

She gave me an amused look. "I'm considering it."

One audience a day, four games of chess. Five days, five gowns. Today she wore a pale lavender, which I didn't think was her best hue. A choker of pearls and amethyst, earrings to match. Over the course of five days, there had been only one constant. I knew; I'd been keeping track. If she was growing bored with chess, it was time for me to make a move of a different sort. I took a deep breath and did it.

"That's an interesting ring, my lady," I said. "Is that the seal of the House of Sarkal?"

"This?" She twisted it on her finger. "Yes. Rather crude work, isn't it?"

"May I see it?" I asked.

Her expression turned quizzical. "If you like."

It slid easily from her finger. I held out my hand. Our fingers didn't quite touch as she dropped it into my palm. I examined the stone, a ruby cabochon engraved with the Sarkal hawk insignia. I peered under my lashes at her. Her expression was unchanged, still puzzled. "A family heirloom, I imagine. It's very old. Do you wear it in honor of your husband?"

"At Astegal's request, yes." Her mouth quirked. "Only in public, to tell the truth. I appreciate its value and history, but it's a bit heavy."

"Ah." A stab of disappointment went through me. I handed the ring back to her. "Your secret is safe with me."

"Oh, he knows." The princess laughed. "He doesn't mind as long as I wear it publicly."

It definitely wasn't the ring, then. The bastard just liked the world to see he'd set his seal on her. The thought filled me with fury and disgust, so much so I lowered my face to hide it, not trusting myself. "I heard he might be sending for you soon," I murmured. "To winter in New Carthage."

"Yes, mayhap within the next fortnight." She slid the ring back on her finger. "Name of Elua, I hope so."

"You miss him." I said it without looking at her.

"Very much so." Her voice softened briefly, then resumed its light tone. "And I'm perishing of tedium. I'm grateful to you for alleviating it."

I did look at her then, looked her hard in the eyes. For the first time, it was the princess who flushed slightly. "I've a fancy to see New Carthage." I forced my tone to match her lightness. "Perhaps you'll invite me as your faithful courtier."

She looked away. "Why don't we venture out, Messire Maignard? As you note, 'tis early yet. I feel I've scarce had a chance to see old Carthage before trading it for the new."

I offered a seated bow. "Your wish is my command."

Within a short time, we were seated in her ornate double palanquin, venturing into the streets of Carthage on the shoulders of her bearers. It was the closest I'd been to her. There was a gap of a mere six inches between us, and I could swear it felt charged with heat.

"What do you wish to see?" I asked her.

"Mayhap we could make an offering at the Temple of Tanit," she said. "It's always wise to honor the gods of a place, don't you think?"

"To be sure," I agreed.

Her bearers were smooth and swift, far more skilled than my lads. The four Amazigh guards flanked the palanquin, silent and menacing in their dark robes and veils. Folk on the street called out good wishes for the princess' health and bowed toward the palanquin, but no one dared approach. Sidonie de la Courcel acknowledged them with the gracious politeness of someone who'd spent a lifetime receiving similar tribute.

The goddess Tanit was akin to Asherat-of-the-Sea, an ancient goddess who had taken many forms and many names. Her ladyship had spent many, many years claiming sanctuary in the Temple of Asherat in La Serenissima. I thought about that when we arrived at our destination, awed once more by her capacity for patience.

The priests scurried and bowed, eyeing the Amazigh warily, offering the princess solicitous advice. One priest was sent running, his sandals slapping against the marble floor. He returned carrying a white rooster by its legs. It was alive, its wings flapping awkwardly. I saw the princess' mask of politeness slip as she recoiled.

"Name of Elua, man!" I said to the priest. "They don't offer blood sacrifice in Terre d'Ange." I fished in my purse for a gold coin. "Surely the goddess finds the scent of incense pleasing?"

He bowed. "Yes, yes, of course."

"Thank you, Leander." The princess was slightly pale. "I'd forgotten they made live offerings in Carthage. That was careless of me."

"I doubt *that* happens often," I said. "You hardly seem the careless type."

"No." My words seemed to strike some chord within her, her puzzled look returning. "Not often."

We made our offerings of incense, gazing at the face of the massive effigy. The goddess Tanit's features were calm and unreadable, her eyes fixed on the unknowable distance. She didn't look like a goddess who craved blood and suffering. *Divine Tanit,* I prayed silently, *if you have compassion and mercy in you, do not suffer your children to do ill in your name. Help me to undo what has been done.*

What prayer the princess offered, I couldn't say. I only knew her face looked very solemn.

And she had called me by name.

I longed to hear her say it again.

Afterward, she seemed oddly melancholy. I directed the bearers to take us to the flower market, where I purchased another absurdly large bunch of roses and laid them at her feet on the floor of the palanquin.

It made her laugh. "Now you're just being foolish."

I bowed elaborately. "If you will not accept it as a tribute to your beauty, accept it as a tribute to your victory today."

"You're magnanimous in defeat. Nonetheless, I cannot accept this gift." Princess Sidonie picked up one of the roses. There were children loitering at a distance, wide-eyed and curious. She tossed the rose to a pretty little girl who caught it with a shriek of delight. The others began to beg. Smiling, the princess tossed the rest of the roses, one by one until they were gone.

It was a nice piece of subtle diplomacy. It was also so damned charming, I caught a couple of the Amazigh guards with eyes crinkled in the suggestion of hidden smiles. "Well played, my lady," I said to her.

She gave me a sidelong glance. "Tell me, Leander Maignard, what game is it you think we're playing?"

"One that I hope will while away the hours and alleviate your tedium." I placed my hand on my chest. "Have no fear, I know how it ends. With you in the arms of your husband and me broken-hearted."

I'd spoken in a light, jesting tone—or at least I'd meant to. But she heard somewhat more in it. Whether I succeeded or failed, there was a bitter truth to my words, somewhat I'd not yet begun to consider. She studied me for a moment, then looked away. "It grows late. I should return home."

"As you wish," I said.

We sat in silence in the palanquin. Gods, I wanted to touch her so badly. Cut through the banter, cut through the spell that bound her. And I couldn't. Not here, not in public, not with guards watching. I needed to get her alone somehow, and I couldn't think how to do it.

I was pondering the problem when the palanquin jolted to an abrupt halt. The two Amazigh preceding us were giving orders in Punic to the bearers, pointing and gesturing. I sensed the princess stiffen beside me.

"Is there trouble?" I asked.

"No." Her expression was unreadable. "I need to . . . no."

It was my turn to be perplexed. "All right."

Whatever it was, the Amazigh and the bearers sorted it out. We changed course and took a different route back to the House of Sarkal's villa. The princess was quiet and withdrawn, and I was fearful I'd made a misstep.

"May I call on you tomorrow?" I asked before I took my leave. "Or have I begun to contribute to your tedium?"

"No, of course not." She gave me a quick, absentminded smile, and I realized that whatever disturbed her, it had naught to do with me. "I've enjoyed your company, Leander. I'll send word."

I bowed. "I will await it."

Thirty-three

When I returned from taking exercise with Sunjata on the morrow, there was word awaiting me—but it was from Bodeshmun, not the princess. He wished for me to call on him immediately at the College of Horology.

Of course, I complied.

I found him distracted and pacing. As before, he was an abrupt and ungracious host, not offering so much as a cup of water. I bowed deeply, keeping my tone light and unconcerned. Harmless. Oddly, it was a great deal easier to do with Bodeshmun than it was with Princess Sidonie.

"You wished to see me, my lord?"

He fetched up before me, glowering. "You took her into the city."

"So I did," I said. "Was that wrong?"

Bodeshmun's deep-set eyes flashed. "I would prefer that you did not, not without consulting me. It is imperative that her contacts be . . . managed."

I shrugged. "She made an offering to Tanit and threw

some flowers to children in the marketplace. There was no harm in it."

"There might have been," he said grimly.

"My lord, she's *bored*." I spread my hands. "I accompanied her into the city at her own request. If you wish to keep her distracted and under the impression that she's not a prisoner for the next fortnight, I suggest you provide her with a few more of these *managed* contacts, because I fear my charming banter and impressive chess skills are wearing thin."

My suggestion earned me one of his quelling looks. "I didn't become Chief Horologist to play master of revels for a bored young princess!"

I stifled a smile. "Nonetheless."

Bodeshmun sighed. "I'll think on it. Until then, you will agree to no further excursions."

"You wish me to refuse her?" I asked.

His broad mouth twisted sardonically. "I'm confident you'll think of some cause. I understand you've done quite well at playing the blushing admirer while dancing clear of any . . . awkward . . . topics. Whoever taught you to dissemble is to be commended."

I inclined my head. "My thanks, my lord."

"Go." He waved one hand. "And remember that if that glib tongue of yours should slip, I'll have it cut out. Keep my warning in mind."

"I always do," I said with perfect sincerity.

The encounter with Bodeshmun didn't trouble me overmuch. At least he was a known danger, and the meeting confirmed he still thought me harmless, a useful fool. But Sidonie . . . Sidonie was another matter. Gods, what was it she'd overheard the Amazigh say yesterday that had disturbed her? I wished I'd had time to learn Punic. If I'd had any idea I'd be in this position one day, I would have learned it years ago.

And what if she didn't send for me again?

The thought of not seeing her made my heart ache. And the thought of failing—of leaving her a spell-bound pawn in Carthage's hands, happily spreading her legs in Astegal's bed—filled me with sick fury.

When a letter inviting me to dine with her that evening came later in the day, I nearly laughed aloud with relief. It was ludicrous. Never in my life had I felt such absurd, soaring joy.

I'd heard it described, though.

That was the awful irony of it. The day I'd accompanied Prince Imriel to the Temple of Aphrodite on Cythera, I'd asked him what it was like to be in love. And impossible as it seemed . . . yes. That was how I felt. As though my heart could burst, flaying my chest. As though I could leap off a cliff and take wing.

And then it changes, he had said. *It becomes a part of you.*

He had been speaking of Sidonie.

She loved him. Not me—him. What I'd said to her yesterday was true. Whatever I felt for her, it didn't matter. Whether I succeeded or failed, this would end with Sidonie de la Courcel in another man's arms, and me broken-hearted. The only difference was whether or not her happiness would be a faltering lie or joyous truth. And astonishingly enough, that had begun to matter to me.

I gazed at myself in the mirror before I departed for her villa. What I'd told Sunjata was true; there was a resemblance between the prince and me, at least a bit. I remembered *his* face well, as it was so much the mirror of her ladyship's. Mine was thinner, more aquiline. My eyes were blue, but

I hadn't inherited that deep, dazzling hue that marked so many of House Shahrizai.

I looked older than I remembered.

Older, and more . . . intense. I wondered if it strengthened the resemblance between us. And I wondered, if it did, could she ever come to love me in his stead?

I reached out and touched the mirror, bracing my fingertips against its cool surface. Gazed at my mirror-fingertips touching my own. "Blessed Elua," I murmured. "I've been away so long, I scarce remember how to pray to you."

Somewhat in my heart stirred. Memories of home. Of fields of lavender and bees buzzing under the golden sun. Drowsing on my belly before our household shrine, the scent of sweet-peas in the air. Elua's enigmatic smile offered in loving benison.

Be worthy of her.

The words floated through my mind, and whether they came from the depths of my unconscious thoughts, or Blessed Elua himself, I couldn't say. I only knew that my eyes stung. "I'll try," I whispered. "Whatever else happens, I *will* try."

I presented myself at the villa as dusk was settling over the city. It was the first time the princess had invited me to dine with her. The steward escorted me to an inner courtyard. It was hung about with oil lamps providing a soft illumination, set with multiple braziers to chase off the evening chill. Sidonie was there, clad in the pale yellow gown in which I'd first seen her. She turned her head as I entered, and our eyes met.

I bowed to her. "Your beauty outshines the sun, Princess."

The words hung between us, echoing strangely. Her eyes brightened as though with tears, and mine stung again. Worthy. I would try to be worthy. I watched her gather herself.

"If you flirt overmuch, I shall have to send you away, Messire Maignard," she said in a cool tone.

Out of the corner of my eye, I saw one of the Amazigh positioned against a vine-decked courtyard wall, his robed and veiled figure almost invisible in the dim light. "I will try to restrain myself, your highness."

She smiled slightly. "Then you may join me."

We sat opposite one another at the dining table. Servants came and went, bringing wine and an array of dishes. Sidonie's manner was guarded and careful in a way I couldn't quite fathom. It was subtle and inexplicable, somewhat only a Guildsman might notice. I made innocuous conversation, speaking of Cythera's fine wines, praising the dishes, inventing delicacies allegedly devised by my late father the chef and describing them in detail. She listened and made all the appropriate comments.

It looked and sounded like a perfectly normal, pleasant conversation. I couldn't shake the feeling that it wasn't.

"Will you have a cordial?" Sidonie asked when the meal was finished and the last plate had been cleared. "There is perry brandy, imported from Terre d'Ange."

"I would be delighted," I said.

A servant approached and poured. "Astegal is thoughtful." She swirled her cup, and a sweet, spicy aroma arose. "He saw to it that I enjoyed a few comforts of home. To be honest, I think he has a taste for it himself. I remembered today that there was a keg in the cellar." She sipped her perry brandy. "Do you like it?"

I tried it. "It's very nice."

"It was distilled on the estate of Lombelon," Sidonie said. "A very small holding owned by a minor lord. Maslin de Lombelon. He served as the second in command of my personal guard for a time."

"It's very nice," I repeated, trying to steer the conversation away from Terre d'Ange. "On Cythera, there is a cordial made from the skins of grapes—"

Her gaze held mine, intense and compelling. "Do you know, Leander, I have been remiss over these past few days. I addressed you in Hellene as an emissary of Cythera. I never thought to inquire . . ." She switched to the D'Angeline tongue. "Do you speak D'Angeline?"

"Yes, of course." I replied in kind, startled. "It was what we spoke at home."

Her voice was light and careless, speaking D'Angeline. "Why do you discourage me from speaking of Terre d'Ange? And why is it, do you suppose, that my guards insisted on routing us around the slave-market yesterday? What did they fear I might see?"

There was a movement in the shadows. I glanced past Sidonie to see the Amazigh on guard lift one hand, his finger wagging in warning. I was not to speak words he did not comprehend.

"I cannot answer you safely." I made myself stumble over the words in D'Angeline, then laughed and shook my head. "I'm sorry, your highness," I said, returning to Hellene. "I know it's my mother-tongue, but I've scarce spoken it since I was a babe. Do you mind overmuch if we continue to converse in Hellene?"

"Not at all." Her gaze was perfectly steady. "I was merely trying to be polite."

Oh, gods.

So that was what this was about, that was what she had heard. The guards had been careless, forgetting she was studying Punic. That was why Bodeshmun was worried about our excursion. Yes, I thought; Sidonie de la Courcel would be disturbed at the sight of Aragonian children for sale in Carthage's flesh markets. And well she should be. Terre d'Ange did not countenance slavery, that was true.

And she was in love with a man who'd been abducted as a child by Carthaginian slavers. Likely it would strike a chord within her.

Like the boy I'd seen.

Is he biddable?

I shivered.

"Are you cold, Leander?" Sidonie asked. "Forgive me, I forget you come from a warmer clime than I do."

"No," I said hoarsely. "Not cold."

I wanted to tell her. I wanted to confess everything. Smash the glass. I didn't dare, not in front of the Amazigh. I had to continue balancing on my high ledge. But everything had shifted. She *knew.* She knew I wasn't what I seemed. Damned guards! I stared helplessly at her, willing her to understand. Fearful that she understood too much.

"I do not mean to bedevil you. Perhaps I should seek answers elsewhere," she mused aloud. "My lord Bodeshmun is a clever fellow."

"Yes," I said. "And a busy one. I myself would not trouble him."

Her quick gaze flicked to mine. "You advise against it?"

I was sweating. I felt my control lapse. I looked involuntarily in the direction of the Amazigh. Thanks to all the gods that were, he wasn't a Guildsman. And neither was Sidonie, but she had been trained very, very well in the art of statesmanship. It might as well have been the same. She saw where my glance went.

"I do," I said.

She inclined her head. "Then I'll not trouble him." She paused, her gaze searching my face. "My lord Astegal will send for me soon. No doubt all will be clear when he does."

I gritted my teeth. "No doubt."

So near, yet so far! Gods, it was infuriating. And exhausting, too. By the time I took my leave of her that night, I felt as though I'd run a distance-race. The only solace I could take from the encounter was that she *was* cautious. Very cautious. And right now, that was a damned good thing. Because once she started voicing her suspicions aloud to Bodeshmun or Astegal or anyone in their service, she was in danger of changing from unwitting pawn to hostage.

And I would be lucky to keep my eyes and tongue.

I slept very poorly that night.

Thirty-four

"It's finished." Sunjata handed me a suede pouch. "Take it. I don't want it anywhere near me."

I opened the pouch and withdrew a ring. Plain gold, shaped like an intricate knot. "Is it a good copy? Good enough to fool Astegal?"

Sunjata gave me a disdainful look. "What do you think? Of course."

I kissed his cheek. "Thank you."

He pulled away slightly. "You'll be pleased to know that I've nearly convinced Jabnit to send me to New Carthage to establish trade for the House of Philosir. The old glutton's rubbing his hands together with glee at the thought of the profit to be made on the back of a looting army."

"That's wonderful!" I was touched. "I didn't think you'd go."

He shrugged. "It was Hannon's idea. He wants Guild eyes and ears on the ground there." Sunjata smiled sourly. "Hannon's a tool of the Council of Thirty, and there's a slow-dawning concern among them that they might not be able to control Astegal once he seizes Aragonia. Not with Bodeshmun at his side."

"Idiots," I said absently. "What did they think? So Bodeshmun's to go to New Carthage, eh?"

"Yes. You'll have them all in the same place, for what it's worth. Any progress?" he asked.

"Some." I sighed. "Dangerous progress." I told him what had transpired with Sidonie.

Sunjata whistled. "You're walking a very, very fine line, my friend."

"I know. I know." I spread my hands. "I need to talk to her alone. But those damned Amazigh are always there."

"You could disguise yourself as an Amazigh," he suggested.

I blinked. "You know, that might come in handy."

"I was jesting," Sunjata observed.

"Even so." I pointed at him. "It's a potential tool. Never set aside any potential tool that comes to hand, right?"

He shook his head. "I should have kept my mouth shut."

I ignored the comment. "What about Bodeshmun? I know he keeps the talisman on him, and I suspect I know where. Does he have any other weaknesses I might exploit? Wine? Women? Boys? Opium?"

"No, no, and no," Sunjata said. "He's vain, but he's suspicious and rigid. And he's not likely to be fooled by a disguise. Leander . . ." He fell silent a moment. "Leander, Bodeshmun's dangerous. More than the entire College of Horologists put together, and more than Astegal. Hannon's afraid of him, the Council's afraid of him, *I'm* afraid of him. When you move against Bodeshmun, I think you'd best be prepared to kill him. And to fly like hell once you do."

I frowned at him. "Why didn't you say this before?"

"I thought you'd give up sooner," he said flatly.

"Your confidence is touching," I commented. "Or is it your loyalty I should question?"

"No!" Sunjata's voice was low and fierce. "Her ladyship gave me my freedom. I would never betray her, no matter how much I doubt the merits of this endeavor." He looked away. "Let us say that I didn't expect you to fall in love at a single glance and become filled with noble purpose and determination." His lips quirked. "Although mayhap I should have known better." He looked back at me. "Ah. No denial this time?"

"No," I said quietly. "What I'm feeling . . . I'm not ready to call it love. By the Goddess, I barely know her! But . . ."

"But there it is." He wrapped his arms around his knees. "Are you seeing her again?"

"Tomorrow." I laughed. "My good lord Bodeshmun's arranged for a hunting party outside the city. I'm invited."

"*What?*" Sunjata's voice rose in disbelief. "A hunting party?"

I grinned at him. "I convinced him he'd best find a way to distract her, or she'd begin asking inconvenient questions. And the gods know that's true enough."

"Nothing like truth to leaven a good lie." Sunjata unwound his arms and rose. "Good luck, then. I'll see you anon."

Jest or no, I thought Sunjata's idea had merit. I summoned Ghanim and spun him a tale about wishing to obtain Amazigh garb, explaining that her ladyship kept some traditions of Terre d'Ange and celebrated the Longest Night with a masked fête. Ghanim listened without comment while one of the Carthaginians translated, his fierce gaze fixed on my face. Although I kept my features schooled to perfect sincerity, I had the strong feeling he didn't believe a word of it.

But to my surprise, Ghanim agreed readily. "There are Amazigh come to the city to trade," the Carthaginian brother translated. "If you give him money, he will obtain Amazigh garments for you."

I gave Ghanim the amount he deemed necessary for barter, realizing full well as I did that there was little to keep him from wrapping the veils around his own face to disguise his slave-brand, and escaping.

He pocketed the money and bowed, both hands pressed together.

"I trust your honor," I said to him.

Ghanim replied without waiting to hear my words in Punic. "Do not insult me," the Carthaginian translated.

I returned the Amazigh's salute. "Of course not."

He was gone the better part of the day. Fortunately, I had no need of my bearers, as I was entertaining one of Lord Solon's acquaintances within the city that afternoon: Boodes of Hiram, a doddering fellow who was the oldest member of the Council of Thirty. His wits wandered with age, although there were flashes of clarity that suggested why Solon had once counted the man a friend.

"Ptolemy Solon," Boodes mused. "By the Goddess, he was an ugly lad! Is he still?"

"Not a lad, I fear." I smiled. "But ugly, yes. Still, he's a mistress any man would envy."

The old fellow nodded; then his head slumped, face crumpling into his white beard. I was just beginning to worry when his head snapped upright. "Yes, of course. Your mother, is she not?"

"No, no," I corrected him. "I'm merely in her ladyship's household."

Boodes peered at me with rheumy eyes. "Are you sure? Betimes my memory fails me."

"Yes, my lord," I said. "Very sure, alas. Tell me, how fares the war in Aragonia?"

"Aragonia." His wrinkled lips worked. "Damn fine oranges they grow there. I used to gorge on them when I was a boy. You like oranges?"

"I do, my lord," I said politely.

"Good." Boodes nodded again. "Moderation, that's the thing. Overreach, and you'll end up with a sick belly. The old Hellenes understood it. Solon does. Astegal doesn't, nor does Bodeshmun."

I hesitated. "Do you speak of the war, my lord?"

He blinked his rheumy eyes at me. "I speak of oranges, young man."

By the time Boodes of Hiram departed, escorted by bearers who clearly bore a good deal of fondness for him, I wasn't entirely sure if he'd been trying to send me a subtle message of the sort Sunjata had mentioned, or if he was merely wandering in his wits. I'd rather liked the old fellow, and chose to believe it was the former. I found it heartening to think that there were those in Carthage concerned about the scope of Astegal's ambitions.

It was a good thing, since it put me in a tolerable frame of mind to deal with Ghanim's return. The Amazigh presented himself at the door of my chambers, his arms filled with dark indigo cloth. He bowed and said somewhat in Punic—or mayhap it was his native tongue—and indicated with pride a bloodstained rip in the fabric.

"Name of Elua!" I said, startled. "Did you kill someone for this?" I mimed a stabbing gesture.

Ghanim grinned. Thrusting out his left arm, he showed me a dagger strapped to his forearm. "Amazigh," he said with satisfaction.

"I see," I said slowly. I thought about calling for one of the Carthaginians to translate, but at need, one can accomplish a good deal without language. I studied Ghanim's face. Whatever he'd done, he reckoned it wholly acceptable with Amazigh culture. I hoped it was, because I wasn't about to inform Carthaginian authorities that I'd commissioned a slave to purchase Amazigh garments for me and discovered he'd killed to obtain them. "Will you show me how to wear it?" I asked, miming.

He nodded. I ushered him into my chambers, and spent a good hour struggling to master the intricate twists and folds of wrapping the head-scarf so that it formed a turban and veiled my lower face.

"Not bad," I said at last, studying myself in the mirror. If I darkened the skin of my face and hands with charcoal and kept my eyes narrowed, I could pass in very dim light. All that fabric provided good concealment.

Ghanim pointed to my waist and mimed drawing a sword. I rummaged in my trunks and fetched out my sword-belt, fastening it about my waist. The sword wasn't the right sort—a slender gentleman's blade, not the heavier weapons the Amazigh carried—but again, it would suffice to pass a cursory glance. Ghanim slapped my shoulder in approval and asked somewhat in a questioning tone.

"Honestly?" I said. "I've no idea, my friend. Not yet. But it seems a useful item to have." I accorded him a bow, pressing my palms together. "My thanks."

He bowed in return.

Once Ghanim had left, I practiced wrapping the head-scarf a few dozen more times, until I felt I could do it in my sleep. And then I took off the robe and burnoose, did my best to scour the stiff, dried blood from the robe with water from the washstand, and buried both items deep within my trunks.

In a single day, I'd acquired a ring and a disguise.

Tools. Dangerous, but useful.

I slept better that night and arose with a renewed sense of purpose. Truth be told, *I* could use the distraction of a hunting party as much as Sidonie. There was a certain measure of safety in Bodeshmun's managed contact. In the company of others, I could count on them to shunt aside any dangerous turns of conversation, and merely play at being the amicable courtier. She knew it was less than the whole truth, of course, but she would have no grounds to question it this day, and I would spend a few precious hours not feeling as though I walked a knife's edge of intrigue.

And I would be in her company.

The hunting party assembled outside the western gates of Carthage. Passing beneath the massive arch, I felt the same reluctant sense of awe I'd felt on first beholding the city. The walls were just so damned vast.

South of Carthage, it was desert; but here near the coast, it was fertile territory, rife with citrus and olive groves. We would be coursing hares today, riding astride and hunting with a breed of dog particular to Carthage, lean and speedy.

"Leander Maignard!" Gemelquart of Zinnrid hailed me, seated astride a dish-nosed grey mare. His wife, whom I had met at his dinner party, was on one side of him. Princess Sidonie was on the other. "I'm pleased you could join us."

I bowed to them. "I am honored."

"You will remember my lady Arishat, I trust." Gemelquart chuckled. "And I am given to understand you have spent some hours entertaining her highness."

I gazed up at Sidonie's face. "I have had that honor, yes."

"Huntsman!" Gemelquart shouted. "Fetch this man a mount and a bow!"

There was a period of milling chaos while all was made ready. I was provided with a stalwart little chestnut mare and a short hunting bow. It seemed there was to be a picnic luncheon. A battalion of servants was dispatched to make ready for it. Along with Gemelquart and his lady wife, there were some half a dozen Carthaginian nobles taking part in the excursion. Most of them, I did not know. Bodeshmun was there, looking distinctly unlike himself in ornate hunting leathers, glowering into his beard.

At last, the horns blew and we rode forth at a jog. The dogs strained at their leashes. I positioned myself beside Sidonie.

"Messire Maignard," she acknowledged me in greeting.

I winced. "Have we returned to such formality, your highness?"

Her brows rose. "Do you not think it wise?"

I wasn't sure how to answer. I made a show of testing the draw of my hunting bow. "I aspire to wisdom, my lady. I do not believe I possess it, not yet. But my lord Ptolemy Solon holds that happiness is the highest form of wisdom." I made a broad gesture. "Today the sun is shining and we are engaged in a pleasant pursuit in the company of friends. If that is wisdom, let us be content."

"You are content with little." Her tone was unreadable. She didn't believe it. I knew; I could feel it on my skin. She doubted me. I had revealed too much when I'd stumbled over speaking D'Angeline the other night, when I'd glanced at the guard, when I'd warned her against questioning Bodeshmun.

I bowed in the saddle. "Today, yes."

Sidonie studied me. "So be it."

So we hunted.

We rode only a short distance from the vast walls of Carthage. The huntsmen sounded their horns and loosed the hounds. We rode after them, whooping in the chase. I felt invigorated. The hounds were graceful, lean-bellied creatures with plumed tails. In an olive grove, they flushed a brace of hare. I shot and missed as the hares dodged and doubled, the hounds yelping. One of the Carthaginian lords I didn't know set out in hot pursuit, followed by others.

"You're not a terribly good shot, are you, Leander?"

Beneath the shade of an olive tree, Sidonie drew rein alongside me, accompanied by Gemelquart and his wife.

"No." I smiled because she'd used my name. "Are you?"

She laughed. "No."

"I am," Gemelquart said. "But I'm under orders not to overexert myself."

"That, and you use your weak lungs as an excuse for laziness," his wife, Arishat, said, but she was smiling as she said it.

"Alais would enjoy this," Sidonie mused. "She likes the hunt, and she loves dogs. She had one for many years—"

"Ah, yes, Alais!" Gemelquart interrupted her. "Your highness, I would be delighted to make your sister a gift of one of these dogs. They are royal Phoenician hunting dogs, a very ancient strain. As you can see, they are possessed of tremendous speed—"

"It was a wolfhound," Sidonie said, frowning. "She was killed."

"Such a sad thing to lose a beloved pet!" Arishat exclaimed. She was a Carthaginian lady some years younger than her husband, with pleasant features and a lovely speaking voice. "Why, I had a cat, a pretty little Menekhetan cat, that I'd raised from a kitten. She used to follow me—"

"Killed by a bear?" Lost in thought, Sidonie blinked. "Or was it a boar?"

"Let me summon the huntsman," Gemelquart said smoothly. He raised one arm and gave a shout, beckoning. "Doubtless he'll be able to advise us on the dogs' qualities and recommend one suitable for a young lady's companion."

In the distance, the huntsman turned, heeding Gemelquart's summons. Bodeshmun heard it, too, and reined his mount in our direction.

"Why can't I remember?" Sidonie reached out and grabbed my wrist without thinking. There was a panicked strength in her grip and slow terror rising behind her black eyes. "Was it a boar or a bear? Leander, why can't I remember how Alais' dog was killed?"

Ah, gods, what in the seven hells did Prince Imriel have to do with the death of her sister's dog? I couldn't even begin to guess. Out of the corner of my eye, I saw Bodeshmun looming nearer. Gemelquart gave me a helpless grimace.

"Sunstroke." I freed my wrist, leaned over in the saddle to place my hand on Sidonie's brow. "Forgive us, my lady, we were thoughtless. The sun is much stronger in Carthage than you're accustomed to. Being raised on Cythera, I forget."

"I don't have sunstroke," she said in a low tone, batting my hand away.

I caught her hand and squeezed it hard enough to feel the small bones grinding together. "Yes," I said. "You do."

She stared at me.

"I fear he's right, your highness," Arishat said in her soothing voice. "Oh, I feel a fool! You feel disordered in your wits, yes? 'Tis a common malady. I've suffered it myself. In the cooler weather, one forgets the sun's strength." She dismounted and took hold of Sidonie's mount's bridle. "Come, let us sit here in the shade together. We'll have the picnic brought to us."

I let go of Sidonie's hand and nodded imperceptibly.

"Sunstroke," she murmured.

"A touch of fever, likely," Gemelquart said with cheerful sympathy. "A cool compress will help. I pray you will forgive us our thoughtlessness. Ah, Bodeshmun!" He greeted the Chief Horologist. "I fear her highness is unwell."

"I'm very sorry, your highness." Bodeshmun gazed down at Sidonie. "I'll send for a physician immediately."

"Thank you, my lord, but that won't be necessary." She returned his gaze, her face pale. "Already, I'm feeling better.

I'm sure if I rest here a little and have something cool to drink, I'll be fine."

"Nonetheless." He snapped his fingers and summoned one of the minor lords. "We can't be too careful, can we?"

A physician arrived in short order. He examined Sidonie and confirmed a diagnosis of sunstroke, prescribing cool baths and rest in a darkened room. Bodeshmun sent for her covered palanquin. While we waited, he strolled some distance from the olive grove, beckoning for Gemelquart and me to accompany him.

"What provoked this?" the Chief Horologist asked us.

Gemelquart shrugged. "Damned if I know. Something to do with her sister's dog getting killed. She wouldn't be swayed from talking about it."

"She couldn't remember how it happened," I added. "It scared her."

Bodeshmun rubbed his chin. "That's not good."

"Well, thank young Maignard here for convincing her it was merely a touch of sun," Gemelquart said with some asperity. "Because I was at my wits' end. Isn't there something you can do?"

"Not without . . . damage," Bodeshmun said slowly.

My blood ran cold.

"So?" Gemelquart retorted. "Do we *need* her undamaged?"

"For the moment, yes." Bodeshmun turned his quelling look on Gemelquart. "You forget, my lord, that her father is the Cruarch of Alba. *He* has returned to Alba's shores, where my spell no longer binds him. It could not be helped."

"I forget nothing," Gemelquart muttered. "I'm merely saying—"

"The Cruarch is bewildered," Bodeshmun continued, ignoring him. "For so long as he believes his eldest daughter is sincere in her marriage, he will remain frozen in inaction, unwilling to commit troops against Carthage. And yes, we *need* that, Gemelquart. We need to keep Alba and Terre d'Ange bewildered and unable to act. We *need* to secure Aragonia. And we *need* to trade on the strength of this marriage to force Terre d'Ange and Alba to bow before the inevitable."

Gemelquart glanced back toward the olive grove. "Yet I fear your spell is weakening."

"Time and distance strain it." Bodeshmun waved a dismissive hand. "Once the princess is reunited with Astegal, all will be well. She will forget her fears. I will see to it that it happens sooner rather than later."

"Do," the other said curtly.

That earned him another quelling look. In the bright Carthaginian sunlight, Bodeshmun seemed to swell and tower, while Gemelquart quailed before him. I clasped my hands behind my back and looked away, doing my best to seem inconspicuous and innocuous.

"Do not presume to give me orders," Bodeshmun said in a voice of quiet menace. "I have wrought my life's work with these spells. The world has never seen their like before. What does the Council know of what is entailed in such magics?"

"Nothing," Gemelquart said lightly. "Nothing at all!" He forced a laugh. "I should return. We don't want to give the princess further cause for suspicion."

Bodeshmun watched him go, resting a heavy hand on my shoulder. "Do you know," he said wistfully, "I almost wish Ptolemy Solon were here. I have no peers capable of appreciating my work, only acolytes and fearful allies." His hand tightened on me. "But you'll tell him, won't you?"

"Yes, my lord," I murmured.

He laughed deep in his chest. "Have you discovered how I bound the princess?"

"No," I said truthfully. "Not yet."

"Ah, well! Keep trying." Bodeshmun laughed again, giving my shoulder a rough shake. "You acquitted yourself well today. You're a useful tool, Solon's pretty little monkey."

I smiled at him. "I try."

THIRTY-FIVE

For a day, I heard nothing. I was in an agony of suspense. Ah, gods! The irony abounded. Bodeshmun, sodding *Bodeshmun*, trusted me. The man Ptolemy Solon himself admired for his cleverness—I'd fooled him. That was good. That was very, very good.

But it was Sidonie's trust I needed.

And that, I feared I was in danger of losing.

Such a difficult game it was. Lies and a marrow of truth. Everything I'd said cut close to the bone. Again and again, I relived that moment in the olive grove. Her hand clutching my wrist, the quiet panic rising. She had listened. She'd heeded me. But she didn't trust me. Why should she? I'd seen the fear dawning in her eyes.

I was afraid, too.

For the first time in years, I drilled with my sword. I practiced in the privacy of my chambers, feeling woefully inadequate. I wasn't a swordsman, wasn't a warrior. I knew how to hold a blade, a few rudimentary thrusts and parries. Nothing more.

Still, I drilled.

"My lord." It was Kratos who interrupted me. "The princess has sent word wondering if you would care for another game of chess."

"Has she?" I snatched the letter from his hands.

"So I'm told," Kratos said laconically. "Not succeeded in bedding her yet, have you, my lord?"

I lifted my gaze from the vellum. "That would be an offense against General Astegal, would it not? Against Carthage itself?"

Kratos shrugged his heavy wrestler's shoulders. "Do I care?"

"I don't know," I said. "Do you?"

He laughed. "Not much."

"If you value your tongue, you'll watch it," I said in warning. "I mean it."

Whatever Kratos saw in my face, it impressed my seriousness on him. He merely gave a brief nod and went to fetch the other bearers.

By the time I arrived at the Sarkal villa, my stomach was in knots. Whatever Sidonie wanted, I didn't think it was a game of chess. And as pleasant as the thought was, I was fairly sure it wasn't a dalliance. I suspected she wanted answers. And while I would like nothing more than to give them to her, I didn't know how in the name of Blessed Elua I could accomplish it without alerting her guards.

In the salon, the chess board was set on the table. The ranks of onyx and ivory figures faced off across the board, their ruby eyes glittering. Sidonie stood beside it, her back very straight, her features calm and controlled. Behind her, one of the ever-present Amazigh stood with his back to the wall.

"Good day, your highness," I greeted her. "I'm pleased to see you're feeling better."

"Thank you." She turned to the Amazigh. "Masmud, you may go."

His eyes widened between veils of cloth. "General Astegal has ordered us to protect you at all times."

"Messire Maignard is a concerned friend and no threat." A hint of steel crept into her voice. "And in Astegal's absence, I command here. I am commanding you now. *Go*."

The Amazigh hesitated.

Sidonie's voice cracked like a whip. "*Now*, or I will have you dismissed!"

He went.

She rounded on me. "Now. Tell me. What is it that passes here? What is it you know that I do not? Why do I find myself unable to recall simple things? And what is it you fear from Bodeshmun and my guards?"

Oh, gods.

There was so much, I barely knew where to begin. And I had a feeling there wasn't much time. I didn't know to whom the Amazigh reported directly, but I desperately hoped it wasn't Bodeshmun.

"Sidonie," I whispered. "All is not as it seems. You've been ensorceled. Parts of your memory are missing. Parts are false. Terre d'Ange is not allied with Carthage. And you are not in love with Astegal."

Her face was rigid. "I don't believe you."

"It's a spell," I said helplessly. "There's somewhat on you, somewhat on your person, some token of Astegal's that binds you. I thought it was the signet ring, but it must be somewhat else. If you can find it, remove it; it will weaken the spell."

"There's nothing *on* me!" Her voice rose. "I'm passing familiar with my own person, Leander, and I think I would know! Who *are* you? What do you want? What does Cythera want?"

"I'm trying to help you!" I hissed. "And if Bodeshmun

finds out, I'll be lucky if he settles for killing me. For the love of Elua, my lady, you're in *danger*! Please believe me. You cannot let them suspect."

"Suspect *what*?" she demanded in frustration.

"That you know about the spell!" I ground my teeth. "All right, mayhap Ptolemy Solon was wrong about part of it. But the ring, Astegal's ring—"

"Take it if it concerns you that much!" Sidonie wrenched the heavy signet ring from her finger and hurled it at me. It bounced off my chest and fell clinking to the floor, rolling beneath the table.

"No!" I took a deep breath. "Not that ring—" There were footsteps hurrying in the hallway outside the salon. I dropped to my knees. "Sidonie de la Courcel, in the name of Blessed Elua and his Companions, by all that is holy, by all that I've ever held dear in my life, I swear to you that I mean you no harm and all I have told you is true. In your heart, in your deepest heart, you know somewhat is amiss. Please, please, please, if you do nothing else, do *not* let them suspect it. Bring me to New Carthage with you. I swear to you, I will prove my words and my loyalty. I am begging you, please, to look into your heart and trust me in this."

Sidonie stared at me without answering.

"Your highness!" The steward bustled into the salon, his voice distraught. "Forgive me, but it is unseemly . . ." He paused. "Is all well here?"

"Yes," Sidonie said slowly. "I'm afraid I dropped my ring. Messire Maignard was retrieving it for me."

"I see." The steward eyed me with relief as I reached beneath the table and found the signet ring. I rose without comment, bowed, and handed it to Sidonie. She examined it, then slid it onto her finger. "Is it damaged?"

"Happily, no." She smiled briefly at the steward. "Why

are you here, messire? Is there somewhat that demands my attention?"

"No." He swallowed. "But the guard . . . Forgive me, your highness. In my lord Astegal's absence, it is unseemly that you should meet alone with another man."

Her brows rose. "Surely you do not suspect me of dallying with Messire Maignard?"

"No, no, of course not!" The steward wrung his hands. "And I am sure that if his lordship were here, he would countenance it without a thought. But in his absence, it falls to me to ensure that there is no cause for misunderstanding or idle gossip. I merely seek to do my duty, your highness. I beg of you, please do not punish me for it."

"I see." Sidonie gazed at him for a long time, during which the steward went white, then red. "You must understand, in Terre d'Ange, matters are very different. But I suppose I am in Carthage now, albeit for only a few more days. Very well, since you have such concern for semblances, you may stay and observe our game for yourself. I'm weary of my lord's Amazigh guards hovering over me as though to dispatch an assassin at a moment's notice."

The steward sighed. "A thousand thanks, your highness."

Sidonie and I sat at the table opposite one another. I felt strung tight, quivering like a plucked harp-string. Oh, gods, that had been a near thing! I'd never known fear before, not like that. Fear for me, fear for her. As long as it served his plans, Bodeshmun wanted her undamaged. But I didn't doubt for an instant that he would throw her to the wolves the moment she was no longer useful to him.

A moment I was trying to hasten.

I played very badly. Sidonie was quiet, concentrating on the board. I watched her annihilate me piece by steady piece. It seemed impossible to believe that no more than a week had passed since we'd played our first game. I didn't feel like the same Leander Maignard who'd sat opposite her that day and blushed at her teasing barbs. The stakes had grown far too high.

"Have you had word from Lord Astegal?" I inquired presently. "You mentioned leaving within days."

"Yes." She captured one of my knights without looking up. "A courier came this morning. It seems matters have progressed swiftly. King Roderico has surrendered."

"Then Aragonia has fallen?" I asked.

Sidonie shook her head. "There was a coup. One of his young cousins has declared himself regent in exile." She watched my move. "Actually, he's a distant kinsman of mine, too. Serafin L'Envers y Aragon. We're related through my grandmother on my mother's side."

I didn't know if that was a safe topic or not. "Ah."

"Astegal says he's holed up in Amílcar with what's left of the Aragonian army. He doesn't expect the fighting to resume until spring." She deftly captured another piece. "I imagine Serafin will attempt to negotiate with the Euskerri and promise them the sovereignty Roderico refused to consider in return for their aid. I don't know why we didn't try to settle that matter earlier when . . ."

Her voice trailed off.

I saw it again, the perplexity and fear. There was a memory missing here. I had no idea what it was, some piece of political intrigue. All I knew was that I wanted to cup her face in my hands, shower her with tender kisses, whisper all of her missing secrets in her ear until the fear and uncertainty were gone.

"I'm sure that all will be well," I said gently. "If King Roderico has surrendered, no doubt this young rebel kinsman will see his wisdom in time and follow. When do you leave?"

"In three days' time." With an effort, Sidonie focused her attention on the board. Her hand trembled slightly as she moved a rook. "So I fear this is our final game, Messire Maignard. Unless . . ."

I sacrificed a pawn in a hopeless gambit. "Unless?"

Her black gaze lifted to meet mine. "Unless you wish to accompany me." Her tone was light, lighter than I could have managed. "You said you'd a fancy to see New Carthage, and a D'Angeline princess ought to have courtiers. Might your lord Solon see fit to allow it?"

Despite the fear, despite the tension, my heart soared. "I'm sure he would. I'm here to obtain Carthage's goodwill, and I've obtained all the assurances he could hope for. I'll dispatch them forthwith and place myself at your disposal."

"Very well." Sidonie declined my pawn's gambit, moving her queen decisively. "Check and mate. I will be pleased to have your company."

"And I to provide it," I murmured. I studied the board, then tipped my king.

"So our game continues?" she inquired.

I wanted to say to her, *It's not a game; it's in deadly earnest*. But Sidonie knew. I didn't need to hear her say it. I *saw* her, saw all of her. The raised chin and the firm, demanding brows, at odds with the delicate bones of her face. All the pride and determination, all the rising fury and suspicion, terror and vulnerability. A measure of trust I hadn't earned. Fault-lines created through cruel artifice. It made my heart ache and my throat tighten.

I loved her.

No point in denying it, no point in doubting it. It was unlikely, improbable, and true. If I had to lay my broken heart on the altar of love and let it be destroyed in a glorious blaze to secure her happiness, so be it. I would do it.

"Always," I said hoarsely. "*Always.*"

There it was again, that word.

The word lodged like a stone in my chest. It felt like a stone in my mouth, heavy on my tongue. Always. Always and always. Why did it make my eyes sting? I looked away. Sidonie looked away. Her steward, Astegal's steward, cleared his throat.

"Then I will see you in New Carthage," she murmured.

What I wanted to say was *I will follow you to the ends of the earth. I will be whatever you ask of me: courtier, savior, lover, and husband, master and slave. Anything, everything.*

Only ask.

What I said was, "Yes."

"Good." She nodded. "To New Carthage."

Thirty-six

I spent three days putting my affairs in order.

I wrote out a lengthy letter to Ptolemy Solon, employing one of the codes her ladyship had devised, one that owed naught to the Guild, but merely to her own prodigious intellect.

I met with Maharbal and haggled over the terms of ending my lease of his cousin's villa earlier than expected. I thanked the steward Anysus for his service and gave him a purse to share amongst the household.

I wrote out letters of manumission as I had promised for my bearers and had them witnessed and stamped by the city official in charge of such matters. I presented them to the lads and asked what they willed.

Ghanim received his letter with fierce joy. Through one of the Carthaginians, he made me to understand that he would be returning to the desert to seek vengeance against the brother who had wronged him. I wished him well. In turn, he uttered a lengthy prayer on my behalf in the Amazigh tongue that no one could translate.

I'd never thought before what a strange thing it was the way lives intersected. I had changed the course of Ghanim's life, while the only trace of his impact on mine was a blood-stained robe hidden in the depths of my trunks. Passing strange.

The brothers elected to remain in Carthage, working as porters or bearers on the docks. It didn't surprise me. They were young enough to be resilient. A couple weeks' worth of a good diet had given them a measure of strength and, more important, hope.

Kratos . . . Kratos was the surprise.

"If it's all the same to you, I'll stay in your service," he said, pocketing his letter of manumission. "Might be you could use a loyal man."

I dismissed the others, then studied Kratos' homely face. "How loyal?"

He shrugged. "I'm not a fool, my lord. Most people don't see that. You did. I know you're up to something. But you kept your word. I'll keep mine. You're not buying my loyalty this time. I'm giving it freely."

"Why?" I asked. "You're the one was clever enough to be concerned about my business being dangerous."

"True." A broad smile spread over his face. "Truth be told, I don't rightly know. I'm curious. You're not what I took you to be."

"And what was that?" I inquired.

"A shallow fellow," Kratos said frankly. "A smooth-tongued politician delighted by his own cleverness. Now . . ." He shrugged again. "I don't know. You seem different, or mayhap there's more to you than I gauged. I'm long past my prime. I've got nowhere to go, no family left to me. Those lads, the Carthaginian boys . . ." He jerked his thumb at the door. "They're young. They've a chance to build lives for themselves. Might be they'll succeed; might be they'll fail.

Me, I'm a broken-down wrestler with only a few good working years left in me. Might as well satisfy my curiosity. Good enough?"

I put out my hand. "Good enough."

Kratos clasped it. "Care to tell me about this danger, my lord?"

"Not yet." I shook my head. "For the moment, suffice to say that as far as you're concerned, I'm exactly what you took me to be. And no careless remarks about the princess." I released his hand and pointed at him. "I meant my threat."

He grinned at me. "Not so effective now that I'm a freedman, my lord."

"I don't think General Astegal's Amazigh guards will be concerned for such niceties," I observed. "My lord Bodeshmun has made it clear to me that a similar threat hangs over my head, the mantle of Cythera's protection notwithstanding."

"Point taken." Kratos sobered. "So why is it you're doing . . . whatever you're doing?"

I sorted through the reasons I'd once believed. None of them seemed adequate. Sidonie's face surfaced in my memory, filled with that terrible mixture of fear, vulnerability, strength, and unlikely trust.

"Because I have to," I said simply.

Kratos nodded. "I understand."

I laughed. "That, my friend, makes one of us."

I'd told my bearers that their freedom would take effect the day I sailed. To that end, I called on Captain Deimos and informed him that I required passage to New Carthage. He took the news with equanimity. We discussed the necessary preparations, including dispatching my letter to Ptolemy Solon by some other means. Happily, Deimos knew of an Ephesian merchant-ship that would be making port at Paphos, and promised to arrange for the letter's delivery.

"What do you know of matters in New Carthage?" I asked him when we'd finished. Sailors always had the best gossip.

Deimos smiled briefly. "On the docks, they're saying that Astegal's set himself up like a king there. Every city and village within a hundred leagues is paying tribute and pledging loyalty to him. He's not going to be content to wear the Council's yoke for long. Is that what you mean?"

"Indeed," I said. "What of this rebel, this Serafin?"

"Ah." Deimos glanced around. "A stubborn fellow with a hopeless cause. I imagine he'll be crushed in time."

"No doubt." I clapped his shoulder. "No doubt."

As I returned from the harbor, I paid a visit to Jabnit of Philosir, ostensibly to inquire if he had an interest in purchasing a necklace set with rubies and seed-pearls that had been among Ptolemy Solon's tribute-gifts, an item for which I'd found no suitable recipient. We haggled for a time and drank sweet tea. When I mentioned that I was bound for New Carthage and needed coin more than gems, Jabnit's eyes lit up.

"At the invitation of the princess!" he exclaimed. "Such an honor. Will you sail under the auspices of the House of Sarkal?"

"No, no." I sipped my tea. "My lord Ptolemy Solon has vouchsafed me the usage of a ship and crew for as long as I require." I laughed. "'Tis a great deal of ship for a lone emissary, but his eminence has his foibles!"

Jabnit pressed his hands together, his eyes twinkling. "You know, I have a most excellent idea."

I listened while he proposed to purchase the necklace for a generous price. In turn, Jabnit asked that I provide passage for his assistant, Sunjata, and once we reached New Carthage, hire out a few of my crew to serve as bodyguards while Sunjata went about the business of acquiring looted gems and jewelry at an advantageous price.

"Think of it!" Jabnit said. "Your men would otherwise be sitting idle in port, spending your wages on dicing and wenching. This way, they will spend *my* wages. And it is a very short journey between old Carthage and new. If your ship will ferry precious cargo for the House of Philosir, I will give you a percentage of the profits." He gave me a broad wink. "And I do not think you will mind Sunjata's company."

"Not at all." I smiled at the fat gem-merchant. "What an excellent idea, my lord."

He chortled. "I knew you were a clever fellow!"

Sunjata was summoned from the rear of the establishment and given the news. He gave me a long, slow smile that could have meant anything. "I'll make ready to leave at once," he said to Jabnit. "How very clever it is of you to have conceived of this opportunity."

Jabnit smiled complacently. "It is, isn't it?"

Clever. I thought about what Kratos had said of me. He was right; a mere two weeks ago I would have been falling all over myself with inward delight for having arranged this so neatly. Now I was merely relieved to have it done.

How odd.

It was the difference, I supposed, between training and being engaged in the actual practice of the arts of covertcy. They say callow soldiers either become men or die quickly on the battlefield. This was a different field of battle, but the stakes were no less high. I'd never known real danger before. Bored and idle on Cythera, a hawk on a tether, I'd thought to crave danger and excitement.

Now I'd had a surfeit of it.

And then there was Sidonie.

That was the oddest thing of all. I truly hadn't believed

one could form such strong feelings for another in such a short time. It seemed an impossible fancy, a poet's tale. Now I was awash in emotion, fairly drowning in it.

I sent a letter to notify her that my own plans for travel to New Carthage were in readiness. She sent a reply in short order, confirming the time of departure. A total of six ships would be escorting her to New Carthage, and she invited me to join their small fleet in the interest of safety. I sent a polite reply accepting with thanks, and dispatched Kratos to notify Captain Deimos.

Gods, I wanted to see her.

And it would be worse in New Carthage. I had to prepare myself for that. There was somewhat between us, and I *knew* Sidonie felt it. That spark of desire when she had touched me. Even when she'd grasped my wrist in fear the day of the hunting party. I could still feel her grip. On my flesh, in my bones.

But time and distance strained the spell, Bodeshmun said. He was convinced that she would forget her fears once she was reunited with Astegal. I wasn't, not entirely. Bodeshmun saw her as a pawn, not a person. Her curiosity was merely an annoyance to be managed. He hadn't truly seen the sharp intellect struggling against the magics that bound her thoughts. Beyond whatever purpose she served, he couldn't have cared less about Sidonie herself. And for that, I was profoundly grateful, because if he had, Bodeshmun might have seen what I did.

Still, it wasn't likely he was entirely wrong, either. Likely the spell *would* exert new strength.

And Astegal . . .

I'd have to see her with Astegal, this ambitious Carthaginian general styling himself a king in Aragonia. The man she thought she loved. I would have to witness it and smile pleasantly. The thought was unbelievably galling.

On the night before our departure, I went through my things once more. One of the trunks her ladyship had given me had a false bottom, a standard practice as such things went. It was there that I'd stowed the Amazigh garments and the ring Sunjata had made for me.

I took a moment to study the latter. I hoped to hell it was an accurate copy. Like as not it was. Sunjata had had the original in his possession, and he had an eye for detail trained by her ladyship.

A simple thing, a knot of gold. A love-token. Sidonie had given Prince Imriel the original. I slid the copy on my finger, wondering what it had meant to them. Some bit of girlish folly, I'd assumed when Ptolemy Solon had explained it to me. That seemed a very long time ago, when I'd been a different Leander Maignard, a callow young man still capable of imagining a Sidonie de la Courcel prone to girlish folly.

Lamplight gleamed softly on the gold. I felt a knot tighten in my throat, tighten around my heart. I tightened my hand to a fist.

"Astegal," I said aloud. "I'm coming for you."

Thirty-seven

We departed for New Carthage on a sullen day, the skies grey and cloudy, spitting fitful bouts of rain. I stood beside my borrowed palanquin, watching hired porters carry my trunks onto Captain Deimos' ship. Everything was packed away, the Amazigh garb and the false ring safely hidden once more.

I'd arrived early, hoping for a glimpse of Sidonie. A glimpse was all I got. I saw her ornate palanquin in the midst of a considerable entourage, flanked by her Amazigh guards. They escorted her aboard the House of Sarkal's flagship. Her figure was cloaked and hooded against the chilly drizzle.

Still, I knew her.

I knew her by the way she moved, at once controlled and deft. There was a neatness to it, a precise grace. I'd seen it every time she left or entered a room. I'd seen it sitting opposite her, a chess board between us, in the way she had made her choices and moved the pieces.

Oddly, it made me think of the time my father had taken

me to see the Cruarch's entourage pass. They'd had that quality, some of Drustan mab Necthana's Cruithne warriors. The Cruarch himself had had it. I'd shouted along with all the other children, tossing petals in his path. He'd glanced my way. His eldest daughter had inherited his black eyes, too.

Beside me, Sunjata shivered. "Gods, Leander! You are truly a man besotted."

I jerked my chin at the ship. "Go aboard, then."

"I will," he said, suiting actions to words.

On the flagship, Sidonie vanished from view. On Captain Deimos' ship, all my things were loaded. There was no more reason to linger on the quay. Kratos waited patiently to accompany me, blinking against the drizzle, his grey-brown hair plastered to his skull. I'd paid one of the porters to take his place at the palanquin, returning it to the villa of Maharbal's cousin. Once that was done, my briefly held slaves were all freedmen. Ghanim eyed me hungrily, eager to enjoy his freedom and pursue his vengeance.

"Go," I said gently to them. "May Blessed Elua hold and keep you."

They went at a swift jog.

I watched them go, wondering. Wondering what had prompted me to speak the words of a blessing I hadn't uttered since childhood. Wondering what private tale of great and terrible romance Ghanim inhabited. Wondering whether the Carthaginian brothers would turn freedom into success or sink back into abject poverty. Wondering what story the hired porter had to tell. All four of them trotted lightly, carrying the empty palanquin. Soon they were out of sight.

Gone.

I sighed. I had the strangest feeling that I'd been here before, done this before. That there had been too many leavetakings in my short life. It wasn't true, but I felt it all the same.

Kratos put his hand beneath my elbow, steadying me. "Ready, my lord?"

I gazed at his stolid face. The squashed nose, the shrewd eyes. "Yes."

He nodded. "Then let's board."

As Jabnit had indicated, the journey was a fairly short one. New Carthage was an old name; the port city had been founded by a Carthaginian conqueror before Blessed Elua walked the earth. Aragonia *had* been part of Carthage's empire, that was true. And then it had been a Tiberian holding, even as Terre d'Ange itself had been long ago. But Tiberium's star had set, and like Terre d'Ange, Aragonia had been an independent and sovereign nation for many centuries.

At least until now.

Throughout the short journey, the weather continued to be miserable. It wasn't truly cold this far south, but it was cool enough that the rain made one feel dank and chilled. Sunjata and I spent a good deal of time taking refuge in my cabin and speculating, while Kratos entertained himself by dicing with the sailors.

"Do you suppose Ptolemy Solon was wrong about Astegal's token being hidden on Sidonie's person?" I asked after I'd told Sunjata about my last encounter with her. "She seemed quite convinced it wasn't."

"It's possible." Sunjata reclined in a hammock, one foot braced on the floor, rocking himself gently. "As I understand, there's more than one way to construct a spell."

"You're the one secretly apprenticed to a horologist," I observed. "Your guess is likely to be better than mine. Why do they call themselves that, anyway? It seems to me that they study a good deal more than the cosmos."

He smiled. "True. It didn't begin that way. The study of arcane arts have flourished since Bodeshmun was appointed." He rocked in his hammock for a moment, then added, "You know, it may well be Solon's inquiries long ago that piqued Bodeshmun's interest."

"That's a dire thought," I commented.

"Mayhap it's one of the reasons he agreed to help you," Sunjata said. "Who knows what goes through the Wise Ape's head?"

I snorted. "It's not *me* he agreed to help. I'm the one taking the risks, that's all."

"Yes, of course." Sunjata smiled crookedly at me. "You just seem to have grown singularly . . . invested . . . in the cause."

I ignored the comment. "So what do you think? About the spell?"

"Hmm." He pushed with his foot, rocking. "Leander, what if it's not one thing you're looking for? What if it's *everything*?"

"How so?" I asked.

Sunjata gazed fixedly at me. "Everything. What if Bodeshmun's managed to stitch and bind the spell into every garment, every piece of jewelry the princess possesses?"

I thought about it. "Is that possible?"

"Yes," he said. "I believe it is."

"There's bound to be some point . . . the bath, mayhap . . ." I thought more about it. "Well, no. I suppose it could be managed if her attendants were careful and clever. Hairpins, earrings, nightgowns."

He nodded. "So you'd have to get her mother-naked to break the spell. Or at least that half of it." Another crooked smile. "That's a prospect you shouldn't mind."

"Yes, well it would have been a great deal simpler to remove a single ring," I said.

"Oh, like Astegal's will be?" Sunjata raised his brows at me.

I shook my head. "That's different. I don't expect that

to be easy. But if his token had been the House of Sarkal's signet ring, I tell you, Sunjata, half the spell that binds her would already be broken."

"And you a happier man," he said.

"I can't help how I feel." I gazed at him. "I'm sorry, I never meant to hurt you. Are you jealous?"

"Jealous." Sunjata folded his arms behind his head. "I'm not sure that's the right word for it. We've been friends for a long time, you and I. Lovers when it suited us. I never expected anything more than that, and I daresay you didn't, either. So, no. And yet . . ." He stared at the ceiling. "What you're feeling, I've never felt. Let us say I'm envious."

"Don't be," I said. "Remember, if I do succeed in breaking the spell, the first thing she'll remember is Prince Imriel."

"There is that." He glanced at me. "Are you so certain she's not capable of loving more than one man?"

"I don't know." I sighed. "Believe me, I wonder about it every day."

"*I* think you need to believe it, Leander." Sunjata smiled with surprising gentleness. "Will it truly hurt all the more if you're wrong?"

"Yes," I said. "It will."

The weather cleared at last on the day we sailed into the port of New Carthage. I nearly wished it hadn't, since it felt almost as though the weather itself was in league with Astegal. Still, it meant we were able to be comfortable above the deck, gazing at the city that was our new temporary home.

It wasn't nearly as formidable as old Carthage, but it was imposing enough. The harbor was large, with heavy fortifications on either side, fortresses mounted with engines of war. Here and there, one could see foundered ships that had not yet been salvaged. But most of Carthage's fleet had survived intact, and the waters were thick with war-ships.

"What happened to the Aragonian fleet?" I asked Sunjata.

"Destroyed," he said soberly.

"The whole thing?" I asked. He nodded.

Like old Carthage, New Carthage was walled, although the walls were a fraction of the size. And too, the city was built on a hill, sloping down to the harbor. Unlike old Carthage, here the hill was topped with a sizable palace, dominating all it surveyed.

That, I thought, would be where Astegal had ensconced himself.

We were stopped and our papers examined. New papers, stamped with the seal of the House of Sarkal, courtesy of Sidonie's steward. The captain who examined them shrugged quizzically, but he let us pass.

There was a procession of mounted Carthaginian soldiers in full regalia making its way toward the quay to meet the flagship. As we waited our turn to dock, I studied the fellow at the head of the procession.

"Astegal?" I asked Sunjata.

"That's him."

He was a tall man, but he sat lightly in the saddle. Black hair bound with a gold fillet. Strong features in the hawk-nosed Carthaginian mold. A narrow beard dyed a striking scarlet. Above it, he was smiling broadly, watching as the flagship was moored. His teeth were very white.

I hated him already.

Trumpets blared as Sidonie appeared at the top of the ramp, flanked by her Amazigh guards. Today it was warm enough that she needed no cloak. She was wearing the pale yellow gown. Sunlight gleamed on her hair, sparkled on the diamonds at her ears and throat.

My heart ached more than I would have thought possible.

Astegal's smile widened as she descended. He made her a courtly bow, a cloak of Tyrian purple swirling around him. He didn't need a cloak, either. It was just for show. The trumpets blared again. To the accompanying cheers of his soldiers, Astegal swept Sidonie into his arms and kissed her.

"Easy, my lord," Kratos said at my left shoulder.

I hadn't realized I was gripping the railing with such force that the wood was splintering beneath my nails. Sunjata gave me a worried look. I forced myself to breathe slowly and relax.

We had to wait some time to dock and disembark, but a second delegation arrived, composed of Aragonian peers with stilted smiles and hatred in their eyes. Foremost among them was a tall, slender old fellow with silvery hair and beard.

"Roderico de Aragon, I'll wager," Sunjata remarked.

Kratos whistled. "The deposed king?"

"He's a political hostage . . . ha!" Sunjata nudged me with his elbow. "Well, well. Look who's here. Justina."

I followed his gaze to spot an old childhood companion in the midst of the Aragonian peers. Justina. I hadn't seen her in the better part of five years. Long ago, she, Sunjata, and I had all trained together under her ladyship's aegis.

"I didn't know she was in Aragonia," I said.

"Neither did I," Sunjata replied. "But her ladyship casts her nets far and wide. Well, that's a gift from the gods."

"Good," I said. "Because we're going to need all the divine providence the gods have to offer."

Kratos glanced from one to the other of us. Over the course of the voyage, I'd assured Sunjata that he was trustworthy. Still, it was the first time we'd spoken openly in front of him. I could see the flicker of curiosity in his gaze, but he kept his mouth shut. Good man.

The throng was still there when we finally disembarked.

I paused at the top of the ramp. On the dock, Sidonie turned her head, gazing in my direction. I felt a sinking sensation in the pit of my stomach as our eyes met. What if she had changed her mind? But no, she tilted her head slightly and made a beckoning gesture.

"You do plan on introducing me, I hope," Sunjata said.

"Yes, of course."

We left Kratos and the sailors to keep watch over our things while Captain Deimos made inquiries regarding lodging. I felt lightheaded and sick making my way along the crowded quay. We waited our turn amid other well-wishers, and then there they were before us.

Sidonie and Astegal.

"Messire Maignard." She smiled at me. "I'm pleased you were able to join us."

"So this is the chess-playing Cytheran D'Angeline." Astegal studied me, then chuckled. "I suppose I must thank you for providing my wife with a harmless diversion. She has an impatient spirit."

I bowed. "The pleasure was mine, my lord."

"You'll lodge at the palace, of course." Astegal waved a careless hand. A gold knot glinted on one finger. "There's ample room, and I fear Sidonie will find it no less idle here, at least until we come to terms with the rebels."

Her brows rose. "Or you could do the sensible thing and leave me to administer New Carthage while you settle the matter."

A muscle in Astegal's jaw twitched. He smiled at Sidonie. "When the last rebel has surrendered, my dear, I will shower cities at your feet and you may administer them to your heart's content. Until then, a man's firmer hand is needed."

"No one ever died of tedium, your highness," I said lightly. Her quick gaze flicked to meet mine.

"I suppose not," she said slowly.

So it was still there, gods be thanked. Her wits, her lingering fears and suspicions. I presented Sunjata to them, explaining my partnership in a business venture with the House of Philosir.

"Ah, yes." Astegal's gaze rested on Sunjata's face for a few heartbeats. "Good old Jabnit's assistant. You did us a good service as I recall." He laid his hand on Sidonie's shoulder, the ring glinting. "Do you remember the painting of gems I presented to your mother, my dear? The House of Philosir procured the gems."

Sunjata bowed. "It was our honor."

"I remember you," Sidonie said to him.

Astegal's hand tightened on her shoulder. "I'm sure you're mistaken."

"No." She shot him a puzzled look. "You were with Messire Maignard, were you not?" she asked Sunjata. "On the street outside the villa."

"Ah." Although his reaction wasn't visible, I could feel Sunjata relax beside me. "Yes, your highness. I was among your admirers."

"Then you must come to the palace as well," Astegal said smoothly. "My lady wife should be surrounded by admirers. Speak to the chamberlain; he will see to everything."

With that, he turned away, taking Sidonie's arm and steering her. I hoped she'd look back at me, but she didn't. I forced myself to look away, willing myself not to show the hatred and jealousy raging inside me. Some yards away, I saw Justina winding her way toward us, attended by a pair of Aragonian servants.

She had been a pretty girl, and she'd grown into an attractive woman. Quick-witted and quick-tempered, I remembered. Dark hair and olive skin. Her mother had been a Hellene slave in the household of a Tiberian merchant, and she could pass for any one of a half dozen nationalities.

To my surprise, Justina spat at my feet.

"What brings a *D'Angeline* to New Carthage?" she demanded in flawless Aragonian. "Do you come to spy and mock for your traitorous Queen while Astegal sets her daughter over us?"

A few Aragonians in earshot murmured with approval. Others sought to hush her, glancing anxiously in Astegal's direction. I was so astonished, I could barely frame a reply. "No, my lady," I stammered in Aragonian. "I am D'Angeline in heritage only. I come as a citizen of Cythera, an emissary of my lord Ptolemy Solon."

"Cythera!" Justina sneered. "What does Cythera want?"

"Peace, generally." I took a deep breath. "My lady, I am Leander Maignard, and I will be lodging at the palace. If you will grant me the courtesy of an audience, I will be pleased to discuss how Cythera might be of assistance to Aragonia in this difficult time." I smiled ruefully. "I fear we are an island with considerable experience in the matter of being conquered and occupied."

"You're blunt," Justina said. "I'll think on it."

She flounced away. Sunjata and I gazed after her. "Well," he said presently. "Welcome to New Carthage and a whole new set of intrigues."

Thirty-eight

Life in New Carthage was agonizing.

Astegal was generous in his hospitality. Sunjata and I were given a suite of rooms to share, with a servant's chamber for Kratos. Space was found in the barracks for a handful of Captain Deimos' men to serve as guards for Sunjata as he went about the business of the House of Philosir, acquiring looted gems and jewelry at prices little short of robbery from unwitting soldiers. Astegal, it seemed, was eager to ensure that peers of old Carthage like Jabnit of Philosir thought themselves fatted on the spoils of war.

While he ruled like a king.

And that he did.

Every night there was feasting and revels in the great hall of the palace. Wine flowed freely, and platter after laden platter emerged from the kitchens. There were dancers and musicians and comedians. Some were Carthaginian, imported along with his household. Most were Aragonian. Some performed with bitterness scarce concealed behind stoic expressions. Some with philosophical indifference.

Astegal didn't care either way.

All of it entertained him—all of it.

He laughed and clapped regardless, tossing coins for the performers to scramble after. And every night, every damnable night, Sidonie sat beside him. For the most part, she was quiet and withdrawn. She was struggling, I could tell. Sorting through her thoughts and fears and confusion, trying to put them in order. Sometimes she would glance my way, and I could see the quiet panic. At other times, Astegal spoke soothingly to her, stroking her face with his ringed hand, and I could see the fears abate.

And every night, every night, she went willingly with him. His strong arm resting around her waist or draped over her shoulders. His hardened soldier's hands. Touching her, possessing her. Guiding her to their bedchamber, over and over.

I thought I would lose my mind.

My only consolation was that Bodeshmun himself seemed disturbed at Astegal's excesses. He attended the revels, grim and funereal in his black horologist's robes. From time to time, I saw him murmur in Astegal's ear. The Carthaginian general merely laughed, waving away his concerns. Well and good, I thought, you reap what you have sown, Bodeshmun.

Still, it was cold comfort.

I waited for Sidonie to send for me, waited and waited. But it was Justina who sent for me first, inviting me to dine privately with her. It seemed she had a villa of her own, not far from the palace.

"Leander Maignard!" This time, in private, Justina greeted me with a kiss. "I'm sorry, I wanted to send for you or Sunjata sooner, but I had to be cautious. I'm treading a narrow path here. Tell me, do you have word from her ladyship? What game is afoot?"

I glanced around, wary of her servants.

"I've dismissed them for the evening," Justina said, reading my face. She reached up to toy with my braids. "The table's already laid. As far as they're concerned, this is likely a dalliance I don't want known. So come dine, and tell me."

I did.

Justina listened in fascination, her eyes widening. "Dire magic," she said when I had finished. "That explains a great deal."

I stabbed my fork into a piece of overcooked fish. "Can you help?"

"I *could* have." She eyed me wryly. "Gods, Leander! I wish you'd come here first. Until her demure highness arrived, I'd managed to position myself nicely as Astegal's mistress."

"Oh?" I savaged my fish. "Then why did you spit at me on the docks?"

Justina blinked. "I told you, I'm treading a narrow path. As far as Astegal and Carthage are concerned, I'm a young Aragonian widow, an eager opportunist playing at being a double agent. As far as loyal Aragonia is concerned, I'm a spy in Serafin's service." She shrugged. "Before this I was eyes and ears, nothing more. Now I'm merely awaiting word on whom, if anyone, to betray. I haven't been able to get word out to her ladyship since the war began."

"It's Astegal," I said curtly.

"You won't mind if I confirm that with Sunjata, will you?" Justina rested her chin on one hand, studying me. "Because I'll be honest, Leander. You seem . . . odd."

I set down my fork. "Odd how?"

"I don't know." Justina blinked again. "Just . . . odd."

I sighed. "Oh, hells! Justina, I *feel* odd. And her highness . . . I assure you, Sidonie de la Courcel is *not* demure."

"Well, she's barely said a word in public," she observed.

"I assumed she felt too guilty over Terre d'Ange's betrayal of its alliances. Aragonians despise her more than Astegal. Naked ambition, at least, they understand. But when Terre d'Ange was invaded, Aragonia was the only country to send troops to its defense. When our turn came, Terre d'Ange turned its back on us and the D'Angeline heir married our conqueror."

I shook my head. "It's not their fault, any of it. Justina, can you still get access to Astegal?"

"Mayhap," she said warily. "Why?"

"Sunjata made a copy of his ring." I picked up my fork and pointed it at her. "And *you* are perfectly positioned to make the exchange."

Justina was silent a moment. "I want to talk to Sunjata."

"Fine," I said. "Do."

The interminable days wore onward. Astegal amused himself, Bodeshmun brooded, the Aragonians quietly seethed. Sidonie continued to be withdrawn. Sunjata was close-mouthed about his discussion with Justina, and there was no word from her.

If it hadn't been for Kratos, I think I truly might have lost my wits in those days. Like old Carthage, the city had a public bath-house with a palaestra, although it was much smaller. Sunjata refused to take exercise there, as it had been overtaken by bored Carthaginian soldiers given to shouting crudities at him. But Kratos, sensing my rising frustration, decided to teach me to wrestle there.

It was a good release, although it left me bruised and scraped. At first the soldiers who used the palaestra as a training field were amused. They shouted crudities at me, too, but I didn't care. And Kratos allowed I was a much better pupil than he'd expected me to be. After a few days' worth of training bouts, the soldiers weren't laughing.

"You're quick," Kratos said after the first time I nearly

managed to pin him. "Stronger than I would have thought for a wiry fellow. Someone taught you before, eh? It's coming back to you."

"No." I grinned. "Quick, and a quick study, that's all."

It didn't take long for word to spread that Kratos had been a professional wrestler in Hellas in his youth. Once it did, a handful of soldiers challenged him to bouts. Kratos permitted himself to accept one a day, and although he must have been well into his fifties, he won with skill and cunning. I couldn't help but wonder what he'd been like in his prime and how he'd come to lose enough matches to fall into penury. When I asked him, he shrugged.

"I got careless after I'd worn a champion's crown a few years running. Squandered my winnings on women and wine. Let myself get soft." Kratos dusted his hands. "By the time I realized it, there was a new generation rising, younger and more fit."

"I'm sorry," I said honestly.

"Not your fault." He clapped my shoulder. "Take it as a lesson."

It was after Kratos had won five or six bouts that Astegal strolled into the palaestra, accompanied by a retinue of Amazigh guards. We watched him spar with his soldiers, laughing and jesting as their blades flashed in the wintry sun. Whatever else was true, the bastard was a gifted swordsman.

"He's good," Kratos muttered. "Careless, though."

"How's that?" I asked. I might not have been handy with a blade, but I knew enough to know Astegal was very good.

Kratos jerked his chin. "Letting victory go to his head. He's won a battle, not a war. He ought to be drilling his troops in the field, not playing cock of the walk in the bathhouse."

"Don't give him any ideas," I said, and Kratos laughed.

Someone *did* give Astegal an idea, though, albeit of a different nature. After sparring for a time, he strolled over to the corner where Kratos and I trained.

"Leander Maignard," Astegal said pleasantly. "You've been an absent courtier. I brought you under my roof to entertain my wife, not roll in the dust with an aging Hellene slave."

I gritted my teeth and bowed. "Kratos is a freedman, and I do but await a summons from your lady wife, my lord. It seems for the moment you've kept her well entertained."

"Yes." Astegal smiled, heavy-lidded. "It does." He changed the subject. "I wrestled in my youth, freedman," he said to Kratos. "And I hear you're undefeated among my soldiers. Care to give me a bout?"

"Do you jest, my lord?" Kratos asked in surprise.

"Not at all." Astegal stripped off his tunic. "Not at all."

Astegal wasn't boasting; he had considerable skill at the game. And he had twenty years on Kratos and the advantage of reach and leverage. It was a hard-fought bout, but in the end, Astegal won. And he won ugly, wrenching Kratos' arm behind his back with such force that Kratos cried out in pain. Astegal leaned one forearm on the back of Kratos' neck, grinding his face into the dust. It was an unnecessary humiliation.

"Do you concede, freedman?" he asked.

Kratos made a muffled sound of agreement. Astegal released him to the cheers of his men. He gave them a brief bow of acknowledgment.

"Carthage's supremacy is restored," he said lightly.

Kratos didn't say anything then, only got to his feet with an obvious effort, rubbing his wrenched shoulder in pain. Later we had a good, long soak in the caldarium, which Kratos claimed would help the injury heal. We could see Astegal in a private room beyond the caldarium, the doorway guarded by a pair of ever-present and vigilant Amazigh. He was taking a massage, his muscles loose and languid, his eyes closed, his olive skin glistening with oil.

There was no one else in the pool at the moment. I entertained thoughts of killing him then and there. If I could have devised a plan that didn't involve me getting spitted on an Amazigh blade, I might have tried it.

"My lord," Kratos said thoughtfully. "Please tell me it's your life's work to destroy that man."

"Why?" I asked.

The expression on Kratos' homely face was calm, but there was hatred in his voice. "Because I would very much like to assist you."

I nodded. "Excellent."

THIRTY-NINE

It was some days before the Longest Night when Justina finally sent for me.

"What in the seven hells took you so long?" I hissed at her when we were alone in her villa. I expected a flare of the temper I remembered in reply, but Justina surprised me.

"I needed to think," she said quietly. "It's a grave danger."

"Did Sunjata not confirm the truth of all I told you?" I inquired.

Justina looked at me for a long time. "Yes," she said at length. "Yes, he did. But he's worried that you're being hasty and careless." She smiled wryly. "I didn't realize you were . . . enamored . . . of her."

"Strong feelings cloud the wits," I said, quoting her ladyship. "Yes, I know. But a task is a task. And hasty . . . Name of Elua, Justina! The Longest Night is nearly on us. We don't have forever. Come spring, Astegal will move against Serafin's rebels, and the opportunity will be lost."

"I know." Justina sighed. "Astegal plans a fête to honor

D'Angeline tradition. I've managed to get invited. I'll approach him then and tell him I've been missing him. Beyond that, I can make no promises."

"My thanks," I said. "It's a great deal to ask, I know."

She gave me another long look. "'Tis an unlikely task. I'd no idea her ladyship had such . . . strong feelings . . . for her estranged son."

"Nor does anyone else," I observed. "Her ladyship is clever enough to use her own reputation and advice against her adversaries. By the Goddess, even Astegal and Bodeshmun think me an ally! Which makes it a perfect gambit, do you not think?"

"I don't know," Justina mused. "I truly don't."

"But you'll help?" I pressed her.

She sighed again. "I'll try."

I didn't know what to expect of the Longest Night. In her ladyship's household on Cythera, we simply celebrated with a masqued ball. I had vague memories of celebrating it in Terre d'Ange as a child. Pine boughs and beeswax candles, snatched sips of *joie*. I'd been permitted to stay awake long enough to witness the pageant of Winter's Queen and the Sun Prince the year before we had departed to prepare a household for her ladyship on Cythera. I remembered music and adults glittering in masks. I couldn't imagine Astegal would seek to re-create it for Sidonie's sake. Surely there were too many dangerous memories of Terre d'Ange attached to it. He would not take the risk.

In that, I was right.

In some ways, it might have been any other night in New Carthage under the rule of Astegal the First. No masks, no pageant. No Sun Prince entering by chariot with his gilded spear to restore light to the world. There was much of what there had been every night at the palace: wine and feasting. All the guests had been carefully selected, so that there were none who would dare strain the fragile veil of illusions that bound Sidonie.

But there was music.

And dancing.

As the Chief Horologist, Bodeshmun himself declared the hour in a deep voice. The balance of the world had tipped, darkness giving way to light. The musicians struck up a measured tune. At the head table, Astegal arose and bowed to Sidonie, extending his hand to her. She rose and took his hand, and they danced together.

I swallowed bile.

They looked well together, loath though I was to admit it. Him so dark, and her so fair. She looked smaller in his arms. His hands, possessing her. Resting on her waist, caressing. Her face lifted to his, his head bent over her, solicitous.

"Sidonie," I whispered, miserable.

But then there was another tune and another. Others danced. I saw Justina approach Astegal and curtsy, voicing a request. I saw him accept, laughing. White teeth, wagging jaw. A narrow strip of crimson beard. The musicians picked up their pace. Justina glanced at me over Astegal's shoulder, her eyes flashing.

I approached her, ignoring the ever-present Amazigh.

Sidonie.

"Will you dance?" I asked simply.

Her hand slid into mine. "All right."

Oh, gods.

We *fit*; we fit so well together, I felt dizzy. Every step she took, I knew before she took it. Her body fit itself to mine. I led her and she followed. Effortless. I wanted to crush her against me. I was fairly trembling with the effort of not doing so.

"Why?" I whispered hoarsely in her ear. "You asked me to come here. Why do you disdain me, Sidonie?"

She shivered. "I don't."

"You do!" I said in anguish.

Her head had been bowed, but she lifted it now. Her black eyes met mine. "When first we met, I spoke of temptation and its lack. At the time, I spoke honestly. But this . . ." Another shiver ran through her. "I thought it would go away, and it hasn't. *Why*?"

"I told you why in Carthage," I murmured.

Sidonie shook her head. "Even if that were true, it doesn't explain this."

I didn't know what to say. I couldn't very well tell her that I reminded her of the love she had forgotten. It would only add another layer of unbelievable madness to my tale, and it wouldn't advance *my* cause with her. If I succeeded, she'd remember soon enough. I shifted her hand from my shoulder, laying it on my chest so she could feel my heart beating fast and hard. "Mayhap the gods have their reasons."

She pulled her hand away. "Please don't make this more difficult."

"Just don't shut me out altogether," I whispered. "Please."

The song ended too soon. There was another of Astegal's hand-picked lords there, Gillimas of Hiram, waiting to claim a dance of her. He was a Guildsman, Sunjata had told me. I'd not had occasion to deal with him. My diplomatic mission had ended in Carthage. So far as anyone here was concerned, I was a lap-dog, a harmless courtier . . . and a failed one, at that.

But they were satisfied it was because of the spell, because Astegal kept her contented. They were wrong. Although she didn't understand why, Sidonie was being wary because she *did* have feelings for me.

Strong feelings.

The knowledge filled me with elation. It lent me strength.

I made myself play at being a perfect courtier that night. I danced with a good many Carthaginian ladies, and with Justina, who was one of the few Aragonians present—or at least, a seeming Aragonian. She played her part so well I forgot myself.

"Well?" I asked her, smiling falsely. "Any luck this evening?"

Justina laughed as though I'd said somewhat witty. "Oh, yes."

"Good," I said, still smiling. "Excellent."

If the night had ended there, it would have been perfect, or at least as near to it as it could be under the circumstances. Unfortunately, it didn't. After the dancing, Astegal decreed a spectacle, announcing that the Amazigh would perform a ritual for us.

All of us returned to our seats at the long tables, clearing the floor. Two Amazigh took their places. They bowed to one another, then unwound the lower portions of their head-scarves, rewinding them in such a fashion that their eyes were bound and covered. With that, they drew their blades and commenced to spar.

What the point of it was, I couldn't say. A reminder of their skill, I suppose. To be sure, it was an impressive spectacle. Robed and faceless, they hardly looked human. They fought with a sword in the right hand and a dagger in the left, flowing back and forth across the floor. Their blades crossed and clashed, glinting in the light of many lamps and candles.

At length, one gained the advantage of the other. Feeling the other's sword-point against his throat, the defeated Amazigh dropped his blade, pressing the palms of his hands together in a curious gesture of surrender. I clapped politely along with everyone else.

"Do any among you think to best my loyal Amazigh at

their game?" Astegal called. There were general utterances of denial. "Ah, but someone must try." He made a show of glancing around the room, his gaze settling on me. "Leander Maignard!" he said brightly. "You were invited here to provide entertainment. Do so."

I spread my hands. "I'm no swordsman, my lord."

Astegal laughed. "That will make it all the more entertaining! Don't worry, my pretty little friend. My men are skilled; you'll take no serious hurt."

The Carthaginian peers laughed. Even Bodeshmun allowed himself a sour smile. I glanced at Sidonie. She wasn't amused. If Astegal thought to lessen me in her eyes by humiliating me in public as he'd humiliated Kratos in the palaestra, he was mistaken.

I rose and bowed. "As you wish, my lord."

One of the Amazigh loaned me his sword and dagger. Someone else bound my eyes with a length of cloth. I stood very still, focusing my breathing. The noise in the great hall was distracting, voices bouncing off the walls. They were making wagers, not on who would win, but how long I would last.

Strangely, the dual blades in my hands didn't feel entirely wrong, only . . . unbalanced. The Amazigh sword was heavier than the one I was accustomed to wielding, and it felt mismatched against the dagger.

"Go!" Astegal shouted.

I took a silent, sliding step to my left and felt the wind of a blade's passage where I had been. I'd always been good at her ladyship's training games. I could navigate the entire villa blindfolded, and I had sharp ears. I concentrated. Beneath the noise of the onlookers, I heard the soft scuff of my opponent's sandals as he advanced, thinking I'd retreated. I poked him blindly with the tip of my sword, moving farther to the left as I did.

A great roar went up.

Circles, I thought. The Amazigh had battled to-and-fro in a straight line. If I could keep circling, I could keep him off guard.

For a while, it worked. Longer than anyone expected, I daresay. Long enough that the tables were turned, and the crowd began laughing at the sight of the Amazigh spinning, his robes flying as he tried to guess which way I'd gone. I kept my blades crossed before me, concentrating on defending myself.

But while the Amazigh may have been fierce in battle—who else would devise such a dangerous ritual?—they were patient, too. My opponent stalked me until he began to catch my rhythm. He landed a blow with the edge of his sword on my dagger-hand, scoring a nasty gash and causing me to drop my blade.

His dagger swept my sword aside. I sensed the blow to follow and whirled away, instinctively taking up my heavy, borrowed sword in a two-handed grip. For a moment, we were both disoriented. The crowd grumbled as the Amazigh resumed his patient stalking.

I listened for him. This felt right, the sword angled across my body. The memory of Prince Imriel practicing in the garden flashed across my thoughts, watching him move through a fluid series of movements. *What do you call it?* I'd asked him. *Telling the hours.* He'd moved in circles. Blood trickled down the back of my left hand, tickling my wrist. I concentrated, trying to remember more.

I wondered if . . .

Careless. The Amazigh blade clattered against my sword. I pushed back in a panic and felt the prick of a dagger at my throat as he slipped inside my guard. I dropped my sword and put my hands together in surrender.

There was good-natured applause as I removed my

blindfold. My Amazigh opponent readjusted the folds of his head-scarf. I bowed to him, my palms still pressed together. He returned the bow impassively.

"Well done!" Astegal chuckled and tossed me a gold coin, as if I were one of his hired performers. "Spinning and dashing like a cornered hare. I've never seen the like. You were right, my dear," he added to Sidonie. "He *is* entertaining. I can see why he made you laugh."

"Yes." Her expression was unreadable, but there was somewhat working behind her eyes. Another memory stirred. "Thank you, Messire Maignard."

I bowed to her. "For you, your highness, anything."

Astegal waved a dismissive hand. "Go, go. Enjoy the revel."

I went.

That night, I couldn't sleep. Although I'd bound it, the gash on the back of my hand throbbed, keeping me awake. I played out memories of the night over and over in my thoughts. Dancing with Sidonie. The feeling of her in my arms, the inexplicable *rightness* of it. The duel with the Amazigh. Wondering if by some miracle I might have been able to re-create the elegant, deceptively simple movements I'd seen Prince Imriel perform. Realizing that it was a damned good thing I hadn't.

Harmless. I had to appear harmless.

It was all right, I'd put on an amusing spectacle. All that Carthage had seen was a cornered hare—and that's all I'd been, really. Still, I tried to remember what I knew of the Cassiline Brotherhood.

Not much, really. Tales from childhood; but the Cassiline Brothers had fallen out of favor not long after I was born. I knew they were stern and celibate, and that they held strange beliefs. That they trained from the age of ten to be the best bodyguards in the world.

And I knew that Joscelin Verreuil, the consort of Prince Imriel's foster-mother, had been one such. In Terre d'Ange, he was reckoned a hero. In her ladyship's household, he was reckoned an almighty irritant. I'd forgotten all about the fact that he was a Cassiline. It must have been he who trained the prince.

And somewhat about a vigil . . .

Yes, there had been a vigil. It wasn't long after her ladyship had arrived on Cythera, where we had assiduously prepared for her. We got word her son the prince had taken sick after kneeling the whole night, the Longest Night, in the bitter cold. I remembered her ladyship being uncommonly distraught, uttering scathing words about the Cassiline Brotherhood in general and Joscelin Verreuil in particular. I remembered my mother commenting that it was likely one of the few things on which her ladyship and Phèdre nó Delaunay might agree.

At the time, I'd agreed, too. It seemed utter folly.

Now . . .

Well, it was folly. But it held a strange, stark appeal. I was a stranger in a strange land, truly and figuratively. I didn't know if I was D'Angeline or Cytheran. I was in love, and I didn't know *how* to love. Blessed Elua did. And the longer I thought on it, the more the notion of laying this burden in his hands, of appearing before him in humility and subjecting myself to his will, appealed to me.

I rose quietly and dressed in darkness. The door to Sunjata's chamber was firmly closed. He had been invited to attend the festivities on this night, but he had declined the invitation. I didn't even know why. We were growing distant to one another, and it saddened me.

Kratos—Kratos was snoring in his chamber.

The sound made me smile. I slipped from our quarters into the hallway. It was late and the palace would be locked and guarded for the night. Still, there was an inner courtyard that would suffice.

Torches were burning low along the corridors. There were guards at every corner, but they let me pass. I was Leander Maignard, harmless. The last one yawned, opening the brass-bound door onto the courtyard. Cool night air washed over my face. Overhead, stars spangled the sky, dimmed by a full moon. In the courtyard, flames danced from four torches arrayed in a square.

In between them, a figure knelt.

"Sidonie," I whispered.

Her back was to me. It didn't matter. I knew her; I would have known her anywhere. I took a step forward. One of the torches peeled away. Indigo robes, flowing toward me. Intent Amazigh eyes in a narrow strip of visible face.

"This is not for you," he said briefly in Hellene.

Her bowed head rose and turned. Sidonie gazed over her shoulder at me.

"It is a D'Angeline custom," I said softly. "Like her highness, I do but seek to keep Blessed Elua's vigil."

The guard's finger wagged. "Not here. Not tonight."

I looked past him. Torchlight streaked her face. Like me, Sidonie prayed for guidance. She was frightened and confused. I wanted to go to her, wanted to embrace and kiss her. I wanted to tell her everything, and soothe away her fears with truths instead of subtle lies.

Instead, I bowed to the Amazigh.

"Forgive me for disturbing her highness' prayers," I murmured. "I will go elsewhere."

"That would be wise," he said briefly. "Go, then."

I went.

And with every step I took, I felt her watch me go.

Forty

So it was that I kept Elua's vigil in my own way. I kept it in the privacy of my bedchamber, kneeling before the narrow slit of a window that illuminated it, my knees aching on the flagstones as I sat on my heels.

I watched the moon move across the skies and prayed.

For what? I couldn't even have said. I just prayed. And somewhere, in the dim hours before dawn, I felt a presence surround me. It settled over me like a cloak of feathers, warm and golden. There was brightness, so much brightness; and somewhat blocking it. A sob caught in my throat, jolting me awake.

I straightened stiffly.

"Will you break your fast, Leander?"

I squinted at Sunjata, leaning on the sill of my window. "What are you doing here?"

He moved away with careless grace. "Keeping watch over you."

I broke my fast with bread and honey and strong tea imported from Bhodistan, and told Sunjata most of what had passed on the Longest Night. He listened without comment until I was finished.

"So she feels it?"

I drizzled more honey on another piece of bread. Thin loops and coils of gold, sinking into itself. "Yes."

"And Justina agreed to exchange the ring?" Sunjata pressed.

"Yes." I gave him a sharp look. "Sunjata, why didn't you attend last night? It would seem to me a passing good opportunity to forge new connections."

"Yes." He sighed. "Yes and no. Whatever connections I make here will be no use to me if you succeed, and if you fail . . . Leander, hear me. This business has me uneasy, and the longer it goes on, the less I like it. If it goes awry . . ."

"There's naught to implicate you," I said. "And I would have thought you of all people would wish to see Carthage brought low."

Sunjata gave me a bitter smile. "Will it restore what was taken from me?"

"No." I was silent a moment. "Do as you wish. Go, if you like. There's naught you can do to aid me here, anyway."

He ran a hand through his hair. "It's not that simple."

"Of course it is," I said.

"No." Sunjata studied me. "It's not."

"Name of Elua, man!" My voice rose. "Either tell me why, or stop moping!"

"I can't," he murmured.

"Which?" I asked wryly.

That, at least, made him laugh. "Ah, gods! All right. I'll try."

It was passing strange. Justina had said I seemed odd. Well and fine, I hadn't denied it. I knew full well I'd changed on this journey. But Sunjata was behaving oddly, too. He had almost from the beginning. And I'd no idea why.

Since there was no merit in worrying about it, I left off. At last, we were getting closer to attaining our goals. Mayhap it made him nervous. Me, it filled with hope.

I dispatched Kratos to Justina's villa with the copy of Astegal's ring. And then, alas, it was back to the agony of waiting. I didn't know how long it would be before Astegal chose to call on her. Not long, I hoped. He was capable of patience, but he didn't strike me as a man fond of waiting to take his pleasures in life.

Gods, I couldn't think about that.

A day passed, then two. On the third, there was no word from Justina, but one of Sidonie's attendants, a Carthaginian girl with a sullen face, brought an invitation to a game of chess. I accepted with alacrity.

We met in the study of the chambers she shared with Astegal. It made me uncomfortable to see evidence of his presence there—a half-written letter in Punic script, a map depicting the harbor of Amílcar. And a looming Amazigh guard, of course. That at least I'd expected.

And Sidonie. She was wearing a gown of deep burgundy red today. The color suited her better than I would have thought.

"Messire Maignard," she said in a measured tone. "Thank you for coming on short notice."

"Of course," I said in surprise. "My lady, as your husband noted, I have no purpose here but to entertain. Truth be told, I'd rather serve at your whim than his." I rubbed the back of my bandaged hand. "Chess is a bloodless sport."

She winced. "Were you badly hurt?"

"No, no." I glanced at the Amazigh on guard and smiled. He didn't smile back, at least not that I could tell. "Shall we play?"

The board was set. As before, we sat opposite one another and began a game. For a time, we played in silence. Sidonie played badly from the beginning, and I could tell her thoughts were elsewhere. Ah, gods! I would have given anything for ten minutes alone with her. But no. Justina had the ring; she would have her liaison with Astegal sooner or later, and if she succeeded, the situation would be greatly changed. Now was *not* the time to take any unnecessary risks.

So instead I took them on the chess board, playing recklessly and foolishly. She was sufficiently distracted that she missed several opportunities I left her and presented me with unwontedly careless openings.

"Ah, Elua!" Sidonie said in disgust as I took advantage of one such, capturing her second rook. It was the first genuine display of emotion she'd shown that day; one of few since coming to New Carthage. "Why did I do that?"

I made as though to tip her king. "Shall I or will you?"

"Wait." She studied the board a moment. "Oh, fine. Do it. But I want a rematch."

"Will you actually *play* this time, my lady?" I inquired.

Sidonie made a face, wrinkling her nose at me. It made her look as young as she was, and it was so uncharacteristic that it made me laugh aloud in delight.

We played another game, this one more evenly matched. "I'm sorry about the guards turning you away the other night in the courtyard," she said some way into it. "They didn't understand."

"That's quite all right." I advanced a pawn. "Did you have a pleasant vigil?"

"No," she said frankly. "Did you?"

"I fell asleep," I admitted.

She laughed and moved her knight. "You're honest."

"I'm trying," I said.

Her quick gaze flicked up at me. There was a question written there. "Yes, well, I'm waiting," she said lightly. "It's your move, Messire Maignard."

I nodded. "I know, my lady. I know."

That was all we said of the matter. We both concentrated on our games. It took long enough that I saw the Amazigh's veil sucked inward in a yawn. In the end, the game was a draw.

"Well." Sidonie raised her brows. "That doesn't happen often."

"No," I said. "No, it doesn't."

There was a sound in the outer chamber, Astegal returning from wherever he'd been. I heard him exchange a few words in Punic with one of the other Amazigh. Shortly afterward, he entered the study, looking sleek and very pleased with himself.

I rose and bowed. "Well met, my lord."

"Ah, young Leander!" Astegal clapped a careless hand on my shoulder. "Fulfilling your duties at last, eh?" He moved past me, caressing Sidonie's cheek. His ring glinted. "I trust he was the perfect courtier?"

"Of course." She glanced up at him. "Always."

Always and always.

Astegal gave a less-than-subtle glance at the Amazigh. The swathed face nodded imperceptibly. "Good man, good man!" Astegal smiled at me and made a shooing gesture. "Run along, then."

Vowing silently to kill him myself, I returned his smile politely and withdrew.

When I returned to my own quarters, there was a message from Justina asking me to call on her. Sunjata was there, sorting through new acquisitions and scribbling out a manifest.

He glanced up as I read the message. "Good news?"

I frowned. "No news, just a summons. Did her messenger say anything?"

Sunjata shook his head. "No."

Well, I thought, mayhap Justina was being discreet, which was wise. Still, I had a sinking feeling. I'd been with Sidonie all afternoon. If Justina had been with Astegal, if she'd succeeded in exchanging the rings, there should have been some change, some shift.

There'd been a small one, I supposed. Sidonie had bestirred herself after losing that first game. That lively spark of intelligence that had been burning dangerously low since Astegal had taken her arm on the docks of New Carthage and steered her away had reasserted itself.

Was it enough?

It didn't feel like it.

So I summoned Kratos to escort me and made my way to Justina's villa. She was there, awaiting me. As before, she had dismissed her servants. This time, there was no kiss of greeting. Justina was restless and pacing, seeming at odds with herself.

"Here." She thrust the suede pouch that contained the ring into my hand.

"Is it . . . ?" I hesitated.

"No." Justina's eyes were bright with tears and anger. "No. I'm *sorry*, Leander. I couldn't do it."

I closed my hand on the pouch, feeling the hard knot of gold within it bite into my palm. I forced my voice to gentleness. "Why?"

"Because I was scared!" She rubbed impatiently at her eyes. "Oh, gods! You don't know; you have no idea. You've been . . . well, no. No, never mind. I have a life and a role here in Aragonia, and I've built it very carefully."

"And you said you were poised to tip the balance," I reminded her. Gently, gently. "What for, if not for this moment?"

"Not like this!" Her dark eyes blazed. "I'm not some marketplace trickster, skilled at sleight of hand. If you want me to send a covert message to Serafin, yes, I can do that. If you want me to engage Astegal in leading pillow-talk, yes, I can do that, too. There's a lot I can do. But I tell you, it's not as easy as you might think to tug a ring from the finger of a man bent on love-making without his noticing! I hoped he'd fall asleep, but he wouldn't stay. He's a glutton for pleasure, but I don't think he's lacking in satisfaction where his D'Angeline bride is concerned. And if I'd tried it and he did notice . . . gods, Leander, do you have any idea how many loyal Aragonians would suffer for it if Astegal suspected me?"

"No," I murmured. "I'm sorry, Justina."

She shuddered. "Don't be. Just . . ." She closed her eyes for a moment, then opened them. "What if this is all for the best? Do you ever think on it?"

"Carthage ascendant?" I asked.

Justina nodded. "Does it really matter to *us*?"

There was so much in the question. We were both protégés of her ladyship, awed, admiring, and grateful. And yet we knew her one weakness. Her son, Imriel. I was here because Melisande Shahrizai loved her son. I was here because Ptolemy Solon loved her ladyship. I had assurances from the Council of Thirty that Solon's goodwill was accepted. Two months ago, this question would have been easy to answer.

Not now.

I sat uninvited, bowing my head. "Yes. It does to me."

She came to stand beside me, stroking my braids. "I'm sorry. I just can't."

I looked up at Justina. "You're sure?"

"Yes." She swallowed. "I *am* sorry. I know . . ." Justina paused. "No, I don't. Not really. But I can't do this. Not for you, not even for her ladyship. Can you forgive me?"

I smiled bitterly. "I'll try."

On that note, I took my leave of Justina, the false copy

of Astegal's ring heavy in my pocket. Kratos walked beside me. They didn't use palanquins in New Carthage, or not yet, at least. I was glad of it. I took a grim satisfaction in feeling the muscles of my calves laboring as we climbed the hill toward the palace.

"So." Kratos pursed his lips. "There's a ring, eh?"

I shot a sidelong glance at him. "I don't know what you overheard, but the less you know, the better for you, my friend."

He snorted. "Friend, is it? Well, if you care to trust me, I've an idea."

Overhead, the full moon was waning. I stopped and regarded Kratos. He returned my gaze evenly, his homely features silvered in the moonlight.

"Tell me," I said.

Kratos did.

Forty-one

All the way back to the palace, I mulled over Kratos' idea. We didn't speak of it again until we were safely behind closed doors in my quarters.

"It's a huge risk," I said to him. "What if she betrays us?"

Kratos shrugged. "If I understand rightly, it's no bigger a risk than you asked the lady Justina to take."

"I'd need your help. I'd need you to stand guard."

He nodded. "I know."

Sunjata blinked at us. "What in the world are you talking about?"

I told him about Justina's refusal, which didn't surprise him. And then I told him about the idea Kratos had proposed. Sunjata's dark skin turned ashen.

"You'd risk everything to seek the aid of a *bath-house attendant*?" he asked, aghast.

"Do you have a better plan?" I asked.

"No." Sunjata glanced at Kratos, swallowing hard. "You're . . . you're that sure of the girl?"

"Astegal's favorite?" Kratos shrugged. "I'm sure he always chooses the same one. And I'm sure she'd gladly see him and every other Carthaginian on the face of the earth dead. His men are getting bored. And they're not gentle. They take more than massages."

I hadn't been back to the palaestra since Astegal had wrestled Kratos, but Kratos himself had continued to take exercise there. I'd given him license, since we were all suffering from inaction and there was always the hope he'd pick up some useful piece of gossip. I'd known Astegal had been going more regularly and training with his men. I hadn't known he had a favorite attendant.

I hadn't known his soldiers were abusing the attendants, either. Not a surprise, I supposed. Still, it made me angry.

"Does she hate him enough to take such a risk?" Sunjata was asking.

"Have you ever been forced to play the whore for a large group of increasingly bored soldiers?" Kratos asked laconically. "Risk, risk, risk. That's all I ever hear any of you talk about. Mayhap it's time to quit talking and take one."

I made my decision. "He's right."

Sunjata looked at me, then looked away. "Leander . . . don't take this amiss. I disagree with this choice. And I don't think we should both risk being exposed. With your permission, I'd like to borrow Captain Deimos and your ship to run a load of cargo to Carthage." He cleared his throat. "I was thinking of asking anyway."

"You don't need my permission," I said. "Go."

He looked back at me, his expression softening. "I'll return in a week's time."

I shrugged. "As you wish."

So the matter was decided. Sunjata made his preparations to travel. Kratos haunted the bath-house, observing the daily movements of Astegal's favorite attendant. And I tormented myself with second-guesses, trying to think of another way.

The problem was, there wasn't one. Right now, everything hung in stasis. New Carthage's port was closed to foreign trade under Astegal's orders and we weren't getting news from elsewhere. Insofar as I knew, the game that Carthage had set in motion was at a stalemate, albeit a temporary one.

And it wouldn't last long.

We waited until Sunjata's ship had sailed. I didn't blame him for wanting to be gone when this took place. As Justina had noted, the Aragonians hated D'Angelines almost more than Carthaginians. The girl at the bath-house might agree to aid us. She might refuse. Or she might say anything we wanted to hear, and then betray us.

Under ordinary circumstances, the bath-house would close its doors for some hours overnight, opening at dawn. In occupied New Carthage, it never closed. There were soldiers who had taken up permanent residence there. Still, Kratos had noted that it was at its quietest in the hours before dawn when the attendants crept about the place, trying to clean and tidy it.

"They must have had pride in their work once," he'd observed.

It was still dark when we left the palace. By the time we reached the bath-house, there was merely the faintest suggestion of charcoal-grey in the eastern sky. Our footsteps echoed slightly in the marble halls. All the lamps were burning low. Here and there, soldiers slept, snoring. The pool-rooms were empty and unlit, dark water shimmering eerily.

Kratos led me directly to the girl. She was in the chamber where I'd seen Astegal taking a massage, carefully filling small flasks of scented oil from a large jug. Another woman was with her, neatly folding clean linen towels. Both of them jumped when they saw us.

"Go," Kratos said to the second woman, jerking his thumb at the door. He didn't speak Aragonian and she didn't speak Hellene, but his meaning was clear enough. She gave us a glance filled with contempt, but she went.

"Where do they take them?" I asked Kratos.

He pointed at a storage closet with a slatted wooden door.

I grabbed the girl's arm and dragged her into the closet. She went without protesting, though I could feel her reluctance. Inside, I pressed her up against the shelves and put my hand over her mouth. Her face was striped with dim light filtering through the slatted door, and I could see the glaring hatred in her gaze.

"Listen to me," I said in a low voice. "Terre d'Ange did not betray Aragonia willingly. There are dark magics at work here. You have a chance to help us undo them. Will you hear?"

Her eyes widened and she nodded.

I took my hand away and fetched the suede pouch from my pocket. I showed the ring to her. "Have you seen this?"

"Astegal wears it," she breathed.

"He wears one like it. It is one of the sources of his power." I'd thought it wiser not to try to explain further. "Every time he comes here, he takes a massage from you. Do you think you could exchange the rings?"

"Yes." She gave me a calculating stare. "I want money."

"How much?" I asked.

"Enough to leave this place until the soldiers are gone," she said. "Ten gold doubloons."

I nodded. "Done. You'll get it when I get Astegal's ring."

A look of world-weary cynicism settled over her face. "You'll cheat me."

"Hold out your hand," I said. She obeyed cautiously. I put the ring in her palm and closed her fingers over it. "What's your name?"

She looked wary. "Esme."

"Esme," I echoed. "Esme, you're holding my life in your hand. If you choose not to trust me, show this to Astegal and tell him what I asked of you. He will have me tortured and killed. He will likely reward you, mayhap with more than ten gold coins. And Aragonia will lay beneath Carthage's yoke for the next hundred years, with Terre d'Ange and other nations like to follow. If you believe nothing else in your life, believe this. I will not cheat you."

Her hand clenched on the ring. "This will weaken him? You swear it?"

"In the name of Blessed Elua and his Companions, I do," I said.

Esme gave a sharp nod. "I will do it."

I touched her cheek lightly. "Be careful, Esme. May Blessed Elua hold you in his hand and keep you safe."

So it was done.

I left the bath-house in a strange state of heightened awareness, Kratos at my side. Either I'd just advanced a pawn in the deadliest game I'd ever played in my life, or I'd sealed my own fate along with Kratos' and the girl's. It was a terrifying sensation. Oddly, it was an enlivening one, too. The sun was rising and the light felt brighter and clearer than I remembered. *This*, I thought, was what it was like to play the game as her ladyship played it. At the highest possible levels, with the greatest possible stakes.

And with fearful repercussions for innocent lives.

I will own, that part troubled me more than I liked to admit.

Kratos read the thought in my face. "She's been around

those men day in and out, my lord. She knows the risk as well as you do. Mayhap better."

"Still," I said.

"I know." He laid a hand on my shoulder. "It's hard."

"My thanks." I laughed. "Gods, Kratos! You were the best purchase I ever made in my life."

He smiled wryly. "It's an odd compliment, but I'll take it."

It was another piece of irony in an affair fraught with it. I'd arrived in New Carthage with one highly trained ally at my side. I'd thought I'd stumbled over a piece of great good fortune to find another in place, poised to do exactly what needed to be done. But for all the Guild training and skills her ladyship had imparted to her people, my fate now hinged on an idea conceived by an aging wrestler and executed by a young bath-house attendant.

I wished I were better at praying.

We wandered the streets of New Carthage for a time, buying spicy sausage pastries in the market once it opened. They were hot enough to burn my fingers and scald the roof of my mouth. I ate slowly, savoring the taste. If Esme betrayed us, it might be the last meal I enjoyed. And if she failed and was caught . . . well, I'd have to confess. There was nothing else for it. If the girl didn't confess my role immediately, Astegal would have her tortured until she did. I would take the blame on myself, claim to have threatened her. Claim that Kratos had obeyed me with no knowledge of my plans. Mayhap Astegal would be merciful.

Although I doubted it.

After eating, we returned to the palace. Bodeshmun passed us in the great hall. He actually gave me a curt nod of acknowledgment. Astegal, hells! I hoped *Bodeshmun* would be merciful. Ptolemy Solon had told me what the man had done to create his demon-stone. He'd slit open an infant's belly and stuck a gem inside it, managed to keep the babe alive long enough for a demon to devour it. I suspected the Chief Horologist was a fellow who knew a thing or two about inflicting hideous torment.

Astegal didn't go to the bath-house that day. The next, he spent most of the day closeted with Bodeshmun and other trusted advisers. I knew, because Sidonie told me when she invited me to call on her for another game.

"Are they nearing terms for a full surrender?" I inquired.

"No, I fear not." She frowned at the board. "It's to do with some grievance of King Roderico's. Astegal says he's addled. I met him when we arrived and he didn't *seem* addled."

"No doubt this has been a trying time for him," I said diplomatically.

Sidonie captured one of my pawns. "Well, I wish Astegal would permit me to join his conferences. Wait, wait, he keeps telling me. For what?" She gave me a level look. "I'm perishing sick of waiting."

"Patience is a virtue worth striving for, my lady," I said. "I'm sure your husband knows what he's about."

"I hope to Blessed Elua someone does," she murmured.

To that, I made no reply. Since no one had come to take me away in chains, it seemed that for the moment, Esme had not decided to betray me, for which I was profoundly grateful. It might still happen, or like Justina, she might simply lose her nerve. But the thought had struck me that if she tried and failed, this might be the last time I saw Sidonie.

The notion was so ungodly painful, I felt unexpected tears sting my eyes.

"Are you all right, Leander?" Sidonie asked in surprise.

"Yes, of course." I forced my voice to lightness. "Your beauty dazzles, your highness. Nothing more."

She gazed at me a moment, then shook her head. "Some days I think everyone here is addled but me."

We played out our game, which I lost. I wished I could make the time last forever, slow the passage of the sun in the sky. But in time I had to take my leave of her. I went with a heavy heart and slow steps.

The next day, all hell broke loose.

Kratos and I were both losing our wits with the suspense of waiting. He went to the bath-house to seek a bout to distract himself. I went to the market, having conceived the notion of purchasing some romantic token for Sidonie that I could leave in my things to be found if matters went awry. At a bookseller's, I found an Aragonian translation of a famous correspondence between a pair of star-crossed D'Angeline lovers. I'd not actually heard of it, but the bookseller assured me it was a popular gift among courting couples.

At any rate, he was eager to make a sale, eager enough that he treated me with more courtesy than most Aragonians I'd encountered in New Carthage, and eager enough that he gave me a good price. I daresay Astegal's men weren't doing much to keep the fellow in business.

So I bought the book, and then spent another hour wandering the streets and pondering what inscription I would write.

I returned to the palace to find it in an uproar.

Astegal was in a fury, shouting at Bodeshmun in the great hall. The Chief Horologist stood with folded arms and bore it, but his deep-set eyes glittered with rage of his own.

"I did my part," Bodeshmun said ominously when Astegal finally paused to draw breath. "Why didn't you forbid her?"

"Because she was *compliant*!" Astegal roared at him.

There was a considerable crowd gathered. I spotted Kratos' hulking form and made my way to his side. "What's happened?"

He gave me a sidelong glance. "Seems a short time ago, the princess took it in her head to go call on King Roderico."

"—precious Amazigh should have stopped her!" Bodeshmun retorted.

"They're not—" Astegal gritted his teeth. "No mind. The damage is done. And you"—he pointed at Bodeshmun—"you need to trot over there and fetch her back before it worsens, cousin."

Bodeshmun went still. "Do not speak to me thusly, cousin."

Astegal took a step toward him. "I'll speak as I please."

They were both big men, both dangerous men in different ways. We all went quiet as they faced off against one another. Astegal's face was suffused with blood, his handsome features distorted. His hand hovered over his sword. Bodeshmun radiated dark, brooding rage. If Astegal moved against him, I thought, he'd best kill him quickly. Because if he didn't, Bodeshmun would make him suffer. I didn't know how, but I knew it would be unpleasant.

A faint voice broke the tension. "My lords, why do you quarrel?"

Astegal whirled. "Sidonie!"

She stood in the entrance to the great hall, four Amazigh flanking her. Her face was very pale, and she was unsteady on her feet. "Is somewhat amiss?"

"No." Astegal strode to her side, the crowd parting for him. "I was frightened for you," he said, cupping her face. "You shouldn't have done that. I keep telling you, it isn't safe yet. Are you all right?"

Sidonie shivered. "No." She fixed her gaze on his face. Her eyes were like pools of darkness, wide and fearful. "I'm sorry. Astegal, you were right. Roderico's mad. He said things, terrible things . . ."

"Hush." Astegal unclasped his purple cloak and slid it solicitously over her shoulders. "I know. I kept trying to tell you. I'm sorry, my dear. I was trying to spare you that ugliness."

"I know." She shivered again. "I'm sorry. I should have trusted you. I think . . . I think I would like to lie down. I haven't felt quite myself since the sunstroke. Do you mind?"

She was lying.

She was lying, and she was doing it so damnably well that I wanted to cheer and shower her with flowers. Oh, she was frightened and shaken, that was no act. And there was nothing she was doing to give herself away, not even anything a trained Guildsman could spot. But I could tell. I *knew* her.

Astegal steered her through the crowd, his hands on her shoulders. The Amazigh guards trailed behind them, looking as crestfallen as veiled warriors could under Bodeshmun's withering glare. When their procession passed me, I bowed.

"Messire Maignard." Sidonie paused long enough to give me a tremulous smile. "You were kind to me before when I was ill. Mayhap when I feel stronger, we'll have another game. It seems chess calms my nerves."

Behind her, Astegal gave me a curt nod.

"Of course." I inclined my head. "As always, your highness, I am at your disposal." Once again, I forced myself to adopt a tone of levity. "I shall hope and pray for your restored health, my lady. In the parlance of chess, I shall await your move."

"Indeed," she murmured. "Indeed."

Forty-two

Here you are, my lord." Kratos dropped the ring into my hand.

I examined it. A simple band, a gold knot. To all intents and purposes, it was identical to the ring Sunjata had created. For all I knew, it *was* the same ring. I hadn't dared set any distinguishing mark on the copy. I slid the ring onto the fourth finger of my right hand. It fit very well.

"So Esme succeeded?" I asked.

Kratos chuckled. "Ah, the lass was brilliant! Yon Astegal does love to be cozened and pampered. She oiled him and worked him down to his fingertips." He kissed the tips of his own fingers. "The ring slid loose like a charm. I could see it all from the caldarium. You remember?"

"I remember," I said briefly.

"Yes, well." Kratos smiled broadly. "It fell to the floor and bounced. *Ch-chink, ch-chink!* Our Esme scrambled after it in a panic. Astegal hadn't even begun to worry before she shoved the copy on his finger, babbling apologies. I watched. She retrieved *his* ring later."

"This?" I raised my right hand.

Kratos nodded. "That. So what happens now, my lord?"

I sighed. "Unfortunately, we wait. I need to speak to Sidonie alone, and that's the one thing I can't fathom how to do."

"That, and getting Bodeshmun's talisman," Kratos observed. Over the past days, I'd taken him fully into my confidence and told him everything. "Is he really as dangerous as all that?"

"Ptolemy Solon thought so," I said, removing the ring and stashing it in the trunk with the false bottom. "And so did Sunjata."

He shrugged. "Doesn't seem like it."

On that score, Kratos was wrong. The following morning, Astegal summoned Roderico de Aragon and his entourage to the great hall. The elderly former king struck a tragic, forlorn figure, standing with the remnants of his court in his former palace while Astegal paced back and forth like an angry lion. Bodeshmun stood behind him, silent.

"My wishes were clear," Astegal said. "No one was to give audience to my wife without my express permission. You defied me."

"She is the Dauphine of Terre d'Ange," Roderico said with dignity. "Was I to refuse her when she was at my doorstep?"

"Yes," Astegal said. "You told her lies that upset her. Last night, she could find no peace without the aid of a sleeping draught. Even now, she is too ill to rise."

Roderico's eyes flashed. "I told her no lies."

"The truth is what *I* say it is." Astegal's voice hardened. "Carthage and Terre d'Ange have always been allies. Aragonia provoked this war by permitting its fleet to prey unchecked on Carthaginian trade-ships. *That* is the truth, and from this moment onward, any man or woman who claims otherwise is guilty of treason. Is that understood?"

The former king didn't answer. One of the members of his entourage, a young man who couldn't have been much past his majority, muttered an expletive.

"You!" Astegal snapped. "Come here." After a moment's hesitation, the young lord obeyed. Astegal surveyed him. "There are rumors circulating that Carthage is capable of wielding dire magics. Observe and learn fear."

He beckoned to Bodeshmun, who stepped forward. The young Aragonian stared at the Chief Horologist with hatred, a muscle jumping in his cheek. Bodeshmun raised one hand, palm upward, until it was level with the man's face. He blew out his breath gently over his palm. A brief puff of dust arose.

The young Aragonian gasped. One gasp, no more. His hands rose frantically to scrabble at his throat. His face worked. Not a sound emerged from his mouth.

"Enough!" Roderico said sharply. "It shall be as you say. Spare the lad."

Astegal folded his arms. "What is done cannot be undone. If you wish others to be spared this fate, remember this moment."

It was an awful thing. The great hall was filled with onlookers. Astegal meant this event to be witnessed. And in front of all of us, the young Aragonian lord slowly choked to death for no apparent cause. His face turned dark and his eyes bulged. It was a mercy when he finally sank to the floor. Several members of Roderico's entourage were weeping audibly, and silent tears ran down the former king's creased face.

"Is it understood?" Astegal repeated.

"Yes, my lord." Roderico's voice cracked. "The truth is whatever you say it is."

"Good." Astegal nodded. "You may go."

They went.

I let out a breath I hadn't realized I'd been holding. Kratos and I exchanged a glance. Well, that was one question asked and answered. Yes, Bodeshmun *was* that dangerous.

The memory of it made my skin crawl. There was no word from Sidonie, so Kratos and I proceeded to the bathhouse. We engaged in a few training bouts, which left me bone-jarred and bruised. It didn't erase the memory of the Aragonian's strangled face, but it helped a bit. Afterward, I went to soak in the caldarium while Kratos accepted one of his friendly wagers.

There, I managed to spot Esme and catch her eye. She pointed to the table in her chamber. I nodded and emerged dripping from the bath. No one was around at the moment; the idle soldiers were cheering on their comrade in his bout against Kratos. I went to fetch the purse I'd hidden in my things.

Esme gave me a startled look when I handed it to her. It was heavier than she'd expected. I'd doubled the amount.

"You did well," I said.

She tucked the purse away quickly. "Lay down. I'll massage you."

I shook my head. "Better if you're not seen with me. Vanish well and be safe until this passes, Esme."

"I pray it's soon," she whispered.

As matters transpired, it *was* soon, at least where Esme was concerned. By the time Kratos and I returned to the palace, there was a whole new uproar in progress. Astegal and his councilors were closeted away once more and the place was abuzz with gossip.

"What passes?" I asked one of the guards I knew by sight.

His face was grim. "We've had ships lying off the harbor at Amílcar. One of them intercepted an Aragonian ship bound for Terre d'Ange. Serafin's pleading for aid from the D'Angeline fleet." He lowered his voice. "Trying to trade on their old alliance."

"I thought the D'Angeline fleet was incapacitated," I said.

"Not the bulk of it," he said glumly. "Looks as though we'll be fighting a winter war after all."

"Hard luck," I said.

The guard shrugged. "It's a soldier's lot."

Better than a bath-house attendant's lot, I thought, but I kept my mouth shut. This particular guard seemed a decent enough fellow. Inwardly, I was pleased. If Astegal pulled his army out of New Carthage, the task of gaining access to Sidonie seemed marginally less insurmountable.

Things were finally beginning to move.

Forty-three

Once things began to move, they moved quickly indeed. By the time Sunjata returned from old Carthage, he was astonished at all that had transpired in his absence. Astegal might have enjoyed playing cock of the walk and being pampered, but when he moved, he moved swiftly and decisively.

Everywhere, plans were afoot. A small standing army would be left under Lord Gillimas' command to guard New Carthage. Bodeshmun would be in charge of administering the city and the surrounding areas, and after his display in the great hall, I doubted there would be much in the way of an insurrection.

Most of the Carthaginian fleet would be moved to blockade the harbor of Amílcar, leaving a handful behind to secure the harbor here. After studying the city's defenses, Astegal had determined that it would be best assailed by land. He himself would command the siege.

Well and good, I thought. Go. Go far, far away, Astegal.

Of all the events that had transpired, the one that astonished Sunjata the most was that Esme had succeeded in procuring Astegal's ring.

"You're sure?" he said. "Did it have an effect?"

I nodded. "Oh, yes."

Sidonie had sent for me the day after Bodeshmun had killed the young Aragonian with a single breath, although of course the knowledge of that event had been kept from her. I'd found her pale and guarded. I'd brought the book of love letters with me and presented it to her as a gift. She'd gazed at it for a long time, her brows furrowed.

"I know this correspondence," she murmured at length. "Somehow. Thank you; it will be a pleasure to read the Aragonian translation."

I bowed. "I hope it may provide solace in your husband's absence."

"My husband's absence." She raised her gaze to meet mine. The fear and uncertainty in her eyes had doubled. Underneath it was a terrified determination that nearly broke my heart. "Yes."

We had played our usual game. At first, I'd thought that Sidonie was playing badly, walking into a rather obvious trap I'd set. Then I felt the pressure of her foot against mine beneath the table as she studied the board.

"I'm in a very precarious situation here, aren't I, Messire Maignard?" she inquired.

I moved a piece, returning the unseen pressure. "Indeed, my lady."

Her hand hovered over her queen. "I confess, I don't fully understand what it is that you've done. Will you be gallant enough to advise me?"

I shook my head. "I cannot divulge my secrets."

Sidonie's head moved imperceptibly in the direction of the Amazigh guard. I gave the briefest possible nod. The guard stared past us, bored half out of his wits. I'd wager they drew straws to avoid this posting.

"Well," she said lightly. "Mayhap I'll find a way to make you talk."

"Mayhap you will," I said. "But not today."

That was all, but it was enough. She knew. She knew something was very, very wrong. Bodeshmun's spell had been weakened. And Sidonie de la Courcel, terrified and uncertain, was nonetheless playing a cautious and meticulous game of her own.

It was hard, so damnably *hard*, not to be able to tell her.

Elua, she had courage! I broke into a cold sweat conversing under the Amazigh's bored gaze. How much worse must it be for Sidonie? She knew, but she didn't *know*. Missing memories, false memories. At least I had the surety of my own wits and a loyal ally or two.

Sidonie was all alone.

I didn't see her again until after the majority of the Carthaginian fleet had set sail and Astegal departed with the army.

The latter was an affair rife with pageantry. It was a vast army. Most of his troops were Carthaginian, but there was a sizable contingent of Nubian mercenaries with striking zebra-hide shields and long spears, and a mounted company of robed Amazigh. We assembled outside the gates of the city to see them off.

"Bastards," Kratos muttered.

The ceremony began with the sacrifice of a white heifer, a singularly gory and unpleasant ritual. Once the poor beast's struggles had ceased, the priests slit its belly and withdrew the steaming entrails for inspection. They pronounced the augurs to be good and invoked the blessings of Tanit and Ba'al Hammon on the venture.

Astegal gave a stirring speech full of lies about the glorious era of peace and prosperity that would follow on the heels of Carthage's victory. His voice carried well, and the army cheered. Clad in gilded armor, he looked every inch the heroic general. Sidonie stood beside him, blank-faced as a doll. Astegal didn't care. He swept her into his arms and kissed her farewell, proclaiming the hope that he would return victorious to news that she was providing him with an heir to the vast new empire of Carthage. There were more cheers and long blasts on the trumpets.

Then he turned her over to Bodeshmun, who made a speech declaring that the Princess Sidonie and New Carthage alike were under his protection. When it was finished, Astegal mounted his horse and drew his sword.

"Onward, Carthage!" he shouted. "Onward to victory!"

The army roared its approval, soldiers beating their shields and stamping their feet, trumpets blaring. Astegal nudged his mount, and they were off, rank upon rank of soldiers falling in behind him, supply wagons groaning. It was a long time before the last column passed us.

I sighed. "Good riddance."

Without an entire occupying army, New Carthage seemed much emptier than before. We returned with the remnants of the procession that had accompanied Astegal to the gates. On every street, Aragonians stared at us with bitter hatred, but it was hatred tempered by fear. Not a one of them dared speak. Perversely, I found myself glad for the presence of Bodeshmun and the remaining forces. I didn't doubt but that every man and woman we passed would gladly see all of us dead.

In that, I was more than right.

On the morrow, I received a message from Sidonie inviting me to accompany her on a stroll in the gardens. I met her at the appointed hour. It was an incongruous sight, the D'Angeline princess surrounded by four veiled Amazigh.

"You look well, your highness," I greeted her. "Are you feeling better?"

"A bit." It was true: she didn't look quite as pale. "I thought the fresh air might help clear my thoughts."

The gardens surrounding the palace were actually quite lovely and extensive. We strolled through them, passing lemon and orange groves, eucalyptus trees, and others I couldn't name. Here and there, we passed Aragonian gardeners at work, pruning the trees and culling weeds. Like the bath-house attendants, I thought, they must have taken pride in their work once. Now they merely looked sullen.

"Everything is so green," Sidonie observed. "It's hard to believe it's winter."

"Southern climes," I said. "On Cythera, the first orchids will be blooming soon."

We continued for some time in this vein, exchanging meaningless pleasantries. Bit by bit, Sidonie's pace increased, until we were walking quite briskly. I realized she was trying to put some distance between us and her guards.

It didn't work. The Amazigh quickened their own pace, trailing behind us like so many indigo spectres. Sidonie gave an imperceptible shrug and slowed.

"Mayhap we might sit for a moment," I suggested, nodding at a marble bench beside a fountain in the shape of a fish spewing water. I was hoping that the sound of splashing water might provide some cover.

It wasn't enough to drown out our conversation. Gods, this was ridiculously frustrating! After a few more moments of inane talk, Sidonie sighed. "Thank you, Leander, you've been very patient. Mayhap I should return."

I rose and bowed. "Of course, my lady. You shouldn't tire yourself."

We returned the way we'd come. And what happened next, I couldn't have said for the life of me how I knew. A lifetime of training to be observant, I suppose. It was the second gardener we encountered, one we'd passed before. This time it was different. Somewhat about him, the way he peered furtively at us as we approached. The way his hands slid and twisted on the pruning shears he held. The way he collected himself and set his shoulders. It wasn't until we'd actually passed him that it all came together in my mind. I glanced over my shoulder.

Between two of the Amazigh, there was the gardener behind us. He held the blades of his pruning shears by the tip, poised for the throw. His arm shot forward. Metal flashed.

"*Elua, no!*"

I flung myself on Sidonie without thinking, my weight bringing both of us crashing to the earth. Somewhat sharp stung my scalp as we fell. I landed hard atop her, driving the breath from her lungs. Her startled eyes stared into mine. Wet warmth trickled though my hair. Behind us, there were shouts of alarm and fury.

Oh, gods.

The feeling of her body beneath mine.

Neither of us moved.

And then strong hands yanked me off her, pulled me upright. The Amazigh surrounded us, asking questions in a garbled panic. Behind them, the gardener's body was slumped on the ground. His head was a few feet away.

"I'm fine." Sidonie's voice shook. "That man—*why*?"

They exchanged glances.

"It doesn't matter," I said. My heart was racing, and I couldn't tell if it was fear or the sudden shock of desire. "You're safe, love. That's all that matters."

She searched my face. "You're hurt."

I touched the back of my head. My fingers came away bloody, but not terribly so. "It's just a nick. Scalp wounds bleed a lot."

"He tried . . ." Sidonie swallowed. "Oh, gods."

"I know." I rounded on the Amazigh. "Name of Elua! Why did you kill him? You should have taken him alive to be questioned!"

One of them shrugged. "Desert justice."

"Desert idiocy, more like!" I wrestled my temper under control. "No mind. Let's just get the princess safely back to the palace. *Now.*"

The Amazigh formed a tight square around us. Sidonie clung to my arm, holding it pressed hard against her. I could feel her trembling. This time, I didn't think it was feigned, not in the least. Oh, gods, that had been a near thing! Fury and terror and tenderness broke over me in waves.

I loved her.

I loved her so much.

And I'd nearly lost her.

Pandemonium broke loose the minute we entered the palace. One of the guards was dispatched at a run to fetch Bodeshmun, who came with alacrity, his black robes swirling around him.

"Are you harmed, your highness?" he asked Sidonie grimly.

"No." Her nails bit into my forearm. "Leander saved me. He's hurt."

"Escort her highness to her quarters," Bodeshmun said to the Amazigh. "Send for the physician. After he's examined her, have him report to me." To me, he said, "Come."

I accompanied him to his quarters. There, Bodeshmun bade me sit and tell him all that had transpired. He listened intently, nodding into his black beard.

"Idiots," he said when I told him the Amazigh had killed the gardener. "They're fierce and loyal enough, but they've no head for intrigue." He sighed. "I'll have every Aragonian attendant on the palace rounded up for questioning."

"Good," I said, angry enough to mean it. "Why do they blame *her*? Surely they must know—"

"No," Bodeshmun interrupted me. "No, they don't, young Maignard. They may suspect something amiss, but they do not *know* it. Not for a surety. And I'd prefer to keep it thusly. Folk are a good deal easier to control when their anger is scattered and misplaced."

I nodded. "I understand."

"You did well out there." He narrowed his eyes at me. "How did you know? How did you notice what trained warriors failed to observe?"

"Warriors are trained to fight," I said. "I'm trained to observe."

"Ah, yes." Bodeshmun gave a thin smile. "The Guild's infamous arts of covertcy. Well, it was well done."

I inclined my head. "My thanks, my lord."

The Carthaginian physician arrived in short order. He reported that Sidonie was unharmed, but distraught in the extreme, demanding that Astegal and the army be returned to protect her.

Bodeshmun snorted. "Give her a sleeping draught."

"I tried," the physician said. "She refused."

The Chief Horologist waved a dismissive hand. "See to this young man's head and try again. Tell her if she's breeding, she needs to rest for the child's sake. There is a good chance of it, is there not?"

The physician bowed. "'Tis too early to tell, my lord. But her highness' weariness and distress augur well for it."

I swallowed, tasting bile.

I took my leave of Bodeshmun and went with the physician, whose name was Girom, to his quarters. There, he undid my braids and cleaned the wound, swabbing it with something that stung like hell, then closed it with two stitches using a needle and waxed silk thread, which also stung like hell.

Once it was done, Girom dismissed me. I returned to my quarters and washed the drying blood out of my hair in the basin, telling Kratos and a wide-eyed Sunjata what had transpired.

"Name of Elua!" I said in disgust. "Sidonie's as much a victim in this as any bath-house attendant. What are they thinking?"

Sunjata shrugged. "They're thinking they saw her kiss General Astegal farewell outside the gates of the city before he rode off to conquer the rest of Aragonia. What else?"

I yanked a comb through my damp hair. "We need to speak to Justina. If this is part of a larger conspiracy, she may be able to find out. She can help spread the word covertly that Sidonie's no more to be blamed than—"

There was a knock at the outer door that made all three of us startle and fall silent. Kratos went to answer it.

"My lord Maignard." It was Girom, the physician. He looked harried. "Forgive me, but I require your assistance. Her highness has consented to take a sleeping draught if you will sit at her side until she sleeps." He cleared his throat. "It seems she feels you are the only one to protect her in General Astegal's absence. My lord Bodeshmun has consented."

Oh, clever girl.

I rose. "Of course. I'll come immediately."

Forty-four

"*Out!*"

An earthenware cup shattered against the wall of the bedchamber. One of the Amazigh dodged flying shards. Girom the physician raised his hands pleadingly. "My lady—"

"All of you, *out*!" Sidonie said in a perfect fury, pacing. She was wrapped in a dressing-robe, clutching it to her. Her hair was loose and unbound, falling over her shoulders. Her face was stark white, save for two spots of hectic color on her cheekbones. "Everyone but Leander! You're worthless, all of you!"

"Go." Girom gestured to the Amazigh.

Sidonie pointed at the physician. "You too."

"Yes, yes," he said in a soothing voice. "As I promised, once you drink the sleeping draught."

Her breast rose and fell with sharp breaths. "You'll go, then? You'll go if I do?"

"As I promised," Girom repeated.

"I want him to stay." Sidonie pointed at me. "I want

Leander to stay until I fall asleep. And then I want him to keep watch outside my door. He saved my life, and you won't bring me Astegal."

The physician sighed. "Drink your draught, your highness."

Sidonie fixed her gaze on me. "You won't leave?"

"I swear it," I said to her. "I'll stay at your side until you sleep, and then I'll guard your door until you wake. No one will pass."

"And you'll go if I do?" she asked Girom.

"Yes," he said wearily. "Please, your highness. It's for your own good."

"All right." Sidonie picked up another cup from her nightstand, this one brimming with dark liquid. Her hands shook and the liquid trembled. She eyed Girom with suspicion. "You promise?"

"Yes, your highness!" he said in frustration. "I *promise*."

She drank. "There. Now go."

Girom heaved another sigh, this one filled with relief. I didn't envy him. "Thank you, my lady," he said to her. "Now lie down and rest. Leander will stay by your side. It's a potent draught; it will take effect swiftly."

She sat obediently on her bed. "All right. Go away now."

He backed through the door, closing it behind him.

We were alone.

Sidonie buried her face in her hands and shuddered. I crossed the room swiftly, kneeling before her. "Are you all right?" I whispered.

"No." She dropped her hands. "Not really." Her tone was unwontedly dry. "I'm scared half out of my wits, and that was the single most mortifying performance of my life." She touched the back of my head with infinite gentleness. "Are you?"

"Yes," I whispered. "How long until the sleeping draught takes effect?"

Her fingers slid through my hair, trailed along my cheek. "The one I poured into the vase hidden behind the chamber-pot under my bed and replaced with unwatered wine? A few more minutes at least if I'd actually drunk it. Talk fast."

My entire body shivered beneath her touch. "I'll try. Only—"

"I know," Sidonie whispered, cupping my face with both hands now. There were tears in her black eyes. "I know."

The lover showers kisses on the face of the beloved . . .

It was gentle, it was frantic, it was terrified, all at once. I knelt before her, my face upturned. She kissed my eyelids, my temples, my cheeks, the corners of my mouth. Sweet, so sweet! I hadn't imagined so much sweetness existed in the world. She kissed my mouth.

My lips parted beneath hers, the tip of her tongue touched mine.

Imriel.

Ohgodsohgodsohgods! Knowledge and memory burst like a ripe seed-pod inside my skull. It filled me to overflowing.

Imriel.

I was Imriel.

I gasped and tore myself away from her, huddling and clasping my own arms, rocking on my knees and shuddering.

I was Imriel.

Sidonie drew back from me in alarm, her eyes widening. "*What?*"

It flooded me; it flooded every part of me. Memories, crashing and churning. I remembered everything. I knew myself. I knew what had happened. Everything. All the plans, all the risk, all the uncertainty. All the fear and horror. My madness. My quest. Ptolemy Solon and his needle, stitching and stitching. Leander's voice, stitching a new tale, binding his memories to my flesh. I drew a breath, ragged and raw. "Oh, Sidonie!" I murmured. "It's me. I'm *me*. Imriel."

She shrank back against the headboard of her bed. "Leander?"

She didn't know me.

Of course she didn't know me.

"I love you," I said in anguish. "Oh, Name of Elua, Sidonie! I've loved you since you were sixteen years old. I'm what you're missing. I'm what you've forgotten. You and I."

"No!" She hissed the word at me, eyes showing the whites all around in sheer terror. "Leander, *please*! Don't do this to me. I can't do this!"

I reached for her. "Sidonie . . ."

She shrank back farther. "Go away! Please, go away!"

I sat back on my heels. "Will you just please listen?"

"No." Sidonie shook her head, squeezing her eyes shut as though to block out the world. A pulse in the hollow of her throat beat frantically. "No, no, no, no. I thought you were . . . I don't know, but you're not. Just please, go away."

Ah, Elua.

I knew everything.

"*Sidonie,*" I said, desperate to reach her. "Alais' dog was killed by a bear!"

For a long moment, she didn't speak or react. I knelt silently, waiting, acutely aware of time dwindling. And then slowly, slowly, Sidonie's eyes opened. She watched me without speaking, breathing hard through parted lips.

"It happened in Alba," I said. "But you were right; there was a boar, too. Years earlier, at a hunting party. We stumbled over a boar. Your horse bolted. Alais' dog, Celeste, was gored, but she survived. I stitched her wound in the woods using Amarante's embroidery kit."

"I remember . . . parts," she murmured.

Oh, gods, it nearly broke my heart to look at her. "Something Bodeshmun did pulled a whole thread out of your memory," I said gently. "And everything that's left is partly unravelled. Is that what it feels like?" She nodded slowly. "Sidonie, I can undo it. If you can find a way for us to be alone together again, for a little while longer, I can explain everything."

Her dark eyes dwelled on my face. "I don't know."

I didn't dare push her. Not now. I was barely holding myself together. "Think on it," I whispered. "Try to sleep. I don't dare stay any longer. But I'll be on the other side of the door, guarding your dreams. And I promise you, Princess, no one will ever harm you while there's breath in my body."

I rose slowly and carefully. Sidonie looked so damnably vulnerable. My doing, my fault. It tore me up inside like I'd swallowed broken glass. Still, it had to be done. I left the room quietly, closing the door behind me.

"She sleeps?" Girom inquired.

"Yes." I leaned against the door, my knees trembling. My voice sounded strange to my ears. I'd entered that room as Leander Maignard, and left it as Imriel de la Courcel. "Yes, she was agitated for a time, but the draught took effect."

"Good." The physician nodded. "I'll return in the morning to examine her." He hesitated. "Are you actually planning to stay? You needn't. It's a powerful draught; she won't wake for hours."

"Yes." I let my knees give way and slid down the door, hoping I looked more like a man settling in for a long vigil than a man collapsing. "I promised." I tried to find Leander Maignard's insouciant tone somewhere inside me. "One should always keep a promise to a lady, messire."

Girom shrugged. "As you like. Send one of the guards to fetch me if there's any difficulty before I arrive."

With that, he took his leave. The Amazigh regarded

me with impassive disinterest. There were two of them on guard. They exchanged a few words in their native tongue. One went to stir the fire in the hearth, then took up a post where he could keep an eye on both me and the outer door. The other stretched his length on a couch, clearly prepared to nap.

I couldn't have cared less.

Imriel.

I was Imriel.

The knowledge pounded through me, over and over. I remembered everything. My madness, the flight to Cythera. My mother. Ptolemy Solon's spell. I remembered everything I'd done as Leander, vividly. I even remembered Leander's own memories, although they'd grown faint and ghostly, like somewhat read in a tale. But I remembered what *I'd* felt as Leander.

And it was nothing to what I felt now.

I was going to have to act fast. Ptolemy Solon hadn't thought a mere semblance would fool Bodeshmun, and that was all I had now. I leaned the back of my head against the door, staring into the dim salon. The gouge in my skull throbbed. I had to get Sidonie out of here.

And I had to get Bodeshmun's talisman.

Ah, gods! What was happening at home? There hadn't been word of Terre d'Ange since Carthage. The thought made me shiver. Leander Maignard hadn't cared overmuch.

I did.

It was a long night. I stayed awake, thinking. At some point, the Amazigh warrior on guard yawned and woke the other. They traded roles. Some hours later, another pair came to relieve them altogether. I watched the process through slitted eyes, thinking about the Amazigh garb hidden in my trunks.

A little after dawn, a Carthaginian chambermaid came

with a tray of tea and fruit. She made to pass me and enter the bedchamber. I shook my head at her.

"No one passes," I said. "I promised."

The door opened behind me. "It's all right," Sidonie said quietly. "Elissa may enter."

I got stiffly to my feet. "Did you sleep well, your highness?"

"Yes." There were violet shadows under her eyes, but her gaze was clear and calm. Sidonie de la Courcel had come to a decision. "Thank you, Messire Maignard. Your presence helped. Would it be too much to ask you to return tonight?"

"No, my lady," I said, bowing. "Not at all."

Forty-five

I made my way wearily to my own chambers, praying I didn't encounter Bodeshmun on the way. For a mercy, I didn't. I was going to have to avoid him, at least up until the minute I killed him.

And I was still working on that plan.

Sunjata was there, muttering over his latest manifest. The gem trade had fallen off since Astegal had pulled the army out of New Carthage. I stopped dead, staring at him and remembering.

"You knew," I said.

His head jerked up and he stared at me, recognition slowly dawning. "You . . . ?"

"Imriel," I said. "Yes. I know myself."

"Ah," Sunjata said. "Yes. It was in her ladyship's letter."

I regarded him with a convoluted mixture of Leander's fondness and my own bitter memories of his voice whispering in my ear, the stab of a long needle, his hand tugging a ring from my finger. "Why did you have me strip?"

He looked away. "I had to know. To see."

I raised my brows. "You could have refused me."

"Leander would have been hurt," Sunjata murmured. "It would have been hard to explain. And . . . you nearly *were* him, at least at first. Even after I saw you." His throat worked. "This is a lonely business, your highness."

"Call me Imriel," I said wryly. "We've been lovers."

Sunjata's dark skin flushed darker. "I have something for you," he said, rising and going to his own bedchamber. He returned with the trunk I'd brought from Cythera, the one inscribed with his name. "These are yours."

I was just opening the trunk as Kratos stumbled from the servant's chamber, yawning and scratching himself. "What's all this?" he asked as I withdrew a pair of fawn-colored woolen breeches.

"My things," I said. Beneath the few items of clothing I'd brought on my flight lay the rest. My sword and dagger, my rhinoceros-hide sword-belt, shiny with wear. A purse with nothing in it but a polished stone with a hole in the middle that I carried for luck and remembrance. My eyes stung. "Kratos, my friend, it seems I'm not who I thought I was."

"Oh?" Kratos rubbed his stubbled chin. "Who are you, then?"

"Imriel," I said, withdrawing the vambraces Dorelei had given me, engraved with the image of the Black Boar of the Cullach Gorrym. A golden torc. "Imriel nó Montrève de la Courcel."

Kratos stared. "Has he lost his wits?" he asked Sunjata.

"No," Sunjata said. "Found them."

I stood and drew my sword. It rang faintly. It was a well-tempered blade, longer and heavier than anything Leander Maignard had owned. I moved softly through the first few forms of the hours. "Sunjata, how much of Leander's attire must I wear to preserve the semblance?"

"At a guess?" He shrugged. "The more you can manage,

the better. Once someone's seen you as Leander, they won't *unsee* you, not unless you remove everything of his. But I wouldn't take any unnecessary risks."

"All right." I sheathed the blade. Kratos was still gaping at me. "Is that why you came back?" I asked Sunjata. "For this moment?"

"Yes," he said quietly. "I owed you that much."

I nodded. "You should go now, Sunjata. I'm going to have to act quickly. And I'll need Captain Deimos' ship. Can you arrange passage back to Carthage elsewhere?"

"Yes." He cleared his throat. "Yes, there are ships carrying information and supplies between old Carthage and new. It should be no trouble."

"Good." I turned to Kratos. "My friend, you ought to go with him. I'll give you money to book passage to Cythera from thence." I smiled. "I suspect my lady mother will find you a joy and a delight the likes of which she hasn't known since a clever and fearless fellow named Canis was in her service."

Kratos closed his mouth with an audible click, then blinked a few times. "Why are you dismissing me, my lord?" he asked in bewilderment.

I laid a hand on his shoulder. "You've been a better ally than I could ever have dreamed. I ask for no more. The risks I've taken thus far are nothing compared to the ones I mean to take."

"Huh." Kratos scratched his chin again. "That's some well-sounding noble folly, my lord. You prepared to risk yon golden-haired princess' life for it?"

I hesitated.

"Didn't think so." A complacent smile spread over his homely features. "By all the gods, why shouldn't I stay? Whoever you are, you're an interesting fellow. What do you need me to do?"

"You're sure of this?" I asked in a hard voice.

Kratos' heavy shoulders moved in a shrug. "I said it, didn't I?"

I paced the room, thinking. "More than anything, I need a way out of the palace that's lightly guarded. Do you reckon you might find one?"

He laughed. "Oh, aye! I reckon."

I closed my eyes briefly, thinking back on that day in the slave-market. The Aragonian boy with the curly hair and the stricken face. So much depended on this: his life, the lives of so many others. Not just mine, not just Sidonie's. More than the fate of even Terre d'Ange hung in the balance. Blessed Elua had guided my hand—or Leander's—the day I'd chosen Kratos. And he was right. If I didn't want to bring this all crashing down on our heads, I couldn't afford to be soft-hearted.

"My thanks, Kratos," I said. An unexpected yawn overtook me. "I need to take a few hours of sleep. Will you wake me around midday?"

"Will you explain all this when I do?" he retorted.

"I will," I promised.

With that, I took to my own chamber and fell onto the bed, exhausted in mind and body alike. I fell asleep almost instantly and slept like the dead until Kratos shook me awake. It felt like no time at all had passed, but the room was filled with afternoon sunlight.

"It's later than I asked," I commented, shaking myself awake.

"Aye." Kratos' face was grave. "I reckoned you needed it. And the eunuch saved you some time. He explained it all to me." He gave a short, wondering laugh. "Never thought to find myself living something out of a bard's tale."

"No?" I rubbed my eyes. "Well, let's just hope we live to hear the end of it, my friend."

Accompanied by Kratos, I made my way to the inn near the harbor where Captain Deimos and his men were lodging. Since the army had left, the inn was empty save for their presence. I bought a jug of wine and met with Deimos at an isolated table while Kratos stood watch. There, I told the captain that I needed him to ready the ship to sail on a moment's notice.

"To Carthage?" Deimos asked.

I shook my head. "Marsilikos."

The captain was no fool. "That's a damned dangerous passage this time of year, my lord, even if we hug the coast all the way. Is it necessary?"

"It will be," I said.

Deimos eyed me. "What are you asking me to do?"

"Right now, better you don't know the details. If you're asking if it's dangerous, yes. And if you're not willing to do it, tell me now, Deimos. I'll not hold it against you." I touched the hilt of my sword. "But I swear to Blessed Elua, if you turn against me at the last minute, I'll make sure killing you is the last thing I do."

His mouth twisted. "Do you know, Ptolemy Solon made me swear a binding oath that I'd render you any assistance you asked. I wondered why the old ape was being so adamant."

"Will you do it?" I asked. "I promise you, if you do, Terre d'Ange will reward you beyond your wildest dreams."

"I'm not an oath-breaker," Deimos said curtly. "You don't need to bribe me. The ship will be ready by tomorrow."

"Good man," I said, sighing inwardly with relief. What I would have done if Deimos had refused, I couldn't say. Sunjata had been right about one thing. I was indeed lucky that my mother loved me.

After the harbor, Kratos and I stopped at the bath-house. It felt strange and empty without the presence of scores of soldiers, and I felt acutely self-conscious as I stripped. I'd done it a dozen times without even thinking. Today, it was different. I could hear the faint echo of Ptolemy Solon's voice in my memory, a pinch at my earlobes. *Surely they will serve as a last line of defense against the perils of nudity.*

Elua have mercy, what an insane risk.

I washed and dressed quickly, feeling safer once I was clad. Back in my chambers at the palace, I sorted through my things, trying to decide how much risk I *was* willing to take. I needed to prove myself to Sidonie, but I had a feeling that if the first thing I did was strip mother-naked in front of her, it would strain her fragile trust. In the end, I donned a pair of my own breeches and underclothes, but everything else I wore was Leander's.

Sunjata had been gone, but he returned before nightfall. I admitted him when he knocked on the door of my chamber.

"I'm sailing for Carthage on the morrow," he said directly. "I've come to bid you farewell."

"My thanks." I put out my hand. "Be safe, Sunjata."

He paused, then clasped it. "And you. Be careful, my lord. Don't forget that you still need to wear Leander's mask for a time, at least in public." He gave me his wry smile. "A little less . . . intensity . . . mayhap."

I nodded. "Duly noted."

Sunjata's smile turned wistful. "I wish you luck."

At that moment, Kratos' voice came from the far chamber, informing me that the physician had sent for me to attend the princess.

"My thanks," I said to Sunjata a second time. I rummaged in my trunk and found my gold-knotted ring, sliding it on my finger and turning it inward to hide it. My heart began beating faster with a mix of hope and fear. I sensed it would be a long time before it slowed. "I fear I'm going to need it."

With that, I went to Sidonie.

Forty-six

In Sidonie's bedchamber, we reenacted the same ritual as the previous evening, only with considerably less drama. She drank the sleeping draught without protest, seeming weary and defeated. It wasn't until the physician Girom withdrew and closed the door that her demeanor changed.

"You can't stay long," she warned me.

"I know." I took a deep breath. "I'll do this as quickly as I can. Forgive me if it sounds—"

"No." Her lips curved in a faint, tired smile. "I made the guards drink a toast to Astegal's health when Girom went to fetch you. If his infernal draughts are half as effective as he claims, they'll be sleeping in minutes. You've got to dispatch Girom before it happens."

I stared at her. "You are a wonderment."

Her slender shoulders moved in a shrug. "Desperation provides all manner of inspiration."

So it was that I waited quietly for only a few moments before going to inform the physician that she slept.

"So soon?" Girom remarked in surprise.

I spread my hands. "Gods, man, can you blame the lass? She's worn to the bone with fear and loneliness. My lord Astegal would have been kinder to leave her in Carthage until Aragonia was truly settled."

He sighed. "Yes, well, Astegal wants his heir. I pray that's the cause of her highness' uncertain moods."

One of the Amazigh was already blinking conspicuously. "Well, whatever it is, I pray her highness calms soon," I said, sinking cross-legged to take up my post before her door. I forced a yawn. "I'll sleep better in my own bed. Go on. I'll send word if there's any difficulty."

Girom took his leave.

I waited.

After a muttered exchange, the blinking Amazigh stretched out on the couch. He was snoring within minutes. The other fellow was bigger. It took longer for the draught to affect him. I watched out of the corner of my eye, praying the draught Sidonie had poured into their wine had been large enough for both of them.

It had been. He paced for a while, shaking his head. Then he sat in a chair, as though thinking a few minutes' rest would refresh him. It wasn't long before his body grew slack and relaxed, head tilted back.

I got to my feet and crossed the room quietly. I shook first one, then the other of the Amazigh. Neither man woke.

I opened the door to Sidonie's chamber. She was sitting on her bed, watching the door fixedly. I entered and closed it behind me.

"So," she said. "Tell me about this spell."

There was a mirror above a dressing table on the opposite wall. I glanced involuntarily at it and saw Leander Maignard's face return my gaze. It gave me a shiver. I hadn't known until that moment what I'd see; but of course, the semblance hadn't been broken for me.

"There were three spells," I began slowly. "The first one bound everyone in the City of Elua the night the Carthaginian horologists displayed their marvel, convincing them that Terre d'Ange and Carthage were allies, and that you had consented to wed Astegal. It binds them still, but only those who were in the city. The last I heard, Terre d'Ange was on the verge of civil war."

Sidonie's face paled. "And the second?"

"The first spell holds only on D'Angeline soil. The second one bound you to Astegal and convinced you that you were in love with him." I twisted the ring on my finger and showed it to her. "This was half of it. It . . . you gave it to me, Sidonie. It was a love-token." I saw doubt in her eyes and hurried onward. "It doesn't matter. You do know the ring, yes?"

She nodded. "Astegal always wore it."

"He still thinks he does," I said. "But a few days ago, the day you took it into your head to call on Roderico de Aragon, I arranged to have it exchanged for a copy. And something changed in you that day, didn't it?"

"Yes." Sidonie looked away, frowning. "It was strange. It was as though I'd been startled out of a daydream. And I thought, why have I been waiting so obediently when I know I could be of use here? So I went to see Roderico . . ." Her voice trailed off.

"And he accused you of betraying Terre d'Ange's alliance with Aragonia," I said gently. "That's when you knew somewhat was truly amiss."

"Yes." She looked back at me, her dark eyes wary. "And I was willing to trust you wholly until yesterday."

"It was the third spell. One wrought by Ptolemy Solon to disguise me so well I didn't know myself. It was the only way I could safely enter Carthage and find you. Bodeshmun would have seen through a mere semblance." I licked my lips, which had gone dry. "Sidonie, this one I can prove to you."

"Then do," she said.

"I have to take off most of my clothes." Gods, it sounded mad.

She raised her brows. "Find another method."

"I can't." I shook my head. "The charm's bound into Leander Maignard's entire wardrobe. Everything, every stitch of clothing, every gem and bauble. And I think that's what was done to you. I thought it was just one thing, like Astegal's ring, but it's everything. Just like it was with me. Let me show you."

It seemed to take her forever to weigh the decision. "If you lay a hand on me, I swear to Elua, I'll scream loud enough to wake the guards."

"I promise," I said fervently. "I'll not move from this spot."

Sidonie didn't comment, only watched. I pulled off my boots and stockings, then removed the ruby eardrops and several gaudy rings. I unbraided my hair, dropping the ties atop the pile.

"The breeches are my own." I undid Leander's sword-belt and dropped it. "Sunjata had them, along with the rest of my things."

"The gem-merchant's assistant?" she inquired.

"Yes." I untucked my shirt and smiled wryly. "That's another story. There's a part of it like to amuse you one day. At any rate, the shirt's the last of it."

"And when you remove it—" Sidonie began.

I did.

I didn't need to look in the mirror. I saw it in her face, eyes wide and awestruck. Neither of us spoke. I kept my promise and stood where I was. It was Sidonie who rose and came to me, slowly and wonderingly.

"Imriel," she said softly, as though hearing the word for the first time.

I nodded.

"I know you." She splayed her hand on my chest. "I don't . . . I don't remember. But I *know* you." She gazed at the pink furrows that raked my flesh. "There was a bear."

"The bear that killed Alais' dog." I covered her hand with mine. "Yes. It did this to me. That's why you can't remember it clearly."

She raised her gaze to mine. "And this spell . . . you think what's stolen my memories is the same? That it's bound into everything I possess?"

"I do," I said.

Ah, Elua! I wanted to hold her so badly, but I didn't dare. I stood there, watching the thoughts flit across her features, watching her come to a decision.

"Very well." Sidonie pulled away from me and began untying the sash of her robe. "Let's find out." Beneath the robe, she wore only a thin shift of sheer linen. She'd already prepared for bed. Her hair was loose, all her jewels removed for the evening. I held my breath as she pulled the shift over her head and dropped it atop the robe.

"Sidonie?" I whispered.

Her jaw tightened. She shook her head in wordless denial, embarrassment and despair in her face. My heart sank. Sidonie averted her face, then bent over to pick up her discarded clothing, her hair falling forward over her bare shoulders.

That was when I saw it.

"Oh, gods!" I blurted.

Her head came up fast. "*What?*"

I closed my eyes briefly and swallowed hard. "Oh, love. I'm so sorry." Moving gently and carefully, I touched her arm and turned her, then gathered her hair and tucked it over one shoulder. Lightly, lightly, I touched the spot between her shoulder blades where the falcon insignia of the House of Sarkal had been tattooed indelibly onto her fair skin. "It's here."

Sidonie shot me a single stricken glance, then crossed over to the mirror, craning her head to peer over her shoulder. When she looked back at me, her expression was adamant. "Cut it out of me."

"I'm not sure—" I began.

Her eyes flashed. "*Cut it out of me.*" She scrabbled on the top of the dressing table and came up with a sharp little knife for paring nails. "*Now.*"

I took the knife, feeling sick. "Do you have any idea how much this is going to hurt?"

"Yes," she said shortly, retrieving her robe and tugging the sash loose. She folded the sash into a thick wad. "Just do it. Please."

I nodded, willing my hands to stop shaking. "Brace yourself against the table and try not to move." Sidonie shoved the wadded sash into her mouth and obeyed. I tried to swallow, but my whole mouth had gone dry. "Arch your back," I said thickly, and she did. "All right," I whispered. "I'll do this as quickly as I can. And please don't ask me to stop, because I'm not sure I'll have the nerve to try it twice."

She made a muffled sound of assent.

My stomach roiled.

The tattoo wasn't very large, not much bigger than the engraving on Astegal's signet ring. It was stark and black against her skin. I laid the blade alongside it, breathing slowly and deeply. I could do this. I *had* to do this. Before I was born, the Skaldi warlord Waldemar Selig had attempted to skin Phèdre alive on the battlefield of Troyes-le-Mont. If a man could do such a thing for spite, I could do it for love.

I cut into Sidonie's flesh.

Her entire body jerked and she uttered a stifled cry that

brought tears to my eyes. Blood flowed, making the hilt of the little blade slippery. Cutting and cutting, all the way around it, shaking my head to clear my eyes of the tears that blurred my vision. Gods, it was awful. It was the most awful thing I'd ever done.

But I did it.

I set the paring knife and the bloody disk of skin and flesh on the table. "It's done."

Sidonie spat out the sash, but her hands remained braced on the table, knuckles white. For a long moment, she didn't move or speak, only breathed hard, her ribcage heaving. Blood trickled down her spine.

"I'm going to kill him," she said at last in a low, savage voice. "Kushiel bear witness, I swear, I'm going to kill him myself!" She straightened and turned so quickly I had to step back. I saw the full helpless fury of the knowledge of what had been done to her written in her face. Everything, every violation.

Every night in Astegal's bed.

And then her expression changed.

"Imriel," Sidonie breathed, tears welling in her eyes. "Oh, Blessed Elua! How could I forget you? In a thousand years, how could I forget you?"

"You didn't," I said, my heart aching for her. "Neither of us did. Sidonie, you found me inside Leander when I didn't even know myself. And I fell in love with you all over again. All the magic in Carthage couldn't stop us from loving one another, any more than all the politics of Terre d'Ange could. You were right when you said Blessed Elua must have some purpose for joining us, because here I am—"

She reached up to me and stopped my mouth with a kiss, with a dozen kisses. I groaned aloud and gathered her to me, sinking one hand into her hair, wrapping my arm around her waist.

"Erase him from me," Sidonie whispered against my lips.

"You're hurt," I murmured.

"I don't care." She shook her head. "I need you."

I slid both hands down to grasp her buttocks and lifted her gently. She clung to me, legs wrapped around my waist, arms twined around my neck, kissing my face as I carried her to the bed. I found clean towels by the washbasin.

"Every trace," I promised, bathing the blood from her skin while she knelt on the bed. The wound was still seeping, but slowly. I'd made the cut as shallow as I could. "Every trace of him, gone."

"You promise?" Sidonie whispered.

"Always." My throat was tight, my heart overflowing. "Always and always."

There was no part of her I didn't touch that night. I kissed the top of her head, the nape of her neck. Behind her ears, and every inch of her face. I laid a trail of kisses down her spine, blowing softly on the raw wound where Astegal had laid his mark on her. I kissed her throat, her arms. The insides of her wrists, the palms of her hands, every fingertip.

With every kiss, I willed her to be whole.

I kissed her breasts, and the valley between them. I kissed her belly. I knelt beside the bed and kissed her feet, her calves. Her inner thighs. Whole and healed.

All of her.

It hadn't begun as desire, not truly. It was a more complicated need. But with every kiss, it grew simpler and simpler. Kneeling between her thighs, I tasted her desire, feeling it echo through my own body, sweet and insistent.

Sidonie tugged at my hair. "Come here."

I rose and shed my breeches. There was a trace of uncertainty in her eyes, a lingering fear.

"Imriel," she said hesitantly. "Does it trouble you . . . ?"

"No." I took her hand and guided it to my erect, aching

phallus, curving her fingers around it. "I'm yours, Sidonie. I love you. You belong to me, and I to you. Every part of me. I won't let anyone take that from us. Not Bodeshmun, not Astegal. No one."

The last uncertainty vanished.

And . . . oh, gods.

It was everything, everything. All at once. Sidonie shook her head impatiently, straddling my lap with an inarticulate sound. My phallus throbbing in her fist. She fitted me to her.

Everything.

I felt the impossibly glorious glide of entering her, slick and tight. And I felt . . . ah, Elua! I felt *everything.* All of it. I felt myself entering her, a wanted invasion. Full and stretched and welcome.

"Name of Elua!" I whispered in awe.

There was no end to it.

It went on and on, pleasure doubled and redoubled. Mirrors reflecting mirrors. Bright, dark. Which was which? It didn't matter. Sidonie rocked atop me, rising and falling, her breasts pressed hard against my chest. I clutched her shoulder blades, struggling to be mindful of the wound between them. I captured her mouth with mine, my tongue seeking hers. I felt her pleasure rise and spiral, felt her breathe my breath. I felt the core of her. I felt myself inside her. Fullness. Opening, opening, convulsing. Over and over.

So good.

I cried aloud at the end. Sidonie's eyes widened. What I felt, she felt. The drive, the need, the acute, prolonged spasm of release. Still, she had the presence of mind to clamp one hand over my mouth.

I collapsed onto my back.

"Imriel." Still straddling me, Sidonie leaned on my chest. Her black eyes gazed intently into mine. "How do we save Terre d'Ange?"

I started laughing.

"I'm not jesting," she said.

"No, I know." I sank my hands into her hair. "It's just . . . I was afraid. Afraid of how you'd react once you knew. Afraid of the damage done." I stroked her hair, winding it around my fingers. "Heart of my heart, I didn't expect you to emerge from this ready to kill Astegal, make love to me, and rescue the realm."

Sidonie smiled ruefully. "I may well fall to pieces later. If I do, I pray you'll be there to gather them. But for now—"

"Talk fast?" I suggested.

She nodded. "Please."

Forty-seven

I sat on the bed cutting Sidonie's shift into a long strip of bandage and told her everything I knew that had passed since the night of Carthage's spell, including my month of madness. She listened in horrified wonder, but she didn't comment until I mentioned seeking Barquiel L'Envers' aid.

"And he *gave* it?" she asked in amazement.

"Seems he loves Terre d'Ange more than he hates me." I told her the rest, tearing the linen carefully. Cythera, my mother. Ptolemy Solon. The details of the spell—the *ghafrid-gebla* and Bodeshmun's talisman.

"Your mother and my uncle," she mused. "Elua have mercy, I never thought I'd have cause to be grateful to either of them, let alone both at once. You've no idea what's happening in Terre d'Ange?"

"No." I shook my head. "There's been no word for weeks. I don't know if L'Envers found the gem that holds the *ghafrid.* I don't know if he got the rest of the country to rally behind Alais. I've no idea. Lift your arms."

Sidonie obeyed. I wound the long strip around her body,

covering the seeping gouge between her shoulders. I had to crisscross the bandage between her breasts, wrapping it around her twice before I tied it.

"It's lucky you're handy with knots," she observed. I glanced up to see a faint spark of the old humor in her eyes.

"Indeed." I finished and went to rummage in her clothes-press for another shift. "It's going to be a problem hiding that from your attendants, love. And it really ought to be dressed by a proper chirurgeon."

"I know." She frowned in thought. "There's nothing to be done for the latter, but I can hold my attendants off for a time. They're fairly well convinced I'm deeply distraught. They'll leave me to bathe and dress myself in peace if I insist on it."

"Girom thinks you might be with child," I said softly, holding out the garment. "Lift your arms again."

She didn't protest, letting me help her on with the shift. "What if I am?"

I sat back on the bed and looked into her eyes. "I had to answer that question for someone else, once. Lucius Tadius, you remember? Sidonie, I'm the child of two traitors, and I'm the man I am because Phèdre and Joscelin loved me despite it. Any child of your blood, I will love." I paused. "Are you?"

"No." Sidonie smiled wryly. "I married Astegal in Carthage. The rites were all Carthaginian. There was no invocation beseeching Eisheth for fertility." Her expression turned quizzical. "And I never said a word about it. I must have known, somewhere deep inside me, that I didn't love him."

I laughed humorlessly. "So Astegal's efforts to get an heir were all in vain?"

"Mm-hmm." She nodded with bitter satisfaction. "Though considerable."

I took her hands in mine. "Did he harm you? Because I swear in Kushiel's name, if he did, it means the difference between Astegal dying and Astegal dying slowly."

"No." Sidonie gave her head a little shake, her gaze sliding away from mine. "No, he wasn't cruel and he didn't force me. He didn't have to. I was willing." Her throat worked as she swallowed. "That's what sickens me the most."

"You *weren't* willing." I squeezed her hands. "Sidonie, they took your will away and turned you against yourself. It's not your fault. None of it."

She glanced back at me. "I can get to Bodeshmun."

I opened my mouth to say it was too dangerous, then thought better of it. "How?"

"The same way I dealt with the guards." Sidonie nodded at the door.

I did say it then. "It's too dangerous, love. The Amazigh are going to be on alert after tonight. And Bodeshmun's twice as suspicious as any desert tribesman."

"The guards won't talk," she said. "After the incident in the gardens, Bodeshmun put the fear of whatever gods they worship into them. I wouldn't risk it twice, not with them, but I'd wager anything that they'll cover for one another rather than admit to Bodeshmun that they fell asleep on duty."

"What if he sees that the spell's broken?" I asked. "Ptolemy Solon told me he'd see through a mere semblance."

Sidonie shrugged. "He didn't notice when you broke the first half. Mayhap it's not the same. After all, I'm still myself. I was all along. And Bodeshmun doesn't *look* at me, Imriel. I'm just a necessary nuisance to him. I was a bored, pestering nuisance, and now I'm a dithering nuisance."

I considered it. "And you actually believe he'd drink a toast at the request of a dithering nuisance?"

"I do," she said. "If I brought him the great good news that I was carrying Astegal's heir, and that in the absence of the father, it was D'Angeline custom that his nearest kinsman drink a toast to the health of the babe . . . yes. Particularly if I threatened to get hysterical if he refused."

"Let me think on it for a day," I said. "If you're sure of it, then I believe you. But I still need to find a way to get you safely out of the palace and onto Deimos' ship. You're a bit hard to disguise."

"So are you," Sidonie noted.

"I'm free to come and go." I twined my fingers with hers, thinking. "Is it always at least four Amazigh who escort you?"

"Inside the palace, betimes it's only one. But outside, yes." She tilted her head. "Why?" I told her about the Amazigh garb that Ghanim had obtained for me. "It won't work. Not outside the palace, not after the attack. We'd be stopped." Sidonie got up and paced the room restlessly, grimacing at the pain of her wounded back. I glanced out the darkened window. Once again, time was dwindling. Soon I'd have to take up my post outside her door. I rose and began cleaning up the mess at the dressing table, gathering the bloodstained rags and ringing them out in the basin. I'd have to take them with me, hidden under my shirt.

"What do you suppose we should do with this?" I asked, reluctantly picking up the ragged disk of skin and flesh marked with the Sarkal insignia.

"Burn it," Sidonie said briefly.

The brazier was burning low, but the coals flared when I blew on them. I laid the piece of flesh carefully atop them. It seared and sizzled, smelling disconcertingly edible. Sidonie shuddered with disgust, watching it blacken and shrink, her fingers unconsciously rolling and unrolling the sash of her robe.

It gave me an idea.

"Sidonie, did you ever hear the tale of the deposed

Menekhetan queen who had herself smuggled before a Tiberian general rolled in a carpet?" I asked.

She stopped and stared at me. "You're brilliant."

"No." I grinned at her. "But between the two of us, we manage to shine fairly brightly, love. If Kratos can find a discreet way out of the palace, I'm willing to sling you over my shoulder and carry you to the harbor."

"When?" she asked simply.

"Give me a day," I repeated. "Send for me tomorrow like you did tonight. Don't risk drugging the guards. A few moments will be long enough to confer." I glanced at the window. "And I don't think I ought to stay any longer. The second team of guards will be arriving soon."

"Tomorrow, then." Sidonie took a deep breath. "Will you hold me first?" I gathered her into my arms, wishing I never had to let her go. She clung to me, pressing herself hard against me. "I wish you didn't have to go," she whispered against my chest. "Imriel, once this is over, I never, ever want us to be parted again."

"I know," I murmured against her hair. "Believe me, love, I know."

Leaving her that night was one of the hardest things I'd done. It felt like I was tearing my heart out of my chest. I had mad fantasies of staying and barricading the door, holding the world at bay; or seizing Sidonie and trying to fight our way clear of New Carthage.

But I didn't.

Instead, I forced myself to let her go. She clung to me for a few heartbeats longer, then released me. I turned away reluctantly and left.

Outside her bedchamber, the Amazigh were snoring and the fire was burning low in the hearth. I stirred the fire back to life and laid another log on it, then took up my post outside Sidonie's door. There I sat, trying to contain the storms of emotion churning in my heart, trying to remember how to be Leander Maignard.

It wasn't long before fresh guards came to relieve the others. They startled at the sight of their sleeping fellows, then shook them awake after a hushed exchange and several darting glances my way. The Amazigh woke groggily, but they awoke. There was another hushed conference, this one with a furious undertone, and more anxious looks in my direction.

"You've naught to fear on my account, lads." I shifted and stretched as though my limbs were stiff from a long night's inaction. "Believe me, I've been on the receiving end of Lord Bodeshmun's threats." I yawned, covering my mouth. "And I do believe I caught a few winks myself. My silence for yours, good fellows?"

"It will not happen again," one of the new guards said curtly, his Hellene heavily accented.

"I'm sure it won't," I agreed.

Well and good, Sidonie was right. The Amazigh might be fiercely loyal, but their personal loyalty was to Astegal. They obeyed Bodeshmun for his sake, but they didn't do it gladly.

As before, I waited until the chambermaid arrived a little after dawn with her breakfast tray. This time, I knocked on the door for her. Sidonie opened it. Our eyes met, a silent spark passing between us. But if nothing else, we'd had a good deal of practice dissembling together in public.

"Good morning, my lady," I said. "Did you rest well?"

"Well enough," she said. "Once again, I thank you for your kindness, Messire Maignard."

I bowed. "It is an honor, your highness."

I lingered long enough to watch her turn and walk back into her chamber. I'd carved a divot of flesh out of her back, and I knew she was hurting badly. It didn't show, not in the slightest.

That was my girl.

After what was surely the longest night of my life, I made my way to my own chambers. I was so exhausted as I was descending the tower stairs, I barely heard the deep rumble of Bodeshmun's voice in time. My pulse leapt like a startled hare, and I plastered myself against the inner wall of the stairwell. There I froze, praying like hell that Bodeshmun wasn't headed for the stairs.

He wasn't.

Out of the corner of my eye, I saw him pass below me, his black robes swirling as he addressed Lord Gillimas. And for the first time, the thought occurred to me that it would be infinitely easier to get Sidonie out of New Carthage if we ignored the business of Bodeshmun and the talisman altogether.

Of course, that would leave a dangerous enemy at our backs.

And Terre d'Ange in chaos.

I made it the rest of the way without event. In my chambers, I found Sunjata had already departed, and Kratos was all smiles.

"Good news, my lord," he said in greeting. "I think I've found your passage. Will you see it?"

"Later." I sat heavily on the couch and shrugged out of my shirt. A damp wad of bloodstained rags fell out.

Kratos' eyes bulged. "What in the name of all the gods have you been up to?"

I yawned. "'Tis a long story. My thanks for your good work, though." I pried off my boots. "Let me sleep a few hours and I'll tell you everything," I promised, peeling off my stockings. "My head hurts, and I'm perishing tired."

Kratos didn't answer.

I glanced up at him and cursed myself. Kratos simply stared at me, his lips working soundlessly. I'd taken off Leander's shirt, boots, and stockings. His rings, ruby ear-drops, and the ties that bound his braids were in the pocket of my breeches. *My* breeches. I'd pocketed the items without thinking, more worried about cleaning the bloody mess in Sidonie's chamber.

"You're . . ." Kratos stammered at last. "You're . . ."

"Imriel de la Courcel," I said quietly, rising. "Well met. Forgive me, Kratos. That was careless of me, very careless."

He stared blankly past the hand I extended. "I know what the eunuch said, but . . ."

I nodded. "It's a shock. I know. I apologize."

Kratos shook himself all over like a wet dog. "You understate the case considerably, my lord." He did clasp my hand then, peering at my face in wonder. "You do have a bit of the look of him. Leander. Only . . . different. A lot different, somehow." He gave a short laugh. "I'll wager you're a fellow knows how to wrestle. Bears, by the look of it."

"That, my friend, is truer than you know." I released his hand. "Give me a few hours, and we'll talk."

"As you wish, my lord," Kratos said with uncommon deference in his voice.

I took to my bed and dreamed of Sidonie.

Forty-eight

Kratos gave a subtle nod as we strolled past the heavy wooden door to the cellar where kegs of wine and ale were stored. The guard posted at the corner of the corridor stared straight ahead, incurious. I glanced to my left and saw the narrow servants' stair that led to the second floor. We kept walking, circling around and returning to our chambers.

"So," I said. "One guard."

"Not bad, eh?" Kratos grinned.

"Not bad at all, my friend," I said. "Are you sure the outer door to the wine cellar isn't guarded?"

"Oh, aye." He nodded. "Except when they're taking deliveries, it's kept locked tight from the inside."

There was no outer defense wall around the palace in New Carthage, only roving patrols of Astegal's men tasked with keeping order in the streets of the city. The guards at the palace doors might question a lone Amazigh leaving in the small hours of the night with a rolled carpet slung over his shoulder. But out on the street, it would be a different matter. Elua knows what manner of errand Bodeshmun might have devised.

"Well done." I clapped Kratos on the shoulder. "Does anyone suspect you?"

He grinned again. "Only of being a wine-sot looking to steal a way into the cellar."

It could be done, I thought. And it would be a hell of a lot easier if Sidonie simply coaxed her guards into drinking another drugged toast. Then all I'd have to do was wait for them to fall asleep and spirit her out of her chambers. There was still the guard in the hallway to dispatch, but I'd be able to take him by surprise. Once I got Sidonie safely away, we could flee to Terre d'Ange to seek aid from whatever army Barquiel L'Envers had mustered. And there was Alba, too. Surely our combined forces would suffice to join Serafin's Aragonian rebels and defeat Carthage. Then we could deal with the spell.

That night, I proposed the idea to Sidonie.

She looked at me like I was mad. "No."

"Love, consider it!" I pleaded. "It's a lot less dangerous."

"For who?" Her brows shot up. "Us, yes. But how many hundreds or thousands of men would have to die before we got this close to Bodeshmun again? And who knows what manner of dire spell he might devise in the meantime? No." Sidonie shook her head. "Believe me, I don't harbor any romantic ideas about sacrificing myself for the good of the realm. But I couldn't live with myself if we didn't try, Imriel."

"I had a feeling you'd say that," I murmured. "All right. Tomorrow, then. It's only going to get more dangerous the longer we wait. Go to Bodeshmun as late as possible. I'll have Kratos keep watch after the dinner hour. It would help if you can convince the guards only one needs escort you."

"The other will grow suspicious when we don't return," Sidonie observed.

"I know." I nodded. "I'll take care of him, too. But it will be easier to take them one at a time."

"Can you?" she asked.

I understood the question. I'd killed men before in self-defense. This would be different. If I were quick and lucky, it would be outright murder. "Yes."

"Good." She was pale, but her face was resolute. "You'd best go. I'll see you tomorrow."

I nodded again. "If things go awry—"

"Just know I love you," Sidonie finished the thought for me. "Always."

There wasn't anything else to say. I kissed her quickly and left to take up my post outside her door, fearful that if I lingered, it would be too agonizing to part. I didn't have to explain it to Sidonie. She understood.

That night, it was I who dozed under the watchful eyes of her Amazigh guards, my head propped against Sidonie's door. I'd kept their secret, so I reckoned they'd keep mine. And I would need every ounce of energy I could hoard to make it through the following night.

In the morning, Sidonie and I went through our cordial routine, both of us achingly aware that it could be the last time we saw one another alive. And then I took my leave of her once more, feeling lightheaded and hollow, as though I'd left the better part of myself in her keeping.

I went to the harbor to inform Captain Deimos that we would be sailing on the morrow, as early as was humanly possible. He heard me out in laconic silence until I finished. "Care to tell me what this is about?"

I glanced over at Kratos, who was keeping watch. No one else was in earshot. Even so, I lowered my voice further. "Rescuing the heir to Terre d'Ange."

Deimos stared at me, a muscle in his cheek twitching. "From what I hear, the lady in question has no wish to be rescued."

"Your information is wrong," I said. "Ptolemy Solon sent me to break the spell that bound her to Astegal. It's done. Now we're both in danger. So I will ask you one last time, will you do this or not?"

His look turned hard. "I told you, I'm no oath-breaker. But I won't sail until I hear it from her own lips."

I nodded. "Done."

After that, there wasn't much to be done except wait. I sent Kratos to procure clean bandages and a healing salve at an out-of-the-way chirurgeon's shop, worried about Sidonie's injury. I mixed grease and ashes from the hearth, testing it on the skin of my hands, until I had obtained a mixture that darkened my skin enough to permit me to pass as Amazigh, at least on brief, dimly lit inspection. I practiced tying the head-scarf and swathing my features. I practiced telling the hours. I packed the few items that mattered to me into a single trunk. I tried to sleep, and failed.

Waiting was always maddening, and this time it was compounded by a sense of helplessness. That day dragged onward like no other I could remember. But at last the daylight began to fade. Kratos and I dined in our quarters. I hadn't dared risk a meal in the great hall since I'd known myself. Astegal, with his eternal revels, would have noticed my absence; luckily, Bodeshmun hadn't cared to continue the tradition.

Once we'd finished, I dispatched Kratos to keep an eye on Sidonie's door. This was the first step in our end of the plan, and the most dangerous one for him. Her quarters and Bodeshmun's were both on the second story of the palace; ours were on the ground floor. There was no reason for Kratos to be lingering upstairs, but he had assured me he could manage it, and I had to trust him. I simply couldn't do everything myself.

I darkened my face and hands, donned my Amazigh garb over enough of Leander Maignard's clothing to maintain both guises.

An hour passed, and then another.

I was beginning to feel a quiet sense of panic rising when Kratos finally returned, red-faced and panting so hard he could barely speak.

"What's wrong?" I asked sharply.

"Nothing," he wheezed, bending over and bracing his hands on his knees. I let him catch his breath, swallowing my impatience. At last Kratos straightened. "Sorry. I started to get suspicious looks. Had to pretend I was running the stairs to work out leg cramps. Good cure, you know."

I made a concerted effort not to shake him. "Sidonie?"

"Gone to see Bodeshmun," he confirmed. "One guard. He stayed posted outside Blackbeard's door. Gods, you look just like one of them!"

"Good." I didn't relax, but my panic and frustration ebbed, my thoughts slipping into a cool, calculating mode. I nodded at the trunk. "Can you make it to the ship with that? You look knackered."

Kratos snorted. "I'll manage."

"Be careful." I paused. "Kratos, I mean to be there well before dawn. If I'm not there by the time the sun's clear of the horizon, it means this has gone very, very wrong. Tell Deimos to sail, and go with him."

"Where?" he asked briefly.

"Marsilikos," I said. "Find Jeanne de Mereliot, daughter of the Lady of Marsilikos. Tell her everything you know, everything we've discussed."

"You imagine she'll believe me?" Kratos asked in a dubious tone.

"Tell her Imriel de la Courcel said to tell her that he was grateful for the offer she made him before he sailed for Cythera," I said softly. "Even though I refused it, I was grateful for her kindness and Eisheth's mercy."

"Ah." Kratos nodded and put out his hand. "Gods be with you, my lord."

I clasped it. "And you."

With that, Kratos shouldered my trunk and exited our quarters. He paused in the hallway, glancing to make sure it was clear, then gave me a brief gesture of affirmation. I slipped through the door, clad in my Amazigh garb. Kratos strode toward the front of the palace without looking back.

I went in the opposite direction.

There weren't as many guards as there had been when Astegal was here. Bodeshmun had increased their number after Sidonie was attacked, but they were still spread thin. Mostly, he'd settled for purging the palace staff of any Aragonians, having uncovered no organized conspiracy, but a deep vein of seething resentment when he put them to questioning.

None of the guards I passed gave me a second glance. If they had, they might have noticed small details amiss. The ash-dark hue of my skin, the color of my eyes. The cut of my sword-belt, the hilts of my blades. But they didn't. The guards were accustomed to letting Astegal's Amazigh pass without question. They saw what they expected to see, and I passed them like an indigo ghost and climbed the stairs.

I'd decided to take care of the guard waiting in Sidonie's quarters first. He would be the safer kill, and the less I needed to move about the palace, the better. And too, I needed to allow time for the sleeping draught to take effect. Outside her door, I drew my dagger and held it reversed, the blade hidden under the flowing sleeve of my robe.

I knocked on the door.

There was a shuffling sound within, and then one of the Amazigh opened it. He asked me somewhat in his own tongue or in Punic; I couldn't have said. I shook my head and pressed a finger to the fabric muffling my mouth. He shrugged and admitted me, closing the door behind me.

He *did* take a second look.

I saw his eyes widen in the narrow strip of visible face, and didn't hesitate. I whipped my arm up, sleeve falling to bare the hidden blade. Plunged the dagger hilt-deep in his chest, one hand smothering his muffled mouth.

Quick.

I'd always been quick.

The Amazigh died almost without a sound, his expression of alarm still fixed around the eyes. Somewhere far away, I felt a little sickened at the discovery that I'd make a skilled and effective assassin. I pushed the thought farther away and concentrated on doing what needed to be done, dragging his body into Sidonie's bedchamber and hiding it on the far side of the bed where it was unlikely to be spotted at a careless glance. If anyone raised an alarm, every moment could be precious.

Once that was done, I yanked the dagger from his chest. His heart had long since stopped, and the wound didn't even bleed much. I cleaned my blade on his robes and gave it a quick whetting.

By now, the sleeping draught should have worked.

If it had worked.

I took a moment to gather myself, breathing slowly. The second guard, the one posted outside Bodeshmun's door, would be harder. I let myself into the corridor, listening. It was late and the palace was quiet. Downstairs, I could hear a few murmurs, but it seemed quiet upstairs. I soft-footed my way to Bodeshmun's quarters, holding the dagger low and hidden at my side.

I didn't give the second Amazigh guard time to react. I simply walked right up to him and pressed him against the door, shoving the dagger under his ribs, angling upward for his heart, clamping my left hand over his veiled mouth. He struggled briefly. I shoved the dagger harder, until I felt him shudder and go limp. With my left hand, I felt for the handle of the door and tried it.

Locked.

I cursed silently, then listened intently for a moment. There were no sounds beyond the door. I eased my dagger from the guard's body, struggling to keep him braced upright. Worked the dagger in between the door and the frame, prying hard until I felt the latch give way with a brittle groan.

That done, I froze. If Bodeshmun *wasn't* unconscious, he would have heard the sound, and like as not, the scuffle, too. He might well be waiting on the far side of the door for me, smiling into his beard, prepared to blow a handful of death into my lungs.

For a mercy, the door opened inward. Still holding the guard upright, I pushed the door open with one foot and heaved the guard's body inside, jumping quickly backward.

The guard's body fell heavily to the floor.

No Bodeshmun.

I glanced quickly around to confirm no one had come, then stepped inside, closing the door behind me. The narrow antechamber was empty but for the figure of the dead Amazigh. It was a dreadful thing to know how easily men died, fierce warriors or no. I didn't doubt the Amazigh's skills, but Bodeshmun had been right. They had no head for intrigue. I daresay Astegal had chosen them for their imposing and mysterious appearance, the very thing that had allowed me to deceive them.

There was a fire burning in the hearth beyond the

antechamber, bright and merry. I thought about appearances and deception and drew my sword, approaching with care. A few paces before I reached the room, I paused and unwound my scarf.

I remembered Phèdre's training.

Leander's memories of my mother's training were with me, too.

I could smell wood-smoke and beeswax. Traces of a familiar aroma, sweet and faintly spicy. Perry brandy, doctored with herbs. An unexpected smell of soap.

And a sour odor beneath it.

Vomit.

I stepped into the salon, the blade angled before me. The fire crackled. Two chairs had been drawn up before it, a table between them. An open flagon of perry brandy sat on the table, two empty cups.

Sidonie was slumped in one of the chairs, her head draped over one arm, a loose coil of hair dangling dangerously close to the fire. My heart leapt into my throat at the sight. I couldn't even tell if she was breathing.

As Bodeshmun would have planned.

He was slumped in the other chair, his bearded chin resting on his chest. One hand lay loose on his knee. The other arm hung at his side, fingers curled. I took a sharp breath, my thoughts racing like quicksilver.

"Sidonie!" I whispered.

There was the merest sliver of a glint beneath Bodeshmun's eyelids.

I hurried to her side, stooped over her, and tucked the fire-heated lock of hair behind one ear. Felt at her throat for a pulse and sighed with genuine relief when I found it. Only then did I take a deep, surreptitious breath and hold it, turning toward Bodeshmun.

He was already rising from his chair, one palm cupped and raised, eyes glittering with triumph.

Lungs full, lips pursed.

But I was ready, and I blew first.

I'd always been quick.

Dust and ashes, a handful of gritty grey matter. What it was, I couldn't have said. Ptolemy Solon would have known. Bones of an innocent man hanged for a crime he didn't commit, mayhap. Gathered under a full moon, burned in a furnace fueled by heartwood, ground to dust by virgins with a mortar and pestle. It didn't matter. Bodeshmun expelled his breath in shock and gasped for air.

One gasp.

I didn't. I stepped backward with alacrity, wrenching Sidonie's chair out of the way. I held my breath until the dust settled, and then I watched Bodeshmun die.

He knew me.

Even dying, he saw through the semblance. I watched his face darken with recognition, fury, the onset of death. I waited, sword at the ready, until I was certain he carried no antidote to his own poison. Then I smiled.

"You know me, don't you?" I said to him. "You know who I am."

Bodeshmun glared, his chest heaving impotently.

I stooped over him, rummaging in his robes. I found it. *It*. The talisman, hidden in an inner pocket of his robes. A stiff piece of lacquered leather, wrought with an image. A whirlwind sprouting horns and claws. A word inscribed beneath it in Punic script.

A word I couldn't read.

Bodeshmun saw it; Bodeshmun knew. I read the bitter satisfaction in his dying face. I leaned down close to him.

"Don't worry," I whispered. "As it happens, Sidonie's been studying Punic. You've only yourself to thank for it.

And in case you wonder as you die, *she* was the architect of your downfall, not me." I settled onto my knees, my Amazigh robes puddling around me. "If you take no other thought into your next life, my lord, take this. It is not wise to meddle with D'Angelines in matters of love."

Bodeshmun's eyes rolled into his head.

Bodeshmun's heels drummed.

Bodeshmun died.

Forty-nine

The sleeping draught was a problem.

"Wake up, love." I patted Sidonie's cheek gently, then not so gently. Nothing. I called her name sharply, as loudly as I dared, but she didn't respond. When I grabbed her shoulders and shook her roughly, her head only lolled in an alarming manner.

Her breathing was even and her heart beat steadily. Girom had said his draughts were potent. Elua willing, she would awaken; that I had to believe. But for the moment, she slept like the dead, and I was fearful that if I rolled her in Bodeshmun's carpet and hauled her all the way to the harbor, I was like to smother her in the process. Even if I didn't, I wasn't sure how Captain Deimos would react to the fact that I'd abducted the Dauphine of Terre d'Ange, drugged insensible.

And if she didn't awaken by dawn . . .

Well, we had a few hours' grace. I'd sooner have left the palace immediately, but no one was likely to notice aught amiss until the second shift of Sidonie's guards came to relieve their fellows.

I resolved to wait as long as I dared. I stowed Bodeshmun's talisman safely in my purse. I propped a chair under the door with the broken latch, lest anyone attempt to enter. I dragged the bodies of Bodeshmun and the guard into the far bedchamber. I cleaned and whetted my dagger a second time.

I waited.

Although it didn't seem to trouble her in the least, Sidonie's position in the chair looked uncomfortable. I eased her down to the carpeted floor, then cleared the carpet in preparation. I sat cross-legged, settling her head on my lap.

She looked younger sleeping, scarce older than the girl I'd fallen in love with. We'd known one another since we were children. I stroked the soft curve of her cheek, remembering. She'd been a reserved child, unnervingly composed from an early age, regarding me with cool distrust. How not? She'd grown up with the weight of the kingdom hovering over her, aware of the schisms that threatened to divide it.

And I . . . I'd been damaged and brooding, filled with fierce passions and loyalties. How not? By the time I was eleven years old, I'd seen and endured things no one should ever suffer.

Neither of us could possibly have understood the other.

It seemed so very long ago.

Ysandre used to force us to spend time together, the scions of House Courcel, hoping we would further our acquaintance. It made me smile now to think on it. Alais and I used to play cards together under the watchful eye of the Queen's Guard, while Sidonie ignored us and read a book.

I wished I could travel backward through time to address those childhood selves. To tell Sidonie that one day she would defy her mother and half the nation for the sake of this proud, wounded boy whom she regarded with such misgivings, that he would grow into a man she trusted beyond all reason. To tell my young self that this cool, haughty girl who galled him so would one day be the most precious thing in the world to him, that she would become a woman for whom he would willingly lay down his life.

I wished Sidonie would awaken.

An hour passed, then another. For a mercy, no one came to call on Bodeshmun. But Sidonie showed no signs of waking, either. I shook her, coaxed her, whispered and pleaded to no avail. Once, she sighed in her sleep and my heart leapt, but she only seemed to settle deeper into slumber.

At last I gave up. If I delayed any longer, I wouldn't reach the harbor in time. The palace would awaken and the alarm would be raised. I shifted Sidonie to the edge of the carpet.

"Sun Princess." I knelt beside her and kissed her sleeping lips. "We have to try this now. Don't you dare die on me, or I swear to Blessed Elua, I'll haunt you through a thousand lifetimes."

There was no answer. I raised her arms and crossed them in front of her face, hoping and praying that it would create a pocket of air that would keep her from smothering. Carefully, carefully, I rolled the most precious thing in the world to me into a carpet.

That done, I rewound the Amazigh scarf around my head and face. I moved the chair blocking Bodeshmun's door and checked the corridor.

Empty.

Good.

I stooped and hoisted the rolled carpet with an effort, slinging it over my shoulder. It was heavy, heavier than I'd reckoned. Sidonie sleeping was dead weight, and the carpet itself was dense and tightly woven.

It didn't matter. I could do it.

I carried her into the corridor, closing the door behind

me, and made swiftly for the servants' stair. It was narrow and winding, and the ends of the rolled carpet scraped harshly against the stone walls. I had to use both hands to keep my burden balanced, navigating the narrow steps awkwardly. By the time I reached the bottom, the guard posted on the lower floor was already looking curiously toward the stairwell. Keeping my head averted, I laid down the carpet and beckoned to him, moving as though to unroll the carpet and reveal somewhat of interest.

"What in the name of Ba'al—" he began, bending over to see.

In one swift motion, I unsheathed my dagger and drove it under his chin, angling for the brain. He made a choked sound, and I covered his mouth. His wide, terrified eyes met mine.

It was one of the Carthaginians, one I knew by sight. The guard who'd told me that Astegal was likely to move against Serafin, one of the more decent fellows. I wished it hadn't been him. I remembered him grumbling about fighting a winter war. He must have thought himself lucky when he'd gotten this posting.

"I'm sorry," I whispered.

His body went limp with death. Blood dripped onto the rolled carpet between us. I stepped over the carpet and wrestled him over to the wine cellar door. This one was unlocked; Astegal had preferred to set a guard on the wine-cellar rather than suffer any delays in his revels, and Bodeshmun hadn't bothered to alter his order. I dragged the guard's body into the dark cellar, then sprinted upstairs to retrieve Sidonie.

Still dead weight.

Once I closed the cellar door behind us, it was pitch black. I paused for a moment, willing my eyes to adjust, but there was simply no light. Step by step, I descended, balancing Sidonie and the carpet on my shoulder.

At the bottom, I stumbled over the guard's legs. The carpet lurched. I caught myself and steadied my burden. Kratos hadn't said where the outer delivery door was located, and I hadn't thought to ask. I wished there had been more time to go over the details of our plan with Sidonie. With her practical mind, it would have occurred to her that I'd be mired in darkness here.

Gods, I hoped she wasn't suffocating.

I began making my way blindly through the cellar, one hand steadying my burden, the other outstretched. I blundered into kegs, barked my shins. I had to turn this way and that, losing all sense of direction.

No good.

I closed my eyes and breathed slowly. Darkness within darkness. I could do this. Leander Maignard could do it in his sleep. A child's training game, nothing more. I lowered the heavy carpet to the cool stones of the floor, turning it in such a manner that Sidonie's face was sideways—or at least so I hoped.

"Love," I whispered. "I have to leave you for a moment. But I'll be back."

Without the burden, I was able to move more swiftly, both hands extended. Five paces forward, and my way was blocked by a wall of wine-kegs. I turned to the left. Seven paces, another wall of kegs. Right, and then right again. Step by step, I negotiated the mundane labyrinth until my hands encountered cool stone. I sidled along the wall until I felt wood beneath my fingertips.

A door.

I threw the bar and wrenched it open, feeling a blast of cool night air on my veiled face. Elua, it felt good!

There was no moon, but there were hazy stars. What light there was was faint, not nearly enough to illuminate the cellar, but I could make my way to it. All I had to do was retrace my steps in darkness. I sidled back along the wall. Twelve swift steps; I'd counted. Left, then left again. Right, seven paces. Five paces forward. I stooped, feeling along the floor.

No carpet.

I closed my eyes again and fought off a wave of panic. What was wrong? I'd been cautious on the outward journey. I'd hurried back. I'd taken bigger steps. Somehow, I'd reached a wrong aisle.

I made my way back to the open door and tried again, taking careful little steps. When my reaching fingers brushed the rolled carpet, I nearly wept with relief. Once more, I shouldered my burden.

Outside, the air tasted so sweet, I had to loosen my scarf for a moment and breathe it deeply. I thought about laying Sidonie down, unrolling the carpet to make certain she was alive. But then I heard Carthaginian voices muttering in the gardens—some of Astegal's guards, making their rounds. So instead, I retucked my scarf and set out at a brisk walk.

The carpet was still dead weight.

It wasn't long before my left shoulder began to ache. I shifted my burden to the other shoulder, heaving and ducking. Heavy, so heavy! I'd carried Sidonie in my arms a dozen times, a hundred times. But this was the one that mattered.

Blessed Elua, please let her live.

At least it was downhill. We entered the streets of New Carthage. There were no Aragonians abroad at this hour, only Astegal's patrols. I strode past them, acknowledging their curious greetings with curt nods. I was a veiled Amazigh bent on some unspeakable errand.

I was a ghost.

An aching ghost.

I carried Sidonie. I carried my guilt—*our* guilt. The murdered guards. My slain wife, Dorelei. Our lost son. All of it.

I carried all of it, tired and terrified. I kept going. I thought about the night that Phèdre, Joscelin, and I had rowed to Kapporeth. Joscelin, his bleeding hands on the oars. We had both known failure once. In Skaldia, he'd surrendered to despair. In Vralia, so had I.

Not there.

Not here.

I prayed to Blessed Elua and his Companions, making every step a word in my litany. And as I neared the harbor, with the night sky dimming, I felt the burden on my right shoulder stir feebly. I hurried my steps, hurried to the wharf.

"Hey!" I shouted at Captain Deimos' ship. "Lend a hand!"

Kratos hustled down the plank, blessed Kratos, his blunt-featured face suffused with alarm. He eased the carpet from my shoulder, carried it in both arms aboard the ship. I followed. Deimos was waiting, watchful, arms folded. On the deck of his ship, Kratos and I unrolled the carpet with reverent hands. I knelt beside it, anxious.

A very tousled Sidonie blinked sleepily at me. "Imriel?"

My eyes stung. "Yes, love."

She blinked again, touching my veiled face. "Look at you. I'm sorry. I didn't want to drink, but Bodeshmun was suspicious. I had to do it. Are we aboard the ship? Why aren't we fleeing?"

I nodded at Captain Deimos. "Tell him."

Deimos leaned over her. "Your highness?"

Her eyes flashed. "Name of Elua, *go*!"

FIFTY

Ptolemy Solon had chosen well in Captain Deimos. He was in truth a man of his word, and he knew a royal command when he heard one. By the time I escorted Sidonie down to the ship's hold, where we'd both be out of sight until we passed the harbor patrol, the oars were out and the ship was moving.

Safe at last, at least for the moment, we held one another for a long, long time.

"How's your back?" I murmured at length.

"I don't know. It hurts." She gazed up at me. "How's your head?"

I laughed. "Fine. I'd nearly forgotten about it. Let me send Kratos to fetch my things. I brought salve and clean bandages."

Sidonie glanced around the hold and wrinkled her nose. "It can wait until we've cleared the harbor. I daresay it's cleaner above-deck. Imriel . . ." She hesitated, almost afraid to ask. "Did you get the talisman?"

"Yes." I fished the piece of lacquered leather out of my purse and showed it to her.

She perched on a water barrel, studying it. "Such an insignificant scrap of a thing," she mused. "'Tis hard to believe it's the key for undoing a spell that put the entire City of Elua under its sway."

"Like as not it's far more complicated and disgusting than it looks," I observed. "Hide tanned from the skin of a stillborn babe or somewhat. At any rate, according to Solon, it's the word of binding that matters. Can you read it?"

"Elua, I hope so. I can speak more than a little, but I can't read much. I was only just beginning to learn the Punic alphabet." Her lips moved as she studied the Punic script. "Emmen . . . emmenghanom. *Emmenghanom.*" Sidonie looked up in triumph. "It means beholden."

I cupped her face and kissed her. "Gods be thanked that you're not one to suffer tedium in idleness, love. I told Bodeshmun you'd know."

"Is he dead?" she asked.

I nodded. "Very."

There was somewhat adamant in her expression. "Tell me how. Tell me everything."

I told her all that had transpired. When I told her how Bodeshmun had died and what I'd said to him at the end, she smiled with grim satisfaction. "Good. How did you know what he was going to do?"

"He killed a young Aragonian lord the same way." I kept forgetting there were gaps in her knowledge. "In front of an entire hall full of people."

Sidonie shuddered. "Elua! No wonder they hated me so, thinking I'd betrayed Aragonia to subject them to *that.*"

"You didn't," I said.

"They didn't know that. And I didn't give them any reason to think otherwise." She gazed into the distance, and I knew she was thinking of things she'd rather not remember. I kept my silence, waiting until her gaze returned to me. The familiar spark leapt between us. Sidonie took my hand and kissed it. "Thank you. I'm sorry for what you had to do."

"And I for what you endured," I said.

"Ah, well, my end of it was easy." A little of her humor returned. "After all, I slept through most of it."

"So I noticed." I kissed her.

She returned my kiss. "Do you know, I even love you covered in . . . Imriel, what are you covered in?"

I rubbed at my face with one flowing sleeve. "Pork grease and ashes." I glanced down at my Amazigh robe. The dark indigo hid the stains, but the second guard had bled freely on me. "And a fair amount of blood."

"Ashes and blood." Sidonie traced a line down my face. "I pray this is the last of it."

"I too," I murmured.

"My lord?" Kratos poked his head into the hold. "We're well under way; it's safe now." He cleared his throat. "Captain Deimos wants a word with you."

We emerged from the hold to find the sails full and the ship moving briskly. The Cytheran sailors went about their business, casting curious glances at us, or more accurately, at Sidonie. Deimos was pacing the foredeck, his hands clasped behind his back. He fetched up before us, offering Sidonie a bow.

"Your highness," he said briefly. "Welcome. I am Deimos Stanakides, in the service of his eminence Ptolemy Solon, the Governor of Cythera. I presume you are Sidonie de la Courcel?"

"I am." She inclined her head. "Well met, my lord captain. On behalf of Terre d'Ange, I extend our most profound gratitude to you and to Ptolemy Solon. The service you have rendered us today will never be forgotten."

Deimos smiled tightly. "Save your gratitude. We're not safe yet. And I'm not satisfied." He fixed his intent gaze on me. "Solon doesn't suffer fools, Leander Maignard. Why did the princess call you *Imriel*?"

I sighed.

"Because it's my name," I said simply. I unbuckled my sword-belt and let it fall. Dragged the Amazigh robes over my head. "Do you require proof of my words, my lord? Ptolemy Solon himself wrought this semblance with his magics, all the better to undo what Carthage has done." I pried off Leander's boots and stood barefooted on the deck. Undid the laces of Leander's shirt and hauled it off me. Once again, I'd worn my own breeches. "There. See and believe."

Deimos paled.

An excited murmur ran around the ship.

I bowed. "Imriel de la Courcel, my lord. Well met."

"Her ladyship's son," Deimos whispered.

"For better or for worse, yes," I said dryly.

He glanced at Sidonie. "And you . . . ?"

"Love him?" she suggested. "Yes, very much so. As much as I love my country and wish to save it from the same foul magics that bound me." Her hand reached for mine, our fingers entwining. "My lord captain, I implore you. Make haste for Marsilikos. Lives beyond our own hang in the balance."

Captain Deimos licked his lips. "I'll do my best."

Once Deimos was convinced, all seemed well. We sailed northward, hugging the Aragonian coast. Three days passed without incident.

Sidonie and I shared the master cabin. The first thing I did was scour myself with soap and fresh water, washing the guise of grease and ashes from my skin. The second was to inspect the wound I'd inflicted on her.

"Is it bad?" She craned her neck, trying to see.

"It's not good." The patch of raw flesh between her

shoulder blades was red and angry, weeping clear liquid. I bathed it with unwatered wine, making her hiss between clenched teeth. I swabbed it with the salve Kratos had bought, bound it with clean bandages. "You need a proper chirurgeon."

"Marsilikos," Sidonie said. "I'll live."

I nodded. "You will."

I made love to her at her insistence. Careful, always careful. Elua knows, it wasn't that I didn't want her, but I feared hurting her worse. I'd injured her badly a-purpose, and I never wanted to do it again. But she knew us better than I did. Knew what she needed, knew what I needed.

Her.

Us.

Kratos was enchanted by her. It made me laugh. He'd grown tolerably fond of Leander and some of that had passed on to me, mixed with a measure of newfound respect; but Sidonie enthralled him.

"Imagine!" Kratos marveled. "Here I was thinking my best years were behind me, prepared to die a broken-down useless slave, and instead I helped rescue a princess who's as brave as she is beautiful."

Sidonie smiled at him with genuine warmth. "And you're as gallant as you are clever, messire. Imriel told me you were the one conceived the plan to get Astegal's ring. For that alone, I'm forever in your debt."

He turned red. "It was an honor, my lady."

"You never spoke that nicely to Leander Maignard," I observed to Sidonie. "In fact, you teased him rather mercilessly."

She gave me a sidelong glance. "Well, not at the end. But you must admit, that pomade made a rather absurd first impression."

I laughed. "Oh, I know. I've not forgotten the stench of it."

Mostly, during those first days, Sidonie and I spent long hours talking—or at least I did. She wanted to know everything, wanted all the gaps in her knowledge filled. And she wanted to know about Cythera and my mother and Ptolemy Solon. I talked myself dry, exploring feelings I hadn't had time to consider. I told her what it had been like believing myself Leander, and about the way he'd changed. About the things that had affected him: her, the Aragonian boy in the slave-market. Sidonie listened gravely, although she didn't try to hide her amusement when I told her about Sunjata.

"Did you enjoy yourself?" she asked, eyes dancing.

"Leander did," I said wryly. "Which is a passing odd memory to hold."

At that, Sidonie looked away. "Yes, I know."

"Love." I took her hand lightly. "You can speak of it. Believe me, there's nothing you could say that I couldn't bear to hear."

"I know." Her fingers stirred in mine. "One day I will. Not yet."

"Let it take as long as it takes." I stroked her fingers. "I didn't speak of what the Mahrkagir did to me for months, and then only to Phèdre. After that, it was years before I spoke of it again. Just don't close me out."

Sidonie squeezed my hand. "I won't. But it's not the same."

"No," I said. "I know. It's awful in a different way. I was there, I saw. And I have the misfortune of having escorted Astegal to Jasmine House, where his performance appeared to be received with considerable satisfaction by not one, but two adepts. So if you think you're going to shock and horrify me, don't."

Her mouth quirked. "There's a question most men would have asked by now."

"Ah." I took her chin in my hand, turning her reluctant face toward mine. "Do you want me to ask it?"

"No." Tears stood in her eyes. "I'm afraid you wouldn't believe me."

"When you said what?" I asked gently. "That you never felt the very gods themselves were attendant on your love-making with Astegal? That you never experienced his feelings as surely as your own, as though you were one person in separate skins? That it wasn't intimate and glorious and terrifying all at once?"

She smiled through her tears. "Well, yes."

I shook my head. "Sidonie, if I didn't know that without having to ask, I might as well go back to Carthage and take up with Sunjata."

That made her laugh and the moment passed. It was all right, I thought. Sidonie had borne the first blow of knowledge with amazing resilience, but she'd warned me it might not last. It was good that we'd begun to speak of it.

In time, she would heal.

And I knew a thing or two about dealing with the burden of unwarranted guilt. As long as we were together, we could survive anything.

Thus was my positive state of mind on the fourth day of our journey, when our luck changed.

It was Captain Deimos who summoned us to the aft deck of the ship and pointed toward the south. I shaded my eyes and squinted, making out the distant form of a warship riding the choppy grey waters behind us.

"We're being pursued," he said grimly. "And they're fast."

Fifty-one

"You're sure?" Sidonie asked, her voice strained.

Deimos gave a curt nod. "Fairly. The captain Astegal left in charge of the harbor reserve is no fool. I doubt it took him long to realize he granted us passage on the very day the princess and Leander Maignard vanished."

"What can we do?" I asked.

He took a deep breath. "You've three choices. We can try to outrace them long enough to put ashore at the next port, but I reckon we're only a couple of leagues south of Amílcar, and it's blockaded. We can take to open water and pray they're not foolhardy enough to follow. Or we can surrender."

"No," Sidonie said.

We glanced at one another. "Open water?" I asked.

She nodded. "Please, my lord captain. It's very, very important."

Deimos' lips moved in a silent prayer. "I'll try."

He strode along the deck, shouting orders. His sailors scrambled to obey. The ship's prow swung toward the east, nosing away from the Aragonian coast.

Sidonie shivered. "I thought we had enough of a lead to get away."

I took off the cloak I was wearing—Leander's cloak, striped and gaudy—and draped it over her shoulders. I didn't like her color. Her face was unwontedly pale, hectic slashes of pink high on her cheeks. "So did I. Lord Gillimas must have known enough to realize we took Bodeshmun's talisman and sent one of their fastest war-ships after us." I felt at her brow. "You're hot."

She shivered again. "I feel cold."

"Let me have a look at your back." I led her to our cabin and examined her. The wound was worse, swollen and inflamed. I bathed it and dressed it as best I could, wishing I were one of Eisheth's scions with healing in my bones and trying not to let her hear concern in my voice. "Just think, if you were an *anguissette*, this would be healing cleanly."

Sidonie made a face. "Yes, and you'd have to worry about me bedding your mother."

I shot her a mortified look. "Perish the thought!"

She laughed. "Well, at least mayhap I'd be racing toward Terre d'Ange with the Name of God rolling like thunder on my tongue, prepared to grapple with a servant of the One God himself, instead of hoping to free a demon from a stone using a term from my latest Punic language lesson."

"Beholden," I said. "Lift your arms."

"*Emmenghanom*." She said the word aloud. "Say it, Imriel."

"Emmeghamon," I echoed, winding the bandages around her.

"Em-men-gha-nom." Sidonie enunciated each syllable with deliberate clarity. "Say it."

I tied the last knot and met her overbright gaze. "Em . . . *Emmenghanom*."

"Say it again." She pulled up her gown and began lacing the bodice.

"You're going to survive this, Sidonie," I murmured. "Both of us are."

"I'm just being practical," she said. "Say it again."

She was right, of course. Practical and right. I said the word over and over, Sidonie correcting my accent and inflection.

When I had it to her satisfaction, she nodded. "Good. You won't forget?"

"No," I said. "I won't."

It was a long, unsettling day. Not long after we'd turned into the open waters, a fierce headwind sprang up against us. There was a good reason Captain Deimos had feared this passage, a good reason precious few ships undertook major journeys during the winter months. Our ship bucked and surged like an unbroken horse, riding the waves, struggling to sail in the face of battening winds.

And our pursuer followed.

There was no doubt of it, not now. By the time the shrouded sun sank below the horizon, it had drawn near enough that we could all see the crimson-striped sail that marked it as Carthaginian and the triple bank of oars that lent it speed.

I slept fitfully that night, holding Sidonie in my arms.

Her skin was too hot, worrying me.

In the morning, our pursuer had drawn nearer. Our oarsmen rowed, groaning. Captain Deimos paced the deck. It didn't matter; none of it mattered. The headwinds from the north were too strong. The Carthaginian war-ship with its striped sail gained steadily on us.

I prayed for something, anything. I prayed for good winds. I prayed we'd find the balance of the D'Angeline fleet awaiting us.

No luck.

The Carthaginian ship overtook us. It came along broadside, blocking our passage. A trebuchet mounted on its central tower thrummed, sending bolts our way. One tore through our topmost sail.

We turned tail and fled.

Back, back the way we'd come, racing before the wind now behind us. Deimos tried to make for land, but the Carthaginian ship raced alongside us, herded us onward. In the distance, I saw the harbor of Amílcar, blocked by a solid blockade of Carthage's fleet. Our pursuer was driving us into their arms.

"We're done." Captain Deimos accorded Sidonie an exacting bow. "Forgive me, your highness. I did my best."

Her voice rose. "My lord, we *cannot* surrender!"

"You'll not be harmed," Deimos said. "Either of you. You're too valuable as hostages."

"Once, mayhap." Sidonie shook her head in impatient despair. "Not now. Astegal would never let either of us go, not knowing we have the key to undoing Bodeshmun's spell. The only reason to keep us alive is to keep Terre d'Ange and Alba from acting by threatening them with our deaths." She eyed the rough seas. "At this point, I'd serve my country better by drowning than being taken alive."

"You're feverish, your highness," Deimos said to her, and to me, "Talk sense to her."

"Captain, she's right," I said. "Is there no chance of running the blockade? At least in Amílcar we'll find sanctuary of a sort."

He gestured. "Look at it."

"You might be able to make it." Sidonie clutched my arm. "You're a strong swimmer, Imriel. One man might be able to slip past the ships."

"It's too far," Deimos said. "The water's too cold."

I gauged the distance. "Even so. If it's our only chance—"

"Fire the ship," Kratos said abruptly behind me.

I turned. "What?"

Kratos jerked his chin at the fast-approaching blockade. "You want to break their line? Set fire to the ship and bear down on them at full speed. I guarantee you, they'll move."

"Would that work?" I asked Deimos.

He looked ill. "Mayhap. It's dangerous as hell."

"Kratos, I adore you!" Sidonie planted a kiss on his cheek. "My lord captain, *please.* A slight chance is better than none. You're not like to find much mercy from Astegal either."

A muscle in Deimos' jaw twitched. "By the Goddess," he muttered. "I'm never swearing another oath as long as I live."

He gave the order, though. His men worked frantically, breaking open kegs of strong spirits and dousing the entire ship, others finding a last surge of strength at the oars. When it came down to it, I daresay no one wanted to be taken by Carthage after assisting in the abduction of Astegal's wife.

"I want you to wait near the landing-boat," Deimos said to us in a taut voice. "The timing of this is going to be difficult." He pointed. "There are catapults on the fortress at the end of the mole. That's the point beyond which Carthage's ships don't dare venture. If we can get past it without foundering, we'll drop the landing-boat and row for shore."

"Thank you, Captain Deimos." Sidonie met his gaze. Shivering and feverish, she was still very much in possession of her faculties. "I'm very sorry to have put you and your men in this position."

His face softened. "You didn't, my lady. My lord Ptolemy Solon did. But I reckon if I were D'Angeline, I'd be proud to serve you."

I fetched my things from our cabin, or at least what I could wear. My sword-belt, Dorelei's vambraces, the torc the Cruarch had given me. I found a piece of oilcloth and carefully wrapped Bodeshmun's talisman in it, stowing it in my purse along with the croonie-stone and a handful of coins.

"What if we founder?" Sidonie asked. "You'll be weighted down."

"What if we don't make it past the blockade?" I countered. "I don't mean to be taken alive."

She swallowed. "Did Joscelin ever teach you how to perform the *terminus*?"

"No." It was the act of last, desperate measure for a Cassiline Brother unable to protect his charge, one that ended in the death of both protector and protected. "Sidonie . . ."

"Imriel." She took my hand and laid it against her heart. "Believe me when I tell you I would far rather die by your hand than be restored to Astegal. Even if he is tolerably good in bed."

I didn't know whether to laugh or cry. I settled for nodding.

"Thank you." Sidonie released my hand.

We watched the blockade approach. All along the ship, Deimos' men stood by with lit torches. Gods, it was going to be a near thing. If he gave the order too soon, we'd go up in a blaze before we reached the harbor. Too late, and the Carthaginian ships wouldn't have time to maneuver out of the way.

"Where's Kratos?" Sidonie asked.

I glanced around. "I don't know."

"*Now!*" Captain Deimos shouted.

The fire caught instantly in a dozen places, sudden and terrifying. It raced along the railing, crawled along the hull, raged upward along the lines. Now Deimos' men ran wildly to-and-fro, dashing buckets of water on the flames. It wasn't for the sake of show; the ship was at risk of becoming an inferno.

We were still under sail, bearing down on Carthage's blockade, close enough that we could hear shouts of alarm ringing out over the water. Through the flames and billowing smoke, I could see banks of oars churning the waters and ships moving, getting hastily out of our way. My eyes were stinging and my lungs starting to burn. I wrapped my arms around Sidonie as though I could protect her from the fire.

"Here, my lord!" Kratos' voice, harsh and coughing. He flung a sodden bed-linen sheet over my shoulders. "Drape yourself and her highness. Cover your mouths."

I obeyed gratefully, then saw he hadn't one for himself. "What about you?"

Kratos shook his head. "No time."

It was a piece of madness. Sailors dashed, hurling buckets, but they'd done their job too well. The entire ship was ablaze. The sails were on fire, and our progress was faltering. We'd won our way past the blockade, but we hadn't cleared the mole.

High overhead, one of the yardarms gave way, crashing to the deck in a flurry of fiery sparks. Someone cried out in agonizing pain. Sparks landed and sizzled on the damp linen wrapped around us. The ship wallowed, flaming.

And behind us, looming through the smoke and flames, the Carthaginian war-ship that had dogged our wake passed the blockade and continued its pursuit.

"To the landing-boat, men!" Deimos' voice roared. "To oars!"

They came, staggering, soot-blackened and singed. Not all of them. There were at least seven Cytheran sailors who didn't survive that desperate gambit. Those who did worked with frantic hands, undoing the knots that held the landing-boat, lowering it into the water. Two held it in place with grappling poles. Others clambered over the railing, dropping into the smaller vessel. The first to gain his feet reached up, gesturing to me.

"Ready?" I didn't wait for Sidonie's answer, but swung her over the railing, lowering her. The sailor below caught and steadied her. Kratos' linen sheet slipped from my shoulders. I felt a blast of heat against my back. Deimos was already in the boat, ordering his men to the benches.

"Go!" Kratos shouted, shielding me.

"You first, old man!" I stooped and caught him under the knee in a wrestling move he'd taught me himself, heaving him unceremoniously over the railing. There were shouts below from the men who broke his fall. The sailors holding the landing-boat in place with grappling poles grimaced. I vaulted the railing and let myself drop. One of them followed suit.

The other didn't. The flames had caught him.

"Go!" Deimos shouted. "Go, go, *go*!"

They were good men, Ptolemy Solon's men. They bent their backs to the oars, churning the grey waters to a frenzy. Behind us, the wreck of the ship foundered and burned, throwing off sparks of fire and burning matter. The Carthaginian war-ship was forced to give it a wide berth.

Before us, a scant twenty yards away, lay the mole and the fortress.

"Go, go, *go*!" Deimos chanted.

I wanted to reach Sidonie, but I didn't dare. There was an open bench near me. I slid into it and grasped the oar shaft. I bent my back with the others, dipping and hauling for all I was worth. The light landing-boat shot across the choppy waters.

The massive trireme bore down on us, its sails full-bellied, propelled by three banks of oars.

From the fortress on the mole came a resonant thrumming

sound. Amílcar's defenders were loosing the great catapults. The first missile, a boulder large enough that two men's arms couldn't have circled it, passed low over our heads and landed behind our stern. A geyser of water shot up.

"Row, lads!" Deimos shouted. "*Row*, damn you!"

We doubled our efforts.

I'd taken a shift the night we'd rowed to Kapporeth, Joscelin, Phèdre, and I, following the stars. And I'd pulled my weight on a Vralian ship during the storm that led to a shipwreck. Those had been long, grueling affairs. This was short and urgent. Life or death would be decided in a matter of yards. The wood of the oar shaft felt hot beneath my hands, burning from the friction of my skin.

We surged past the fortress.

The catapults thrummed and thudded.

But not against us. Amílcar's defenders were well-armed and determined. They might not know who we were, but they knew Carthage was against us. They loosed a barrage against our lone pursuer. At least one missile struck true. The Carthaginian ship slowed, taking on water.

"Keep going," Deimos said grimly. "Row!"

The port grew closer. We were well inside the mole. I spared a glance over my shoulder and saw the wounded Carthaginian ship beginning to founder. I whispered a prayer of thanks to Blessed Elua.

Our pace slowed as we drew into the harbor.

Amílcar.

Even in the midst of terror and urgency, it made me feel strange seeing it again. I'd seen it as a child. It was here that the Carthaginian slave-traders had sold me to a Menekhetan merchant. It was from this very harbor that I'd set sail toward horror; and now I was back, seeking sanctuary in a besieged city. Strange, indeed.

There was a large contingent of armed men awaiting us

on the dock. Archers with crossbows were arrayed in two ranks, one kneeling, one standing behind them. All held their weapons cocked and ready. A mounted man watched us intently, a lean fellow, his cheeks pitted with old pox scars.

"Peace!" I called in Aragonian. "We come seeking sanctuary!"

His eyes narrowed. "Why?"

Fifty-two

I got carefully to my feet, raising my hands to show they were empty, and made my way forward to where Sidonie was shivering in the prow. "Are you all right?" I whispered to her.

She nodded. "Cold."

I helped her stand. None of Deimos' men moved. The archers on the dock kept their crossbows trained on us. "We bear her highness Sidonie de la Courcel, the Dauphine of Terre d'Ange," I called. "Freed from Carthage's grasp."

The mounted man spat. "Carthage's bitch!"

"No longer." Sidonie was wavering on her feet, but her voice was steady. "Messire, if you bear any love for either of our countries, you will welcome us ashore."

For a long moment, he hesitated, surveying our exhausted, singed, sooty human cargo. Kratos was huddled in the prow, grimacing. Sidonie and I stood. Everyone else, Deimos included, simply leaned on their oars.

"Down," the mounted man said at last to his archers. "I am Vitor Gaitán, captain of the Harbor Watch," he said to us. "I will take you into custody. What happens then is for Serafin to decide."

"He's my kinsman," Sidonie said. "I need to speak with him immediately."

Vitor Gaitán eyed her. "That's for Serafin to decide."

"She needs a chirurgeon is what she needs," I said. The man opened his mouth to reply. "And no, that's not for Serafin to decide."

Gaitán's men secured the landing-boat and helped us ashore, then marched us through the streets of Amílcar. Gods, we were a sorry lot! Kratos was among the worst, blisters rising on his back, his shirt scorched to holes. To compound matters, he'd broken a rib or two in the fall when I'd heaved him over the railing. Still, he shrugged off my apologies. "One of the last fellows didn't make it," Kratos said soberly. "Like as not that would have been me. I'm not as quick as you, my lord."

There were a good many folk on the streets, watching with curiosity. The mood in Amílcar was markedly different than New Carthage. It was a city holding out in the early stages of a siege, tense, jubilant, and defiant.

That, I thought, would change.

Vitor Gaitán led us to a park where a makeshift infirmary of tents had been erected and called for chirurgeons to attend our wounded.

"I'm off to report to Serafin," he said to us. "What happens then—"

"Just go," Sidonie said wearily.

I sat with her on one of the cots while we waited. There were two chirurgeons on hand, but she wouldn't allow either of them to examine her, insisting that they tend first to the injured among Deimos' men.

"How many of them died?" she asked me.

"Seven or eight," I said. "I'm not sure." I took her hand.

"Sidonie, Bodeshmun threatened to have my eyes put out and my tongue cut from my head if I was merely careless. Astegal might have kept you alive as a hostage if they'd caught us, but I think the rest of us would have been dead or wishing we were. And if we succeed, far more lives will be saved than lost."

"I know." She gazed into the distance. "It's still a hard cost to bear. None of them had any stake in this. They were just obeying orders."

"I know," I said.

She glanced at me. "Thank you for not trying to soften it."

It wasn't long before we heard the sound of a carriage approaching, and then a woman's voice angrily addressing the guards Vitor Gaitán had left posted to watch over us. It was a voice I knew, and one I never thought I'd be so grateful to hear. We got to our feet as Nicola L'Envers y Aragon entered the chirurgeons' tent.

"Name of Elua!" She stopped short, staring at Sidonie. "It *is* true."

"Well met, Lady Nicola," Sidonie said a bit unsteadily. "I regret the circumstances."

"What . . ." Nicola paused, then shook her head. "I don't even know where to begin."

"It was a spell," I said. "Dire magics. Half of Terre d'Ange hasn't gone mad, and Sidonie didn't willingly betray Aragonia. We'll gladly explain the entire matter to you, but Sidonie needs to be seen by a chirurgeon. She has an injury that's healing badly and she's burning up with fever."

Nicola looked at me in bewilderment. "Who are you?"

I'd forgotten half of my scorched attire was yet Leander's. Ptolemy Solon wove a tight spell. "Imriel, my lady." I sat on the cot and began hauling off Leander's boots. "'Tis another piece of sorcery—"

"Wait." Sidonie touched my arm. "You'll only have to go through it again. Better to do it all at once, so they'll believe. Your son Serafin's taken charge of the resistance and declared himself regent in exile?" she asked Nicola.

"Yes." She regarded us with continued bemusement.

Sidonie took a deep breath. "Then we need to speak with him and whoever else is in command here."

"After you see a chirurgeon," I added.

I daresay Lady Nicola thought we were both mad or fevered, but she escorted us both quickly from the tent and into her carriage. There the three of us sat in awkward silence. Sidonie was still shivering. I read the doubt and uncertainty on Nicola's face.

"You gave me a spotted horse," I said to her. "You said his name was . . ." I searched my memory. "Hierax. Hierax, but the Tsingani who bred and trained him called him the Bastard."

Her violet eyes widened. "Blessed Elua! *Imriel*?"

I nodded. "I know it's hard to believe. But please, trust us long enough to hear us out."

Nicola leaned out the window and called to the driver. "Hurry, please."

She took us to the Count's palace—or what had been the Count's palace. Count Fernan had been killed in a skirmish outside New Carthage. It was a solid building of grey granite, located in the Plaza del Rey at the heart of the city. There, she led us to a pleasant guest-chamber where we were able to wash the worst of the soot and smoke from our skin, and sent for her own chirurgeon, a capable Eisandine woman named Rachel. Lady Nicola stayed in the room while Rachel examined Sidonie. She caught her breath at the sight of the inflamed wound.

"What did this to you?" the chirurgeon asked.

Sidonie met my eyes. "A paring knife. Does it matter?"

"I suppose not." Rachel swabbed the wound. "I need to apply a poultice to draw the poisonous humors. You'll have to be still for a full day and not disturb it."

"Not yet." Sidonie shifted restlessly. "Not until I've addressed Serafin and the others."

The chirurgeon made a disapproving sound.

"It's important," I said to Rachel.

She sighed. "I'll clean and dress it, and give you willow-bark tea for the fever. But mind, if you don't heed me quickly, it will start to putrefy. And once that happens, a mere poultice won't suffice. I'll have to induce maggots into the wound to devour the rotten flesh. Do you understand?"

Sidonie merely nodded. "My thanks."

The chirurgeon Rachel sent her young Aragonian assistant to brew the tea, then finished binding the injury. Sidonie was sitting up and drinking the willow-bark tea obediently when a man who could only be Serafin L'Envers y Aragon entered the room unceremoniously. His olive-skinned features and straight black hair were Aragonian, but he had the violet eyes that marked so many of House L'Envers.

"Why didn't you await my orders?" he asked his mother.

Nicola raised her brows. "To receive my kinswoman, the Dauphine of Terre d'Ange? I wasn't aware it was necessary."

"We're at war with the woman's husband, Mother." Serafin turned to us. "You're Sidonie?"

"Yes," she said. "Cousin Serafin, I presume?"

He ignored the question. "You've one hell of a nerve coming here to beg sanctuary."

"You've no idea," Sidonie said dryly. "Would you care to summon a council to find out what Carthage has done to both our nations, and what we might do about it, or do you wish to berate me a while longer?"

Serafin's nostrils flared, but he held himself in check.

"You've knowledge that might shed light on this ungodly affair?"

"I do," she said. "We both do."

He gave me a hard look. "Who are you?"

I gave him a brief bow. "Imriel de la Courcel."

We'd never met, so Serafin took me at my word, but it startled him nonetheless. "The missing prince?"

"More often than not," I agreed.

"Call a council, Serafin," Nicola murmured. "Whatever it is they have to say, I suspect we'll all want to hear it."

He nodded brusquely. "Escort them to the great hall." With that, Serafin took his leave, accompanied by a handful of guards.

"He seems a touch . . . intemperate," I volunteered.

"Terre d'Ange's betrayal took everyone hard," Nicola said soberly. "Serafin more than most. It's half his heritage. You won't find a lot of goodwill here, I fear. I've felt the brush of suspicion myself, and I've lived a good deal of my life in Aragonia."

Sidonie finished her tea. "Lady Nicola, do you know what passes in Terre d'Ange these days?"

"You've not heard?" Nicola inquired.

Sidonie shook her head. "There was no information passing through New Carthage. Before that, I was kept ignorant."

"We've been isolated since the siege began," Nicola said. Her expression was deeply troubled. "But at last reckoning, Terre d'Ange was divided against itself. Barquiel sought to install your sister, Alais, as Princess-Regent, using troops he raised and some of Alba's forces. Ysandre decreed them in rebellion against the Crown. They've established a base at Turnone, while Ysandre holds the City of Elua."

I felt sick. "Are they at war?"

"Not yet—or at least they weren't. But it seems a precarious stalemate." She shifted her worried gaze to mine. "No one's known what to believe. I'd never have thought Ysandre would grow power-mad, but there's an ambitious strain in the L'Envers bloodline. Elua knows Barquiel's always had it."

"It's not ambition," Sidonie said. "Not this time." She rose and I took her arm to steady her. She gave me a fleeting smile. "Let's go take your clothes off for the Aragonian council."

"I'm beginning to think you enjoy that part," I observed.

Her smile deepened briefly. "I do, actually."

The council wasn't large. It consisted of Serafin and eight others, all men. His father, Ramiro Zornín de Aragon was among them. I wondered how it was that Serafin had claimed the regency over his father's right, and suspected it had somewhat to do with ambition. Phèdre had always said that Ramiro, a minor member of the House of Aragon who'd long served as King's Consul, had a good deal of charm and little ambition.

I supposed she ought to know, since Nicola had been her lover for many years, which was why I'd never liked her. Those feelings seemed distant and petty now.

The other members of the council consisted of Vitor Gaitán, the captain of the Harbor Watch; a grizzled veteran named Liberio who was in command of what remained of the army; and five other Aragonian lords whose names blurred together in my memory.

"So few," Sidonie said in a low voice.

"Many followed the King when Roderico surrendered," Nicola said quietly. "And many others have accepted Carthage's terms."

Sidonie and I were ushered into chairs at the long table in the great hall, facing the council. To a man, they looked disapproving. I was glad that Lady Nicola stayed, unobtrusively taking a seat at the far end of the table.

"Speak," Serafin said with a curt nod.

Sidonie rose, resting her hands on the table. Elua, she looked young in those surroundings! She *was* young. But she was the daughter of the Queen of Terre d'Ange and the Cruarch of Alba, and the only person in the room raised from birth to rule a nation.

"My lords," she said in a clear voice. "Thank you for hearing us. I am Sidonie de la Courcel of Terre d'Ange, and for our mutual benefit, I wish to tell you what befell my country."

The youngest of the Aragonian lords actually had the temerity to hiss. Serafin shot him a look. "Shut your mouth, Jimeno," he said. "Go on."

She inclined her head. "Last summer, we received a suit from General Astegal, Prince of the House of Sarkal, wishing to pay tribute to Terre d'Ange on behalf of Carthage. With some misgivings, Parliament voted to receive his delegation. My mother took the precaution of bringing the Royal Army within the City's walls and ensuring the Carthaginians were escorted by Admiral Rousse and several of his war-ships."

"That we know," Liberio said laconically.

Sidonie ignored him. "During the course of his visit, Astegal made an offer for my hand. He implied that Carthage, Terre d'Ange, and Alba might together force Aragonia into a peaceable surrender and build the beginnings of a mighty empire. That offer, we refused."

No one hissed this time. They listened.

"Astegal appeared to accept our refusal with good grace." Her voice hardened. "But he had promised that his horologists would show us a marvel on the night that the moon was obscured. He insisted on keeping his pledge. We allowed it."

Sidonie paused. "My lords, I cannot tell you what marvel I witnessed that night. It seemed to me that I saw somewhat wondrous, but when pressed to describe it, I cannot. All I can tell you is this: Blessed Elua knows, gossip carries. Much of this part of the world has known that for the past year, Terre d'Ange had been divided over my desire to wed my royal kinsman, Imriel de la Courcel. I ventured out that night very much in love with him. I awoke the next morning with no memory of his existence."

There was a short, shocked silence.

"That," Sidonie said thoughtfully, "I believe was unique to an intimate spell that bound me, and me alone. But no one noticed, because we'd all been caught in a greater magic. One that bound the entire City of Elua, man, woman, and child. I awoke that morning believing that Carthage and Terre d'Ange were allies. That Aragonia had committed an act of aggression against Carthage. And worst of all, that I'd fallen in love with Astegal of Carthage and gladly agreed to wed him." She glanced up and down the table. "So I believed. So everyone in the City of Elua believed. I had no memory that things had ever been otherwise. And two days later, I was escorted to the harbor with great fanfare, where I boarded a Carthaginian ship without a single D'Angeline guard, without a single attendant, and sailed away to marry Astegal." She paused again, steadying herself. "Which, as you well know, I did. And I didn't begin to truly suspect aught was amiss until a man named Leander Maignard entered my life."

My turn.

I rose, while Sidonie sat gratefully, careful not to rest against the back of her chair. "My lords," I said. "My name is Imriel de la Courcel, but the face I wear belongs to Leander Maignard. Listen, and hear what befell me."

They did.

I told them what had befallen me the night of the marvel, although I glossed over certain details. The Unseen Guild, Sunjata's identity. But I told them of the needle and the whisper, the stolen ring. The madness that followed. I told them about seeking Barquiel L'Envers' aid and fleeing to Cythera. My mother. Ptolemy Solon and his knowledge, how he had deciphered the spells that bound Sidonie and Terre d'Ange. The spell he'd wrought to conceal me from myself.

"A spell undone with a kiss," I said.

One of the Aragonian lords scoffed. "A poet's tale! Why should we believe any of this nonsense? Simple greed's a lot more likely."

Sidonie and I exchanged a glance.

"Now?" I asked.

She nodded. "Now."

This time I played it for dramatic effect. I removed Leander's shirt first, smoke-scented and scorched. I knew what Serafin and his council saw. Leander Maignard, bare-chested before them, his torso smooth and lean. I'd put in his ruby eardrops, and I made a show of removing them. I wasn't wearing much else of his.

"You know me," I said to Lady Nicola. "Imriel. You told me once to know myself. Do you see me?"

Nicola shook her head, eyes wide and wondering. "I see a man like to have Shahrizai blood in him. Not Imriel de la Courcel."

Ptolemy Solon wove a tight spell.

I dragged off Leander's boots and stockings, then stood bare-footed and -chested in the great hall of the Count's palace. There are few merits to having survived an attack by a bear—or a shapeshifting magician in a bear's form—but it makes for a fairly strong impression.

Nicola gasped and covered her mouth.

Liberio came out of his seat.

"What you see, I saw!" Sidonie's voice was urgent as she rose to join me, standing before them. "And I knew him. I didn't remember, but I *knew.* So I stripped myself bare, thinking the same had been done to me." Her mouth twisted. "It hadn't. Astegal set his seal on me in a different way. He had the insignia of the House of Sarkal etched into my skin. A mockery of the marques the Servants of Naamah bear. The mark that made me his willing bride." She shuddered. "I begged Imriel to cut it out of me. He did. And I knew myself at last and what had been done to me."

There was another stunned silence, this one longer. It broke at length in a multitudinous clamor of questions and statements.

". . . can we be sure this isn't a Carthaginian trick?"

". . . about the spell binding the City of Elua?"

". . . *seen* the wound with my own eyes!"

"*Enough!*" Serafin L'Envers y Aragon pounded on the table. He leaned forward, his gaze intent. "Why was Carthage pursuing you? Were you discovered?"

"Not exactly, my lord." Out of the corner of my eye, I could see that Sidonie was racked by a fresh onset of shivers. Whatever good the willow-bark tea had done, it wasn't enough. "We killed the horologist who wrought the spell and obtained the key to undoing it, then fled. Carthage seeks to thwart us. But if it lies within your power to get us from Amílcar to Terre d'Ange, we can undo the spell and restore our alliance with Aragonia."

"We don't need Terre d'Ange," Liberio muttered.

"We need *some* ally," another voice countered.

"Do you swear to this?" Serafin asked without heeding them. "Both of you. Do you swear to it in the name of all your gods?"

"I do," I said.

"Yes!" Sidonie got the word out in a gasp, her knees buckling. I caught her before she hit the floor.

"Do you really doubt?" I asked Serafin with disdain.

"No." He met my gaze squarely. "But we need to discuss this amongst ourselves all the same."

"Do," I said, cradling Sidonie in my arms and exiting the hall.

Fifty-three

"Imriel, I hate this." Sidonie lay on her belly, chin propped on her hands, her face suffused with impatience.

"Too bad," I said ruthlessly. "You're not moving."

The chirurgeon Rachel had applied a poultice the evening before, a disgusting mess of bread mold and mashed burdock root. She'd ordered Sidonie to remain motionless for a solid day, allowing the poultice to work undisturbed. Over the course of the night, it had done a great deal of good, and now Sidonie was restless.

She made a face. "I feel much better."

I drew a lock of hair away from her brow, feeling her skin. It wasn't nearly as hot as it had been, but it was still overly warm. "So you do. But you fell into a dead faint in front of Serafin's council yesterday. You're not moving until sundown."

There was a knock at the door, and I went to admit Lady Nicola.

"How is she?" she asked.

"Better," I said. "Irritable."

Nicola smiled. "I would have expected Ysandre's children to be strong-willed."

"My lady, will you *please* come tell us the news!" Sidonie's voice called from the bedchamber.

We went into the chamber. It tugged at my heart seeing her like this. She wore a shift of fine white linen with the back cut out, a thick crust of dried poultice slathered between her shoulder blades. The garment also had a disconcertingly low decolletage that tugged at other parts, particularly when Sidonie propped herself on her elbows as she did now, revealing the cleft of her cleavage.

I cleared my throat. "Don't do that, love. You'll crack the poultice."

She shot me an amused look. "It's fine. What news?"

"Not much, I fear." Nicola sat in the chair I drew up for her, brows knitted. "The trouble is that Amílcar's a city under siege. You've seen the blockade at the mouth of the harbor. Would that I could tell you there's some secret egress from the city proper, some tunnel escape into the foothills, but there's not."

"What about a sortie?" I asked. "Is there any chance we could slip past Astegal's lines in the midst of a sally?"

Nicola nodded. "'Tis the only chance, I fear. Not everyone is willing to take that risk."

I frowned. "Why not? It doesn't seem like Amílcar's got many choices here, my lady. Forgive me for speaking bluntly, but Astegal's got a good portion of Aragonia well in hand. He's not lacking for supplies. Unless the current balance tips somehow, he can afford to wait you out until you starve."

She sighed. "Yes, and for the moment, Amílcar is amply supplied. Betimes it takes desperate times to drive men to desperate measures. In the eyes of some, we're far from it. And then there's the problem to the north."

"What problem to the north?" Sidonie asked suspiciously.

"The Euskerri," Nicola said. "They've ranged far enough to hold all the mountain passes."

"*What?*" Sidonie stared at her, lips parted. "Do you mean to tell me that despite everything that's happened, Aragonia is *still* at odds with Euskerria?"

"You speak of it as though it's a sovereign nation," Nicola said dryly.

Sidonie swore softly and made to rise from the bed. "I swear to Elua—"

"Oh no!" I grabbed her by the nape of the neck, pinning her down. "You're *not* going anywhere. Not until the chirurgeon grants permission."

She glared at me. "Imriel . . ."

I shook her. "Promise."

She blew out her breath. "Fine. I promise."

Lady Nicola was staring at both of us. "You two are oddly well suited to one another, aren't you?"

"Oddly, yes," I agreed.

Sidonie settled back down, propping her chin on her fists again. "Tell me why Serafin hasn't sought an alliance with the Euskerri, my lady."

"He was planning to make overtures," Nicola said. "But he changed his mind when he learned they were continuing to negotiate behind our back. The Euskerri offered to betray us to Carthage in exchange for sovereignty."

"Why do they want sovereignty so badly?" I asked.

"They're an ancient folk," Sidonie said. "Like the Maghuin Dhonn in Alba, they were here long before the Tiberians or the Carthaginians settled in Aragonia. They have their own language, their own laws. For centuries, they had an agreement with the kings of Aragonia that they'd be given the right to govern themselves according to their own customs, but that was broken too many times for them to trust. Now all they want is sovereignty at any cost."

It was my turn to stare at her.

"I sat in on the negotiations my mother oversaw," Sidonie reminded me. "Don't you remember me asking what you knew about them the night . . ."

Her voice trailed off.

"Oh!" I was struck by the sudden, vivid image of Sidonie kneeling, naked and obedient, her hands clasped behind her head. That was a conversation we hadn't ended up having. "Um. Yes."

"So Carthage wasn't willing to meet their terms?" Sidonie inquired of Nicola.

Nicola shook her head. "No. No, Astegal was confident that once he had Aragonia under his thumb, he could roll easily over the Euskerri. I suspect he underestimates them. There were a good many skirmishes between us before Carthage invaded. The Euskerri won as many as they lost. They're not terribly well organized, but they're fearless, stubborn fighters."

"Do you think the Euskerri's forces combined with Aragonia's would be able to defeat Carthage?" Sidonie asked.

"Possibly," Nicola allowed. "I'm not a military strategist."

"What are you thinking?" I asked Sidonie.

"They're not asking for much," she said slowly. "It's a very small territory. Part of it lies on D'Angeline soil, and my mother was willing to cede it. No deal was brokered because King Roderico's ambassador refused to do the same, and the Euskerri refused to accept aught less. I'm thinking Serafin is a fool not to make the offer. Begging your forgiveness, my lady."

"No need." Nicola shrugged gracefully. "Men tend to be

proud, stiff-necked, and impractical. I agree. Unfortunately, my son is not as easily influenced as my husband."

"And more ambitious," I observed.

"Yes." She glanced sidelong at me. "That too. But I think he might be convinced to relent on this point after what you've told us." She was silent a moment. "My younger son, Raul, was in the City of Elua that night, wasn't he?"

"Oh, gods!" I'd forgotten. "Yes. I'm sorry, my lady."

"I wondered why I'd had no word from him for so many months," Nicola murmured. "So, yes. I think it possible that Serafin might be convinced to make a treaty with the Euskerri once he's had time to think on it. It won't sit lightly on him, thinking of his brother bound to Carthage's thrall. 'Tis the others will be harder to convince."

"Can you sway your husband?" Sidonie inquired.

Nicola didn't mince words. "Yes."

"That's two votes," Sidonie mused.

"General Liberio's will depend on whether or not he believes we could defeat Carthage with the Euskerri's aid," Nicola said. "If he doesn't, there's no chance the others will agree to it."

"And if he does?" I asked.

"There's a chance they could be persuaded," she said. "Not a good one, but a chance."

Sidonie pushed herself back onto her elbows. "I'd like to address them."

"Give me time to speak to Ramiro and Serafin," Nicola said to her. "Let them take Liberio's measure, and we'll proceed from there. Prince Imriel is right; you're not to leave your bed today."

"You'll tell me as soon as you know anything?" Sidonie pressed.

"Yes, your highness." Nicola smiled at her. "You have my word."

Sidonie nodded, the gravity of her expression almost sufficient to offset the distracting display of cleavage. "And you my thanks. Terre d'Ange is fortunate to have someone with your presence and wits here in Amílcar."

"Rest." Nicola rose. "Terre d'Ange is also fortunate to have an heir of such singular will and determination, and I suspect they'd wish to keep it that way. Of a surety, I have no wish to inform Ysandre that her valiant daughter succumbed to an injury from a paring knife."

I laughed and Sidonie smiled reluctantly. I escorted Nicola to the door, pausing there in the corridor.

"My lady," I said. "I've behaved very rudely to you in the past, and I wish to apologize. All I can say is that I was young, and there was a great deal about love that I didn't understand."

"There's no need," Nicola said quietly. "I knew what you'd suffered. I understood."

It was true. Nicola L'Envers y Aragon was the one person in whom Phèdre had confided, the one who knew the worst details of what she'd endured in Daršanga.

"Nonetheless," I said. "I do apologize."

"Then I thank you for it." She touched my cheek. A garnet seal dangled from a gold bracelet on her wrist, bearing an incised dart. Kushiel's Dart—the only lover's token Phèdre had ever bestowed on a patron. "We *will* see this undone, Imriel. Carthage will not prevail. Not here, not in Terre d'Ange."

I took her hand and kissed it. "Blessed Elua grant it will be so."

Nicola took her leave, and I returned to tend to my restless beloved, pouring a cup of water from a jug beside the bed.

"Here." I handed it to her. "The chirurgeon Rachel said

you should drink a good deal of water to help flush the poisons."

Sidonie drank obediently. "Imriel, if I promise to behave and lie abed, will you go to the infirmary to see how Kratos and the others are? I'm worried."

"You already promised," I reminded her. She gave me a look. "Yes, of course. I'm worried, too." I stroked her hair. "Sidonie, if it helps to think on it, when I was in Bryn Gorrydum, after Dorelei was killed, I had to lie abed a long time and obey the chirurgeon's orders. I did everything he said, thinking that the sooner I was mended, the sooner I'd be free to seek vengeance."

"I know," she murmured. "But you were nearly disemboweled by a bear, not nicked by a paring knife. And in the end, it was more than vengeance."

"True." I glanced at the poultice on her back. "And that was no nick, love. But at the time, it helped. That's all I'm saying."

She sighed. "Will you find me a book to pass the time?"

I was leaving to do just that when Sidonie called me back.

"Imriel."

I paused in the doorway. "Yes?"

She gazed at me with those dark, dark eyes. "I meant it. I want to kill Astegal myself. I want to feel him die."

I bowed. "Sun Princess, if it lies within my power, I will grant it."

I found the palace's modest library and selected a tome for Sidonie: an Aragonian history that appeared to contain detailed and violent descriptions of various battles. I thought it might suit her mood.

Fierce.

Alais had said that once. It was during that terrible

time when I was recuperating from the injuries Berlik had dealt me, the day I'd let myself grieve for the first time: for Dorelei's death, for the death of our unborn son. I'd wept savagely, racked by sobs and regret. And afterward, for the first time, Alais had spoken openly of Sidonie and me. *I think she must love you very much,* she'd said. *She's very fierce, even though it doesn't show.*

Alais knew her sister well.

Gods, poor Alais.

Thinking on it, I nearly wished I believed myself Leander Maignard still, blithely unconcerned about the fate of Terre d'Ange. It would have been a good deal easier than knowing myself Imriel and thinking with wretched horror of the stalemate Nicola had described, with the lives of those I loved hanging in the balance. Phèdre and Joscelin, loyal to the Queen and ensorceled. Alais, the sister of my heart, struggling to hold the rest of the realm together.

"Here." I stooped and presented Sidonie with the book.

"Thank you." She reached up to tug on my hair, tugging my face down to hers, and kissed me with fierce ardor. "Go. Tell Kratos I expect him to dance with me at our wedding."

I smiled. "I will."

I made my way to the infirmary in the park, leaving a trail of stares and whispers behind me. Clearly, news of our performance and revelations had spread throughout Amílcar. At least the mood wasn't openly hostile, not like New Carthage. Still, I kept my hand hovering over my sword-hilt.

"Prince Imriel!" Captain Deimos hailed me outside one of the tents. "What passes?"

"Precious little," I replied. "Are your men well?"

"Those that lived, aye," he replied soberly.

I winced. "I'm so sorry, my lord captain."

"So am I." Deimos jerked his head at the tent. "Among

the survivors, I daresay your manservant bore the brunt of it. He's within."

Inside, I found Kratos lying on his belly on a cot, his back covered with damp bandages. He was a more complacent patient than Sidonie. He lifted his homely face with pleasure, regarding me. "My lord! How fares her highness?"

"Well enough." I sat beside him, cross-legged in the dirt. "And you?"

Kratos shrugged his meaty shoulders. "It hurts to breathe. But I reckon I'll live."

I thought about Gilot, who had been one of Montrève's men-at-arms, the companion of my youth. He'd died from injuries he sustained while trying to protect me: cracked ribs, a bone splinter. There in a gatehouse in Lucca, in the midst of a quarrel none of us had held stake in. If Gilot had stayed out of it, he might have lived. He'd spent his life on the mechanism that raised or lowered a drawbridge. His efforts caused that splinter of bone to shift and pierce his lung.

Gilot had died a hero.

Elua, I was sick of heroes.

Once, I'd wanted to be one. I'd harbored glorious dreams of styling myself a hero in the manner I believed Joscelin to be. I'd lost those illusions a long time ago, but I hadn't understood until now how much *heroism* meant living in terror that you wouldn't be able to protect those you loved.

Ptolemy Solon was right.

Happiness *was* the highest form of wisdom.

"You will." I gripped Kratos' shoulder firmly, feeling the solid meat and muscle of him. "You have to live, my friend. Sidonie is expecting you to dance with her at our wedding. And it's bad form to disappoint a lady."

Kratos blinked at me. "Truly?"

"Truly." I released his shoulder, rubbed my eyes with

the heels of my hands. "May I give her your promise that you will?"

Kratos nodded. "I'll do my best, my lord."

I smiled at him through blurred eyes. "Thank you, Kratos. That's all any of us can do."

Fifty-four

The following morning I held my breath as the chirurgeon Rachel eased the poultice from Sidonie's wound. She'd changed it the night before and refused to comment on the healing progress, which I suspected was as much as anything a ploy to keep Sidonie quiescent. Today she relented.

"Better," Rachel said with grudging satisfaction. "*Much* better."

Even I could see it was so. The swelling had subsided and the angry red flesh had turned pink.

"Am I free, then?" Sidonie asked impatiently.

"No." The Eisandine healer gave her a stern look. "Now it needs air and sunlight, highness. Give it another day. You need not remain confined to your bed, but do not cover the wound. I will give orders that for an hour after noon, the courtyard will be reserved in privacy for your usage. Sun is healing. Seek it."

Sidonie sat upright and made a disgusted sound.

"Even the stunted tree seeks sunlight," I said to her. "Hear and obey, Princess."

"Obey." She wrinkled her nose at me. "You like that part, don't you?"

"No." I smiled, sliding my hands up her arms as she straddled and kissed me, her shift riding high on her thighs. "Yes."

The chirurgeon cleared her throat. "I'll return in the evening to examine you once more, your highness."

"Thank you, Rachel," Sidonie said absently, gazing at me.

"You shouldn't overexert yourself," I said when the chirurgeon had left.

"I'm not." She wriggled further astride my lap. "But I can't bear being kept idle, and I can't *go* anywhere if I can't cover this thing, except to take sun in the courtyard. So . . ." She kissed me again, her tongue darting between my lips. "I want to feel like myself, Imriel. Stop treating me like I'm made of glass. I won't break."

I traced a line down her throat into the cleft between her breasts. "No?"

Sidonie shook her head, her eyes grave. "No."

"All right." On a whim, I reached for the cup of water on the bedside table. I poured it slowly over the thin linen of her shift, soaking it until it became transparent. "You know you're driving me mad wearing this thing."

She smiled. "Oh, good."

The sheer fabric was plastered to her breasts, pink nipples jutting against it. I slid my hands down to her buttocks, pulling her hard against me, then lowered my mouth, sucking and biting at her breasts through the linen. Sidonie sank her hands deep into my hair, sighing with pleasure.

"More," she whispered. "Please."

"Mmm." I reached up and tore the neckline of her shift open, the thin, soaked fabric giving way easily. Sidonie made a small, startled sound of delight, then a deeper one as my mouth returned to her breasts, gliding over her silken, wet flesh. She pressed herself harder against me, hips moving involuntarily. When I felt her begin to shudder all over, I lifted my head and captured her mouth, forcing her to moan her pleasure into mine. I felt the sweet vibration of it all the way to my core.

It almost drowned out the knock at the outer door and the sound of Lady Nicola's voice. It seemed to be true that certain events in our lives were fated to be relived. We looked at one another.

"You'll have to answer that," Sidonie said breathlessly.

I grimaced. "Let me fetch you a clean shift."

Her eyes danced. "There isn't one."

"Where's your gown?" I asked. "You can wear it with the stays undone."

"Taken to be laundered," she said. "No one's returned it. I thought it was a ploy to keep me from leaving my quarters."

"Tell me you're jesting," I pleaded. Sidonie just laughed. With a groan of dismay, I shifted her from my lap and went into the antechamber, closing the door of her bedchamber behind me.

"Good morning, Imriel," Nicola greeted me, looking pleased. "Rachel tells me that Sidonie's much improved."

"Yes," I said wryly. "Much, much improved. My lady, we have a . . . garment crisis."

Nicola raised her brows. "Oh?"

"We escaped the ship with the clothes on our backs," I explained. "Sidonie's gown was taken to be laundered and hasn't been returned."

"I asked my seamstress to take her measurements from it and alter a gown or two to fit her," Nicola said mildly. "I had some of Serafin's clothing that would suit for you, but nothing for Sidonie. I'll send someone to investigate. But if she didn't mind receiving me yesterday clad in—"

"It's torn." I flushed. "Rather badly."

"Ah." Her lovely face lit with mirth. "Much, *much* improved, I take it."

"Oh yes," I murmured.

Nicola laughed. "Well, 'tis good to know that love and laughter flourish even in the midst of war. I suspect we need it now more than ever, and I thank you for your unwitting gift of the latter. I can return later."

"No."

The bedchamber door opened to reveal Sidonie artfully draped in a bedsheet. It looked almost like a Hellene peplos.

"How did you learn to . . . ?" I gestured vaguely.

She looked at me with amusement. "Play-acting with Alais when we were children. Lady Nicola, if you will forgive our state of considerable disarray, I would very much like to hear your news."

Nicola L'Envers y Aragon was a diplomat's wife—and like as not, twice the diplomat her husband was. She inclined her head. "Of course."

So I ushered her inside, where she told us that Serafin and Ramiro had both come around to thinking it was worth risking a sortie and attempting to send a delegation to treat with the Euskerri.

"They're willing to grant sovereignty to Euskerria?" Sidonie asked.

"If the Euskerri are willing to wage war on Carthage, yes," Nicola said. "Ramiro thinks several of the southern counties might renege on their treaties with Astegal and rise up against him if we're able to do this. And that if we don't make the effort, Aragonia will be devoured piecemeal, Euskerria included. After long thought, Serafin has agreed."

"What about General Liberio?" I asked.

Nicola spread her hands. "They'll speak to him today. I'm afraid that's one decision I stand no chance of influencing."

"My lady, you might remind them . . ." Sidonie searched briefly, then came up with the book I'd procured for her yesterday. She flipped through it and found the place she wanted, passing the volume to Nicola. "Some centuries ago, Alfonso the Second sought to gain control of Euskerri territory," she said. "His army outnumbered theirs ten to one, but the Euskerri harried his forces and drew them into the mountains where they suffered a terrible rate of attrition. The war went on for years and ended in a negotiated truce. But if there were a force ready to fall on the rearguard, as in Amílcar, the same tactics might be used to more immediate effect."

"I'll do that." Nicola sounded a trifle startled.

"I didn't know you'd such a head for battle," I said to Sidonie.

She raked an impatient hand through her hair. "My mother assumed the throne and inherited a war. She never wanted either of her daughters to be utterly reliant on the wisdom of others."

Gods, I loved her.

"I'll do what I can." Nicola rose, gazing at both of us, her expression complicated and unreadable. She gave her head a little shake. "Blessed Elua have mercy! Astegal of Carthage truly grasped the tiger by the tail when he sought to divide the two of you, didn't he?"

"Yes." I reached for Sidonie's hand without thinking.

Her fingers tightened on mine. "This is for all of us, my lady. Aragonia and Terre d'Ange, too."

"Even if Liberio agrees, there will be others to be swayed," Nicola warned her.

Sidonie nodded. "I know. Will they give me leave to address them again as an emissary of Terre d'Ange?"

"I believe so," Nicola said. "But I'm not sure how much

weight your words will carry, my dear. With Terre d'Ange divided against itself, you're not in a position to promise anything with certitude."

"Then I'll have to be eloquent," Sidonie said calmly.

"Very," Nicola agreed.

The balance of the day passed without incident or further news. An assortment of clothing arrived for Sidonie, resolving the garment crisis. I accompanied her to the courtyard, where she sat in the sun for an hour, the stays of her bodice undone to expose her healing wound. She was quiet and withdrawn, thinking. I said nothing to disturb her thoughts. Diplomacy was her strong suit, not mine. If the council was to be swayed, the burden rested on her slender shoulders.

Afterward, she sent me on a quest to find a detailed map of Aragonia and paper, pen, and ink.

"Would you mind leaving me for a few hours, Imriel?" she asked apologetically when I'd returned with the items. "I need to compose my thoughts."

"Of course." I grinned. "Are you saying I'm a distraction?"

Sidonie eyed me. "Thoughts of unfinished business between us, yes."

I laughed and kissed her. "I'll go see how Kratos fares. I need to speak to Lady Nicola about making more permanent arrangements for him, and for Deimos and his men."

I left her sitting cross-legged on the bed, her head bowed over a writing tablet, her back bare in obedience to the chirurgeon's orders.

In the infirmary, I found Kratos in good spirits. His ribs were swathed in bandages, but he reported that he was able to move around a little and there was less pain when he breathed. It made me hopeful.

"So what's to become of us, my lord?" Kratos asked.

I told him what we were hoping to accomplish with the council and the Euskerri. He listened sagely, nodding.

"They'd be fools not to agree," he said when I'd finished. "All of 'em. Wrestling's a good way to take a man's measure, and Astegal's ruthless. If they don't stand together, he'll take them down one by one."

"I know," I said. "I pray we can convince them."

"You will." Kratos took a deep experimental breath. "So we're bound for Euskerri territory, eh?"

"We?" I shook my head at him. "Oh, no. Elua willing, Sidonie and I, yes; and then on to Terre d'Ange. But you, my friend, are staying in Amílcar to recover."

"My lord!" he protested. "Put me astride a horse and I'll be fine. You can't abandon me here. I don't even speak the language."

"No." I laid a hand on his arm. "Kratos, I've been responsible for too many good men losing their lives in quarrels not their own. I'm not risking yours again."

His jaw tightened. "You gave me my freedom. It's not your choice."

I gazed at his face: the blunt, worn features, the squashed nose. There was pride there, pride and courage and a canny intellect. Kratos had found hope and purpose long after he'd thought it lost. It would be cruel to take it from him.

So be it.

"It *is* my choice," I said in a hard tone. "I'm responsible for Sidonie's safety. And I'm sorry, Kratos, but you're not fit for travel. You might be able to ride, but could you mount in a hurry? Could you scramble over rocks if we had to flee on foot? No. You're staying here."

Kratos bowed his head. "As you will."

I felt bad for him, but not as badly as I would have felt if he'd died like Gilot. "We'd never have gotten this far without you, my friend," I said more gently. "Think on that while you heal."

He grunted. "I'll try."

I took my leave of Kratos and found Captain Deimos. His men were restless and concerned, trapped in a besieged city with the threat of Carthaginian reprisal hanging over them if Amílcar should fall. I promised to speak to Lady Nicola about dispersing them throughout the city so that they might not collectively be identified as the crew of the Cytheran ship that assisted in abducting Astegal's bride. Beyond that, there wasn't much else I could do.

When I returned to the palace, Lady Nicola was in conference with several Aragonian lords' wives, doing her best to persuade them to sway their husbands, I reckoned. Since I gauged it too early to interrupt Sidonie, I went to the palace stables and begged the loan of a horse.

Ever since we'd arrived, I'd wanted to get a look at Astegal's forces. I rode to the northwestern edge of the city.

Over the course of a day, word had spread of Sidonie's and my initial address to the council, and I found myself greeted with curiosity and wonder more than hostility. The squadron of guards posted in the northwest tower were glad enough to introduce me to their captain, who took me out onto the walls himself.

"There the bastard sits, your highness," the captain announced with a wave of his arm.

I gazed at the scene before me. There was the army we'd sent off with fanfare from New Carthage, spread out across the plain at the base of the foothills. Amílcar was situated between two rivers, and Astegal's army occupied the ground between them, fortified by defensive trenches and earthworks. Soldiers bustled about, digging the trenches deeper and building the earthworks higher.

"No siege engines?" I asked.

The captain, whose name was Aureliano, shook his head. "Thus far he's not bothered. I reckon he thinks he can wait us out."

"Do you?"

Aureliano pursed his lips. "Unless something gives, aye. Are the rumors true? Are you and the princess able to put an end to the madness in Terre d'Ange and send aid?"

"I don't know," I said honestly. "If we could get there, yes. But we're trapped here as surely as you are." I paused. "What would you think of aid coming from another quarter? Euskerria, say?"

He shrugged. "Better the devil you know than the one you don't. I'd welcome the Euskerri if they could deal with Astegal."

I peered at the forces arrayed against us. "Is he here?"

Aureliano laughed. "Himself? No, not today." He pointed toward the south. "We heard he's taken the palace of Montero for himself. Most days, he's there, living the good life while his men work and toil."

"Careless," I murmured.

"He was here the day you arrived, though," Aureliano added. "And the day after. Storming around on a big black horse, looking a fury."

"Good," I said.

The sun was growing low on the horizon, so I thanked Aureliano for his kindness and rode back to the palace. This time I found Lady Nicola free. There was no word yet regarding General Liberio's decision, but at least she readily agreed to send someone to ensure that Kratos, Deimos, and the others were taken care of to the best of Amílcar's ability. In a few days, I'd come to depend so heavily on her generosity and competence, I felt guilty that I'd ever thought ill of her.

That done, I returned to find Sidonie, still in her pensive mood.

"Finished, love?" I asked.

"I think so." She moved a sheaf of paper. "Elua willing, there'll be an opportunity to address them again. Is there news?"

"Not yet." I sat beside her. "Would you like to rehearse your words? Shall I play the audience for you?"

Sidonie hesitated. "I think not. What I'm planning . . . Imriel, I'm afraid I'll lose my nerve if I tell you ahead of time. Afraid it will sound foolish once I say it aloud."

"You?" I tilted her chin up and kissed her. "Never."

She smiled ruefully. "Well, I've done a number of things I would never have thought I'd do. Fall in love with you. Defy my mother. Wed Astegal."

"The latter doesn't count," I said.

"There's just so much at stake." Sidonie shivered. "Elua! I've addressed ambassadors and statesmen before, but there was never anything like this at stake. And I was always a representative of my mother. If they thought I was too young and inexperienced to listen to, she was always there to intercede. It's just so much damned responsibility. And I don't know what we'll do if I fail. Do you?"

I rubbed her shoulders, bare beneath the unlaced gown. "Spread the word *emmenghanom* until it's on the lips of every man, woman, and child in Amílcar, trusting that someone will carry it to Terre d'Ange and Alais and L'Envers to complete what we've begun. And then lock the door and make love until Amílcar falls and Astegal comes to reclaim you. At which point I will take your life and my own, and we will die in a final flourish of terrible, wonderful romance about which the poets will sing for centuries."

Sidonie laughed, tears in her eyes. "I'd much rather live a long and blessedly uneventful life with you. Although the part about the love-making sounds good."

"In that, I can oblige." I took her hands. "Sidonie, if you're given the chance, you won't fail. You won't."

She searched my face for signs of doubt, but there weren't any.

I believed in her.

"Thank you." Sidonie touched my lips. "Always."

"Always and always," I echoed.

Fifty-five

Lady Nicola was brief and to the point. "Liberio agreed."

I closed my eyes, a wave of relief washing over me. That was the one hurdle that *had* been cleared. I offered a silent prayer of thanks to Blessed Elua.

"And the council?" Sidonie asked.

"Several of the remaining five are opposed. But they're willing to hear the argument. There will be an open audience this afternoon." Nicola studied her. "Have you taken a turn for the worse? You look pale."

"No," Sidonie murmured. "Merely anxious. My lady, can you spare a chambermaid to assist me this afternoon?"

"Of course," Nicola said gently.

We waited out the long, dragging hours until the council met. Lady Nicola's chambermaid arrived and I was temporarily banished from our quarters while she helped Sidonie dress and arrange her hair. Sidonie emerged just as a courtier came to fetch us. She wore a dark green Aragonian gown with a square neckline that had belonged to Nicola, a shawl of rich golden silk over her shoulders.

"Those are nearly Montrève's colors," I commented. "A good omen."

Sidonie gave me a brief smile. "Let's hope."

The council met at the same long table in the great hall, but this was an open meeting with the hall filled with onlookers, murmurs rising to the rafters. Serafin motioned for us to be seated facing the council, our backs to the throng.

"My lords, ladies, and gentlefolk," he announced. "I am Serafin L'Envers y Aragon. In the abdication of Roderico de Aragon, the absence of ranking nobility and with the blessing of my father, I have assumed command here. Does anyone wish to gainsay this?"

No one did.

"Very good." Serafin laid both hands on the table. "We are here to debate the merits of two grave issues. One is the possibility of assisting our kinswoman, the Dauphine Sidonie de la Courcel, in escaping Amílcar and fleeing to Terre d'Ange. The other is the prospect of seeking an alliance with the Euskerri with her aid. I believe both issues possess the potential for desirable outcomes that outweigh the risks and costs. Here is my reasoning."

Serafin made his case in strong, calm terms, better than I would have reckoned, explaining that unless the balance of power tipped, Amílcar would eventually be forced to surrender. That this was a long chance, but it was a chance. I'd called him intemperate, but he had some of his mother's cool-headed competence in him. The crowd listened to him in silence.

After he spoke, one of the opposing members was given a chance to address the council and the crowd: Rafael de Barbara. He was an older Aragonian lord with a dignified bearing and a tutored rhetorical style. He spoke of Sidonie's youth and lack of experience in terms that were at once disparaging and sympathetic, reminding everyone that with

Terre d'Ange in disarray, its heir was in no position to negotiate with the Euskerri for safe passage over the border, let alone a major treaty.

"So send your own ambassador," I muttered. Sidonie hushed me.

Rafael de Barbara held the floor for a long time, recounting the long history of animosity between the Euskerri and Aragonia, culminating in recent battles. He reminded them that when the most recent skirmishes had erupted, Terre d'Ange's only concern was that it not spill over the border into Siovale. And he finished by urging them not to undertake a desperate measure that would destroy the very realm in the process of attempting to save it. At that, there was scattered applause.

When he had finished, Serafin's father, Ramiro Zornín de Aragon spoke out in support of the plan, confirming his belief that other cities would seize the opportunity to rise up against Astegal. He wasn't eloquent, but he was precise, with names and facts and figures at his disposal. I saw Lady Nicola smile with quiet pride.

After Ramiro, there was another opposing member, an undistinguished, mousy fellow who made many of the same points as Rafael, only with less skill. Still, I could hear murmurs of agreement in the crowd behind me. I wished I could turn in my seat and gauge their faces.

General Liberio, the grizzled veteran, followed him. He stood to speak. "What we are facing is a choice between a slow loss or a desperate victory," he said bluntly. "In my opinion, this can be done. And we can use it to our advantage." He pointed one thick finger at Sidonie. "What is the one thing we need to draw away some of Carthage's forces? A bait Astegal cannot resist. His wife."

I felt the blood drain from my face. I hadn't considered *that.*

At my side, Sidonie met Liberio's gaze without flinching.

She'd considered it.

The instant Liberio sat, the last opponent was on his feet, Jimeno de Ferrer, the youngest of the council. "Precisely," he spat. "Astegal's *wife*. Serafin, I know she is your kinswoman, but can you ask us to trust to this tale of madness and parlor tricks? If there's an ounce of truth to it, it's that an impetuous young woman agreed to an ill-advised marriage. Now she seeks to flee home. Shall we spend precious Aragonian lives to help her?" Jimeno shook his head. "I think not. And I think there is no more to the tale than that."

He sat to mixed applause.

Serafin nodded at Sidonie. "You may speak."

She rose and inclined her head toward the council, then walked to the corner of the table, turning so she could address council and crowd alike. "What is more likely, my lords and ladies?" she asked. "That I am a fickle bride, or that half of Terre d'Ange was plunged overnight into madness and betrayal for no reason whatsoever?"

There was a tense, waiting silence. Sidonie let it stretch until I could feel my heart thudding in my chest.

"I have spoken to the council of the spell that bound us," she said at last. "Hear now of my first suspicion that somewhat dire was amiss. I had ventured out to make an offering at the temple of Tanit. As I returned through the streets of Carthage, I overheard my guards directing my bearers to turn aside lest our route take us through the slave-market. At that moment, I began to know fear."

She swept her gaze over them, letting it rest last on Jimeno de Ferrer.

"Prince Imriel told me later what I would have seen there," Sidonie continued. "What *he* saw. Aragonian folk taken as spoils of war at the sack of New Carthage, sold into slavery. A ten-year-old boy. There was a noblewoman looking for a pretty child to adorn her household. She declined to purchase him because he didn't speak Hellene. There was no way to determine whether or not he was sufficiently *biddable*."

There were hisses, but they were meant for Carthage, not her.

"That is the war you are fighting, my lords and ladies," she said steadily. "That is the opponent you face. Amílcar has resisted Astegal. The siege has only just begun and your spirits are high. But there is no help coming from any quarter. *None*. And if none comes, week after week, month after month, your spirits will gutter. You will face the slow loss of which General Liberio spoke. Amílcar will be forced to surrender. When it does, Astegal will not be merciful."

"What if we surrender *now*?" Jimeno challenged her. "Others have accepted his terms." He smiled, thin-lipped. "And we've something to offer in exchange. You and your paramour."

A gabble of comment arose. Sidonie waited it out until they fell silent once more, awaiting her reply.

"Yes," she said mildly. "You could do that, my lord. It may even be that Astegal would be merciful for that price. And Aragonia as you know it would cease to be. You would become a Carthaginian vassal state, subject to Carthage's laws, Carthage's customs, Carthage's demands for tribute. Astegal's rule and whims. Is that your desire?"

There was a roar of protest.

"It's no one's wish," Serafin assured her.

"Then what cost *are* you willing to bear for freedom?" Sidonie asked, raising her voice, clear and carrying. "Is the cost of a sovereign Euskerria too high? It is a minor territory that the Euskerri have inhabited time out of mind and will continue to do. Will Aragonia truly be destroyed if a small chunk of land is gouged out of its holdings?" She faced the council directly and let the silk shawl slip from her shoulders onto the floor. "I did not think so when I paid the price for my freedom."

The crowd broke into pandemonium, stamping and shouting. Sidonie turned to acknowledge them, and I saw Serafin catch his breath. I twisted in my seat to see that she'd had the back of her gown cut low enough to reveal the still-raw wound, proof of her tale.

It was a long time before order was restored. Sidonie took her seat quietly. I retrieved her shawl, settling it over her shoulders.

"Enough!" Serafin finally succeeded in shouting the crowd silent. "Has anyone aught else to say?" he asked the council. No one moved. If any of the others yet opposed it, they weren't willing to follow Sidonie's performance. "Shall we vote?"

Another outburst erupted.

"We want a voice!" someone shouted.

"Give us a voice!"

Ramiro leaned over and whispered to his son, who nodded in agreement.

"Forgive me," Serafin said in a low voice. "But this is an Aragonian matter, and I think it must be decided by Aragonians. It's going to be mayhem if you stay. Let us have this debate, let the people have their say, and let the council vote. I will send word."

"Thank you, my lord." Sidonie rose, and I accompanied her.

"Wait!" Rafael de Barbara said sharply. "I note that you did not address my concerns regarding your fitness as an emissary, young highness."

She met his gaze. "Did I not?"

He gave a sour smile. "That was a cheap theatrical gesture at the end."

"Indeed." Sidonie inclined her head. "I would not have resorted to it were there not urgent need. I would expect a man of your rhetorical skill to understand."

We left the great hall unescorted; no one wanted to leave the debate. A guard closed the doors behind us, and we could hear a fresh clamor arise.

"Gods." Sidonie shuddered. "What do you think?"

"I think you swayed the crowd. And I pray the crowd sways the council." I cupped her face in my hands and kissed her. "I think you were splendid. Sidonie, if they fail to aid us, it can be through no fault of yours."

"I did my best," she murmured. "Cheap theatrics and all."

"You were splendid," I repeated. "And later, we can discuss this matter of serving as *bait* if they accede."

She gave me a tired smile. "How else did you suppose Astegal might be persuaded to divert his forces?"

I sighed. "I hadn't thought on it."

"Pray we get the chance," Sidonie said soberly.

Fifty-six

There was no word forthcoming that afternoon or evening. We stayed awake late into the night, hoping to hear. The chirurgeon Rachel came to examine Sidonie's injury, decreeing at last that it might be bandaged and covered, but she had no news. I fell asleep at length with Sidonie in my arms, waking briefly at the sound of her murmuring the word *emmenghanom* in her sleep.

Later I was told the debate raged late and long. After the commonfolk had given voice to their wishes and the council had voted, members were up until the small hours, hammering out details of the agreement they reached and laying the foundations of a plan.

We didn't find out what it was until Serafin sent for us.

Along with General Liberio, Serafin received us in the quarters that had once belonged to the Count of Amílcar. His violet eyes were bleary for lack of sleep, his face looking creased and older. Liberio was the fresher of the two. As an old military hand, I daresay he had experience doing without sleep. Sidonie appeared calm, but I could sense the tension in her.

"Tell us what was decided," she said. "Please."

Serafin yawned. "Forgive me. In principle, everyone more or less came to agreement, with a notable exception or two. 'Tis too valuable a chance to waste. And yet, 'tis too desperate a chance on which to risk much."

"What does that mean?" I asked warily.

He tossed a sheaf of paper at Sidonie. "Read."

She skimmed it briefly. "It's a charter granting sovereignty to Euskerria."

Serafin nodded. "Of course, it's contingent on their full support against Carthage. And my continued regency."

Ambition, I thought.

Sidonie glanced up. "Will I be representing you as well as Terre d'Ange, then?"

"Therein lies the 'more or less'." Serafin smiled wryly. "Yes. All the necessary assurances are in the charter. We'll do our best to give you a chance. What you make of it is up to you." He gestured. "The both of you."

"You sound as though you're sending us off on our own, unaided and alone," I observed.

Serafin and Liberio exchanged a look. "Nearly," Serafin admitted. "You'll be assigned a guide, of course."

"Imriel, me, and a guide?" Sidonie asked flatly. "That's all?"

General Liberio cleared his throat. "Your highness, I'd send an entire squadron if I thought they could protect you. I don't. Astegal knows that you're here and he knows you're desperate to get to Terre d'Ange. The moment we send out a sortie, he's going to be on the alert. This escape can succeed by only one of three means." He ticked them off on his thick fingers. "Strength, speed, or guile. We don't have the strength. He's already routed this army once. If we had the numbers to meet him on the battlefield a second time, I'd have done it."

"What about speed?" I asked, remembering what I'd seen atop the battlements. "Astegal's got his cavalry pinned behind his infantry, trapped between two rivers. They'll have to get through their own defenses to reach us."

Liberio gave me an approving look. "True. However . . ." He reached for a sketch on Serafin's desk. "There's an embankment here, and defensive trenches here and here. The bridge across the Barca River lies here, between the trenches. Astegal's cavalry will have to pass the embankment and a trench to reach it, but you'll have to cross a trench, too. We're still working out that part."

I studied the sketch. "So we'll not have much of a lead."

"No," he said bluntly. "And every mount in Amílcar's been on siege rations for the past weeks. Unless I miss my guess, Astegal will send his Amazigh after you. Those desert-bred horses they ride are swift, hardy, and well-fed. I don't like your chances in a foot-race."

"So where does guile come into play, my lord general?" Sidonie inquired.

"Ah." Liberio nodded. "We mean to capture and hold the nearest trench long enough to get a small mounted company across it and over the bridge. Half of them will scatter, bound for the cities Ramiro discussed. The other half, with you among them, will race northward." He exchanged the sketch for a map and traced a line. "Astegal will expect you to make for the nearest pass. They will. But you'll take your leave of them before his cavalry catches you and make your way secretly through the mountains to Roncal." He tapped the map. "Here. It's a Euskerri stronghold with a pass beyond."

"I remember," Sidonie said absently. "Janpier Iturralde was from Roncal."

"Who?" I asked.

"The Euskerri ambassador," Serafin said. "Or as near as they have to one. That's who you'll treat with, Sidonie."

"So I take it we're no longer serving as bait?" I inquired.

The other two men exchanged another glance. "I'm afraid that's not changed," Liberio said somberly. "I expect the Amazigh will catch the men they're pursuing, your highness. And when they do, my men will have orders to betray you, leading the Amazigh into a Euskerri ambush. You'll have a lead on them, nothing more."

"You mean to force the Euskerri's hand," Sidonie observed.

He shrugged. "Into the ambush, aye. Whether or not they'll agree to more is anyone's guess."

"I mislike this." I frowned. "Would it not be simpler to abandon the notion of forging an alliance with the Euskerri altogether? All we need to treat for is safe passage over the mountains. If Sidonie and I can reach Terre d'Ange, we can undo Carthage's spell. Terre d'Ange and Alba alike will send aid."

"Yes." Serafin poured a cup of water from a ewer and drank. "There is that option. And there is fear among certain quarters that you will take our aid and do exactly that." He set the cup down. "The Euskerri are near. Despite the hostilities between us, they are a known quantity. Terre d'Ange is far. And despite the long alliance between us, it is currently very much an unknown quantity. The consensus was that at this juncture the Euskerri are a better wager. And that is the price of our aid."

"I see." Sidonie was quiet a moment. "So Imriel and I and a lone guide are to make our way to Roncal, where I will inform Janpier Iturralde that I've brought a hostile Carthaginian force into Euskerri territory, then expect him to treat gladly with me."

"I don't expect you to succeed." Serafin met her gaze squarely. "Only to try. The Euskerri want sovereignty very badly. And there are those still very much opposed to granting it. You were the one tipped the balance. Are you unwilling now to stand by your words?"

Her eyes flashed.

"Sidonie." I held up my hand. "You don't have to agree to this. Neither of us expected it to be quite so dangerous."

"If there were a safer way, I'd offer it," Liberio murmured. "There isn't. As it is, a good many men may die for this venture."

"I don't see any other choice, Imriel," Sidonie said simply. "Other than staying and awaiting defeat. I was quick to speak of sacrifice yesterday. How can I refuse to take the risk? I'd give a lot more than a few ounces of flesh for Terre d'Ange."

"You're sure?" I asked.

She nodded. "I'm sure."

So it was decided.

We wouldn't be able to act immediately. In accordance with General Liberio's plans, it would be a night sortie, the better to sow confusion. In order to see well enough to execute his plan, we'd need to await a tolerably clear night with a good moon, and the moon was yet a waxing sliver. He counseled patience and put his men to work building a portable gangplank to bridge the defensive trench.

I spent a good deal of time telling the hours in the palace courtyard, honing the skills that had been neglected during my tenure as Leander Maignard. I was keenly aware that in the days to come, I would be Sidonie's sole protector. And that was the one area of the Cassiline discipline that Joscelin had neglected to teach me—the sphere of defending one's ward. He'd taught me everything I needed to know to ward *my* life. Neither of us had dreamed that one day I'd be playing such a role.

At least I'd learned how to fight from the saddle. Gods, it seemed like a long time ago that I'd advised Claude de

Monluc to trick Barquiel L'Envers into lending his own Akkadian-trained Captain of the Guard to teach the Dauphine's Guard. It hadn't been much more than a whim that had led me to train with them, posing as an anonymous guard among guardsmen. Now I was glad of it. With Liberio's permission, I visited the armory and appropriated a small buckler, a leather hauberk with metal scales, a helmet with a peaked crest, and a short bow and quiver.

For her part, Sidonie spent long hours in the palace's library, reading everything she could find on the Euskerri. Whether or not it would prove of use, I couldn't say, but it helped pass the interminable waiting.

Blessed Elua be thanked, her wound continued to heal cleanly. At her insistence, some days after the council met, I took her to see Kratos. With Lady Nicola's assistance, he'd been lodged in a boarding-room where a good-natured Aragonian widow was paid to look after him.

"Your highness!" Kratos looked thunderstruck when he answered our knock. "You came to see *me*?"

Sidonie laughed at his expression. "How are your burns, Kratos?"

"Healing." He peered over his shoulder as though he could see through his tunic. "And your injury? You were passing feverish, my lady. I worried."

She gave me a sidelong look. "Much, much improved."

"What about the ribs?" I asked Kratos.

He took a deep breath, his chest swelling. "Better."

I was glad.

We passed a pleasant hour talking with Kratos. Somewhere in the back of my thoughts, I'd hoped he'd have some clever perspective on our plan for escape that no one had conceived; but he didn't. He merely shook his heavy head, running one hand over his cropped, greying hair.

"You were right, my lord," Kratos said soberly. "I'd only slow you down. It's dicey, but I don't see another way."

"Pray for us?" I asked.

"To all the gods I know," he affirmed.

Sidonie stooped and kissed his cheek. "Remember your promise."

A blush suffused his homely face. "To dance at your wedding?"

She smiled. "To dance with *me* at my wedding, Kratos. I mean to make it a point not to forget those who've saved my life. And the other thing, too. The word I taught you. Keep the knowledge quiet, but don't forget."

"*Emmenghanom,*" Kratos said softly.

Sidonie nodded. "Exactly right."

We didn't spread the word throughout the entire city. At this point, it was dangerous. Blockaded, besieged Amílcar was a hotbed of gossip. If it were to fall in our absence or failure, if word were to leak that we'd disseminated the key to undoing Carthage's spell far and wide . . . well, it was Sidonie's fear that Astegal would have every man, woman, and child put to the sword rather than risk word carrying to Terre d'Ange. And with that, I agreed.

But we made sure it wouldn't be lost.

General Liberio agreed in a bemused fashion that those soldiers serving as couriers carrying word of Amílcar's plan to neighboring cities would carry it. I'm not sure he believed, not entirely. He was a pragmatic fellow. Still, he agreed. And Sidonie and I taught the word to half a dozen bright-eyed, impassioned young men. If any of them survived, the word would be passed onward.

Emmenghanom.

Beholden.

We taught the word to Captain Deimos, lodged in a harbor inn, posing as the captain of a fishing vessel. He didn't want to hear it, not really, but he'd been Ptolemy Solon's man too long. In the end, the desire for knowledge won out.

"*Emmenghanom,*" he whispered, closing his eyes.

"If all else fails, the Wise Ape of Cythera will know what to do with it," I said. "And if we succeed, I will keep my promise. Terre d'Ange will reward you."

Deimos shuddered. "Goddess save me from wisdom. I hope to be an ignorant man in my next life."

We gave the word unto the safekeeping of Nicola L'Envers y Aragon. To her, I showed the talisman; the scrap of lacquered leather filched from an inner pocket of Bodeshmun's robes. A whirlwind sprouting horns and claws, a word inscribed in Punic.

"This is it?" Nicola inquired. "On *this* you pin your hopes?"

Sidonie and I nodded.

"*Emmenghanom,*" Nicola murmured. "I'll remember."

"Write it down," Sidonie said, fetching pen and paper. "Write it as it sounds when I speak it, my lady." She knelt beside Nicola's chair, her face earnest and pleading. "I know it sounds absurd. But if we fail—"

Nicola cut her off. "You won't fail."

Sidonie shrugged gracefully. "But if we do . . ."

"*Emmenghanom,*" I echoed. "Beholden. We are beholden. We will all be beholden to you. Sidonie and I, Ysandre, Alais, Drustan, Phèdre and Joscelin, your son, Raul, the whole of Terre d'Ange . . ."

Nicola raised her hand. "I understand."

She wrote the word, mouthing the syllables to herself.

There was little else we could do, save wait.

Fifty-seven

Slowly, slowly, the moon waxed. At its halfway point, it would have shed enough light to stage a sortie, but the weather was foul: cold, grey, and drizzling. The mood in the city grew tense and strained. When the weather showed no sign of breaking, Lady Nicola decided to hold a fête.

"Are you sure that's wise?" I asked her. I couldn't help but think of Gallus Tadius' orders during the siege of Lucca. He'd have been apoplectic at the waste.

"People need something to keep their spirits up," Nicola said pragmatically. "And my husband's wine-cellar can withstand the blow. Besides, there's someone who'd like to meet you, but he's felt awkward about it. This will provide a nice opportunity."

I was intrigued despite myself. "Who is it?"

She smiled. "You'll see."

It wasn't an extravagant affair. With Carthage's troops camped outside the walls and the spectre of death hanging over those who hoped to assail them, that would have felt unseemly or desperate or both. But it was a pleasant affair.

The food that was served was modest and less than abundant, but the wine flowed freely. Skilled musicians played in a distinctly Aragonian style, rapid rhythms punctuated with clapping. An air of defiant gaiety permeated the great hall.

A young Aragonian lieutenant begged leave to teach Sidonie one of their national dances. I watched her try to follow his lead and master the quick, intricate steps, laughing when she tripped over his feet. He was flushed and nervous. She looked bright and beautiful, her color healthy. I thought about that last day on the ship, her skin fevered and hot to the touch, and I was filled with gratitude.

"So that's Ysandre's daughter," a melodious voice beside me murmured.

I turned and blinked. For a moment, I thought I was seeing an older version of my cousin Mavros with lines at the corners of his twilight-blue eyes and his black hair threaded with silver. Then I realized who he must be and tensed. "Marmion," I said. "Marmion Shahrizai."

Many years ago, after Skaldia's invasion, Marmion had placed country over family and betrayed my mother into the Queen's custody. He in turn was betrayed by his sister, Persia, who placed family over country and helped my mother escape. In the end, Marmion's men had unwittingly set fire to Persia's manor house in a botched spying attempt. Marmion himself was stripped of his title and sent into exile. I wasn't sure what to expect of him.

He read it in my face and smiled wryly. "I bear you no ill will, Prince Imriel. But I must confess myself terribly curious to meet Melisande's infamous son."

"Am I infamous?" I asked lightly.

Marmion's gaze shifted back to Sidonie. "I thought so when I heard you'd seduced the Queen's heir. Now it seems mayhap I was mistaken." He shook his head. "Melisande's son risking life and limb on behalf of Ysandre's daughter. Who would have thought to see the day?"

"No one," I said. "But mayhap the gods themselves have ways of redressing old wrongs."

He turned a measuring look on me. "You look a lot like her, you know. You must hear it often."

"Not so very often," I said. "People seldom speak of my mother to me unless they're telling me what horrors her actions visited on their families."

Marmion laughed without mirth. "I suppose so. Is it true that you've seen her?"

I nodded. "On Cythera."

"Melisande." He was silent a moment. "Is it true that her sentence was commuted to exile in exchange for her aid?"

"Yes," I said.

He shook his head again. "So after all she's done, our sentences are the same."

"I'm sorry, my lord," I said quietly. "I understand that your sister's death was an accident. It was a terrible tragedy."

"Yes." Marmion gathered himself. "Tell me, is she happy?"

"My mother?" I thought about it. "I think she has found a certain calm and acceptance. I wouldn't call her *happy*."

Whether or not the answer pleased him, I couldn't say. Marmion studied me. "I see a good deal of House Courcel in you, too. It's not as obvious, but it's there. You've a look of Prince Rolande, Ysandre's father. I remember him from when I was a boy. Too impetuous for his own good, but he had a streak of high nobility." He touched my arm, light and unexpected. "I wish you well, of course. All of us pray you succeed. But it would please me to know you restored honor to House Shahrizai's name. That's all I desired."

It touched me. "I'll do my best."

"Imriel!" Sidonie joined us, eyes sparkling. She greeted

my exiled kinsman. "You must be Lord Marmion. Well met, my lord."

He bowed. "Just Marmion, your highness."

"Then I will be just Sidonie," she said. "Since it is my hope that we will be near-kin one day."

Marmion smiled. "I do believe that would please me, too. Blessed Elua hold and keep you, Sidonie. And when you see your mother . . . tell Ysandre that I think fondly of her."

"I will," Sidonie promised.

With that, he took his leave of us. I gazed thoughtfully after him. "Do you suppose he was ever your mother's . . . ?"

"No." Sidonie shook her head. "No, I actually asked her about that one of the few times we spoke about you without acrimony. I remembered hearing that he was one of her favorite courtiers before he was exiled. She was fond of Marmion. He made her laugh. But she never took him as a lover." She gave me one of her quick, flickering smiles. "'Tis a pity. She might have been more sympathetic toward us if she had."

I slid one arm around her waist, pulling her against me. "Do you suspect your mother of harboring perverse desires?"

Sidonie looped her arms around my neck. "Doesn't everyone?"

All in all, Lady Nicola's fête was a considerable success. We were all strung tighter than overtuned harps, and we needed the distraction. None of us forgot about Carthage's army camped outside Amílcar's walls. None of us forgot that come the first clear night, we would attempt a desperate venture. But for now, we were alive and free, and we celebrated that fact, Aragonian and D'Angeline alike.

If the food was scant and the great hall dim and a trifle cool for a scarcity of lamp-oil and hearth-wood, it didn't matter. Keg after keg of wine was breached, and Ramiro

Zornín de Aragon urged folk to drink with mournful enthusiasm, making everyone laugh and Lady Nicola smile with fond indulgence. The musicians played until sweat dripped from their brows.

We were alive.

We were free.

And at the end of the night, I got to retire with my beloved.

"Imriel." In our darkened bedchamber, Sidonie breathed my name. I found her mouth and kissed her. She tasted like wine and honey on my tongue.

"What's your desire, Sun Princess?" I whispered.

"You." She sank to her knees, her hands gliding over my chest. I felt her fingers undoing my breeches. I felt my taut phallus spring free. I groaned as she licked the underside, swirling her tongue around the crown like a child with a sweet. Groaned louder when she took me into her mouth, sinking my hands into her hair and freeing its coils, feeling her nails digging into my buttocks.

"Stop!" I gasped.

Sidonie's eyes gleamed in the faint light. "Is that a *signale*?"

"No." The word emerged as a growl deep in my throat. "Come here, Princess."

Beneath her gown, Sidonie was still bandaged, clean strips of white linen laced across her shoulders, crisscrossing her breasts. For the first time since I'd wounded her, I ignored her injury. I laid her on her back and spread her thighs, fitting myself between them, propped on one arm. I teased her, taking my phallus in my hand and rubbing its swollen crown against her slick cleft until she gasped and begged, her back arching, hips thrusting helplessly.

Then I took her.

Deep.

Hard.

"*Elua!*" Sidonie's last ragged gasp burst in my ear, her inner muscles milking my shaft. I burst in her, spending myself, seeing a sparkling darkness behind my closed eyelids. Good, so good. Where did Sidonie begin and Imriel end? I couldn't even tell anymore. This could be the last time. I didn't know.

I never wanted to know.

Our bodies quieted in the aftermath of pleasure.

"Your back?" I murmured.

"I think it's all right." Her voice was low and different. It always was after love-making. "If it's not, it was worth it."

I rolled off her, sliding my arm beneath her. "Sleep, love."

Sidonie lay in the crook of my arm. "Look at the window. It's almost dawn." We watched the light seep through the shuttered window. "It looks as though the weather might have cleared."

"Mayhap," I agreed.

We looked at one another. "Right." Sidonie nodded. "Sleep."

In the morning—or later in the morning—when we arose, we found it was true. The weather had broken and the day was clear and bright, giving every promise of a clear, cloudless night.

"I don't think they'll do it tonight," I said to Sidonie. "Not after the fête."

I was wrong.

In the early afternoon, Captain Aureliano, the soldier I'd met atop the walls of the city, sought us out, finding us in the palace library. He'd struck me as a competent, easygoing fellow when I'd met him. Today he was as serious as death.

"Well met, your highness," he said when I introduced him to Sidonie. "General Liberio sent me to confer with you."

Sidonie paled. "Is it tonight?"

"It is." Aureliano took a deep breath. "The general had us let the word slip to Astegal's men that there was a fête last night. We do a fair bit of taunting back and forth, you know. Not much else to do. But he reckoned that in the event the weather cleared today, they'd never expect us to pull a stunt tonight."

"Clever," I said.

"Liberio's a clever fellow," Aureliano said. "I'll be in command of your company. He's sent me to go over every instruction with you to be sure there are no mistakes made tonight."

"Tell us what we need to know," Sidonie said in a resolute tone.

Aureliano went over the plan step by step. Saddlebags would be delivered to our quarters. We were to pack our things and be ready by nightfall—nothing more than we could carry on horseback. That part at least was simple—neither of us possessed more than we could carry.

"What about supplies?" I asked.

He shook his head. "Your guide will be carrying enough to get you through the first night or so. Once you're north of Amílcar, you'll find villages willing to trade. Carthage's sway lies to the south yet."

The sortie was to take place some hours after midnight. Aureliano and his men would come to fetch us and escort us to the western gates of the city.

"You're opening the gates?" I asked, startled.

"No choice," he said grimly. "There are sally ports to the north and south, but they're too small to admit aught but foot-soldiers. Not horses, and surely not that movable gangplank."

The balance of the plan was simple. Liberio's infantry men would essay a pair of sorties; the first from the southern sally port to provide a distraction, and the second from the northern port. Once the latter had secured the trench, the gates would be opened. A company of soldiers would rush forth with the gangplank to bridge the trench. As soon as it was in place, we'd follow. A second company, the one that would scatter across Aragonia, would follow in our wake.

"Getting across the plank's going to be the worst of it," Aureliano warned us. "We'll have to go single file. Do you ride well, your highness?"

"Tolerably," Sidonie said.

"Good." He gave a brusque nod. "Getting to the bridge proper is the second worst. We'll be crossing ground held by Carthage. With luck, they'll be too confused and in disarray to act swiftly."

"And Astegal will be fuming his way from Montero," I observed. "Where he's been careless enough to ensconce himself."

"Indeed." Aureliano smiled briefly. "There are ten of us escorting you. Once we've crossed the plank, I want you to fall into the following formation. Four lines of three abreast. Your highness, you'll be in the middle of the second rank, directly behind me. Prince Imriel, you'll be in the middle of the third rank. The last rank will form your rearguard. Is that too difficult to understand?"

The question was directed at Sidonie. On any other occasion she would have shot him a cool look. Today she shook her head somberly. "No, my lord captain. I think I can manage it."

To his credit, he took her at her word. "Good. Once we've crossed the bridge, we ride like hell. There's a squadron of archers will try to follow in our wake. They'll hold the bridge behind us as long as they can to delay pursuit. When your guide Paskal gives the word, you'll split off from the company. Do you have any questions?"

"No," Sidonie said.

"I do," I said. "You and the men who drew this assignment . . . how were you chosen?"

Aureliano met my eyes. "We volunteered. What do you reckon our odds are?"

I thought about the Amazigh guards beheading the assassin in the garden. Desert justice. "Do any of you speak Hellene?"

"I do," he said.

"Give yourselves up before the Amazigh catch you of their own accord," I said. "Don't give them an excuse to kill you out of hand. Try to convince them you've information you'll give only to Astegal."

"And tell Astegal you were forced into cooperating," Sidonie added. "Tell him Serafin and Liberio threatened to kill your wives and children. Tell him you want to swear loyalty to him."

"Will it work?" Aureliano asked.

Sidonie shrugged. "It might. He takes a certain pleasure in getting folk to betray their loyalties."

"My thanks." He bowed. "I'll see you anon. Take some sleep if you can. It's going to be a grueling night."

Fifty-eight

At the hour of midnight, we gathered in the great hall to wait.

The mood was quiet and subdued, the palace nearly empty. Most folk were either sleeping or elsewhere along the city walls. But Lady Nicola waited with us, for which I was grateful.

"You've everything in readiness?" she asked for the third or fourth time. It was unsettling to see her unsettled.

"Everything," I assured her.

"I'm sorry." Nicola shuddered and wrapped her arms around herself. "It's the waiting. It drives one mad, doesn't it?"

Sidonie didn't comment. I watched her gathering herself, gathering her courage. Mostly I just watched her, etching her features on my memory over and over again. I wasn't afraid for myself, but I was terrified for her sake. I wondered if Joscelin had felt that way. Probably, I thought, and with a great deal more regularity.

Still, it was awful.

It almost seemed too soon when Aureliano and his men came for us. He introduced us to Paskal, our guide. Paskal was a short, dark, broad-chested fellow who seemed disconcertingly young. I'd hoped for someone steady and authoritative, someone like Urist. But Paskal's mother was Euskerri. He knew the language and the territory. I supposed that was more important than age.

"Ready?" Aureliano asked.

"Yes." Sidonie glanced at me, then reached for my hand, gripping it hard. "Let's go."

We bade farewell to Lady Nicola, who embraced us both. "I'll not say good-bye to you," she said steadily. "We'll meet again. But yes." She forestalled Sidonie's question. "*Emmenghanom.* I remember. And I have it written and saved in a safe place."

Sidonie smiled quietly. "Thank you, my lady."

Another leavetaking.

Gods, I hated them.

We rode through the moon-silvered streets of Amílcar, the city silent and tense. The first sortie hadn't been launched yet. General Liberio wanted to be certain every element was in readiness. Once they struck, things would move very quickly.

Our company gathered inside the western gate, behind the stalwart company of soldiers responsible for maneuvering the gangplank into place. I didn't envy them their task. They'd be slow-moving and exposed.

A runner went to inform the General that we were ready. We waited. My horse shifted under me, cocking one hip. I wished I had the Bastard. He'd make a target, though, his speckled white hide gleaming in the moonlight. We rode dark horses, wore dark clothing. Our armor was darkened with ash and grease. Sidonie was shrouded in a man's black cloak, the hood drawn up to hide her hair.

We waited.

The first sortie struck.

On the far side of the wall, a clamor of chaos and confusion arose to the south of us. The sound of bowstrings twanging. Shouts of pain and anger, battle-cries. A clash of weapons. Horns blaring an alarm. I wished I could see what was happening.

Then the second sortie.

The sounds of battle intensified. South and north. Men screaming, men dying. We'd be riding through it. I glanced at Sidonie. She met my gaze, her eyes wide: twin pools of blackness in her pale face.

"Whatever happens, I love you," she said.

I nodded. "Always."

"You won't let Astegal have me?"

I shook my head. "Never."

More horns blared—ours, in the tower of the gatehouse. "Be ready," Aureliano said briefly.

It was a proper portcullis, massive and heavy. Somewhere in the gatehouse a gear cranked, raising the grate. Two men wrestled with the heavy bar of the inner gates. Four men in concert shoved at the doors themselves, hurling them open.

"Go, go, go!" someone shouted.

The infantry soldiers carrying the portable bridge raced forward, dashing for the trench some thirty yards away. The fighting was north and south. Before us, the moon-shadowed ground was open. At Aureliano's signal, we moved forward into the open gateway. He raised one hand, bidding us wait.

We waited.

Liberio's soldiers scuttled under their burden. Dim figures peeled away from the fighting on both fronts. I couldn't tell if they were Amílcar's men or Carthage's. Both, I thought. Metal clashed on metal. I settled my buckler on my left arm and drew my sword. Our fellows wrestled the gangplank into place, bridging the trench.

"*Now!*" Aureliano shouted.

He led the charge, spear lowered. One by one, we followed.

Single file.

This was the hardest part, the worst part. I fell in behind Sidonie. The speed of our passage had blown her hood back, loosened her hair. It streamed, silver in the moonlight. I saw a figure racing to intercept her on foot, wielding a throwing-axe. I dug my heels hard into my mount's flanks, passing her. I rode him down before he had a chance to throw, trampling him. My mount balked and shied.

"*Go!*" I shouted at Sidonie, pointing with my sword toward the improvised bridge.

She went.

Several of Aureliano's men passed me. I wrestled my mount under control, cursing him. The rearguard checked their horses, yelling at me. I rejoined the column. We thundered toward the trench, toward the gangplank. Overhead, the moon shone, placid and bright. All around us, men fought and died.

One, two, three . . . I was the ninth to cross. I could feel the planks dip and give under the weight of my mount, but they held. A Carthaginian soldier veered out of the darkness unexpectedly, jabbing at me with a thrusting spear. I kneed my horse hard and it swerved.

"Fall in!" Aureliano was shouting. "Fall in!"

We obeyed, all of us. Falling into the formation he'd ordered: four ranks of three. Or mayhap three ranks. I didn't know if the rearguard had made it, and I didn't know if the archers meant to hold the bridge were following. I didn't dare look. All that mattered was that I could see Sidonie in front of me, alive. And in front of her was Aureliano and his line, clearing the way with lowered spears. Astegal's infantry fell away before their onslaught, unprepared.

And beyond, the bridge across the Barca River.

Somewhere, more horns were raising an urgent cry. Ahead of me, a racing figure hurled a javelin. The soldier to the left of Sidonie went down, his mount rolling and squealing horribly.

"Move!" I shouted at the soldier on my left. "Move up!"

He hesitated.

I swore and urged my mount past him, cutting him off. Not such a bad horse, really. I fell in beside Sidonie, taking my place at her side. I saw a Carthaginian archer kneel, taking aim in the moonlight. His bow twanged. I twisted in the saddle, leaning low, and caught the shaft on my buckler.

And then there was the bridge and a double line of men determined to defend it. Aureliano rode them down without hesitation. The soldier to his right went down. I chopped mercilessly with my sword, hacking at blurred faces in the moonlight, shoving at them with my arrow-pierced buckler.

We cleared the line.

We crossed the bridge, dark, moonlit water sliding beneath us.

Behind us, more bows twanged. Ours or theirs? I couldn't tell.

"Ride!" Aureliano's voice rose. "Ride for your damned lives!"

It was a strange and surreal flight, hurtling ourselves across the moon-drenched landscape. We rode at a hectic pace, clinging to our saddles. Bit by bit, the sound of fighting faded. Pursuit was coming, but not yet. We followed the road as it curved along the coastline, rising into the foothills.

Within a quarter of an hour, there was dense pine forest crowding the western edge of the road. Not long after they appeared, Paskal drew rein and whistled sharply. Our company halted.

"Here?" I asked Paskal.

Our guide shrugged. "Better sooner than later."

"Good luck," I said to Aureliano. "Give them a good chase."

"Thank you," Sidonie added soberly. "More than I can say. May the gods be with you and your men."

Aureliano gave a brusque nod. "And you, your highness."

That was all. There was no time to waste or spare. Aureliano raised one hand in farewell and ordered his men to move. Paskal beckoned for us to follow, turning his mount into the forest.

We had to travel slowly. The dense pines blocked out the moonlight until there was barely enough to see by. Branches reached for us, prickling and tangling as we made our way between the trees. The foothills weren't steep, but the grade was deceptive. Our horses had been ridden hard, and I could feel mine laboring. The slow pace made my skin itch.

But we were alive.

And the very factors that slowed us protected us. The road had been utterly blocked from our view within twenty paces. The thick pine mast muffled the sound of our horses' hooves. There was no way the Amazigh could suspect we'd turned off the road, no way they could track us here at night.

Not long after we entered the forest, we heard the sound of hoofbeats in the direction from which we'd come. Many hoofbeats, racing along the road. The sound rose and rose, then faded as they continued onward.

"Astegal's cavalry," Paskal said in a low voice.

"Likely," I said. "Pray for your friends and press onward."

I don't know how long we rode that night. Hours. I found myself haunted by the memory of my long search for Berlik, wandering through the endless Vralian forests. And I thought, too, of the night that Clunderry had staged a cattle-raid, the night that my bindings had broken and I'd ridden into the woods alone, compelled by Morwen's summons. And then there was the night I'd entered the standing stones with Morwen, that terrible night, and the race through the woods afterward.

It was a relief when the grey light of dawn began to filter through the trees. Paskal halted. "The forest should break in another league." He pointed westward. "Unless I've led us astray, there is a shepherd's hut where we can take shelter for a few hours. Can you keep going, your highness?"

"Yes." Sidonie looked weary, but her voice was adamant. "Thank you, messire, but you needn't ask. I can ride as long and hard as need be. Just don't let the horses founder."

Paskal glanced at me for confirmation.

"She means it," I said. "On both counts."

So we pressed onward. The going was easier in daylight, and despite my misgivings about his youth, Paskal was a good guide. We emerged from the pine forest to bright green hills, a stone hut visible in the distance.

"Well done!" I commended him.

He smiled with pride. "I can always find my way to anyplace I've been. My mother says it is because birds sang to me in the womb while she carried me."

"That's lovely," Sidonie murmured.

Paskal's smile widened. "Thank you, your highness."

He led us down the valley and up the far side to the shepherd's hut. After being trapped in besieged Amílcar, I had to own, I felt my heart rise at the sight of all that open space surrounding us, green hills as far as I could see. We were exposed, but no one could come upon us unseen, that was a surety.

There was a little stream where we were able to water the horses. Paskal carefully laid out the contents of his packs: a measure of grain for our mounts, bread and cheese and sausage for us. I bade Sidonie sit on the lumpy pallet in the hut and set about building a small fire in the pit in the middle of the floor. Elua knows, after Vralia, that was a skill I'd mastered beyond compare.

"Do you want to take first watch or shall I?" I asked Paskal after he'd fed the horses.

He looked surprised. "I will keep watch, my lord."

"Oh, no." I shook my head. "Paskal, we're dependent on you to reach Roncal before Astegal's men. Once they discover they've been tricked, they'll ride like the devil. We need you with your wits and astonishing bird-sense about you. That means we're sharing duties, you and I."

"My lord!" he protested.

"Imriel," I said. "How old are you?"

Paskal flushed. "Nineteen."

"Gods," I muttered. He seemed younger; but then, I doubted he'd lived through anything close to what I had by the time I was his age. "Just do as I say, please."

"First watch, then." He glanced at Sidonie. "I daresay her highness would appreciate it."

With that settled, Paskal went outside to keep the first watch, while I joined Sidonie on the lumpy pallet. "Are you all right, love?" I asked softly, folding my arms around her.

"I'm fine. I could keep going if we didn't need to breathe the horses. And I don't mind taking my turn at watch." She shivered a little. "My first real glimpse of war, that's all."

"I'm sorry." I tightened my arms around her. "Sorry you had to see it."

"No." Sidonie was quiet a moment. "No, I think it was important that I did. Important that I understand what it is that I've asked Aragonia to do and what I will ask the Euskerri to do. Not only in abstract terms of freedom and country, but the real cost of blood and horror."

I pressed my lips to her hair. "You're going to make a remarkable Queen someday."

Sidonie rested her head on my shoulder. "Not for a long, long time, I hope. My mother's a remarkable ruler in her own right. I'd be more than happy to spend the balance of my days as a remarkable heir."

"That, my love, isn't in question," I observed.

After that we slept for a time. It felt like only a few minutes before Paskal came to wake me with a tentative shake, but I could see that the sun had shifted. I freed myself gently from Sidonie. Paskal curled up in a blanket on the other side of the hut, and I went outside to keep watch for another hour or so.

I hated to wake them. The little fire I'd built had warmed the hut until it was almost cozy and they both looked so peaceful: the Dauphine of Terre d'Ange and the nineteen-year-old soldier-lad with a good sense of direction on whom our lives currently depended. But the horses were rested, the day was fleeting, and we had nearly a hundred leagues to cover before we reached Roncal.

"Time to go," I said.

A short time later, we were on our way.

Fifty-nine

We pushed the horses as hard as we dared on that journey. It was far from the worst trek I'd known in my life, but it wasn't pleasant. The little villages that clung to the sides of the hills were few and far between, and those we encountered offered nothing in the way of comfortable lodgings.

In the villages, we were greeted with a mix of suspicion and awe. I was apprehensive each time we entered one, remembering the hostility in New Carthage and the attempt on Sidonie's life. Here in the north, it was better. They hadn't felt the sting of defeat yet. But neither were they willing to wholeheartedly believe a wild tale from the lips of two D'Angelines and a lone half-Euskerri guide riding out of the hills. And even if I'd been inclined, I couldn't play out my transformation from Leander Maignard's semblance. I had abandoned the last of his tattered, scorched attire in Amílcar, and I didn't trust a pair of eardrops and a couple of gaudy rings to sustain Ptolemy Solon's spell for any length of time. I'd pushed my luck far enough.

So Paskal and I continued to sleep in shifts, in villages or out of them. There were several nights when we were forced to make camp in the open, sleeping on the cold, hard ground. I didn't mind on my behalf and Paskal seemed a hardy sort, but I knew Sidonie was uncomfortable. She wasn't accustomed to this sort of hardship. Still, she bore it without complaining.

On one such night, she came to join me while I kept watch during my shift, wrapped in my cloak.

"Unable to sleep?" I asked.

Sidonie nodded. "It's perishing cold without you to warm me."

"You could huddle with Paskal," I suggested.

She smiled. "I'd rather sit with you."

I opened my cloak. "Come here, then." We sat together in companionable silence until I could feel her growing warmer and relaxing beneath my arm. "I wish I had my flute," I said. "I could charm you to sleep."

"Do you still remember the tune?" she asked.

I tried to hum the charmed melody with which Morwen had haunted my dreams in Alba, the song that had won my freedom in Vralia, sending my gaolers to sleep. But the notes and the cadence were gone, slipping from my memory. My voice faltered and at last I shook my head. "I'm afraid it's gone."

"Too bad," Sidonie said. "It might have been useful."

"Mayhap D'Angelines weren't meant to meddle with magic," I said.

"Mayhap," she mused. "Or mayhap we never bothered, content with the magic that lay within ourselves and the arts Elua and his Companions taught us. If we'd known more, if we'd been wiser in the ways of the arcane arts, we might not have succumbed to Bodeshmun's spell."

"Or I might have been able to protect myself from Morwen's charm instead of having to rely on the *ollamhs*," I agreed.

Sidonie stirred. "We could found an academy to study it. That could be our legacy, you and I."

"Oh?" I smiled into the night. "I thought our legacy was going to be ensuring the enduring survival of House Courcel by providing it with a multitude of heirs."

"I see." She laughed. "How many?"

"Hordes," I said promptly. "Hordes and hordes of brooding boys and haughty girls who will grow up and surprise everyone, including themselves."

"Well, I don't see why we can't do both," Sidonie observed. "After we finish saving the realm."

I squeezed her shoulders. "There is that."

Another silence settled between us. I was beginning to think mayhap she'd drifted into sleep when she broke it, her voice low. "Do you often think about the son you lost?"

"Yes." I swallowed. My unborn son, the child who would have grown into a tyrant. "Not so much as I did in the first year, but yes. Of course." I tried to make out her face in the dim light. "Does it frighten you to think on it?"

"No." Sidonie gazed at me with that expression of utter trust that nearly split my heart in two. "You asked me that once before, and my answer is the same. No. There's nothing that lies between the two of us that frightens me, Imriel. We defied Blessed Elua's precept and others paid the price for it. We have to live with that, you and I. If we survive this, I think we might at least reckon ourselves forgiven in part." She smiled slightly. "I'm not sure how I feel about *hordes*, mind you. But I think we could manage a brooding boy and a haughty girl or two. 'Tis a pleasant thing to contemplate."

"Life and hope," I murmured, holding her closer.

"And love," she added.

Two days later, we reached Roncal.

That last leg of our journey was the most difficult and the most beautiful. The hills grew ever steeper, the views breathtaking. In the distance, to the north, we could see snow on the peaks of the mountains; and yet, the slopes themselves were a bright, vivid green, even in winter, except where they were blanketed with darker pines. The air was crisp and cold, and our breath came short. Still, I could understand why the Euskerri loved their territory.

"There it is," Paskal pointed as we crested the seventh peak of the day, our mounts huffing. "Roncal."

As strongholds went, it didn't look like much. It was a village of charming red-roofed buildings nestled in the valley. But the river that snaked through the valley had carved a passage through the mountains beyond, wide enough to be easily traversed, yet narrow enough to be easily defended. I could appreciate the strategic value of the place. The best thing of all about it was that there was no sign that Astegal's cavalry had arrived before us.

We descended into the valley. The houses were whitewashed with red or green shutters, designs and words painted over the doorways. I asked Paskal what they meant.

"Those are the names of the houses," he said. "Of their families. And the symbol of the sun to greet the dawn."

"Eguzki," Sidonie said, half to herself. "The sun."

Paskal gave her a startled look. "Yes."

Curious faces peered from a few of the houses and a man with a large wheel of cheese on his shoulder passed by, giving us a hard stare. Paskal led us along the valley, reading the names of the houses aloud. At one of the largest, he halted.

"This is the house of Iturralde," he said with shy pride.

"Paskal, you're a genius," I said.

"No." He grinned. "Just lucky like a bird."

Sidonie took a deep breath. "Well, 'tis time to face the

second test of diplomacy." There was a trace of dismay in her voice. "Would that I could bathe first."

There weren't many folk in Euskerri territory who would recognize the Dauphine of Terre d'Ange if she turned up on their doorstep, but Janpier Iturralde was one of them. It was a woman who answered Paskal's initial knock. Sidonie and I waited. I'd dismounted and stood holding her bridle, which was as close as we could come to presenting any manner of formal appearance. But she sat upright in the saddle, her posture regal and her expression composed.

The woman glanced over at us, eyes widening. She and Paskal exchanged words in the Euskerri tongue, and then she vanished. Paskal returned to join us. A few moments later, a man emerged. He was a sturdy, barrel-chested fellow with black hair and dark eyes set close to a long, straight nose. He stood on the doorstep for a long moment, staring at us, then at last approached.

"I did not believe it," he said in accented Aragonian. "But it is true."

Sidonie inclined her head. "Greetings, *etxekojaun*. It is a pleasure to see you once more."

His mouth quirked. "The daughter of the Queen of Terre d'Ange comes to my house and greets me with a Euskerri courtesy. Why? I thought your country had gone mad and you'd run away to marry the Lion of Carthage."

"It has and I did," Sidonie said. "Now I come bearing a tale of dire magics, a pursuing army, and an offer for Euskerria's sovereignty on behalf of both Aragonia and Terre d'Ange. Will you hear them?"

The blood drained from Janpier Iturralde's face. "Do you jest?"

"No." She shook her head. "Blessed Elua bear witness, I have never been more serious in my life."

He ushered us into his home with alacrity. Several hasty

introductions were made, and then Sidonie poured out our tale to the Iturralde clan, while Janpier offered hurried translations for those who spoke no Aragonian.

It was hard to gauge their reaction. It was intense, but I couldn't say whether they were hostile or sympathetic. Janpier's pallor darkened ominously throughout the telling of our story. His wife covered her mouth with one hand and sat staring wide-eyed. Their eldest son clenched and unclenched his fists. When Sidonie had finished, there was a burst of Euskerri exchanged.

"How long before Carthage's men come?" Janpier Iturralde demanded.

"I don't know," Sidonie said steadily. "A day, mayhap. Mayhap hours. We saw no sign of them, but they'll be riding hard."

"How many?" he asked.

"Astegal's cavalry numbers three hundred horse. I don't know how many he'll send."

"Three hundred!" His brows rose. "That's all?"

"It's a siege army," I observed. "There are thousands of infantry troops and a massive naval force."

"Bah!" Janpier waved a dismissive hand. "But they're not here, are they?" He turned to his sons—there were three of them all told—and issued a stream of orders in Euskerri. The lads nodded and departed in a hurry. The women of the household began bustling about without any orders given.

"What passes?" I asked Paskal in a low tone.

"They're marshaling the village," he replied.

"Yes." Janpier Iturralde overheard us. He pointed a finger at Sidonie. "Euskerria's hand will not be forced. We are not children to be bought by a simple bribe. We will defend ourselves and slaughter these men of Carthage. Only *then* will we decide."

"Fairly said, *etxekojaun*," Sidonie agreed. "I'm sorry. It

was not my wish to imperil Euskerria. But Carthage would have come for you sooner or later. And if Amílcar falls, it will not be three hundred horse. It will be ten thousand on foot. Can you stand against them?"

He ignored the question. "Go with Laida and the girls. They will take you to a safe place." He pointed to Paskal and me. "You and you will fight with us."

"My lord!" I protested. "It is imperative that her highness Sidonie and I continue on to Terre d'Ange. Will you not grant us passage?"

"Oh no." Janpier shook his head. There was a spark of righteous fury in his gaze. "You have led this army to our doorstep. Either you stand beside us to fight them, or we will give them what they want. You."

"I'll fight beside you!" Paskal sounded eager.

Sidonie and I exchanged a glance. "'Tis a fair request," I murmured.

"Imriel . . ." Her eyes glistened. "I couldn't bear to lose you."

Janpier Iturralde overheard that, too. "What makes you think I could bear to lose a single Euskerri life?" he asked in a cold tone. "Do you imagine you love your kinsman more than I love my own sons? My own flesh and blood?"

She closed her eyes briefly. "Of course not."

"Then he stands with us," Janpier said.

Sixty

There was a point north of the village where the pass narrowed so that the Amazigh would be forced to ride no more than three or four abreast, their line strung out and attenuated. It was there that we waited, hidden in the pine forests that flanked the pass on both sides.

Unorganized, Lady Nicola had called the Euskerri. Elua knows, that was true. There was little in the way of a command structure or a battle plan. A few of the younger lads were posted on lookout, perched high on the pines. When the Amazigh arrived, they'd whistle sharply. We were to rush out with slings and javelins and slaughter Astegal's men.

That was the plan.

The women and children of Roncal had been evacuated to a campsite high in the hills above us where they would be safe, Sidonie among them. We'd parted an hour before sundown. I could still feel her anguished farewell kiss lingering on my lips.

We waited.

The Amazigh didn't come that night. The sentries in the

treetops kept their vigil. Those of us on the ground dozed, spread throughout the forest. I reckoned there were less than three hundred men of fighting age in the village, but the Euskerri seemed unconcerned about numbers.

"Prince Imriel?" Paskal's voice reached out to me in the darkness, sounding young and uncertain. "What's it like?"

"Battle?" I tilted my head in his direction. "Much like escaping from Amílcar."

He rustled. "No. Love."

"Ah." I remembered Leander Maignard asking me the same question outside a temple in Cythera. I leaned back against the trunk of the pine tree beneath which I was sitting, the rough bark snagging my hair. "It's a force to make a man yearn for a lifetime of peace, Paskal."

His reply sounded bewildered. "I don't understand."

"Pray you have the chance to do so," I said.

It wasn't long after dawn when the lookouts' sharp whistles roused us. I bounded to my feet, snatching my dagger from its scabbard and holding it by the tip. Since I didn't have a javelin or a sling, it was the best I could do. Ululating cries burst through the forest, men racing forward. I ran, too.

Astegal's Amazigh.

They were strung out in a long line throughout the pass. Nowhere to go, nowhere to maneuver. The Euskerri fell on them, hurtling javelins and stones from the high embankments. I threw my dagger as Joscelin had taught me and one of the Amazigh rocked back in the saddle, slumping. I leapt down and darted between horses, yanking at the reins of a second opponent whose panicked mount had him half-unseated. He cursed and chopped at me with his sword, trying at the same time to regain his balance. I parried with my arms raised above my head, vambraces crossed. Dorelei's gift. His blade skittered off their surface.

I caught his robes and jerked.

He fell.

I had my sword out before he hit the ground. I plunged it into his heart. His riderless horse reared above me, hooves flailing. I ducked under it, catching a glancing blow to the helm I'd borrowed from Amílcar's armory. Before me, another man clutched at the javelin sprouting from his ribcage and toppled from the saddle, falling hard and bearing me down in a swirl of indigo robes. I scrambled out from underneath him, a little dizzy, and dealt him the mercy-blow.

Another figure sought to ride me down, sword swinging. I stepped sideways and parried in the Cassiline manner, my sword angled over my head. An unexpected maneuver, meant to defend against a foe on higher ground. His momentum carried him onward until a flung stone from an unseen enemy knocked him insensible.

Javelins and stones.

Ululating cries.

After that it was over very quickly. Janpier Iturralde hadn't been boasting. The Euskerri won that day, and they won handily. This was their territory and they knew every inch of it. There was no mercy. They swarmed the narrow pass with brutal efficiency, dispatching any who lived. They gathered the horses, herding them back toward the village. They tended their own dead and injured with care. They dragged the Amazigh dead into mounds.

"So." Janpier studied me, blood-spattered. "You kept your word."

I jerked my chin at the piled dead. "You might want to strip the corpses. If you've any thought of accepting Aragonia's offer, believe me, those robes make an almighty disguise."

He regarded me inscrutably, then issued an order in Euskerri and strode away.

They stripped the dead.

So many men! Faces laid bare, tawny limbs flopping. Some of them were a good deal younger than one would have reckoned behind the veils and robes. It was such a vulnerable thing, mortal flesh. I thought about Ghanim, the Amazigh slave who had extended such fierce loyalty to me when I'd promised him his freedom. I wondered what bribe it was that Astegal had given these tribesmen in exchange for their loyalty, and I wondered if they'd reckoned it worth the cost as they died.

The women emerged from their secret encampment. Wails of mourning for the Euskerri dead arose. Their losses had been light—I'd not counted more than a dozen—but dead was dead. It was a small village. Every man slain was someone's brother or son, husband or father. In the midst of it Sidonie and I found one another.

"You're alive," she whispered with profound relief. "Are you hurt?"

I shook my head. "A few bruises." I wanted to hold her, but I didn't dare. I was covered in blood and filth.

"Paskal?" she asked.

"He's fine," I assured her. "Helping with the wounded."

"Your highness!" Janpier hailed her, picking his way back toward us through the dead. "You should be proud. Your kinsman fought well."

"He's skilled with a blade." Sidonie's tone was neutral. "I congratulate you on your victory, *etxekojaun*, and I grieve for your losses. What passes now?"

Janpier Iturralde fixed her with a hard gaze. "Today we celebrate and mourn. Tomorrow we send word of our victory and your offer throughout Euskerria. The day after, the debate begins. You will remain here until the matter is decided, of course. Laida will show you to the guest-house."

To the north, the empty pass beckoned. I had an

overwhelming urge to snatch a pair of horses yet milling around us, grab Sidonie, and flee. I couldn't, of course. Sidonie had come to them as an emissary of Terre d'Ange and Aragonia. She had to play the role in good faith on behalf of all the parties involved. Still, I yearned to move onward.

All together, we made the long trek back to the village amid mixed jubilation and despair. There was more of the former than the latter. The women were somber, but the young, untried men among the Euskerri were filled with excitement, reliving the battle, while the older ones smiled with dour pride. The Amazigh horses were reckoned a serious prize.

And beneath it all, everyone was buzzing at the prospect of a free and sovereign Euskerria. Even without understanding the language, I could feel it. I prayed they would reach a swift decision in the days to come.

For a mercy, there actually *was* a guest-house in Roncal. Paskal explained to us that it was used during times of celebration when Euskerri from neighboring communities would come to stay and mingle. A good many marriages were arranged that way. But for now, its lodging-rooms were at our disposal. Through Paskal, Janpier's wife, Laida, introduced us to the *etxekoandere*, or mistress of the house, a dignified woman named Bixenta. And through Paskal, Bixenta assured us that we would be cared for in a manner befitting our stature.

"Is it possible to have a bath?" I asked with longing.

Bixenta unbent enough to smile a little when Paskal translated the question. "This will be arranged," Paskal told us. "She recommends that I do the same once you have finished."

True to her word, Bixenta took good care of us. The hospitality was homely, but it was warm and unstinted. Sidonie and I took turns bathing in the wooden washtub in a tiny room off the guest-house's kitchen. Sidonie insisted on letting me go first.

"I didn't fight a battle today," she murmured, undoing the buckles of my vambraces. "I want to see for myself that you're all right."

I was.

I had myriad bruises blossoming and a knot on my skull where a horse's hoof had dented my helmet, but my skin was whole. I let Sidonie examine me to her satisfaction before I clambered into the tub and scrubbed myself thoroughly. Elua, it felt good. Afterward, the water was so filthy it had to be changed. While fresh water heated, Bixenta took my dirty things to be laundered and brought clean, simple clothing in the Euskerri style: black breeches and vest and a white shirt with loose sleeves. There was a shadow of sorrow in her dark eyes, and I wondered who the clothes had belonged to.

And then it was Sidonie's turn.

"Let me see your back, love," I said gently to her, unwinding bandages that hadn't been changed for two days.

"Elua," she muttered, leaning forward in the bath and wrapping her arms around her knees. "Imriel, I look forward to the day when neither of us has to examine the other's wounds."

It looked good. The disk of scabbed flesh between her shoulder blades was beginning to crack and peel, revealing pink new skin underneath. I soaped it carefully, kneeling beside the tub, watching water and suds run down her spine. "So do I."

Bixenta had brought clean attire for Sidonie, too. The dress had a fitted black bodice embroidered with elaborate needlework and a two-tiered skirt of white and crimson below. After I'd applied fresh salve and clean bandages that Rachel had given us, I helped Sidonie don the dress. It smelled of cedar, as though it had been carefully preserved in a clothes-press.

We ventured out of the bathing-room to find Bixenta waiting. She pressed her hands together, raising them to her lips when we emerged. Her large dark eyes were bright with tears.

"*Etxekoandere.*" Sidonie hesitated, then framed a halting question in the Euskerri tongue, augmented with many gestures. It seemed she'd put her time in the library of Amílcar to better use than I'd reckoned. Bixenta replied in a torrent of Euskerri, her hands flying and gesticulating.

They communicated as women do, better than men. Bixenta pointed between the two of us, raising her brows and clasping her hands.

"I think it was her wedding dress," Sidonie said to me in a soft voice. "She reckoned it was the only finery that would suit the occasion. I'm not sure whether those are her husband's clothes or her son's that you're wearing. If I understand rightly, she's lost both."

"Will you tell her I'm grateful?" I asked.

She nodded and did. Bixenta merely shook her head and urged us into the kitchen, where she fed us an ample meal of stewed red beans and spicy sausage.

That evening there was a celebration in the town square. As in the City of Elua, the square was dominated by a large oak tree. Paskal explained to us that the Euskerri reckoned any agreements made beneath the oak tree to be sacred and binding.

Tonight, though, there were no politics or debate, only music, song, and dance, fierce in expressing joy and sorrow alike. We watched while our hosts pressed cup after cup of strong cider on us. Some of the instruments seemed ancient and strange: high-pitched horns made from the horns of oxen, thick staves used to beat out a complex rhythm that echoed from the sides of the valley. One could well imagine that the Euskerri had been here from time out of mind, honing their arts long before Blessed Elua wandered the earth.

As the sun was beginning to set, a group of Euskerri men performed the final dance of the evening: a sword dance accompanied by flute and drum. The men faced one another in a double line, moving in deliberate, complex steps. Their blades glinted as they maneuvered them, periodically bringing them together with a loud, metallic clash. The lowering sun stained their white shirts with ruddy light.

The dance ended with a final flourish, clash, and shout at the precise moment the sun's lower rim touched the western edge of the mountains lining the valley. The drums and flutes fell silent. Everyone turned as one toward the west, touching their brows and breasts in a salute to the dying sun.

It gave me a shiver, even as Sidonie and I followed suit. There were traditions in Terre d'Ange older than Blessed Elua, such as the arrival of the Sun Prince on the Longest Night.

This was a living embodiment of a very, very ancient faith.

And then the celebration was over. Along with Paskal, Sidonie and I returned to the guest-house where Bixenta had laid the beds in our chambers with linens smelling of soap and a hot iron's touch. It had been an arduous journey, a long night, and a fierce battle, and it was a blessed relief to lie in a warm, clean bed, feeling the silken warmth of Sidonie's bare skin against mine.

I meant to tell her, but I was asleep before I could get the words out.

Sixty-one

On the morrow Euskerri from all across the mountains began pouring into Roncal.

I was surprised at how quickly the news had travelled. Paskal explained to us that the beating-staves used at the previous night's celebration had carried word as far as two leagues. Dozens of messengers had departed at first light to spread the news farther, riding the swift Amazigh horses captured in the battle.

More and more Euskerri came.

They were all cut from a similar cloth, men and women alike. A dark-haired, dark-eyed folk, proud and rugged. Very few of them spoke aught but their own tongue. I wished I could understand them.

"I know," Sidonie said ruefully when I voiced the thought. "'Tis frustrating. I understand only a little myself. I'll have no way to gauge whether or not my words have swayed them, no way to gauge what they're saying."

"Do you think the outcome is in doubt?" I asked in surprise. "I have the sense they're hell-bent on gaining sovereignty."

"True." She knit her brows. "I don't know. Mayhap I'm overanxious. I can't stop worrying over what's happening at home. It goads me somewhat fierce to be so close."

On the following day, the debate began.

It was held in the village square, crowded to overflowing. A small dais had been constructed at the base of the oak tree. Sidonie stood atop it, flanked by Paskal and me. In the midst of a sea of dark-haired folk, she stood out like a beacon, far more than I did. She told our tale in a strong, clear voice, pausing after every few sentences for Janpier Iturralde to translate her words into Euskerri.

There were no interruptions. We had been told that the debate would follow on the heels of her words. Sidonie talked and they listened.

She told the story well. There were no dramatic embellishments; it was compelling enough on its own merits and any clever twist of rhetoric or theatrical gesture would fail to translate. She expressed regret for leading the Amazigh to Roncal while making it clear that the situation in the south was growing desperate, and that if the Aragonians and the Euskerri didn't stand together against Carthage at this juncture, they would fall separately. She enumerated Astegal's forces in succinct terms.

I didn't think the Euskerri doubted her, at least not in a broad sense. We might not have had a parlor trick to play to lend credence to our tale of ensorcelment, but the essential reality of the situation was self-evident. Terre d'Ange was in disarray to the north and Aragonia besieged to the south. The Amazigh had come in pursuit as Sidonie had said they would. Janpier Iturralde could vouch for her identity.

She presented Iturralde with the written charter of sovereignty that Serafin's council had prepared and described it in clear detail for the benefit of the audience. She recited from memory the terms of the accord to which her mother had been willing to agree well over a year ago, detailing the D'Angeline territory to be ceded. She gave her word on behalf of Terre d'Ange that not only would the accord be kept if the Euskerri agreed to it, but that Terre d'Ange would use its sway to ensure that Aragonia didn't break faith with Euskerria.

When Sidonie finished, a great roar arose, not cheers, but merely the sound of thousands of voices rising in simultaneous argument as the Euskerri turned to one another in the square, taking up their individual concerns and ignoring her presence. She blinked, taken aback.

Janpier Iturralde moved closer to us. "There will be debate for many hours," he said frankly. "Perhaps for days, as others come to Roncal. There is nothing more you can do. Wait in the guest-house and I will send word if there is a decision or further questions."

I glanced involuntarily toward the north. "My lord, is it not possible—"

Sidonie laid a hand on my arm. "We will await your word, *etxekojaun*," she said calmly.

In the days that followed—and it *did* take days—the debate raged heatedly. If there was a system of governance in place among the Euskerri, I failed to grasp it. Of a surety, there was no single ruler. It didn't appear that there was a formal parliament or governing council, either, nor any form of elected republic. As best I could determine, each village had its own headman or woman, but they were not allowed to represent the views of the village until concord was reached.

And once it was, the headmen and women of the villages argued the matter all over again amongst themselves. Only when they had come to agreement did they select spokespersons to carry out their will.

There was a certain fairness to it, but it was a messy process and a frustrating one. Like Sidonie, I chafed at our nearness to the D'Angeline border. Along with every other house in Roncal, the guest-house where we were lodged was now filled to overflowing, half a dozen women aiding Bixenta in cooking and cleaning for the contentious horde. Every night, I entertained thoughts of laying claim to a pair of swift horses and fleeing north.

"We *can't*," Sidonie said irritably when I proposed the idea for a second time. "Imriel, I agreed to this. If we flee, it undermines all our credence. There will be no agreement, no alliance. The best we could hope is that Amílcar holds until we can send aid. And then we're talking about sending D'Angelines to fight and die in the Euskerri's stead. In the end, I'm accountable to *our* people."

I groaned. "I know! It's just—"

"*I know.*" She blew out her breath in an impatient sigh. "Gods! I think about it every hour of every day. Do you think it's not killing me, too?"

"No." I grasped her shoulders hard, rubbing her collarbones with my thumbs. It calmed me. I could feel her body yielding beneath my touch, ceding what her determined sense of honor and propriety wouldn't. "No, I know. I do. I'm sorry."

Sidonie shook her head and reached for me.

We took out our frustrations on ourselves, on each other. In the midst of turmoil and uncertainty, we found surety. Helpless to rearrange the world to my liking, I was at least able to control *this*. Unable to relinquish her role, Sidonie was at least able to surrender in our bed. We made love like war. I pinned her wrists high above her head with one hand, feeling her arch beneath me. I plowed her relentlessly, driving her to climax after climax, until I had to release my grip and spend myself deep within her. I felt her nails score my back, her thighs tightening around hips.

"So Astegal didn't take that from you," I murmured into the crook of her neck.

"Astegal took *nothing* from us!" Sidonie whispered fiercely in my ear. "You promised me that."

"And I meant it." I propped myself on one arm. "Nothing he did could ever alter my love for you. But—"

"You wondered if having my innermost will perverted would curb my penchant for violent pleasure." Her mouth twisted wryly as I nodded. "So did I, actually. But it seems I'm still reclaiming bits and pieces of myself."

"I'm glad," I said honestly.

"You were so gentle and beautiful when that was what I needed." Sidonie wound a lock of my hair around her fingers. "Thank you."

"Always," I said.

She gave me one of her quick smiles. "Or not, as it happens."

I laughed and planted a kiss on the inside of her wrist. "You're going to have bruises."

"Mmm." Sidonie touched my cheek, her expression turning serious. "That's a part of me Astegal never touched, Imriel. I don't . . ." She hesitated. "I'd like to think that somewhere deep inside, I knew enough to withhold my trust from him, to keep the most vulnerable part of me safe. But in truth, I don't know." She lifted one shoulder in a slight shrug. "It may simply be that he never knew me well enough to suspect it was there. Although in a way, I don't suppose he could have when there was so much we could never discuss."

It was the first time she'd spoken of what had passed between her and Astegal. "No?" I asked quietly.

"No. The first night . . ." Sidonie pulled away from me to sit upright, drawing her knees up and wrapping the sheet around them. "On the ship. I remember I asked him if he'd ever been in love before. He laughed and told some tale of a married woman he'd adored when he was little more than a youth. Then he told me that he wasn't going to ask the same question. That as far as he was concerned, whatever lay in my past, it was all washed clean away the moment he laid eyes on me. That we were born anew for one another, and only the future mattered."

"Very romantic," I observed.

She shot a glance at me to see if I was mocking, but I wasn't. "I thought so at the time. But it was just a means to keep me from discussing the past, lest I realize how much my memory was lacking."

"So what did you talk about?" I asked.

"The future." She gave another wry smile. "The glorious, peaceful, and just alliance of nations we would build. He laid out a bold, sweeping vision of the reforms he imagined for Carthage's role in this empire, such as eliminating the slave-trade. Nothing that could be accomplished immediately, mind you, but things that would come in time if we were patient and diligent."

"He played to the best in you," I said softly.

"Mayhap." Sidonie raked a hand through her disheveled hair. "Or mayhap to a strain of that L'Envers' ambition I didn't know I harbored. Noble aspirations are no excuse for conquest. I don't know. It shames me to remember it."

I didn't say anything.

"I believed him, though," she said. "In him, in his vision. And there's a part of me that wonders . . . in the beginning, when it was all new and fresh, it truly seemed Astegal believed it, too."

"When did it change?" I asked.

"I suppose it started in Carthage." She hugged her knees. "On the ship, he'd led me to believe I'd be involved in matters of import once we were there. That I'd have a voice, responsibilities as I'd had in Terre d'Ange. But once we arrived, he kept telling me that the Council wasn't ready, that it wasn't Carthage's way. That I had to be patient, and everything would change after Aragonia fell. So I was. Dumb, patient, and obedient."

"Not to hear Bodeshmun tell it," I said.

"It got worse after Astegal left," Sidonie said. "That was when I became restless and bored. But I didn't begin to doubt until you entered my life." She smiled wistfully. "Or at least Leander Maignard did, reeking of pomade, beating me at chess and stirring strange thoughts and yearnings in me."

"Not to mention gazing at you like a lovelorn pup," I added.

"Yes." She glanced at me, tears in her eyes. "That too. And I'm so grateful that you came for me, but . . . oh, gods! I wish none of it had ever happened. I wish I could forget it. And I can't."

I slid behind Sidonie and embraced her, holding her while she wept, her body shaking with an anguish she'd not let herself feel until now. My heart ached for her and I wished there were words I could say that would ease the pain, but there weren't. That was one truth I knew all too well. Hurting was part of the healing.

"It gets better, love," I said. "That, I promise."

She laughed through her tears, sniffling. "Good. Because I hate this."

I smiled against her hair. "I know."

Afterward, Sidonie slept. I stayed awake for a time, watching her and thinking a thousand thoughts. But at length, I slept, too.

In the morning there was word.

The Euskerri wished to meet with us in the hall of the guest-house.

Sixty-two

What?" Sidonie's voice cracked with outrage when she heard the Euskerri's terms. A few of them flinched. There was no sign of last night's wounded young woman in her. This was Ysandre de la Courcel's heir in a rare fury. "Why in Blessed Elua's name would you insist on such a thing?"

The Euskerri were demanding that she accompany them to Amílcar.

And that I join them in battle.

"You said you would ensure that the Aragonians keep their word," Janpier Iturralde reminded her. "We do not trust them. If we are victorious over Carthage, the agreement with Aragonia must be witnessed. As the arbiter of this accord, it is your duty."

She struggled for control. "I pledged my word, not my person. I have a duty to my country. And Terre d'Ange's role in this will be meaningless if we're not able to free her from the spell that binds it."

Janpier translated her words. There was a rapid spate of

argumentative Euskerri, resulting eventually in nods. "Terre d'Ange's role may be meaningless anyway," Janpier said calmly. "We do not believe that you have the authority to speak on behalf of Terre d'Ange, not with your country divided against itself. It is Aragonia that concerns us. What passes for leadership in Aragonia has granted you authority on their behalf. Your presence is our surety."

"My presence," Sidonie said. "As your hostage."

He colored slightly. "I would not use that word."

"I would," I said grimly.

There was another long exchange in Euskerri. "It is not so simple," Janpier said. "Aragonia seeks this bargain because they are desperate, but they have betrayed us in the past. We long for our freedom, but the price is very high." There was sympathy in his face. "It will take a very great gesture of good faith for us to accept this offer. That is what is required of you. Without it, we must decline."

I rose from the table. "Then decline. We will be on our way and wish you well." A pair of brawny men moved to block the door to the hall. I stared at Janpier. "You would refuse to grant us passage to Terre d'Ange?"

He shrugged in apology. "We *do* long for freedom."

Sidonie made a strangled sound. "Ah, gods! Do I understand this aright? If we agree to accompany you, the Euskerri will take arms against Carthage's army? And if we refuse, you will turn us away in spite? Despite the fact that it's in your own best interests to let us pass?"

"Yes." Janpier's face hardened. "Who are you to tell us what is in our best interests? You led an army to our doorstep, highness. In the minds of my people, if you are not willing to do this thing, you have acted in bad faith and we would rather take our chances with Carthage."

"Astegal will never grant you sovereignty," she said. "Never."

Janpier offered another stoic shrug. "Then we will fight him here in the mountains. Nothing will have changed but the enemy's face."

She raised her gaze to the rafters. "I begin to understand why Aragonia has been so reluctant to deal with the Euskerri."

He nodded. "We are a proud and stubborn folk. Those are our terms."

"There are other passes through the mountains," I observed.

"Yes." Janpier glanced at me. "All of which we hold, Prince Imriel."

Sidonie steepled her fingers and bowed her head. I saw her chest rise and fall as she took a deep breath and composed herself. When she spoke, her voice was quiet and even. "*Etxekojaun*, I understand. Please understand that I, too, love my country. Imriel and I hold the key to her freedom. Grant us this compromise. I will accompany you willingly. But I pray you let Imriel continue onward to Terre d'Ange."

"Sidonie . . ." I murmured.

She shook her head at me. "Don't argue."

It didn't matter. The point was moot. Janpier translated her words for the others. There was a long, heated argument. At the end of it, he turned back to us. "No," he said simply. "I am sorry, highness. If the decision were mine, I might grant your request. But there is anger and fear."

"Anger and fear," she echoed.

"Anger because twelve men have died already," Janpier said soberly. "Anger at the thought that your kinsman, who is a valuable warrior, would refuse to share our risk while others died. Fear because your country is in the grip of strong magic. We do not doubt this, highness. We know such things in the mountains. I myself am afraid. I fear that if we allow your kinsman to pass, matters will worsen."

"My lord." Sidonie closed her eyes briefly. "We hold the key to undoing the spell."

"Or unleashing war among your people," Janpier said. "Can you swear it will not take that to accomplish your ends? Can you swear that it will not end with the army of Terre d'Ange arrayed against us?"

I felt sick.

Of course we couldn't swear to it. We knew far too little of what had passed in Terre d'Ange since I left; and of what little we knew, none of it boded well. We had no idea if Barquiel L'Envers had succeeded in finding the demon-stone, no idea what transpired save that madness yet reigned, and Ysandre had declared Alais, her own daughter, in rebellion against the Crown.

"No," Sidonie said quietly. "I cannot."

Janpier nodded. "Then we shall deal with what is known and nothing else. We have Aragonia's offer. You have our terms. In an hour, we will convene in the square. You will give us your decision and your word beneath the oak."

With that, we were dismissed.

In the small room we shared, I could feel the fury radiating from Sidonie like heat from an overstoked oven. Elua knows, I was angry, too, but I'd had more experience with life's unfairness, and I hadn't been raised to carry the weight of the realm on my shoulders.

"They've left us no choice, have they?" she said in a tight voice.

"Not much," I said. "Assuming they're not actually planning to restrain us, we could go southeast and try the coastal towns north of Amílcar. We might be able to find a ship willing to carry us to Marsilikos in another month's time."

"In a month's time, Astegal's likely to have discovered

what happened here. Do you imagine he won't have his navy patrolling the coast?" Sidonie asked. "Like as not he already does after our last attempt. He's not stupid."

"What about the western coast?" I asked, thinking. "Does he have ships there?"

"Not as many." She scowled. "But the goddamned Euskerri control the northernmost ports on the western coast and those to the south have agreed to Astegal's terms."

"Not happily," I observed.

Sidonie glanced sidelong at me. "He'll be looking for us. And you and I aren't exactly the most inconspicuous people in Aragonia."

"I know." I frowned. "Sidonie, I'm not afraid of battle. I don't like it, but I'll do it. If that were the only term, I'd swallow my bile and accept it. Risking your life and the whole of Terre d'Ange for no good reason is another matter. And the only way I'm willing to accept their terms is if the Euskerri pledge to have a company standing at the ready to whisk you north and across the border at the first sign of defeat."

She searched my face. "Do you think that's our best option?"

"Truly?" I nodded. "I do."

She sighed. "I want a courier. That's my demand. A courier sent north immediately bearing a letter for Alais and my damned uncle in Turnone. I don't care if the Euskerri are frightened. If we can do nothing else here, we can send the key home. After all, that's what truly matters, isn't it?"

"Yes," I said. "And if the Euskerri don't agree . . ."

". . . we take our chances elsewhere," Sidonie finished my thought. Her anger had drained away, leaving weariness in its wake. "Blessed Elua grant they see reason. I have a feeling that's not the first time those words have been uttered."

A short time later we returned to the village square, escorted by Janpier Iturralde and the committee of Euskerri we'd met with an hour ago. The square was thronged with people, even more crowded than it had been the other day. As we pushed our way through to mount the low dais beneath the oak tree, it gave me an uneasy memory of the night we'd gathered in Elua's Square to witness a marvel promised by Carthaginian horologists.

Janpier raised his hands to quiet the crowd. "Have you reached a decision?"

"Yes." Sidonie faced him. "We will agree to your terms if you will agree to ours. There is one condition without which I will refuse. There is one condition without which Prince Imriel will refuse."

He nodded impassively. "Speak."

Sidonie presented our terms. Janpier Iturralde translated them for the crowd, and the now-familiar roar of argument arose, delegates on the dais shouting back and forth with the villagers they represented. I studied Janpier's face. He met my gaze squarely, but his nostrils flared in a defensive manner.

"We're not bluffing, my lord," I said to him. "You have forced our hands, but we *will* walk away from this agreement."

"There is—" he began.

"Anger and fear." I cut him off. "Yes. Believe me, I am passing familiar with the emotions this day. Whatever it is you fear from Terre d'Ange, it will come more surely without the key than with it. It is a malevolent magic that binds our realm. Do not be a fool."

Janpier pointed at Sidonie. "And her? Is her safety worth more than the safety of our wives and sisters and daughters?"

"It is to me," I said calmly.

He bristled. "You would dare to claim—"

"Yes!" I raised my voice. The blood beat in my ears,

clashing like bronze wings. "Yes, Iturralde. As surely as you place Euskerria's concerns far, far above mine. And *your* wives and sisters and daughters will be far from the battlefield. I pledged my loyalty to Sidonie de la Courcel long ago. Even before I knew I loved her, I swore to lay my life down in her defense." My hand hovered over my sword-hilt. "If you want me to fight and mayhap die at your side, that is the price. Her safety. I will not be forsworn."

Janpier looked startled and impressed. "I will tell them."

I relaxed a little. "Thank you."

Whether or not that made the difference, I couldn't say. All in all, we were asking little compared to the sacrifice the Euskerri asked of us. The price they would pay for their freedom was like to be high, yes. But in the end, it was their choice. Ours was forced upon us, and it made me ache inside to turn my back on Terre d'Ange when we were so very close.

And after another hour of clamorous discussion, they agreed to accept our terms.

There beneath the oak tree at the center of Roncal, we swore our oaths. Sidonie and I swore in the name of Blessed Elua and his Companions, I that I would fight at the side of the Euskerri, and she that she would bear witness to the signing of the agreement that granted Euskerria sovereign status in Aragonia's eyes in the event of our victory. The Euskerri called the sun to bear witness and pledged to fight Carthage unto the death.

The matter was settled.

Once again, we were at war with Carthage.

SIXTY-THREE

Once the matter was settled, things moved quickly.

The Euskerri who had descended on Roncal dispersed like the wind, carrying word to every town and village perched in the mountains. There would be a great force amassing, Janpier Iturralde assured us. Six or seven thousand, he thought, although the Euskerri had never mustered in force before.

Sidonie and I wrote a letter to Alais on a piece of much-scraped parchment Janpier procured for us.

I watched her outline the important details in her neat, precise hand. The truth of what had befallen us, the accord to which we had agreed. The key to undoing the spell: the word, *emmenghanom*. Beholden. And then I watched her falter.

"What do you say, Imriel?" Sidonie asked me in bewilderment. "How do you say it?"

I'd written too many such letters.

"Tell her you love her," I said gently. "Tell them all. I will, too."

I liked the courier Janpier found for us: a bold-faced fellow named Nuno Agirre whose family originally hailed from the D'Angeline side of Euskerri territory. His grandfather had been an ardent scholar and all his descendants spoke fluent Caerdicci along with their native tongue. He swore without hesitation beneath the oak tree that he would do his utmost to see the letter delivered.

"It will be an honor," he added. "Is there any sign by which they will know it is genuine?"

I glanced at Sidonie, who looked dismayed. I thought about how I'd sent my ring, the gold knotted ring, back to her from Skaldia. Alais wouldn't know the significance of the ring, but there was another item that would suit. I eased the gold torc from around my neck.

"Here." I handed it to Nuno Agirre. "Alais will know this. Her father the Cruarch gave it to me with his own hands on my wedding day. I wear it in honor of the wife and child I lost."

Nuno stowed it in his packs along with the letter. "Very well, your highness. May the sun shine brightly on your venture!"

"Blessed Elua hold and keep you," Sidonie said in reply.

With that, Nuno mounted and departed, lifting one hand in farewell. He was riding one of the swift, tireless Amazigh horses; Janpier hadn't stinted. We watched his figure dwindle as he reached the far end of the valley and began to climb toward the longed-for and forbidden pass. Sidonie's lips moved in a silent prayer. I uttered one myself in my thoughts.

"Do you think he'll make it?" she asked me.

I took her hand. "Of course. He knows the territory, and he strikes me as a man with his wits about him. I reckon his odds are better than ours."

We sent another courier in the opposite direction during

those days of preparation. Paskal had been a great help to us in Roncal. With Janpier's permission and all the enthusiasm of youth, he had managed to recruit a score of men to serve as Sidonie's personal guard. A few of them were no older than he was, inflamed by the romanticism of the notion, but I was pleased to find that most appeared to be solid fellows, family men to whom the idea of beating a safe retreat to the mountains appealed more than dashing into battle. And two of them spoke Aragonian, which was a blessing.

Once that was done, Paskal approached us with his idea. "Send me ahead to scout," he suggested. "General Liberio sent men to the cities nearest Amílcar, to Badalon and Coloma and Tibado, begging them to rise up against Carthage. If any of them got through, I can tell them the Euskerri are coming. Perhaps it will convince them."

It was an excellent idea, albeit a dangerous one. And so Paskal was dispatched, brimming with enthusiasm. I watched him go, shaking my head and praying he'd find his way safely.

Two days later we departed Roncal.

Sidonie and I bade farewell to Bixenta, who had taken such good care of us. She embraced us both and uttered a blessing in the Euskerri tongue. And then we saddled our mounts and rode south with the others.

There was no fanfare, no great proclamation. The Euskerri had gotten all of that out of the way during their debate. The decision to go to war had been made, so to war they went.

There was also precious little in the way of a plan. Euskerri from all over the mountains were to make their way to the foothills above Amílcar. Mayhap there *would* be six or seven thousand of them. Janpier was convinced of it. If it was true, we would have numbers to equal Astegal's, as there were a good four thousand Aragonian soldiers in Amílcar itself, and thousands more dispersed across the country, subject to the terms of Roderico's surrender.

But even so, we had no way of mounting a coordinated attack; and the Euskerri's idea of warfare was to swarm their enemy from a position of strength. We wouldn't have that on the plains surrounding Amílcar. What we would have was a ragtag army of thousands with no form of organized leadership. As more and more Euskerri trickled toward the south, it became increasingly obvious that we would be mismatched on open ground.

"If we simply fall on Astegal's forces from behind, I'm afraid it will be a slaughter," I said to Sidonie as we rode. "He might have gotten lax about drilling in New Carthage, but they're disciplined enough to hold formation."

"I know." She frowned in thought. "I get the sense the Euskerri are simply hoping to lure them into the hills and ambush them. I'm not sure Astegal's going to be so easily lured."

"Any suggestions?" I asked. "You know him better than anyone, and it seems you've got as good a head for battle as anyone here."

Sidonie gave me a wry look. "Do you imagine the Euskerri would actually listen to me?"

"No." I smiled. "But they might listen to me."

"I'll think on it," she said.

Our journey back to Amílcar took a day longer than our flight from it. Euskerri from east of Roncal had already reached our destination and made camp in a deep basin of a valley some half a league from the city. I was glad to see that at least there were sentries posted atop every hill. Still, it made me feel anxious and exposed, being so close to Carthage's army and so unprepared to engage it.

Roncal's company made camp in the farthest northern end of the valley. I spoke to Gaskon, the Aragonian-speaking member of Sidonie's guard I reckoned the most sensible, and made it clear to him that if there was any sort of attack, they were to flee without hesitating. He understood and agreed.

And then we spent several agonizing days waiting.

It was a tense and strangely lonely time. Little by little, in dribs and drabs of a hundred men here, two hundred men there, Euskerri arrived. Janpier was right, their numbers did swell into the thousands. And none of them shared our language or our cause. They were here to fight Carthage, but they would just have gladly fought Aragonia if they'd thought it would gain them sovereignty.

At least they treated Sidonie with deference and her guard was decent. On the very first day, Gaskon brought a crude oilcloth tent he'd bartered for among some of the other soldiers. When Sidonie thanked him, he smiled quietly into his mustaches.

"I have a daughter no older than you," he said. "I would not want her sleeping exposed among so many men."

Then you shouldn't have dragged her here, I thought; but I bit my tongue on the comment.

On the third day we got a piece of good news. Paskal rejoined us, beaming from ear to ear. The word he carried spread quickly throughout the camp. He'd encountered no luck at the first two cities—they were fearful of Astegal's ire—but the Duke Leopoldo of Tibado was a crusty firebrand seething under Carthage's yoke. He'd pledged a thousand men to the cause. Several dozen Euskerri headmen commenced to argue about the best method to mount a joint attack.

"How swiftly can he marshal them?" Sidonie asked Paskal.

He shrugged. "Immediately."

She turned to me. "Can we have a look at the battlefield?"

"If Paskal knows a route to a safe vantage point," I said.

"Oh, I do," Paskal said cheerfully.

We left the Euskerri to argue and rode out of the camp, crossing several valleys and heading up a wooded slope. On Paskal's orders, we left the horses and climbed the remaining yards on foot. At the top of the slope, the woods ended. We lay on our bellies and peered downward. We were northwest of the city, but we could see Amílcar spread below us and Astegal's army much as we'd left it, except the trenches had grown deeper and the earthen bulwarks were higher.

"Where does Tibado lie?" Sidonie asked.

Paskal pointed south. "A day's ride. If there's to be an attack, the Duke would ford the river to the west and position his troops between the rivers."

"I wish there was some way of alerting Amílcar," she said absently.

"You're *not* thinking of trying to slip through Astegal's camp," I warned her.

"Like Phèdre did at Troyes-le-Mont?" She gave me a quick smile. "Elua, no."

"I imagine they'll be on the lookout," I said. "They know there's a chance that aid is coming. But there's no way for them to mount a full-scale counterattack if we can't draw off some of Carthage's forces."

"There's three hundred Amazigh horse and all those robes and veils," Sidonie said. "Three hundred men could cross the bridge and ride right up to the camp in guise."

"True," I agreed. "That's good for one strike, love. Then they'd have to flee or die. I'm not sure it's worth it."

She looked at me. "What if they stopped short?"

I shook my head. "I don't understand."

"Astegal's clever," Sidonie said. "And he's vain. He likes knowing things and he likes being in control of things. You told me to think about what might lure him out of his camp,

Imriel. What if his three hundred loyal Amazigh rode up to the verge of the river and stopped short there? Simply waited?"

"It would gall him," I said slowly.

She nodded. "It would drive him mad. I don't think he'd do anything foolish, not right away. He'd send a small delegation. But if you killed them and fell back—"

"He'd send a larger delegation," I finished. "And if we continued to fall back—"

"You could lead them into ambush," she agreed.

"And then the Duke's men could fall on the others from behind!" Paskal's eyes gleamed.

"They'd be horribly outnumbered," I observed.

"Well, what if we divided our forces?" Sidonie suggested logically. "We could send the bulk of the Euskerri to join the Duke of Tibado and keep a thousand in reserve for the ambush. I can't imagine more than that could maneuver efficiently in those woods anyway."

"And if the ambush succeeded, we could capture the bridge and mount a rearguard attack on Astegal," I said. "Mayhap hold the ground long enough for Liberio's forces to get free of the city."

"It's possible," Sidonie said. "If Tibado and the Euskerri stage a slow retreat of their own, it might create more of an opportunity to . . . Imriel, why are you staring at me like that?"

"Awe," I said. "Awe and adoration. I'd no idea you'd prove quite such a brilliant strategist."

"Thank my mother and Leander Maignard." She gazed down at the city. "To be honest, I doubt such a risky notion would ever have occurred to me if your Leander hadn't forced me to play a better game of chess." Sidonie shivered. "Although it's a good deal more terrifying when the players are real. Do you suppose it might work?"

I shrugged. "Well, I've not heard a better idea."

We retreated carefully back down the slope, retrieved our mounts, and returned to the campsite. The argument was still in full sway, joined now by hundreds. If the din was any louder, they would have heard it in Amílcar. I shook my head.

"Listen," I said to Paskal. "I'm going to propose our plan. You're going to translate. And so far as you know, this is entirely *my* idea. Do you understand?"

He glanced at Sidonie. "I believe I do."

I kneed my horse forward and rode close to the loudest knot of arguers, then took a deep breath. I thought about Gallus Tadius who had commanded the Red Scourge in Lucca through sheer force of will. "Right!" I shouted over the uproar. It dimmed slightly, heads turning in my direction. "Here's the thing, lads. You're a disorganized, contentious, piss-poor excuse for an army. These aren't your precious mountain passes. If we don't have a decent strategy, we're all dead. Lucky for you, I have an idea."

Paskal translated.

I talked.

They listened. And somewhat to my shock, the Euskerri came to agree with me without a great deal of argument. There was a certain sense of relief once it came to it, as though they'd been waiting for someone to assume command here. We settled in quickly and began sketching maps in the dirt and working out the details.

By the end of the day we had a plan.

Sixty-four

Two days later our plan was ready to be implemented.

Elua knows, it wasn't perfect. It was messy and dangerous and difficult to coordinate. But it was ready.

The bulk of the Euskerri army had withdrawn to the west, taking one of Paskal's careful routes through the hills to a point where they could ford the Barca River unseen and establish a new camp within a reasonable striking range of Astegal's forces. Paskal was to continue onward to alert the Duke of Tibado, whose men would join them there. And there, they would post sentries and await our move.

I was to be among the disguised Amazigh. After some discussion, we had decided it would be best if the majority of the apparent Amazigh were on foot. It would give Astegal greater incentive to give chase and the horses would be more effectual on the primary battlefield. Only thirty of us would be mounted, that we might move swiftly to secure the bridge if we were successful.

Come dawn, we would find out.

The Euskerri gave Sidonie and me a wide berth that night

before the attack was to be launched, for which we were both grateful. I'd spent the better part of the day teaching three hundred men how to secure their Amazigh head-wraps and face-scarves. The balance of the day, I'd spent tending my mount and checking my gear. Dusk fell all too quickly.

"Imriel." Sidonie lay in my arms inside our rough tent. "Promise me you won't do anything foolish and heroic. That you won't take any unnecessary risks."

I stroked her hair. "I'll try."

She lifted her head to gaze at me. "It's awful. I feel like there are so many things I should say, but I don't know what they are except that I love you."

"It's enough," I said. "It's all I ever needed. Sidonie, if this goes awry, promise me you won't hesitate. Don't think about me. Don't wait in the hopes of finding out what happened. Just flee with Gaskon and his lads, as hard and fast as you can. Don't pause until you reach Terre d'Ange." I traced the line of her brows, so similar to my own. "Please? It's the only way my mind will be at peace."

She hesitated only a heartbeat. "I promise."

I kissed her. "Good girl."

"You should sleep." Sidonie touched my lips. "As much as I'd like to make love to you until the sun rises, I'd sooner have you go into battle well rested."

I caught her hand and kissed her fingertips. "Blessed Elua grant us a thousand more nights, Sun Princess, that I might make this one lost night up to you a thousandfold."

Her black eyes glittered with tears. "Only a thousand?"

"Ten thousand," I vowed. "A hundred thousand."

She laid her head on my shoulder. "I pray he does."

We lay like that for a long time, neither of us moving. I held Sidonie in my arms, listening to her breathe, feeling the heart beating steadily in my breast. And I prayed that Blessed Elua would prove merciful on the morrow. I prayed that our plan wouldn't fall to pieces; I prayed that Astegal would take our bait. I prayed that this ragtag band of Euskerri wouldn't be slaughtered, that Amílcar's forces would recognize us as allies and rally in time. I prayed that Sidonie would be safe.

And at the end, I allowed myself one selfish prayer that I would survive the coming battle. That I would live to see Terre d'Ange free of ensorcelment, to see my loved ones once more. To see the wondrous light of love in Phèdre's eyes, the pride in Joscelin's face.

All of them.

And to wed the woman I loved and spend a lifetime of peace with her.

Blessed Elua grant us mercy.

I slept.

The day dawned grey and drizzling. The foot-soldiers committed to ambush were the first to depart, slipping over the hills and into the pine forests that lined the road to Amílcar. Two of Sidonie's guards went to take up vantage points and serve as sentries observing the course of the battle. Three hundred Euskerri fussed and fidgeted with their Amazigh robes and scarves, making ready to stage our appearance. I checked my gear and my mount's hooves one last time.

All was in readiness.

It was time to go.

"Come back to me," Sidonie said quietly. Fine raindrops glinted in her hair. "May Blessed Elua and his Companions watch over you all and grant us victory."

I kissed her, then fastened my scarf in place. "Be safe, love."

That was all. I mounted my horse—one of the Amazigh horses, a spirited bay with a strongly arched neck and a willing gait. I glanced around at my three hundred veiled and robed companions. Fearless Euskerri eyes gazed back at me in the slits between their indigo scarves. I adjusted my flowing sleeves to hide the gleam of my vambraces beneath them.

"Let's go," I said.

Janpier Iturralde echoed the command in Euskerri.

Atop the crest of the first hill, I turned and looked back. Sidonie was standing, watching us, a small figure in the far end valley, determinedly regal and upright. Her guard surrounded her. Their mounts were saddled in the picket-line, ready to flee on a moment's notice. Good. I raised one hand in farewell, then rode out of sight.

We crossed the green hills, then plunged into the woods. I could hear men muttering and swearing as pine branches plucked at their robes. I told Janpier to bid them be silent, and he did. After that there was only the soft tramp of hooves and feet on the pine mast. I could smell the rich loam beneath. The earth was growing warmer. Spring was coming.

I prayed I'd live to see it.

The journey that had seemed endless by night went quickly by daylight. We made our way down the forested hills north of Amílcar and emerged from the woods to find the road empty. Beyond it stretched the sea, grey and wrinkled beneath the cloudy skies.

South lay Amílcar.

We went south. Thirty horsemen in the front, riding five abreast. I was in the center of the front rank. I'd assumed a position of command. It was expected; the plan we were executing was mine. The others followed on foot. We passed the pine-covered slopes where our comrades were hidden. I looked for them, but there was no sign.

And then there before us was the Barca River, cutting a wide, winding course through the plains. There was the bridge across which I'd fled with Sidonie and Paskal and

Captain Aureliano and his men, our valiant decoys. I wondered if they'd survived. I prayed they had.

And beyond it . . . Amílcar and Astegal's army.

There were sentries posted at the near end of the bridge. They hailed us with shouts as we came into view. We made no reply, but advanced steadily. Some fifty yards shy of the bridge, I drew rein. Our company halted.

There we made a stand and waited. The skies spat a fitful rain at us and gusts of wind tugged at our damp indigo robes. The Carthaginian sentries at the bridge conferred in consternation. One left his post and headed for the main encampment. Another came forward at a jog, approaching us. I lifted my hand, bidding my company to wait.

"My lord?" Janpier Iturralde muttered urgently beside me.

"I'll take him." I drew my sword and heeled my horse. He sprang forward eagerly, hooves clattering on the road. The Carthaginian sentry slowed, uncertain. Beneath the brim of his helmet, his face was young and perplexed. It was uplifted toward mine, a span of bare skin showing under his chinstrap.

I didn't slow.

I leaned in the saddle and beheaded him at a single stroke. Desert justice, the Amazigh had called it. Out of the corner of my eye, I saw his head bounce. His headless body slumped. I wheeled my horse and returned to the line.

"Wait," I said briefly.

Janpier translated.

We waited, as still as statues. We watched the news ripple through Astegal's encampment. Horns blared a summons. A pool of blood ebbed from the headless trunk of the dead sentry's neck. Astegal took to the battlefield himself: Astegal of Carthage, Prince of the House of Sarkal. Riding a black charger, his gilded armor the brightest thing under the grey skies. He rode back and forth along the river, gauging us. I knew him by his splendid arms, by the crimson strip of his beard. All too well, I remembered the satisfaction in his heavy-lidded eyes. I stared at him between the folds of my Amazigh scarf.

"Do it," I whispered. "Let me make your wife a widow today, Astegal."

He didn't.

Sidonie was right; Astegal was no fool. I wished he was. I longed to cross blades with him. Longed to erase her shame. But no, he wasn't going to commit himself. Still, I could tell by his restless movements that curiosity was eating at him.

We waited for at least an hour before he made his first move. The Euskerri might be a contentious folk, but they were capable of great patience, too. No one threatened to break our ranks. No one spoke. At last Astegal sent a small company of archers across the bridge to test our resolve.

We retreated out of bowshot. For every pace the archers advanced, we retreated, until I could see their uncertainty and reluctance. I had to smile behind my veil. They were increasingly isolated from their comrades. They might get off a flight or two, but we could take them.

It took another hour for Astegal to lose patience with that particular game of cat and mouse and call his archers back. I promptly ordered the Euskerri to advance and we returned to our initial position.

In the end, I don't think the gambit would have worked if it hadn't been for the Amazigh guises. Astegal had sent his loyal Amazigh on a mission of crucial import to his plans. He *had* to know they'd failed. He *had* to know this was a trap. But our silent, veiled presence maddened him. I watched him stare across the river. I watched his gestures grow more and more curt.

I watched him come to a decision.

Astegal wasn't taking any chances. When he committed forces against us, he did so in a large way. At a guess, I'd reckon he mustered a good two thousand of his troops. And I had to own, the sight of the endless line of them snaking over the bridge and advancing toward us made my blood run cold.

"Retreat," I said. "Slowly."

Step by step, we did. The Carthaginians broke into a jog and began closing the distance between us, their armor rattling. I could feel the Euskerri's resolve beginning to weaken. Beneath my Amazigh robes, cold sweat trickled. My mount grew restive, sensing my fear. I waited until I could see the dense pine forests to the west out of the corner of my eye.

"Go!" I shouted. "Go!"

The Euskerri didn't wait for a translation, breaking into a dead run. I could hear the roar behind me as I eased my horse into a swift trot. Carthage was in full pursuit.

A poorly thrown javelin soared over my right shoulder and clattered harmlessly on the paving stones in front of me. The skin between my shoulder blades itched. I was wearing my hauberk beneath my robes, but I wasn't sure it would turn away a well-thrown weapon. I fought the urge to heel my spirited mount to a gallop and flee.

Two thousand. I hadn't thought Astegal would send so many against so few.

Still, the Carthaginian line was strung out the length of the road. When the Euskerri troops hiding in the forest burst forth with their fierce, ululating cries, I thought I'd never heard a sweeter sound.

This was the Euskerri's preferred method of battle. Hundreds of Carthaginian soldiers were slain during that first onslaught, brought down by javelins and stones. But there were hundreds more yet coming.

There was no question of risk or heroism. It was an ugly,

bloody melee. I fought from the saddle, chopping and hacking on both sides, simply doing my best to stay alive. Men cried aloud, fell, and died. Our men. Their men. The roads grew slick with blood and gore, cluttered with bodies. Somewhere in the distance, horns were blaring an insistent alarm and that sound too should have been sweet to my ears, for it meant the rearguard attack had begun. But at the moment, I was too busy trying to survive.

If it hadn't been for the horns, I'm not sure we would have won our skirmish. Astegal's soldiers fought hard and they were more skilled than the Euskerri when it came to hand-to-hand fighting—more skilled and better armed. But when the horns grew ever more strident, several hundred of those closest to the city peeled away in answer to the summons, mayhap suspecting that this attack was a mere decoy.

The rest we killed.

Gods, it was a grim sight. I'd seen battle, but never carnage on this scale. Over a thousand Carthaginian dead and hundreds and hundreds of Euskerri dead or grievously wounded. I reckoned there were no more than four hundred yet fit for battle.

And this was only the beginning.

"Right," I said wearily. "Janpier?"

Janpier Iturralde was dead. The surviving Euskerri argued among themselves and finally produced a boy younger than Paskal who spoke Aragonian. He looked to be in a state of shock, his eyes stretched wide enough to show the whites, but he translated obediently for me.

"Here's the thing, lads," I said in tones far more gentle than aught Gallus Tadius had ever used. "We need to take the bridge and the ground outside Amílcar's gates between the trenches. We have to give Aragonia a chance to mount a full attack on the rear of Astegal's forces, or there's going to be a slaughter. So gather your courage and strip the dead of any arms or armor you can use."

It was an ugly business. I dismounted and shed my damp Amazigh robes. I used the head-scarf to bind a deep gash in my left thigh. Working quickly, I scavenged a helmet, a pair of greaves, a shield, and a spear. The Euskerri followed suit and outfitted themselves with the spoils of the dead. We were a desperate, ragtag bunch, but at least we could no longer be mistaken for Amazigh.

I mounted. "Let's go."

We went. All four hundred of us.

Short of the river, we paused. Astegal *wasn't* a fool. There was a battle raging in the distance that dwarfed our skirmish, and Astegal himself must have joined it, for he was nowhere in sight. But he had left a company of archers to defend the bridge; and beyond them was another company holding the ground between the trenches: his Nubian mercenaries with their long spears and zebra-skin shields, a thousand strong. Their dark faces were set and grim. I thought of Sunjata with an unexpected pang. Atop the walls of the city, I could see Aragonian sentries watching and waiting for an opening. I prayed they'd be swift to seize it when we gave it to them.

Someone asked a question in Euskerri.

The boy translated. "What do we do?"

In the distance, I could hear the hue and clamor of war. I gazed at the blank stone walls surrounding Amílcar, the waiting archers, the waiting soldiers. I thought about Sidonie in the valley. Safe. She would be safe. She'd wanted me to promise I wouldn't take unnecessary risks. This wasn't. Without Aragonia's full aid, the Euskerri and the troops from Tibado would be slaughtered, and Astegal's hold on the nation more certain than ever.

I had to do this.

I had to try.

"We charge the bridge. And then we fight and live or die." I settled my spear like a lance. "Riders to the fore. Infantry follow."

We charged.

Astegal's archers knelt and shot. I caught the first arrow on my shield. The second took my horse. I was pitched over his head as he went down hard, poor valiant beast. I lost my shield and my spear. I rolled and came up fighting, ripping the sword from my sheath. The Euskerri surged after and around me.

We took the bridge and plunged into enemy territory.

In a poet's tale, every thrust and blow, every individual act of heroism would be catalogued and recorded for posterity. This was no poet's tale. It was war. Just war. I fought well because it was what I'd been taught to do. It didn't matter that it wasn't a style suited for the battlefield. Not in the midst of this chaos. I told the hours over and over—beyond fear, beyond weariness, beyond thought. I defended the sphere of my own person and the bodies mounted around me.

Our Aragonian allies answered my prayers. They rushed from the sally ports to join the fray, scrambling to clear the first trench. Gears ground. The portcullis lifted to admit the bulk of Aragonia's army onto the battlefield.

What an ungodly mess it was.

It stank. It stank of death and desperation. Gore churned into mire, bowels spilled in death. We heaved bodies into the trenches, forging a gruesome causeway. Sharp hooves carved dead flesh. Onward, onward. Feet trampling the dead. Horns blowing. Men scrambled in and out of trenches. Aragonia's army seized control of the ground between them. They hewed at the earthen bulwarks with battleaxes to forge passages. They raced over open ground, falling on Carthage's army from the rear.

And in the end, we won.

I never saw the main part of the fray. When the last of the Aragonian army had passed, the surviving Euskerri asked me if we should follow them. We'd lost half our remaining number before the Aragonians had emerged and there wasn't a survivor among them that wasn't trembling with exhaustion. In the aftermath of battle, I could feel a profound weariness settling into my bones.

"No." I shook my head. "We're done."

When we heard the horns blowing a retreat, I wasn't sure who it was signaling. It wasn't until a lone Aragonian rider came racing back bearing the news that we knew. Astegal had been captured alive, brought down by a Euskerri javelin that had struck his helm hard enough to knock him insensible. Additional troops from nearby Coloma had arrived, defying their leaders to join the rebellion.

Pinned between two forces, leaderless, the Carthaginian army had mounted a concerted attack and broken through the western line. Even now, they were fleeing, likely to retreat to New Carthage and make a stand there.

There was cheering from atop the walls of the city and, impossible as it seemed, from the devastated Euskerri. But I was surrounded by dead men, many of whom I'd led into this battle. I was weary and soul-sick, and I couldn't feel aught but a grim relief.

"Is General Liberio pursuing?" I asked.

"No." The courier's battle-grin faded. "We can't afford to. We took too many losses."

"The Euskerri?"

He nodded. "They were hit hard."

The news had spread through the city. It wasn't long before every manner of chirurgeon, physician, and healer in Amílcar came pouring out to tend to the injured. I reckoned my leg could wait and helped as best I could, setting aside my weariness to serve as a bearer for litters ferrying the maimed and wounded to the makeshift infirmary in the park. They'd prepared well; there were hundreds of new tents erected. They would be needed.

The surviving remnant of the army came trickling back, many carrying injured comrades. I missed seeing Astegal escorted into the city with his arms bound behind his back, which I regretted. I kept an eye out for Sidonie and her guard. Their sentries must have reported the news, but I knew she'd be worried for me.

It was nearing sunset when they came. I was sitting with Miquel, the young Euskerri who spoke Aragonian, giving him sips of water from a skin and waiting for a litter. He had a broken spear-head lodged in his ribcage.

I rose when I saw them.

"Go," Miquel said in a hoarse voice. "I'm not going anywhere."

I couldn't, though. All I could do was stand and watch as they rode toward us. No one had even begun to tend to the dead; the task was too enormous. I watched the blood drain from Sidonie's face as she took in the extent of the horror. Her gaze met mine. Not even the relief of finding me alive could alleviate it.

"Gods have mercy," she whispered. "This is victory?"

I couldn't find my voice to answer and I didn't try to stop her when she dismounted, when she reached up to touch my cheek. I needed her too badly. I needed the one bright and shining thing in my life to believe any of this was worthwhile. I wrapped my arms around her and held her close, pressing my face against her hair.

"Cousin," a tired voice said. "You bring us cause to rejoice today."

I looked up to see Serafin L'Envers y Aragon seated on a fine chestnut horse. Aragonian soldiers were bringing the last of the wounded to the city. It was to his credit that he'd not left the battlefield until it was done. I could tell he'd fought hard; his gilded armor was splashed with blood.

Still.

"You're an ambitious man, my lord," I said, releasing Sidonie. "So is Astegal of Carthage. Behold the cost of his ambition. Look on it well. And if you find that greater Aragonia is not so willing as you had believed to anoint you the king's successor, or if you find yourself thinking to break faith with the Euskerri, I bid you remember this sight."

Serafin nodded curtly. "I take your meaning."

"I pray we all do," Sidonie murmured.

SIXTY-FIVE

Once more we were ensconced in the palace of Amílcar.

In the great hall, Lady Nicola wept at the sight of us. "Blessed Elua! Why in the name of all that's holy did the Euskerri insist on sending you back here?"

I shifted, leaning on Sidonie's shoulder. My leg had begun to stiffen and it hurt badly. "Because they are a proud and stubborn folk who don't trust Aragonia. Also a very brave folk. My lady, when your chirurgeon has seen to those in urgent need, I'd be grateful for her attention."

"Of course," Nicola said. "I'll send her immediately."

"Lady Nicola." Sidonie hesitated. "What's to become of Astegal?"

Nicola's face turned grim. "He'll be executed at dawn in the Plaza del Rey on the day after tomorrow. Surely you don't plead for clemency?"

"No," Sidonie said shortly.

"She wanted to kill him with her own hand," I said.

Nicola looked startled, but only for a moment. "I can understand. But he's responsible for the deaths of thousands of

Aragonians. I suspect the council will wish for justice to be administered in the Aragonian fashion."

I felt Sidonie's shoulders tighten beneath my arm. "Then I'll settle for watching him die," she said.

"I can understand that, too," Nicola murmured.

We were given the same room in which we'd been housed before; indeed, the clothes-press still held clean attire that Lady Nicola had provided for us, which was a mercy. Servants came to fill the bath, which was also a mercy.

"Elua!" Sidonie breathed when she unwound the Amazigh scarf and peeled away my blood-soaked breeches. I glanced down. It looked worse than I'd thought, muscle welling in the deep gash. She sank to her knees and covered her face. "No more, please. I can't bear this."

"Love." I grasped her shoulders and raised her. "It's over. After today I never want to draw a sword again, I promise you. Whatever's happening in Terre d'Ange, we'll see it settled peaceably."

Sidonie nodded. "We will."

It was awkward bathing, but I managed; and shortly afterward, the Eisandine chirurgeon Rachel came to tend me. She offered no comment, washing the gash with unwatered wine and sewing it in neat stitches. It hurt like fury. She spread salve over her work and bound it with clean bandages.

"You should take rest," Rachel said when she'd finished. "Stay off it for a week. But you won't, will you?"

I shook my head. "We have to go home."

"*Emmenghanom.*" Rachel said the word softly and smiled at our surprise. "I was one of the people Lady Nicola entrusted with it lest aught go awry. When nations fall, healers are among the first to be spared. Our services are always needed. And I am D'Angeline. My loyalties will always lie with Terre d'Ange."

"Elua willing, the key has already been delivered," Sidonie said. "But we need to be sure. We'll stay to ensure that the accord with the Euskerri is fairly concluded. I gave my word. And then we must go."

Rachel bowed her head. "As you must."

She left us then. I lay on the bed, my head in Sidonie's lap. She ran her fingers through my hair, rhythmic and calming. My leg throbbed. Every part of my body was bruised and aching. Behind my closed eyelids, I saw only carnage. Myself in the midst of a raging storm of violence, my sword rising and falling. Men dying. I'd no idea how many I'd killed that day. But I'd a good idea of how many I'd led to their deaths.

"Do you wish to speak of it?" Sidonie asked in a low voice.

"No." I concentrated on the soothing feeling of her hands stroking my hair. "One day. But not today."

"One day," she echoed.

"One day," I agreed, my eyes still closed. "One day we'll tell our horde of brooding boys and haughty girls how their parents fought for freedom against a man who would be a tyrant. One day we'll discuss the terrible price the Euskerri were willing to pay for their own freedom. One day it will make a wondrous tale, Princess." I opened my eyes and gazed at her inverted face. "But not today."

"No." Sidonie leaned down to kiss me. Her lips lingered on mine, soft and sweet, a promise of Blessed Elua's mercy. "Not today."

I sighed and slept.

On the morrow we learned further details. The losses were staggering, especially among the Euskerri. Of the nearly six thousand who had gone into battle, no more than fifteen hundred survived. The troops from Tibado and Coloma had taken heavy losses, too. Until the forces from Amílcar had arrived, it had been very nearly what I feared—a slaughter. But in the end Carthage hadn't fared much better. They hadn't been prepared for the speed and ferocity of the attack on their rearguard. Astegal's troops had been slow to respond to orders. Duke Leopoldo of Tibado had taken advantage of the confusion and rallied his men, and the Euskerri had done the same. Carthage found itself caught between the hammer and the anvil. When Astegal had fallen, their resolve broke.

I thought about Astegal in New Carthage, playing at being a king. Feasting and tossing coins to dancing-girls in the evenings, sparring and jesting with his men in the palaestra during the days. I remembered what Kratos had said. If Astegal had been more diligent in drilling his army, he might have been victorious yesterday.

The war wasn't over. Astegal's wounded army would retreat to New Carthage, where they held the city and a good number of potential hostages. We'd arisen to find that the navy blockading Amílcar's harbor had fled, likely for the same destination.

But Bodeshmun was dead and Astegal soon would be. It was the arcane skills of the former and the determined ambition of the latter that had driven Carthage to seek empire. There had been men uneasy with the scope of Astegal's goals. After my time there as Leander Maignard, I thought there was a chance the matter could be resolved diplomatically.

I prayed so.

There was a ceremony that afternoon to mark the historic transfer of sovereignty to Euskerria. It broke my heart to see how few of the village headmen who had pledged their acceptance in Roncal were there to see it.

Serafin spoke well. "There has long been enmity between our people," he said. "Yesterday that history was erased in a tide of blood. If we take no other lesson from this tragedy, let it be this: We have learned we are alike. We suffer and bleed alike. We grieve alike for our lost brethren. And we value our freedom above our safety." He paused. "Euskerria has earned the freedom we bestow on her this day. As you well know, it is not wholly mine to give on behalf of Aragonia. But I pledge to you on behalf of all here assembled that we will accept no terms that do not honor this agreement. And that which Euskerria has earned that *is* mine to grant, I pledge freely. My friendship, honor, and respect."

There were tears in the eyes of many of the Euskerri present when his words were translated. One of them rose to speak.

"Yesterday we gained a nation and lost the flower of a generation," he said simply in accented Aragonian. "We will strive to make Euskerria into a nation worthy of their sacrifice."

"Your highness?" Ramiro Zornín de Aragon said to Sidonie.

She rose. "On behalf of Terre d'Ange, this concord is heard and witnessed. Like my kinsman, I lack the full weight of authority to speak for my country. But as I am my mother's heir, I swear in the name of Blessed Elua and his Companions that while my memory lives, I will do all in my power to see that this accord is kept in good faith."

So it was done.

There was no rejoicing among the Euskerri; the cost had been too high. And Amílcar was a city torn between victory and loss, aware of the struggle that lay ahead. But it was done.

Afterward I yielded to wisdom and retired to my bed to ease my leg. The wound appeared clean enough, but it felt as though someone were holding a hot poker to my thigh. And I reckoned if there were any folk who could be trusted to make travel arrangements with swift efficiency, it was Sidonie and Lady Nicola. I slept fitfully and woke to find Sidonie perched on the side of the bed and gazing at me.

"Well?" I asked.

She smiled for the first time in days. "I found Captain Deimos. With Lady Nicola's aid, he's procured a new ship and reassembled his crew, and he's willing to carry us to Marsilikos."

I pushed myself upright. "Truly?"

"Truly," Sidonie said. "He's impatient to be free of Amílcar and he thinks the seas will be calm enough. He also thinks your mother will have his head if he doesn't see you home safely."

"That's good news," I said. "Did you find Kratos?"

"Oh, yes." Her smile deepened. "He was very excited. He embraced me and turned fifty shades of red while apologizing for the importunity. His burns are well on their way to healing. He wishes to travel to Terre d'Ange with us and plans to meet us tomorrow."

"Can Deimos make ready to sail on the morrow?" I asked.

"He thinks so," she said. "At least by noon."

"After Astegal's execution," I said.

Sidonie took my hand. "I spent an hour in the infirmary visiting the wounded. It's . . ." She shook her head. "It's awful, Imriel. I'm willing to cede my own need for vengeance. But I need to see him die. For everything he did." She was quiet a moment. "I talked to several of Duke Leopoldo's men in the infirmary. Paskal fought alongside them after he brought word of our plan. One of them remembered seeing him slain on the battlefield. And I asked after Captain Aureliano and his men, the ones who helped us escape. They never returned."

"Ah, Elua!" I whispered.

"I know." Sidonie sighed with sorrow and regret. "Do you know, I begin to understand my mother better. I pray to Blessed Elua that the likes of this never comes again in our lifetimes. But if one of our haughty girls declared herself in love with Astegal's son, I suspect my reaction would be less than rational."

I squeezed her hand. "Your father tried to tell me as much."

"He's a wise man," she murmured.

My throat tightened. "Are you sorry?"

"About you?" Sidonie gave me a quick look. "No! Gods, no. About a thousand other things, yes. I wish I'd had the courage to trust in Blessed Elua's precept years ago and defy my mother. I wish I'd argued more forcefully against letting Bodeshmun show us his damned marvel. I wish I didn't have the weight of thousands of dead Euskerri on my conscience." She freed her hand and laid it on my breast. "But I will never, ever regret loving you."

"Nor I," I said.

"Always and always," Sidonie said. "I understand more, that's all."

"All knowledge is worth having," I observed. "So on the morrow we watch Astegal die, then sail for home?"

She nodded. "That's the plan."

Sixty-six

We greeted the dawn in the Plaza del Rey.

There was a massive crowd in the main square at the center of Amílcar. Everyone in the city—everyone within ten leagues of the city—wanted to see Astegal of Carthage executed.

A certain macabre enthusiasm pervaded the square. I understood it, although I didn't share it. Not quite. It wasn't just that I'd had my surfeit of death. I *did* want to see Astegal die. He'd earned his death a thousand times over. But I would take no joy in it. As with Amílcar's hard-won victory, there would be only a grim satisfaction.

It would be done.

Finished.

The skies were still leaden when we assembled. Sidonie and I would be very close to the executioner's block, standing with Lady Nicola and her husband and son, with the council members and Duke Leopoldo of Tibado, his weathered face seamed by a sword-cut. There were a good many of the walking wounded in that crowd. I myself leaned on a gilt-headed walking stick that the chirurgeon Rachel had procured for me, and I was grateful for its aid.

Dawn broke in the east, streaking the skies with fire. Along the route from the palace's dungeon, drums began to beat. The crowd chanted.

"As-te-gal! As-te-gal!"

I glanced at Sidonie; her chin lifted, her profile achingly pure. "Are you all right, love?"

She nodded, wordless and pale.

The executioner waited, his heavy broadsword angled over his shoulder. His face was impassive. The wooden block, with a niche for Astegal to lay his neck, sat at his feet. I thought about Berlik kneeling in the swirling snow, baring his neck for my blade. This was different, so different. When all was said and done, I'd understood why Berlik did what he did. Why he'd killed Dorelei, why he'd killed our unborn son. And I had wept for his death.

No one here would weep for Astegal.

The drums continued beating, steady and unrelenting. The blood beat in my veins. A rush of sound in my ears, a bronze clash of wings. I saw Astegal of Carthage drawing near.

His hands were bound behind his back beneath his battle-frayed purple cloak, but his head was high, his eyes glaring. Proud. He was a proud man. The crowd pushed and shoved, clamoring for his blood. Astegal ignored them. There was only one person his gaze sought. As the guards ordered Astegal to halt before the executioner, Sidonie took a step forward.

I would to Elua she hadn't.

Everyone there knew the tale that lay between them. A hush fell over the crowd. And in that moment, Astegal moved, quick and sure. His shoulders jerked and the ropes binding his wrists parted and snapped. Somehow he'd managed to fray his bonds during his imprisonment and hide his handiwork. Astegal grabbed the executioner's sword by the blade with his bare hand and wrested it from him, heedless of the wound it inflicted. In two swift strides, he seized Sidonie and held her pinned against him, the blade to her throat.

"Don't!" Astegal shouted at the surging guards. His face was suffused with rage. "She'll be dead before you can strike!"

My head rang.

"Hold!" Serafin ordered the guards. He ground his teeth. "What the hell do you think to accomplish, Carthaginian?"

"I am a Prince of the House of Sarkal and I'll not be executed like some common galley slave," Astegal spat. "Bring me a horse or I'll cut her throat."

I gazed at Sidonie. She wasn't struggling; he had the blade pressed hard enough to her flesh that a thin line of blood was visible. But she wasn't frightened, either. She was furious. Our eyes met and the ringing in my head quieted, leaving a strange sense of calm in its wake.

I dropped my walking-stick and stepped forward. "Let her go, Astegal."

"You!" His eyes widened. "How?"

I'd forgotten Astegal didn't know. "I've been here for a while. You knew me as Leander Maignard in New Carthage. Your cousin Bodeshmun isn't the only man on this earth to master sorcery." I drew my sword. "Let her go, and I'll grant you what you don't deserve. A warrior's death."

He bared his teeth at me. "I think not."

"Look around you, Astegal." I gestured with my blade. Members of Vitor Gaitán's Harbor Watch had pushed through the crowd to surround us, crossbows drawn and trained on Astegal. "You're a dead man. Do you think you can mount a horse without withdrawing that sword from Sidonie's throat?"

"Then we'll walk," Astegal said grimly. "My dear *wife* and I."

Sidonie's eyes flashed with fury.

Elua help me, I almost smiled. "All the way to New Carthage?" I asked. "Then you'd best not lower your blade for an instant, because one of us will be there to kill you the moment you do. And you'd best not sleep, because Sidonie will slit your throat herself." I watched the knowledge sink into him and spread my arms. "Come. Surely you're not afraid?"

"Of a man half-crippled?" he asked in contempt. "Ba'al have mercy, no." Astegal tightened the blade against Sidonie's throat. "Make it worth my while, D'Angeline. Because right now, I've no reason to do aught but die knowing I caused you grief."

"All right." I nodded. "Kill me and you'll be given a sporting chance to live. A swift horse and an hour's lead."

The crowd had been spell-bound and silent, but that raised a gasp. "You can't make that offer," Serafin said in a tight voice. "Aragonia will not countenance it."

I looked at him. "I won't lose."

There were a hundred debates we could have had, but I couldn't marshal the will to argue them. The ringing in my head had quieted, but I could feel Kushiel's presence over me like a mantle. This was what I was meant to do. I was as certain of that as I'd ever been of anything in my life. And Serafin L'Envers y Aragon was half D'Angeline. There was Kusheline blood in the line of House L'Envers. He returned my gaze for a long moment, and mayhap the bronze wings beat faintly in his blood, because in time he nodded.

"A swift horse and an hour," Serafin said. "I swear it."

There was a roar of protest at his words, but Astegal jerked the blade again. Blood trickled down Sidonie's throat and she closed her eyes. The roar faded. "I don't trust you," Astegal said to Serafin.

Serafin shrugged. "Bring him a horse."

It was done. I watched Astegal weigh the decision, wondering if he could trust Serafin's word, wondering if there was some other way. I picked my words carefully, driving them like a wedge into the fault-lines on his soul. "I killed your kinsman, Astegal. I watched Bodeshmun die. I led your Amazigh into ambush and killed three of them with my own hand. Are you sure you're not afraid?"

He lowered the sword and shoved Sidonie violently from him. "Come and see!"

Fingers tightened on the triggers of crossbows. "Hold!" Serafin shouted. "Give him his chance!"

"Are you all right?" I asked Sidonie, steadying her.

"Yes."

"Good." I kissed her lips and went to fight her husband.

Astegal was waiting for me. He'd wrapped his cloak around his left arm to serve as a makeshift shield. The end was dangling and I thought he might try to use it to foul my blade or distract me. He had the hilt of the executioner's sword firmly gripped in his bleeding right hand. I wished I'd donned my vambraces and I wished my leg didn't hurt so damnably much. It would slow me down, and my speed had always been one of my advantages. Astegal was reasonably quick, too. I'd seen him spar. And he was a tall man. He had a few inches of reach on me.

I looked forward to killing him.

He circled around to my left, angling to get the rising sun in my eyes. It made me smile. Elua knew, Astegal wasn't going to defeat me that way. I pivoted right on my good leg and positioned myself behind him. He jumped to face me before I had a chance to land a blow.

"What the hell are you smiling at?" Astegal growled.

"You," I said simply.

His left arm snaked forward, folds of cloak unwinding in the direction of my face. I ignored it and parried the low thrust I knew would come beneath it. His breathing quickened as he took a step backward and rewound his cloak around his arm. For the first time, I saw fear in him.

We traded a few blows, testing one another. If Astegal had had a shield, we might have been evenly matched. We weren't. I didn't press him yet. I didn't want to risk making any mistakes, fearful that my leg would give out beneath me if I made a careless move. But when I parried his blows with ease, I saw the realization dawn on him that he was truly in grave danger.

He was good with a sword.

I was better.

Still, Astegal was a fighter. He sought to goad me as I'd goaded him, sending a pointed glance in Sidonie's direction.

"Very romantic, seeking to defend your beloved," he said smoothly. "She's a wanton little thing, isn't she?"

I didn't answer.

He essayed a quick jab at my face, hoping to force me off balance. I held my ground and parried, sweeping his blade to one side. "So willing and eager," Astegal said, taking a step backward to regroup. He licked his lips. "She tastes sweet like honey."

I kept silent, holding my sword angled before me.

Astegal's expression hardened. He came at me fast and our blades crossed and locked. Both of us strained for leverage. My left leg trembled. I tensed my muscles and willed it to steadiness. He leaned toward me, close as a lover. "She suckled my root like no one has ever done," he whispered in a confidential tone. "I miss that."

I held my tongue.

Patience.

"Betimes . . ." Astegal raised his voice. "Betimes when I was finished with her, she would beg me for more." The crowd around us murmured. He searched my face for a reaction and found none. I felt frustration weaken his resolve and took a quick step backward, resettling myself. "Gods!" Astegal spread his arms slightly, dropping his guard. "And you call yourself a *man*?"

I plunged my sword hilt-deep into his belly. "I do."

Astegal's mouth gaped. The executioner's sword dropped from his nerveless right hand. For a moment he merely stood and swayed. Then he sank slowly to his knees. And as he sank, I withdrew my blade with a ruthless wrench.

"All that passion you're so quick to boast of didn't belong to you, Astegal," I said in a cold voice. "It never did. You took it and twisted it to your own ends, you and Bodeshmun. And I will tell you what I told him while I watched him die. It is not wise to meddle with D'Angelines in matters of love."

On his knees, Astegal grimaced and clutched the wound in his belly with both hands, holding his entrails in place. "You promised me a warrior's death," he said hoarsely. "Grant me the mercy of the battlefield and make it swift."

"Mercy." I placed the tip of my blood-stained blade over his heart. "Mercy is not mine to grant." I turned my head toward Sidonie and addressed her formally. She was my beloved, but she was also the Dauphine of Terre d'Ange. "Your highness?"

If there was anyone present who would have denied her the right, they stayed silent. I would have given her the sword if she had wished. Instead, Sidonie approached and laid her hand over mine on the hilt.

We would do this together.

She gazed down at Astegal. When she spoke, her voice

was cool and venomous. "How fitting that in the end you should plead for the sweet release of one final thrust."

Astegal didn't reply. Through the pain that racked his features, I saw a complex mix of emotions: anger, shame, bitterness, and regret. I couldn't see Sidonie's expression, and mayhap it was just as well.

Sidonie's hand tightened on mine.

Together we drove the blade home and granted Astegal mercy. I could feel a shudder the length of the blade as he died. Sidonie never flinched.

Sixty-seven

On the heels of Astegal's death, there was a great outcry of bloodthirsty cheers in the plaza. It hadn't been Aragonian justice, but it had been a spectacle beyond their wildest dreams. The executioner dragged Astegal's lifeless body into place, positioning his head on the chopping-block. He retrieved his sword with grim determination and hewed Astegal's head from his body.

At that Sidonie turned away and hid her face against my chest. I held her gently. Astegal would have been a tyrant, but she'd believed herself in love with him for long months. In the beginning she had seen glimmers of nobility in him about which she still wondered.

I understood.

The executioner mounted Astegal's head on a long pike. I found myself thinking once more of Berlik. He'd looked peaceful in death. Astegal didn't. He looked sad and foolish, his face fixed in a grimace. His mouth hung open, his narrow crimson beard looking like blood drooling over his chin. His heavy-lidded eyes were half-open, showing the whites.

"Behold!" Serafin L'Envers y Aragon shouted. "*This* is the fate of those who would seek to conquer Aragonia!"

The crowd roared their approval. Sidonie shivered and raised her head.

"Are you—" I began.

"I'm all right," she said. "Or I will be." She searched my face. "You could have killed him cleanly, couldn't you?"

"Yes." I didn't elaborate.

"You keep your promises," Sidonie murmured. "Thank you."

"Shall we go home?" I asked.

She nodded. "Please."

It was a few hours before we were able to depart. Captain Deimos didn't have his new ship in full readiness. Lady Nicola insisted that her chirurgeon tend to the cut Astegal had inflicted on Sidonie's throat. It wasn't serious, but it was deep enough to warrant bandaging.

"I am so perishing *sick* of blood," Sidonie said as I washed the dried residue from her throat and chest while we waited for Rachel.

"So am I, love," I said. "So am I."

It was a bit before noon when Kratos came from the harbor to report that Deimos' ship was ready to sail. I greeted him with pleasure. His blunt, homely face was filled with awe.

"I wasn't able to get close enough to see," Kratos said. "But I heard how you killed that bastard."

"It's done," Sidonie said.

"Done, and done well." He pointed a thick finger at her. "You and my lord here did exactly what was needful. Don't you ever be ashamed of it, your highness. Not for one instant of one day."

It made her smile, which gladdened me. "Thank you,

Kratos. I'm not. I just want to go home and see my own country safe."

A sizable party assembled to escort us to the harbor. We said our farewells there on the docks. Another leavetaking, but at least this one wasn't fraught with deadly peril. Elua willing, we would live to see one another again in times of peace.

"We will pray that the news be swift and joyous," Lady Nicola said. "For all our sakes. It will be much easier to effect a diplomatic resolution with Carthage if Terre d'Ange stands behind us once more."

"We will do our best to make it so," Sidonie promised.

In the end there was little left to say that hadn't already been said. We boarded the ship and Captain Deimos gave the order to raise the anchor. The rowers leaned their backs over the banks of oars. Within a few minutes, we were under way, leaving the harbor we'd entered in flames. Sidonie and Kratos and I stood on the deck and watched the figures on shore dwindle.

"Terre d'Ange!" Kratos marveled. "Not a sight I ever thought to see."

Sidonie looked worried. "Pray we find her whole."

It was a slow journey. The sea was far more calm than when we'd essayed it before and the winds less forbidding, but it was still rough going. Deimos kept us in sight of land and we crawled up the coast of Aragonia. During the days, Sidonie and I passed the time by beginning to teach Kratos the rudiments of D'Angeline.

The nights, we had to ourselves.

On the first night, she was quiet and withdrawn. I let her be and waited for her to speak. She'd learned what it was like to feel a man die by her hand that day. No matter how much Astegal had deserved his death, it was a grave thing. And I had a good idea that it wasn't the only thing troubling her.

"I keep thinking on it," Sidonie said at length. "Watching him die. Betimes it sickens me. And then I think about what he said to you today . . ." Her jaw tightened. "And I wish I could kill him all over again."

"He said it only to goad me," I said.

Her shoulders moved in a slight shrug. "It was true, though."

"I know." I ran a lock of her hair through my fingers. "I know, love. And I'm so very sorry for it. I swear, while there is breath in my body, I will never suffer anyone to hurt you again in word or deed."

She sighed. "Do you suppose that when we tell our brooding, haughty horde the glorious tale of their parents' exploits, we might leave that part out of it?"

I smiled in the dim light of the cabin. "I think we might."

The following day dawned as fair as the previous one. I hobbled through my Cassiline exercises on the deck, reckoning it was better to keep the muscles of my leg from stiffening. Sidonie commented on the likely folly of such a notion, but she didn't try to dissuade me. Instead she watched. As I told the hours, I caught glimpses of her standing against the railing, the sea breeze tugging at her honey-gold hair and the pretty blue scarf Lady Nicola had given her to hide the bandage around her throat. When I finished, I limped over to join her.

"You look pained," she observed.

"It hurts," I admitted.

Sidonie cocked her head. "How badly?"

I felt the blood quicken in my veins. "If you're asking what I think, not *that* badly, Sun Princess."

"You promised me a hundred thousand nights if Blessed Elua spared you." She took my right hand in hers and raised it to her lips, kissing my knuckles. "Imriel, Astegal is dead.

Whatever he said, whatever he did, whatever *I* did . . . it doesn't matter. It's over. And I mean to begin putting it behind me."

"With my help?" I inquired.

She nodded gravely, but there was a wicked spark of humor and passion lurking deep in her black eyes—still there, wondrously unextinguished. "Oh, yes. A great deal of it."

The days passed slowly.

The nights fled.

It was a strange time, suspended between one thing and another. Both of us were grateful to be alive. Both of us were fearful of what we would find in Terre d'Ange. We were both haunted by our memories. Some of them, like our flight from New Carthage and the terrible carnage outside the walls of Amílcar, were shared. Some weren't. Sidonie bore the stigma of her time as Astegal's willing bride. And the nearer we drew to Terre d'Ange, the more I remembered my time of madness there, the awful things I'd said to those I loved.

But we were able to lose ourselves in each other.

It was a gift of Blessed Elua, and of Naamah, whose blessing I'd sought before our first liaison. I felt their presence attendant on our love-making, which was by turns tender and violent. Once nights had been my bane, the province of bloody nightmares that woke me screaming.

Now they were my joy.

It lasted all the way up the coast of Aragonia and well after we'd passed the mountains and caught sight of Terre d'Ange's coastline, a sight that made my heart swell. It lasted until the morning we drew near the mouth of the Aviline River and saw a fleet of dozens of war-ships clustered there, anchored offshore outside the harbor of Pellasus. The town was smaller than Marsilikos, but it did a lively trade with ships bound up the Aviline. These weren't trade-ships and the pennants flying from their masts were not the silver swan of House Courcel, but solely the lily-and-stars of Terre d'Ange itself.

"What does that mean?" I asked Sidonie.

She wore her troubled look. "I'd say it's an indication that they're not in the service of the Crown. It's not an auspicious sign. Do you think Nuno failed to deliver the key?"

I shook my head. "I don't know."

One of them raised its sails and hailed us, heading out in our direction. "Your highness?" Captain Deimos inquired. "What will you?"

Sidonie and I exchanged a glance. "If the country's still torn apart, we're better off dealing with those *not* in the Crown's service," I said. "And it's not as though we could outrun an entire fleet."

"Wait for them," she said to Deimos.

We lowered our sails and waited as the D'Angeline war-ship made its way alongside us. I felt ungodly tense, and although Sidonie's face was composed, I knew she felt the same way.

"Hey!" A sturdy fellow aboard the war-ship shouted through cupped hands in crude Aragonian. "What passes? Is anyone speak D'Angeline?" And then the ship drew nearer, the gap closing between us. He caught sight of Sidonie and me. His hands fell and he stared. Everyone on the war-ship stared.

Separately, they might not have known us, not for a surety. None of them had seen us before. But I bore the unmistakable stamp of House Shahrizai on my face, and Sidonie looked enough like her mother that they'd seen the like of her profile on a thousand coins.

And we were together.

The war-ship drew alongside and men scrambled to secure the ships—ours heedless of the stares, theirs wondering.

"Who's in command?" I called.

A brown-haired man in the tattered jacket of the Royal Navy approached the railing. "Captain Henri Voisin," he said hesitantly. "Your highness?"

"Imriel de la Courcel," I said in confirmation. "We come bringing her highness Sidonie de la Courcel, the Dauphine of Terre d'Ange, home."

"So I see." Henri Voisin's gaze slid toward Sidonie. "Is she . . . ?"

"Sane?" Sidonie inquired. "Mercifully, yes. What passes here, my lord?"

His expression was torn between hope and doubt. "A great deal. We thought you were a ship out of Aragonia. You're flying Aragonian flags. We hoped you'd have news."

"We do," Sidonie said. "Come aboard and we'll share it in exchange for yours."

With some difficulty, Voisin made the crossing. He was breathing hard as he clambered over the railing onto our ship. The realization that our crew was not Aragonian did nothing to alleviate his trepidation. I couldn't blame him. Insofar as I was aware, the last he knew of either of us, Sidonie had gone off to wed Astegal, and I'd vanished after screaming my throat raw in a month-long fit of madness. Still, he gathered himself and made a careful bow. "Well met, your highnesses."

"And you, my lord," Sidonie said. "Tell me, who do you serve?" He didn't answer. "Is Terre d'Ange at war?"

"No," Henri Voisin said. "Not yet."

"But it's divided? And growing worse?" She read the answer in his face. "Who do you serve? My mother or my sister?"

His throat worked. The fact that the question could put a man in fear made my blood run cold. "Your sister."

"So the City of Elua remains under a foul enchantment?" she asked. "No key to undoing the madness was found?"

The D'Angeline captain licked his lips, glancing from one to the other of us. "No. There was some talk, some wild rumors of magic, after . . ." He nodded at me. "After you vanished, your highness. But it came to naught."

"Let me be swift," Sidonie said. "There *was* a spell cast, a dire spell. I was bound by it myself. It was Imriel who freed me from it." I started, struck by an awful realization. Sidonie continued. "Since then, we have been working to undo what was done. Carthage's forces were dealt a grievous defeat at Amílcar. General Astegal is dead." Her face hardened. "Even now, his head adorns a pike in the Plaza del Rey. And Imriel and I possess the key to undoing the spell that binds the City of Elua and all who were in it that fateful night."

"Sidonie." I touched her arm. "You can't go ashore."

She stared at me. "What?"

I felt sick. "I'm a fool. In all that's happened, I forgot. You're free of the spell that had you believing yourself in love with Astegal. The one that was worked on you alone. Not the other, not the *ghafrid-gebla*. The demon-stone." I could see Henri Voisin's expression out of the corner of my eye and I realized I sounded mad, but it couldn't be helped. "Ptolemy Solon said it would reassert itself if you—or anyone—returned to D'Angeline soil."

Sidonie closed her eyes. "Ah, gods!"

Sixty-eight

If it hadn't been for what had befallen Drustan mab Necthana earlier in the year, I daresay Henri Voisin would never have given full credence to our tale.

It wasn't swift. In the end, all of us talked ourselves dry. Sidonie and I related the entire tale of what we had endured. In turn, Voisin told us what had happened in our absence.

Some of it, we knew. Barquiel L'Envers had raised a delegation and sent for Alais. She'd come. All together, they'd sought to persuade Ysandre and Drustan that they and the entire City were ensorceled. Ysandre had declared them in rebellion against the Crown. Alais and L'Envers had retreated to Turnone and begun the reluctant work of raising an army. Since late autumn, Alais had served as the de facto ruler of Terre d'Ange, aided by a shadow Parliament of lords and ladies from the Lesser Houses, with L'Envers serving as her Royal Commander. Throughout much of the realm, Turnone was regarded as the new seat of rule.

The Royal Army was ensconced in the City of Elua, guarding it fiercely. Quintilius Rousse and his six ships were blockading the harbor of Marsilikos, monitoring who came and went. L'Envers had ordered Henri Voisin and his ships, those who had not been present in the City the night of the marvel, to ward the mouth of the Aviline River, fearing an assault from Carthage should they prevail in Aragonia.

As far as an incised emerald gem went, Voisin knew nothing.

But what he did know was that Drustan mab Necthana had returned to Alba with the intention of bringing an Alban army to Terre d'Ange to support the Queen. And there, his wits had cleared.

Until he returned to Terre d'Ange with a larger force at his back, bent on talking sense into Ysandre.

"It's only rumors," Voisin said. "But they say the Cruarch went mad again once they landed. Him and the honor guard that had travelled with him the first time. When his officers tried to reason with him, he accused them of treason and lit out for the City with his guards. No one tried to stop him."

"It's the spell," I murmured. "It's malevolent at its core."

"Mayhap," he said cautiously. "As her highness said, matters are growing worse." He paused, then delivered the worst news yet. "Last week, at the spring equinox, her majesty issued a threat." He spoke the words as though they pained him. "She said if her highness Alais and your uncle and every man and woman aiding them did not surrender and plead for clemency by the next full moon, she would declare war on them."

I stared at him in shock. "That soon? Was she serious?"

"I don't know," Voisin said. "But I'm afraid it's possible."

"Ah, gods! That means we've precious little time. We need to talk to Alais and my uncle," Sidonie muttered. "We need to *know*. We don't dare ride blind into the City of Elua."

"You *can't*, love," I observed. "I'll have to go alone."

Her eyes glittered. "Is there no way?"

I opened my mouth to say no, and my thoughts went to the croonie-stone I carried in my purse—smooth and polished granite, a hole at its center. A reminder of what I had endured. A reminder of what I had lost—Dorelei and our son. I remembered its weight around my neck, the bindings of red thread around my wrists and ankles. Alban magic. It had been given me by an *ollamh*. It had protected me from the power of a talisman wrought of my own aching desire.

I didn't know if it would protect her.

"Mayhap," I said, as cautious as Henri Voisin.

"Tell me," Sidonie demanded.

I told her.

Henri Voisin looked sickly fascinated by it all. I don't know how much of it he believed. Enough to give us a chance.

"I mean to try it," Sidonie said with grim determination. "If it works, so much the better. Our stories are stronger together. If it fails . . ." She lifted her shoulders in a shrug. "I'm the only one it will affect. I give you leave to overpower me and haul me back to Amílcar. At least it will give proof to our claims."

"You're sure?" I asked.

She nodded. "We have to try. My lord captain, will you hear my orders?"

He gave her a dubious look. "I'll hear them."

"I would have you keep our presence here quiet for the time. Bid your men to do the same. Find us a discreet escort to Turnone, then take your fleet to Amílcar," Sidonie said in a steady tone. "With or without me, depending on how matters fall. There's naught to be done at sea here. I would have Terre d'Ange honor her alliances. The presence of a D'Angeline fleet will hasten negotiations with a weakened Carthage."

It heartened him. "I believe your sister and uncle would agree."

"Good." She looked at me. "Shall we attempt the charm?"

I racked my wits, trying to remember the items the *ollamh* Aodhan had used when he wrought the charm of protection that warded me against all who sought to bind me. "I need salt. Salt, and rowan and birchwood." I closed my eyes, grateful for Phèdre's training, and recalled the scent of camphor. "And pennyroyal. Oh, and red thread, of course."

"Of course," Henri Voisin echoed doubtfully.

In the end, he had to return and put ashore to collect some of the items—and failed to find them at that. Salt, we had aboard the ship, and Sidonie picked red threads out of the Euskerri wedding dress that Bixenta had given her, braiding several lengths. Voisin found incense imbued with oil of pennyroyal in a small Temple of Azza, but rowan and birch were a lost cause. He returned with dried bundles of juniper and wild rosemary instead, claiming an old herb-wife in the marketplace insisted they held protective properties.

"It's worth a try," I said.

There was a stone firebox on the deck of the ship used for what little cooking was done; mostly we subsisted on sailor's fare of hard biscuits and salt cod. I kindled a fire with the fragrant wood under Captain Deimos' watchful eye and cast a handful of incense on it. I had Sidonie remove her shoes and stockings and stand barefooted on the deck while I poured a line of salt around her in a circle. Henri Voisin and his men watched the proceedings as though we were absolutely mad, for which I didn't blame them; but Deimos and the Cytherans took the matter in stride. They served Ptolemy Solon.

Kratos merely shrugged. "After what I've seen, I'll believe most anything."

"I don't recall the exact words of the invocation," I said to Sidonie. "But I'm praying it doesn't matter. When Firdha had to renew my bindings, her invocation wasn't exactly the same as Aodhan's. She said it was due to differences between the traditions of the Dalriada and the Cruithne. But they both worked."

"Do as you think best," Sidonie said, her face pale.

I knelt and bowed my head before I began. I prayed silently to Blessed Elua and his Companions that they would guide my hand this day. And I prayed to all the gods of Alba, great and small, that they would lend me their magic. I had honored them and done my duty as a Prince of Alba in joy and in sorrow, and Sidonie was the Cruarch's eldest daughter. I prayed to Dorelei's merciful shade to intercede with Alba's gods on our behalf. I prayed they would listen. I held the solid weight of the *ollamh*'s croonie-stone in my hand and prayed that it retained enough of Aodhan's magic and learning to anchor my fumbling spell.

I thought of Berlik bidding me do my duty with a humble heart, and I prayed to sea and stone and sky as the Maghuin Dhonn did. I prayed that there was some debt owed for the honorable death I'd granted him.

I made my heart humble.

I prayed without words for a miracle.

And then I began.

"*The charm of Nerthus ward thee, the charm of Lug defend thee, the charm of Brigit protect thee, the charm of Crom shield thee,*" I chanted. There was a faint stirring in the air. The trickling smoke rising from the fire smelled sharp and pungent. I thought it would be meet to include the gods of Terre d'Ange. "*Blessed Elua and his Companions hold thee and keep thee from all harm.*"

I circled her three times. "*To ward thee from the back,*" I said, tying the red threads around her right wrist. "*To guard thee from the front.*" I tied another length around her left wrist, then stooped and did the same to her ankles. "*From the crown of thy head to the sole of thy foot, be thou protected.*"

I stood and hung the croonie-stone around her neck, its weight settling into place. "*From all that seeks to bind thee, be thou protected!*"

I clapped my hands as Aodhan had done.

Unlike me, Sidonie didn't jump. "Is that all? Is it done?"

"All I can remember," I admitted. "I think so. Do you feel anything?"

"No." She shook her head. "But then I suppose I wouldn't, would I? Not until I set foot ashore."

I rubbed my sweating palms on my thighs, then began to scoop up the circle of salt, giving it back to the sea from whence it had come. "I reckon we'll find out."

Henri Voisin returned to his ship and preceded us. We would be putting ashore at the harbor of Pellasus. Voisin would secure the harbor and procure an escort from among his men, then signal us to make landfall.

I spoke to Captain Deimos and thanked him for his service, which had gone so far beyond aught he could have imagined when he gave his oath to Ptolemy Solon. "I'll ask no more of you, my lord," I said to him. "Return to Cythera and tell my mother you saw me safely delivered to Terre d'Ange." I hesitated. "And . . . thank her for me."

Deimos smiled wryly. "Mothers, eh?"

In the matter of Melisande, it was such an understatement it made me smile in return. "Tell her I'll send word when I can, Elua willing," I said, surprising myself by meaning it. "As well as a generous reward for you and your men. Terre d'Ange owes you a great debt."

He put out his hand. "Luck, your highness. I gather you'll yet have need of it."

I clasped it. "Safe travels to you."

I spoke to Kratos, too, giving him one last opportunity to return to Cythera with Deimos and his men to take service with my mother rather than continue on into unknown danger with Sidonie and me.

"You'd be safe," I said. "I've no doubt my mother would be delighted by you. And they speak Hellene."

Kratos looked at me as though I'd gone mad. "My lord, after all this, do you think I'd miss seeing the tale through to its end?" He shook his greying head. "Oh, no! Besides, without me, you'd still be trying to figure out how to get that damned ring off Astegal's finger."

I smiled. "All right, my friend."

It was late in the afternoon before Henri Voisin's ship signaled us, the slanting sun turning the harbor's waters to gold. The oarsmen brought us to the wharf and secured the ship's moorings. The ship rocked gently on the protected waters. Voisin was waiting ashore. He had managed to clear the harbor of onlookers and to procure an unmarked carriage and mounts and pack-horses for a dozen men.

"Resourceful fellow," I commented.

Sidonie shivered beside me as the gangplank was lowered. "If the charm doesn't work, you promise you'll send me back to Amílcar no matter how much I rage and protest?"

"I promise," I said.

"I don't want to lose you again," she said. "I don't want to lose *me* again."

"Sidonie." I grasped her shoulders. "You don't have to do this. I have the key. *Emmenghanom.* I have Bodeshmun's foul talisman in my purse. You can go back to Amílcar with Voisin and his men. Or even stay anchored in the harbor if he's willing to spare a ship."

"I can't." She looked past me at the land beyond the city,

the gentle hills beginning to green with the advent of spring. "What if we're both needed, Imriel? I have to try."

I released her with a sigh. "As you will."

We said our farewells to Captain Deimos and his men. Henri Voisin and his were waiting. Better if we didn't delay. Every minute gave rumor a chance to spread. Kratos went before us, carrying the trunk that held our few possessions and lashing it to the carriage.

Sidonie caught my hand in a terrified grip. Her face was white, black eyes stark. "Let's find out."

We descended.

Nothing happened when we stepped onto the wooden docks. When we stepped off the dock onto the cobbled stones of the harbor square, her body jerked and her hand tightened on mine. "They itch and burn," Sidonie said in wonderment. She lifted her free hand and regarded the binding of red thread around her wrist. "And this . . ." She touched the croonie-stone lying in the hollow of her throat. "It feels heavy."

My throat tightened. "And you?"

She let go my hand and reached up to cup my face, kissing me in answer.

She knew me.

She knew herself.

I kissed her back with relieved, desperate ardor, then lifted my head to find that every D'Angeline sailor in the harbor had gone to one knee and bowed their heads. To her. To *us*. I saw tears in Sidonie's eyes.

"Your highnesses." Henri Voisin rose to his feet, his face grave. "I am not entirely certain what has transpired here this day, but I sense the hand of Blessed Elua in it. Tell Princess Alais and his grace the Duc that the Royal Navy of Terre d'Ange has obeyed the orders of the Dauphine. We wish you the gods' own speed."

Sidonie drew a deep, shaking breath. "And you, my lord. And you."

Our escort mounted.

Kratos opened the carriage door and ushered us inside. The stiff cushions creaked as we settled ourselves. Kratos himself took a seat atop the carriage alongside the driver. A whip cracked and hooves drummed on the paving-stones.

We were off.

SIXTY-NINE

We made our way in haste to Turnone.

The city lay some sixty leagues west of the City of Elua, perched atop a steep hill. Marc Faucon, the sensible young lieutenant that Henri Voisin had appointed to lead our escort, told us that Barquiel L'Envers had selected it because it was easily defensible.

"So he would make a stand if my mother makes good on her threat?" Sidonie asked soberly.

Faucon, riding alongside the carriage, glanced through the window at her. "Nothing is certain, your highness. If it comes to it, he's chosen a place that could be defended for long months without engagement. But in the end . . ." He shrugged and didn't finish the thought.

"She couldn't possibly succeed." I felt sick at having to utter the words. "Not against the entire country."

"No." Faucon's expression was grim. "But her majesty has a very large, very well-trained army at her disposal. If she will not relent, we face the choice between suffering ourselves to be ruled by madness and lies or enduring terrible bloodshed."

Sidonie buried her face in her hands. "Oh, gods! It's not their fault. The spell . . . it's like an awful sickness."

"Then I pray your highnesses possess the cure in truth," Faucon said gently. "Because if you don't, I fear thousands may die of this disease."

We eschewed the towns and made camp along the roadside, choosing isolated stretches. Neither Sidonie nor I wanted word of our return to be known—not until we knew what we were going to do. Marc Faucon apologized profusely for the discomfort. Sidonie, who had endured worse during our sojourn among the Euskerri, waved his apologies aside. For my part, I couldn't have cared less.

At night we watched the moon rise.

In a little less than three weeks, it would be full; and Ysandre would make good on her threat.

War.

I checked Sidonie's bindings obsessively, still half-disbelieving that the charm had worked. It seemed too good to be true. I'd seen the hours and hours that it had taken Ptolemy Solon to wreak his charm of semblance, and I knew the horrific measures to which Bodeshmun had gone to create his vast spell. It was true that Aodhan's charm had been wrought as swiftly as mine, but he was an *ollamh*. It took years and years of study to attain that rank.

"Mayhap the magic lies in the croonie-stone," Sidonie offered. "After all, it was an *ollamh*'s gift."

I shook my head. "It wasn't enough alone. Morwen was able to summon me when one of the bindings broke."

"Well, mayhap there's an untapped gift for magic in your bloodline," she said. "Or mayhap it was some arcane gift of the Maghuin Dhonn in exchange for granting Berlik a noble death and urging mercy for those who remained. Mayhap it's because the spell that lies over the City wasn't meant for me and me alone." She rubbed her left wrist. "Or mayhap it's simply that every now and then the gods do grant our prayers. Whatever it is, I'm grateful."

"Does it still itch and burn?" I asked.

"All the time," Sidonie said. "Yours didn't?"

"No." I frowned. "Only when Morwen summoned me or when I thought of you. It was all tied to my desire and longing."

"I suppose Bodeshmun's spell is a constant." She glanced involuntarily toward the east. "It does seem to get a little easier to bear as we travel. Or mayhap I'm merely growing accustomed to it."

"It's possible," I said. "At any rate, we've plenty of quandaries for the academy of magic you envision us founding for our legacy to study."

Sidonie shuddered to the bone. "At this point, I'd be overjoyed to earn the legacy of having averted civil war in Terre d'Ange."

It took us three days to reach Turnone. We arrived shortly before sunset and waited at the base of the steep, winding road while Marc Faucon and a couple of his men went to alert the palace and ensure our entry into the city was secure. I leaned out the window of the carriage and gazed up at the forbidding walls. It would indeed be a difficult place to besiege; in that L'Envers had chosen wisely. But in the end that would only prolong the inevitable.

Dusk was falling as Faucon rode back to inform us that all was in readiness. We closed the carriage curtains and began our ascent, jolting upward in muffled darkness. It seemed to take forever, but at last the road leveled. We heard Faucon exchange a word with the guards in the gatehouse, then the creak of the gates being opened. The carriage moved forward.

I could hear the sound of other horses, other carriages, occasional voices calling out greetings to friends. Not many. For a D'Angeline city at nightfall, it was quiet. Then again, I suppose there wasn't much revelry in the cities of Terre d'Ange these days. I remembered the uncertain mood that had gripped Marsilikos before I left. That could only have deepened.

Our carriage drew to a halt.

"Put up your hoods," Marc Faucon said in a low voice beyond the window. That had been part of Henri Voisin's resourcefulness; he'd provided us both with heavy cloaks with deep, concealing hoods.

I tucked an errant lock of Sidonie's hair into hers. "Mind it doesn't blow off this time, love."

She nodded without smiling.

I couldn't see much of the palace as we entered. I kept my head lowered, and the hood obscured the sides of my vision. It was large enough that our footsteps echoed. By the chill that permeated the place, I guessed it was old and poorly heated. It smelled like stone. I could hear Kratos' heavy, familiar tread behind me. His presence felt reassuring. He believed more strongly than anyone that this unlikely tale into which he'd found himself thrust would end happily. I wished I had his faith.

Faucon spoke to another guard. A door opened and Sidonie and I were ushered into a warmer room while the others waited. I could hear a fire crackling. The door closed behind us.

"It's safe," a man's voice said. I recognized it.

I lifted my head and drew back my hood. Beside me, Sidonie did the same.

"Oh, *Elua*!" Standing before us, Alais covered her mouth. Her violet eyes glistened with tears as she gazed at both of us. "Is it true? Is it really true?"

"Yes, dear," Sidonie said softly.

Alais caught her breath on an indrawn sob, took a step forward, and flung her arms around Sidonie's neck. Sidonie closed her eyes and embraced Alais, whispering words I couldn't hear into her ear. When all was said and done, I might regard Alais as the sister of my heart, but Sidonie was her flesh and blood. They were Ysandre and Drustan's only heirs and the bond they shared ran deep.

I found myself left to meet Barquiel L'Envers' gaze: the same lovely eyes as his niece and grandniece, set in a lined face grown ten years older since last I'd seen it. For the first time in my life, there was nothing but respect in it.

"So you did it," he said. "You found her and freed her."

"Yes," I said simply.

Alais released Sidonie, although she caught her older sister's hand in a hard grip. With the heel of her other hand, she rubbed at her tears. "I'm sorry. It's just been so awful. You can't imagine."

"I know." Sidonie squeezed Alais' hand. "But I've a passing good idea, love. You need to tell us everything. Did our messenger not arrive?"

"The Euskerri lad?" L'Envers inquired. "Yes, he did."

"He bore the key," I said. "A word, *the* word." I fumbled in my purse and fetched out Bodeshmun's talisman. A scrap of lacquered leather, a whirlwind sprouting fangs and horns. "*Emmenghanom*. What happened? Did you not use it?"

Barquiel L'Envers spread his arms. "On *what*?"

Sidonie and I exchanged glances.

"You didn't find the demon-stone," I said quietly.

"No." L'Envers' face was set and hard. "I received the letter you sent from Cythera. Before matters with Ysandre came to a head, I searched to the best of my abilities. So did others. We found no emerald gem inscribed with sigils on the premises of the Palace or anywhere in the City."

"It's there." Sidonie freed her hand from Alais' clasp and scratched impatiently at her bindings. "It *has* to be. Did you search the whole of the treasury? Did you—"

"Sidonie." I interrupted her. "Once we start this conversation in earnest, I suspect we'll be at it all night. I know time's short, but I'm road-weary, dirty, and hungry, and my leg aches. I imagine Kratos and Faucon and his men are waiting on us, too. Do you think it might wait an hour?"

"Elua!" It was Alais who answered in a guilt-stricken voice. "I'm so sorry. Of course you are! I ordered a room made ready for you and there's space in the barracks for your men . . . Let me tell the chamberlain to have a bath drawn, and I'll have supper served here so we can speak privately, and . . . Imri, do you need a chirurgeon?"

"No." I smiled at Alais, my heart aching for her. "But I need a proper greeting."

"I'm sorry," Alais whispered. She wrapped her arms around me. I rested my chin atop her black curls and returned her embrace, feeling a measure of nervous tension ebb from her. Her body felt thin and frail. The months of strain and uncertainty had taken a fearful toll on her.

"It's all right, love." I forced all of Kratos' assurance into my tone. "We'll see everything put right. Don't worry."

Alais sniffled. "Don't patronize me." Still, when she pulled away, I could see she'd taken heart from it.

"And he *does* need a chirurgeon," Sidonie added acerbically. "Even if it's healing clean, I imagine it's time for those stitches to be pulled."

Her sister nodded. "I'll send Nathaniel Montague. He can be trusted. Almost everyone here can. How were you wounded, Imriel?" Alais paused, knitting her brow. "And why do you both want to be so secretive? It would bring everyone a great deal of hope and joy to know that you've returned safely."

"Imriel was injured in a battle. And we're being careful because we're not safe, dear," Sidonie said in a gentle voice. She turned out her hands, showing the bindings on her wrists. "Imriel's charm is the only thing standing between me and madness."

Alais gave me a startled look. "You wrought an *ollamh*'s charm?"

"So it seems," I said. "And if we survive this, I'd love to hear your thoughts on it. But it's not just that, Alais." I took a deep breath. "We need that gem. And if it means Sidonie and I have to go to the City to search for it, I'd sooner your mother think us allies than enemies."

"The grieving widow and her deranged but harmless cousin," Sidonie murmured.

"Widow?" L'Envers asked sharply. "Is Astegal dead?"

"Very," I said.

"So you really did marry him," Alais said to her sister in wonderment. "You sailed away to Carthage and married him."

"Yes." Sidonie didn't offer anything further.

After a moment, Alais gathered herself. "I'll go speak to the chamberlain."

In a short while, Sidonie and I donned our hooded cloaks and were shown to a bedchamber where a steaming bath awaited. When I asked Alais if the household staff would find our mysterious presence suspicious, she gave me a look that was world-weary and old beyond her years.

"These days? No."

Once we'd bathed, there was a discreet knock at the door. A voice beyond it announced himself as Nathaniel Montague. I admitted the chirurgeon, who was a slight fellow with blond hair and brown eyes that lit with a spark of hope at the sight of us. He bowed low. "It is my very great pleasure, your highnesses."

The gash was knitting cleanly, and Montague confirmed that the stitches should be pulled. I sat on the bed while he knelt and snipped each stitch with a tiny pair of shears, then tugged the lengths of black thread out of my flesh. Sidonie stood at my side. When Montague had finished, he remained on his knees, gazing up at us like a supplicant.

"We've tried," he said simply. "All of us who follow Eisheth's teaching. Tried and tried to find a cure for this madness. Tried and failed. Is it true you bring hope?"

"A very slender thread of it," Sidonie said.

He kissed both our hands, then rose. "I will pray."

I glanced at Sidonie when he'd left. Her shoulders had slumped under the burden of so many folks' hope, but when she saw me looking at her, they straightened. She lifted her chin. The warm lamplight illuminated her fair skin, the mark of Astegal's sword healing but visible on her bare throat.

"I'm not giving up," she said. "No matter what happens."

"Good." I kissed her. "Nor am I."

Seventy

I was right; we talked until dawn.

Sidonie and I told our story first. If anything happened to us, it was important that the truth be known. And I don't think I'd ever seen Barquiel L'Envers astonished, but he was astonished that night. Alais gasped aloud when Sidonie told of bidding me to cut the mark of the House of Sarkal out of her flesh.

"And you did it?" she asked me in horror.

"I had to," I said.

Alais looked at her sister. "May I see?"

It was an odd request, but I understood it. It was such an outrageous tale, I didn't blame Alais for needing to see the physical truth of it. Sidonie must have understood it too, for she didn't answer, only turned her back to me. I unlaced her stays carefully, parting the back of her gown. Her hair was coiled in a loose chignon. The slender line of her back was bare, the disk-shaped scar showing like a brand between her shoulder blades, fresh and pink.

"Gods!" Alais breathed. Barquiel L'Envers hissed through his teeth.

I laced Sidonie's stays and we told the rest of the tale. Bodeshmun's death, finding the talisman. Our flight from New Carthage, our desperate entrance into Amílcar and our violent escape from it. The Euskerri and their insistence on an act of good faith. That part, they had learned from Nuno Agirre.

"I nearly throttled him," L'Envers said shortly.

"It wasn't his fault," Sidonie murmured. "And the Euskerri paid an awful price in the end."

The war.

Astegal's death.

I told that portion of our story while Sidonie was silent. I left out Astegal's goading comments, but I told them of Sidonie's role in Astegal's death. That was the part that had Barquiel L'Envers staring in astonishment at his eldest grandniece. Sidonie returned his gaze with equanimity. Alais wasn't surprised. She knew her sister far better than most people did.

And then it was our turn to listen.

Some of it we'd already heard from Henri Voisin, but I listened carefully lest there be some further clue in the details. There wasn't. What there was instead was a palpable sense of how awful it had been when Ysandre had turned on them in a rage, accusing them of sedition and betrayal.

"She's not herself, Sidonie," Alais whispered. "She's just . . . *not*."

"And Father?" Sidonie asked.

Alais shook her head. "He'd left before I arrived and she'd expelled us before he returned. Our paths didn't cross. I never saw him in the grip of it." She shivered. "I'm just as glad."

I swallowed. "Did you see Phèdre and Joscelin?"

"Yes." Alais looked at me with sympathy. "They're not . . . I don't think it's taken them as hard as some. Phèdre wasn't angry or harsh. She's heartbroken at your disappearance. She just kept pleading with us to see reason and seemed hurt and confused when we wouldn't." She looked at her uncle. "And Joscelin was just . . . Joscelin. Only worse."

"I gave them your letter," L'Envers said dryly. "Apparently it wasn't convincing—or at least I was an unconvincing messenger. Messire Verreuil thinks I've disposed of you in some dreadful fashion."

I raised my brows. "Do you blame him?"

To his credit, he answered with candor. "No."

Sidonie sighed. "Well, we're going to have to face them all. Because if we stand *any* chance of averting this conflict, Imriel and I have to go to the City and find this damnable demon-stone before the full moon."

"What if it's not there?" L'Envers asked. "What if it doesn't even exist?"

She glanced unerringly toward the east. "There's somewhat there." Sidonie rubbed unthinking at the bindings on her wrists. "I feel it. I feel it tugging at me. Even here, even now. It's better, but I still feel it."

I laid my hand over hers. "Don't fret at them, love."

She stilled. "Tell us where you searched, Uncle."

To the best of his ability, Barquiel L'Envers had done a thorough job. He'd searched the entire contents of the Royal Treasury. Those folks he'd recruited had scrutinized everyone with whom they came in contact, every inch of the City that they could scour. But a gem was a small thing and the City was large.

And in the end, they'd found nothing.

"So how do you propose to better my search?" L'Envers asked frankly.

"Does my mother know about it?" Sidonie asked.

He shook his head. "She had an inkling I was up to something, but I didn't tell her what it was. When matters worsened, she accused me of trying to loot the Treasury for my treasonous plans."

"Good." Sidonie allowed herself a faint smile. "Then I'll get the entire City searching for it."

"And how do you propose to do that?" L'Envers inquired.

"I'll tell them it's an extremely valuable talisman that Bodeshmun left behind to defend the City against all who would assail it," she said steadily. "And that its charm must be invoked anew after Bodeshmun was foully murdered by an Aragonian assassin. With his dying breath, he bade me to flee to the City and see it done . . . but tragically, he perished before he could tell me its whereabouts."

Barquiel L'Envers ran a hand over his cropped hair. "Not bad, child," he said thoughtfully. "It plays to their paranoia." He looked at her with concern. "Are you sure you're up to the task? It's going to take one hell of a performance, especially on your part. Right now I'm not convinced you can utter Astegal's name without sounding like you're spitting poison, let alone play the grieving widow."

"She can do it," I said.

"I appreciate the feat the two of you managed to achieve in New Carthage," he said. "This will be different. You'll not be dealing with enemies. You'll be dealing with folk you know and love turned horribly against everything they hold dear." L'Envers sounded more somber than I'd ever heard him. "It's going to break your hearts."

"I understand," Sidonie said quietly. "All I can do is try."

"You won't have much time." Alais' brow furrowed with anxiety. "No matter how well you spin your tale, it's bound to be exposed soon. Sidonie, you and Imriel killed Astegal with all of Amílcar watching. Now that they're not under a blockade and trade will be resumed, that news will spread. We can try to contain it, but you know what gossip's like."

"We can contain it until the full moon, Alais," L'Envers said. "If they don't find this cursed gem by then . . ."

He fell silent.

We all did.

I cleared my throat. "I suppose . . . I suppose we need to discuss what's to be done if we fail."

"I believe that decision falls to the Dauphine," Barquiel L'Envers murmured.

It surprised me a bit. It had always irked L'Envers that Ysandre had proved more strong-willed and independent than he'd hoped, and I would have expected him to have wrung every possible ounce of power and control out of this situation. But instead it seemed the opposite had occurred. He looked old and tired and more than willing to let Sidonie take responsibility for the decision. Alais just looked relieved. It wasn't a decision anyone wanted to make.

I watched Sidonie square her shoulders once more. "What are our choices?"

"We can withstand a siege for a few months." L'Envers rubbed his temples. "I chose Turnone with that in mind. To buy time if things worsened. Unfortunately, it seems Ysandre has found a means to counter that gambit." His mouth twisted. "In hindsight, we should never have sent so many delegates. We should never have let her know that the entire country is arrayed against her. I thought it would help convince her, but it didn't. It angered her. She remembers. And she's prepared to . . ."

Whatever it was, he couldn't bring himself to say it.

Alais did.

"Mother's threatened to start sacking villages if we don't surrender." Her voice shook, but she continued. "One a day until Uncle Barquiel and I kneel at her feet and beg for clemency."

I felt the blood drain from my face.

"Elua have mercy!" Sidonie whispered.

"I tried to tell you." Alais shivered. "It *is* worse than you can imagine, Sidonie. We tried everything we could think of. We tried reasoning with her. We offered proof from the archives, testimony from hundreds of delegates from outside the City. All she could see was a vast conspiracy." She shivered again. "We tried pleading, too. Uncle Barquiel and I offered to stand down, to beg for clemency, to do aught that she desired if only she would come with us to Alba. Nothing worked. And it's not just her. It's all of them. Everyone who was in the City that night." Alais fell silent, and Barquiel L'Envers reached over to squeeze her hand.

Sidonie met her sister's gaze. "Do you truly think she means it?"

"I do," Alais said in a broken tone. "This spell . . . it's horrible. It twists everything. And yes, I am very much afraid that Mother means to make good on her threat."

L'Envers nodded in mute agreement.

"I see." Sidonie gazed into the distance for a long time. When at last she spoke, her voice was low and anguished. "Then I think we all know the answer. Do I have to say it aloud?" No one replied. She closed her eyes briefly. "Do we at least have the numbers to prevail?"

"Yes," L'Envers said gently.

"Then if Imriel and I fail, Terre d'Ange must fight." She dashed impatiently at her tears. "Rouse the countryside. Send urgent word to Talorcan in Alba for as much additional aid as he can send. Is there aught the Master of the Straits can do?"

"He's reluctant," Alais murmured.

"Beg him to think on it," Sidonie said. "If you can amass

enough strength and numbers to overpower them, and with his magic, mayhap . . . mayhap you can force them to surrender without giving battle. Take them prisoner. And then you could ferry the survivors and the women and children to Alba."

"Once the army takes to the battlefield, I fear none will allow themselves to be taken prisoner, no matter how overwhelming the odds," L'Envers said. "You can't think about them as though they're rational."

The entire Royal Army, slaughtered. It would be worse than the carnage at Amílcar.

Sidonie shuddered. "The women and children, then."

Barquiel L'Envers nodded. "As many as we can save."

So it was decided. We'd committed to a course that would lead to civil war in Terre d'Ange. I remembered the words of the Euskerri who had spoken at the ceremony in Amílcar. *Yesterday we gained a nation and lost the flower of a generation.* I felt sick and hollow inside.

I daresay all of us did.

Seventy-one

After the awful decision was made, we discussed getting into the City as quickly as possible without arousing suspicion. L'Envers and Alais determined that our best ploy would be to return the way I left, hidden on a merchant-barge. We could tell everyone that we had hired them in Pellasus and travelled secretly upriver.

"The fellow who ferried you before, Gilbert Dumel, knows how to keep his mouth shut," L'Envers said. "He's moored at the village of Yvens. Ought to be a short journey if you meet him there."

He left us for an hour or so to send advance word to Dumel and begin the terrible process of making arrangements for the war; and I think also to give Alais and Sidonie some time alone together, something for which Alais was clearly yearning. When he left, she curled up beside her sister, resting her head on Sidonie's shoulder. I had to own, either Barquiel L'Envers had more sensitivity in him than I'd reckoned, or this experience had altered him. Or mayhap both were true.

"Shall I leave, love?" I asked Alais.

"No, please don't. I've missed you both and been so horribly worried." She gathered herself and sat upright. "I don't mean to act the baby. It's just such an ungodly relief to know this spell *can* be thwarted." Alais traced the bindings on Sidonie's wrist. "I've an idea why the charm might have worked. You've an affinity for its magic in your blood, Sidonie."

"I do?" She sounded surprised.

"Of course. We both do. It comes from Grandmother Necthana's bloodline," Alais said. "The Maghuin Dhonn claim that our gifts, like my dreams, come from *them*. That we intermingled long ago and there's a strain of their blood in ours. The Cruithne deny it, but it's true that a lot of the *ollamhs*' lore, at least the part that's to do with magic and not history and poetry and law, comes from the Maghuin Dhonn."

"If we survive this, Sidonie wants to establish an academy to study magic in Terre d'Ange," I informed her. "It's to be our legacy."

"Truly?" Alais asked.

Sidonie smiled with sorrow. "It's a notion from a time when Imriel and I hoped that the key written on Bodeshmun's talisman was all we needed."

"It's a good idea, though." Alais hesitated. "I've come to a realization over the course of these past months. I do not, *not* want this responsibility. Not here. I never wanted it here. And not in Alba, either. I thought I did, but I was wrong." She met her sister's gaze. "I know my duty. But what if I can fill it in a way no one considered? If we do survive this, I want to return to Alba to continue my studies and become an *ollamh*."

"An *ollamh*," Sidonie echoed.

"In Alba, an *ollamh* is the Cruarch's equal," I said, remembering my first encounter with one.

Alais nodded. "If I could attain that rank, I would wield a good deal of influence, which is all that the carping D'Angeline peers ever cared about. All that business about the succession was only ever about power anyway. And as for Talorcan . . ." She shrugged.

"You don't love him," I said softly.

"No." Alais glanced at me. "He's a good man. But no, I don't."

"Then you shouldn't wed him." Sidonie stroked her sister's unruly black curls. "After this, I suspect the peers of the realm may prove rather receptive to the idea of having a member of the royal family grown wise and powerful in the ways of arcane lore."

"Do you think the *ollamh*s might be able to help us now?" I asked.

Alais shook her head. "Only with charms of protection like yours and that will help only if we're able to get folk across the Straits. But I think the Maghuin Dhonn know things we've lost. You said the demon in the stone was an elemental, a desert spirit. The Maghuin Dhonn's magic is old and wild and rooted in nature. If you should fail . . ." Her voice trailed off.

"We won't fail," I said.

"But if we do, you'll look for further answers among the Maghuin Dhonn," Sidonie said firmly. A glance passed between them.

"We *won't* fail," I repeated, willing myself to believe it.

Barquiel L'Envers returned shortly thereafter to inform us that the preparations were under way. "I sent a swift courier to alert Gilbert Dumel," he said, sounding ragged. "He ought to reach Yvens a half day before you."

I got to my feet. "Is our carriage ready?"

"Sit." L'Envers pointed at me. "There are fourteen members of our shadow Parliament here in Turnone, representing the seven provinces. I've taken the liberty of sending for them." He shifted his gaze to Sidonie. "You need to address them. I know time is short. Alais and I will tell them the whole of your tale later. But they need to see and hear you. They need to believe the madness can be broken. They need to believe that this battle is worth the cost, and to carry that word home with them. They need *hope*."

"Then they shall have it," Sidonie said.

Gods, I loved her.

There was no time for sleep, but it didn't matter. We could sleep in the carriage, jolting our way toward Yvens. We waited for the fourteen members of the shadow Parliament to assemble, woken from their own slumber in the grey hours of dawn. Alais sent her chamberlain to the kitchens. We broke our fast with bread and apricot preserves and many pots of strong tea.

"They're ready for us," L'Envers said.

Sidonie and I donned our cloaks and hoods. We were ushered to another room, a small chamber adjacent to a larger room, one that might have served as a musical salon in happier times.

"Wait here," he said to us; and to Alais, "Do you know what to say?"

She looked ashen but resolute. "I think so."

It wasn't the best of plans. The door to our chamber was thick and heavy, and L'Envers had closed it—all the better to make a theatrical gesture. I supposed it ran in the family. Still, it meant that whatever Alais said, we couldn't hear it, only her muffled voice. But in the end, it didn't really matter. When Alais finished, L'Envers wrenched open the door.

"Go," he said tersely.

We walked out together. I'd emerged bareheaded; it was

close and airless in the storage chamber. Sidonie didn't push her hood back until we emerged. I heard fourteen voices gasp.

There was only one face I recognized: Frederic Guillard, a young Azzallese baron who'd spent a summer at Court some years ago. I'd played piquet with him in the Hall of Games. I didn't know the others. They were peers of the Lesser Houses, man and woman, old and young. It didn't matter. They were there to represent their folk. They stared at us with wonder and uncertainty.

"My lords and ladies," Sidonie addressed them in a somber tone. "I wish to thank each of you for your courage in defending Terre d'Ange in a time of sorrow. And I wish to apologize for my own role in it." She took a deep breath. "You have heard rumors that there is dire magic behind the madness that grips all who were in the City of Elua on that fateful night. We are here to tell you it is true. And we are here to tell you that it *can* and *will* be defeated."

I saw the first glimmers of hope in their faces.

"The tale is long and time is short," Sidonie continued. "I will leave the full telling of it to my royal kin. But know this: For months on end, I was in the grip of the same madness. I believed lies. Neither my wits nor my will were wholly my own. And yes, in the grip of this madness, I wed Astegal of Carthage." She glanced at me, her eyes bright. "But love, true love, is a persistent and abiding force. Imriel de la Courcel found a way to break the spell and save me." There was a second collective gasp. Sidonie held out one hand. "It is a method that will work only if the victim has been removed from D'Angeline soil," she said gently. "It will not work on those poor afflicted souls in the City. But there is another method that may succeed and yet avert the shadow of war that hangs over us."

They listened hungrily.

"I will make no false promises," Sidonie said. "The challenge is a difficult one. Imriel and I will depart immediately for the City. We will do everything in our power to succeed. If we fail, the burden will fall to you—to you and to all the folk of Terre d'Ange." Her voice was strong and steady. "And if we do fail, I call upon you to rise up and prevent the slaughter of innocents. To do whatever is necessary. I call for war."

There were nods and murmurs, looks of grim determination. As awful a choice as it was, there was a certain relief in hearing it stated aloud.

"I call upon you to do so knowing that those who can be captured *can* be saved." Sidonie gestured, showing her bindings. "There is magic in Alba that can shield against the effects of this foul spell. One way or another, it *will* be broken. And know this." She took another deep breath. "We go forth in every hope of success. Over the past weeks, I have witnessed great and terrible things. And I bear glad tidings out of them. Carthage's army has suffered a great defeat."

That caught them by surprise; I'd forgotten that they didn't know. But we were the first bearers of the news, and we'd bade Marc Faucon and his men to stay silent.

Sidonie smiled grimly. "Astegal of Carthage is dead. Even now . . ." She had to raise her voice to be heard above the rising excitement. "Even now, his head adorns a pike in the Plaza del Rey in Amílcar! And even as I speak, the bulk of the D'Angeline fleet hurries to Aragonia to honor our alliance and make *war* on those who sought to divide our fair country against itself!"

It stirred their blood like strong spirits and brought them to their feet, cheering. And Elua, yes, it gave them hope. A fierce, proud, violent hope, but hope nonetheless.

"We go now to the City in an effort to save her!" Sidonie shouted above the noise. "We ask that your prayers ride with us! We pray to Blessed Elua and his Companions that we may show the world once more that there is no magic so dire that love cannot defeat it!"

I don't think anyone heard her final words. It didn't matter. They surged forward to offer their support and gratitude, weeping and laughing and clamoring. I couldn't even see Sidonie in the throng that surrounded her, but they acknowledged me, too. I found myself embraced, my cheeks kissed, my hands clasped. It struck me more forcibly than I could have reckoned, and somewhere beneath it, I realized that for the first time in my life, I was being wholeheartedly accepted by my fellow countrymen.

"I've thought dreadful things of you, Prince Imriel," a beautiful old L'Agnacite woman whispered to me, tears on her wrinkled cheeks. "I'm very sorry for them."

I swallowed against the lump in my throat. "That's all right, my lady. Just lend us your prayers."

"I will." She pressed my hands between her soft palms. "I will."

At length the crush subsided. Barquiel L'Envers pushed his way through with Alais at his side. "I fear their highnesses must depart," he announced. "Time *is* of the essence. But they have endured grave dangers to be here today. Let us take heart from their words and resolve to be no less worthy of Terre d'Ange!"

The cheer was resounding.

My heart ached.

And then it was time for one more damnable leavetaking. This one hurt. Marc Faucon and his men came to fetch us. They had Kratos in tow. I introduced him to Alais and L'Envers, reckoning he deserved no less. They'd heard the tale, they knew his role and treated him with respect. Still, I took a certain pleasure in the bemusement of the watching peers, wondering what in Elua's name an aging Hellene wrestler with a squashed nose was doing in the midst of everything.

And it drew out the inevitable a few precious moments longer.

"Good luck," Alais whispered fiercely against my neck when I hugged her. "Be safe. *Please* be safe. And keep Sidonie safe."

I held her hard. "I will."

Barquiel L'Envers clasped my hand. "I misjudged you," he said bluntly. "I'll not apologize for it. Blessed Elua knows, your mother was a pox on this land, and you struck fear into our hearts when you turned my sensible grandniece's head."

It made me smile. "I know."

L'Envers snorted. "Never thought that you might actually love her." He watched Sidonie and Alais say their farewells, clutching one another's hands and speaking in low tones. His face softened. "I suppose I should have. Never approved of Ysandre and Drustan's union either, but it seems to have produced a remarkable pair of offspring."

"Yes," I said. "It did."

"Ah." He snapped his fingers. "Speaking of Drustan, I nearly forgot." L'Envers untied a silk pouch from his belt and handed it to me. "The token you sent with the Euskerri messenger. It was a gift of the Cruarch, was it not? He'll expect to see you wearing it in his niece's memory."

I opened the pouch to find the torc that Drustan had given me the day I'd wed Dorelei in Alba. I'd always admired Drustan. I'd been proud to receive it from his hands. What an awful thing it was to contemplate all his quiet strength and dignity twisted awry. "Thank you, my lord."

Barquiel L'Envers offered a curt bow. "Blessed Elua hold and keep you. I wish you all the luck in the world."

Time to go.

Again.

Sidonie and I raised our hoods and shrouded our faces. We left as we'd come, cloaked and anonymous. I kept my head lowered, watching the foot-worn granite blocks as I passed. I felt fresh air on my face, damp with spring's promise. I climbed into the carriage, sliding across the horsehair seats. Sidonie joined me. I felt the carriage dip as Kratos took up his post alongside the driver. Someone drew the curtains. I pushed back my hood. Beside me, Sidonie did the same.

A whip cracked; a voice issued a command.

The carriage lurched forward.

Gods, I was tired. I hadn't reckoned how much so until I took my place in the carriage. I hadn't slept and I could feel the weight of all that *hope* riding on my shoulders. And if I was feeling it, I knew Sidonie was feeling it more. I slid my arm around her and she nestled close against me.

"You were magnificent," I murmured against her hair.

"I'm scared," she said quietly. "I'm afraid of what we'll find in the City. I'm afraid of facing it, Imriel. And I'm afraid of failing."

"I know." I drew her closer. "But they didn't."

"No?" Sidonie lifted her head and gazed at me, yearning for reassurance.

"No." I shook my head. "They didn't. You did what you promised. You gave them hope."

We paused at the gates of Turnone, and then the carriage nosed steeply downward. The horses plodded steadily, the carriage creaking and groaning. Sidonie yawned and settled her head on my shoulder. I held her, reveling in her warm presence, feeling the undercurrent of exhaustion tugging at the both of us.

"Sleep," I whispered. "Sleep, love."

She did.

So did I.

Seventy-two

The farther we went toward the City of Elua, the more Sidonie's bindings troubled her. She didn't complain, but she answered honestly when I asked. She said it felt as though her wrists and ankles were twined with stinging nettles.

It worried me.

It worried me a lot.

"I can bear it." She shrugged. "The itching's worse than the pain, and it's actually starting to hurt more than it itches. It's an improvement."

"I'm not worried about your ability to endure pain, love," I said. "I carved a chunk of flesh out of your back on your orders. But what if Bodeshmun's spell overwhelms the charm when we reach the City?"

Sidonie looked away. "We can't let ourselves think thusly."

"We can't afford not to!" I raised my voice. "Sidonie, if you fall prey to Bodeshmun's spell in the City of Elua, I'm not going to be able to wrestle you kicking and screaming back across the sea. I'm going to be surrounded by folk in the grip of the same cursed spell, and they're not going to allow mad Prince Imriel to lay violent hands on you!"

"I know," she murmured. "You needn't shout."

I forced myself to speak calmly. "I think we should discuss the possibility of your staying out of the City. You could go to Amílcar or Alba. Anywhere far, far from that cursed demon-stone."

"And how is mad Prince Imriel going to convince everyone in the City to search for that cursed demon-stone?" Sidonie looked back at me. "You need me. We have to take the chance." She paused, frowning. "Imriel, if anyone should stay outside the City, it's you."

"Me?" I stared at her.

"What happens if the spell *does* reassert itself?" She searched my face. "Will it wipe away my memories of these past months? Or will it merely twist them? Will it have me believing that you ensorceled me against my will? That you conspired with your mother and Ptolemy Solon to work some dark charm to seduce me, to abduct me, to persuade me to help you kill my own beloved husband? What happens to you if I denounce you before the entire City?"

I closed my eyes. "Ah, gods. I hadn't thought of that."

"You worry about me, and I worry about you," Sidonie said softly. "And between the two of us, you'll be in worse danger, mad Prince Imriel. Can I persuade you to stay safely away?"

I opened my eyes. "No."

"I didn't think so." She touched my cheek. "I'll tell you if there are further changes in the bindings. And of a surety, I'll warn you if I feel my wits are about to crumble."

"If you have the chance," I said.

"And I pray I do," Sidonie said. "In the meanwhile, let me bear the pain without fretting over what it might betoken, because there's naught either of us can do about it. Not if we stand a chance of averting this war. And you know damnably well both of us will take any risk to make that happen, no matter how long the odds." Unexpectedly, she summoned a hint of a smile. "I'm trying to imagine that it's a pain associated with somewhat far more pleasant. Somewhat involving you and tightly knotted ropes. It helps, actually."

I raised my brows. "Oh, indeed?"

Her eyes glimmered. "Mm-hmm."

Gods, I wished there was *time*. I wished we could halt the world for a day and banish all that surrounded us. The looming war. The jolting carriage, the jogging guards surrounding it, Kratos sitting alongside the driver, singing tunelessly in Hellene.

A day, one day . . .

We didn't have a day. Not even an hour. Only duty and hope and the desperate prayers of a nation. There on the stiff horsehide cushions, I settled for pulling Sidonie against me, kissing her until I felt her soft lips part, her body yielding sweetly, arms around my neck.

"We *will* prove it," I whispered. "There is no magic so dire."

Sidonie kissed me again. "None."

I found myself thinking about the day when everything had changed between us: the day of the hunt when a boar had gored Alais' dog and Sidonie's horse had bolted and thrown her. I'd flung myself atop Sidonie, thinking to protect her. As it happened, my effort was unnecessary; but in that moment, a spark had been ignited. I could still remember the thrilling shock of it. The feeling of her body beneath mine, the sight of realization dawning in her dark eyes.

"Do you remember the hunt?" I asked, not bothering to explain.

She smiled. "Oh, yes. You know I do. Gods, I thought about it for days and days. 'Tis no wonder that when Leander

Maignard saved my life in the garden, I felt so strongly for him. For you." She was silent a moment. "It's so very peculiar the way the events in our lives cast reflections."

"I know," I said. "I've thought it since Cythera. Phèdre and Joscelin went on a quest to find the Name of God and bind an angel. You and I seek to free a demon with a word."

"And if we succeed, Terre d'Ange will be indebted to Melisande Shahrizai," Sidonie added. "It feels as though we've been on a long, strange journey to bring the circle around to a full close."

"My mother persuaded Ptolemy Solon to aid me for her own reasons," I reminded her. "It doesn't erase the past."

"No, but it changes the future," Sidonie said. "If we *do* come out this whole, I don't think anyone will ever ever dare question your integrity again." Her voice softened. "And our horde won't have to grow up knowing their father was responsible for having his own mother executed. Elua help me, but I'm glad of that."

I thought about my last glimpse of Melisande: standing at Ptolemy Solon's side on the docks of Paphos as she watched me sail away into danger, believing myself to be Leander Maignard. About her parting words. *Be safe. Just be safe.* Almost the same words Alais had spoken. There had been genuine love in them. Whatever else was true of her, I didn't doubt that my mother loved me.

"So am I," I murmured.

Sidonie cocked her head. "I'd like to meet her someday."

I tried to envision it and couldn't. My cool, regal beloved with her startling streak of hidden fire; my damnable mother and the deep, ineffable spell she cast. "I suppose anything is possible."

The doubt in my voice made her laugh. "We'll see."

At night we made camp in isolated areas as we'd done on the journey to Turnone. We talked strategy with Kratos, explaining the situation in the City of Elua to him in detail. Kratos listened and nodded sagely.

"So all in the City believe you mad, my lord?" he asked.

I stared at the campfire. "Yes."

Until we'd caught sight of the shores of Terre d'Ange, I'd avoided thinking about it; but the nearer we drew to the City, the more it preyed on my mind. I still bore traces of scarring on my wrists and ankles where I'd chafed my flesh raw against my restraints, screaming horrible threats at those I loved and plotting their deaths. Scars. An echo of the bindings I'd once worn to protect me against Morwen's talisman, an echo of the increasingly painful bindings that protected Sidonie against Bodeshmun's spell. And that in itself was an echo of the ropes I'd knotted around Sidonie's willing wrists more than once, the memory of pleasure that helped her endure the pain.

The bright mirror and the dark.

The things I'd said in my madness . . . ah, Elua!

"Kratos." Sidonie touched his thick forearm. "No one in the City knows you. 'Tis my thought to tell them that you were my lord Astegal's most loyal bodyguard, the cherished comrade of his boyhood. That he trusted you with my safety, and that you have repaid it a thousandfold. That I now trust you with my poor deluded kinsman's care. Are you up to the task of playing this role?"

Kratos bent his head toward her. The firelight danced over his blunt features, his bristling hair. "I will arise to any challenge her highness sets me."

"We don't deserve you, Kratos," I murmured.

He turned his hard, shrewd gaze on me. "Don't say that, my lord. I was plucked from a slave-market by a foppish young D'Angeline to serve as his bearer. I saw something in him worthy of serving. When I spoke, he listened. *You* listened."

"Leander listened," I said. "By the time I knew myself, I'd already seen the measure of your worth."

"Ah, well." Kratos glanced back at Sidonie. "I suspect there was a fair bit of you in there all along, my lord."

On the third day, we reached the outskirts of Yvens, an unassuming little village on the Aviline known for its olives. As before, Sidonie and I waited while Marc Faucon and a couple of his men rode ahead to secure the way.

It was a lovely spring day, clear and almost balmy. We waited alongside an olive grove. They were venerable old trees with gnarled trunks. The afternoon sun slanted through their leaves, through the clusters of delicate white flowers blooming on their branches. Sidonie and I walked in the grove while Kratos and Faucon's men kept watch.

"It seems impossible to think of war on such a day," Sidonie said wistfully.

"I know." I laid my hand on a sun-warmed trunk, thinking about the night years ago when I'd stood atop the walls of Lucca with Deccus Fulvius, watching the ancient olive groves outside the city go up in flames. "But even without magic's urging, men will make war despite all the beauty in the world."

"As a child, one of my favorite stories was hearing how my mother averted a civil war in Terre d'Ange." She glanced unerringly toward the north. "How she refused when Lord Amaury begged her to raise an army in Caerdicca Unitas and rode toward the City with only a small escort, throwing coins to the folk along the way that they might know her face, that they might know their Queen had returned, alive and well."

"And a throng of people trailed after her," I said softly. "Farmers and weavers, beekeepers and chandlers."

"And children." Sidonie's voice broke on the word.

"And children," I echoed. "And when they reached the

City of Elua, they never halted. Arrows rained down upon them, and they answered with showers of coin. Ysandre de la Courcel rode forward, flanked only by the ranks of the Unforgiven. The rebel soldiers gazed at the coins in their hands and wept, knowing they'd been fed a lie. They laid down their arms and knelt."

"Yes." Sidonie wiped her eyes.

I was quiet. I knew the tale well; indeed, the coins had been Phèdre's idea. But it was different for Sidonie. Ysandre was her mother as well as the Queen. If Terre d'Ange went to war, it would be on her order. To have that great legacy of courage and valor lost forever was an ache too deep for words.

And Phèdre and Joscelin . . .

That, I couldn't bear to think.

"They averted a war and restored peace," I said. "We will do the same. We'll bring the circle around to a full close. We won't fail them, Sidonie."

She didn't answer, only nodded.

Shortly thereafter, Marc Faucon returned with word. Gilbert Dumel had received L'Envers' message and he was prepared to ferry us into the City, but he advised that we wait until nightfall to enter Yvens. And so once more, we waited. Faucon's men had brought savory meat pies, fresh bread, and goat cheese back with them from the village, but the thought of food made my stomach churn.

Come nightfall, we entered the village.

It had the same eerie quietude as Turnone and every other town we'd passed through on our journey. Through a gap in the curtains, I could see that lamplight glowed in the windows of the houses, but the streets were empty. We passed Yvens' single inn and it appeared almost empty. On a pleasant spring evening like this, the village should have been alive with music, young lovers turning out in droves to court one another.

"Elua!" Sidonie whispered. "It's like the realm's already in mourning."

"I fear it is," I said soberly.

The barge was waiting at the wharf. I remembered its captain, Gilbert: a taciturn fellow who'd given me a wide berth when he'd brought me to Marsilikos, the tales of my raving madness fresh in his mind. I must have looked godawful, worn to bone and sinew from a month of deprivation, my wrists scabbed. Now he gazed at our hooded figures in wonderment as we boarded the barge. Once he'd escorted us to a cabin, he asked the question it seemed nearly everyone did. "Is it true?"

Gods, there was so much pain in the question. He didn't gasp when we shed our hoods, but tears glittered in his eyes.

"It's true," Sidonie said to him. "We're here to try to undo the madness."

Gilbert Dumel was a man of few words; he went to one knee and bowed his head, then left us.

My injured leg was aching. I sat on the narrow bunk. Sidonie stood in the cabin. Both of us listened to the sounds of the barge making ready to depart. Kratos' heavy tread, other footsteps. Faucon and six of his men would accompany us to the City of Elua, posing as barge-hands. If there was any news to impart, good or ill, they would serve as couriers. We listened to the soft calls of the real barge-hands, Gilbert's terse orders.

And then there was the sound of oars dipping. The barge slid slowly into the darkened river.

"How long do you suppose?" Sidonie murmured.

"About a day and a half," I said. "We're like to reach the City on the morning after tomorrow."

A single lantern hung from a hook in the cabin's ceiling, swaying gently. "Imriel." Sidonie gazed at me. "Will you forgive me in advance for all that I might have to say or do to convince them of our tale?"

"Need you ask?" I said.

She smiled sadly. "For my sake, yes. I fear Alais and my uncle are right. This is going to be harder than either of us imagine. And I fear . . ." She laughed, but it was a tired, broken sound. "I fear I'll have to find a new way of thinking about the pain of these damned bindings. Once we're in the City, I don't think I can allow myself the risk of thinking about you as I do."

"Not while playing the grieving widow," I said.

Sidonie nodded. "I'll need to pull away from you. Elua knows, I don't want to. I need you beside me now more than I ever did. But I'm afraid I can't do this if I don't."

"I understand." I reached out and she came over to take my hand. "And yes, I forgive you in advance for aught you might have to say or do."

"Thank you."

"Always." I squeezed her hand. "Do you need me to leave you alone tonight? I can sleep in the bunks below."

"No, not yet, please." Sidonie shivered. "If you don't mind, tonight I'd like you to hold me and tell me for the hundredth time that we *will* succeed, because the closer we get, the more frightened I am."

"Then I will," I said.

And so I did, over and over, while the barge glided through darkness, bearing us toward the City of Elua and our fears. I spun a tale of gladness and joy and made promises there was no way I could possibly keep. It didn't matter. If we failed, no one in the world would care that for once I hadn't kept my promise. And Sidonie knew my promises for lies, but the words comforted her nonetheless.

At length, she slept.

I lay awake and prayed to Blessed Elua and his Companions to grant mercy to their children and turn my lies to truth.

Seventy-three

The next day, Sidonie withdrew from everyone, spending long hours in the prow of the barge, cloaked and hooded, kneeling in a private vigil.

"Is her highness wroth?" Marc Faucon asked me with concern.

"No." I shook my head. "Only preparing for what lies ahead. Leave her be."

I passed the day helping Kratos acquire a few more words of D'Angeline. All along the banks of the Aviline, there were signs of spring's return: trees bursting into green-leafed glory, flowers blooming. Any other time the sight would have gladdened my heart, but it didn't. Last night's false promises tasted like ashes in my mouth. I was frightened, too. Elua knows, I'd known fear before, but not the kind of fear that accompanied having the fates of so many people I loved riding on my shoulders.

And my role was easier than Sidonie's. She had to convince the entire City she was mourning a man who had violated her very will, had to convince them to believe an intricate web of lies and truth. All I had to do was let them go on believing I was disordered in my wits. We'd considered telling them I'd been cured in Carthage, but that raised in turn the problem of explaining why the rest of the realm couldn't be cured of their own apparent madness. In the end we had decided that the simplest, safest course was to let them continue believing as they did.

When the sun was sinking low on the horizon, Sidonie rose. She paused briefly to address us. "I'll be retiring for the night. Kratos, would you be kind enough to bring me something to eat?"

He rose. "At once, my lady."

Her gaze shifted to meet mine. She gave me a quick, sad smile that broke my heart. "I'll see you on the morrow."

"On the morrow," I agreed.

That night I made my bed belowdeck on a narrow bunk, surrounded by the snores and wheezes of men deep in slumber. And if I'd let myself, I could have lain awake all night in futile thought or desperate prayer, but there was no merit in it. My thoughts would only turn in helpless circles, and if Blessed Elua hadn't heard our prayers by now, he never would. So instead, like a soldier preparing for battle, I forced myself to sleep.

By the time I rose and made myself break my fast, the City was in sight.

Like spring, the sight of those white walls shining in the distance had always been cause for gladness. Not today. I remembered all too well watching them recede as this very barge had carried me away. It had been summer then. Three seasons had passed since I'd left. The spell that gripped the City was malevolent at its core.

How much worse had it gotten?

Some distance from the City, Gilbert Dumel ordered his oarsmen to cease progress. We waited until Sidonie emerged into the sunlight. She looked pale and hollow-eyed. I didn't think she'd slept like a soldier. She gazed toward the City, expressionless.

"We'll not be able to enter unchallenged, your highness," Gilbert informed her. "They'll raise the chain and insist on searching the barge before we're allowed to enter the harbor."

"I'll speak to them," Sidonie said.

Gilbert gave a curt nod. "We'll take our lead from you, highness."

The oarsmen resumed their stroke. Before long, we could see that the massive chain used to protect the harbor from invasion was already raised. A swift, sleek galley with a ballista mounted on its prow hailed us.

"State your business!" came the shout.

Sidonie was silent.

We followed her lead.

The galley bore down on us fast. As it drew nigh, I saw there were additional ballistae mounted on the sides and aft. Every one was manned, and there was a sizable contingent of armed men aboard, a thicket of crossbows pointing at us.

"Halt the barge," Sidonie said quietly. Gilbert gave the order. As we drifted slowly to a halt, the galley turned broadside to us.

"State your business," the galley's captain repeated. He had a hard face. They all had hard faces. Sidonie stood in the prow without moving, Kratos and I a few paces behind. Although the captain didn't notice me, I watched his face as he recognized her. It only got more grim. "Your highness."

"My business is the business of Terre d'Ange." There was a raw edge to Sidonie's voice, but it held a note of command, too. "And I will state it only to her majesty the Queen."

The captain gestured and his men lowered their crossbows. "You bring tidings out of Carthage?"

"I bring tidings of woe," Sidonie said, low and savage. "Tidings of death and defeat and bitter betrayal. But I will not deliver them to you, messire. Lower the chain and let us pass, or you may go join my *sister* and her rebel army."

If the captain harbored any doubts, those words erased them—that, and the unfeigned emotion behind them. She didn't have to pretend. All of the very real grief and fury at what had befallen Terre d'Ange was there.

"Lower the chain!" the captain shouted. "Send to the Palace! Tell them the Dauphine has returned! *Now*!"

Unseen gears ground somewhere ashore. The mammoth chain sank beneath the waters. Our would-be adversary became our escort as the galley swung back around to precede us into the harbor. As our progress resumed, Sidonie stood motionless, her black cloak hanging in folds around her. The garment that had served as a tool of concealment now appeared a badge of mourning.

Our oarsmen bent their backs. The barge slid past the white walls.

We entered the City of Elua.

I couldn't sense any immediate change, but I saw Sidonie's shoulders tighten and I knew the pain had gotten worse. I prayed that was all it was. "Are you all right?" I asked under my breath.

She nodded without turning. "Thus far."

Gods, it was hard not to go to her, to offer the simple comfort of my presence. To share the burden. But I couldn't, or at least Sidonie couldn't accept it if I did. Not with the eyes of the City watching.

So I didn't.

The response to the galley captain's order had been swift. By the time we were docked at the wharf, there was a royal escort awaiting us: a company of soldiers led by Ghislain nó Trevalion himself. His broad, good-natured face was set in harsh lines. And unlike the galley captain, Ghislain noticed me immediately as we disembarked, his eyes widening in shock. "*You!*"

"Have no fear, my lord," Sidonie said. "He's no danger."

Ghislain's face darkened, but he proffered a bow. "We will see, your highness. I would welcome you home, but I fear your return portends ill."

"Yes." She met his gaze squarely. "I need to speak to my mother. Immediately. Is my father in residence?"

"He is."

She nodded. "So much the better. Take me to them, please."

There was a carriage with the insignia of House Courcel waiting. When I made to follow Sidonie into it, Ghislain caught my arm. "I think it best if you ride, Prince Imriel."

"My lord Ghislain!" Sidonie's voice was sharp. "I tell you, it's fine. Imriel labors under the delusion that he's enamored of me. It is inconvenient, but he poses no threat." She pointed to Kratos. "And Kratos here is . . . was . . . my lord Astegal's most trusted and loyal bodyguard. No harm will come to me while he is present."

Kratos folded his arms and looked impassive.

Ghislain hesitated, then shrugged. "As you will."

Inside the carriage, we sat in silence for most of the ride. Unlike the rest of Terre d'Ange, the City of Elua was abuzz. People thronged the streets, staring as our entourage passed. But there were no greetings shouted, only a rising tide of speculation. It held an edge of anger that made my skin prickle.

"Feels like a hornets' nest," Kratos muttered. "This isn't how I imagined one of the great cities of Terre d'Ange."

"It's *not* how it is." Sidonie glanced at him, pain in her eyes. "All that you will see and hear in these days . . . it's a lie, a foul lie wrought by Bodeshmun's magic. I beg you to believe me."

"I do," he said gently.

And then there was no more time for talk. We clattered into the courtyard of the Palace. There were more guards on duty than I ever remembered seeing, and the ostlers who came to attend to mounts and carriage-horses worked with martial efficiency.

"This way." Ghislain snapped his fingers and his men formed a cordon around us, ushering us into the Palace.

It was another moment come around full circle. Members of the Court turned out to stare, wondering at Sidonie's unexpected return, wondering at my unexpected presence. There were hard-eyed guards posted everywhere. When we passed the Hall of Games, there was a scuffle taking place. A woman's voice rose to a shriek, haranguing some unseen companion with accusations of cheating. It should have been a shocking breach of decorum, but no one batted an eye.

Sidonie was right.

This was *not* our City.

We halted outside the door of one of Ysandre's private salons while Ghislain exchanged a word with the guards. I watched Sidonie's shoulders rise and fall as she took a deep breath, bracing herself. Kratos placed himself at her side, unbidden. She gave him a look of gratitude. Good. That was all right. No one had cause to believe he was aught but Astegal's loyal man. He could lend her the support I couldn't, and no one would think twice at it.

The door was opened.

We were ushered into the salon.

Ysandre and Drustan were awaiting us. They stood side by side: the Queen of Terre d'Ange and the Cruarch of Alba, united. I saw Ysandre take in my presence, and I saw suspicion dawn on her features. Drustan's expression was unreadable behind his woad tattoos. Ghislain and a dozen of his men remained as the door was closed behind us.

"Sidonie." Ysandre uttered her daughter's name without a trace of warmth. Drustan said nothing, only watched his eldest, the black eyes she'd inherited hard and appraising. "What is the meaning of this?"

"Your majesties." Sidonie curtsied deeply and held it. She spoke without lifting her head. "My husband Astegal, Prince of the House of Sarkal, General of Carthage, is dead."

As before, there was a world of grief behind the words, not for Astegal, but for the City of Elua, for her mother and father, and all who dwelled in the City. It didn't matter. It was real. It sufficed.

Ysandre paled. "How?"

Sidonie straightened. "It was the Euskerri. Serafin L'Envers y Aragon made a treaty with them. Together they defeated Astegal's army outside Amílcar. Astegal . . ." She paused. "I am told . . . I am told he was captured and executed. He had left orders for me to flee for my own safety. And there is more—"

"House L'Envers!" Ysandre hissed the word, nails digging into her own forearms. "I should have known it. This conspiracy grows vaster by the day. I swear to Blessed Elua, I could claw that cursed blood from my own veins if I could!"

"Hold." Drustan lifted one hand. "You said there was more," he said to Sidonie. "Speak."

"A ray of hope." She gazed at her father. "One last gift of my lord's kinsman Bodeshmun. It is why I was sent swiftly and in secret."

Ysandre and Drustan exchanged a glance. "Then let us hear this tale in its entirety," Ysandre said. She pointed at me. "And you may begin with how and why Melisande

Shahrizai's oft-vanished son comes to reappear in your company."

There were nods and mutters of agreement among Ghislain's men.

Sidonie inclined her head and began to speak.

In the end, I daresay it was Barquiel L'Envers' long-standing and well-known dislike of me that sold my end of the tale. They knew he'd helped me get out of the City. When Sidonie stated her belief that he'd done it to get me out of the way for good, it struck a chord. We already knew Joscelin believed it to be true.

"No doubt Uncle Barquiel believed Astegal would be swift to dispatch Imriel when he showed up in Carthage with this mad fantasy of rescuing me." Sidonie's voice softened. "But he didn't know my husband. Astegal took pity on Imriel and had his physicians treat him as best they could. He was kind that way. He had a generous, noble heart."

Everyone nodded.

I swallowed my bile and tried to look humble.

"And what do you believe *now*, Imriel de la Courcel?" Drustan asked in an implacable tone.

I spread my hands. "I believe whatever Sidonie tells me. I know there are thoughts in my head that are wrong. I know Sidonie doesn't love me. I saw that in Carthage. But I believe whatever she tells me, and I would never do anything to harm her or any of you. I just don't want to be sent away again."

I sounded like a simpleton to my own ears, but they seemed willing to accept it.

"This is Kratos." Sidonie switched to Hellene, laying a hand on Kratos' arm. "He was my lord's most trusted bodyguard, the companion of his childhood. At Astegal's command, he has seen me safe these long weeks. Now that we are here, he has agreed to keep watch over poor Imriel."

Kratos bowed.

Ysandre eyed him coolly and spoke in fluent Hellene. "I do not recall seeing this man when General Astegal's delegation was here, and he has a rather memorable face."

Beads of sweat broke out on my brow. It wasn't a challenge any of us had anticipated. Gods, this was hard! They might have been in the grip of madness and paranoia and easily misled in some ways, but neither Drustan nor Ysandre had lost their faculties.

"No, your majesty." Kratos offered another bow. "I was a wedding gift."

Her brows rose. "A wedding gift?"

"My service was to the greater House of Sarkal." Kratos pressed a fist to his chest. "My lord Astegal's mother released me into the service of her son's household that he might have one retainer he trusted beyond all doubt to watch over that which was most precious to him."

If I hadn't known better, I would have believed he spoke with absolute sincerity and conviction. Ysandre relaxed, and I thanked the gods for Kratos and his quick wits.

"And a wise woman my lord's mother proved to be," Sidonie murmured in D'Angeline. "For in the end, the House of Sarkal *was* betrayed."

Although the rest of the tale was almost entirely a skein of lies, Sidonie spun it artfully, telling them how when word of Astegal's death reached New Carthage, the city devolved into bitter factions grasping for power. That was a familiar notion that fell on willing ears. She told them that on Astegal's orders, she was to flee with his kinsman Bodeshmun back to Carthage proper; but before it could be arranged, Bodeshmun was slain by the treachery of Gillimas of Hiram, who bribed the Amazigh guards. He'd told her of the protective gem, bade her to flee to the City of Elua instead of Carthage, to find the gem and renew its charm.

Sidonie had witnessed violent death since she'd left her parents' side. Her description of Bodeshmun's end, his gasped words and dying rattle, rang horribly true. And through it all ran that raw thread of genuine anguish, giving the weight of truth to her lies.

"I'm sorry, my dear," Ysandre said when Sidonie finished. The unexpected gentleness in her voice brought a lump to my throat. Ysandre glanced at Drustan. "We didn't mean to doubt you. It's just . . ."

"I know." Sidonie shivered. "Alais."

"You've heard?" Drustan asked gravely.

She nodded. "But *why*? Why would she do it? I don't understand."

"No one does. There are theories. But we'll talk about that on the morrow. You should rest. You must be weary to the bone and grief-stricken atop it." Ysandre rested her hands on her daughter's shoulders and gazed into her eyes. "Sidonie, I am so very, very sorry about Astegal's death."

"Thank you." The words were choked. I had to look away as Ysandre enfolded her in a comforting embrace. I couldn't bear to see Sidonie cling to what was left of her mother's goodness.

Drustan, too, embraced his daughter. "This gem," he said. "Do you truly think it might help?"

"I do." Sidonie dashed the tears from her eyes. "You saw . . . we all saw what marvels Bodeshmun and his horologists were capable of achieving. I think he may have seen that the City of Elua would be in dire need of protection. I think it's terribly important that we find it."

"Then we'll do so." Drustan held her hands. He glanced downward and frowned. "Why are you wearing an *ollamh*'s charms?"

"To keep her safe," I put in quickly and anxiously. "It was my idea."

This question, we *had* anticipated.

Sidonie glanced over her shoulder at me. "I fear Imriel remembers," she said softly. "Alban magic, my cousin Dorelei's death. It's all mixed up in his thoughts. He's afraid. Afraid that's what's behind Alais' and Talorcan's rebellion. He thinks this will help keep me safe from it."

"It won't," Drustan said shortly. "It's ambition, not magic, at stake here."

"I know." Sidonie smiled through tears at her father. "But I don't mind and it brings him peace. Can we not let it be and concentrate on finding Bodeshmun's charm? For *that* I truly believe might prove effective."

Drustan released her hands. "Of course."

"Of course," Ysandre echoed.

There was a discreet knock at the door. Ghislain nó Trevalion went to answer it. He returned, inclining his head. "Your majesties," he said. "The Comtesse Phèdre nó Delaunay de Montrève and her consort Joscelin Verreuil wish to see their foster-son. They have received word of his return."

My heart raced.

"Admit them," Ysandre said.

Seventy-four

The door opened.

I hadn't had time to brace myself. Not against this. The sight of them was like a spear to the gut.

"*Imriel.*" Phèdre breathed my name and my arms opened. She walked into them and I embraced her, willing myself to forget the vile things I'd said in my madness, wanting to believe for a few heartbeats that everything was well.

"Did he harm you?" Joscelin demanded. "*Did he harm you?* Because I swear to Elua, I will butcher him if he did!"

He meant L'Envers. "No." I released Phèdre. "No, no one harmed me. I'm sorry. I'm so sorry. I can't think straight."

"Still?" Phèdre whispered.

I glanced at Sidonie and nodded. "Still."

"When I heard you'd returned, I hoped . . ." Phèdre gathered herself and turned to Drustan and Ysandre. "Forgive us, your majesties," she said in a formal tone. "I apologize for the impropriety."

"Oh, *stop*," Ysandre said irritably. "You know damnably well you don't need to stand on protocol. These are dire times and Sidonie brings dire tidings. Astegal of Carthage is dead and his army has suffered a great defeat."

"Name of Elua!" Phèdre gasped. "Oh, you poor child," she said to Sidonie. "I'm so terribly sorry."

Sidonie looked near tears again. "Thank you, my lady," she murmured. "I'm sorry to bring such awful news."

"You were in Carthage?" Joscelin asked me in bewilderment. I nodded. His right hand closed on my elbow, hard enough to hurt. He shook me roughly. "Why? Why did you flee? How could you do that to us? Do you have any idea how worried we were?"

I closed my eyes. "Yes. I'm sorry."

"Take him home," Drustan said brusquely. "We'll hold a conference on the morrow."

My eyes flew open. "No! I need to be near Sidonie." I wasn't playing a role; I was terrified that her bindings would break or fail. I didn't know what I'd do if they did, but I knew I had to be there.

"The hell you do," Ysandre muttered.

"It's all right," Sidonie said quietly. "It soothes his mind to know I'm close at hand. Imriel, go with your foster-parents, at least for the night. You can return in the morning." She touched the croonie-stone at her throat, her eyes eloquent. "Kratos will stay with me to make sure I'm safe."

I hesitated, misliking it.

"Imriel!" Phèdre gazed at me with reproach. "After all that we've done for you, after all that you've put us through, how could you possibly begrudge us a single night?"

It was true, of course; but in all the years I'd known them, they'd never once thrown it in my face. It wasn't like Phèdre to do it now, believing me to be in the grip of madness as she did. As unkindness went, it was surpassing mild; still, it made me heartsick.

"Of course," I said. "I'm sorry."

And so I went with them, willing myself to be calm and docile. The truth was, there wasn't anything I could do if Sidonie's bindings failed and there was a chance that she'd turn on me if they did whether I was present or not. I felt frustrated and helpless. Mayhap she was right and I should have stayed out of the City, but it would have killed me to send her here alone with only Kratos to aid her. Quick-witted and loyal as he was, he barely spoke D'Angeline.

Above everything, there hovered the pervasive sense that she *needed* me, that I needed to be here. It was the same sense Sidonie had felt on the ship. Blessed Elua had joined us for a purpose. If there was aught we could do, it would require us both.

Once I'd willed myself to docility and we'd entered Montrève's carriage, Phèdre and Joscelin seemed more themselves. Almost.

"So how was Carthage, love?" Phèdre asked gently, as though I were ten years old and I'd gone on a pleasure-jaunt.

"Fine." I forced a smile. "They were very kind to me there."

"Did you . . ." She hesitated. "Did Prince Astegal's chirurgeons examine you?"

"Oh, yes." I leaned my head back against the cushions. "They were able to help a little. They explained matters in a way I could understand. I know I'm not right in my wits. I do."

"It's all right, Imri." Joscelin exchanged a glance with Phèdre. "We'll take care of you. We'll always take care of you."

My eyes stung. "Thank you."

Phèdre's townhouse in the City had always been a place of warmth and joy. Every time I'd returned to it, I'd been received with open arms and tears of happiness. Not this time. Our driver had to give a password before the gate was opened. In the narrow courtyard, Montrève's men-at-arms were arrayed to meet us, hands hovering over sword-hilts.

"Is all well?" Ti-Philippe called in a hard voice.

"As well as it gets," Joscelin affirmed. "Bad news from afar."

We descended from the carriage. There was no Eugènie waiting to fold me to her bosom and accuse me of being heartless, no joyous reunion. Only hard-eyed, watchful men. One of them gave me a terse smile.

"Prince Imriel." Hugues inclined his head. "We're pleased to see you safe."

Hugues, sweet Hugues. He'd always been among my favorite retainers at House Montrève, the strapping shepherd-lad Ti-Philippe had seduced ages ago, long since grown into a beautiful, gentle man with a heart as vast as his shoulders were broad. He'd taught me to wrestle when I was a boy, taught me to wield a quarterstaff as effectively as a shepherd's crook. When I'd wed Dorelei and gone away to Alba, Hugues had given me his treasured wooden flute as a parting gift. He should have been laughing with joy, concocting more bad poetry to declaim in his lovely voice.

He wasn't.

"Thank you, Hugues," I whispered.

Another curt nod. "Of course."

Inside it was worse. The household staff was quiet and furtive—*here*, here in Phèdre nó Delaunay's home, where it wasn't unknown for a stablehand to dine with the Comtesse of Montrève.

"Where . . ." I cleared my throat. "Where's Eugènie?"

Phèdre shot me a puzzled look. "In the kitchen, I imagine."

There I found Eugènie up to her elbows in flour, kneading dough. She bobbed an awkward curtsy. "Prince Imriel," she said in a careful tone. "We had word of your return. I'm making the quince tarts you like so much."

I made myself smile at her. "Thank you, Eugènie."

It was just all so *wrong*, as though I was caught in a waking dream where no one was quite themselves. I thought I'd be better prepared than Sidonie to deal with it, since I'd already experienced their madness. I was wrong. Matters had worsened, and I wasn't recovering from my own bout of insanity this time, questioning my own memories. I had to fight the urge to shake them, shout at them to wake up, to come to their senses. Ptolemy Solon had warned me that any attempt to struggle against the spell would cause it to tighten like a snare. I had to keep reminding myself of it.

It got worse when we dined in the early evening. Shortly after we'd taken our seats at the table, there was a commotion in the courtyard. Joscelin went to attend to it and returned looking somber.

"Queen's courier," he said. "Ysandre's declared a state of mourning. They're announcing it throughout the City."

"Just the City?" Phèdre inquired.

"They'd only make a mockery of it outside the City's walls." Joscelin frowned. "Elua! Would that we knew what Alais and L'Envers did to make them turn against the Crown itself."

"Alais." Phèdre shook her head. "I reckon myself a fair judge of character, but I'll admit, I never expected this of her." She glanced at me. "You were always close to her, Imri. Did you suspect she harbored such ambitions?"

I cleared my throat. "Not . . . not in Terre d'Ange." I saw Alais' weary face in my memory, heard her words. *I do not want this responsibility.* "I knew she aspired to overturn the law of matrilineal succession in Alba. It surprised me."

"It's not just Alais and L'Envers," Joscelin said grimly. "Talorcan's backing them, the treacherous bastard. Somehow he's managed to seize power in Alba. Drustan says he's got seven hundred men in Turnone. If he sends more, this war's truly going to be ugly."

"Must it come to that?" The words were out of my mouth before I could stop them. They both stared at me. "I'm sorry. It's just . . . if the whole country is against us, do we even stand a chance?"

"Yes, of course," Phèdre said firmly. "I have every hope that the support for this rebellion is broad, but not deep. When the commonfolk see the cost of it, I believe they will come to their senses and beg Alais and Barquiel to surrender. And if they do not . . ." Her face took on an expression of stern dignity. "There are things in this world that are worth fighting and dying for, Imriel. Without respect for the rule of law, we are no better than the most savage of barbarians. What did we stand against Waldemar Selig for if not for this?"

I bit my tongue and nodded.

"You of all people should know that, Imriel." Joscelin sounded disappointed in me. "Do you forget your own history?"

"No," I murmured. "I'm sorry."

"Poor boy." Phèdre's face softened. "It's not your fault. He's not himself, Joscelin."

"I blame those witches of the Maghuin Dhonn." Joscelin's jaw tightened. "He's not been right since they sank their hooks into him. And Alais . . . I fear they got to her somehow. You recall, she seemed passing fond of that youngest son of the Lady of the Dalriada, the Maghuin Dhonn harpist's get."

Phèdre shivered. "And through her to Talorcan."

Joscelin nodded. "I fear as much."

The damnable thing was that they made it almost seem plausible. We'd come up with a similar tale ourselves. I licked my dry lips. "I thought so, too. I gave Sidonie the croonie-stone that the *ollamh* gave me to protect her. I tried to copy the charm he wrought."

"Ah, love!" Phèdre gave me a sorrowful smile. "Your heart's in the right place, no matter how misguided the object of its affection. It gives me hope."

"There *is* one hope." I told them about Bodeshmun's gem and his death-bed charge to Sidonie.

Joscelin's eyes brightened. "Do you really think it holds the power to protect the City?"

"I do," I said, meaning it.

"I remember seeing it." Phèdre gestured at her throat. "The Chief Horologist wore it on a chain around his neck. Every facet was inscribed. And there's no denying that he was a man of surpassing gifts. The marvels he showed us . . ." She smiled at me, this time with gladness. "That *is* a piece of hope, love. Whatever happens outside these walls, if the City of Elua can hold, the heart of Terre d'Ange lives."

"For no one, man, woman, nor child, may be rightfully crowned sovereign of Terre d'Ange anywhere but here," Joscelin said.

"Nowhere," Phèdre agreed.

They exchanged glances, remembering. I could guess at their memories. Ysandre de la Courcel riding fearlessly toward the City amidst a shower of silver coins, each one bearing her likeness. They believed they were fighting to preserve her legacy, their legacy.

And they were so very, very wrong.

SEVENTY-FIVE

I endured the night.

It felt terribly strange to sleep beneath the low roof of my boyhood bedchamber. I'd not slept there for years. I'd outgrown it in ways I couldn't even number. And yet it held so many memories. Long nights conversing with Eamonn when he had fostered with us. My own sickly reflection in the mirror as I'd sawed at my Shahrizai braids with a dagger the day after I'd visited Valerian House for the first time. Phèdre adjusting the collar of my doublet on the day I'd wed Dorelei mab Breidaia.

That was the last memory.

As I lay sleepless, I thought about Dorelei and our unborn son. Their spirits slept now beneath a green mound in Clunderry, Berlik's skull buried at their feet. I prayed for their forgiveness and understanding.

And I thought about Sidonie.

Ah, gods! Was simple happiness truly so much to ask? Was it ambitious to dream of a future in which we spent our lives together, taking pleasure in each other, in the bright mirror and the dark? In the heady abandon of love-play, in the homely comfort of watching our children dandled on the loving knees of their grandparents?

"Kushiel," I whispered into the darkness. "I have spent my life trying to be good. I pray you hear your scion's prayers. There is no one here in need of your harsh justice, only your mercy."

There was no answer. Outside my narrow window, the moon inched closer to fullness in the night sky.

Some time after dawn, I arose hollow-eyed for lack of sleep and donned the clothing that the maidservant Clory had laid out for me. Black breeches and a black doublet. Mourning attire. It must have belonged to Joscelin.

It fit surprisingly well.

I descended the stairs to find the rest of the household likewise attired in mourning garb. Joscelin eyed me critically. "You're limping. I didn't notice that yesterday."

I opened my mouth to say that my healing wound stiffened when I slept, then caught myself. "I took a tumble on the ship in some rough waters and got a nasty bruise."

Phèdre cocked her head at me. "Why didn't Astegal's ship continue up the Aviline? What made you decide to transfer to a barge?"

For the first time in my life, I had cause to curse her agile wits. "We thought it would be safer if no one knew Sidonie had returned," I said. "We'd heard the rumors of impending war."

She didn't blink. "How did you know you could trust the barge-captain?"

"I don't know." I was too tired to invent a good lie. "Astegal had made plans for every contingency. You'd have to ask Kratos the details."

It seemed to satisfy her, at least for the moment. I trusted

Kratos would field the question with aplomb if Phèdre chose to pursue it. I hoped he'd slept better than I had.

Word came from the Palace before we'd finished breaking our fast; we were summoned to a funeral service in Astegal's honor that afternoon. It would take place at the Temple of Elua, followed by a reception at the Palace. Ysandre and Drustan were moving swiftly; but then, there was precious little time to spare.

"I should attend as a member of House Courcel," I said, rising from the table. "I'll see you at the temple."

Another glance exchanged.

"Imriel," Phèdre said gently. "I think it's best if you stay with us. I'm pleased that the physicians in Carthage were able to explain your situation in a way you could understand, but Sidonie's in a great deal of pain right now. I fear worrying about your delusions is the last thing she needs."

I gritted my teeth. "Actually, she said I was a solace. That it was a comfort to know that the last kinsman she expected had stayed loyal to the Crown."

"I'm sure she did," Phèdre said. "She's always had a keen sense of propriety, even as a little girl. I never understood why you disliked her, any more than I can understand why your illness turned your feelings inside out." She shook her head. "Nonetheless, give the poor child a moment's peace."

Joscelin's hand closed on my shoulder. "Why don't we spar? It will be like old times."

I turned my head toward him. "Do you mean to keep me here forcibly?"

"Imri." Joscelin's grip tightened, then released. He caught my hand instead and raised it, baring my wrist to reveal the faint scars there. His eyes were grave. The vile threats I could never unsay, never forget I'd uttered, echoed in my memory. "We're trying to help."

I looked away. "I know. All right."

I couldn't begin to count the number of times I'd sparred with Joscelin: here in the inner courtyard of the townhouse, in the gardens of Montrève. The hilts of the wooden practice-swords we used were smooth and shiny with wear. He'd begun teaching me on the deck of a ship bound for Menekhet when I was ten years old. Betimes when I concentrated on my footwork, I could still remember the feel of the warm deck beneath my bare feet. I'd been so grateful for his attention, for his loving patience.

My heart wasn't in it today.

My heart was in the Palace, agonizing for Sidonie as she prepared to hear Astegal of Carthage lovingly eulogized, worrying about the charm holding. It was with Alais and, gods help me, Barquiel L'Envers as they went about the terrible chore of raising an ever-larger army. I fought mechanically. My feet remembered the steps of their own accord. My thigh throbbed. My arms remembered the dull exhaustion I'd felt outside the gates of Amílcar, my muscles quivering with the aftermath of untold blows and parries.

Too many memories.

The dead; thousands of dead. Dead Amazigh, dead Carthaginians, dead Nubians . . . and, ah, Elua have mercy! Thousands of dead Euskerri. The flower of a generation.

"Not bad." We were both breathing hard when Joscelin called for a halt. He smiled at me, his summer-blue eyes crinkling at the corners. "You've kept up your training."

"Yes." I forced the word past the tightness in my throat. "I've tried."

Joscelin clapped my back. "Good man."

When the hour arrived to depart for the Temple of Elua, it was almost a relief. Our carriage was draped with swags of black mourning-cloth and the headstalls of the horses had been dyed black. Our escort of outriders wore the forest-green and gold livery of House Montrève, but each man sported a black armband. We proceeded somberly through the streets of the City. Black cloth, black paint, black armbands. I remembered entering the City with Sidonie . . . how long ago? Almost two years. The black armbands, the down-turned thumbs.

This was different.

That had been a bitter reminder of my mother's legacy. This was a city in mourning. Mourning Astegal of Carthage, who had stolen away the love of my life, whose ambition had turned all those I loved against all they held dear. On the streets, men and women wept openly. I gazed out the window at their faces, my heart aching. And I allowed myself the fierce consolation of remembering the quiver that had run the length of my blade when Astegal had died, of Sidonie's hand firm atop mine on the hilt and her unflinching courage.

And Astegal's damned head on a pike, his slack jaw gaping.

The Temple of Elua was thronged with mourners and guards. In the vestibule, I pried off my boots quickly and slipped through the crowd in the inner garden sanctum to find Sidonie. She was with Drustan and Ysandre and Brother Thomas Jubert at the base of Elua's effigy, Kratos at her side. I saw her head turn as I made my way toward her. The quick flair of relief in her eyes eased a tight knot inside me.

"Imriel." Sidonie greeted me carefully. "I thought to see you at the Palace this morning."

I gave her a brief bow. "Forgive me. Are you well?"

Her shoulders twitched. "I'm enduring."

"Imri!" Phèdre's voice behind me held a note of despairing reproach. "I'm sorry, your highness. I asked him not to trouble you."

"He's no trouble, my lady." Sidonie smiled at her with a mixture of sweetness and sorrow. "I quite missed his presence this morning. In a strange way, I feel I've lost a sister and gained a brother." She laid her hand on my arm. That irrepressible spark leapt between us, giving the lie to her words, but we'd had long practice in dissembling. "I know you've missed him, but I hope you'll spare me his company from time to time."

"Of course," Phèdre said without hesitation. "For as long as you like."

"He doesn't think of *you* as a sister," Ysandre noted suspiciously.

"I'm trying," I said humbly.

Drustan gave me a hard look. "See that your man Kratos keeps an eye on him," he said to Sidonie.

She inclined her head. "Of course, Father. I only wish to have the comfort of family around me on this dark day."

Brother Thomas cleared his throat. "Speaking of which, we should begin, child." He took Sidonie's hands. "Are you prepared?"

"I am, my lord."

The priest released her hands and took his place before the plinth on which Elua's effigy stood. He spread his arms, echoing the pose of the massive effigy behind him. The crowd ceased its murmuring and fell silent. Brother Thomas was a big man. I remembered how he'd reminded me of Berlik when I'd first seen him, with his black hair and light grey eyes. I remembered how I'd spoken to Brother Thomas and an assembly representing all the priesthoods of Elua's Companions in an effort to convince them that my love for Sidonie was genuine. In the end, all of them had acknowledged the validity of our claim.

And now he gave her husband's eulogy.

"We are gathered here today to honor the passing of Astegal, Prince of the House of Sarkal, General of Carthage, husband of the Dauphine of Terre d'Ange, her highness Sidonie de la Courcel," Brother Thomas began.

The crowd gave a collective sigh. "Astegal of Carthage was a man of great and daring vision," the priest continued. "He came courting Terre d'Ange with his arms laden with gifts and his mind brimming with ideas. He captured our imagination and he captured the heart of our young Dauphine . . ."

It went on at considerable length. I daresay it was well done. I did my best not to listen, concentrating instead on the beating of the blood in my veins. I stood behind Sidonie, near enough for her to feel my presence, not so close that it aroused suspicion. I couldn't see her face, but I could feel the pain radiating from her as surely as though it were my own.

At last he ended. ". . . pray that if Blessed Elua is merciful, they will find one another again in another life and live to see their dreams brought to fruition." Brother Thomas bent his head to Sidonie. "You may speak now, my child."

"Thank you." Sidonie took his place before the plinth. Her face was streaked with tears. "I will not . . ." Her voice shook. She clasped her hands together hard and willed it to steadiness. "I will not attempt to elaborate on the eloquent words Brother Thomas spoke. I can but thank him for bringing to life so beautifully the memory of the man with whom I fell in love and for whom I grieve today."

The sentence was delivered with seemingly perfect sincerity, and I knew in the marrow of my bones that those were the hardest words Sidonie had ever spoken. A few of the mourners sobbed aloud.

She paused, collecting herself. "Astegal gave me many gifts during our too-short time together. He was as generous to me as he was to Terre d'Ange. But there is one gift he gave in secret—his greatest gift to me, to us, to the City of Elua. And it is of that gift I would speak on this fearful day, on the eve of a darker tomorrow."

In a clear, steady voice, with tears drying on her cheeks, Sidonie repeated the tale of Bodeshmun's death and the hidden gem.

She had inspired hope in Turnone and she inspired it here. I could feel the mood shift, hearts lifting. I watched Ysandre's eyes shine with pride, Drustan rest his hand on his wife's shoulder, nodding in approval. Ah, gods! They had every right to be proud of their heir. I prayed one day they would know why.

"I beseech you." Sidonie opened her arms, echoing the priest, echoing Blessed Elua himself. "All of you in Elua's blessed City. Take up this search, leave no stone unturned. Amidst the tragedy of his death, let us lay claim to this last, best gift of my Astegal and snatch hope from despair, honor from treason."

They roared.

It went on and on; promises and vows and pledges shouted with ferocious determination. The denizens of the City of Elua would raze the very foundations of the City to find Bodeshmun's gem. Sidonie lowered her arms and stepped away from the plinth, stumbling a little. Kratos caught her, but it was my gaze she sought.

"*My Astegal,*" Sidonie whispered beneath the roar, her voice catching in her throat, barely audible. "I feel sick."

"I know," I murmured.

That was all the comfort I could offer. As in Turnone, the throng pressed forward, offering their sympathies, offering their fierce vows. The guards beat them back, restoring order. I was pushed to the side, unheeded. I found Phèdre and Joscelin beside me once more, Joscelin shoving at the guardsmen with an unwonted curse as they crowded us.

It didn't matter.

All that mattered was that Sidonie had succeeded. She'd

been right; she had a role to play here. She had swayed them as no one else could have done: Ysandre's very well trained heir, Astegal's grieving widow.

I prayed it was enough.

And I prayed it was in time.

Seventy-six

"Look," Phèdre said in wonderment, gazing out the window of the carriage as we rode to the reception following the service. "They're tearing up the city."

It was true.

Word had spread like wildfire. By the time we emerged from the Temple of Elua, it was already racing ahead of us. Men and women thronged the streets, worrying their fingertips bloody as they pried at paving-stones, clamoring to search the premises of merchants and wineshops and threatening violence to any who might forbid them entry.

"Good," Joscelin said briefly.

Phèdre glanced at him. "Surely there must be a more logical way to approach this."

He shrugged. "You're good at figuring out that sort of thing."

"Well, we know Bodeshmun had the gem the night of the fête when the delegation first arrived," Phèdre said pragmatically. "That's when I noticed it."

"He had it the day of the marvel," I added. I was just as

glad to have her mind working on this puzzle and not picking out inconsistencies in our story. "Sid—" I caught myself. Elua, this was hard. "I went to watch the preparations in Elua's Square earlier in the day and I saw it then."

"So if Bodeshmun hid it himself, all we need to do is retrace his steps between the last sighting and the day he departed to limit the possibilities," Phèdre mused. "Unless of course he handed it off to someone else."

"He had runners going back and forth to adjust the mirrors on the walls." I pictured Bodeshmun pacing in his study, absentmindedly touching his chest where the painted leather talisman that held the key to unlocking the demon-stone was hidden. "But I don't think he was the sort to hand off so powerful a charm."

"No?" She regarded me. "Well, that would surely make the task easier. I'll have to ask Sidonie's opinion. Doubtless she came to know Bodeshmun quite well during her time in Carthage."

"Doubtless," I agreed.

"What about the Royal Treasury?" Joscelin suggested. "After all, where better to hide a single gem than amid a thousand others?"

Phèdre smiled at him. "That's an excellent thought."

I stifled a groan. That was one of the few places L'Envers *had* managed to search thoroughly; but I couldn't very well say it, and I couldn't think of a valid reason to discount the notion. I gazed out the window at the folk pelting through the city, spreading the word, searching haphazardly. A gem the size of a child's fist. It could be hidden anywhere. I remembered the icy-hot pain of a needle piercing my kidneys, Sunjata's voice hissing in my ear.

Go to Cythera.

An emerald flash.

"Do you recall what Bodeshmun did after showing you

the marvel?" I asked. "After the shadow had passed from the moon?"

"Everyone went . . ." Phèdre's face went blank. "There was a fête, wasn't there?" she asked Joscelin, who nodded uncertainly. "Elua! Between the wonder and the horror, I swear, the night's a blur." She stroked my hair. "I don't remember much beyond hearing you'd been found unconscious and raving, I fear."

"That was a bad night," Joscelin murmured. "I'm sure others will recall it better."

I wasn't. I already knew Sidonie didn't; we'd discussed it. But I held my tongue on the thought.

The reception took place in the Hall of Audience. The first thing I saw upon entering was the painting rendered in ground gems that had been the centerpiece of Carthage's largesse. It was on prominent display, the frame draped in black crepe. I stood and gazed at it for a long time. Ptolemy Solon had said that the image had defined the essence of the spell. A tall man with black hair and a crimson beard, a blonde woman. Standing before an oak tree, their hands clasped in friendship.

Or love.

I'd assumed the woman was meant to be Ysandre; we all had. It could as easily have been Sidonie. Mayhap it represented both of them. I searched the image for clues, hoping to find an image of the emerald gem buried in the leaves of the oak tree or mayhap a word hidden in the glimmering whorls of its bark, but there was nothing. Like as not it was a futile hope. L'Envers had said he'd searched Elua's Square and the great oak tree itself. It had been barren in winter with no crown of green leaves to hide a gem. If the demonstone was in Elua's Square, it could only be buried beneath the flagstones.

But a word . . . if there was a word hidden in the design,

it was like to be written in Punic. I wouldn't even recognize the alphabet. I resolved to tell Sidonie to examine it herself at the earliest opportunity.

"Cousin." A familiar voice behind me startled me out of my reverie. "A terrible story, is it not? But I hear your condition is improved."

"Mavros!" I turned and blinked at him. He was wearing a doublet of Courcel blue with braided silver trim and the insignia of the silver swan on its breast. "Why aren't you in mourning attire?"

"I am." Mavros showed me his black armband. "Officers of the Royal Army were given orders to remain in uniform."

"Royal Army?" I echoed.

His handsome face hardened. "Do you expect me to stand by and do nothing while that ambitious chit and her snake of an uncle attempt to overthrow the throne? Yes, of course I put in my name for a commission. Every peer in the City with a shred of honor and courage has."

I glanced over in Joscelin's direction. "I'm sorry. No one mentioned it."

Mavros followed my gaze. "Ah. Yes, well, I expect they're being cautious around you. Joscelin *did* put in his name, but the Queen refused to allow it." His next words eradicated any dawning sense of relief I might have had. "Ysandre has sworn that Alais will never take the throne while she lives. We will fight to our last breath, but if it comes to it, if L'Envers takes the City, she's asked Joscelin to remain that he might perform the *terminus* for her."

"Surely not," I whispered. "Phèdre would never consent to it."

His brows rose. "'Tis a grave sacrifice to be sure. But Joscelin Verreuil is the Queen's Champion. It's his duty."

I didn't want to believe it, but I did. I remembered Sidonie aboard Deimos' ship as we prepared to set it afire and attempt the harbor at Amílcar. *Believe me when I tell you I would far rather die by your hand than be restored to Astegal.* There was a streak of fierce pride in the women of House Courcel. Ysandre might make such a vow rather than cede the throne alive. And Joscelin . . . in his right mind, Joscelin would never honor it, nor would Phèdre consent to allow him.

But they weren't.

Mavros misread my expression. "Don't worry," he said kindly. "No one expects you to serve, Imri. You're ill. If your madness returned on the battlefield, it would endanger us all." He smiled. "At any rate, I hear there's hope for the City. Carthage may save her after all."

"Yes." I had to get away from this stranger with Mavros' face. "Will you excuse me?"

I plunged into the sea of mourners, seeking Sidonie. Now that Mavros had mentioned it, I realized there were more familiar faces than I'd noticed wearing military uniforms. I did my best to avoid them, and in the process blundered into one of the few figures not clad in black or Courcel blue. I knew her by the gleaming fall of red-gold hair that hung down her back.

"Amarante!" I said in relief.

Elua, it was so damned easy to forget.

She turned, the crimson silk robes of a Priestess of Naamah swirling gracefully around her. Her brows knit as though she were trying for a moment to place me, and then she inclined her head. "Prince Imriel," Amarante said politely. "I was pleased to hear that you had returned safely."

"Yes." We were within earshot of Sidonie. I glanced at her. Her expression was composed, but I could see the stricken look behind her eyes. From the first dawning of our liaison, even before it had begun, Amarante had known. She had been Sidonie's sole confidante and conspirator.

Amarante moved past me. "Sidonie." Her voice changed, softening. "I'm so very—"

"Please don't." Sidonie laid her fingers gently over Amarante's lips. "I don't think I can bear to hear another word of sympathy today."

"I understand." Amarante took her hand and kissed it. "Would you like me to stay with you for a while?"

"No." Sidonie shivered. "No, thank you. It's a kind offer."

"Of course." Amarante studied her face, frowning slightly. She was a Priestess of Naamah and although it happened precious seldom, she knew withdrawal when she encountered it. For a mercy, whatever she saw, she chose to attribute it to grief. "You know you've only to send word to the temple if you need me."

"Yes. Thank you." Sidonie watched her go. "I'm not sure how much longer I can do this."

"Your highness is weary," Kratos said in Hellene. "You should retire."

She looked at him with hope. "Do you suppose I might?"

He bowed. "I will speak to your lady mother."

Kratos strode through the crowd, gesturing for people to keep their distance from Sidonie. They deferred out of respect for their beloved Astegal's most trusted bodyguard.

"Sidonie," I said in a low voice. "Before you go, I want you to look at the gem-painting that Astegal presented at the fête. It's part and parcel of the spell. See if there are any words hidden in it written in Punic."

"Punic." She nodded, closing her eyes briefly.

"Are you all right?" I asked.

"Yes." She opened her eyes. "But I can *feel* it. And I'm afraid of slipping away."

"Don't." I caught her hand and squeezed it hard. "Stay."

She returned the pressure. "I'm trying."

Across the hall, Ysandre was gesturing and Drustan was shaking his head. Kratos' face was flushed. He offered them a curt bow. Drustan made his way toward us. I released Sidonie's hand and moved a few feet away.

"Sidonie." Drustan rested his hands on his daughter's shoulders. "I understand that you are weary and heart-sore. But you need to be strong." His fingers flexed. "We stand on the eve of war. This is the greatest test any ruler might face. And I know you cannot fathom what that truly means, but you *are* your mother's heir. The people need to see that neither grief nor betrayal will bow your head."

"Yes, Father," Sidonie murmured.

And so she stayed, and I stayed near her, offering the meager comfort of my presence as the reception wore on and on and an endless line of well-wishers came to proffer their sympathies. Over and over, they offered the same regrets and platitudes; over and over, Sidonie accepted them with forced gratitude. Many of them asked if there was a chance she yet carried Astegal's child. Their faces fell when she shook her head.

What another piece of bitter irony it was. The peers of the realm, the lords and ladies of the Great Houses of Terre d'Ange, had always held reservations regarding Ysandre de la Courcel's half-Cruithne heir. If Sidonie had truly fallen in love with a foreign prince, they would have shrieked to the heavens about the sacred bloodline of Blessed Elua being further diluted. And yet here they were, offering her adulation, mourning the loss of Astegal of Carthage.

I willed myself not to hate them. It was the spell, only the spell.

I can feel it. I'm afraid of slipping away.

Those words made my blood run cold.

At last the reception ended, the crowds thinning, departing with multitudinous vows to find Bodeshmun's charm. Phèdre came to find me.

"Will you not come home with us, love?" she asked plaintively.

I shook my head. "I need to stay here."

"Have no fear, my lady." Kratos' arm descended over my shoulders, heavy and solid. Whether or not he understood all the words spoken, he read the situation well. He smiled at her. "As her highness has bidden me, I'll make certain that the prince comes to no harm."

Phèdre cocked her head and replied in Hellene. "You don't have a Carthaginian accent."

"No." Kratos' smile never wavered. "I was born in Hellas and taken in battle many years ago, serving as a mercenary. Bad luck. On the day Astegal was born, his father freed me." He removed his arm from my shoulders and pressed his clenched fist to his heart. "Hence, my loyalty."

Her expression eased. "I see."

Once the hall was emptied, Sidonie went to stand before the gem-painting. She gazed at it for a long time as though lost in contemplation. The guards surrounding her, and even Drustan and Ysandre, waited with respect.

I lingered, hoping.

But no. At length she turned away, giving her head an imperceptible shake. There was no hidden clue.

The hunt continued.

SEVENTY-SEVEN

For five days the hunt for Bodeshmun's gem continued at a frantic pace. The City looked like it had been sacked and looted.

At first the mood was one of fierce jubilation. After conferring with Phèdre and hearing her thoughts on a more logical approach, Ysandre ordered the Royal Army to assist with the search. They began by digging up the whole of Elua's Square, removing the massive paving-stones and hauling them away, sifting through the dirt below.

They found nothing.

The mood didn't sour all at once, but day by day the tension mounted. The search continued. The wing of the Palace in which the Carthaginian delegation had lodged was stripped bare. Following Joscelin's suggestion, the Royal Treasury was moved piece by piece to an array of empty storage chambers, every gem within it scrutinized. Routes from the Palace to the Square were scoured obsessively. Every crack and crevice along the white walls of the City where Bodeshmun's mirrors had been placed was examined.

Nothing.

As hope dwindled, tempers flared. The semblance of looting became a reality and there was widespread fighting in the streets of the City. A rumor went around that a wandering Tsingani *kumpania* had found the gem and stolen it away, sparking riots in Night's Doorstep. A house was burned, an entire family killed in their sleep. The Cockerel closed its doors for the first time in memory.

Rumor ran rampant, fueled by the fact that no one could quite remember the details of the night surrounding the marvel.

Even the Night Court wasn't immune. Someone remembered that Astegal and a group of Carthaginians had visited there. A fresh rumor went around that Bodeshmun had accompanied them, that he had entrusted the gem to the safekeeping of Bryony House, whose treasury was renowned for being more secure than the Royal Treasury itself. An irate crowd stormed the gates of Bryony House, demanding that the Dowayne allow them to search the treasury. When she refused, claiming that her own household had already conducted a thorough search, the altercation turned violent. The Dowayne's skilled guards skirmished with the mob.

The incident killed three and wounded many others.

Every day brought irate petitioners to the Palace: robbed merchants, injured citizens, a furious Janelle nó Bryony. Every day, the Hall of Audience rang with shouting.

Every day was worse than the last.

And worst of all, Sidonie *was* slipping away.

There was never enough time to talk. She sent for me when she could, but we didn't dare spend much time closeted without arousing suspicion. If it hadn't been for Kratos, I'm not sure we'd have managed at all. The members of her personal guard had been recalled from the duties to which they'd been assigned when she left for Carthage. All of the goodwill I'd managed to earn had vanished, lost along with the memories of an affair that had divided the nation. The first time I saw Claude de Monluc, he regarded me with cool wariness. Still, so long as I only met with Sidonie with Kratos in tow, they were willing to allow it.

As long as it was brief.

As long as we did naught to arouse suspicion.

"Imriel." It was on the fifth day that Sidonie greeted me at her door with a momentary look of blankness. She shuddered, her gaze clearing. "Thank you for coming. Please, come in."

I entered, Kratos padding behind me. "How bad is it, Sun Princess?" I asked when the door closed behind us.

"Bad." She sat hunched on the couch, hands gripping opposite elbows. The hollows of her eyes looked sunken and bruised. "It hurts. It hurts all the time, and I'm afraid to sleep. Afraid I'll tear away the bindings all unwitting. I have to think about it every minute of every day."

"You can do this," I said steadily. "You *can*, Sidonie."

She shivered. "I can feel it. It's out there. But it feels like it's everywhere in the City. Nowhere more than anywhere else. It's there and it's here. In my head, buzzing like a beehive. It keeps telling me it would be so much easier to let go and believe."

"It lies," I said.

"I know." Sidonie took my hands, pressed them to her face. Her tears were hot on my skin. "But I can't help it. At least I feel myself starting to believe *our* lies, and not some skewed version of my own memories. Elua! How can we fail after all we've tried? After all who've died for our efforts?"

I held her while she wept. "We won't."

Over the crown of her head, I could see Kratos watching us. For the first time, there was doubt and fear on his broad features.

I fought against despair.

"Sidonie," I whispered. "We will *not* fail."

She lifted her head and kissed me, clinging to me, her mouth hot and desperate. "I love you," she murmured. "I do. I *know* it."

I nodded, swallowing hard. "No magic so dire."

"None," Sidonie echoed.

But there was. Bodeshmun had crafted his spell with care and hidden the demon-stone with consummate skill. Day by day, its influence ate away at Sidonie's resolve, even as it ate away at the foundations of the City of Elua. In the end, Ysandre was forced to declare an end to the search and command the Royal Army to restore order.

"I'm sorry," Ysandre said to Sidonie when we dined that evening. House Courcel, seemingly united, tolerating the presence of poor mad Prince Imriel. "I know you placed a great deal of hope in Astegal's kinsman. But we cannot afford to have the City at its own throat. Not on the eve of war."

Sidonie leaned her brow against steepled fingers. "I understand. But . . ."

"You cannot afford to be soft, child." There was sympathy in Drustan's voice. "I too wish that we had found Bodeshmun's charm. But we must deal with that which is, not that which we wish might be. In these final days, the army must be free to prepare for battle, knowing that we leave the City calm behind us when we go."

"Has there been word?" she asked him.

Drustan and Ysandre exchanged a glance. "Yes." It was Ysandre who answered. "Reports of a considerable force amassing on the plains east of Turnone. It seems our threat worked. Alais and L'Envers mean to make a stand."

"Did you . . ." I hesitated. "Did you truly mean it, Ysandre? Would you have put innocent villages to the sword?" I knew I shouldn't ask, but I couldn't help myself. If there was any chance the answer was no, mayhap this looming tragedy could still be averted.

Ysandre looked at me with pity and sorrow. "That is not a threat one makes in idleness, Imriel. Of course I meant it. No village conspiring to give aid to traitors is innocent. It would have been a grievous measure, but a necessary one."

But you can't win! I wanted to cry the words aloud. I didn't. It wouldn't do any good. "What if Sidonie and I attempted to treat with them?" I asked instead. "Alais might listen to her sister, and you know we've always been close."

On the other side of the long table, Sidonie lifted her head, following my thoughts. If the search for Bodeshmun's gem was a loss, that would at least serve to get her out of the City of Elua, away from the spell's malign influence.

"Why on earth would Alais listen to either of you over the orders of her own mother and father?" Ysandre's eyes narrowed. I could see the suspicion rising in her, abrupt and overwhelming. "Or is there some other scheme behind this, hmm? You'd like that, wouldn't you? A chance to spirit Sidonie away for yourself. I daresay it's exactly what you've been waiting for."

"Mother!" Sidonie said sharply. "He's only trying to help."

Ysandre pointed at her. "You're overtrusting. If you'd learned nothing else from your sister's betrayal and that which befell your husband's kinsman in New Carthage, I'd expect you to be on guard against *that* particular weakness."

"I was only trying to help," I murmured. "I'm sorry."

Drustan regarded me, his face impassive behind its woad markings. "Imriel, you did a great service to Alba after Dorelei's death, and I will always hold your memory in honor. But I fear so long as this delusion grips you, you're not to be trusted. Your words today prove it." His gaze shifted to Sidonie. "And I fear it might be best if you were to avoid his company unless matters of state dictate otherwise."

"Kratos—" she began.

"I don't care about Kratos!" Drustan shouted. It was so out of character that Sidonie simply stared at him, shocked. He wrestled himself under control with a visible effort. "Kratos." This time it was a summons. Kratos, posted by the door like a good bodyguard, came forward in answer to it. "Escort Prince Imriel to his quarters, or wherever it is he wishes to go," Drustan said. "He is no longer permitted to call upon the Dauphine."

Kratos hesitated, not entirely understanding the command. Sidonie repeated it for him in Hellene, her voice toneless. He bowed to her. "As my lady bids."

I rose. "Take me to the townhouse, Kratos. I will place myself in Phèdre and Joscelin's care and free you to return to Sidonie's service. It's her that Astegal bade you to protect, not me." I glanced at Ysandre and Drustan. "I trust that will suffice?"

"It will," Ysandre said curtly.

Gods, it had happened so quickly! After all our care, they'd turned on me for one ill-chosen suggestion. I left the dining hall feeling the weight of their hard stares, and Sidonie's silent despair tugging at my heart.

I gathered a few things from my quarters at the Palace and sent for a carriage. We were on our way in short order, the carriage jolting over the torn-up streets of the City.

"What now, my lord?" Kratos asked soberly.

"Do your best to protect her." I rested my aching head against the cushions. "The charm I wrought . . . it's beginning to fail. And it hurts. She's afraid to sleep for fear she'll tear the bindings loose. You can watch over her, at least give her the solace of sleep. Her guard trusts you; they'll not quibble at it. It might help."

Kratos nodded. "I'll tell her."

"I think . . ." I rubbed my temples. "I think we have to begin to prepare for failure."

"There's a tight lock on the city," he observed. "No one's allowed to come or go without a thorough inspection." Kratos met my gaze and shrugged. "I've been checking. It won't be easy to get her out, if that's what you're thinking."

"I don't know what I'm thinking," I said slowly. The image of Joscelin performing the *terminus* leapt unbidden into my mind. I'd never seen it done, but I'd heard it described. The graceful turn, the steady hands. One dagger hurled, the other slashing his own throat. I closed my eyes, willing it to be gone. Joscelin would do his duty and Phèdre would follow him into death. I knew that as surely as I knew the sun rose in the east. "It's not just Sidonie."

I wasn't sure I could abandon them.

I wasn't sure of anything.

"We can't save them all, my lord," Kratos said gently. "And mayhap none of them. I'm sorry. But we're only mortal. You have to choose."

"I know." I buried my face in my hands and took a deep, shuddering breath. "Sidonie, then. The City's defenses will be stretched thin once the army departs. If she can hold on long enough, at least there may be enough of *her* left to aid us. And mayhap . . . mayhap we can think of some way to help the others."

"Mayhap," Kratos said. "Mayhap, my lord."

The kindness in his voice nearly undid me. "I'm not

giving up, Kratos," I said. "Not while there's breath in my body."

He smiled with sorrow. "I never thought you would, my lord. If it comes to it, I'd be proud to die trying beside you. 'Tis a far nobler death than I'd ever thought to earn these many years."

We rode the rest of the way in silence.

Seventy-eight

Once the Queen declared an official end to the search for Bodeshmun's gem, a strange mood settled over the City: proud, defiant, hostile, despairing. All of these things at once.

War was coming.

The full moon was a week away.

Companies of the Royal Army patrolled the streets, keeping order. They drilled in the City gardens, trampling the new spring growth. Drustan mab Necthana and Ghislain nó Trevalion would be sharing command—the Cruarch of Alba and the Royal Commander of Terre d'Ange. Wherever they went, they were hailed with fierce shouts.

On an unofficial level, the search *did* continue. I took part in it, hoping against hope, desperate for the distraction. On the heels of Phèdre's latest inspiration, I searched the river wharf with a company of Montrève's retainers. Alas, to no avail. I prowled the City, muttering the word under my breath in the hopes that it might unexpectedly release a demon. Ptolemy Solon had said it was needful to take possession of the gem to break the spell, but mayhap he was wrong. Over and over, I whispered the word of unbinding.

Emmenghanom.

Beholden.

And, ah, gods! I was beholden. Every day, rising under Phèdre and Joscelin's roof, I was reminded of it. I owed them my life. Almost everything I was, I owed to them. The thought of abandoning them, of being unable to save them, hurt more than I could say.

Kratos came regularly to the townhouse. When we could snatch a private moment, he reported on Sidonie's condition, his homely face grave, dark circles under his eyes. He was giving up his own sleep to safeguard hers, catching naps during the day.

At first it helped.

And then it didn't.

"We're losing her, my lord," Kratos said simply. "Bit by bit."

I fought down a welling surge of helplessness. "Does she still trust you?"

"Aye. Sometimes she forgets for a moment and addresses me as though I truly were Astegal's man. Either way, she trusts me." He withdrew a flask from the inner pocket of his doublet—new livery in Courcel blue, freshly tailored to fit his broad frame. "She's stubborn. She's fighting it as best she can. This is a sleeping draught she had the Palace chirurgeon prepare." Kratos smiled ruefully. "She bade me use it on her if need be. Use her own tactics against her. She reckons she won't remember them by the time it's needful."

"Sidonie." I sighed. "Kratos, do me a kindness. Have you run of the City unheeded?"

He nodded. "As far as anyone's concerned, I'm General Astegal's right-hand man. No one tells me what to do but her highness."

I handed him a letter. "Deliver this to Lieutenant Faucon. He and his men are lodging at the Jolly Whistler near the wharf. Tell him to get it to Alais as quickly as possible."

"What's in it?" Kratos asked.

"Everything we know," I said grimly. "Our failure to find the gem, all the places that I know for a surety have been thoroughly searched. The fact that Sidonie's bindings are failing. The fact that Queen Ysandre has pledged herself to a death-pact if Alais and L'Envers take the City. Is there aught I've forgotten?"

Kratos shook his head. "Do you reckon any of it will help?"

"I don't know." I raked a hand through my hair. "If they know about the death-pact, they can hold off on entering the City. But what then? Do they remain camped outside its walls while day by day, week by week, month by month, the madness grows? You saw the way the violence has escalated. How long until those trapped within the City begin to turn on one another?"

He didn't answer.

I shrugged. "We do what we can, my friend, and pray."

Kratos delivered the letter and reported back to me to say it was safely done, and that Marc Faucon believed he could get it to Alais without trouble. Their guise as barge-hands had proved effective; indeed, the men who'd ferried Sidonie up the Aviline were reckoned heroes by the City Guard. Captain Gilbert would carry Faucon and his men to Yvens, from whence they would make haste to Turnone.

I wished to Blessed Elua I could think of a way to get Sidonie back aboard that barge. I couldn't. All vessels, incoming or outgoing, were being searched with ruthless thoroughness. I thought Marc Faucon stood a good chance of getting away with hiding a letter on his person. I didn't think there was a chance of hiding the Dauphine of Terre d'Ange on an outgoing barge.

Long ago, Phèdre had been smuggled into the city of La Serenissima aboard a ship, hidden in a chest with a false bottom large enough to conceal her. I'd mulled over the possibility. But fate hadn't seen fit to place such an item at my disposal, and I could only imagine the suspicion it would provoke if mad Prince Imriel sought to commission a carpenter to build him one.

Of course, if I was wrong about Faucon's chances, it was all moot. That letter would damn me for a traitor if it was found.

The following day, Kratos strolled the wharf and came to report that to all appearances, the barge had departed without incident. I breathed an inward sigh of relief. For the moment, at least, I was safe, safe in the knowledge that I'd done all I could think of to do, and safe from the accusation of treason.

Then the Caerdicci idiot came.

His name was Antonio Peruggi, a name that became etched in my memory for its eternal association with sheer stupidity. The details of his story, I learned later; he was a merchant-captain trapped by the blockade in Amílcar with a cargo of silk he was unable to sell during war-time. When the blockade lifted, he decided his cargo would fetch better prices in Terre d'Ange.

And so he sailed to Marsilikos carrying silk and news out of Amílcar.

Barquiel L'Envers had been right; he and Alais had done an outstanding job of keeping the news from the City of Elua. They held the river and they held the roads, and no one they deemed unworthy of absolute trust had been allowed to pass. Unfortunately, Peruggi had heard the rumors in Marsilikos and gotten it into his head that Ysandre would surely reward him for being the first to deliver the news. He'd purchased a horse and hired a guide to lead him to the City of Elua across the countryside, avoiding all of L'Envers' checkpoints.

Stupidity, cunning, and greed.

The first we heard of it was a summons from a Queen's courier bidding me to Court. I thought mayhap I'd rejoiced too quickly at Marc Faucon's successful escape and felt the blood drain from my face.

"Why do you look so pale?" Phèdre asked. "Mayhap the news is good."

I forced myself to smile. "Mayhap."

"Not likely," Joscelin observed.

We arrived at the Hall of Audience to find Ysandre pacing in a fury, her color high and hectic. I glanced at Sidonie. She returned my gaze, but I couldn't read her expression. Beside her, Kratos grimaced in warning.

"Imriel." Ysandre fetched up before me, pointing toward a trembling figure. "Do you know this man?"

I looked at him. He was of average height and middle years, muscle running to fat. Brown hair, a forgettable face. He sported several ostentatious rings, and his chin was quivering. "I've never seen him before in my life."

"His name is Antonio Peruggi," Ysandre said in a taut voice. "He claims to have news from Amílcar. He claims that you and Sidonie conspired to bring the Euskerri to defeat Astegal. He claims you killed Astegal with your own hand, and that my daughter aided you. And he seems to think I will reward him for this knowledge."

I went ice-cold.

"Who paid you to say that?" The words were out of my mouth before I knew I'd thought them. Fear and rage drove my body and wits; I found myself standing before Peruggi without realizing I'd moved. He gaped at me, uncomprehending. I struck his face hard enough to wrench his head sideways. "Who?"

"No one!" Peruggi cried in broken D'Angeline. "It's true! Everyone knows!"

I struck him again. *"Who?"*

"No one!" he cried again.

"Do you know me?" I demanded. "Have you ever seen me before?"

"No!" Peruggi said raggedly. "But I heard the tales—"

I backhanded him across the face. "Was it Alais? Barquiel L'Envers?"

"Enough." It was Sidonie who spoke, her voice cool and commanding. "He speaks sedition," she said to her mother. "I told you as much. I sense L'Envers' hand behind it. It reeks of his tactics. This is some scheme to drive a wedge between us."

Ysandre considered her daughter's words. "Is that so?" she asked the Caerdicci merchant. She sounded eminently reasonable. "Will you hold to your story or shall I have you tortured until you divulge the truth?"

Antonio Peruggi shook his head. There was a trickle of blood at the corner of his mouth where I'd struck him. "No," he whispered. "Please, your majesty."

"So it was L'Envers," Ysandre pressed.

"Yes." He gazed at me, eyes damp. "Yes, the Duc L'Envers."

"Sedition." Ysandre lingered over the word. "You have sacrificed your rights here, Messire Peruggi, and I would be within mine to have you executed." He flinched. She glanced at Sidonie. "What do you say?"

"Let him be flogged." Sidonie fixed the Caerdicci merchant with an implacable gaze. "Let him be put in stocks and given a public flogging, then turned loose to leave the City, his back bloody and bare, that all across the realm might know the price of speaking sedition in the matter of my husband."

Ysandre nodded. "So be it."

Ah, gods! I was torn between relief and horror. Elua knows, the man had spoken the truth, even if it was driven by greed and idiocy. My rage had been unfeigned, although no one would have guessed at its cause.

But Sidonie . . .

I wasn't sure.

Later that day, Antonio Peruggi was flogged in Elua's Square, kneeling on sifted dirt denuded of its paving-stones, his bent head and helpless hands held in stocks, his thick, fleshy torso bare. I watched the Queen's chastiser's arm rise and fall, wielding the metal-tipped flogger. I watched it shred Peruggi's skin as he jerked and moaned in the stocks, blood running freely down his back. I watched Sidonie's calm, appraising gaze.

My heart ached.

When it was done, a watching crowd roared their approval. Members of the Queen's Guard helped a stumbling Peruggi from the stocks, helped him to mount. Slapped his horse's haunches and sent him toward the southern gates. I made my way unobtrusively to Sidonie's side.

"Are you still there, love?" I murmured under my breath.

For the space of a few heartbeats, she didn't answer; but at last her head moved in an imperceptible nod. Wherever she'd gone, it took a long time to come back. "Get out of the City," she said in a low voice. "Save yourself before this truth breaks in earnest."

"Not without you," I said steadily.

A glance, one glance. Anguish surfacing in her dark eyes. Gods, I wished I could make it go away! Instead, Kratos shifted, placing himself closer to Sidonie. Ysandre's suspicious gaze found us. I moved away.

That night I couldn't sleep. I gazed out my narrow window. The moon was very nearly full. Three days. In three days it would be full. I wondered if the spell's strength waxed and waned with the moon. I thought about the emerald flash I'd seen before the madness on Sunjata's needle took me and wondered if mayhap the gem would emit a spark by the rising moonlight.

It seemed no less implausible than anything else, so I rose and went to saddle a horse. In the process, I awoke the sleeping stable-lad, who went to alert the guards. One went to fetch Joscelin, who came to stop me.

"You can't go out there alone, Imri," he said. "It's not safe."

I thought about all the dangerous places I'd ventured alone and I could have laughed until I wept. Instead I told Joscelin my notion about the moon affecting the gem.

"I suppose it's worth a try," he said. "I'll go with you."

And so we rode out together, starting our quest under the moon-shadow of the ancient oak tree in Elua's Square, where the dirt was still clotted with Antonio Peruggi's dried blood. I kept feeling myself drawn to the place where it had begun. But there was no emerald flash, only the rustling of the spring breeze in new leaves.

We rode in aimless circles, making a rough outward spiral through the streets of the City. The City was restless, the sounds of harsh revelry and discordant music pouring from inns and wineshops open well past the usual hour. Atop Mont Nuit, the Houses of the Night Court were all ablaze with lamplight.

"Soldiers," Joscelin said, gazing toward the distant lights. "Bidding farewell to the pleasures of the flesh. One can't begrudge them."

"No." I thought about Sidonie lying in my arms the night before battle. *As much as I'd like to make love to you until the sun rises, I'd sooner have you go into battle well-rested.* I'd prayed to Blessed Elua for a hundred thousand nights to make up for that one. My eyes stung. "But I'm surprised Drustan and Ghislain don't insist on better discipline."

"When did you start thinking like a commander of men?" Joscelin glanced at me. "Ah, well. I imagine they'll have a good long march to sweat out the excesses of debauchery. And in the end . . ." He fell silent.

"In the end it doesn't matter," I finished. "Because they're all dead men."

"If it comes to it. Don't make mock of their sacrifice," Joscelin said in a somber tone. "One day, they'll be remembered as heroes who fought to preserve all that we hold dear in Terre d'Ange. Their deaths will not be in vain if their valor lives on in the hearts of men."

"I'm not mocking," I said wearily. "Just heart-sick."

Joscelin nodded. "So are we all."

I wanted to say no, no you're not. You're all *sick*, poisoned by Bodeshmun's vile spell, poisoned by this cursed demonstone we're trying so hard to find. But I knew it would do no good, so I held my tongue and kept searching, riding the moonlit streets, hoping to spot an emerald spark amid the bobbing torches and spilling lamplight.

I didn't.

We made our way back to the townhouse at dawn. I watched the sun's rays breaking in the east.

Three days.

Only three.

Seventy-nine

For two more nights, I continued to roam the City, accompanied by Joscelin or Hugues and Ti-Philippe. I didn't really have much hope left, but sleep evaded me and I didn't know what else to do with myself.

Phèdre didn't like it, fearing I was in the grip of a new obsession. For the first few days after Ysandre had declared an end to the search, folk in the City had continued to look for Bodeshmun's gem in a furtive manner under the wary eye of the Royal Army. But that had faded as their thoughts turned increasingly to war.

The mania to find the gem vanished as though it had never existed. War was the new mania.

War.

War.

War.

It was all I heard. In the townhouse, in the streets, spewing from the inns. An endless drumbeat of war. The City's mood ranged wildly from fierce, deluded optimism to maudlin sentiment. Theories abounded and were analyzed tirelessly. Alais' and L'Envers' army would desert at the first show of strength. The battle would end in devastation and ruin, but poets would sing forever of the glorious sacrifice of the Royal Army of Terre d'Ange. Folk argued heatedly on every side of the argument; but on one point, all agreed. They were eager for it to begin.

And I continued my futile, lonely search, Joscelin having succeeded in convincing Phèdre that this obsession was at least harmless.

By the dawn of the third day, the last day, I felt hollow inside. I'd done my best. It hadn't been enough. There was one more night. Tonight the moon would be full. If there was any merit to my theory, tonight would be the last, best chance. I took to my bed, willing my weary body to succumb to sleep. A few hours would be enough to sustain me. I had to keep trying.

It felt like my head had scarce touched the pillow before Phèdre shook me awake.

"Imriel." Her face was grave. "There's a delegation from Alais. Ysandre and Drustan are receiving them at the Palace in an hour's time. I thought you'd want to be there."

I blinked. "Yes, of course."

I was still stifling yawns when we entered the Hall of Audience an hour later. It was an open audience and the Hall was crowded, but people made way for the Comtesse de Montrève and the Queen's Champion and, I suppose, poor mad Prince Imriel.

It was a formal affair. Drustan and Ysandre were seated in twin thrones on a dais, emblematic of their shared rule. Sidonie stood between them, the acknowledged heir to Terre d'Ange, her features composed. That damnable gem-painting was displayed on an easel behind her, still draped in mourning crepe. Astegal and a blonde woman, their hands entwined before the oak tree.

I met Sidonie's gaze. She nodded at me with polite courtesy. There was nothing else there, nothing that I could see.

And no bindings of red thread at her wrists.

I'd lost her.

And, ah, Elua! As if that weren't terrible enough, I saw that Alais and L'Envers had chosen to send a delegate that might present no threat, that might move a hardened heart. I recognized her. She was a member of their shadow Parliament, the elderly L'Agnacite woman who had wept and apologized for thinking terrible things of me. She held herself with dignity and grace, surrounded by an escort of some twenty men in humble attire. None of them were armed.

"We recognize the Baronesse Isabel de Bretel as an emissary of the avowed traitors Alais de la Courcel and Barquiel L'Envers," Ysandre announced coolly. "Do you bring word of their surrender?"

"Your majesties." Isabel de Bretel sank into a deep curtsy, then rose. "We come in peace. I bring one last plea for sanity."

"We ask for nothing more," Drustan said with deceptive mildness, resting his chin on one fist. "Have they renounced their mad quest?"

"There is madness, but it does not lie outside the City's walls." Her voice quavered, then strengthened. "Your majesties, we beg you to see reason! These men . . ." Isabel de Bretel gestured. "These men surrounding me, they are farmers and tradesmen and merchants, fathers and husbands and sons. We come to beg you to listen."

"Listen to *what*?" Ysandre's voice rose. "More sedition?"

A thousand voices murmured in agreement.

"You're ill!" The old baronesse's voice broke. "All those outside the City's walls know it." I could tell by the angle of her head that she sought Sidonie's eyes, but there was nothing there she could speak to. "Please, we're searching for a cure. We're all searching. We beg you stay your hand—"

Drustan made an abrupt gesture. "Do you bring terms of surrender?"

Isabel de Bretel bowed her head. "No, your majesty."

"Then there is nothing to discuss." Ysandre nodded to the Palace Guard. "Throw her in chains. Throw them all in chains and lock them in the dungeon." She paused. "No, wait. Save one of these farmer's sons to carry word to our youngest child. We will give no quarter. We will accept no terms save surrender."

Ah, gods! I was cold, so cold. Guards moved forward, chains at the ready. They'd been prepared for this. The outcome had never been in question.

I daresay Isabel de Bretel had expected it. It had been a desperate measure. They knew reason held no sway here, but they'd been compelled to try. I would have felt the same. She said a quiet word to her escort, then stood with her back proud and straight, holding out her hands to accept the shackles.

None of them protested. The guards handled them roughly nonetheless. They wrestled all but one of her party into chains, singled out a lanky young fellow with silken brown hair and cornflower-blue eyes, young enough that he was still rawboned with it.

"You." Drustan pointed to him. "Come here." The lad approached the throne, trembling. Drustan moved swiftly, rising and grabbing a handful of his hair. He stared into the lad's eyes, his face deadly. "I should send you home in pieces, farmer's son," Drustan said softly. "Or at the least have you flogged. But time is short."

"Your majesty," the poor fellow whispered. "*Please!*"

Drustan put his free hand on the lad's chest and shoved him. There was a ripping sound. The lad cried out in pain, stumbling backward and falling hard. "No quarter." Drustan tossed a hank of brown hair on the lad's sprawling form, the roots bloody. "No terms but surrender. Go."

He went, weeping.

I wanted to weep, too.

"Take the Baronesse de Bretel and the others," Ysandre said with disdain. "Get them out of my sight."

The Palace Guards obeyed, shoving them past us. Isabel de Bretel paused before me, seeking my gaze as she'd sought Sidonie's. Her gnarled hands rose, chains clanking at her manacled wrists. I could still remember the feeling of her hands pressing mine in gratitude and apology, the overwhelming sense of forgiveness and redemption that had come with it. But I didn't dare meet her eyes. I turned my head away from her and saw Sidonie's dispassionate face. As I gazed at her, her brows knit. For a second, for the merest space of a heartbeat, I thought mayhap there was a flicker of agonized awareness behind her eyes. Then it vanished and my heart ached anew.

We had given them hope.

We had failed them.

"My lords and ladies!" Ysandre's voice rang clear and true. "You have heard the final word of those who would destroy the rule of law in Terre d'Ange. They are relentless. They are the enemy. I bid you go forth this day. All who will serve, I bid you to say farewell to your families. All who will remain in the City, I bid you remain stalwart in your defense of her. And to all, I bid you reassemble here on the morrow, an hour past dawn, and hear a declaration of *war*!"

The cheers shook the rafters.

My stomach roiled.

I walked out of the Hall of Audience in a daze. People streamed on either side of me, cheering. When I felt a heavy hand descend on my shoulder, I whirled, more than half-ready to fight.

"My lord." Kratos backed away, raising his hands.

"How could you let her remove the bindings?" I hissed. "*How?*"

His broad chest rose and fell. "She pulled them loose in the bath," Kratos said simply. "I can't be everywhere, my lord. I'm sorry."

"I know." I clenched my fists, willing my fury and despair to subside. "You did your best. Thank you."

"It didn't make much difference, my lord," he said quietly. "I think we'd already lost her. At least she's no longer in pain."

"Imriel?" It was Phèdre's voice somewhere behind us, worried.

"Go. Don't give Sidonie any reason not to trust you." I jerked my chin at Kratos and he faded into the throng.

"Why are you in such a hurry to be gone?" Phèdre reached my side, reached up to touch my cheek. "Did you know that woman, Imri? The baronesse? The way she hesitated, it almost seemed she knew you."

"No." I gazed at Phèdre, at her still-beautiful face. The scarlet mote of Kushiel's Dart floated atop the dark iris of her left eye. On the eve of war, I was still her greatest concern. I took her hand, pressed it as Isabel de Bretel had pressed mine. "No, I don't know her," I lied. "May we go home?"

Phèdre nodded. "Of course."

That night, the moon rose full and silver and bright. It seemed far too lovely to be a harbinger of war. I searched the City with Hugues and Ti-Philippe accompanying me. As before, we began at the beginning, in Elua's Square and spiraling outward. I thought about how so many things seemed to have come around full circle, but mayhap it wasn't a circle after all. Mayhap it was a spiral, loop upon loop repeating, ending at the farthest point from where it had begun.

Valor turned to poisoned folly.

Heroes turned to destroyers.

Traitors turned to allies.

I pushed the thoughts away and concentrated on my search. Ti-Philippe and Hugues didn't make much of a pretense of searching, chatting instead of the war to come. The retainers of House Montrève would be staying to defend those left behind in the City of Elua. Both were envious of those who would be serving under Drustan and Ghislain's command.

"I'm sorry you're not able to serve, Imri," Hugues said kindly to me. "That must hurt inside."

"Yes," I murmured. "It hurts."

We finished our winding circuit and retraced our steps. Circles. I thought about training with Joscelin, telling the hours on my own. Riding in an endless circle around the besieged city of Lucca on night patrol with Eamonn. The chambered nautilus shell on Master Piero's desk. Elua, that seemed like a long time ago. A golden ring, a coiled knot. Shackles of love, shackles of madness, shackles of protection, shackles of punishment.

My mind wandered in circles.

It was an hour or so shy of dawn when we arrived back at Elua's Square. No emerald flash, no gem. I dismounted and knelt in the loose dirt, bowing my head and praying to Blessed Elua.

"This is your city," I whispered. "The city you founded, the city that bears your name. These are your people whom you have always loved dearly. I pray, if there be any way to save them, show me. Use me as you will."

And then I prayed to his Companions: to Naamah to spread her grace on true lovers, to Eisheth for the balm of healing, to Azza to avenge the pride of a nation deceived, to Shemhazai for the wits to avert this tragedy, to Anael to restore the sense of care and husbandry that war destroyed, to Camael to stay his martial hand in favor of compassion.

And although it was a thing seldom done, I prayed to Cassiel, the Perfect Companion. "I know you do not like to be beseeched in prayer," I whispered, "but you will lose your greatest servant if we cannot turn aside this fate. If you hold any influence, I pray you wield it."

Last I prayed to Kushiel, echoing the prayer I'd offered the night I'd entered the City.

"Grant them mercy," I pleaded. "Grant us all mercy."

The moon was paling in the sky by the time I rose stiffly. Another perfect circle. I gazed at it while Hugues and Ti-Philippe waited with ill-concealed impatience. They had indulged my madness. They were weary of it.

"Imri," Ti-Philippe said at last. "We're due at the Palace in a little over an hour."

"Yes, all right." I swung astride the saddle and took up the reins. "I'm finished. Let's go."

EIGHTY

At the townhouse, I scoured my face in the washbasin, pressing a cool cloth to my burning eyes. I changed into fresh clothing: more black mourning attire, this time commissioned by Phèdre. I was lightheaded with grief and lack of sleep—and like as not, hunger. I'd been eating as poorly as I slept. I summoned Clory and sent her to bring me bread and honey.

While I waited, I fetched Bodeshmun's leather talisman from my purse. The lacquer had crackled and the ink was fading with wear. I studied the image, the faint inscription in Punic. A whirlwind sprouting horns and fangs, a word to bind or free it.

More circles, a mad gyre of circles.

"I killed you too quickly, Bodeshmun," I murmured. "If you were alive, I'd wind your entrails on a stick until you told me where that goddamned gem was."

Somewhere, in whatever passed for hell among Carthaginians, I imagined Bodeshmun was smiling his dour smile.

Clory returned and I hid the talisman back in my purse.

I drizzled honey on Eugènie's fine, crusty bread, watching the amber-gold coils melt into themselves. I thought about the bee-skeps I'd ordered built in Clunderry. Coils of golden straw. Dorelei's laughter and the round, rising circle of her belly.

Honey and gall.

I thought about Sidonie and the first time I'd awoken in her bed. Tousled locks of golden hair spread across the pillow. Her face, smiling at me in the sunlight, still soft with sleep.

Love.

You will find it and lose it, again and again.

I'd been fourteen years old when a Priest of Elua had said those words to me, and if I'd had any idea how much it would hurt, I might have killed myself to spare the pain. But I wasn't the damaged, brooding boy I'd been. I'd failed Dorelei, and I'd very nearly failed her a second time in Vralia. While my heart yet beat, I didn't mean to accept failure again.

And when it didn't . . . well.

As Kratos had said, it would be a noble death.

So I forced myself to eat, although Eugènie's good bread tasted like ashes and the sweet honey was bitter in my mouth. When it was done, I felt a trifle less lightheaded. I heard Phèdre's voice calling for me downstairs. I buckled my sword-belt around my waist, the old rhinoceros-hide belt that Ras Lijasu had given me many years ago in distant Meroë, a talisman in its own right.

A reminder of heroes.

"Are you ready?" Phèdre asked as I descended the stair. "We're nearly late."

I nodded. "I'm ready."

We rode by carriage to the Palace. The mood in the City had shifted yet again. It had turned proud and somber. Folk saluted as we passed. Our outriders returned their salutes. War. We teetered on the precipice of war.

And the gods remained silent.

Once again, folk made way for us in the Hall of Audience. A heavy silence hung over the hall. The eternal susurrus of gossip and speculation had been stilled. I never thought I'd miss it. Instead, there were only the sounds of people breathing, the rustle of fabric, the creak of armor. An ocean of armor, bright with the crests of dozens of the Great Houses of Terre d'Ange. Almost the entire Parliament had been present the night Bodeshmun wrought his magic, many of them attended by their own men-at-arms. All of their forces would be serving.

We took our places at the head of the crowd. The thrones had been removed from the hall. Only the dais remained, the dais and that cursed gem-painting. Ysandre, Drustan, and Sidonie stood on the dais, still as a tableau. Drustan wore full armor. His breastplate was worked with the twin insignias of the Black Boar of the Cullach Gorrym and the Silver Swan of House Courcel. Sidonie didn't so much as glance in my direction.

The crowd waited.

"My lords and ladies," Ysandre said in a grave voice, "I took the throne at a young age, facing what I believed would be the most dire threat of my lifetime. I was wrong. We have been betrayed. Betrayed by a terrible, cunning cabal. Betrayed by ambition and greed. Betrayed by forces we may never fathom."

The gods alone knew how horribly true that was, I thought.

Ysandre's voice rose. "But if those who poise themselves to strike at the very heart of Terre d'Ange think to bring us to our knees, they are mistaken! Today, this day, in the presence of all here assembled, I declare *war* on Alais de la Courcel, Barquiel L'Envers, their rebel army, and all who support them!"

The silence broke, cheers crashing like waves. I closed my eyes, feeling the blood pound in my ears.

When the noise dimmed, Drustan spoke. "Terre d'Ange is not the country of my birth, but I have come to love her. I have shed my blood for her before. I go forth willingly today to do so once more." He paused. "Whether we succeed or fail is in the hands of the gods, yours and mine. I go forth in the hope that they grant our prayers, that the resistance will collapse and I will return to stand before you and call upon you to send the valiant army of Terre d'Ange to Alba to unseat my usurping nephew. And I go forth in perfect faith that if we fail, the effort will not have been in vain. History will remember this day. History will remember all of us as heroes."

The cheers rose again, loud and deafening. The clamor echoed inside my aching head. My skin felt tight.

Ghislain nó Trevalion stepped forward and bowed toward the dais, then drew his sword in a crisp salute. Drustan drew his own sword and returned the salute.

"Make way!" Ysandre cried. "Make way for Drustan mab Necthana, the Cruarch of Alba, and Ghislain nó Trevalion, the Royal Commander of Terre d'Ange! They shall lead us now to Elua's Square, where we will repeat this declaration for all the City to hear. And thence onward, onward to war!"

The crowd began to part, cheering. The sound battered me. The sunlight slanting from the high windows glittered on a sea of armor. I should have slept more, eaten more. I was swept along with the throng, shoved to the side, dizzy and . . .

No.

The clamor was *inside* me, filling me, all of me. The silent gods were speaking, speaking to me, speaking through me. I listened. A sharp stab of joy went through me . . . and, ah, Elua! Everything changed. I'd begged Blessed Elua to use me as he willed. He had answered. They had *all* answered. Hope and desire and tenderness and pride and ferocity and compassion, all filling me, lifting my heart. Emotions I couldn't name, glorious and wondrous. The brightness was *inside* me.

I was a chalice filled with light.

I walked forward into the corridor, my hands unbuckling my sword-belt without a conscious thought. Before the dais, I let it fall. Behind me, I could hear the familiar murmurs rising. I wanted to laugh for joy.

I gazed at their faces. At Drustan, calm and steady and courageous. At Ysandre, proud and noble-hearted. And, ah, gods, Sidonie! She gazed back at me, a perplexed frown creasing her brow, as though she were trying to remember a dream she'd forgotten. My girl, still struggling deep inside against the spell that had ensnared her. I loved her so much.

I loved them all.

I forgave them all. None of this was their fault, none of it. And the gods were merciful after all.

I spread my arms wide, feeling as though light must be streaming from my fingertips. "Your majesties." My voice seemed to come from very far away and it was filled with gentleness. "You must not do this thing. The gods themselves forbid it."

My words hung shimmering in the air.

Ysandre looked past me and nodded.

And my world went black.

Eighty-one

"You didn't have to stay."

Joscelin's voice was the first thing I recognized as I swam slowly back to my senses. Kratos' was the second, low and rumbling, speaking faltering D'Angeline with a pronounced Hellene accent.

"I don't mind. Her highness cares for him in her way."

My head hurt with a splitting pain. I was . . . where? Their voices had an echoing quality. A vast space, empty. There was cool, hard marble beneath my cheek. My eyelids were too heavy to lift. I lay still and listened.

"He wasn't always like this," Joscelin said with deep regret. "He suffered a terrible ordeal as a child."

Behind my closed eyelids, I could envision Kratos' broad shoulders lifting in a shrug. "As you say."

Echoing.

The Hall of Audience. I was still there; but all of the wondrous brightness that had filled me was gone. All gone. Blessed Elua and his Companions were silent. I had failed.

I was a flawed vessel. My stomach lurched. I swallowed bile and cracked open my heavy eyelids.

I was lying on my side on the dais. Before the easel that held the painting—that goddamned, thrice-cursed gem painting. It loomed over me. And this time, from my unlikely vantage point, I *saw* it. "Oh, gods!" I sat up fast. Too fast. My head swam and my nausea surged. "Kratos. Kratos! It's in the tree. It's *inside* the damned tree."

"Imri?" Joscelin asked cautiously.

I ignored him, reaching for my purse and finding my belt gone. "My belt," I said to Kratos. He looked blankly at me. "My sword-belt. Where is it?"

"Don't—" Joscelin began.

Kratos handed me my sword-belt. I ignored the blade, wrenched open my purse. I pulled out Bodeshmun's faded talisman and turned it sideways, holding it up before the painting. "Look."

The image was subtle, but it was there. Whorls in the bark. Circles. Circles within circles. I'd taken it to be a bole on the oak tree. It wasn't. It was the image of the demon itself; the *ghafrid*, the elemental, turned on its side. Hidden in the design.

"I see it," Kratos said slowly. "But wasn't the tree searched?"

"All over the outside, yes." I touched the image. It was nestled just below a fork in the trunk. "But there must be a niche, a hidden aperture. Somewhat that was missed, somewhat cleverly disguised. If there's a spell that can make me look like Leander Maignard, surely there's one that can hide a hole in a tree." I levered myself onto my feet, waiting for another surge of nausea to pass. "How long was I unconscious?"

"A quarter of an hour or so," Kratos said. "Not too long."

I began buckling my sword-belt around my waist. "Then there's time. The army won't have departed yet. Ysandre may not even have begun to address the City. It takes time to muster an event on that scale."

"Imriel." Joscelin's tone was flat. "You're talking nonsense. And you're indulging him," he added to Kratos. "I'd prefer you didn't."

"Joscelin, *look*." I held out Bodeshmun's talisman sideways again to show him the match . . . and remembered. My heart sank. Sidonie and I had omitted that part of the tale, reckoning it was too difficult to explain what a horned, fanged whirlwind had to do with protecting the City. "It's a symbol," I said. "It's a sign that the demon—" I bit the inside of my cheek, willing the dizziness that addled my wits to be dispelled. "That the gem's hidden in Elua's Oak."

Joscelin put his hands on my shoulders. "You need to sit down."

"Please." I forced myself to breathe slowly and evenly. "I need to get to the Square."

"No." His voice hardened. "Phèdre was right. I should never have let you continue in this mad hunt. It's made you worse."

"Joscelin—"

He shook his head. "I promised Ysandre I'd keep you out of the way. Kratos was kind enough to assist. And it was just barely enough to keep her from throwing you in the dungeon for safekeeping. You're not going anywhere near the Square, now or anytime soon."

I closed my eyes. "I am begging you to please, please trust me, Joscelin."

"I'm sorry," he said. "I can't. Not in this. You're *not well*."

I opened my eyes. "Kratos."

Kratos didn't hesitate. He seized Joscelin from behind, pinning his arms—or at least seeking to. But strong and skilled as he was, he'd not reckoned on the highly trained reflexes of a Cassiline Brother. Joscelin twisted and struggled, working his right-hand dagger free of its sheath, and stabbing backward at a low, awkward angle. It was enough. Kratos grunted as it plunged into his thigh, his arms loosening.

Joscelin broke free, yanking the dagger with him and drawing his left-hand dagger to match it. He settled into a defensive stance, vambraces crossed, eyes wild with sudden shock and suspicion. "What in the hell is this, Imri? Is it treason after all?"

Kratos took a lurching step toward him.

"Don't!" Joscelin flipped his right dagger, holding it by the bloody tip. "One more step and I'll plant this in his throat."

"Hold," I said to Kratos. "Stay back." I raised my empty hands to Joscelin. "I don't want to fight you. Please, just let me pass. I need to get to the Square."

"Is it Alais?" Joscelin asked, angry and bewildered. "Are you in league with her? What are you doing? What scheme is this? Does it have aught to do with your mother?" I glanced past him toward the far end of the hall, thinking that if I could get past Joscelin, I could beat him in a foot-race. "Oh, no." He reversed his dagger again, grasping the hilt and setting himself against me. "You're not going anywhere."

I took a deep breath. "Joscelin Verreuil, as a Prince of the Blood and a member of House Courcel, I am ordering you to stand down."

"I'm obeying her majesty's orders," he said. "You've no authority to countermand them." Kratos attempted to sidle around him, limping. Joscelin took a few steps backward, better positioning himself to guard both of us. "You're staying here until Ysandre and the Palace Guard return." He pointed at Kratos with the tip of one dagger. "And I swear to Elua, if this man moves again, I *will* throw on him."

"He means it," I said to Kratos in Hellene. "He can kill you in the blink of an eye."

Kratos nodded stoically. "What will you?"

What I willed, what I longed for, was the wondrous, glorious certainty that had filled me: the voices of Blessed Elua and his Companions. I wanted it back. I wanted it to have worked in the first place. But mayhap I wasn't a flawed vessel after all. Mayhap words spoken to me long ago in Lucca were true: the gods answer our prayers sideways at best. I had my answer. I had the key to finding the gem, to saving Terre d'Ange.

And the man I loved and honored above all others stood between me and my goal.

I drew my sword. "I don't want to do this."

"Then don't," Joscelin said steadily.

I shook my head. It had gone too far. Kratos was exposed. We'd both be accused of sedition, mayhap of treason. Mayhap they'd still look for the demon-stone and find it. What then? Sidonie's memory had slipped away, and with it, the key to unlocking the spell. Others had it. Alais and L'Envers. They could use it once they took the City if they could find the gem. But by then there wouldn't be much left to save.

"I have to try," I said, and advanced on him.

Elua! We'd sparred so many times, Joscelin and I. I never, ever thought we'd duel in earnest. Not in a thousand years. And it wasn't . . . not quite. Not yet. My sword clattered off his vambraces. Joscelin made a deft move to attempt to trap it with the curved quillons of his daggers. I made a deft move to evade it. We circled one another, trading reluctant blows.

"What did we do wrong, Imri?" There was a note of anguish in Joscelin's voice. "Was there aught you wanted that we failed to provide?"

"No." I feinted at his left. He was slower to parry on his left side where his arm had been badly broken in Daršanga. But my head was still splitting and the dizziness and nausea hadn't gone away. I was slow today. "No, I never wanted for aught."

"Did we not love you enough?" Joscelin asked softly.

My eyes stung. I blinked to clear them. "No! Name of Elua, no!"

Astegal of Carthage hadn't succeeded in distracting me, but this . . . gods. It made me sick at heart, sick enough to break my concentration. Joscelin took advantage of it and made another pass at trapping my blade. This time I barely evaded it. Metal screeched on metal. We both whirled, then parted and fell back. I held my blade angled before me. Joscelin gazed at me, daggers crossed, a world of pain and sorrow in his summer-blue eyes.

"Then *why*?" he asked me.

I swallowed. There was no answer I could give him that he would believe. And I didn't think I could defeat him without getting one or both of us mortally wounded. He was too good. He always had been. Even on my best days, I'd won only one bout in three against him; and today was far from one of my best. And even if Joscelin gave me an opening, I wasn't sure I could bear to take it.

But there was one thing I was sure of.

Even here, even now, in the grip of Bodeshmun's cursed spell, even believing me a traitor, Joscelin loved me. He'd gone for his daggers and not his sword. He was fighting defensively, seeking to disarm me. He didn't want to hurt me any more than I did him, mayhap less.

I dropped my sword.

Joscelin glanced at it. I charged him. I saw his eyes widen, his daggers sweeping up instinctively toward my throat. At the last minute, he grimaced and let them fall. I hooked my right foot behind his left ankle and brought us both crashing to the marble floor.

We rolled, grappling.

On the floor, unarmed, the odds changed. I was the better wrestler. At an age when most boys in Siovale were being taught the art and science of it, Joscelin had been training to be a Cassiline Brother. But Hugues had taught me to wrestle during the long summer days at Montrève. And I'd learned a great deal more at the ungentle hands of a former Hellene champion in New Carthage.

In the end I pinned Joscelin as Astegal had pinned Kratos in the palaestra, wrenching his arm hard behind his back, my legs twined with his. Unlike Astegal, I didn't grind his face into the marble.

"I'm sorry," I whispered. "I pray you'll forgive me." Joscelin glared at me, his head twisted. I glanced up. "Kratos?"

Kratos limped over, snatching up one of Joscelin's daggers along the way. He brought the pommel crashing down hard on the back of Joscelin's head.

I winced in sympathy.

Joscelin's eyes rolled back and his body went limp.

I released my grip on him, breathing hard. I turned Joscelin over and felt at his throat for a pulse. It beat strongly. I knelt and kissed his brow. Kratos eyed me impassively.

"He's my foster-father," I said. "And a hero of the realm." I got to my feet. The hall spun around me, then steadied. "Are there guards about?"

Kratos shook his head. "Not in earshot, I don't think." He nodded at Joscelin. "The Queen put a great deal of trust in him. There'll be guards on the outer doors, I imagine."

"How's your leg?" I asked him. "I'm not sure they'll let me pass alone."

"I'll manage." He continued to eye me. "What was it you thought you were doing, anyway? Did you imagine they'd listen?"

"I did," I said. "But I think the gods answer prayers sideways." I clapped his shoulder. "I'll explain later. Let's go."

Eighty-two

I was right. Without Kratos' aid, I'd never have gotten past the guards. He strode through the corridor toward the main doors of the Palace, shouting loudly for the guards to fetch our horses.

The guards looked dubious. "I thought Prince Imriel—" one began.

"He is god-touched, man!" Kratos roared, grabbing the fellow's doublet. "Not mad! He had a . . . a seeing! You hit him before he could speak it! Do you people know nothing?"

"A seeing?" the guard repeated.

"A vision," I said. "I know where the gem is. Blessed Elua has decreed that it must be found before this war is launched."

They hesitated.

Kratos shook the man he held like a terrier with a rat. "I serve the House of Sarkal. This was Lord Bodeshmun's last wish and her highness' great hope. Go! Now!"

The guards exchanged glances. One unbarred the doors

to let us pass and the other ran toward the stables, shouting for an ostler.

Ah, gods! Quickly, quickly, quickly. I waited in an agony of suspense, terrified at the thought that Joscelin would awaken and come in pursuit of us, terrified that someone would find him, terrified that the guards would grow suspicious at his absence and forbid us passage. But no; Kratos had rattled them and they still regarded him as their revered Astegal's sole representative in the City. The ostlers came at a run, leading the blaze-faced bay I'd been riding and the sturdily built chestnut that Sidonie had given Kratos.

Kratos mounted with a grunt. I could see blood darkening the fabric of his blue breeches and moved my mount unobtrusively to block the sight, then swung astride.

"Do you need an escort?" the guard asked Kratos.

"No," he said curtly. "Just open the gates."

The order was given, the gates were opened. "You'd best take the lead," I murmured to Kratos. "They'll make way for you when we reach the Square."

He nodded and set his heels to the chestnut's flanks.

We burst through the gates and began racing through the City. The streets were as empty as I'd ever seen them. Everyone was gathered at the Square, just as they had been the night of the marvel.

Only this time it was to hear a declaration of war.

How long did we have? I wasn't sure. Kratos thought I'd been unconscious a quarter of an hour. I didn't imagine my head was any harder than Joscelin's. When he woke, he'd be in a fury. Once he denounced us, it would be over.

Kratos didn't ride well and his injury made it worse. He jounced awkwardly in the saddle. His horse wasn't swift. Again and again, I had to check my own mount, fearful of clipping the chestnut's hooves, reining in my own impatience.

When Joscelin awoke, he would ride very, very swiftly in pursuit.

We passed empty townhouses, empty stores, empty wine-shops. The thunder of our passage made my aching head swim.

We glimpsed the outer edge of the throng, ordinary citizens clogging the street. "Make way!" Kratos began shouting. "Make way in the name of Astegal of Carthage!"

People turned and stared. They knew him, knew his homely face with its squashed nose. They knew his heavily accented D'Angeline. They moved, sluggish, their bunched ranks parting with frustrating slowness.

Kratos plunged into their midst and I followed.

People stared after us.

If I failed, if I was wrong . . . Kratos was dead. I didn't doubt it. He'd aided me and assaulted Joscelin. The same twisted malevolence that had led the City to hail him as Astegal's trusted right-hand man would turn on him. They would tear him to pieces for his betrayal.

And likely me too.

The street opened. We had reached the outer edge of Elua's Square. It was packed with soldiers. They were slower to move, but they did, giving way reluctantly at the name of Astegal of Carthage. I gazed above a shining sea of helmets.

Elua's Oak.

It rose, vast and majestic, its spring canopy spreading over the Square. I'd stood beneath it as a boy when Ysandre de la Courcel announced an end to Phèdre's sentence of penance and gave her blessing to the quest to free the Master of the Straits. I'd sat beneath it as a young man, beside a dry and empty fountain, suspected of treason thanks to Barquiel L'Envers' machinations. Almost a year ago, I'd groveled at its roots, succumbing to madness. And only a few hours ago, I'd knelt beneath it and prayed.

I prayed now, sick and dizzy.

A wooden dais had been erected beneath the oak. There they were: Ysandre, Drustan, and Sidonie. Drustan's sword was in his hand. I guessed the speech had already been given, the salutes exchanged.

"Make way!" Kratos called, forging a steady path through the crowd of soldiers. "In the name of Astegal of Carthage, make way!"

I followed in his wake.

Far behind us was the sound of a new commotion arising.

Joscelin.

No time.

No time for fear, no time for uncertainty. No time to try to explain what I was doing. I left that to Kratos. As we reached the oak, I draped my mount's reins over his neck, kicked my feet free of the stirrups. I drew myself up and stood atop my saddle, swaying unsteadily. My heart thudded in my breast. I caught the lowest limb, hauled myself atop it. Below voices rose in furious argument.

". . . sorry, your majesty, but he's had a *vision*," Kratos was saying, his tone stubborn. "Your men were too hasty."

I inched along the thick branch, trying to hurry. To the juncture, to the fork. There was a mossy hollow there. I locked my ankles around the tree limb and plucked the dagger from my belt, probing.

Nothing.

The commotion grew louder. Joscelin was getting closer. I glanced down through the greening oak leaves. I saw Sidonie below me, her face upturned and puzzled. I stabbed at the crotch of the tree, prying away chunks of moss, chunks of bark. Bits and pieces of oak detritus fell like rain.

An arrow whizzed over my head.

"No!" Sidonie's voice. "Hold!"

Moss and bark, moss and bark. And then . . . hardened mud. A crude mortar, packed in a hole, crumbling under the tip of my blade. I kept my head low and dug frantically. My dagger scraped against somewhat hard. I dug harder, prying out large chunks of dried mud. I saw the silver link of a chain glinting. "I have it!" I cried, sticking my dagger in my belt and yanking on the chain. It came loose as a single piece, a dirt-encrusted emerald dangling from silver links. "I have it!"

The crowd below murmured in wonder.

Joscelin's voice rang out, hard and urgent. "Get him down from there! Whatever he means to do with that thing, do *not* let him do it!"

Too late, I thought. I clutched the chain in my fist and whispered the word. "*Emmenghamon.*"

Nothing happened.

"Your majesty, it's a trick," Joscelin called. The soldiers were parting for him now. He reached the dais, breathing hard. "I'm sorry; Elua knows, sorrier than I've ever been in my life."

I tried it again. "*Emmenghamon.*"

"What passes here?" Ysandre's voice could have frozen water.

"Imriel attacked me," Joscelin said grimly. "And this man's in league with him." He pointed at Kratos. "I don't know why, but they're frantic to get their hands on that gem. We've been deceived. Somewhat is very, very wrong here."

"Joscelin, no!" Phèdre's voice, horrified.

"I'm sorry," he said more softly.

My head pounded, sick and throbbing. I clung to the branch, clung to the chain, and tried to shut out their voices. I was saying it wrong. I had to be. I pictured Sidonie in the hold of Deimos' ship, still disheveled from her sojourn in Bodeshmun's rug, her lips working as she sounded out the Punic word. "*Emmanghamon*."

Nothing.

"Imriel de la Courcel." Drustan's voice, the umistakable tone of command. I glanced down to see a bank of arrows trained on me. Sidonie was still almost directly beneath me, gazing upward. "You will descend and place yourself in custody of the Palace Guard. Now."

Sidonie.

Spirals and circles.

I wrapped the chain around my right wrist and drew my dagger. I fished Bodeshmun's talisman from my purse. I took a few slow, deep breaths. Quick. I'd always been quick. I would have to be very, very quick. I whispered a little prayer to Blessed Elua and his Companions and felt a measure of my dizziness and nausea abate. It was a small mercy, but I'd take it.

I inched back out onto the limb, swung my leg over and dropped.

The guards moved swiftly toward me. I moved faster. I grabbed Sidonie, putting the edge of my dagger to her throat and setting my back against Elua's Oak. "No one move!"

No one did. The horror and loathing on their faces went through me like a spear. Sidonie's body was rigid against mine, trembling a little. Whether with fear or fury, I couldn't tell.

"Sidonie," I murmured in her ear. "I know you don't remember it, but you once promised to trust me beyond all reason. And I swear to you that all that I am, all that I possess, including this gem-stone, is yours." With my left hand, I held Bodeshmun's talisman before her face. "I need you. I can't do this alone. Forget your memories. Look into your heart. And if you find somewhat there, some lingering spark of trust and love that owes naught to reason, I beg you to speak the word written here."

She went very still.

"Don't!" Ysandre snapped. "Don't you dare!"

Sidonie reached for the talisman. I let her take it, keeping my blade at her throat. No one dared move as she studied the scrap of leather.

"Always and always," I whispered. "That was the promise."

Her body shifted. I lowered the dagger and let her turn to face me. If my words hadn't reached her, I was a dead man anyway. But she was still between me and the guards and I heard Drustan order his archers not to attempt to shoot over his daughter's head. Sidonie's dark, dark eyes searched mine.

"*Emmenghanom.*"

It was faint, so faint! I could barely hear it, couldn't make out if her pronunciation differed from mine. For the space of a few heartbeats, I thought it must not have. I thought that we had failed, that we'd gotten it wrong. That her knowledge of the Punic alphabet had been too imperfect, that Ptolemy Solon had been mistaken after all, that we'd failed to fulfill the terms of the spell. And then I felt the chain wrapped around my wrist quiver. Sidonie made a startled sound and dropped the leather talisman.

The talisman was smoldering, the edges black and curling.

The emerald was glowing beneath the dirt that encrusted it, the symbols of the Houses of the Cosmos etched into its facets shining whitely.

"Move away from him, Sidonie!" Drustan shouted. "Step away!"

She didn't budge. I could feel heat from the demon-stone rising. The silver chains wrapped around my wrist were growing warm. I dropped my dagger and unwound the chain.

"I think you'd all better get back!" I called. "It's too late to stop this!"

I swung the chain like a goatherd with a rope lariat. The demon-stone left emerald trails of brightness lingering in the air. Circles upon circles. I meant to scare them, and it worked. They scrambled, pushing and shoving, trying to flee in a panic. Pressing outward, clearing a space. The chain was beginning to burn my palm. I prayed to Elua no one got crushed, and tossed the gem and chain into the empty space.

The emerald glare intensified. The gem spun on the trampled dirt, the chain lashing in circles around it. The silver links turned ruddy with heat. Brighter and brighter. The air grew hot and dry and hard to breathe.

The demon-stone burst.

I heard the sound of the first crack and moved without thinking, spinning Sidonie against the oak tree and shielding her with my body. The sound when it burst was like a splintering thunderclap, loud and deafening. Tiny shards flew outward with tremendous force. I felt a spray of them pierce me from behind, lodging in my flesh, needle-sharp.

And then the world roared.

It was a roar of fury, a roar of triumph. A roar of freedom. It seemed to suck all the air from Elua's Square. A hot, dry wind rose—rose and rose. Spiraling. I warded my face with one arm, turning to peer behind me. I could see people struggling to flee, could see their mouths open to shout. I couldn't hear anything but the roaring. But mostly I saw *it*.

It gathered itself out of dirt, sucking up the trampled soil. Desiccating it, pulverizing it, rendering it as fine and dry as desert sand. A whirlwind of earth. Through slitted eyes, I watched it grow, rising into a column fit to rival the height of

Elua's Oak. I watched it sprout horns, wicked and curving, shiny as mica. I watched a dark maw gape open in the whirlwind's midst, revealing jagged fangs the color of old bones.

It grew and grew.

And then it stopped growing. It spun in one place. The dirt spun; the horns and maw didn't. High in the sky, at the apex of the whirlwind, the wicked horns dipped. Toward us, toward Sidonie and me.

I looked at her.

She gazed back at me with awe.

We had freed a demon.

The world roared again. There was a rushing sound. When it moved, it moved quickly. It passed over the Square, passed over the City, scouring everything in its path with a blast of fine-ground dirt. In its wake, it left abraded skin, terrified and weeping folk. A deafening absence of sound. It passed beyond the walls of the City without slowing and continued. Moving south, going home.

Gone.

Eighty-three

In the aftermath of the *ghafrid*'s passage, Elua's Square was hushed.

The folk of the City were frightened; many were injured. And all of them were awakening from a malevolent dream to a terrible, terrible truth. The looks on their faces nearly broke my heart.

"What have I done?" Ysandre said. She was speaking for everyone present. Her voice shook. "Elua! What have we *all* done?"

Drustan fixed me with his dark gaze. One side of his face was bleeding, scored by myriad gashes from flying gem fragments. Here and there, shards of emerald glinted amid the tattooed whorls. "Not all of us."

Now that it was over, I was trembling, too. My head ached and I stung in a hundred different places, shards embedded in my own flesh. Gods, it had been a near thing! "It was a spell," I said. "It wasn't your fault. And you didn't do it. We were able to break the spell in time."

His gaze shifted to Sidonie. "Both of you."

"Barely," she murmured, her face pale.

"Does that . . ." Ysandre shivered. "Does that mean it didn't happen as we believed?" A faint note of hope crept into her voice. "You didn't go to Carthage and wed Astegal? Was that all part of the falsehood?"

"No," Sidonie said gently. "I wish it were."

The sound of mourning arose in the Square, breaking the hush. Some folk were still silent and shocked, but others began keening. I saw soldiers on their knees, rocking back and forth, burying their faces in their hands. I looked at Phèdre. Her eyes were closed, her face shuttered. Joscelin was staring at his hands, turned palms upward. I looked away.

"Alais," Ysandre whispered in horror, the full realization striking her.

"It's all right," I said. "It didn't happen."

The Queen of Terre d'Ange shook her head. What Ysandre was thinking, what she was feeling, I couldn't imagine. I felt sick at heart remembering what I'd said and done in my madness. Ysandre de la Courcel had declared war on her own daughter. On her own nation.

The keening grew louder. I watched Ysandre gather herself with a profound effort of will. She and Drustan exchanged a glance. He nodded, knowing her mind. They bore the same burden of guilt.

Ysandre stepped to the dais. "People of Terre d'Ange!" They quieted. She took a deep breath. "In the presence of all here assembled, I declare myself unfit to sit the throne. I relinquish the throne of Terre d'Ange to my eldest daughter and heir, Sidonie de la Courcel."

Ten thousand hungry eyes turned to Sidonie.

This, neither of us had expected.

"No." Sidonie's voice was quiet, too quiet. She squared her shoulders and raised her voice. "No. I do not accept this charge. I, too, fell victim to Carthage's wiles. I, too, fell beneath the spell's influence. I fell farther and harder than anyone. I stand before you here today only because Imriel de la Courcel rescued me from it, as, in the end, he has saved all of us."

A poet's tale.

I glanced at Kratos and saw tears streaking his broad face.

"Blessed Elua is merciful," Sidonie said. There were tears on her face, too. "He does not join hearts without a purpose. We have all been spared this day. We have all been granted mercy and redemption this day. I acknowledge my mother's wishes. I will serve as regent for a month's time. And as such, this is my order to you."

They hung on her words.

"Go home," Sidonie said, and though her voice was soft, it carried. "Let those with a chirurgeon's training among you come forward to tend to the wounded. Everyone else, I bid you go home. Go home and do penance. Go home and mourn at what very nearly happened. Go home and give thanks that it did not. There is a tale to tell here, and it will be told in due time. Now we need to grieve, all of us. We need to regret. And yet let us always remember, the gods had mercy on us. In the end, love prevailed."

She reached for my hand.

I took hers and squeezed it hard.

No one cheered. It was too somber a moment and they were too dazed by what had happened. By the demon's passage, by the dawning horror of what they'd nearly done. Here and there, a number of folk yet knelt, rocking and wailing. Still, it gave many of them purpose. I saw them take heart from her words.

For the moment, it was enough.

The crowd began to stir, making way for those answering the call for chirurgeons. Ghislain nó Trevalion shook himself from his own shocked torpor, giving orders in a hoarse voice. His men began to clear a space, separating the injured from the hale, facilitating the process.

"You're hurt," Sidonie murmured. "You need a chirurgeon."

I shook my head. "Later."

"Imriel." Sidonie freed her hand from mine, reached up to touch my face. "There are no words. There will never be enough words." Her dark eyes were grave. "Thank you. I love you. Always and always."

"And I you," I said. "We did it, Sidonie. You and I, together."

She smiled through the tears that still welled. "We did, didn't we?"

"Yes." I took her hand, kissed her palm. "I need to speak to Joscelin."

Sidonie nodded. "Go."

I made my way to the edge of the dais and stepped down. Joscelin's head rose slowly, a new world of pain in his eyes. "Imri—" he began, his voice rough.

"Don't." I shook my head at him. "Please don't, Joscelin. I couldn't bear it. I remember my own madness. I remember what I said and did, and it was vile and hurtful. With all that happened, even at the worst of it, you were only trying to protect me from myself."

His eyes shone. "I thought . . ."

"I know," I said. "I do."

Joscelin embraced me, his callused hands firm against my shard-studded shoulder blades. I stifled the pain. Still, he felt it and let go. "I'm proud of you," he said simply. "So proud."

I blinked away my tears. "I sought but to follow your lead."

"*Imriel.*" At Joscelin's side, Phèdre's closed eyes opened.

A sweep of lashes lifting, unshuttered. She looked at me with wonderment. "Blessed Elua joins more than the hearts of lovers," she said. "For surely he knew what he was about when he sent us into Daršanga to find you."

Joscelin glanced toward the south. "What in Elua's name *was* that thing?"

"Ptolemy Solon called it a *ghafrid*," I said. "An elemental desert spirit. I called it a demon. It was trapped in the stone."

"Ptolemy Solon," Phèdre echoed. "The Governor of Cythera?" She furrowed her brow, examining her restored memories. "The one rumored to be your mother's patron?"

"Yes." In the midst of everything her quick wits were beginning to work on the puzzle. Despite my aching head and stinging backside, it made me smile. "It's a very long and very strange tale. And I will gladly tell you the whole of it, but not right now."

"What can we do to help?" Phèdre asked without hesitation.

I looked around at the milling chaos. "Right now, help people stay calm. Tell them it's all right; everything will be all right."

It took a while to get everything sorted out. Dozens of people had been injured by the flying shards or suffered severe abrasions from the *ghafrid*'s passage. The Royal Chirurgeon, Lelahiah Valais, arrived. Although she was no less dazed than anyone else in the City, she took control of the situation at Sidonie's order. Tents and cots were fetched and a makeshift infirmary quickly established in Elua's Square.

Aside from one young soldier who was in danger of losing an eye, most of the injuries were superficial; but it took a long time to remove all the tiny shards of emerald. Teams of chirurgeons worked diligently with tweezing implements, washing and salving myriad punctures or bandaging raw patches of scoured flesh. Lelahiah Valais attended me personally. She would have tended to Drustan first, but the Cruarch insisted that I take precedence. For once I didn't argue. I lay on my belly, listening to the sound of gem fragments plinking one by one into a metal pan.

Sidonie stopped in to check on my progress.

"How are they?" I asked, meaning everyone.

"Scared, confused, horrified." She was quiet a moment. "I understand what they're feeling. I was there, too. If you hadn't found the gem, I would have been part of launching a civil war."

"We knew the risks of entering the City," I said.

"Yes." Sidonie nodded. "It makes a difference. I've already been through the shock of awakening from a lie. I've had time to live with it. I'm talking to as many people as I can, trying to reassure them that it's not their fault. But it will take time."

"Healing does," I murmured.

"Mm-hmm." She cast a glance over my flesh. "You look like a demon's pincushion."

"Don't make me laugh," I said. "My head hurts."

She gave me a weary smile. "Better laughter than tears. Come find me when you're done."

It took almost an hour for Lelahiah Valais to pluck the last shard of emerald from my flesh. I rose and donned my clothing while her assistant went to fetch Drustan. He entered the tent and took my place on the cot, sitting quietly while Lelahiah examined his face. I found myself feeling awkward in his presence.

"I'm sorry this came to pass, my lord," I said to him.

Drustan looked sidelong at me. "I should have known. When I returned to Alba, the spell lost its hold on me. But when I returned, it reclaimed me and I forgot myself." He studied me. "That's why you put an *ollamh*'s charm on Sidonie, isn't it?"

"Yes," I said. "But it worked only for a time. And I'd been warned. You had no way of knowing, my lord."

He shook his head. "I should have known."

I could tell there was no comfort I could offer that Drustan would accept. Not now. I bowed to him, then left in search of Sidonie.

I located Kratos first. He was seated outside one of the chirugeons' tents, his thigh bandaged, telling our tale in broken D'Angeline to a group of wide-eyed soldiers who had suffered minor wounds. I paused, listening to his words.

". . . put her hand on his and *zzzzt*!" Kratos gestured. "They push the sword into Astegal's black heart."

"You saw it?" a soldier asked in awe.

"Oh, yes." Kratos nodded, then caught my eye and shrugged. I smiled and said nothing. Let him tell the story. Let him give them heroes: let him redirect their horror and self-loathing into anger toward Astegal and Carthage. It could only help.

I found Sidonie in another one of the tents, holding the hand of a Namarrese marquise whose brow had been gashed badly enough to require stitching, a young woman with a hereditary seat on Parliament she'd scarce warmed before the night of the marvel. The woman would have been tended to earlier, but she was sobbing too hard for the chirurgeons to do their work.

". . . thought, thought, thought it was *real*!" she gasped.

"I know," Sidonie murmured, stroking her hand. "So did I, so did we all."

"And I don't want to have a *scar*!" the woman wailed. "Every time I look in the mirror, I'll have to see it and remember!"

Sidonie looked up, feeling my presence.

"Yes," I said to the distraught young marquise, sitting on a stool beside her cot. "You will. A very faint, tiny scar." I traced a line on her brow. "And one day you will bear it with pride. You will say to your children and your children's children, 'See? I was there that day in Elua's Square, when Blessed Elua proved that there is no magic so dire it can stand against the force of love. I bear this scar as proof.' "

The marquise looked at me with fearful hope. "Will I?"

"You will," Sidonie promised her.

It calmed her enough that she allowed the chirurgeons to sew her wound. Once they began, Sidonie rose. She looked tired, but steady.

"Are matters under control?" she asked.

I nodded. "Well enough."

"We need to send word to Alais and my uncle." Sidonie shuddered. "They need to know that they're not under attack. We have to send a messenger."

"The Baronesse de Bretel?" I asked.

"Yes." She sighed. "I should have seen to freeing them immediately, but it seemed important to be here. Will you come with me?"

"Of course." I glanced around. "Where's Ysandre?"

Sidonie nodded toward another tent. "Lending comfort. It's the only thing she trusts herself to do right now, and I daresay she won't leave until Father's been seen to. Phèdre and Joscelin are with her. I promised to call an audience as soon as everything's settled."

There was a bit of confusion over who was to attend us. Diderot Duval, the Captain of the Palace Guard, was missing. In the end, Sidonie called for her personal guard. Claude de Monluc flung himself on his knees before her, head bowed, apologizing, to her, to me.

"Don't," Sidonie said firmly. "Just serve."

Claude gathered himself. "Yes, your highness."

We rode through the City to the royal dungeon. Despite Sidonie's orders, there were a good many folk wandering the streets, looking dazed and lost. One might have imagined that some great disaster had struck, that a vast earthquake had leveled the City, leaving its inhabitants to question the will of the gods. Most of them were ordinary citizens who had been too far away to hear Sidonie speak in the Square. On seeing us, they pressed close around our escort, begging for answers, halting our progress. Claude and his men had to push them away with their shields.

"Hold," Sidonie said to him. She raised her voice. "My people, you will have your answers by the day's end. That, I promise. But I beg you now to let us pass. We must send word to let the rest of Terre d'Ange know that the City of Elua is no longer under the sway of Carthage's spell."

They fell back slowly, some still shouting pleas. I looked at Sidonie. Her face was drawn with sorrow and weariness. "How are you holding, Princess?"

"Holding." She glanced back at me. "And you?"

"The same," I said.

Everything was in disarray everywhere. We reached the royal dungeon and found ourselves besieged by bewildered guards, asking the same questions. Sidonie was forced to repeat a variant of the same speech before ordering the release of Isabel de Bretel and the men who had travelled with her.

As a rule, Terre d'Ange is not cruel to prisoners. But when I saw the elderly Baronesse de Bretel and her men blinking at the spring sunlight in the dungeon's courtyard, I knew that at the least they had been confined in darkness since yesterday's audience. The baronesse stopped short, squinting at Sidonie and me. Her men cringed a little.

"Ah, gods," Sidonie whispered in pain.

"It's all right," I said to Isabel de Bretel. "We did it, my lady. We succeeded after all. The spell is broken. Sidonie serves as regent at her majesty's bidding. There will be no war."

Her head rose, her formerly neat coif of white hair lank and disheveled. The baronesse glanced slowly around at the shocked guards, their sudden attitude of humble respect. Her voice broke. "Truly?"

"Truly," Sidonie said. "My lady, I had thought to ask you to bear this message to my sister and uncle, but given your travail, it was thoughtless—"

"No!" Isabel de Bretel flushed, her skin as fine as wrinkled parchment. She gave a short, wondering laugh. She clasped her hands together. "No, your highness. Please, I beg you. Nothing would please me more."

"Are you certain?" Sidonie asked gravely.

"Yes." The baronesse nodded. "Oh, yes. May I . . ." She hesitated. "Forgive me, your highnesses, but may I touch you? May I be certain this is real and not some fevered dream born out of fear and confinement?"

I answered for both of us. "Yes."

With slow, tentative steps, Isabel de Bretel came forward. Her men followed, strides gradually lengthening as they realized their shackles had been stricken for good, that they were no longer prisoners and there would be no war. Isabel de Bretel cupped Sidonie's face in her gnarled hands, then mine. Feeling and believing, her old eyes filled with hope and awe. After all the stricken faces I'd seen, it gladdened my heart to see hers. I remembered the touch of her soft, wrinkled palms against my skin. Then it had felt like redemption. Today it felt like a benediction.

We had given them hope.

And we had not failed them.

Eighty-four

We escorted the Baronesse Isabel de Bretel and her men to the Palace to prepare for their journey and found a new dilemma awaiting us.

"You're not allowed entrance, your highness," the nervous guard at the gates informed us. "Captain Duval's orders."

Sidonie stared at him. "*What?*"

The guard licked his lips. "I don't . . . I don't know. He came riding hell-for-leather from the Square. He said you wrought a terrible spell that's driven everyone mad and we had to trust him and keep you from claiming the throne at all costs." He looked ill. "I don't . . . I don't know what to believe. Have I lost my wits?"

"No," I said. "But it sounds like Captain Duval has."

"I suppose some were bound to," Sidonie murmured. "It's a terrible strain."

Claude de Monluc drew his sword. "Open the gates and stand aside, man! I heard the Queen's words myself. Her highness is in command here."

The guard screwed up his face. Now it looked as though he were about to burst into tears. "I don't know what to do."

"How many of the Palace Guard are with him?" de Monluc asked.

"Forty or fifty?" he guessed.

"We can take them, your highness," de Monluc said to Sidonie. He gave me a grim, sidelong smile. "With Prince Imriel's help, I don't doubt it."

"Elua, no!" Sidonie said in alarm. She glanced at Isabel de Bretel, who had gone ashen. "No violence. It's not his fault. It's no one's fault." She pressed her temples. "Imriel. Do you think you can persuade my mother that her presence is required more urgently here than among the wounded?"

"I'll try," I said. "And I'll drag her here if I can't."

I rode quickly back to Elua's Square, weaving and dodging hundreds of aimless, wandering pedestrians. I found Joscelin outside the tent where Lelahiah Valais was still working on Drustan's injuries, and Ysandre and Phèdre within it. I bowed and explained the situation to the Queen.

"No." Ysandre didn't meet my eyes. "I had Isabel de Bretel cast in chains for speaking the truth to madness. I can't possibly face her. I'm sorry. That's why I abdicated the throne. It's Sidonie's duty now."

"Sidonie refused your charge," I said.

Ysandre shrugged. "She accepted the regency. We will discuss it later."

"Your majesty!" I said sharply. "Will you force her to use violence against your own people?" She winced as though I'd struck her. I beheld the fault-lines of pride and shame in her and exploited them without mercy. "With all due respect, your majesty, your daughter's ordeal has been worse than yours. And yet she has consented to bear this burden until you are ready to resume it. Will you truly weighten her load?"

That stung her.

Ysandre's head rose, her cheeks flushing. "You dare speak to me thusly?"

"Yes," I said ruthlessly.

"Ysandre," Phèdre murmured. Her name, nothing else. The Queen looked askance at her. If there was anyone in the world who knew aught about carrying terrible burdens, it was Phèdre nó Delaunay.

"I'll accompany you," Drustan offered.

"No." Ysandre closed her eyes, then opened them, squaring her shoulders in a familiar gesture. "No, stay. Lelahiah isn't finished. Imriel is right. I need to do this."

Exiting the tent, Ysandre summoned a company of the Palace Guard and placed them under Joscelin's command. He accepted it without comment, bowing in the Cassiline manner. Back to the Palace we rode, a hundred strong. This time, people cleared the streets. Ysandre sat very straight in the saddle, her face stark. No one begged her for answers. Outside the gates of the Palace, she met Isabel de Bretel's gaze without flinching.

"My lady de Bretel," Ysandre said in a steady tone. "I am so very sorry for making you suffer."

The elderly baronesse bowed her head. "Your majesty."

Ysandre looked at the guard. "Open the gates."

He did with alacrity. We entered the courtyard. The guards on the outer doors fidgeted.

"Summon Captain Duval," Ysandre said. "Summon the guard. Summon the Royal Chamberlain Lord Robert and the household staff. I want them all assembled."

They obeyed. We waited while ostlers and stable-lads peered at us, gaping. In a short while, there was a considerable crowd of guards and attendants spreading into the courtyard. I knew Diderot Duval by sight. He stared at us, flanked by uncertain guards, his face working helplessly. I pitied him.

"Hear me," Ysandre said to them. "Until further notice, you will obey her highness Sidonie de la Courcel as the rightful and acknowledged regent of Terre d'Ange. Is that understood?"

Most murmured in agreement.

"Your majesty, no!" Captain Duval cried. "You're ensorceled! This is madness, this is sedition—"

"Take him," Ysandre ordered the guards surrounding him. "Gently. See him to the Palace infirmary." The Palace Guardsmen descended on him as gently as possible, but he struggled. They bore him away, his cries echoing along the empty marble corridors. Ysandre shuddered, then gathered herself and turned to Sidonie. "Am I asking too much of you?" she asked, searching her daughter's face.

"No," Sidonie said softly. "You taught me well. But the people need you, you and Father, too."

"Right now, we all need one another," I added.

"Imriel de la Courcel." Ysandre looked at me and shook her head. "I suppose you're going to insist on wedding him now," she said to Sidonie.

Sidonie gave her a faint smile. "Unless you want to lose your heir *and* regent, yes. Don't you think he's proven himself worthy?"

"Stubborn child." Ysandre reached out to stroke Sidonie's hair, then leaned over in the saddle and kissed her brow. "I do. And I don't want to lose either of you." She straightened. "I'm going to return to your father. But if you've need of aught, send for me."

The Queen left the bulk of the company of guards with us, returning to the Square with only a score under Joscelin's command. She left us with a courtyard thronged with folk: the Palace Guard, the Dauphine's Guard, the Palace chamberlain and his household, Isabel de Bretel and her men, all looking to Sidonie for guidance.

"Well and so." She took a deep breath. "Lord Robert, please prepare quarters for the Baronesse de Bretel and her men and see to their needs. They'll be carrying an important message of peace for us. Please see to it that they have suitable tents, supplies, and attendants."

He bowed. "At once, your highness."

"My lord de Monluc." Her gaze fell on Claude. "Send a man to the Square to search for Michel Carascel. I believe he suffered minor injuries. He's still Captain Duval's second in command, is he not?"

"He is," Claude affirmed.

"Inform him that he's been promoted," Sidonie said. "He's to assume command of the Palace Guard. They are to return to their regular duties." Claude bowed. "Send a messenger to Ghislain nó Trevalion," she continued. "I want an escort of fifty . . . no, thirty. Thirty members of the Royal Army for the Baronesse de Bretel." She glanced at me. "Thirty?"

"Thirty's good," I said. "Enough for safety's sake, too few to seem a threat."

"Thirty, then," Sidonie said. "Prepared to depart for Turnone on the hour. I want all of them given white pennants of peace to carry."

"All of them?" Claude echoed.

"All of them," Sidonie said firmly. "Let there be no mistake about our intentions. Terre d'Ange is at peace. We will escort their company to the gates of the City. On the heels of their departure, we will hold an open audience. Lord Robert, please notify the Secretary of the Presence. Lady Denise should be on hand to record the proceedings. And please alert the Queen's Couriers. I will prepare a proclamation for them to carry throughout the City on the immediate conclusion of our audience."

"Only the City?" the chamberlain inquired.

"For the moment," Sidonie said. "Word of the full tale will spread quickly in the City. I'll prepare a more thorough account to be disseminated throughout the realm, but I'm not sure we've sufficient couriers for such a massive undertaking." She frowned in thought. "The Royal Army might serve, though there's the matter of aid to Aragonia to be discussed—"

"Sidonie." I interrupted her. "There's time."

She caught herself. "That will do for now. I'll be in my quarters drafting a proclamation. Let me know when all is in readiness."

The crowd dispersed in various directions, grateful to be given a sense of purpose. I escorted Sidonie unbidden to her quarters. She dismissed the frightened chambermaid with a kind word of reassurance. Once the girl had gone, Sidonie sank to her knees, covering her face with both hands.

I crouched before her. "Are you all right, love?"

"Yes," she said, muffled. "And no."

I took her shoulders in my hands. "You don't have to do this all at once. And you don't have to do it alone. They're shocked. It will pass in time. Your mother's promised her aid if you need it. In the meanwhile, send for Alais and L'Envers. They've got a shadow Parliament in place: they've been virtually governing Terre d'Ange. And I think it will do everyone good to have a great public reconciliation."

"Yes. That's a good thought." She dropped her hands. Her eyes were bright with tears. "Ah, gods! I'm sorry. I tried. I tried and tried. I wasn't strong enough."

"Sidonie!" I shook her. "Don't ever think that."

"It hurt." She rubbed her eyes with the heel of one hand. "And it was just so damned terrifying to feel my memories slipping away, bit by bit. Then one day I was sitting in the bath, feeling like there were red-hot shackles around my wrists and ankles, and I thought, why am I enduring this? And I couldn't remember. So I took them off. Just like that. And then it didn't hurt anymore and I didn't care. I was gone."

"Not all of you," I reminded her.

"No." She gazed at me. "When I saw you in the hall, walking toward the dais and dropping your sword, telling us the gods forbade the war . . . I don't know. I didn't remember, not exactly, but there was such a strange brightness about you. It tugged at somewhat inside of me. Why did you do it?"

I told her.

"Elua!" Sidonie's eyes widened. "Is that how you knew where to find the demon-stone?"

"No." I smiled wryly. "I woke up in the hall with my head splitting, staring sideways at the damnable gem-painting. And I saw it." I took her hand and traced a spiral on her palm. "The design from Bodeshmun's talisman. It was hidden in the whorls of bark on the tree."

Sidonie stifled an unexpected laugh. "Truly?"

"Mm-hmm." I leaned forward and kissed her lightly. "You have a proclamation to write and a letter to Alais. Can you manage?"

"Yes." Her fingers closed around mine. "I just need . . . I need you beside me. And I need this to be the one place where I don't *have* to be strong."

I smiled again. "I know. And in that, love, I'm more than happy to oblige in any way that will ease your burden."

This time, Sidonie smiled back at me with a trace of genuine amusement. "I can think of quite a few. Unfortunately, the most pressing would be helping me with this proclamation. Will you?"

I rose, pulling her to her feet. "Of course."

Sidonie stood without moving for a moment. I could feel

her gathering her strength, gathering her will. She glanced up at me, somber once more. "Do you think we'll ever truly recover from this? All of us, I mean, not you and I."

"Yes," I said honestly. I placed her hand on my chest. She spread her fingers, feeling the ridges of the scars beneath my doublet. "I don't think things will ever be the same. They can't be. But we've survived. We'll grieve. We'll heal. We'll remember that there's laughter and joy and love and desire in the world. Enough to drive out the grief and sorrow. Enough to banish guilt and shame."

"Do you promise it?" she asked.

"Yes." I slid my arms around Sidonie's waist, pulling her against me. She put hers around my neck and clung to me, fierce and hard. I rested my cheek against her head, breathing in the scent of her hair. "I promise."

EIGHTY-FIVE

My heart rose at the sight of Isabel de Bretel and her escort departing the City of Elua, a thicket of white pennants flying above them. Sidonie had been right to insist on them. It was a strong image, a powerful message of peace. No one cheered—the mood was still far too sober—but there was a feeling like a collective sigh of relief. A step toward normalcy had been taken.

We returned to the Palace to hold an audience.

Mere hours had passed since the demon had been freed from the stone and the spell broken. It felt like a great deal longer. I was weary for lack of sleep. My head ached, a tender lump having risen on the back of my skull. My entire backside stung with a hundred pinpricks. My stomach still roiled.

Given the choice, I'd far sooner have told the tale quietly to a chosen few in a private salon, and I know Sidonie would, too. But it wouldn't have been fair. It wasn't only our story. The entire City was confused and hurting and scared, desperate to learn how they'd been brought to the brink of civil war, to learn what the terrible whirling presence that had fled the City had been, to learn how in the world they'd imagined themselves to be grieving for Astegal of Carthage.

And so once more the Hall of Audience was packed. This time it was Sidonie and I who stood on the dais alone, gazing out at a sea of faces. It felt strange to stand there and see Drustan and Ysandre's faces among them, gazing back at us.

"My lords and ladies," Sidonie said. "Elua's city awoke from a fearful dream today. We are here to tell you who cast us into this nightmare and how our long sleep was broken."

They listened, hushed.

She spoke of Carthage and the night of the marvel. Of the memories all of them shared, of waking to believe herself in love with Astegal. Of sailing away with him while crowds cheered. "Not all your memories are a lie," she said in a low voice. "These things happened. I believed as you did. In Carthage, I wed Astegal of the House of Sarkal."

A sound somewhere between a hiss and a moan arose.

"But there is one among us whose memories of that night differ," Sidonie continued, turning to me.

I told the story as I'd told it in Amílcar, leaving out the details of the Unseen Guild. They already knew about my madness. I told them what had preceded it—the needle and the whisper, the stolen ring. This was Terre d'Ange. When I told them the words Sunjata had spoken—*You're lucky your mother loves you*—there was a gasp. Still, there was no blame in their eyes. I kept going and spoke of waking from my madness to find the City in the grip of a delusion. I told them how I'd sought Barquiel L'Envers' aid and fled to Cythera.

My mother.

Ptolemy Solon, the Wise Ape, picking apart the spells that had been wrought, giving me the key to undoing them.

Leander Maignard and the spell of disguise that Solon had wrought.

Carthage, and Kratos' true identity.

And then Sidonie picked up the thread of the tale and continued it. There were no theatrics this time, no shock of revelation as I shed Leander's guise. Only her voice, steadily recounting the story. The rising suspicion and fear she'd felt, the realization that pieces of her memory were missing. New Carthage. How Astegal had left to beseige Amílcar. The attempt on her life. How I had come to know myself, how she had drugged her guards. How I had shown her the golden ring stolen back from Astegal, how I had told her of the spell, how I had revealed myself to her.

Astegal's mark etched in her flesh.

Begging me to cut it out of her.

"He did," she said simply. "And I remembered." Sidonie fell silent. The hall was so quiet, the only sound was that of Lady Denise Grosmaine's, the Secretary of the Presence, quill scratching softly against paper, recording our history.

"We made a plan." I took up the story. "A desperate plan."

I told them how Sidonie had tricked Bodeshmun. How I'd killed him, how I'd found the talisman on him. Our harrowing escape, our flight on Captain Deimos' ship. The pursuit. Our fiery entrance into the harbor of Amílcar.

When I grew hoarse, Sidonie resumed the tale. Back and forth we traded it. Our negotiations with the council in Amílcar, our escape from the besieged city. The Euskerri's ambush of the Amazigh, the bargain on which the Euskerri insisted. The return to Amílcar and the terrible battle outside its walls. The bloody, costly victory.

Astegal's capture.

Astegal's death.

Here and there I saw nods. Kratos had told parts of the

story in the Square and some had heard bits and pieces of it. We told the whole of it. Sidonie and I wove the story between us, spinning it with our voices. My weariness vanished as I watched all those faces hanging on our words. We gave them the story as a gift. Its origins reached back into the past. A traitoress had given birth to a boy raised to believe himself a goat-herding orphan; two heroes of the realm had rescued a stolen boy and taught him to be good. The rulers of two nations had given birth to two girls and instilled ideals of valor and justice in them.

And it reached back farther into the tales of those who had shaped them: Anafiel Delaunay, Phèdre's mentor and patron. A grandfather I'd never known whose vicious charm had shaped my mother's youth. On and on it spiraled, backward into the mists of time.

But it would go forward, too. I thought of the words I'd spoken to the injured young noblewoman today. The story would go on and on. One day, Sidonie's and my great-grandchildren would stand in the Hall of Portraits, holding their own children's hands. They would point to our likenesses and tell our story.

These were your great-great-grandparents . . .

And they would live tales of their own, spinning it ever farther into the future. On and on without end.

My voice faltered and ran dry. I'd reached the present. The balance of our story was yet to be written.

In the silence that followed, no one spoke. Phèdre was the first to move. She came forward, her eyes shining with too many emotions to name. It didn't feel right to be raised on the dais, so I stepped down to her level, then helped Sidonie down beside me. Phèdre embraced us both in wordless gratitude.

They all came forward then—Drustan and Ysandre, Joscelin. Ghislain nó Trevalion. All the hundreds of peers and citizens and soldiers packed into the hall. They embraced us and they embraced one another. Raul L'Envers y Aragon was there, his face streaming with tears. His wife, Colette, whom I'd known since I was a youth; her brother, Julian, unfamiliar in an officer's livery. Mavros. Courtiers and priests and chambermaids, all mingling together. Kratos, a limping hero.

I embraced them all—I, who had once been a damaged, brooding boy reluctant to be touched. I took them into my heart and held them there.

And through it all, I felt the lingering echo of the presence of Blessed Elua and his Companions—a promise of hope, a promise of healing, a promise of happiness. And always, I felt Sidonie's presence, as sure and unfailing as sunlight, her heart bound to mine by a golden cord.

How long it lasted, I couldn't say. Three hours, four . . . the moment stretched, endless and infinite.

It was what was needful.

It lasted as long as it lasted.

Slowly, slowly, it moved onward. The throng began to thin. They took our story and our blessing and carried it out into the City. The Queen's Couriers took Sidonie's proclamation and rode forth to announce in every quarter that Carthage's spell was broken and the realm was at peace.

In the streets, strangers embraced and wept.

Poets in their chambers began to scribble notes.

The Secretary of the Presence's assistants began to transcribe copies of her record, preparing to send them throughout the realm.

In the nearly empty hall, I sat on the edge of the dais and sighed. Sidonie stood beside me, resting one hand on my shoulder. Apart from the attendant guards standing at a discreet distance and the hovering chamberlain, almost everyone had left. Only those who loved us best remained.

"So." Ysandre broke the long, long silence. Her violet eyes were bemused. "Terre d'Ange owes its freedom to Melisande Shahrizai?"

I nodded wearily. "In a sense."

Joscelin shook his head. "The humors of the gods are perverse."

"Yes." Phèdre's gaze rested on us, on Sidonie and me. "But in the end, they are merciful."

Mercy.

Just the sound of the word felt like the touch of grace. I closed my eyes, feeling the tide of exhaustion returning to claim me, a spiraling weight dragging me downward. And then I forced them open so I could look at Sidonie. Her face was swimming in my vision and there was a sparkling darkness behind my eyes. I'd slept very little in the past few days.

"What will you?" Drustan asked his daughter.

"Food." Sidonie's fingers brushed over the lump on the back of my skull, feather-light. "And sleep."

"Sleep," I echoed.

And then the sparkling darkness took me.

I roused briefly, long enough to allow myself to be assisted to a bed. I was vaguely aware of voices. I let them slip away and slid back into the darkness.

I slept and dreamed. I dreamed of blood and war and fire. I dreamed of showers of rose petals falling. I dreamed of Sidonie's black gaze staring at me through the falling petals, staring with stark fury before a mirror. A vast mirror reflecting the occluded moon. A paring knife. A slippery disk of flesh and blood, more blood. Bodeshmun's chest heaving futilely, his heels drumming. Swords. Men dying, men crying. Astegal's head on a stake, his mouth slack. A golden knot, whorls of bark. An emerald splintering. Whorls of dirt and sand, towering high above Elua's Oak. A gaping maw, horns shiny as mica dipping.

I blinked awake.

Moonlight spilled through the bedchamber, a moon just past fullness.

In the balcony door, Sidonie turned. "Imriel."

I propped myself on one arm. "Did I miss aught?"

"No." She came over and ran a lock of my hair through her fingers. "How's your head? Lelahiah said it was best to let you sleep."

"Better," I said. "I think it was mostly exhaustion. I felt like a candle that had been blown out."

"Can you eat?" she asked. "I'll send someone to the kitchens."

"Later." I folded back the bed-clothes. "Come here."

Sidonie shed her robe and slid into bed, slid into my arms, warm and naked. Her body pressed against mine. She shivered, a shiver that owed nothing to coldness. "I keep thinking about it. The demon. It *bowed* to us."

I tightened my arms around her. "I know. Mayhap even a demon may be grateful."

"Mayhap," she murmured.

There was nothing else to say.

We slept.

Eighty-six

In the days that followed, Terre d'Ange slowly found its bearings.

Sidonie and I met with Ghislain nó Trevalion and determined to dispatch five hundred soldiers throughout the realm, carrying copies of the transcript of our audience to be read in every city and village. She appointed Raul L'Envers y Aragon to head a delegation to Amílcar with a pledge of aid should it be needed. The Siovalese lord Tibault de Toluard volunteered to serve as an ambassador to the fledgling Euskerria, carrying a charter stamped with the royal seal confirming Terre d'Ange's end of the bargain. Together we drafted letters to D'Angeline ambassadors scattered around the world, assuring them that Terre d'Ange had regained its wits.

Drustan sent his honor guard to Alba carrying a message of peace and apology to his heir Talorcan.

Those members of Parliament who had remained ensconced in the City gathered their retinues and departed for their own estates, in many cases reuniting families torn apart by Carthage's spell.

The priesthoods of Blessed Elua and his Companions announced that the month of Sidonie's regency would be a time of contemplation for all. They bade their own members to meditate on the near-tragedy in an effort to discern what divine lessons it might hold.

I kept my word and dispatched a letter to my mother and Ptolemy Solon on Cythera, giving sincere thanks for their aid and including a generous reward for Captain Deimos and his men drawn on the Royal Treasury. It also included an official declaration stamped with the royal seal and signed by the Regent of Terre d'Ange confirming that Melisande Shahrizai de la Courcel's sentence of execution had been reduced to one of exile.

Across the realm, there was no rejoicing, only quiet relief. In the City, a somber mood prevailed.

It was a strange time. I'd returned to the City and been treated with wary care as an invalid, deranged and harmless. All of that had changed. Without being asked, the folk of the realm treated me as an unofficial co-regent. The captains of the Palace Guard and the City Guard consulted me on their decisions. Claude de Monluc, continuing as the head of Sidonie's personal guard, regarded my word as interchangeable with hers. And then there was Kratos, our unlikely hero, loyal to us both.

"Gods be thanked," Sidonie said when I commented on it.

Her workload was heavy. Within two days of the spell's breaking, petitioners began pouring into the City, heedless of the injunction to spend the time in contemplation. It seemed ten thousand petty disputes had sprung up during the time of madness. The judicial system had fallen apart under the strain. Some suits were unsettled and deserved a fair hearing; others had been settled by Alais in a manner the complainants disliked. Sidonie considered refusing to hear them until the month had passed, but after consulting with Brother Thomas from the Temple of Elua, she decided that the realm would be better served by accepting their petitions and hastening the return to normalcy.

Word from Alais and Barquiel L'Envers had been swift and joyous on the heels of our news. Still, it took time for them to arrive. It was a week before we heard that their entourage had been sighted.

That was a glad day.

They came under the white banner of peace, trebling the number of pennants Sidonie had dispatched. I stood beside Sidonie under the arch that spanned the gates to the City, watching them come. All those white pennants fluttering, as though a flock of white doves hovered above the earth. The walls were lined with watchers.

My throat felt tight.

Aside from the pennants, it wasn't an impressive entourage. All the outriders wore mismatched livery, much of it threadbare. This was a fragment of the army we would have fought, cobbled together from commonfolk and the scions of the Lesser Houses. Still, their weapons were sturdy and sharp. It would have been a terrible thing.

"Sidonie." Alais breathed her sister's name, dismounting before the gates. Barquiel L'Envers followed suit. The man behind them remained in the saddle. I looked up with a shock and met Hyacinthe's sea-shifting gaze.

The crowd murmured.

Slowly and deliberately, the Lord of the Straits dismounted. He moved as though to offer a bow.

"No, my lord." Sidonie sank into a curtsy. I bowed low. All our guards dropped to one knee. After a moment, Sidonie rose. "Terre d'Ange gives thanks to her highness Alais de la Courcel and his grace Barquiel L'Envers for serving in her hour of need," she said in a clear, strong voice. "Let it be noted!"

There were cheers then, for the first time, ragged but heartfelt. L'Envers clasped my hand as Sidonie embraced her sister.

"Imriel," he said steadily. "Well done."

I nodded. "And you."

Hyacinthe.

He was slighter than I remembered; still, there was that mantle of power that hung over him, those dark, roiling eyes that had stared into the prospect of a dreadful forever. He clasped my hand, too.

"Thank you," I said to him. "Thank you for coming."

Hyacinthe smiled slightly. "Thank you for rendering my presence unnecessary." He looked past me, searching.

"She's not here," I said, knowing he was looking for Phèdre. "There's to be a ceremony in Elua's Square."

He inclined his head. "Ah."

I hugged Alais. She felt less frail than she had in Turnone. "I'm so glad," she whispered. "So very, very glad."

"So am I, love," I whispered back.

We mounted and rode to Elua's Square. It had been left untouched, bereft of its paving stones, the wooden dais still on the dirt beneath the great oak tree. Drustan and Ysandre stood on it. Instead of guards, they were flanked by Priests and Priestesses of Elua, barefoot in blue robes.

There hadn't been time to issue an announcement, but a sizable crowd had gathered nonetheless. They whispered among themselves as we approached, the rumor of Hyacinthe's presence spreading.

At a word from Sidonie, our company drew rein and dismounted. Alais and L'Envers approached the dais.

"It is not truly my place to perform this office today,"

Ysandre said in a quiet tone. She gazed at her youngest daughter, sorrow etched on her face. "But I think it fitting that you receive this from my hand and no other. It is I who owes you the greatest debt." She held out a gold medallion strung on green ribbon. "Alais de la Courcel, for your service to the realm, I present you with the Medal of Valor."

Alais bowed her head. Ysandre placed the medal around her neck, then kissed and embraced her daughter. Drustan put his arms around them both and said somewhat in a voice too low for anyone else to hear. Alais nodded, her face hidden. A soft sigh of approval ran through the crowd.

Terre d'Ange was whole.

We would endure.

The Medal of Valor was likewise presented to Barquiel L'Envers, who received it with a modesty I didn't think was feigned. This ordeal had altered him, as it had all of us. He looked tired and relieved, a man spared a dreadful burden. But Alais . . . when Alais turned to face the crowd, she gave a smile so bright and dazzling, so utterly genuine, that I felt myself smiling in reply.

We would heal.

The ceremony was concluded. I watched Hyacinthe pay his respects to Drustan and Ysandre. There was somewhat reassuring about his presence there, a reminder that there were benign forces in the world able to match Carthage's magic. I thought about the mysterious journey that Phèdre and Joscelin had undertaken at his behest some years ago. Somewhere, I suspected, the pages of the Book of Raziel from whence his arcane knowledge came lay hidden and guarded. Mayhap they would vanish forever, or mayhap they would become a thread in someone else's tale.

I didn't know for sure.

I didn't want to know.

All that I wanted, I had. I glanced sidelong at Sidonie and caught her doing the same. She laughed.

"What are you thinking, Sun Princess?" I asked.

Her eyes sparkled. "Guess."

I smiled. "I think I can."

"Likely." Sidonie reached up to kiss me, and there were no murmurs of disapproval from the slowly dispersing crowd, no underlying current of suspicion, only quiet smiles and nods. The fact that we were together had become emblematic of the fact that all was well in Terre d'Ange. Our love had been woven into the fabric of the realm.

My arm resting around Sidonie's waist, I watched Hyacinthe approach Phèdre and Joscelin.

"Tsingano," Joscelin said in greeting.

Hyacinthe nodded at him. "Cassiline."

He didn't speak to Phèdre, only folded her in his arms. I watched her cling to him, holding him hard, taking solace in his presence. He was the Master of the Straits, but he was her oldest friend, too. Their story reached back a long, long way. Across the crowd, I met Joscelin's eyes. He shrugged, the hilt of his sword rising over his left shoulder. Joscelin understood.

Everything was intertwined.

If Phèdre had never cared so deeply for Hyacinthe, she would never have set out on a quest to free him from his curse. Never have found herself in Menekhet, where the threads of our stories intertwined. Never have gone to Daršanga to free me. And if Joscelin hadn't loved her beyond all reason, he would never have accompanied her. Never have defended us all in a dark and terrible hall that stank of death and ran red with blood.

None of us would be here.

"Imriel." Sidonie's voice broke my reverie. I realized that the official participants of the ceremony were waiting on us. They wouldn't leave before we gave the signal. That was something else to which I'd have to grow accustomed, a taste of the future to come. Sidonie's regency would end in a month, but I *had* fallen in love with the Dauphine of Terre d'Ange, heir to a throne that my mother had coveted and I had never wanted. One day she truly would rule in her mother's stead, with me at her side. "Are you ready?"

"No," I said. "But I will be."

EIGHTY-SEVEN

The month passed swiftly.

There was an endless amount of work to be done, but the arrival of Alais and L'Envers and their shadow Parliament was a great help. With their aid, we were able to assemble a Court of Assizes willing and qualified to review the multitude of petitions. There were a handful of cases in which Alais admitted to questioning her own judgment—she knew a great deal more about Alban law than D'Angeline—but many could be dismissed out of hand by the Court. The rest, Sidonie agreed to review herself.

The moon waned and waxed. The trade routes grew busy. Life in the City began to resume some of its normal rhythms.

Alais met with her royal parents to speak to them about her desire to end her betrothal to Talorcan and pursue her studies to become an *ollamh.* Sidonie and I attended the meeting. They heard Alais out in silence.

"I am willing to give my blessing to this plan," Drustan said when she had finished. "As an *ollamh*, her stature and influence will be greater than that of a Cruarch's wife. But I do not know if that would be understood in Terre d'Ange."

"Far better than it would have been a year ago," Ysandre murmured. "Though there is still the question of succession."

"I've thought about that, too." Alais hesitated. "Aunt Breidaia . . . we've grown close since Dorelei's death. I think she would be pleased to adopt me as a foster-daughter. And if she did . . ."

"You'd be Talorcan's sister in the eyes of Alban law," Drustan mused, finishing the thought. "Your children would be eligible to be named his heirs."

Alais nodded without speaking.

"Ah, love!" Ysandre studied Alais' face. "Is it truly your heart's desire?"

"It is," Alais said in a steady voice.

Ysandre smiled with sorrow. "Then I think I too must consent to give my blessing. If we have learned naught else, of a surety we have learned the dangers of placing politics over love." Her gaze fell on Sidonie and me. "So one oft-postponed wedding is to be cancelled and one much-thwarted one announced. I think it would be best if we waited until I've resumed the throne to issue both proclamations. I want there to be no question that this was in accordance with my will and done with my blessing."

"And mine," Drustan said quietly.

So it was decided.

The waxing moon grew full. In a small, modest ceremony, Sidonie relinquished the regency and Ysandre reclaimed the throne. The banns were posted announcing our betrothal. The wedding would take place the following summer, in one year's time. All of us reckoned the realm needed time yet to heal, and Sidonie and I would sooner be wed in joy than sorrow. For now it was enough that our betrothal was recognized and accepted.

There were no protests, no mention of Melisande Shahrizai. Carthage's treachery had overshadowed hers. The love affair that had strained the realm had proved its salvation.

The world had changed.

A few weeks after Ysandre resumed the throne, word came from Aragonia. Pressed by the presence of the D'Angeline fleet and fearful of further military support coming from Terre d'Ange, bereft of its ambitious general and his sorcerous kinsman, Carthage was cutting its losses and negotiating for a truce.

Aragonia itself was in disarray. There were factions supporting Serafin L'Envers y Aragon and factions supporting the deposed king, Roderico de Aragon. There were factions that held that the best compromise was for the childless Roderico to name Serafin his heir. There were factions supporting the accord with the Euskerri and factions opposing it. After consulting with Sidonie, Ysandre sent a sharply worded message indicating that if Aragonia failed to honor its bargain with the fledgling sovereign nation of Euskerria, Terre d'Ange would withdraw its naval support, leaving their ports defenseless.

Beyond that, it was their story to tell.

There was talk of retribution against Carthage. As spring wore onto summer, Ysandre convened Parliament to discuss the matter—a Parliament altered and expanded by circumstance. The members of the shadow Parliament who had helped Alais govern had been inaugurated as official members under Ysandre's rule. The debate was waged by old members and new, the bright mirror and the dark.

All voices were heard. Sidonie and I spoke against war. We'd both seen too much bloodshed. We both carried our own scars. No amount of further blood would erase them.

In the end it was Hyacinthe's voice that decided it.

He had elected to stay until Drustan returned to Alba. I daresay there was a part of him that missed the land of his birth. The Master of the Straits was reckoned the equal to the Queen and Cruarch, and his counsel was always welcome.

"It is my thought that our nations have seen enough war for one lifetime," Hyacinthe said, sitting at Drustan's right hand. "I, too, speak against it. You are within your rights to demand some manner of restitution." He shrugged slightly, and the air around him seemed to shudder. "And you are within your rights to decide that the tribute-gift with which Carthage gained entry to the City suffices. As to that, I do not care. But I will say this." His voice rose, threaded with ominous thunder. "Carthage's deeds threatened and damaged the lives of those I love. If that had been known to me, I would not have hesitated to use any and all power against them."

The hall was hushed and breathless.

Hyacinthe smiled grimly. "I consider it a debt owed. If Carthage should ever think to raise its hand against the least citizen of Terre d'Ange or Alba while I live, I *will* sink it beneath the waves."

There was no further talk of retribution.

With the matter settled, Drustan returned to Alba, escorted by the soldiers who'd come to defend Terre d'Ange against itself. Alais and Hyacinthe went with them. Before they left, I'd remembered a promise unkept. I spoke to Phèdre, who sent Ti-Philippe and Hugues to Montrève to see it fulfilled. Unlike in other years, there was no great farewell fête for the Cruarch, but there was a small gathering of family and friends. It was there that I fulfilled my promise. Sidonie laughed at me, but she willingly consented to be part of it.

Alais' eyes widened when she saw us enter. The wolfhound paced before us on a leash, tall and dignified, no longer a pup. "Oh, Imri!" She pressed her cheeks with both hands. "You remembered."

"Ah, Elua," Ysandre murmured in fond despair.

I handed the leash to Alais. "We chose her a year ago. Her dam was one of Celeste's littermates. Artus Labbé said she was the best of the lot. He called her Allegra."

"Allegra," Alais whispered, stroking the dog's head. Its plumed whip of a tail beat. "Thank you."

It was another thing brought around full circle. I'd mocked myself after that day long ago when Alais' dog Celeste, my gift to her, had been gored by a boar and I'd sought to protect Sidonie from a harmless deer. Imriel, savior of dogs, defender against deer. Later, when it truly mattered, I *had* failed. Failed to protect Dorelei, failed to protect Celeste. The bear that had killed my wife and our unborn son had slain Alais' dog, too.

The bear-witch.

Berlik.

So many sacrifices, great and small. Had they been needful to bring us to this moment? I would never know. All I could do was mourn and honor them, great and small. The Cruithne princess who taught me what it meant to love selflessly. The noble-hearted dog who died trying to defend her.

"Thank you," Alais repeated. She gave the wolfhound a hug and straightened, unselfconsciously brushing dog hair from her gown. "I thought . . ." She hesitated. "When I return, I thought I might stay at Clunderry. It was a place of happiness, once. I'm ready to remember it thus."

I smiled. "I'd like that. I'd like to think of you there."

"Not alone, surely?" Sidonie inquired.

Alais shook her head. "No, of course not. Aunt Breidaia and I talked of it before I left. And Firdha or one of the other *ollamhs* would have to consent if I'm to continue my studies there."

"Ah." I raised my brows. "So you might invite Aodhan of the Dalriada, who wrought my bindings. And mayhap his pupil, Conor mac Grainne, the son of the Lady of the Dalriada and a certain harpist?"

"I might in time." Alais flushed. "I told you I believe the Maghuin Dhonn know things we've lost. Mayhap it's time to reclaim them. To work together in peace and understanding."

I eyed her until her flush deepened. "Mayhap."

Mayhap it was, I thought. Mayhap Dorelei's death and Berlik's sacrifice were part of another pattern yet to emerge, one in which Alais played a role no one could have guessed. Or mayhap her role was a bridge to another tale, one that would be told by generations yet to be born.

I hoped it would be a joyous one.

Eighty-eight

Summer gave way to fall. In the countryside, it was harvest time. In the City, the peers arranged hunting parties and began to talk of wintering at the Palace. The endless stream of petitions abated. The D'Angeline fleet returned from Aragonia with the glad news that King Roderico had agreed to honor the Euskerri treaty and name Serafin his heir, settling the discord overseas. The ordinary rhythms of life slowly took precedence.

Terre d'Ange continued to heal.

The paving-stones were replaced in Elua's Square. All across the City, the signs of damage wrought in the quest to find Bodeshmun's gem were erased. People began to gather in wineshops and inns. Trade in the Night Court, which had slowed for all of the Thirteen Houses save Balm House, resumed at a livelier pace.

There were reminders. The swathe the demon had cut on its passage through the City was visible, cobblestones and the sides of buildings scoured clean and smooth. Where it had crossed the outer wall, the stones gleamed especially white.

And there was the charred foundation in Night's Doorstep where a humble dwelling had been burned to the ground and a family of Tsingani killed. During her tenure as regent, Sidonie had ordered it left untouched.

Never forget.

None of us ever would. But bit by bit, we learned to live with the memories.

The plans for Sidonie's and my wedding got under way in earnest. It was to be a grand fête, the greatest celebration the realm had seen since Phèdre had staged a celebration for the entire City on the occasion of Hyacinthe's freedom. Like an idiot, I expected Sidonie to take a deep and abiding interest in the process.

She wrinkled her nose at me. "Why would you think that?"

"Well," I said, feeling foolish. "In my experience, women do. There's naught Phèdre likes better than planning a fête. Your mother, too."

We were lying in bed. Sidonie shook her head, her hair loose over her bare shoulders. "I used to hate formal occasions. All the stares, folk muttering about Ysandre's half-breed heirs tainting House Courcel's pure bloodline. It was worse for Alais because she looks less D'Angeline than I do. I told you how much I hated the fact that I couldn't keep the gossip from hurting her." She traced the scarred welt on my left thigh. "It's different now. I've learned to enjoy fêtes and I'm looking forward to ours. But I'd rather plan somewhat larger. And I'd rather do it with you."

I ran my fingers through her hair. "An academy of magic?"

"Mayhap." She shot me a look. "We could start smaller. I

did promise Amarante to see a new Temple of Naamah dedicated in the City if she would return and stay. And she has."

"Ah." I smiled. "Well, if there's anyone owes Naamah a temple, it's you and I." I circled the pink disk between her shoulder blades. "Kratos is of the opinion that the City of Elua needs a palaestra. I fear he's growing bored."

Sidonie shivered. "Don't, please."

"Talk of Kratos?" I asked.

"No." She peered over her shoulder. "I hate it, that's all."

I flattened my palm against her skin. "It's a badge of honor, love."

"I know." Sidonie sat upright, quick and deft. "But I still hate it. More than I hated gossip." She straddled my lap and stroked my chest, her eyes dark and grave. "Your scars are a reminder of love and loss, of struggle and sacrifice and honor. Mine's just a reminder of Astegal."

I pulled her against me and kissed her. "Who?"

Her gaze softened. "No one."

Fall turned into winter; a quiet season, a fallow season. The Palace was filled with a fresh crop of young peers embarking on the Game of Courtship. The Hall of Games was filled once more with activity, though its jocularity wasn't quite the same.

For the most part, Sidonie and I ignored it. We made love and we made plans. A temple, an academy, a palaestra. Anything and everything was possible. She'd had a taste of what the burden of rulership would be like, and I of what it would be like to share it with her. Now, before the burden fell on our shoulders in earnest, we had time to dream and begin the work of bringing our dreams to life.

Some would be easily brought to fruition, like the temple. We had in mind that it would be a haven dedicated to oppressed lovers, a cozy little sanctuary. It was a fitting tribute. I proposed building it on the site of the burned Tsingani house.

"It would still serve as a reminder," I said. "But it would be a more uplifting one. There's enough guilt and shame."

We debated whether or not that was a good thing, whether or not it would be disrespectful to the memories of the Tsingani who had died. We met with members of Naamah's priesthood and wrote to the Lady Bérèngere, who was the head of the order.

And we went to Night's Doorstep and met with Emile at the Cockerel and spoke with many of the Tsingani who frequented the inn and lived in the quarter. It made me smile to see Sidonie among them, listening gravely to their concerns. In the end, everyone seemed pleased by the idea, and we proceeded to consult with various architects.

The academy would be an infinitely larger and more challenging project. If it were to happen, it truly would be our legacy. For now we merely talked about it, debating where it might be, debating its nature. Would it be an institution of pure academic study or would we seek practitioners of arcane arts to teach the actual practice? Should there be a philosophical component? What rules should govern the practice of magic? To whom should the practitioners be accountable? Where to even begin?

They were questions to be settled over the course of a lifetime, like as not questions that would outlive us.

That was all right.

We had a lifetime.

And we had the nights—a hundred thousand nights that Blessed Elua in his mercy had granted us. Neither of us ever forgot that each night we spent together was a blessing, and long as the winter nights were, they passed swiftly.

The Longest Night came and went, celebrated with somber joy. The nights grew shorter and fled ever more quickly.

Spring came.

The trees greened and flowers blossomed. Workers began clearing the burnt debris from the site where Naamah's new temple would be built. Pledges to attend our wedding began flooding in from far afield.

Some of them surprised me. My Serenissiman cousin Severio Stregazza and his wife planned to come. I'd met him only once, long ago. Some surprised and delighted me. I'd sent word to Lucius Tadius da Lucca, having kept up an intermittent correspondence with him all these years. Lucius was coming. Some of them honored me. Hyacinthe would be attending, the Master of the Straits and his family. And some, like Eamonn and Brigitta, simply delighted me.

"You've touched a good many lives, Imriel," Sidonie observed.

"A good many lives have touched mine," I said in reply.

I thought in those days about the ones who wouldn't be attending. Women killed in the Mahrkagir's zenana; and those who had survived. If I could have chosen one soul among the living, it would have been Kaneka, the strong-willed Jebean woman whose courage had been an inspiration to us all. On that long, grueling voyage with Phèdre and Joscelin to find the Name of God, Kaneka's home village had been the first place I'd remembered what it meant to be happy.

I hoped she was there with a love and children of her own, dandling them on her knee and telling them stories. Telling them of dire magics and unlikely heroes.

And I thought of Dorelei.

Often.

Sidonie came upon me unexpectedly one day in our quarters, sitting cross-legged on the balcony and playing the wooden flute that Hugues had given me. I'd never played it for her. I didn't know she was there until I stopped and felt her presence.

"That's a pretty tune," she said softly behind me.

I lowered the flute. "It's a silly song. I learned it as a child."

"I thought it might be." Sidonie rested her hands lightly on my shoulders. I'd told her things she remembered. How I used to make Dorelei laugh by playing a child's goatherding song. "Will you play it again?"

I did.

She bent down to kiss me. "Dorelei wanted you to be happy."

"I know," I murmured. "That's what hurts."

"I know," Sidonie said.

Private griefs, private shames. There were some we could never share with one another, not wholly. But that was all right, too. We *knew* one another. We bore our scars and carried our memories as best we could. We watched the pale green leaves darken and broaden, spring hurtling toward summer. We watched Ysandre stew and fret over the preparations for our wedding, silk tents blossoming on the greensward of the royal gardens. We made our plans, made love, whispered words of solace and passion to each other.

Elua knows, there was passion.

Less than a week before our wedding, I caught Sidonie conspiring with Amarante in our quarters.

"—don't want to risk blasphemy," she said.

Amarante's voice was tranquil. "I would never have suggested it if I thought it did. But if it eases your mind, my mother agrees that it's not."

"What's not?" I asked without announcing myself.

They both glanced at me and fell silent. Sidonie's dark eyes narrowed; Amarante's, calm and apple-green, her gaze as steady as it had been the day she'd helped me stitch Alais' dog's wounds.

"Nothing," Sidonie said.

"Not yet," Amarante added.

"Fine." I leaned down to kiss them both. "Keep your secrets."

Whatever it was, it didn't trouble me. I trusted Amarante without question. She'd kept Sidonie's secrets for as long as she'd been her companion, and she'd kept our secrets when it would have meant the Queen's wrath on her head. Without her aid, we might never have found the means to carve out enough time to discover that our feelings for one another ran far deeper than the lure of the forbidden. And I daresay there were secrets of Sidonie's that she kept even now. If Sidonie needed to speak of Astegal, to tell someone things she couldn't bear to tell me, it would be to Amarante that she'd turn.

The City swelled. Peers from all over the realm came, guests from overseas. The Palace was a whirl of activity. The inns were crowded and there wasn't a townhouse to be rented. Every night there was a new fête to attend.

Terre d'Ange had come out of mourning.

I was reunited with old friends and introduced them to new ones. Eamonn and Brigitta brought with them a strapping one-year-old boy with bright blue eyes and a thatch of ruddy hair. Lucius arrived with his satyr's grin, unaccompanied by family. Raul and Colette returned from Aragonia accompanied by Nicola, who had played a role in brokering the peace there and ensuring Serafin's succession to the throne. Maslin de Lombelon arrived unannounced, smiling crookedly at my surprise. The Lady of Marsilikos arrived accompanied by both her son and daughter. The Shahrizai came in numbers. The Cruarch's flagship brought Hyacinthe and Sibeal and their two children, grown startling older than my memories placed them. Urist was in Alais' vanguard, serving once more as commander of the garrison of Clunderry.

There was sorrow mixed in with the joy.

But mostly there was joy.

We needed it, all of us. And so we toasted the mourned dead and celebrated the living. I watched Joscelin glower at the sight of Phèdre laughing with Severio Stregazza, who had once offered for her hand, and smiled as Nicola succeeded in coaxing him into a better mood. I heard Maslin's tales of his adventures in distant Vralia and the changes yet brewing there. I watched Mavros flirt unabashedly with an amused Lucius, and decided that Master Piero's best pupil could hold his own against my obstreperous cousin. I listened to Eamonn and Brigitta's animated account of developing their own philosophical academy, making notes in my thoughts.

And I watched Sidonie.

It seemed we were parted more often than not at each glittering affair. There was too much clamor for our attention. But we always knew where the other was. Time and again, I would glance across a crowded room and find her gaze meeting mine.

Two days before our wedding, I didn't see her at all. She departed with Amarante, bound, I thought, for a last fitting with Favrielle nó Eglantine, but day turned into evening without her return. The guards bade me not to worry, but they would say naught of her whereabouts. I attended a fête hosted by Lady Nicola, thinking to see Sidonie there.

"No," Nicola said, her eyes dancing. "Her highness sent her regrets. It is her hope that you might make an early night of it. You'll not be seeing each other on the eve of the wedding."

My pulse quickened. "Ah."

Nicola laughed and made a shooing gesture. "Go to her."

I returned to our quarters to find them ablaze with candlelight and Sidonie awaiting me. All the attendants had been dismissed and the drapes were drawn. The air in the room took on a charge. I could feel the blood beating in my veins.

"You planned this well, love," I said.

Sidonie gave me a quick smile. "I have somewhat to show you."

I raised my brows. "Oh?"

She took a deep breath. "Will you see?"

The words sparked a faint memory of a tale Phèdre had told me long ago about her foster-brother Alcuin and their lord and mentor Anafiel Delaunay. Those three simple words were the formal request made by adepts of the Night Court on completing their marques. The debt was not fully concluded until the marque was acknowledged. I gazed at Sidonie, the air quivering between us. She looked young and a little uncertain.

"Present yourself," I said.

She undid the laces of her bodice and pushed her gown from her shoulders. It fell around her ankles in a shimmering pool of amber silk. She stepped neatly out of it and removed her undergarments. Candlelight made her naked skin glow. I forced myself to breathe slowly. Sidonie gathered her clothing and placed it carefully over the arm of the couch.

And then she knelt as I'd taught her, clasping her hands behind her neck. But there was one difference. She turned and knelt with her back to me.

My breath caught in my throat. "Ah, love!"

A sunburst. Astegal's scar formed the center of it, the pink disk turned to gold. Gold lines radiated outward, edged in black for definition. I walked forward and touched it. It was a bit larger than the span of my hand, perfectly centered between her shoulder blades.

I remembered Amarante assuring her there was naught blasphemous in whatever they were plotting. Now I understood.

"It's *your* mark." Sidonie's voice shook. "Do you like it?"

"No." I circled her, stooped. Took her chin in my hands and tipped her face up toward mine. I kissed her until I felt her body sway toward me, yearning warring with obedience, fear warring with desire. "It's beautiful. You're beautiful. I love it. And I love you."

She made a soft sound and slid her arms around my neck, kissing me. I gathered her in my arms and carried her into the bedchamber where a dozen more candles blazed. I laid her on the bed and opened the door of the cupboard that stood beside the bed.

"What will you, Princess?" I asked gravely.

"My choice?" Sidonie asked.

I nodded.

She withdrew a length of silken gold rope.

"You're sure?" I asked. I'd not bound her since Carthage's spell had been broken. Too many memories of pain and fear, the *ollamh*'s bindings and her wits slipping away. But tonight Sidonie placed her wrists together and nodded.

"I'm sure."

I tied her wrists together, lashing them securely. Lashing them to the bedposts. I placed her on her belly first. I stripped off my own clothes, kissed her from the nape of her neck to the cleft of her buttocks, lingering over the sunburst. I fingered the slick cleft and bud between her thighs until she writhed beneath me, face pressed against the pillow. And then I pulled the pins from her hair and turned her over. The golden cord stretched her arms tight overhead, her breasts taut.

"Imriel . . ." Sidonie said, breathless.

"Ah, no." I spread her thighs wide, sliding downward to taste her. "I'm only beginning."

Kushiel's mercy, cruel and sweet. I had learned the art of

patience making love to her. Mine. She was mine. I took her to the precipice of pleasure and abandoned her there, over and over, until she wept and begged.

So good.

And then I fitted myself between her thighs, propped on one arm. I rubbed the crown of my phallus between her slick nether-lips, over Naamah's Pearl. I slid the tip of my shaft into her, only enough to make her body jerk and strain, then withdrew, over and over.

Sidonie glared at me, her face damp with tears. "I hate you!"

I smiled. "No, you don't."

"Please?" she begged. "I need you."

I clutched my aching phallus, feeling it throb in my fist, rubbing it against her. "Tell me the truth."

"I love you." Her back arched. "Always and always."

I sank into her, deep and true.

"Oh, *gods*." She began to climax, ankles locked around my hips. "Don't stop. Please, don't ever stop."

And I didn't.

Not for a long, long time.

Eighty-nine

Two days later, we were wed.

The day before the wedding, we didn't see one another. I knew Sidonie was being taken to Eisheth's temple, where she would light a candle to Eisheth and beseech the goddess to open the gates of her womb and grant her children. It was a mystery in which men were not allowed to partake.

I thought about that alone in my quarters. I thought about the unborn son who had died with Dorelei. Aniel. We had chosen that name for him. If Sidonie had a boy, I wondered if she'd consent to name him Aniel.

I thought she might.

Whatever fate saw fit to grant us, girl or boy, a lively horde or a cherished few, I thought, we would love them. We would never let a day go by unmarked, unnoticed, without letting them know they were loved. Without letting them know we loved one another. Our lives together were a gift. I would always be grateful for it.

The day of our wedding dawned clear and bright. How not? The Master of the Straits was in attendance. Favrielle nó Eglantine's assistants came to make certain that my attire was immaculate. It was simple, very simple. Black breeches, a white shirt open at the throat, embellished with subtle white-on-white embroidery along the neckline. No doublet. I remembered sweltering when I'd wed Dorelei.

Not today.

They fussed over the lay of the shirt and fussed over my hair and the shine of my boots until I grew impatient and dismissed them. Not long afterward, Phèdre and Joscelin arrived to escort me. Phèdre caught her breath at the sight of me.

"You look—" She shook her head.

I smiled. "So do you."

And then it was time to go. We rode the short distance from the courtyard to the Palace gardens, wreaths of flowers draped around the necks of our mounts. At every step of the way, there were folk flanking our path, cheering and throwing petals. I thought half the flowers of Terre d'Ange must have been stripped bare for this one day. We reached the gardens and dismounted, continuing on foot. Petals fell like a blizzard.

Through the falling petals, I saw her.

Sidonie's dress was white, white on white, matching my shirt. It looked vivid and bright against the greensward and the blue robes of Brother Thomas standing behind her. Her arms and shoulders were bare. There were white roses woven into her honey-gold hair. We smiled at one another. There was a throng of thousands present, but I saw only her.

I walked across the greensward and took her hand.

Another moment in life come around full circle.

Brother Thomas stooped to touch the green, growing grass, then lifted his hands to the blue, blue sky. He invoked Elua's blessing on us. Once more, I felt my brow anointed with oil. I touched the golden torc at my throat, remembering. I saw understanding in Sidonie's dark gaze. And then Bérèngere of Namarre came forward and anointed us a second time in Naamah's name. Her daughter had kept our secrets, but she knew the role desire had played in our union. The oil on the Lady Bérèngere's fingers smelled of jasmine, and her expression was at once solemn and glad.

There were vows then. I repeated the words that Brother Thomas gave me to recite, finding my voice gone suddenly soft and husky. Tears stood in Sidonie's eyes. I watched Sidonie recite the same vows. A thousand memories crowded me. We'd gone through so very much to reach this place, this moment in time.

"Let it be done." Brother Thomas' voice was firm and carrying. He spread his arms wide as though to embrace the world. "In Blessed Elua's name, I bid you seal this union with a kiss."

The cheers rose.

Petals fell.

Sidonie smiled at me through her tears, joyous tears. She slid her arms around my neck. I cupped her face in my hands and kissed her as though the fate of the world depended on it.

It was done.

We were wed. Melisande Shahrizai's son and Ysandre de la Courcel's heir. And the realm rejoiced at our union, their cheers ringing to the heavens. A vast band of musicians began to play. Servants began to circulate bearing trays of *joie*. I downed a glass at one swallow, gasping at the cold fire that burned its way down my throat. Sidonie laughed with delight at my reaction.

The celebration began.

I would that I could have stopped time and preserved that day forever. It was a perfect day. There was the shadow of sorrow, yes. It would always be there. But that was the nature of life. The bright mirror and the dark, reflecting one another. And today there was so much brightness.

So many people I loved were there.

"Dagda Mor!" Eamonn said good-naturedly, folding me into a rough hug. "I don't think I've ever seen you truly *happy* before, Imri."

I laughed. "Elua willing, you'll see a lot more of it."

Out of the corner of my eye, I saw Maslin de Lombelon go to one knee before Sidonie, taking her hand and speaking in a low tone. She listened, then kissed his cheek softly.

Urist came to clasp my hand, his grip hard and strong. We nodded at one another, sharing memories in silence. "She'd be glad," he said simply.

My eyes stung. "Thank you."

Maslin, rising to approach me, his gaze clear of the old bitterness. "I'm happy for you," he said, honest and direct. "Truly. Both of you."

I grinned at him. "My thanks, my bright angel." It made him laugh. "I'm glad you came."

Alais, looking older and self-assured. She hugged me hard and whispered in my ear. "I'm so glad to have you as a brother, really and truly."

I hugged her back. "You always did, villain." She didn't protest at the nickname, only laughed. "No harpist?" I inquired.

"No." Alais pulled away to regard me with amusement. "Not yet."

And then Drustan and Ysandre approached. I bowed. "Your majesties."

"Imriel." Drustan laid his hand on my shoulder. "I told you once that you would always be family to me." He smiled quietly. "I am pleased to find it true."

"As am I," Ysandre echoed.

I bowed again. "I will try to be worthy."

"I think you've managed," Ysandre said wryly; but then she embraced me and touched my face, her touch gentle and lingering. "I did a very good thing when I sought to heal the rifts in our realm by finding you, Imriel de la Courcel. Better than I knew. I'm sorry it took me so long to see it."

I nodded, words failing me.

It went on and on. Mavros and my Shahrizai kin. Lady Nicola. Ghislain nó Trevalion; his wife, who'd sought to have me killed. Their son, Bertran. Lucius Tadius da Lucca. Barquiel L'Envers. Old friends, old enemies.

All happy.

Phèdre and Joscelin.

"Thank you," I said to them. "Just . . . thank you."

For the gift of my life, for the gift of all that I was. For everything. I owed them everything. I always would.

Phèdre smiled. "Your happiness is all the thanks either of us ever needed, love. I pray to Elua it never ends." She turned her head, sensing Hyacinthe's approach. "What does the *dromonde* see today?"

"Happiness, indeed." Hyacinthe's sea-shifting gaze settled on my face. He smiled, too. "Ordinary and mortal and messy. A great deal of it. Will that suffice?"

"Yes," Joscelin said firmly.

"Gods, yes!" I echoed fervently.

The congratulations ended and the fête began in earnest. There was food, an abundance of food. Long tables had been laid beneath the silk tents and they were filled to groaning. Musicians played in shifts, unceasing. There were acrobats from Eglantine House and strolling poets. Sidonie and I sat side by side, reveling in the joyous pageantry. We listened to a thousand toasts, we received a thousand gifts. We made a toast of our own, drinking deep to one another, to all of those we loved who were present. To those who could not be here today. I watched Sidonie fulfill a vow, dancing with lumbering Kratos as the setting sun streaked the sky with fire.

I thought about my mother, far away on Cythera.

And Ptolemy Solon.

Happiness is the highest form of wisdom.

I thought the Wise Ape might be right.

"Your highness," Claude de Monluc's voice said at my ear. "There's a fellow here seeks entrance to your nuptial feast. He says you'll know him. Says he has your horse. Sure as hell looks like it."

I rose, a trifle unsteady. "Did he give his name?"

Claude shook his head. "He said you'd know."

I went to meet him. In the fiery wash of light, the Bastard's spotted hide glowed. He pricked his ears forward at the sight of me. The figure astride him raised one hand, backlit by the setting sun. I looked up at him, shading my eyes, and gazed at a face I'd seen in the mirror, disconcertingly familiar. "Leander Maignard."

"Prince Imriel." He bowed from the saddle, then dismounted with a lithe twist and handed me the reins. "Thought you might like your horse back. He's a fine mount and you seemed passing fond of him."

I stroked the Bastard's neck. The Bastard snuffled my hair. "You came all this way to return my horse?"

"Not exactly." Leander grinned. "I was supposed to be here days ago, but the damned ship was wind-stilled during the passage. Her ladyship's going to be disappointed that I missed the ceremony. She was expecting a thorough accounting."

"I see." I glanced back at the reveling throng. "It would surprise me to learn that she doesn't have other spies in place."

"Ah." He shrugged. "Doubtless. But none who might hope to gain a lengthy audience with the Dauphine of Terre d'Ange that they might report back to her ladyship in great depth and detail on the singular nature of this young woman for whom my lady's only child was willing to take such great risks."

I smiled. "Oh, you reckon, do you?"

"You owe me," Leander said shrewdly. "I loaned you my face, I gave you the clothes off my back. I gave you my memories."

"She's curious, isn't she?" I asked.

He grinned again. "Perishing."

I laughed. "All right. Let me have a word with my captain here." I turned the Bastard over to Claude de Monluc and bade him have someone stable him. "You can put Leander's things in my quarters," I said. "I'll not be needing them tonight." I lowered my voice. "And have a discreet guard set on him. I want him watched while he's here. I'll want to know where he goes and whom he meets with."

"As you will." Claude looked bemused. "He's your mother's spy, isn't he?"

"He is," I said. "But he's right. I owe him."

I rejoined Leander. We crossed the greensward, toward the sound of music and laughter. The servants were lighting the lamps, sunset's glow giving way to blue twilight. The scent of thousands upon thousands of flower petals crushed underfoot and thousands more blossoms blooming hung in the air.

"It's beautiful," Leander mused. "I'd forgotten."

"Imriel!" Sidonie came toward me, holding Lucius by the hand, her eyes sparkling. "Lucius has been telling me tales from your days in Tiberium. I knew about your dalliance with his sister, but you never told me you posed . . ." Her voice trailed off as she stared at my companion. "Leander Maignard," she said in wonderment.

Leander bowed. "Her highness Sidonie de la Courcel, I take it?"

"Well met, messire." She laughed. "Again, as it were."

He straightened. "The honor is a first for me, your highness. I offer my congratulations to you and Prince Imriel on this joyous day."

"He's here to spy for my mother," I informed her. "She's perishing of curiosity."

"Well, he's welcome here today. We wouldn't be here if not for his aid." Sidonie took Leander's hands in hers. "Thank you, Messire Maignard," she said gravely. "Terre d'Ange owes you a great debt. *I* owe you a great and personal debt."

"I didn't—" Leander began in a modest tone.

Sidonie reached up to tug his head down and kissed him. There was enough ardor in it that Leander flushed to the roots of his hair when she released him. "I didn't, I just . . ." he stammered; then blew out his breath. "Um. Thank you."

I raised my brows at her. "Are you trying to unsettle him?"

"Would I do such a thing?" She flashed me a wicked smile. "I reckon I owed the real Leander Maignard at least that much." She kissed him again—lightly, on the cheek. "Enjoy yourself, messire. I'm sure we'll speak more during your time here. Lucius, I would very much like to hear the end of your tale."

Leander stared after her.

"She's not what you expected," I said to him. "She wasn't in Carthage, either."

"No." He gave himself a shake. Such a strange thing it was to be standing beside a man whose memories I shared, whose life I'd lived without his sharing in it. "No, I suppose she wasn't. I guessed that much when Deimos returned and told us how you'd ended Astegal's life together." Leander gave me a sidelong glance. "Did she come to care for me?"

"She did." I clapped a hand on his shoulder. "And if you wish to know her better, I suggest you ask her to play a game of chess ere you depart."

"I'll do that," he said, bemused.

I laughed. "Come. There are others you should meet."

I introduced him to Drustan and Ysandre, who received him with wary courtesy. To his distant kin in House Shahrizai, who regarded him with interest. To Kratos, who shook his head and marveled, remembering.

To Phèdre and Joscelin.

Leander gazed at Phèdre for a long, long time, as though he were seeking to memorize her features. At length, he sighed. "I have a message for you from her ladyship, my lady." He beckoned her close and whispered in her ear. I saw Phèdre's dart-stricken gaze shift, coming to rest on me. After a time, Leander drew back. "Have you any reply?"

"Yes." Phèdre smiled. "Tell her she's welcome. Tell her it was my honor and my privilege." She glanced at Joscelin, who smiled back at her with his wry half-smile. The saviors of my life, the heroes of my heart. "*Our* honor. *Our* privilege. And we are no less proud than she."

Leander bowed. "I will."

Twilight into dusk, dusk into night. The revels continued. The musicians played, tireless. We danced, trampling the greensward. I could not count my partners. I only knew, as the sky began to lighten in the east, that the last one was the one that mattered. I held Sidonie in my arms. The prophecy an old Priest of Elua had spoken for me so many years ago had proved true. I had found love and lost it, over and over again.

This time I meant to keep it.

Weary-looking servants began making the rounds,

handing out gilded baskets filled with rose petals. One last ritual, one last gift for the merry-makers who had stayed to usher in the dawn. There were more of them than I would have guessed. The musicians laid down their instruments. Someone—Mavros, I thought—started a bawdy chant. A hundred more voices took it up.

"Are you tired?" I asked Sidonie.

She shook her head, eyes gleaming. "No."

"Good." I scooped her into my arms and started toward the Palace. The crowd followed, cheering. "Neither am I."

"Imriel!" Sidonie laughed and wound her arms around my neck. "Surely you're not planning to carry me all the way to our bedchamber?"

"Mm-hmm." I kissed her without pausing. "It's not as far as the harbor in New Carthage, and you're a good deal easier to handle when you're awake and not wrapped in a carpet. I don't ever want to lose you again, Princess. I might never let you go." I kissed her again, hard and demanding. "Nothing and no one will ever come between us again."

She kissed me back. "Do you promise it?"

The crowd swirled around us, pelting us with petals, laughing and shouting, offering traditional blessings and bawdy jests. Love. It was all done in love. I gazed at Sidonie, at the mixture of love and desire and perfect trust in her black eyes, rose petals caught in her hair. My unlikeliest of loves, found in the last place I would ever have thought to look.

My sunlight.

My heart swelled, my happiness feeling too vast for my body to contain. I felt the touch of divine grace brush us both like a mighty unseen wing, setting somewhat deep inside me to quivering, filling me with brightness.

It felt like a promise.

"Always," I said. "Always and always."

About the Author

JACQUELINE CAREY is the author of short stories, essays, the nonfiction book *Angels: Celestial Spirits in Legend and Art*, novels *Godslayer*, *Banewreaker*, and *Santa Olivia*, and the nationally bestselling series Kushiel's Legacy. Carey lives in Michigan.

Don't miss the first novel in

JACQUELINE CAREY'S

saga!

Please turn this page

for a preview of

Naamah's Kiss

Available in paperback

Naamah," I breathed.

"Naamah," Cillian agreed, his finger hovering over the page.

Our gazes met in triumph. It had taken a year for him to gain proficiency in the D'Angeline tongue and teach it to me. A year to find the right text, and for me to draw painstaking details from my recalcitrant mother. She glanced over our shoulders at the illustration of a priest in red robes, bestowing a careless remark on us.

"Oh, aye. That bears a likeness."

Cillian rolled his eyes. I giggled.

Naamah; desire. The bright lady had a name.

I studied the page. I studied all the pages. I mouthed the D'Angeline words to myself. Here was the tale my mother had sketched for me long ago, told in full.

Elua; Blessed Elua. First and foremost of their gods. All the rest had followed him. Fallen from heaven, fallen from the skies. They gave up their immortal heritage for him. Why? I traced his likeness. Born of the earth, nurtured there.

Conceived of the blood of a lone deity's mortal son and the tears of his mortal beloved, essences that mingled in the soil. Claimed by neither earth or sky, nor stone and sea.

He wandered.

The others left heaven and followed him.

I didn't understand it; I couldn't. It was too strange, too foreign. I couldn't grasp the tales. Were they gods or servants? Was Elua their *diadh-anam*? My mother had said he wasn't. But if not, what was he?

Why did they follow him?

When he hungered, Naamah lay down with strangers to get coin that he might eat. And then they came to Terre d'Ange, where the people welcomed them with open arms. There they stayed and got many children until the lonely god relented and invited Elua and his Companions back to heaven. But he refused, and went to a different place instead, and all his Companions went with him.

I looked at the illustrations again. One of them showed a priest in brown robes pouring out an offering of grain at the feet of a statue. The statue was of a man holding a seedling in the palm of his hand.

"Anael," I said aloud.

" 'Anael, also called the Star of Love and the Good Steward,' " Cillian read. " 'He gave unto them many gifts of husbandry, and taught them to grow good things and care for the land.' What's he to do with anything?"

"I don't know," I murmured. I'd never told him about that small bit of magic I could do. "If my father was a priest of Naamah, do you reckon he's descended from her line?"

Cillian shrugged. "Mayhap. After so many years, I imagine the lines are muddled. Why?"

"No reason." I closed the book. "Well. Now we know."

"I could try to find out his name for you," he offered. "I'm sure there's a register of important foreign guests who attended my father's coronation. Mayhap the priest's name is recorded in it."

I glanced at my mother's face. Her expression was unreadable. "No," I said slowly, stroking the cover of the book. "No, it's enough to know this much. Thank you, Cillian."

He smiled. "You're welcome, little frog."

And for a time, it *was* enough. Knowledge, I decided, could be a fearsome thing. I knew who I was: Moirin, daughter of Fainche. I did not wish to become other. And so I locked the name of the bright lady my father served away in my heart along with the name of the man with the seedling whom they called Star of Love and Good Steward, and I prayed instead to the Maghuin Dhonn Herself that I should be one of Her children and no one else's.

In the autumn, Cillian began his formal studies at the Academy and I saw less of him. Still, he came when he could. By spring, he'd grown another three inches and his head was full of all manner of new tales and histories, as well as gossip about the young men and women studying with him.

"You must come when you're of age, Moirin," he wheedled. "It's only two years from now, is it not?"

"One," I said, offended.

"Oh, aye?" He looked surprised. "That's right, I forgot. My sister looked older at thirteen."

It needled me that he should see me as such a child. I was old enough that I could survive in the woods alone. I could read as well as Cillian, and I'd learned D'Angeline as fast as he could teach it to me. But now he was reading works by Caerdicci scholars and learning skills like astronomy and mathematics. Wherever he was going, I was being left behind.

I said as much to my mother.

She gave me her wry look. "Wait."

"For what?"

"You'll see."

Oengus came that summer. He'd come a few times since our pilgrimage to Clunderry. This time, he eyed me critically.

"She's not started her woman's courses?" he asked my mother.

She shook her head. "No. I'd have told you."

I flushed. "Whatever for?"

They exchanged a glance. "It would mean you're eligible to be courted," my mother said. "Time enough and more for that," she added in a firm tone, putting the subject behind us.

That night, she went with Oengus. I lay awake in my nest of blankets, listening to the sounds of the night forest, trying not to think on what they did out there. When I closed my eyes, I saw the bright lady. Naamah, whose gift was desire. She held her hands cupped at her waist, then raised them and smiled at me. *Soon*, she said in a voice like honey, and opened her hands. A shimmering grey dove burst into the air, its fluttering wings echoing the fluttering deep in my belly.

Soon.

Soon came that autumn and winter. My woman's courses didn't start, but my body changed nonetheless.

I grew tall; or at least taller than my mother. At first I was reed-thin with it, but then that changed, too. My breasts and hips swelled. Where once my body had been quick and nimble, it now acquired a lithe, nubile grace.

I felt strange in my skin.

Good, but strange.

A world of sensation abounded. I craved it. I could become absorbed for hours in the softness of a piece of rabbit hide, running the down-soft fur over my cheek. Drawing a comb through my hair. The way my clothing rustled against my skin. The sensual warmth of thawing my hands over the fire after a day afield could make me shiver with pleasure.

"Ah, Moirin mine," my mother murmured, watching me. "You're a beautiful girl."

"Am I?" I asked, startled out of a reverie.

She kissed my brow. "You are."

When Cillian came that spring for the first time in long months, I saw it reflected in another's eyes. I was boiling tender lily buds over the hearth-fire and sensed him coming long before he arrived, a trail of disruption in his wake. He bounded into our campsite on long legs, his voice turned deep and booming.

"Moirin!" he shouted. "Moirin! I'm sorry I've been away so long, but there's the most amazing news—"

I stood. "Oh, aye?"

He blinked. "Moirin?"

In that moment, the balance of power shifted between us forever. I crossed my arms, folding them under my young breasts, and saw his gaze flicker over my body. "And who else might I be?"

"Ahh . . ." Cillian flushed. "You've grown, that's all."

"So I have," I agreed.

"Aye." He stood stupidly, staring.

"What news?" I prompted him.

"Oh!" He started. "Oh, aye." He made a sweeping gesture toward the west. "There's a whole new land that's been discovered across the sea. An Aragonian explorer found it. It's all the talk of the Academy."

"Is it now?"

"It is." Cillian came toward me, dropping the satchel he carried. His hand rose as though of its own accord to touch my face. "Dagda Mor!" he breathed. "Have I been gone so long?"

I leaned away from him. "You have."

"Forgive me?" he begged.

"I might." I ducked and picked up the satchel. "What have you brought me?"

It wasn't much. Stale oatcakes; the dregs of last season's honey, crystallized in the comb. A smoked ham that was nearly rancid. An illustrated history of the Master of the Straits.

"Hmm."

Cillian flushed again. "I'll bring whatever you like next time."

I stepped close to him, until we were nearly nose to nose. "What I *want* is my friend back."

"Moirin." His voice was husky. He clasped my upper arms, his hands strong. It felt good. His dark grey eyes were intent on mine. I'd never noticed how handsome he was. "Have I not always been your friend?"

I shrugged. "When it suited."

"It suits."

He kissed me. His lips were firm, but softer than I expected. Over and over, Cillian kissed my mouth. And then there was his tongue, probing tentatively. At first the invasion startled me, and then I welcomed it. I teased it with my own; teased and retreated, forcing him to delve deeper into my mouth.

Yes, I thought. *This.*

The bright lady agreed, amused.

There was a sound of my mother clearing her throat. She was standing near the hearth, a brace of grouse dangling from one hand.

Cillian sprang backward.

I eyed her.

"So," she said wryly. "Already?"

"We were just—" Cillian began.

"I can see well enough what you were about," my mother said. "Moirin . . ." She sighed. "Grown as you may have done, you're a child in a woman's body yet. Have a care with it, will you not?"

I didn't want to have a care with it and I didn't want to be told I was a child. What I wanted was for Cillian to kiss me again and find out what happened next. But there was a shadow of worry behind my mother's eyes that made me nod reluctantly and keep my peace.

And so I sat plucking grouse while Cillian spoke of the rumors surrounding the new land that had been discovered across the sea; of fabulous cities rising up from lush jungles, folk who dressed themselves all in jade and feathers, and gold beyond telling. It was all very interesting, but I'd rather have been kissing him.

When it came time for him to leave, I walked with him to where his mount was tethered on the outskirts of the woods, feeling my mother's gaze boring into my back. Cillian's stalwart pony had been replaced by a tall chestnut gelding, another sign that he was edging toward manhood.

"He's a beauty." I blew softly into the chestnut's nostrils. He whickered and lowered his head that I might scratch his ears. "Will you teach me to ride him?"

"Moirin." Cillian caught me around my waist. He turned me around and kissed me again. "I'll do aught you wish, my witch-girl," he whispered against my lips. "Only tell me you're not wroth and I'm welcome here."

"Hmm." I pulled back in the circle of his arms. "I *am* wroth. But only because I missed you."

"I'll come again," he promised, pulling me toward him and showering my face with kisses. "I promise."

"Shall I make sure of it?" I teased, tasting my newfound power.

"How?"

I slid my hands into his auburn hair and kissed him in reply, long and deep, pressing my body against his. Cillian groaned into my open mouth. I broke off the kiss and slipped from his arms with a deft twist. The blood was beating hard in my veins and I wanted more as surely as he did; but I knew just as surely that this was *my* gift and I was in control of it.

"Will that do?" I asked innocently.

"Aye," he said in a daze. "That will do it."

“A postmodern fable of enormous scope and force”*

Santa Olivia

By Jacqueline Carey

There is no pity in Santa Olivia. And no escape. In this isolated military buffer zone between Mexico and the U.S., the citizens of Santa Olivia are virtually powerless. Then an unlikely heroine is born. She is the daughter of a man genetically manipulated by the government to be a weapon. A “Wolf-Man,” he was engineered to have superhuman strength, speed, stamina, and senses, as well as a total lack of fear. Named for her vanished father, Loup Garron has inherited his gifts.

Frustrated by the injustices visited upon her friends and neighbors by the military occupiers, Loup is determined to avenge her community. Aided by a handful of her fellow orphans, Loup takes on the guise of their patron saint, Santa Olivia, and sets out to deliver vigilante justice—aware that if she is caught, she could lose her freedom . . . and possibly her life.

“A terrific book . . . both a romantic romp—and a deep piece of literature that left me breathless and cheering.”

—Patricia Briggs,
#1 *New York Times* bestselling author

Please turn this page for more rave reviews for Jacqueline Carey

"A postmodern fable of enormous scope and force . . . a cautionary tale of people caught in a web of lies and creeping terror, and a love song to the beauty and power of being different."

—Eric Van Lustbader, bestselling author of *The Bourne Sanction**

"Fabulous . . . *Santa Olivia* draws you in, compels you to enter its well-built world, daring you not to turn away as you are captivated by every single page.

—LA Banks, author of *The Vampire Huntress Legends* Series